URBAN GOTHIC
THE COMPLETE STORIES

Bruce Benderson

ITNA

ITNA PRESS
Los Angeles, CA
www.itnapress.com

This is a work of fiction. Names, characters, places, and incidents are a product of the author's imagination. Locales and public names are sometimes used for atmospheric purposes. Any resemblance to actual people, living or dead, or to businesses, companies, events, institutions, or locales is completely coincidental.

Cover art courtesy of **Scott Ewalt** Copyright © 2022

Urban Gothic: The Collected Stories. -- 1st ed.
ISBN 978-0-9912196-3-6

Library of Congress Control Number: 2022939099

ACKNOWLEDGEMENTS

This book has taken me on a 50-year journey encompassing my entire career as a writer. Putting it together was like paging through an album of the memories, thoughts, fears, dreams, desires, joys, resentments, disappointments, and triumphs that define me as an artist and make up what most would call my "identity." In consequence, a true list of acknowledgments should include nearly everyone who played a significant role in my life.

Rather than attempting such a daunting task, I'll instead warmly thank those who advised me during the compilation and editing of these stories: Cathleen Peters Saito, Dale Corvino, Drew Zeiba, Travis Jeppesen, and Scott Neary. I've always been awed by the talent of the person who created the art for the cover of this book: Scott Ewalt, a great artist whom I also have the privilege of calling a friend. I appreciate the efforts of Jerry Wheeler, who copyedited this manuscript in record time. Warm appreciation many years later to Eddie Mercado for collaborating with me on a story that appears in this book. And finally, a huge expression of thanks to the publisher and editor of ITNA, Christopher Stoddard, without whom this book would never have existed.

CONTENTS

Preface 1

Call It Love

The Ring 7

Dust, Angel 13

Blades 23

Fraulein 33

James 41

Persistent Patsy 49

The Buttoned Lip 91

A Libertine 95

The Worst Place in New York 101

Myra 109

The Puerto Rican 131

The Romanian Boy 135

Pseudo Noir

The Old Switcheroo 143

Recommendations for the Mass Production of Teenagers 195

Recovered Memory 247

I Murdered My Sim 267

Time-Worn Tales

Pinocchio 275

Stations of the Cross 285

She 293

The Sea 297

The Sacred Art of Breeding

A Visit from Mom 301

Family Romance 315

When Crack Was King

A Happy Automaton 333

King of the High Con 353

Suicide Ecstasy 361

The New York Rage 373

Pretending to Say No 387

Casio Like the Keyboard 403

Apollo's Curse 409

Counterfeit John 415

The Other Maria 425

The Reformers

They Had Stories Then 433

Why Oh Why, My Brother? 439

Take My Advice 447

Time-Warped Vision 449

Hosting Made Easy 451

A Hero 455

An Anarchiste de droite 463

A Closet Catholic 465

Weird Trips

The Grandstander 479

Return to San Francisco 527

Lost in Bucharest 543

Convalescence 547

Mouth of the River 563

Deep Springs: Blood and Brains in the California Desert 581

Goodnight, Manhattan 587

Old Europe 593

Times Square Redux 601

Times Square Obituary 611

Blackout 615

Fear of Fashion

A Black Boxes Alibi 621

A Fashion Enthusiast 629

Sort of a Fashion Journalist 635

An Eden of Fashion...639

A Genuine Star Sapphire 641

Dangerous Minds

Gore 647

My Body: Design and Architecture..................................649

Intern's Incantation..657

Friday the Thirteenth 663

Preface

WE LIVE IN EXCEPTIONAL TIMES. If I may be permitted an easy simile, it's as if a giant, not overly sharp blade is cleaving the old relationships between ethnicities, genders, and sexual pairings in the hopes of rearranging the unbalanced power dynamics inherent in them. Yes, I'm referring to a sensibility that those made uncomfortable by these radical changes are calling "cancel culture." I myself welcome and accept such long-awaited adjustments in equality; but, as most blades are double-edged, one aspect of the new mentality has not at all won my support, and that is the rewriting of history to match contemporary value judgments.

This collection of 59 texts—21 of which have never been published before—includes every finished short literary piece I created between 1970 and the present. Unsurprisingly, many of them reflect the values and, especially, the language of their time, back when pronouns reflected a male bias, descriptions of minorities were created by the minds and perceptions of majorities, and the current incarnations of feminism and gay liberation were less developed. It would be an injustice—especially in terms of the education of those born after these historical periods—to pretend such mentalities were nonexistent despite the fact that the erasing of offensive—call them triggering—yet realistic details and language from accounts written or taking place in the past is becoming more and more common. To put it simply, I have not edited or changed any language in these older texts to reflect current norms.

The only other issue this complete collection may occasion has to do with the kind of texts that can be called "short stories." This issue can be traced all the way back to the invention of the novel—or, more properly, fiction—in anglophone literary culture in the second half of the seventeenth century.

Most studies accounting for the birth of the novel in English cite Paul Bunyan's *Pilgrims Progress* (1678) as providing a template for what would become the contemporary novel. This *spiritual autobiography*, or detailed account of an individual's fall and redemption, influenced the majority of fictional narratives that followed. So powerful was the mandate of the spiritual autobiography that it eventually infiltrated nearly every narrative, or story, that exists in America—from contemporary short stories and novels to many forms of journalism and even the steps blueprinted by today's recovery movement—a purely Protestant mentality that depends almost entirely upon the same narrative of fall and redemption.

I find it curious that critics currently trying to reform our language or make it more politically correct have proven no match for this deep-seated characteristic of narrative—the mandate of structuring one's story as a spiritual biography. Even the most radical, "woke" reformers have not questioned the redemptive narrative itself, only the details of its moral imperatives and habits of language. More disappointing is the fact that America's reliance on the spiritual narrative when it comes to telling stories has placed draconian strictures on the division between what can be thought of as fiction and what can be thought of as "facts." Even creative nonfiction has become subject to such an interrogation, despite the obvious need such narratives demonstrate for many of the techniques and mechanisms of fiction.

There do, however, exist other literary cultures in which the redemptive narrative does not necessarily hold sway. The one with which I am most familiar is the French literary tradition; and because the French definition of stories, or "textes," is unhampered by the demands of the redemptive narrative, their definition of what constitutes a "story" is much roomier. In many cases, French prose neglects to define a text as either fiction or nonfiction, aware as most French writers are of the high degree of imagination needed to tell any story that touches on the truth, whether fact-based or wholly fantastic.

I now come to my motive for initiating this discussion. Many of my texts were either influenced by French literature or—in a few cases— were originally written directly in French by me and then translated by me into English for this collection. In the process, I have included a few brief texts that might actually be categorized as essays and whose purpose is to extend and deepen the vision that materializes in my stories. Those who doubt the appropriateness of such inclusion might only glance at the short texts in Baudelaire's *Paris Spleen*, which may seem like essays, but for Baudelaire and his scholars ended up being termed "prose poems." To collapse this issue into its crux, I will say that the stories in this collection are about reality as I see it, and the few short essays that help connect them are just an extension of my lifelong search to come as close to that reality as I possibly can—by any means necessary. I hope you enjoy them.

Bruce Benderson
New York City
2022

Call It Love

The Ring

OF ALL THE GANGSTERS and hustlers, the crack-smokers and dealers, I only made one friend during my entire fifteen years in old Times Square. It was a sixteen-year-old boy, a frail little hustler from a middle-class family who had fled a sadistic father and alcoholic mother in Grosse Pointe, Michigan, one of the most exclusive enclaves in the Midwest. Aside from the johns, he was the only white besides me in the bar we frequented; and his appearance was so extraordinary, mostly because of his ultra-blond hair, his enormous amber-colored eyes that looked yellow in the sunlight, his arms like matchsticks, and his pale and translucent skin that others, intimidated and overcome by his beauty, tried to ignore him. He was so slender and so smooth-cheeked that he looked like a young girl before her breasts have developed; and in summer, his tank tops revealed his shoulder blades, which seemed sculpted from meringue. He was, without a doubt, immensely popular with the johns in this place, but he possessed a combination of coolness and placidity that insisted on respect—or a sense of embarrassment and unease—on their part.

I myself felt not the slightest sexual desire for him. It would be more accurate to call what I felt an irresistible reverence for his beauty, which filled me with tenderness. It is true that I wanted to caress his thick masses of fluorescent curls or touch his whipped-cream skin from which emerged his prominent skeleton, but I did not dare and, in a sense, did not want to. After a period of nine months, he'd become my best friend there, the only one to whom I could lend money with the certainty that he'd pay it back and the only person to whom I confided the details of my life, career, and desires. In contrast, the other hustlers were almost like adversaries, whom I desired and whom I paid for pleasure, but in whom I couldn't trust.

In the entire bar, there was only one other person with whom I'd developed a casual friendship. She fascinated me largely because of her image. It was a very small Vietnamese woman, a transsexual who operated a transgender brothel in Atlantic City. Once a month, she came to New York to see her boyfriend, a Puerto Rican hustler, and I would see them in the bar.

My first encounter with the Vietnamese had left me fascinated by her rings, her black Issey Miyake fashions, her jet-beaded capes, her lustrous black hair cut Louise Brooks style, and especially her eyes, which shone like onyx jewels and which were framed by eyebrows tweezed into immense, thin half-circles.

Like the blond boy, she was a better conversationalist than most of the people in this bar. After some time, I'd find myself talking with her and the little blond while the Vietnamese's boyfriend left to find drugs. The blond boy and the Vietnamese were in the habit of talking to each other to some extent, but I had the impression I was the principal link between the two.

Perhaps the most striking thing about these experiences was, again, the Vietnamese's eyes when she'd glance at me from time to time while I was speaking with the blond boy. Just the hint of an ironic smile would compress the corners of her lips, and her eyes said that she was aware of the wealth of friendship I felt for the blond. But she never mentioned this observation, and my friendship with her always remained on the same level.

I love rings. For several years, I had been collecting them. I don't know why, but when I wear a ring that I like a lot, I feel as if I'm under the beneficent power of a protective star. It calms me and gives me the impression of possessing power. I have a friend who insists on putting the rings I buy—always secondhand, never new—in a solution of water and kosher salt. According to my friend, this rids these jewels of the "bad vibrations" imparted to them by their previous owners. But I don't believe in these notions, and I always discover good energies in my rings.

One day I was alone in the bar with the blond, and he admired a gold ring with a sapphire I was wearing. When he told me, I took off the ring and offered it to him. I suppose it was a flamboyant gesture—the sacrifice of one of my favorite rings—but as I've already explained, this boy had something that inspired respect, and perhaps even more than that.

The boy accepted in his dignified and nearly silent way, and the invigorating effect that comes from the accomplishment of a truly generous act spread through me. Two days later, when I saw him in the bar, he was wearing the ring.

That winter, I left New York for three months for some literary projects. Old Times Square had a quality that you couldn't bring to mind when you weren't there. I could never completely recall its ambiance. I suppose that was the reason I didn't think about the place much during my trip. But from time to time, I would find myself thinking of the boy and wondering how he was doing.

One of the first things I did upon my return to New York was to visit my bar. I was a bit disappointed that the boy wasn't there that evening. The Vietnamese was, but I sensed a coldness coming from her, and her ironic smile was a little more pronounced. I wasn't at all surprised. In that world everything changed so quickly, your usefulness for someone could evaporate in an instant. There were too many factors interfering with friendship. Who knew? Maybe she was dealing with HIV now, or handling a legal problem. However, I made the mistake of speaking to her even so. And during the conversation, I mentioned my friendship with the blond boy and said I was disappointed that he wasn't there that evening. And to exhibit my high esteem for him, I explained how I had given him a very expensive ring.

As the months passed, and the boy's absence became normal, I began thinking of him less and less. I admit I nearly forgot about him completely. It wasn't until just before the month of May that I saw his little back in its yellow tank top not far from the entrance to Port Authority. The traffic was making too much noise for him to hear me, but I ran after him and touched his shoulder. The face I saw when he turned his head was covered with a torrent of shredded skin, scarred into thin ribbons of dead flesh. And one of his amber eyes was no longer an eye but a pink and gray hole. We conversed politely while I made an effort not to look him in the face, and then he left. But, overcome by pity and an unexplainable sense of disgrace, I shouted after him, "Give me your telephone number!" He came back and scribbled it on a piece of torn paper.

I ran to the bar for a double scotch, and when the bartender, a worn-out, hardened guy, noticed my face, he asked in an offhand way what was going on. "Have you seen the face of that little blond boy who was always here last year?" I said, forgetting the folded-up scrap of paper and leaving it on the counter.

"Oh yeah," said the bartender. "His career as a hustler is over, I'd say." He offered a gruesome smile.

"But what happened to him?" I asked. "Who did that?" The bartender lit my cigarette and pointed to the back of the bar with his chin. When I turned to look, I saw the Vietnamese.

"But why?" I asked in shock.

"Don't know," said the bartender curtly, "something about a ring. You do know, don't you, that pathetic little blond was her great love?"

I nodded weakly.

"He even gave a pricey ring to that Oriental slut, and she wore it all the time, showing off her jewels in this scummy bar. But like a lot of people, she forgot he was only a prostitute. When she discovered that the ring hadn't been bought for her but that it came from one of the kid's admirers, she threw acid in his face."

My cigarette went tumbling from my lips. With a filthy, wet rag, the bartender wiped up the crumpled scrap of paper and my cigarette and tossed them in the ashtray. Then, brusquely, he threw all of it into an enormous trash can.

Dust, Angel

REAL POWER: I'm talking about you and me. Us wearing tuxedos and me showing up in a white one. You got to dress up this way for this restaurant, it's the most high-class one you can think of. You're a big coke dealer and so am I. Though I show up smiling, it's just that I don't want to get my white tuxedo dirty, but somebody is giving you lip, so I have to take his fucking face and make mincemeat out of it.

Nobody talks to you that way, not to you. You understand what I mean when I tell you we were all *padrinos*. It was a bugged-out dream, I can't remember all of it.

The first one I ever had about you.

You never think I'm ever thinking about anything, do you? But you don't know how much I'm always thinking, thoughts spinning around like a revolving door spitting things out.

Making people do things to me they wouldn't do really, dressing them up and peeling them down, putting weapons in their hands, making them too nice or ready to murder me, saying you lied to me yesterday.

Did you?

My mind so full of so much shit like bees buzzing round and round the same branch.

Have you ever seen that? A whole colony of bees settling on a branch.

Lucky you didn't walk into it, 'cause I wouldn't want to see you get hurt.

And there would be too many bees all at once to punch each of them out.

Can you see me spinning round and round, knocking those bees off one at a time like a wheel that goes *whirr?* My mind churning out cartoons into the black air.

One of them's my dog Kuchi, used to yap around my mother's ankles, yapping and yapping at our old man because he's beating her up.

One of them's my little brother with his pants falling off his butt.

The other's a fish that used to be in a tank in somebody's house. If you stick your lips right up against the glass, this fish would come and stick his lips against the glass, too, right up to you.

The glass would feel cold.
Wonder where the fish is now.
Probably dead.

You keep thinking about things, and you don't know why. The thoughts swim around looking for a place to get out, but they can't find it, maybe you made them up.

Like this one: I'm so little, I'm in a shoebox: that was my little bed. The shoebox is on the floor and Kuchi's coming over to see what's in it, then he begins to lick me and at first it feels good.

Did you ever get licked all over?
Now it's kind of weird 'cause Kuchi has taken a little bite of me.
Now he's going to eat my leg off, somebody's got to stop him.

When a dog tries to eat a baby it doesn't really hurt. The teeth sink right through the soft skin, you know, sometimes a cat will eat her baby but when they found that they took me away from my mother.

Then when I was four they gave me back.

Hand me that pillow. Now let me tell you what I was thinking about that dream.

The coolest Mafia man. The best scarface walking into a restaurant that's so shiny you need sunglasses to look at the silverware. He's on his way to meet the godfather because he's his ace and number one boy walking right in just as they bring out the steak on the silver plate, or is it a snake? Maybe it's a snake on a silver platter coiled up like rope. You're wearing a black tuxedo and I'm wearing the white one, remember. Can I have some coke, I say.

You pull out your silver blade and open up the diamond-studded box and fix me a line, everybody in the restaurant is watching but nobody dares to say anything, nobody except one person who is thinking of saying something. It's a guy that's so jealous he just can't stand to see us set up like this and I feel—

Did you ever look in the mirror and what you saw in the glass, suddenly for a moment you pretended it was someone else and he makes a face at you and you have to keep from smashing your fist into the mirror—

Well, I felt like that when I looked at this dude that's jealous of us. It's as if I saw him in the mirror and I really didn't like what I saw.

It's the worst feeling you can imagine.

I'm glad I remembered to bring my piece.

That's what this bulge in my tuxedo pants pocket is, by the way.

I had asked you to carry it but you said, if I had a big bulge in my pants pocket everybody would look because they're not used to seeing it, but you, kid, they're used to seeing a big bulge there anyway, so you put it in your pocket.

And you keep looking at that bulge in my pocket and feeling safe—'cause you know what's in there and it's going to keep anybody from giving us any trouble.

Hairy scary moby dick, that's what's in there.

So we take some more coke, you open the diamond box—was it diamond or gold?—and give it to me until the wheels spin in my head and a dog is yapping there. I wish he'd shut up, he's making the walls spin, we hated what was going on, which is why he used to run around her ankles yapping.

And now the guy in the mirror, he's standing in front of you, sir, and my hand's on my piece, I've got to protect you.

But what I can't understand, what I can't even look at, is you're reaching out and laying your hand on him, nice: the way you do to me. So that he looks more and more like me till I can't stand it anymore, and now I'm the one who's jealous, I want to smash the mirror with my fist that, fucking traitor. I'd like to cut off his ears and stuff them in his mouth because he's not worth hearing a kind word from you, he doesn't deserve it, don't let him near you, he doesn't deserve it, don't listen to him because he's rotten.

He might bite your balls off.

Don't get mad at me, it was only a dream. Press your hand against my forehead like that, it makes me feel better.

I should start working out more, shouldn't I?

Then I could take you easy, if I wanted to.

Only kidding.

I'd protect you.

Except sometimes I feel a little mad at you because you're always telling me what to do—yap-yapping at me all the time, till I get a little sick of hearing it or you want to have sex when I don't which to be perfectly honest is quite a few times even though I say okay and you say if you don't want to and I say just let me finish this beer.

Don't get mad.

I do have feelings for you.

I appreciate all you did and shit.

Pass me a beer, would you?

Yapping and yapping in my head until the nightmare was finished, 'cause there's nothing you can do while it's happening, if somebody you care about is wearing a black tuxedo in the most high-class Mafia restaurant in the world and you are his ace and the two of you are ruling the fucking world but suddenly he is reaching out to touch the fucking asshole that does not even respect him, there's no way of waking up from the nightmare.

Just leave me alone when I get like that, don't take it personally, I don't even know you're in the room, I can't get the dream out of my head and I begin to believe that it's really happening, I know it's not your fault but I'll kill you if you come near me.

I didn't mean you, I meant him.

Give me a kiss.

I'll tell you about that fish—listen to me—I'll tell you all about him: he can't see. That's why he comes up real close when you put your lips on the glass, he comes to see what it is. Then when he does, there's something in his lips that makes them stick to the glass, and he's stuck there—isn't that bugged out—and you think he's kissing you. But he's stuck there and can't get away.

If I was that fish, and I had a fist, I'd smash it right through that glass, then the water would come spilling out all over that guy's kisser and wouldn't he be surprised, maybe his mouth would fall open, and I'd slide inside it—swim right through him and punch him in the guts with my fins.

Or bite his balls off.

Imagine a fish biting a guy's balls off. It's bugged out, isn't it?

I suppose I should tell you that when I was in the bar the other night I met this dude and he said I have cocaine, why don't you come over we'll do some. When I came over he did have coke and he kept trying to tell me to take off my gloves and I wouldn't. He even got my pants off, but I wouldn't take off the gloves. Then finally he said why don't you take off one glove I promise you won't have to take the other off.

I took it off.

We got it on and he gave me some money which I gave most of it to you, you remember you asked me have I got any of the cash you gave me and I gave you back three fins? Well, that wasn't what you gave me I spent that, but what I gave you back I got from him.

Then tonight I saw him in the bar and I said hey I want my glove back, I left it at your house, I forgot to take it.

And he said, I threw it away.

You couldn't have thrown it away I said because you made me take it off. You couldn't have thrown it away.

Well, I did he said that money I gave you was worth a lot more than that stupid glove anyway.

I grabbed him by the shirt and slammed him up against the bar, said give me my fucking glove, you stole my fucking glove you bastard.

And he said, what's the big deal about a glove. Then he got scared for a second and pulled out a twenty and said here will this take care of it, and I took it and said it would, but I didn't really feel that way.

And he said, can I buy you a drink my friend?

And I said I'd love one thank you.

And he said I really had a good time with you.

It'll be better the second time I said, and he went and talked to somebody else.

To tell you the truth I had another dream. We were at a shopping mall and you were going to buy me a new pair of Adidas. Where are they I said, I want to try them on, give me the box, oh you said I left the box inside the store. So I went to wait for you in the parking lot and then I kept walking, there was a tree by the side and on a branch hanging from it was a whole bunch of bees. The bees had formed in the shape of a head like your face and the mouth was open like a big hole as if to kiss me and I laughed.

Sometimes I wish they'd put me in a shoebox and leave me there for a while with the cover on it—just leave me alone—I don't want to watch what some people do to other people. That little pup always knew when something wasn't right.

I guess I should tell you I went home with that guy again tonight. Please don't be mad at me. You remember you bought me those gloves.

After he gave me the bill and bought me the drink and then he came back he was a little high and he said maybe I should, maybe I should try it again. Let's go I said.

We went over to his place.

And what do you think: there was the glove lying right there on the couch where I had left it.

But I thought you threw it away.

I thought I did, he said, go ahead take it. Take your pants off.

But I wouldn't and I made him suck my dick with my pants on this time.

Afterward he said that wasn't so good, it was better last time.

I didn't say anything so he said that again. Okay, he said then no hard feelings. But I've got to get up early.

Okay, I said. I took the glove.

He said see you.

Aren't you forgetting something, aren't you forgetting to give me the money?

But I gave you twenty in the bar he said.

That was for the glove.

You got the glove back.

Look, are you going to give me some money? You said you threw the glove away.

I already gave you money. Now take the glove and get out, you lied to me anyway, it wasn't better the second time.

You lied to me, you said you threw the glove away, I said, now give me my money or I'll work your face over.

Get lost he said.

I hit him so hard he fell over and I worked his face over really good with my boot.

You're not mad at me, are you?

To tell the truth that fish was in my house. We had quite a big tank, all us kids got together and bought it and put rocks in the bottom and we bought a whole bunch of fish little by little, that tank was something, but my favorite was that fish that couldn't stop kissing.

One night, the old man came home drunk and they had a fight so he picked up the tank and smashed it. The water went all everywhere and the fish were flip-flopping on the floor, but do you know that one fish's lips were still stuck to a piece of glass?

He didn't flip at all.

He was like stone stuck to glass. I guess he was scared.

I had to work that smartass over. There's no respect in this world.

He'll wake up with a face the size of a watermelon and he'll know better next time. He'll know not to cross me when I'm thinking of you.

I mean when I'm thinking about protecting you.

Sometimes you make me feel like I can't take it anymore, you never let up. There's a wheel in my head spitting out nightmares. It's taking everything I got to fight those nightmares. Bees are stinging me in every part of my body and I've got to take care of them one by one. But your voice is out there saying pay attention to me, can't you hear what I'm saying, I told you before.

Pay attention to you? I've got a whole hive of bees on me and I've got to punch out each of them with my fist. Get away from me or I'll kill you too.

I was talking to the bees, I mean I was talking to one of them.

Open up another beer, *padrino,* turn out the light, let's stop thinking about this. Now that's better.

In the dark like this your face hanging over me keeps changing. Something is crawling over it making it look different each moment that passes. I'd like to kiss it, too, touch it, but it keeps getting away from me.

Blades

IT'S A CLASSIC cowhide purse for a middle-class lady, brown and unremarkable, with a simple gold-plated clasp. It took a leather worker's thick, curved needle and some fishing tackle to sew the razor blades along the inside, like a circle of jagged teeth above the open straight razor at the bottom.

Flip the purse open. The upscale odor of sour tanning is all you'll notice before the icy slice of the razor's edge makes you howl. You yank out a bloody hand—learn to keep your hands to yourself.

Her own dark hand is nimble. Its bones can collapse past the defense zone of razor blade teeth to the big roll of bills perched next to the straight razor. They thread twenties from the purse like magic tricks, smoothing them into a limp curve over the knuckle of a big forefinger, letting them float onto the bar counter to the tinkle of her silver bracelets.

In this dim light, she seems to be a big-boned lady over six feet tall, with a provincial hairdo tapering at the earlobes, dressed in a tidy silk shift appropriate for the office, and a single strand of real pearls. It's only the span of many silver bracelets on the big wrist that seems slightly odd, and the fact that she's sitting in this dank, dark hole.

The hole is of the disappearing center-city sort, where mostly male prostitutes or transgenders sell sex to older men to get the drugs they want. Homosexual behavior pays the bills, even though the atmosphere seems hyper-hetero. Queens snap at sulky homeboys wearing gold jewelry or the bead necklaces of gangs, while lustful, mostly drunken businessmen still carrying attaché cases ogle one or other from the shadows. But she is imperiously beyond the darkness, supposedly immune to all the excitement over strong contrasts of genders, miles above the seedy envy of money, in her very perfect world of idealistic romantic interests.

He is slouched by her side in a concave curve, his wiry legs dangling from the bar stool; his full, curvaceous mouth welded to the bone structure of a lean face. Dead almond eyes under gleaming licorice strips of hair yanked back wolfman style. His sixteen-year-old chin sports just enough hair for a scraggly goatee. For those with unarmed purses, this is the archetypal WANTED bulletin. The nerves that control the face muscles are already dead to scrutiny, the eyes apathetic to the camera flash at Central Booking. From the dark drapery of the oversized clothing poke big, adolescent bones. In this dim light, within the black walls, from certain angles, the clothes make the body look puffed for challenge, similar to a threatened cat raising its fur like porcupine quills to look bigger and fiercer. The clothes could also be hiding a weapon, lost to potential friskers in the folds, or a second set of clothes worn underneath by someone with no fixed place to live.

The teeth are jagged. The upper row, anyway. They're rotting, chipped by accidents or brawls. But then the lower row… they're all gold. Sleeves of gold molded perfectly over the contours of his real teeth. All nine in front. So that his real teeth are probably rotting underneath.

The gold teeth flash their predatory grins at the big, pleasant-looking Black lady with the new purse from which money keeps appearing to pay for alcohol. They are drinking Amaretto. There is a feminist bravado in her warm brown eyes under the copper eye shadow. Her voice is sibilant but a little schoolmarmish. With soft, curt remarks and dismissive gestures, she makes known what kind of woman she is. In charge of her own life. Undaunted by the fact that he is half her age and three-quarters her height. Never paying for sex, by the way. But maybe she'll cook a feast for him later, when they get hungry. He'll be hungry real soon, he mentions, scanning the bar with blank eyes and poking a thumb into a pocket of his oversized jeans, while the fingers splay impudently across the top of his thigh toward the crotch.

Two days ago, she recovered from that fever. A fever she would never mention here. She only comes to this hole to avoid the censure of a world that faults her for being too tall. That's all there is to it. So why give wind of the elaborate procedures that were carried out two days ago?

Two days ago, she turned her kitchen into a sterile laboratory. With the help of her girlfriends, she rinsed the sink and fixtures with boiling water and scrubbed the countertops with bleach. A friend who works as a plastic surgeon's assistant was visiting. She and the friend laid out the sterilized instruments, the plastic bladders of silicone, and the syringes of estrogen on gauze-padded sheets, set out alcohol and cotton for prepping. A long line of customers snaked out of her kitchen into the hallway of her building. Some had self-anesthetized with medications ranging from crack to Percodan. The first of many wanted loose silicone added to her breasts, which had already been created two years ago using silicone bags. But this procedure was cheaper. Others wanted prominent cheeks or chin extensions to make the outline of their faces more heart-shaped. Then there were those who wanted enormous buttocks or hips to appear even more curvaceous. She herself only wanted more shapely thighs as her legs tend to look too gangly and male.

The injection of the silicone causes enormous bruises. In some places, layers of plasma surface and smart like a bee sting. She had to sleep with a pillow under her knees because even the slightest pressure in the swollen area of the injections was excruciating.

But the worst was the fever. It spiked up and down hourly for two whole days. It burned her eyes in their sockets as if they had been replaced by acetylene torches. Her tongue felt heavy and sandy against her dried-up palate. Slowly, the fever melted the fear into a hot trickling. The trickle became a sun-warmed brook. She began to float on this lightly rippling brook. Her body was weightless. The rivulets became cool, flowing through her limbs and swirling around her splayed fingers. The waves were like the satiny skin of an adolescent against which one slides one's hand. There'd be no harsh sex to contact at the end of the long stretch of rippled skin, only this endless sliding. This was the clean love for which she was in search, and now she had found it, but as she had expected, she could not in the face of it move her body. No one but no one need know about this fever. How could they ever understand?

The flat, oval face of the romantic interest is watching the new-smelling purse with veiled curiosity. The long, dark hand with tinkling bracelets slides inside the purse again and comes out with another bill earned from the silicone sessions. The boy's eyes gleam with interest. She asks him to go to the store and get both of them packs of cigarettes and mints. He slides off the bar stool to attention. His hand curves over the fresh bill. Her prideful eyes sparkle with Amaretto as she watches him shuffle toward the door. She loves the stiff, thrusting walk, the ill-intentioned slouch, the pants hanging from his skinny hips. She imagines, mistakenly, that all eyes are fixed on the line of sight linking him to her proprietary gaze.

What she doesn't know is hidden under the drapery, crisscrossing the lean, nearly hairless chest and severing his nipple, fanning out from his ribcage almost all the way to his navel: a vast constellation of welted scars, still tender to the touch after almost a year. And inside his brain is the muffled memory of a searing incident: black sky in a dark park. An overheated crack pipe quickly stashed in his pocket, so hot that it burns its way to the flesh of his lean thigh. He's trying to hide the smoking crack pipe from the olive eyes of a rageful dealer to whom he owes money, as a quick, dull stampede of feet approach from behind. In the park with the broken street lamps, he feels the pressure of metal against his muscles as he is backed against a wire fence. It bulges behind him like a hammock while his feet scud uselessly forward.

Then there are the endless jabs and slicings—like children poking curiously with sticks at a big dead animal—the points sinking in and popping out, edges of blades making ribbons of the T-shirt and cross-hatching the skin of the chest, and a close-up of crusted knuckles around a knife handle, while another big calloused hand encircles his neck and presses the back of it against the fence.

He tries to drop his jaw low enough to bite one of the fingers. But the grip tightens, the slicing keeps happening until he feels himself slump down slow-motion. Liquid is seeping out in a pissing feeling, a warm weakness, like a brook trickling in the sun. His limbs flow deliciously away like a hand sliding down the satiny skin of the most beautiful girl's body. And there'll be no recriminations at the end of the long stretch of rippled skin, only this endless slide.

He stops at the entrance to the store, feeling the bill against the pads of his palm. A magnetic pull is coming from the corner where little magic vials are sold. But the black bitch's purse constantly giving birth to those twenties has a stronger shimmer.

He pokes the bill through the scratched slot of the plastic anti-theft shield, and two packs of Newport and a roll of mints spill back, followed by clattering coins and some folded, grimy bills.

Back where the purse is, the hole has swollen full of people. Boisterous and impatient. They push by him without so much as a "sorry." They really should watch themselves as somebody could end up in the toilets with a skull split open. The tall black bitch who claims to be a real woman doesn't bother telling him to keep the change when he holds out the coins and crumpled bills with the mints and Newports. And she seems to want to sit here all night. If she is a woman, there'll be a slippery pussy into which to plunge, but at the very least, tits to suck and the padding of an ass against his thighs. There'll be an apartment somewhere, a bed and a shower, and maybe a full refrigerator.

Then there's that purse.

Much later, it is nestled between their hips on the back seat of a taxi, upon which her long-boned body is folded into thirds, her pressed-together knees improbably high. The not very serious fantasy of reaching across her lap to open the door and shoving her out of the taxi as the light changes flashes through his mind. Then all of it is erased by the murky row after row of faceless buildings, his body moving through night…

Entering her apartment like they now are, you might remark that her sober middle-class image was being compromised. It's not just the many feminine icons replacing genuine accoutrements of a woman's life, as in the bathroom. It's the shabby compromises of the city outskirts poking through the brave attempts at upper-class ascendancy: that laminated breakfront imitating a European antique or the knock-off country flower print on cheap curtains and couch covers; the sound system with its many luminous readouts showing itself off in a corner.

He is wild about that sound system. There are CDs piled everywhere. The latest ones. He rifles through them, letting out gasps when he discovers some of his favorites of the moment. Her mascaraed eyes glue themselves with sullen suspicion to his hand movements. He feels the look but pretends not to, rakishly poking the first CD into the system and then striding toward her. As he grinds against her to the music, her eyes peer vigilantly from above, on the lookout for the hand that might reach for a weapon. She is caressing him through the baggy clothes with the covert agenda of frisking. But the hard curves of his body and the flat stomach remind her of those delicious, dizzy slidings. His calloused hands clasp her flesh, and the lush padding of his lips suffocates her. Her tongue begins to swirl against the gold teeth, and the musty smell of his body makes her feel weak with intimacy.

He, for his part, is quickly surveying her body, spanning different parts of the skeleton with his caresses to make a diagnosis. Is it a real woman? The buttocks feel too sculpted, but the arms snaking over his back have the creamy, yielding texture of femininity. The tops of the thighs feel pliant and meaty.

He decides not to worry about it. When he pushes her backward, she obeys, collapsing onto the big matching-print bedspread. Looking down, you'd see her long, twisting figure cradling his smaller clenched body, which is lunging. Then her pantyhosed legs rise, opening along either side of his narrow hips, as the skirt hem inches up her thighs. The legs hover in the air, then snake around the narrow waist, expertly edging the pants and undershorts down to reveal smooth, hard buttocks dimpled at the teardrop tops.

What a fool she is. Not to have had him remove all his clothes before her body got trapped underneath his. Not to have had him put the clothes away from the bed. Out of the pants he still wears, the weapon will pop. Or from his socks. He'll hold the point of the blade to her neck while she is pinned beneath him and leave her bleeding like a pig.

Just let him try it. At the least sign, she'll lunge upward with superhuman strength. He'll go flying off her and hit the wall. She'll pounce on him and hold him by the hair while her fist smashes cartilage and gold-sleeved teeth pop from the blood-gushing mouth. And what will she do with all that gold? Should she have it melted down? Make that plain heart-shaped locket she'd been thinking of getting?

The pants are already off and kicked to the foot of the bed. The room is a cavern of thickened breath. Hands are reaching behind her to unzip her dress.

He won't find out. *Ever.*

Her passion will overrule all his explorings. As he lies naked on his back, his body will be claimed by her hungry mouth. She's already flipped him. He's stretched his arms over his head. His legs dangle submissively from the edge of the bed. It's safer this way, she tells him. You won't get the rest of me until I know you better. The teasing tongue and slippery mouth glide in cool pleasure over his thighs and crotch, tracing their way through the thicket of his groin to—

No! He grasps both of her ears to keep her head from moving. Not up there.

A feeling of insult gushes through her. Molten offense. *He knows.* Isn't she good enough? Why's she got to keep her mouth below the waist?

He just… doesn't want to take his shirt off.

Teasingly, she pinches the hem of the T-shirt and begins to lift it. His hand locks over hers. His mouth compresses.

She swings her feet to the floor and cups her chin in her hands. The unzipped dress slips from one shoulder.

Take your shirt off, she orders sulkily.

No!

Her hand snakes to his thigh and slides onto his crotch, begins its rhythmic stroking. Harder and harder his penis gets, deeper and more rhythmic his breathing…

Take your shirt off.

No. Never.

But this time, something tells her not to withdraw. Her hand lingers at his thigh, caressing it reassuringly. The story of the scars unfolds. The scars were an unzipping. His skin shredded like ripped clothes, letting life out through the seams. An enormous loss. And even when the blood had been replaced and the wounds had closed, he never got everything back. All of it went down a size.

In fact, he doesn't take his shirt off. He wears it even when he's alone, quickly shedding it to wash and then putting one on again. The sight and the memory of vulnerability are too much for him…

A barely audible hum deep in her throat. Her warm, brown eyes flooded with a look of compassion. How unconcerned with scars she is, how eager to lightly caress his whole body with her hands and mouth. How she dreams about and prays for that moment of trust. How this chance for him to get used to his new body couldn't be better. With the help of someone who really likes it…

The shirt slowly peeling upward… Past the flat nub of the navel and the bloom of almost invisible hairs leading toward the sculpted chest, under the wide net of crosshatched scars.

They hurt a little, he says.

Breath held. Her hand barely grazing the skin, contacting the net of welts.

Both of them breathing. Stooping, she runs her moist lips over the pattern, stops to tease the intact nipple, the soothing hum still vibrating in her throat. Over and over, she lathes the chest with an adoring tongue, the sides of the rib cage, the burn scar at the hip.

The moistened chest feels healed, he thinks. She's reforming it for him with her mouth. Slowly but surely his breath comes easier and the muscles relax. The suction on his body sends waves of soft pleasure coursing; his hands encircle her neck and pull her toward his crotch.

Afterward, her head is cradled on his chest. Their guards drop. She drifts into sleep with the feeling of being in the natural world. A small sigh of ease from his gently parted lips. I bet I'm going to be here for a while, he's thinking as he loses consciousness, his chest naked for the first time since…

The middle of the night. A scarred angel in her arms. Against her cheek in the darkness, the edges of the welts. Waves of tenderness are enveloping her. She is thinking, tomorrow… after she has cooked breakfast for him…. he will discover that she has given him some money. Not for sex. But because she knows he has no cash.

The best idea would be to get a fifty from the roll of bills now and slip it into the pocket of his pants lying at the foot of the bed…

No embarrassment. She can put the purse somewhere safe and not have to think about it.

She slips out of bed and feels her way to the corner of the couch where the purse is lying, pausing a moment to think of what has been lulled into sleep on the bed. Her eyes are full of astonished tears of gratitude, reverence for her rescued child. She feels woozy with tenderness as she sticks her hand into her purse too carelessly.

It nicks her finger.

She puts the purse in the bottom dresser drawer and tiptoes to the bathroom for a bandage. Then she sinks beside the unveiled beloved, who has shifted his back to her so she can't see his open eyes, which are staring at the bottom dresser drawer.

Until his lids fall closed.

And the orbs begin to twitch.

And he dreams yet again of shrieks slashing the black air.

Fraulein

SHORTLY AFTER Christine Jorgensen shocked the world by flying to Copenhagen and changing her gender, an unhappy office worker in Munich decided to follow in her footsteps. However, whereas Miss Jorgensen had welcomed publicity and flaunted her sex change to the media, eventually developing a nightclub act to which audiences came to gawk, the depressed and disenfranchised Fraulein considered her greatest ally to be privacy. All she thought about before deciding on her surgery was how to hide it from family, friends, and the media. In fact, her sole objective for her upcoming adventure was to ensure the world would see her and treat her unquestionably as a "real woman," a woman who had been born with her female sex intact; and thus, the Fraulein decided not only on a new name and surname, but on a completely new identity that could not be traced to her past. This was accomplished as soon as she'd saved up enough money to immigrate to America, where she did not know a soul, and began organizing a series of clandestine trips from her small apartment in downtown Manhattan to Baltimore, where Johns Hopkins University hospital was quickly becoming pre-eminent for top-of-the-line sex reassignment surgery.

The fruits of the Fraulein's efforts and strategies were mostly internal. Becoming a woman for her did not lead to any approximation of a normal heterosexual life. It did not improve her social or romantic chances or help to integrate her into society. The Fraulein had changed her body to please herself alone, and her pleasure over that accomplishment was more than enough. Any side benefits resulting from it would only distract her from the joy she felt thinking about her body and examining it in the mirror. She pasted old German newspapers to the windows of her ground-floor apartment on East 15th Street to keep out prying eyes and began her love affair with her mirror, which reflected an increasingly feminine image enhanced by more and more makeup and more and more accessories, even if there was nothing she could do about her overly large hands and men's size twelve feet.

Perhaps because the Fraulein had been born before the war, in 1974 she was still inspired by a decidedly old-fashioned aesthetic consisting of ankle-strap platform shoes, some slinky black Chanel cocktail dresses, and hair cut pixie style and dyed jet-black Roaring Twenties style. The look was completed by a thick layer of foundation to conceal the large pores caused by months of electrolysis, very pronounced eye makeup with lashes unnaturally long, and brows plucked thin to yield the effect of a Theda Bara vamp. These dramatic details kept onlookers at bay by intimidating them, even if many still stared with startled curiosity at the overly made-up middle-aged woman in red lipstick and dark stockings who possessed such large feet.

But at home, in front of her mirror, the Fraulein's heavily made-up face and fashions seemed to transform into a perfect incarnation of her lifelong dream, and although she was well aware of the pain, sacrifice, and complicated procedures she had subjected herself to in order to achieve her ideal image, during such mirror gazing she enjoyed pretending it had all come at once, as if some fairy godmother had merely needed to touch her with a magic wand to bring out her real identity.

Such magical thinking was undoubtedly the reason for other kinds of romantic fantasies, most of which she pushed to the back of her mind out of a fear of losing the discipline she had relied upon to forge her new life. Willpower mattered, she was well aware, and must not be weakened by romantic fantasizing. Willpower was the stuff that accomplished dreams. Despite this emphasis, however, on fixity of purpose, there was one dream she had never been able to extinguish completely. It floated at the back of her mind eternally, although she rarely allowed herself to indulge in it. It was another magical, fairy-tale idea, the idea that someone somewhere who would fall in love with her instantly would suddenly appear in some unexplainable way.

On that Christmas eve in 1974, a cold, snowless, gray day that had waned into night, this imagined reward of true love instantly seemed to have forced itself into her consciousness more powerfully than usual as she prepared to entertain the only tenant in the building whom she spoke to, a woman with twenty-three cats who was *persona non grata* to everyone else. The Fraulein's easygoing attitude toward the cat lady could perhaps be explained by the fact that the woman lived on the sixth floor of the building and the Fraulein on the first. The first floor was the only place where the overwhelming ammoniac odor of cat litter and urine, which made others gag as they passed the cat lady's door, was close to imperceptible.

It wasn't as if the Fraulein was unaware of the stench the cat lady was causing with her animals. She'd even overheard one neighbor talk about getting a glimpse of the front room, despite the cat lady's habit of never answering her door. The neighbor had taken advantage of a rare chance for a peek inside the cat lady's apartment when the latter returned with an unwieldy shopping cart holding the many bags of litter she'd purchased and dropped her keys just as the door to her apartment swung open. The glimpse inside only lasted a second, but that was enough time to observe that the front room was filled with wads of newspaper saturated with urine and cat turds. In fact, rather than using litter boxes for her twenty-three cats, the cat lady seemed to have turned her entire front room into a giant litter box by scattering the newspaper and litter granules on every surface of the floor.

Even after hearing this, the Fraulein remained convinced that there were far worse people in the city, and wasn't the cat lady a victimized outsider just like she was? Someone whose life style was so offensive—whether it be by sight or by odor—to others that she had been driven into a sort of exile? The cat lady only went out at night for fear of the other tenants, and often it was to dump enormous bags of used litter and urine-soaked newspaper in the garbage. Living by night was another sacrifice with which the Fraulein could identify. She also had confined herself to her apartment in the day and only ventured out at night for food and other necessities during the entire period in which she was transitioning.

The Fraulein was edging the carp, *kartoffelpuffer*, and *sauerkraut* onto separate platters and arranging a plate of fresh and fragrant *lebkuchen* next to them to be served with her mulled wine when she heard the bump and rattle of the cat lady's grocery cart on the marble stairway. She'd obviously decided to do her nightly dump first before coming to the Fraulein's door. Then she heard the woman's knock and swung the door open. "*Frohe Weihnachten!*" she announced brightly.

The cat lady looked at her confusedly until the Fraulein translated the words. "I'm telling you Merry Christmas in German!" she explained.

Not knowing what else to do, the cat lady curtsied, folded her shopping cart, and set it against the wall near the entrance.

For lack of any better idea, the Fraulein handed a glass of mulled wine to the still confused cat lady and explained she was about to introduce her to traditional German Christmas Eve food. But it was obvious from the look in the cat lady's eyes that she was far from adventurous with cuisine, and although she brought the proffered glass of mulled wine to her lips and took a tiny sip, she winced at the overwhelming flavor of spices but tried to smile appreciatively, except that it came out as a grimace.

Both ladies were painfully aware of how ill-suited they were to each other and how little—as two near recluses—they had to talk about with anyone; and just as had happened during the cat lady's previous visit, conversation was extremely halting. Not only that, but the cat lady was very worried the Fraulein would return to their previous conversation in which she'd exhibited another old-fashioned characteristic of her upbringing: an ingrown sensibility of resentful anti-Semitism that had flourished in her country as the prewar German economy was tanking; and—to the cat lady's great alarm—that was indeed the dreaded topic the Fraulein launched into once again.

The cat lady's shyness was so deep-seated, it could have easily been characterized as social phobia, but because she was more intelligent than the Fraulein, she'd been able to generalize her own disenfranchisement across a wider sphere. The Fraulein might have been able to feel compassion for her, but the cat lady was also able to empathize with nearly all minorities, to the extent that she found these expressions of anti-Semitism grotesque and began objecting to them with a voice that was becoming shrill.

"I have nothing against Jews," she pleaded. "Don't judge a whole people by the individuals you don't like!"

"You don't know them like I do," scolded the Fraulein, having suddenly adopted the tone of a schoolteacher sternly counseling a misinformed pupil. "They are opportunists and betrayers, filthy people," she advised.

As these words left her lips, both ladies were seized by an identical and desperate emotion: it was an unbearable feeling of loneliness and forfeit catalyzed by the reality of spending Christmas Eve with someone who couldn't possibly be more inappropriate. In the Fraulein's case, this yawningly wide abjectness loosened the restraints with which she normally controlled her unrealistic fantasy of love at first sight, and as this mad hope for love suddenly welled up within her, an uncanny coincidence occurred. The fading German newspapers blocking her windows from a view of the street began to bulge in one place, and the window they were attached to began to creak in its frame, until the window shattered and a body came crashing through it.

It was a young British sailor on leave, still dressed in the regulation whites and navy cap of the deckhand, who must have been so inebriated that he'd collapsed against the window. Whether he'd passed out before he'd fallen through the window or at the moment he hit the floor, the young man was comatose, lying face up between the couch and the television, while the astonished Fraulein gaped down at him, her bony fingers clutching her chest, her mascaraed eyes thrown open in wide circles in her black-banged face pancaked pale by makeup. From the sailor's ankle poked a shard of glass through a dangling tendon.

As the cat lady stood frozen in horror, trying to grasp what had happened, the Fraulein carefully extended a hand and gingerly picked the shard out with thumb and forefinger. She put the shard on an ashtray and looked at the coating of blood on it. The thing that she had to do was call an ambulance. But medics would be so meddlesome. She saw their contemptuous eyes scanning the apartment with its Makassar doilies and porcelain bibelots and imagined them studying her hands and feet with mocking irony in their eyes.

"I'll call 911," offered the cat lady, but the Fraulein looked at her severely.

"Go home," she insisted. "Christmas Eve is over, and let's keep this evening between us if you don't mind?"

Gazing at her again confusedly, the cat lady reluctantly nodded in agreement, then walked to the entrance for her shopping cart and slipped quietly out.

The Fraulein ran to the bathroom and saturated a washcloth with hydrogen peroxide, then came back to the prostrate form and gently cleaned the wounded ankle. The tendon was almost completely severed, and the foot turned askew in her hand, frightening her. But calling 911 was out of the question because she thought she knew at the bottom of her heart what had happened. Her precious fantasy of love at first sight—the very one she had chided herself for entertaining—was happening. True love had been delivered to her by the strangest machination of fate. She stared down at the face of the young English sailor and took in his large convex eyelids, whose skin looked so delicate in the sallow, bony face. The graceful liverish lips had a vulnerability and a purity that shocked her. She didn't want uncaring doctors and underpaid nurses rudely adjusting or cutting into his body, and she also had to work quickly or he would lose too much blood.

She went back to the bathroom and found a roll of gauze, then took a needle from her sewing kit and held it under hot water, before wiping it with cotton and rubbing alcohol and then threading it. As she hurried back to the prone sailor, emotions about the fact that she held the power to save him fused with the formerly forbidden fantasy of instantaneous true love. She hoped he'd remain unconscious during the procedure of sewing up his leg, because she had no anesthetic. She was confident her ministrations would probably stop the bleeding, but the thought also occurred to her that her attempt to reattach the tendon with such primitive tools could leave the sailor crippled or with a limp. Even that fear was transformed by her repressed hunger for love and welling passions into something positive. If the sailor ended up crippled, he would need her even more.

James

I HAVE A DREADFUL FASCINATION for James, a husky, depressed nineteen-year-old with skin the color of tobacco.

James has a fixation for his dead father, who taught him to shoot heroin when he was twelve and whom he watched die from an overdose three years later in an abandoned lot. He shoots dope just like Dad did, and he's proud of being able to handle a higher dose.

James refers to his addiction as "my wife" and to me as the only friend he ever had. A month after I met him, I decided he needed a methadone program to save his life, and I took him to a for-profit clinic in midtown after a major hassle getting him ID. I sat in the clinic reading while he doubled over in spasms of withdrawal, until they gave him a little paper cup of purple liquid to drink. The plan after that was for him to move in with me after picking up his clothes. However, the methadone made James even higher than the dope did, and he fell asleep somewhere in a park for a day and a half.

My father was dying of heart failure in upstate New York, so I left town without finding out exactly where James had nodded out. The death of my father shortly after and the sleep of James are permanently superimposed in my mind.

My thoughts of James are full of delicious sensations, though I've never seen him take a bath. I doubt he gets to take a shower more than once a week or so, but I've never noticed an unpleasant odor coming from him. His smooth skin is often clammy and of so fine a grain that it reminds me of latex coated with sea water. On the other hand, his armpits, each with a tiny clump of coarse black hair, smell like honey, though there is a slight staleness that makes me start licking and biting.

Under James's coarse, shiny pubic hair is a large, torpedo-shaped penis of a liverish color. His balls are surprisingly full and hearty for someone his age, for I've noticed that many adolescents have testes that are small, hung high, and extremely sensitive to handling.

One thing that makes James comfortable having sex with me is that I remind him of the older guys he encountered in jail. This is merely a reference to my dumpy, middle-aged body and to the fact that I seem to him to conduct myself with a certain amount of authority.

Despite our rapport from the first moment we met, I've suffered extreme anguish from James's various symptoms of heroin addiction. More likely than not when we meet by chance in a midtown bar, he is sweaty and shaking. The assumption at such times is that I will "help him." This never seems like the optimum moment to stop being an enabler. One would have to be a better philosopher than I to see the larger purpose in not rescuing him from the cramps, vomiting, and diarrhea that take hold of him in the sleazy washroom.

Reverse peristalsis has become an established circuit of James's heroin-infused digestion. We can be anywhere with the music playing and the quips flying, a surly smile gashing his handsome adolescent face when—oops!—James spins quickly to the side, grabs an empty glass and vomits into it, coming back refreshed.

Despite these constant exudations, James's body and even his breath never lose their pleasant odor.

Upon my return from my father's funeral, I went to our midtown bar carrying my suitcase. My intention was to see if James would appear so that I could immediately take him home. Eventually, he strolled into the bar but in much worse shape than I'd imagined. His face was wan, and his tank top was covered with bloodstains. I'd assumed he'd continued with the methadone for which I'd made a week's advance payment. Instead, he'd gone back to shooting after only two days. With logic typical of the addict, James blamed me for not being there when he finally came to and leaving him homeless in the winter weather as a result. He said I'd broken a promise about letting him move in with me and that he'd had to spend four nights in the park.

As we talked, his mouth became sullen in the bar's shadowy mirror. His scowls leapt at me in white-toothed flashes from the mirror's muddy water. His butch clarinet of a voice honked rude answers to my prying questions.

Because James didn't like the schoolmarmish tone of my voice, when I tried to touch him, his meaty forearm convulsed. It jerked back to strike me... but caught itself just in time.

He hoisted my suitcase, and we walked down the block to a hotel frequented by hookers and drag queens. I studied his arm's recent puncture mark with its ragged collar of purple. James said he'd stayed at the hotel last night on the basis of a deposit and could only redeem his clothes or watch or wallet by paying the balance.

So, he went upstairs, and I forked out the sixty-four dollars. Then he came down holding a few worthless clothes, followed by a slim, young gay guy in new clothes and blond hair cut in a longish style that looked provincial. This made it clear that I hadn't paid just for James but for his friend as well, who kept the room for another night.

I told James he might as well spend the night at the hotel. When he eagerly agreed, I said I hoped that "you two faggots" would sleep well in each other's arms. His blunt hands clenched into fists and began swinging. They made wet smacking sounds against my cheek and temple and screeched across my teeth like fingernails across a blackboard. The blond shrieked, "No, James!" as I stumbled toward the exit stairs. But James followed and swung one more time, making me tumble down all six.

I picked myself up, and he pursued me into the street, after which the blond came running and managed to drag him back inside.

My lip was slightly cut, but my calf suddenly inflated, sections turning a hideous purple. I began a fast hop toward the corner, fearful he would reappear. Then he came toward me holding my suitcase, one arm spread in a gesture of supplication. His coat was shedding stuffing in the places where I had wrenched it. His pale face was furrowed and suctioned by sobs.

The blond was trying to tug him away from me by the hem of his coat, but James put down the suitcase and wept into his hands. Neon from the lingerie sexshop saturated the drop of blood on his knuckle with extra color. This made him look like a statue of a religious prophet transfigured by an awful revelation. Drag queens on their way to a club picked daintily around him. The blond decided to settle for the free room and went back inside.

We fell into a cab. My calf throbbed but my mind didn't dwell on the beating I'd provoked. Anyone who knows street people knows never to challenge their image. People from James's world own nothing but the strength or appeal of their bodies, which must always be represented as decent and of value to society.

What shrieked in my thoughts was the realization that James hadn't bothered even to ask how my father was. So I told him he had died. James exploded into girlish tears again, burying his wet face in my armpit. His bruised hands clutched my sleeve, staining it with blood. As his temple pressed against my neck, I felt his pulse racing, and his body oozed sweat. We headed for the copping block on East 113th Street where he could put a stop to his withdrawal.

The cab driver refused to wait. With a curse, I climbed out and sat on my suitcase perched against a store window. My ankle had inflated to such girth that the pressure of my pant leg smarted. I hoisted it and removed the shoe and sock. Junkies passed by with only a sideways glance at the chubby white guy with the dark bladder for a calf. There I sat, propped on an Eddie Bauer suitcase in the middle of an East Harlem copping block.

At my apartment, James cooked up the dope. I lay on the bed with my leg raised, balancing a load of ice cubes in a twisted towel. Though the pain began to freeze away, the leg had become macabre. Concussed blood had swelled into so dense a pool that the skin seemed thin and ready to burst.

James grazed the leg with a kiss. The spike was still hanging from his arm by a pinch of skin. When his nervous system catapulted into the rush, he pulled out the spike and spilled out of his clothes, then onto the bed. I rolled on top of him, and he began to devour my face with his wet, cushiony lips. His mouth gaped open, and our tongues began to wrestle. I let my bad leg hang over the edge of the bed for fear of placing pressure on it.

Those who have had sex with junkies know about their hypersensitivity. They compensate for dulled nerves by a taste for meticulous pleasure. James's flesh pricked alive to contact like an arm that has lost circulation and is suddenly massaged. As I gnawed his nipples, I imagined the sparks shooting through him like hot sand. His head felt welded to mine as I yanked at a handful of his short, kinky hair. When his arms fell above his head, I licked his armpits with the flat of my tongue. His dick hardened against my belly; it was the "dope stick" phenomenon. The penis engorges more slowly than when the body isn't high, but once the blood is there, it's stuck. It allows endless stimulation, and orgasm builds slowly. The waves increase and break like the proverbial multiple female's.

His cock in my throat was like an electrode that seeped some of this slurred desire. Then it rushed into me so I, as well, felt I was becoming high. On and on I worked with the game of feeling and desensitization, leaving behind the thought of my hurt leg. James's necro-withdrawals were erased by sudden surges of feeling. My hands, mouth, and weight trampled his beached body in a simulacrum of his earlier battering of me. He began to groan.

Street people have topsy-turvy personae. His voice, which was usually a growl, had become a thin, womanly moan. There were hulks with long prison records who'd lurched into my bed and somersaulted into the passive role in much the same way. It all had a certain logic as the thrust of machismo broke through the membrane to its subconscious opposite. The piercer became the pierced.

He hopped off the bed and posed before the mirror, separating his ass cheeks with his callused hands. His cock wasn't hard, but his haunches undulated. Energy coursed through my thighs and into my groin.

I fucked James for the first time, though we'd fantasized about it before. But we had never thought I'd be one-legged. All I could do was lie on my back while James slipped on a condom and sat on it. Then I pumped my pelvis upward as my calves hung over the bed.

Like a switch flicked to off, both of us popped into unconsciousness. I jerked awake a couple of hours later, around dawn. My leg throbbed as if blasted by a blowtorch. He stayed passed out beside me, his breath fast and shallow in the junky's accelerated REM. sleep.

With the light, my anger ignited. I saw myself limp to the closet in search of a baseball bat to smash the sleeping body until every bone was broken.

But I hadn't even gone home with James, though I had been beat up. The second part of this tale is a fantasy. He'd gone to bed in the hotel with his blond faggot, and I'd hopped in cowardice to my cab. I spent the night alone in anger and shock with handfuls of ibuprofen. The next morning I went back to find my suitcase.

The fantasy is a symptom of what I wish I was, something more masochistic that is larger and more open. But even then I'd need a James who'd want to come back to me, and who would know how to transform into a pious model of remorse, after viciously wielding his fists.

Persistent Patsy

PATSY HATED the new crop. Every time they passed her desk over which her head hung almost as if to hide it from view (for nearly nineteen years), what she knew they were thinking scrolled through her head like an electronic ribbon. *What's... That... Senior... Citizen... Doing... Here?* She could see it ticker-taping across their own brains in an endless loop of contempt, sometimes spelled out in yellow LEDs ready for her proofreading skills, while she wondered, first of all, what font it was. It looked like that moving strip of news wrapping the edge of a building in Times Square, the one people stared at with their heads bent back. *What's... That... Leftover... Baby... Boomer... Doing... Here?* Wasn't it the old Terminal font from the DOS years, VT-100, with its Pac-Man associations? She had to admit choosing retro lettering to speak of the outmoded was a savvy "marketing strategy." What they didn't know was that she herself could easily have come up with such an idea—if they'd ever let her become a copywriter instead of demoting her to checking the figures borne of their questionable ethics. Regardless, it was too late now. Her company had switched from advertising to data mining for the Feds.

Nineteen *fucking* years at this firm. *Thirty,* she bet they thought as they glanced down at the top of her fifty plus-year-old graying head and bounced "millennially" past her. Past Patsy, that faithful old company girl, the sole office anomaly with no alibi, who wasn't an actor working part-time or a previously booted manager who'd had to come back as a low-paid receptionist after her rent spike. Patsy was just somebody who really had no excuse for still being around. Her only occupation, from what they could figure, was claiming a paycheck every month to finish her theft of their future Social Security fund, while also remaining busy developing an odor between her legs to broadcast her coming barrenness.

"Old maid," she'd heard one of the young and glib managers chortle as he marched authoritatively past her desk, and Patsy was convinced it was meant for her. The word had been used less humorously when she was a child, and those sporting such monikers obligingly donned orthopedic Oxfords to march in self-abnegation toward a hole in the ground. "Spinsters," like the one in Bette Davis's *Now, Voyager*, with mustaches and laughably outmoded names like Ida or hers—Patricia: a failed dabbler in the writing of amusing ad copy, with jokes no one had gotten.

A TV commercial

BATHING-SUITED WOMAN, standing poolside.

BILLIE HOLIDAY'S VOICE, singing: "Ain't Nobody's Business If I Do."

WOMAN: "Extra-absorbent Tampons® won't reveal even the heaviest flows…"

Close-up on her face, whispering: "… They're just too busy doing their job."

She dives into swimming pool. Every drop of water is sucked up.

WOMAN stands up, looks around: "Oops."

HOLIDAY'S voice returning: "… nobody's business if I do…"

Clever, she'd thought. "You don't respect the client's product," they'd accused. Whereupon they kept her proofreading their inane copy until the increasing ease of product exposure through the internet lost them one client after another. In the old days, the company had flourished selling what they called "paid advertising." Now it had been abandoned by manufacturers who relied on what they referred to as "earned media," covert viral injections of branding into psychographically analyzed social networks. What to do? The new batch of much younger directors took the reins and made a hairpin turn for big bucks. On behalf of government intelligence, they suspended all ad copywriting in favor of invading unsuspecting minds. All that was left for Patsy and her dreams of copywriting was checking numbers whose top-secret purpose no one even bothered to reveal to her.

You'd think cred came automatically from having any kind of job at this with-it firm, which was now a CIA-funded data brokerage offering cleaner, faster results for a mere six figures rather than the high seven demanded by old farts in suits at established companies like Lockheed Martin. The new management of T-shirted marauders didn't own suits and were hell-bent on making every one of those dinosaurs completely obsolete. Using the latest Google engineering as artillery, they blasted open every encrypted pixel on the web. Nosey and amoral as their internet espionage was, everybody doing it bore respectable scientific credentials—the way a gun sports a silencer.

The new media managers went about unlocking their information silos, which Patsy finally learned were insular systems of encrypted data to which they applied their gangster hacking skills, until they'd pried every last byte out of them. Not one of those bushy-tailed sneak thieves ever expressed the slightest opinion regarding the later use of such data. Their apolitical alibi—"just doing my job"—halted all self-examination on the spot. Their flippant irony and flimsy hipness kept them quite buoyant and perky, despite the fact that these were based on the most fragile smidgen of confidence. What was more, she thought a kind of post-AIDS Tweedledee neutering was showing at the edges. When Patsy, who'd just turned fifty-four, glanced at one of their crotches, all she could picture was smooth blankness, like Barbie's. How trenchant could their celebrated wit be when they lacked any strong opinion? How far could they travel on the notion that just making money was some kind of "cause"? Under their with-it urban carapaces roiled a repressed jumble of confused feelings, guilt about sex they confused with ultra-sophistication about it. If they really were looking for irony, there it was in the mirror. What was more satirical than a CEO in a trucker cap and rolled-cuff jeans, an accountant convinced granny dresses were radical camp, or a crew of live-juice guzzlers obsessed with avoiding contamination? "Take the stairs!" a young tech had shouted disapprovingly at her as she waited for the elevator. Apparently, she was wasting his electricity and raising health insurance rates by not being interested in prolonging her life through aerobic exercise.

These days, Patsy's pet peeves about her co-workers' false superiority were echoing nonstop through her increasingly tormented mind, like ears suffering from deafening tinnitus. For some reason, the words were now continually spelled out in that retro Terminal font. She also could not stop rehearing and respelling the *spinster* word or doubt that it had been a reference to her. Then she overheard something in the ladies' room that really set her teeth on edge.

"Hey Caitlin, ever get down with that dude Noah? I hear he's a ten-second spurter."

Spoken in a falsely blasé tone, as if from one hooker to another. It was clear they weren't talking about her this time, but couldn't those six-figure-earning pubescents who were so oedipally conflicted (they had to be since so many lived at "home"—their parents' places) fathom that she still knew what it meant to "get down"? Not on your life. Those castrates hadn't the slightest idea she'd probably been poked by a lot more phalluses than they had, even if most of her eggs were gone, and taking her pleasure was currently limited to self-fondling. Which didn't at all mean her multiple orgasms were any less seismic! Patsy froze mid-track in her stall with a few sheets of toilet paper in her raised fist, exerting all her strength not to blurt out, "I've fucked oodles more than you, honey—while you were still browning your diapers!"

"Fucked to death," a sardonic conscience in her brain added, seconds after those arrogant bitches had left the ladies' room and it was safe to wipe and flush without being overheard. To *death?* Well, kind of, if she was being honest with herself. Throughout the reckless decades of the eighties and nineties, she and her girlfriend Doebee had raised hell—three, four, five nights a week for almost twenty years. They'd even had a contact at *Page Six* who'd plant their photos in a few gossip items that covered the more notable moments of nightlife.

Photo: Patsy and Doebee mugging for the camera in classic movie bombshell poses.

Caption: *This old-style legendary nightlife duo came inches from being pulled in for indecent exposure, after they showed up at 2AM in matching cellophane-wrap raincoats and little else. Go, girls!*

Those were the days, she thought ruefully. Nowadays, you were likely to find lead-ins on that page like, "Eighty-year-old Jane Fonda says she has 'closed up shop down there.'" In the old days, club crawling had been her temporary stopgap against the tedium of this job, which had been her only reason for maintaining a more "appropriate" wardrobe. Doebee had called those work rags "aseptic drag." (Doebee herself didn't need to change her club look to match her work look because her job was in the business of fashion.) Despite a radically younger management, you still couldn't show up at Patsy's company today with pink hair or fishnet stockings or ripped jeans, or packed into a vinyl dominatrix dress and teetering on stiletto heels, not even on so-called "casual Fri-days." Patsy's "real" clothes were now permanently stored in a trunk in her closet along with a rainbow assortment of wigs she'd used to trans-form her prematurely graying head into Barbarella's, Bettie Page's, or a host of Marvel Comics and anime characters—in the good old days.

Not *to* death but *toward* death? That was a lot closer to the truth. It had been a slow, involuntary wasting she couldn't blame on her worst enemy. At the age of fifty-four, aging was no trip to Bountiful but to the inevitable stultification of brazen sensuality, kind of like when the cheese removed from its wrapper softens too much because somebody forgot the Zip-Loc® and finally reaches *deliquescence*. That was the loveliest word she could find for her unpreventable, uneventful and dismaying decline. None of her coworkers would be able to suss out the aesthetic or semantic powers of such a word. The new breed of anyone working with words had absolutely no interest in them. At the moment, honesty was the best policy… and it kept her sitting on the toilet long after she'd flushed… thinking back again to more of the sample copy she'd dared to submit to the bosses in hopes of a promotion…

A TV commercial

Blaring honky-tonk music.
Voiceover: "Think all canned meat belongs on the
wrong side of the tracks?"
Medium-shot: *row of ramshackle houses*
on poverty row street.
Pan: *across railroad tracks to*
street of upper-middle-class homes.
Sounds of a string quartet.
Zoom: *to window. Inside, a well-dressed*
woman is making canapés with Spam®.
Behind her, an elegant dinner party in progress.

Voiceover:

"Then meet ©Hormel…

  and pamper your guests' palates."

The bosses hadn't been into that one, either. Even though her talent for repartee had been considered legendary in the club scene—especially when enhanced by blow—it had never acquired a single professional perk here.

By the time Patsy met Doebee on Friday at the end of that same week, she was still smarting from such self-avowals. She knew her friend was bound to guess something was awry. Lunch together was a once-a-month ritual since everyone else from the old days had passed on to the Great Beyond, or married and settled down with children, or "closed up shop" like Miss Fonda. Only the two hell-raisers still espoused the live-fast-die-young creed—high-risk sex, oodles of booze, drugs, and occasional tricks turned for get-high money—although neither of them was doing any of that these days. By the late 90s, when club after club succumbed to the pressures of the new antiseptic urbanity and closed its doors, the girls had stubbornly continued an escalating quest for hot boys. The age gap between them and these love objects had widened to the proportions of mother-son pairings, so they began referring to their unreliable cuties as "sardines"—scared little fishies meant to be caught and devoured. Efforts at triumphing in the world of counterculture fashion were now more cutthroat than ever, not to mention colored by uglier envy. Between them, the two girls passed band members (including one who really had become a rock star) as casually as the aluminum bra, fur-trimmed panties, clear plastic skirts, fifties handbags, coke spoon earrings, psychedelic paisley blouses, or chevron fishnet stockings that one or the other borrowed or boosted. I mean, they were on a budget. Both had passed the forty mark, too; not to say that each did not still have access to drugs and dealers for coke, molly, ice, mescaline or an occasional snort of *mantega* (heroin)—all of which they pooled as blithely as their outfits. Patsy and Doebee were proud of sharing everything, even the crabs Doebee caught from a hot drummer and left behind on Patsy's couch.

Doebee finally ended up in the emergency room after a coke binge and made the decision to go to Narcotics Anonymous. Once she was out of the picture, nothing was the same for Patsy, whose hunger for The Life gradually faded into the start of her current deliquescence. Unlike Doebee, she'd never made a life-changing choice. She merely succumbed to the attrition of growing older; but at least, in her mind, her libidinal juices were still a-rage. She hadn't changed when it came to desire, just gotten tired of that scene. Nevertheless, she succumbed to the pressure of derisive smiles and began to dress in a more mature way, hoping never to become one of those left-behind ladies she fearfully studied on the bus, who seemed not to have changed perms, shoes, lipsticks, shoes, or nylons for decades.

A sober Doebee began rising in her career as a fashion photographer's assistant and eventually opened a company with her own stable of shutterbugs to rep. She was beginning to take in the shekels. Her oral needs had always exceeded Patsy's, whose stronger addiction was promiscuity, so Patsy kept her figure, aside from a little drooping here and there, and Doebee became unbelievably obese. On Friday, when Patsy walked into the Italian restaurant where they always lunched, Doebee had already opted not to wait any longer for her friend and had gone for the dessert before the main course. Over cheeks bulging with tiramisu, her eyes widened considerably. She gulped the stuff down as fast as she could in order to exclaim, "What in fuck's wrong with you, paleface? Come on, spit it out."

Patsy picked up the oversized menu to shield her face and gazed guiltily over the top edge. "Why don't *you* spit it out?" she mocked, gesturing at Doebee's mouth with a tip of her head. Then she explained, "You know I tend to dwell."

"On all the wrong things. How's the job?"

"Sucks. How's the diet?" Might as well swipe back again, she had figured; but Doebee had defiantly plunged her spoon into the tiramisu and was shoveling it into a grotesquely wide-open mouth, baiting Patsy to produce her usual look of feigned disgust.

"Unlike you, I don't turn away chubby chasers!" fired Doebee defensively.

"Yours is not to reason why?"

"Not when copping cock or pie."

"But what's the sense if there's no elegance, beauty, or meaning?"

Doebee tried again. "Would you fucking tell me what the fuck is fucking going on? You really think you can hide it? I already know you wouldn't demean yourself getting laid by somebody who's only satisfying a fetish, like I do. But your mind must be ragging on office politics again, am I right?"

"Not exactly," answered Patsy ruefully. "I was, uh, reviewing the past is all."

"Shit."

"Am I supposed to go on in some glazed state of mind like everyone around me seems to do? I mean, doesn't everything start with being totally honest with yourself?"

"Yeah, if you have a whole roomful of other people who made the same mistakes and will help you accomplish that gargantuan task," instructed Patsy, "not to mention a higher power to rely on when you finally admit you're powerless. You know, I never understood why you wouldn't go to NA with me. You can't do this shit alone is what I found out."

Patsy didn't want to put down her friend by saying what she was really thinking, that the Anonymous movement was just a reductive crutch too close to the evangelical conversion process to provide any deep insights; and anyway, the idea was too complicated, so she just answered, "Some sisters are doing it for themselves."

"Thanks for the tip, Aretha. Now clue me in to your epiphany."

"Working with those shallow automatons who think therapy is a phone call to their life coach has made me feel as if my own life may have been little more than a cop-out."

"Hmm. Keep spilling."

"All those years we frittered away. Fun as they were, I suddenly think I was just avoiding bigger issues."

"Such as?"

"Love, for example. We never learned to love."

"Huh? What was Traherne, chopped liver? You were with that motherfucker for five fucking years."

"You're not being serious, are you?"

"*You* certainly were, my dementia-compromised friend. I should replay some of the thirty-page monologues about destiny and passion and transcendence you fed me to justify that tragic affair. Meanwhile, he stood you up more times than he ever put his tongue in your mouth, much less his dick in any other receptacle. What a total asshole."

"Exactly. And I spent five years on it, without achieving anything. I ended up right where I started, alone and depleted. Nor did I ever advance my career, as you certainly have. For me, a great love seemed enough."

"Which is why I want you to come and work for me. We do marketing brochures too, you know, all that stuff to promote our photographers' skills, their bios. You'd be great at that."

"I would have agreed yesterday. But I've been thinking back to some of the ads I concocted. They really weren't that good, Doebee."

"Bullshit."

Patsy finally picked up the menu and signaled to a young waiter. She ordered a Caesar salad and sparkling water. Doebee ordered a main course of gnocchi with a side of sausage. As the guy jotted down the order, she leeringly lowered her eyes to his crotch. The waiter scampered away.

"Jeez, Doebee, that guy was so light in the loafers, I was afraid he was going to float away with our orders."

"You never know," said Doebee. "Anybody could be a chubby chaser. As for the gay part, at this weight you can conceal a lot. Maybe I'd ask him to roll me in flour and look for the wet spot while I blew him. He could think I was a fat dude with a very little weenie."

"Stop!"

"Well, I had a friend who used to smuggle in a pint of rum when she visited her man in prison. Just hid it under one of her folds, and they never found it during inspection."

Patsy's thoughts wandered back to Traherne, her final boyfriend, who'd been twelve years younger than she, and the calamitous *coup de grâce* that had permanently pushed her out of the running. She wincingly considered the amputated end of that affair the way you'd study the mangled remains of a car accident involving family members. "My one and only experiment with a millennial…" she mumbled to herself. It had taken her more than a year to stop looking at pictures of him or purposely walking by the places where their affair had taken place and then bursting into tears. She'd finally succeeded, but now an image of him came swooping into her mind without warning. She remembered how shamelessly she'd chased that pansexual, metrosexual drunkard who dabbled in Ritalin and Special K and insisted on covering up a large port wine stain on his cheek with a heavy layer of foundation makeup. It was something nobody had questioned in his club kid days, which he'd already outlived by several years and a few pounds when she met him.

What had attracted her was his beautiful skin and rather exquisite bone structure featuring exaggerated cheekbones and a frontier-man jawline, as well as his enormous frightened eyes, not to mention ample, cushiony lips. These features were transformed into a macabre version of themselves when he had a hangover, however. His mouth didn't change, but the eyes sank into their sockets and were ringed with dark circles, making him look like a skull with luscious lips glued on. The cirrhotic fluids seeping from his liver temporarily discolored his complexion and produced a kind of Gothic bilious glamour-pallor, a common problem for substance abusers who had severely sculpted faces and delicate skin and therefore could not even work as models. Her friend Doebee heaped scorn on the problem by dubbing him Edie Munster—Edie after the doomed Warhol superstar Edie Sedgwick, because he often affected her hair styles as well as her eye makeup, and Munster in reference to an old TV show that spoke for itself. When the relationship endured longer than Doebee had hoped, she began ridiculing him with a second nickname: "How's the Groovy Ghoul?" She loved pointing out that no matter how hip the look or tight the pants, hungover he was no more enticing than a Young Frankenstein.

Twenty-something men from the club scene like Traherne were often hobbled by excessive narcissism. That meant that anyone with enough patience who was proactive enough could get them, even if it did reduce them to passivity close to a corpse's. Once captured, they could be trained in the scenario of being lovers, which is exactly what Patsy had done. The Traherne brand of narcissist seldom wants to be outdone on the physical plane by his partner and generally ends up with a much more lackluster mate who is also more intelligent. At that point in her life, Patsy fit the bill on both counts. Traherne used her to explain to him who he was and could be, preferably in the most hopeful terms. Time with Patsy was a much-needed hiatus for him from "life as runway." She was someone to hold and comfort him when he arrived at 5 a.m. with his makeup smeared and part of his port wine birthmark show-ing, while coming down from that evening's drugs and convinced—although only temporarily—that he was far from the fairest of them all. Because he was obsessed with the fact that he'd outgrown his image of himself, he ate up her claim that he also had a soul that might come in handy in a few more years. The truth was that he had traded all that in long ago by deciding there was no path in life that didn't involve com-petition and *schadenfreude*. His only weapon for that battle was an extremely developed talent for passive aggression that took the form of a kind of erotic jiu-jitsu. Tender-eyed and satin skinned as an ephebe, as adept at sex as a porn star with an abused childhood, he'd also mastered an incredible passivity that manipulated her better than any identifiable aggression, because it made everything that went wrong seem to be based on her choices because, to all appearances, he made none.

His most subversive ploy was his infernal text messaging. Traherne always texted her right before a definite date and didn't show up unless he got an answer, even though the evening had been previously estab-lished as absolutely on the calendar. Patsy would stare unblinkingly at the screen of her phone for the last hour before leaving her apartment, because if she missed his confirmation text, he wouldn't appear and would claim he'd thought she must have canceled. He always got to their destination after her, anyway; and while he was on his way, he'd text at every corner about his location and expect her to acknowledge she was aware of it. He certainly didn't come off as very observant, either. Dur-ing their entire relationship, he never learned the location of any of the light switches in her apartment. She came home one night from an art opening from which he'd demurred and found him prostrate on the couch in pitch-blackness because he didn't know how to turn on the lights or the TV.

Traherne's degree of commitment was the same when it came to the abortion she'd scheduled after she became pregnant from him. She was under the anesthesia before he finally texted "to confirm" but, worse still in her eyes, he never called afterward to see how it had gone. She phoned him a few days later to read him the riot act about his lack of concern, and he countered with, "I don't really believe in abortion."

Instead of fizzling, their affair was blown to smithereens. A week after the abortion, on his way to meet Patsy at McDonald's to "discuss our relationship," Traherne was already having trouble with his balance. A cop took one look at his foundation makeup, ripped jeans with fishnet stockings poking through them and antique Mary Quant mod blouse—as well as the can of beer he was guzzling—and nabbed him for drinking on the street, which was illegal. The fragile lad in the inappropriate costume was shipped to the Tombs while Patsy waited in McDonald's for over three hours, nursing a black coffee and staring at her phone screen with increasing fury.

Traherne called the day he got out of stir to explain what happened, and they rescheduled their discussion for later that same evening. This time he appeared at her apartment on time but looked traumatized, with wild eyes and a mottled complexion, as if still in shock. Patsy later understood that he was expecting to be coddled and comforted because of what he'd just endured, but her final mistake was insisting instead that he fulfill his promise of relationship talk, even if he was in no state of mind to handle it. She quickly discovered that he actually had no awareness of the many things he *hadn't* done—it had all been unconscious—or how hurtfully she'd experienced his pathological passivity. When his amnesia became more and more offensive, she lost it and viciously hurled a shoe with a spiked heel at his head. It did miss him, but he was absolutely devastated by what he termed her "unprovoked cruelty." For the first time, his rage found direct expression and detonated to the tune of smashing her television screen and punching holes in the wall with his fists until his hands were bleeding, and she began to fear for her own life…

"Oh, sorry." Patsy excused her vacant expression to Doebee. "I was just thinking… about—"

"Weren't we talking about 'love'?" said Doebee, enclosing the word in quotation marks she formed with two fingers of each hand. "If you figure out where to find any of that, I hope you'll clue me in. Lemme grab the bill. As Eleanor Roosevelt once recommended, when you sit down to a meal, always consider those less fortunate."

What neither friend realized was that the chance both were hoping for currently existed closer than either had thought. Patsy returned to the proofers' pool from lunch, and there was a new employee sitting at a desk in the third row. If you stood at that threshold and looked over heads bent over desks and checking figures—a vast, stagnant puddle of mostly brownish hair—your eyes, well, her eyes, fastened upon a miracle. They ground to a halt on the left of that row, four desks in from the aisle and nearest the window, where blond perfection shimmered like an apparition. Later she'd be able to tell you that the row in which he was sitting was almost exactly nine feet from the open entrance to their proofers' pool, although the precision of such information made her feel ashamed. In between proofreading tasks, idle periods that sometimes lasted more than a half hour, as she walked back and forth between her desk and the ladies' room or the kitchen, she had quietly amused herself by counting her steps between his row and the threshold of the proofing pool. Later, at home in her studio apartment, she measured and then averaged the length of her stride and came to the conclusion that there were almost exactly nine feet between the open, arched proofing-pool entrance and his row.

Beginning on Monday, she was able to verify that the left side of his body was near enough the window to be touched by the sunlight streaming in, which for the next nine work days skimmed him exactly between 12:03 and 12:06 p.m. and then crept along his body inch by inch as the afternoon progressed, cutting him precisely in half by 2:35. From her own desk, she kept a log of the sun's progress as it crowned the object of her obsession. After more days accumulated, the raiment enlarged and managed to fully envelop him fully by 4:55 p.m. all the way from the top of his glorious golden head to his surprisingly slender Oxford-shoed feet, which were both planted unmoving on the floor as he stared into his computer screen. This was all she was granted for the entirety of each afternoon: his back and the blazing cap of hair fully illuminated, for about thirteen minutes.

About two weeks later came a miraculous day when they found themselves alone together in the elevator at the end of work. Was he British? His voice sounded so, although it could have been South African. At any rate, she surmised, he had to be a foreigner because he was bothering to talk to her. Perhaps her age had made him assume she was one of the bosses. Or maybe he was gay and simply bored by the ride down and also unresponsive to differences in female appearance, which she had to admit was unlikely—especially for a gay guy. Certainly, she was making too much of this, but the post-contact glow was exquisite enough to erase most verbal details of their encounter. She struggled to remember. He'd introduced himself as Jude and taken the trouble to explain that, although he was temporarily seated in the proofreading pool because of a lack of desks in the other room, he was actually a data researcher, developing a new algorithm that promised to mine more penetratingly. Absurdly, the last word in his sentence caused the color to rise in her cheeks. Nor did she think she'd sensed any one-upmanship in the admission. It was not designed to put her in her place as a lowly figure checker. Haughtiness and irony had been missing from the way he blandly offered it. It felt more like "Getting to Know You…", the song. And that's really how it felt: set to music. Subsequently, she seized it as license to mumble "hello" whenever she arrived at work after him and walked past the desk where he was enthroned.

Their second encounter turned out to be life changing—again, in her opinion. She encountered him in the company kitchen during a coffee break and told him about going from proofreading advertising copy to checking rows of figures for accuracy, as well as her resentment regarding that "demotion"—as she saw it, even if her salary had been raised. Perhaps her remarks had sounded articulate enough to give him the hunch that she could do more, because the following Monday, there was a different sort of proofreading work sitting on her desk, a top-secret report exploiting statistics on terrorism that the company had mined, covered with red stamps reading *Absolutely Confidential.* Consequently, she was unable to ask him if this more interesting work was the result of his recommending her, because if he turned out to know nothing about it, she would have violated the warning of all those red stamps. Happily, he was the one to mention it first, explaining that he'd been dissatisfied with the proofreader they'd been using and had suggested her. Then he handed her a surprisingly thick stack of papers, which turned out to be an endlessly detailed confidentiality agreement she was supposed to sign, and he was gone.

Of course, part of the thrill (all superlatives were relative in this boring place) was being privy to firsthand information about the various leaks, phishing schemes, data thefts, extortions, and political trolling happening on the DarkNet, such as those hackers, probably Russian, who had conquered the entire city of Atlanta for more than a week with SamSam ransomware, during which everything digital in that city ground to a halt. Utility bills were impossible to pay, online banking disappeared, parking fines couldn't be collected, and police reports had to travel back a half-century to being recorded by hand on hard copy. Patsy was treated to complex, detailed theories about how this might have been accomplished, little of which had been shared with the public and about half of which she was able to understand. As she scanned the rundown of such misdeeds squirming through the net like high-powered insect borers, a malicious anti-establishment thrill she'd long thought dead began to stir in her. On the street at lunch hour, she found herself suddenly stopping to stare at a black leather motorcycle jacket in a chic store window before catching hold of herself in time not to go in and buy it. Her mood brought back an ancient memory of the hymen broken when she was fifteen by a body builder, who'd taken her on a risk-filled motorcycle spin through heavy traffic after she'd gone AWOL in L.A. from a namby-pamby high school trip, and had convinced her to go all the way in the wave-dampened sands of moonlit Venice Beach.

When she got back to the office, she found an even thicker manuscript waiting on her desk with a Post-It® bearing the word, "RUSH." Normally such a message would have made her sullen, but this time it felt "rock and roll." It was a report about video conferencing scams in the Balkans, one of which had lured its target, a high-level Romanian politician, into a sex chat room with a performing prostitute, who convinced him to meet her in the flesh after which he was kidnapped and tortured to reveal classified government information.

For the first time in her proofreading career, Patsy's speed and focus were becoming influenced by her level of interest in the material, despite the fact that she knew she was being trusted to approach all of it objectively and coolly to ensure accuracy. Even though her new lack of professionalism distressed her, she found herself galloping yawningly through reports about ISIS or WikiLeaks and giving detailed and affectionate attention to reports heavy with sexual descriptions. Struggling against their erotic power, she eventually went so far as to suspect that Jude was funneling those particular texts to her to excite her. Doebee, or anyone else, would have clued her in to it being an unlikely possibility, but she found herself rubbernecking the object of her obsessions when she walked past his desk to the ladies' room, in hopes of offering him a leering wink to signal that she knew he'd recognized her as a fellow connoisseur of the dark side. Each time she did this, he was no less fixed on his screen than before and never looked in her direction.

It made sense, she thought to herself. Obviously, her age and current appearance concealed the fact that she'd started her adult life in a bohemian context, replete with promiscuity, recreational drugs, and mostly unexamined radical politics. In other words, she'd led a life that prioritized impulse and pleasure, like so many who belonged to her generation. Sadly, the thrill of rebellion had trickled away like her egg supply, and as her hormones diminished, she'd slipped into this grayed-out life of bitter celibacy and resentful loneliness. Did it have to have happened? Regardless, she was through giving into it. She was all but convinced that her encounter with the golden data programmer was an invitation to come back to pleasure.

The new man in Patsy's life—as she already labeled Jude—became the one who was turning her juices back on. Objectivity and reason marinated in the flow of desire and softened, as happens when you fall in love—a different sort of "liquefaction." Alone in the company kitchen for her afternoon coffee, which she recklessly sweetened with three whole packets of sugar rather than the usual Splenda®, and lightened with a more pragmatic spoonful of Cremora®, Patsy obsessively reviewed her active years with the dry ruthlessness of an accountant. She compared them to the present, trying to determine whether, unlike Humpty Dumpty, she really could put herself back together.

She had never learned traditional feminine wiles like the ones her mother had known but hadn't needed them when she and Doebee had been on the prowl flouting every convention. Aside from the outrageous outfits she'd worn to the clubs, she really hadn't known how to dress, and she'd dispensed with the problem of stringy, prematurely gray hair by wearing wigs that were obviously wigs but that she didn't even remove in bed with men. She was the bearer of a lot of lucky endowments: intelligence; a wild sense of humor; long, still shapely legs; and small breasts that had retained some buoyancy. As a teenager, she'd tried to convince herself that her pale complexion had a pre-Raphaelite allure. She certainly still had the hands for it. Placing her palms on the table, she studied their paleness and thin, elongated fingers and verified that there were only two liver spots in sight. At the end of work, she'd get a jar of Porcelana® Skin Lightening Cream at Wal-Mart, where it was only $4.97. Maybe her hands had become a bit fluttery recently, but they were still slender in width with delicate wrists unmarked by creases. She next subtracted some of what had been lost, trying to determine the cause: innocence and hope, pale beauty replaced by a new mousiness, and clear eyes now marked by crow's feet. For some reason, these thoughts brought up the day she'd discovered what her mother had been hiding from her all her life. Patsy had so admired her elegance and grace, provincial as it might have been. She'd hoped she'd grow up with the same serene confidence in her appearance, the same regal walk. And then one day, as she was paging through a scrapbook of old black-and-white family photos, she came to a photo booth picture of her mother taken thirty years ago as a college girl, which she'd seen hundreds of times before. "I thought I was so ugly back then," said her mother, looking over her shoulder. "I looked at that picture and thought I was hideous." A trapdoor opened in Patsy's stomach, and part of her heart fell through it.

None of it mattered now, because she had a mission. Most exciting was the fact that she'd never fallen in love with or even been attracted to such a straight arrow of a man, with impeccably white shirts, starched collars, and clean pressed chinos worn over tight buttocks below a lithe, athletic torso. The precise cut of his soft blond hair never looked messy, and even his somewhat nerdy watch with its stainless-steel chain-link band was a kind of turn-on. She couldn't remember ever being with a man who'd worn a watch. So much of what excited her was in his Delft-blue eyes whose irises were ringed by a corona of silver-gray sparks.

They had a clarity that spelled total honesty and acute awareness. Just the thought of them cleared the haze of her decadent past exploits with doped-up drummers or unwashed artists wearing paint-spattered jeans. Imagining him above her, looking down into her eyes as her arms were wrapped around his clean body produced a sharp, thrilled intake of breath. And there was that smile, too, the most easy, unexaggerated smile, which revealed—but just a little—his gleamingly white, even teeth.

More remarkable than any of that was one of the feelings he was beginning to provoke in her. As if by magic, he was bringing her back "into the light." It took Patsy a while to acknowledge what that light was because her pride fought against it: the light of the *present*, which equally illuminated the new generation of co-workers she'd so maligned in her thoughts. Catapulted into the here and now with everyone she'd felt exiled from brought, at moments, a new and sudden ease. But there was also a problem. Despite the fact that the top-secret reports continued to accumulate on her desk, Jude himself remained no more than minimally accessible. The few times they ran into each other in the hallway or kitchen, he blinded her with his light, his intent listening, the way he addressed her so frankly with his eyes, and the smile, of course. Men just didn't do that unless they were interested. If that was the case, why had weeks passed without anything happening?

Patsy decided to take the bull by the horns. Maybe it would be a turnoff for him, but she vowed she would ambush Jude right after work at the entrance to the building. She'd create some visual excuse for standing there, not tying a shoe, since she didn't want to be bent over like that when he came out of the building, but perhaps checking for something in her purse, trying to find her cell phone, for example. She had only to look up suddenly and beam confidently and delightedly upon seeing him and then extend the encounter with some chatter.

She didn't recognize him for almost a full second as he approached the glass outer doors of the building from the elevator, probably because of the late afternoon traffic reflected in them. On the other hand, just those transparent overlays didn't seem enough to make him look unfamiliar. At that brief moment, it looked like the light had gone out of his alert, affable, outwardly directed eyes, his easy, open smile. Then he saw her and the thought passed out of her head as all of it turned back on; or maybe it was because he had come through the doors, and nothing was now confused by reflections.

"Hey!"

"Hi, Jude. Boy, I gotta get this bag organized! Oh, there it is, my cell phone!"

He was silent, merely observing her with those steady, uncomplicated-looking eyes, something she suddenly found a tiny bit unsettling. "Oh," she filled in chirpingly, "I never even thanked you for taking the horror and boredom out of this job as a galley slave. (She pronounced *horror* in a tone of irony she hoped sounded facetious.) I even like coming to work now. I mean, almost… it's almost… entertaining."

As soon as she said it, she realized her faux pas. At the word "entertaining," he'd looked askance for the first time and shifted his eyes from hers. However, the smile hadn't changed, and it was high time for her to go for broke. After a sharp intake of breath, she blurted out, "Hey, I know the coolest tapas place near here, with a full bar, too. Why don't we stop by for a bite—not to mention a nip."

"I know that place," replied Jude, as if he'd thumbed through a card file in his head and instantly pulled out a profile.

"Then you're in?" she asked a little too quickly. "I'd love to hear more about all you do."

He didn't agree verbally but began walking in the right direction. Patsy scooted forward to reach him, and they navigated the rush hour crosswalk together as her heart beat wildly. But the tapas place was crowded and noisy, with a live, loud *cantaor flamenco* singing over an amplified guitar.

"Hey, we're here to talk," she immediately snapped at the hostess. "Anything in a quiet corner?" Then she took Jude into her peripheral vision to check on whether the directive had made him uncomfortable. It didn't seem to have.

Patsy ordered a vodka gimlet straight off, and Jude just shook his head when the waitress asked him what he was having. The waitress picked up the menu and strode away. "Gotta have my after-work chill pill," Patsy offered as an alibi. He nodded; and immediately after, the strangest thing happened. It felt like somebody had flipped a switch connecting current to a bot. The somewhat vacant cast that had slightly unsettled her as Jude had walked toward the glass doors shifted, as if an electronic reshuffling had taken place. Jude's features and body language composed into an entirely different manner. Now he was radiating full-blooded interest and hearty benevolence in her direction while he studied her intently.

"You must have been quite a wild one," he suggested. He wasn't exactly leering; the expression felt more permissive. In fact, wasn't it what Patsy had been waiting for? She decided to take it as a compliment.

"Yeah," she giggled. "You probably wouldn't have recognized me. I was a real club kid."

She could feel him considering that information before offering, "From party girl to government employee, huh?"

She hadn't really thought of herself as one. This wasn't a government job. She just worked at a company whose biggest client was the government. "Jude, I was just a lowly figure checker before you came along, and originally, I had wanted to become a copywriter. You know, product ads... I still hardly know anything about the stuff we do."

"Then it was never your ambition to deal with such material?" he interrogated. Well, it wasn't really an interrogation. She ascribed such a feeling to her usual paranoia. "I meant, what we're doing now must be awfully dry and dreary in comparison with the publicity days," he coaxed.

Seeing her chance—yet again—she jumped on it. She arched her eyebrows, hoping it would be taken as mildly seductive. "Not any more, thanks to you. Some of that classified stuff you've been sending my way is pretty X-rated." She giggled, tempered it with a blush, and searched his eyes for verification that with that material he'd been courting her rakishly if indirectly; but all she saw in his eyes was that they were fixed more intently on her.

"Have you been telling your friends about it?" he said.

"Of course not! Remember? There's a confidentiality agreement."

"Exactly. So, uh, what do you do for fun?"

Was her chance back again? "I'm still somewhat of a... risk-taker," she intimated, without even considering he looked less like a risk-taker than anyone she'd ever met.

"Ooh, la la."

"What?" She certainly hadn't expected that. Maybe another switch had been flipped, but he actually was leering now.

"I suspect you're kind of a bad boy yourself."

His eyes went blank. "Really?"

Patsy was getting frustrated. Who was this dude? Some male version of a cock-teaser? At one moment, it felt like he was coming on to her, even a bit indecently. Then, suddenly, he was back to that bland, benevolent, enthusiastically accepting manner he'd exhibited the first time in the elevator.

"Mind if I ask you something?"

He nodded.

"You're gay, right?"

Jude smiled as if he'd been asked, 'Where'd you get that cool watch?' before answering, "No."

Things wound down to a standstill once she had a second drink and the two of them had eaten an assortment of tapas. The flamenco singer was really beginning to annoy her. She had to focus through the sound, and it was giving her a headache. When she and Jude parted cordially in front of the restaurant, she still felt like she hadn't gotten to know him at all. The small amount of information they'd exchanged was all about her. What was this, some kind of interview or something? For what?

Vigilant as Patsy was in the coming week, her data on Jude never increased. His manner had warmed, she assured herself. Any time they ran into each other in the company kitchen, he greeted her almost as if she were a close friend, and they talked mostly about trivial matters. She had yet to catch him chatting with anyone else. She even brought up the black leather jacket she'd seen in that store window and asked him if he thought it was "too young a look" for her. "Not if you like it," he'd answered generously. Patsy was at a loss. Either this guy led the most boring life in the world, or he was extremely shy and private, but that didn't match his increasingly affable manner. Late one night as she lay in bed, a sudden thought sparked through her. Maybe he was married, and happily. It was certainly possible. But what kind of married man was as curious about her private life as he was, especially the mildly off-color details? He encouraged little anecdotes from her about her daring adventures in Club Land, asked what kind of buddy Doebee had been, whether they'd ever gotten into any scary scrapes with the boys they dated or had ever supplemented their get-high expenses with a bit of drug dealing. Patsy loved talking about her past adventures because it made her feel a little like she was still that person, something that was backed up by her hope—waning though it was—that his enthusiasm for listening to such tales was actually fueling a subtle but increasing fire in him that he was bound to act on eventually. If that was the case, then her new splurges, directed by Doebee, were probably a good idea. For the first time in years, she was enthusiastic about shopping for clothes and began dressing her slender figure in vampish garb that was still within the spectrum of working girl respectability. She showed up in heels and a couple of chic suits with tight skirts, in Italian wool blends and colors that attracted attention. They certainly did. To her satisfaction, she caught more than one of her millennial co-workers glancing at her tightly outlined butt, and another momentarily distracted by the cleavage she displayed in the pink satin bodice by Chloe she wore under a jacket in place of a blouse.

Nothing happened. Was he just a voyeur, a man in a stable marriage who needed a few vicarious thrills? What a depressing theory.

It was the wrong theory according to the only other friend Patsy still had from her club days: Alejandro, a once handsome, still impossibly effeminate makeup artist with an over-the-top Spanish accent (think Charo). He may have been worn out from a twenty-eight-year passage through the cruel wringer of discos, backroom bars, and circuit parties, but he hadn't lost his style. During his salad days in the 80s and 90s, he'd instructed friends to refer to him as the "High Priestess of Love," a flawed reference to the 1955 film flop *The Prodigal,* loosely based on *The Gospel According to Luke* and starring Alejandro's favorite sex goddess, Miss Lana Turner. But these days, the High Priestess was nearing sixty and had become a lot plumper. He was more apt to identify with corseted dowager actresses from the 30s and 40s, such as Dame May Whitty, who'd played the elderly but nimble spy in *The Lady Vanishes.* Dame May was, in fact, the name with which he answered his cell on the very day when Patsy, in search of advice for the lovelorn, desperately rang.

"Suffering girl, let the Whitty woman loosen her girdle, take a look in her crystal ball, and discover the fate waiting for you with this dreamboat. Didn't you call him Jude? At least it isn't Judas. I'm already praying this love doesn't turn out like it did for Lana when she got gored in the womb by a bull in *Love Has Many Faces*. Hurry over, la daughter. Don't forget to bring some liquid refreshment to oil the Dame's divining powers."

When Patsy arrived, Alejandro was still in the kimono he wore as a bathrobe and in a very buoyant mood, which he ascribed to the house call of a burly Dominican plumber's assistant whom he'd led to the source of a leak by sashaying his hips in a come-hither motion stolen directly from *Gilda*. The strategy had paid off after the promised addition of a tip, and Alejandro, who hadn't yet recapped the tube of KY lying on his flower-patterned couch cushion, was glowing with fulfillment. Patsy had to shift the sticky tube to the coffee table in front of the couch before she could sit down beside him and take the bottle of Prosecco out of its bag.

"Ooooh, Miss Girl," he purred contentedly while wriggling, "what an engine of desire that laborer was. Such a tireless torpedo he was packing! It's a true miracle, and I've been reborn. I feel like I can have children again." Suddenly he shuddered and added in mock terror, "Pray to the gods that I'm not experiencing what happened to poor Rosalie in the Thomas Mann novella *The Black Swan!* The one who fell in love with a much younger man after going through menopause and thought she'd been rejuvenated because her period came gushing back, only to discover she had cancer of the uterus!"

"Not familiar with that one," said Patsy.

"You certainly are, daughter! I gave you a copy!"

"Oh, yes, well, don't worry. Didn't that character have a club foot?"

Alejandro had already passed on from that subject. "Lady, precious daughter, listen to Mother and stand up! Let your mother take a good look at you."

Patsy stood with a sigh and twirled around for him as he examined her carefully, stopping at her red patent leather heels and forcing his eyes to mist over. "Thank the gods! Your suffering has been a boon! The fires of love have transformed my little brown wren into a chic femme fatale. What a happy mother you have made me!"

Patsy flopped wearily back on the couch and slipped out of her heels. She stretched out her legs and propped them on the coffee table. "Mind my taking these off? They're killing me."

"Go ahead, *chérie,* of course. *Mi casa es tu casa.* Now. You're saying the blond demigod gracing your office might be turned on by you but never sticks the key in the ignition?"

"Right. I mean, I barely know a thing about him, but I can't shake the hunch that he's into me some way. I don't know how he does it. He gets everything out of me; the more off-color, the more into it he seems. Then, suddenly, he blanks out, and it doesn't go anywhere. He's completely private."

"Did you say *private?*"

"Yeah."

"Hmm." Alejandro stood and headed for the bookcase. "I'm going to have to consult my Book of Hours for this one, girl, go right to the top." He pulled out a hardcover book that Patsy noticed held a great number of Post-It® bookmarks and came back to the couch. "The Old Testament," he explained, showing her the cover, which pictured Joan Crawford in her living room with her two poodles in front of a glamor portrait of herself. It was *My Way of Life,* the advice book she had written in the early 70s. Alejandro began paging devotedly through it and then looked up sharply. "Did it ever occur to you that this stud is so mum because you haven't shown any curiosity about his interests?"

"But I want to! He doesn't talk about them, and I just can't figure out what they are."

Alejandro lowered his gaze and read a few more paragraphs of his handbook, then raised his head again. "You sound just like those wives Joan lowers the boom on for not making nearly enough effort," he said severely. "If I remember my catechism correctly, Saint Joan thinks it's the wife's job to figure out what her hubby's interests are. Just stopping by the office to ask for more money to get your hair frosted won't cut it. Nor does hubby really want to admire the new hat you bought. No, no, no, my good woman. If, for example, the head of your household is a trader, it's up to *you* to run out and buy *Investors for Dummies* on the sly and read up on the subject. Then, when he comes home, he won't want to hear about the woman who tried to rip a camisole out of your hand during a stampede at a Macy's sale that morning or how sweetly you treated the maid after she broke the floor polisher. No. Without, of course, neglecting to prepare an entire dinner and making sure your hair and makeup are absolutely flawless, you must sit down across from him in candlelight and casually drop a few pearls of wisdom about 'the market.' Make him think you were fascinated by it all along and check the market every day with thoughts of him, but that you never wanted to bother him. From then on, he'll be delighted to talk to you about what happened at work. And you'll be thrilled he isn't complaining about his boring evenings with you to his secretary at some Happy Hour. *Whatever* he is into isn't the point. *You* get into it, too, and act like you've always been. Even baseball!" At the last word, Alejandro couldn't help wincing.

"What if he's into snuff films?" asked Patsy.

Alejandro wasn't phased. "Miss Crawford would insist you visit the set of one of them to take notes," he claimed imperiously. "*Anything* for your man!"

"Okay. But how the fuck do I find out what he's into if he never mentions it, or changes the subject when I ask?"

"Use your *imagination*," said the former High Priestess of Love with a mysterious air. "You'll figure it out." Then he looked at Patsy with frustration. "O.k., why don't you start with Facebook. You can handle that, can't you?"

Patsy couldn't believe she'd never even thought of it. She popped up from the couch. "Okay, gotta get cracking. I appreciate your advice."

"Thanks for the divination fluid," said Alejandro.

"Huh?"

"The Prosecco!" he snapped rather irritably. "I need it to get into mental oracle drag."

As Patsy headed for the door, in a sadistic schoolmarm's voice he cautioned her with a Joan Crawford quote from *Queen Bee*. "And remember, Miss Betsy Palmer: Do *not* oppose me!" Patsy recognized the quote. It shortly precedes the scene in which the Betsy Palmer character hangs herself.

As Patsy had kind of suspected, when she got home and checked Facebook, there was no profile for Jude. He wasn't even on LinkedIn. The thought occurred that somehow she must have been aware of the unlikelihood of finding out about him that way, which was probably why she hadn't bothered to consider checking. She closed her laptop cover with a gesture just short of a slam and leapt angrily onto the bed. She was so enervated by her obsession that she succumbed almost immediately to sleep.

When Patsy arrived at work the next morning, another bulky manuscript was sitting on her desk, bearing the usual "Extremely Confidential" stamp. This one had to do with international espionage hacking efforts that had bypassed several crucial levels of Pentagon security. Before she went any further, she glanced up to see if Jude was sitting at his desk yet. He hadn't arrived when she'd come in and still wasn't there. Patsy's mouth composed a slightly sullen frown as she returned to her proofreading task somewhat haphazardly, skipping notations of algorithms she had no way of verifying and checking only words and punctuation. That was all she did until she got to page ten, the beginning of a detailed explanation of the method the hackers had used to bypass sophisticated military encryption and several-factor authentications. Something dawned on her. She returned to the beginning of page ten and began reading more carefully this time. Strangely, the tools the hackers had used weren't that dependent on high-level coding, although you would need a basic knowledge of Terminal Unix to understand them fully. The only instruments they had added to that to accomplish their sleazy undercover activities were ready-made algorithms found in the deepest realms of the DarkNet, all of which had been fingered and revealed by the investigators in this report.

How aware of future plans was Patsy when she slipped thirty-eight sheets of paper about these hacking methods between the pages of an industry magazine she'd retrieved from the kitchen and set the magazine to one side of her desk? Her only thought at the time was that she'd stumbled upon some material that—unlike most of the other texts she'd proofread—could probably teach her to understand some of this stuff, as well as the fact that there was an excellent chance the subject would dovetail with Jude's interests and preoccupations. Joan Crawford's advice had been right, it occurred to her. If you really want your man to value you, learn something about his calling and show him that you're not only sexy but smart enough to understand what matters to him—although, not quite as well-versed at it as he is, of course. *Thank you, Miss Crawford*, thought Patsy to herself. She knew Joan would look darkly on competing with your man. It was just a matter of sharing his concerns and excitements, sharpening your skills at becoming the "woman behind the man." Such an inner dialogue was enough to make her decide to skip lunch and wait until the proofers' pool was nearly empty. Jude was sitting at his desk now, but something perverse told her she had the least to fear from him. Unlike the others, he knew something about her, and for that very reason, he would never in a million years guess that she was capable of the strategy she was about to put into action; she was capable of it now only because her love for him had made her into a different person.

It took only a few moments to take the pages from between the magazine and photocopy them. Then she strolled casually back to the proofer's pool, not bothering to check on whether Jude was looking at her when she walked by his row, because his eyes were always glued to his screen and he never did. That evening at home, after downloading a Kindle book about basic Unix commands, she began trying to match lessons in it to sections explaining the methods the hackers had used to breach Pentagon protections. This turned out to be fairly easy because they had not relied much upon their own expertise to succeed. She took a pen and a piece of paper and made a list of terms that pertained to the information, then educated herself a bit further about their meanings so she'd be able to bring them up in conversation. She had no intention of revealing anything from the report to Jude, not only because it was confidential, but also because it may have come from the work of another employee. The last thing she wanted him to think was that she'd violate security and couldn't be trusted. His life seemed devoted to entrapping such individuals. Suddenly the queerness of her attachment struck her. 'I'm in love with a kind of cop,' she thought to herself. All in all, such people had been "pigs" in the enemy camp during her bohemian years.

Easy as it had been to learn some of the Unix commands, understanding the algorithms the hackers had stolen from the DarkNet turned out to be a lot harder. Patsy reread the information in the report about these algorithms over and over and looked up some of the terms. Eventually, she came to a conclusion that made her feel anxious. The only way to become articulate about that part of the operation, which was probably the most interesting material, was to go into the DarkNet and actually see the sites from which they'd been lifted. Of course, all of them had already been busted by the investigators. If she was going to do this, she had to collect details from the report about alternate domains known to harbor similar information.

Patsy's nighttime research continued for almost a month; and, although she finally located websites on the DarkNet that were still disseminating such destructive code, she couldn't understand the first thing about them. She had hit a brick wall and still had nothing hot with which to pepper her conversations. During the day, her "friendship," or whatever it was, continued with Jude, who even consented to go to lunch with her on two occasions but still revealed practically nothing about himself. She came away from the second occasion with a dreadful hunch. Maybe Jude never told her anything interesting about himself because he just *wasn't* interesting. He was just a dull research scientist from some place like MIT, who had nothing to talk about but algorithms, Java, and other kinds of coding; and, perhaps, unlike Patsy with her underground origins, he got no kick out of the kinky descriptions in the research and just thought of them as part of criminal evidence.

She began to realize how unrealistic it had been to believe he'd sent her sex-laced reports to turn her on. Regardless of her fantasies about being Angelina Jolie in some adventurous caper, her prankish Brad Pitt was still missing. The realization was deeply depressing, which is probably why she decided to splurge at a Fifth Avenue spa for the sheep embryo face mask she'd been pining after. She called Doebee and made her promise to meet her there at lunch hour the very next day.

Patsy lay on a sheet-covered table under blinding light while the cosmetician opened her derma with a micro-needling wand, an electric baton with a bunch of small needles at the end, used to make tiny punctures in the skin, which was supposed to allow the sheep placenta to seep deeper into its layers. She had been unaware of this stage of the treatment, and even though her face had first been covered in numbing cream, she was feeling very uncomfortable.

Doebee sat beside her, paying little attention to the beautification process while she made short shrift of a couple of bagged calzones. Before Patsy's entire face, including her mouth and cotton-ball-protected eyes, was covered with a thick layer of the serum, she tried to spin out the entire story of how she'd made a gargantuan effort to learn enough about her inamorato's field to impress and interest him, until she collided with the more technical aspects of her quest and came to a standstill. Ignoring the censorious look of the cosmetologist, who'd pointedly asked her to please take it outside, Doebee went ahead and lit a Virginia Slim, taking a deep puff.

"Doebee, you can't smoke in here!" protested Patsy, whose voice now came through the layer of serum in a barely distinguishable gurgle.

"Give me a break. How many times have I told you that we were put on this planet to seek gratification? As far as I'm concerned, an after-lunch stogie is well worth the chance of being booted out of any snob spa." The cosmetologist offered her a furious look and began peeling off the facial, which had hardened to a plastic-like mask.

Patsy sat up. "So, do you still think there's any chance with Jude?"

"What I think is that you're a pea-brained idiot! *Fuck* Joan Crawford! Why in Satan's name would you want to have conversations about that shit with anybody, even if he was your number one interest? How much fun would it be discussing programming with him after sex?"

"All I know about him is that he invents algorithms to catch criminals."

The cosmetologist tried to ignore the conversation and instead forced a bright smile at Patsy. "All right, dear, all done. Why don't you take your friend out to the roof patio until your face dries and you can come back for the wax and sealing."

"What is she, a sports car?" quipped Doebee, which earned another daggered look.

When they got to the roof patio and its improvised garden, the two women stretched out on chaises longues. Doebee lit another Virginia Slim and continued her counsel. "I think you can assume that he happens to be a human being. Even a mathematician could be into watching football. Or cars. Or motorcycles. Or threesomes, for fuck's sake! Or breeding goddam Shih Tzus, as it were! And he might even be married, which is something you should find out *pronto.*"

"But how?"

"You gotta find a way to get into his computer, honey. Anybody who has to work in an office has personal emails, website histories, maybe even porn sites on their computer to take advantage of during breaks. Who doesn't need contact with their real lives at least once during those goddam endless eight hours a day? He's gotta have something on there."

Doebee was right. Of one thing Patsy was now certain: she had to find out more. There was still the possibility there was a side of him that jibed with her. She didn't mind shy, private guys, she told herself. More times than not, they turned into dynamos when they were horizontal. His easy manner and animal magnetism suggested other interests, even if he did keep things close to his vest. Such considerations cleared her head and changed her strategy, but she was going to have to take a chance.

That evening, seated at the kitchen table with her laptop, Patsy spread out her notes and carefully re-followed the instructions for plunging back into the DarkNet. Then she located those illegal hacking sites (marveling at the fact that their creators had so little imagination they'd designed all of them with the same visual: Guy Fawkes in a mask) and downloaded the algorithms. If she had the nerve or enough knowhow, she planned to use them to hack into Jude's computer. It obviously couldn't be as protected as the Pentagon's, which had been penetrated using the same strategies. Maybe she didn't understand the algorithms, but they were executable files. She would probably just have to click on them. What was more, she was already familiar with the company's VPN, which employees used to upload documents when they were working at home. From there, she would surf past all the individual desk stations and slip into Jude's using those hacking tools.

It took her thirteen hours to bypass the various encryptions and multi-level password verifications protecting the cyber-brain of the man she loved (she had to think of it as that personal and fleshly in order to keep going). By 7:08 a.m., she had finally slipped from the office server into his operating system and had even constructed a fantasy metaphor for it in her mind. Against a black background of vast negative space, the Jude she'd liberated was slipping out of his clothing and coming toward her with outstretched arms. What she hadn't bargained for within the hundreds of files to which she suddenly had access was the amount of code she had to plow through, none of which she understood and all of which seemed endless. There were hundreds, even thousands, of pages of it. Worse still, Jude's Outlook folders were all encrypted, so she couldn't access any of his email. There was no sign anywhere of personal messages of any kind. Maybe it was a good thing and meant that he wasn't married.

Anxious to get this over with, she started on his web history and bookmarks after verifying that he only used one particular browser. Here as well there were few footprints left behind except for several URLs he seemed to have visited repeatedly. The names of each were scrambled with encryption, too; so, without knowing what it was, she merely clicked on the first one; whereupon a video of Honey Boo Boo filled the screen.

Patsy watched the chubby ten-year-old's exhibitionist antics for about ten minutes. Holding a liter of Mountain Dew and a quart of ice cream, she was laugh-screaming hysterically as her panting mother, at a time when she was over 300 pounds, chased her frantically to wrest the booty from her hands. So, one of Jude's extracurricular activities was being a Honey Boo Boo fan? It was too unbelievable, so she clicked on the next bookmark, which turned out to be TLC's canceled reality series, *Here Comes Honey Boo Boo*. It just didn't make sense! Nevertheless, the next three websites were discussion boards about Honey Boo Boo, and it looked like Jude had even highlighted some favorite postings in pink.

That was the moment when it dawned on Patsy that there was no way out. She'd always thought most scientists were square, but that wasn't the point. Did Jude have a daughter, possibly from a failed marriage? If that was the case, would an educated man like him be encouraging her to get off on Honey Boo Boo's white trash charm in some ironic or contemptuous manner? Or maybe his daughter was from a very early marriage, a one-night stand; and Jude, being the principled man he was, didn't feel it right to abandon her or judge the culture she had to grow up in. He'd conceived her at seventeen when he lost his virginity with a girl in a trailer park; and the daughter he'd left behind didn't feel any irony watching Honey Boo Boo but related to her, even envied her. What could he do about it?

Still, even that didn't justify watching *Here Comes Honey Boo Boo*, thought Patsy. If it was for his daughter to enjoy, regardless of the girl's environment, Jude was a lousy parent for exposing his kid to negative behavioral models. What was next, reruns of *The Anna Nicole Show*? Likewise, even if there was no child in his life and all this was just for his fun—well… you could start by calling him classist or sexist and then move on down the line to deranged and/or unbelievably idiotic!

Patsy's 7:15 cell phone alarm rang out with an app that produced a gong of increasing volume over a ten-minute period; but she just let it go on, so that its sustained Zen temple notes became the soundtrack for her increasing stupefaction. There had to be an explanation, something she could relate to, something that truly denoted what was best in him.

She clicked on the next bookmark. This time the screen filled with garish, infantile colors that formed the phrases:

MY LITTLE PONY
FRIENDSHIP AND LOVE

"MY" was enclosed in a cartoon heart. A quick search revealed that it was a TV cartoon about six Technicolor ponies who promoted friendship and foiled enemies, and now it was also a blockbuster movie. She read on about *My Little Pony* and soon discovered another strange phenomenon. Apparently, a lot of good-tempered dads watched the show with their young daughters, and this had produced a parasitic culture of grown men who were obsessed with the show and called themselves "Bronies." They had clogged 4chan.org with Brony postings that included images of pastel horses until they enraged many on that website, and then they had even started attending Brony conventions where they collected and traded memorabilia.

It was as if an inflated dirigible in human form had suddenly been punctured and was flattening before her eyes, revealing a shocking lack of a third dimension. The euphoria that she'd experienced at the thought of him up to this moment began to trail away like vapor as the reality leaked out of it. Was he a Brony?

The time was 8:50, and she hadn't slept all night. Nor had she any intention of taking a sick day after what she'd just discovered. She wanted to look Jude straight in the eye and ask him for an explanation of these bizarre discoveries. He couldn't really hold her invasion of his privacy against her if she made it blatantly clear how deeply interested she had been in him and how eager to share his interests.

Given the lack of time, she took a taxi to work, aware that she was still going to be about a half hour late. Bursting through the glass doors at the entrance, she swiped her card through the reader and sailed past.

Once in the elevator, a crazy mood came over her. What had just happened had injected her obsessive quest with such ridiculousness that it was close to comedy. Reviewing what she'd discovered on his computer, she felt almost as if she were straying into an alternate universe. She wouldn't have been the slightest surprised if the elevator stopped at a floor and Pee Wee Herman or a hookah-smoking caterpillar stepped in. With sudden hysterical hilarity in the face of such surreal absurdity, she threw her head back and let out a long manic laugh that filled the elevator car just as it stopped at her floor.

Reaching the proofers' pool, Patsy marched toward her desk past Jude's row and saw him sitting in front of his computer as always; but this time, instead of the perfect posture he always exhibited, he was hunched forward and had brought his face so close to the screen that he seemed to have suddenly become very near-sighted. Was he trying to hide or something? Then Patsy noticed six people gathered around her desk. One of them was her boss, who was in intense conversation with a severe-looking woman in a navy blue pantsuit that looked more like a uniform. Listening intently to their conversation was a man dressed in a similar way, but his suit jacket had fallen open, revealing a holster strapped to his side. The other three were men wearing rubber gloves, and one of them was kneeling to break the lock on one of her desk drawers. "Take it slow," the woman instructed in a clipped tone. "Could be booby-trapped."

Another man had disconnected Patsy's computer, which he was lifting toward an empty insulated box. The last was packing away the contents of her other drawers, including a collection of advice paperbacks Patsy felt so demeaned by that she hadn't even mentioned them to Doebee. They included *Straight Talk, No Chaser: How to Find, Keep, and Understand a Man* and her most embarrassing of all, *How to Get a Boyfriend and Keep Him—The Bulletproof Strategy: FOR WOMEN ONLY.*

As soon as the six glimpsed Patsy, they froze for an instant; and because Patsy stopped suddenly and backed away, the woman and man in navy blue strode purposefully toward her. The woman pulled out a badge and held it in her face. "Patricia Willoughby?" Patsy nodded, and a split second later, the woman had bent her over a vacant desk and was holding her head pressed against it with such force that her nose was crushed sideways. She felt her arms yanked behind her and cold steel encircle her wrists as the handcuffs were snapped shut.

Less than a half hour later, she sat next to Agent Nickel, the woman from the CIA who had arrested her. They were in the back seat of a car heading toward an undisclosed location where she was told she'd be interrogated. The charge? Unauthorized access of a government computer with intent to compromise top-secret information. It turned out Jude was no employee of her company. As is the case with most firms that have government contracts related to the fight against terrorism and coordinated with Homeland Security, this company had been assigned Jude as an undercover CIA agent to oversee security and safeguard sensitive information.

Ms. Nickel had seemed exceedingly severe during Patsy's arrest, but she really wasn't the harshest or least sympathetic of federal agents. She even felt a little sorry for her naïve charge.

"All I was trying to do was find out if Jude and I had anything in common," Patsy said plaintively, sniffling a bit. "I was… kind of in love with him, you know? I was only looking for personal stuff."

Nickel let out a rough chuckle. "What federal agent would leave the slightest personal material on their computer? It's against regulations. Are you going to tell me you weren't aware of that?"

Patsy shook her head piteously. Nickel looked at her with a smidgen of disbelief.

"But he did have it," protested Patsy. "He had all this Honey Boo Boo and My Little Pony stuff."

Agent Nickel's expression darkened. "If I were you, I'd shut my mouth right now, Miss. You're digging yourself in a lot deeper by showing inordinate interest in the only two pedophile investigations this agent was involved in. By the way, Jude isn't his name."

"What is it?"

"I cannot reveal that. But maybe you should have spent more time on the web rather than digging into his files. You might have found out how many adult males are fans of My Little Horsey or obsessed with Honey Boo Boo. Now that sure isn't normal! I advise you stay away from the subject when we get downtown."

"Pony."

"What?"

"It's My Little Pony, not Horsey."

"Whatever. There's just one thing I can't get over. How did a rank amateur like you manage to get past all those encrypted protections and three-factor log-ins?"

Patsy considered the question in silence for several moments and, finally, in a rather brave little voice answered, "Don't you know that love always finds a way?"

The Buttoned Lip

THE TWENTY-ONE-YEAR-OLD from Manchester is unshaven, with an almost skinhead-short, close-cropped pate. It's a very masculine face, with a sturdy symmetrical nose and warm amber eyes, except for the mouth, which is trim, buttoned. Maidenly is the first word that comes to mind.

Despite that mouth, this appears to be the head-butting face of a mosh pit boy, a working-class Brit, you find yourself thinking, before you let your eyes move downward to discover that the chest is shirtless, that the over-broad shoulders are skeletal as the blade of a sailboat rudder, that they sprout long pipe-cleaner arms clutching a skateboard, and that the chest is emaciated enough to outline the breastbone.

He first came at you some three or four weeks ago, through the glaring flatscreen of a computer, during a night of substance abuse as you sat naked before your camera, accepting anyone who dared log on. The virtual tangle of limbs that ensued was so hypnotic, mixed with the sparkling trail of drugs through brain cells, that when he typed that he was coming to New York for the first time and suggested you meet him at the airport, you found yourself typing, "I'll be there."

Now here you sit in a recklessly racing taxi with the stranger, ready to install him in your apartment at least for a night, just to get a taste of the real thing. What you hadn't bargained for were his rail-thin limbs or his voice, which is pea-thick Manchester, so full of indie music neologisms that you wish you had subtitles. Still worse, sensing the unfamiliarity of this speech to your ears, he's quickly lapsing into an unnerving, catatonic silence, a buttoned lip.

Nothing unbuttons it even when you get to the apartment, where he sits on the most comfortable chair, knees apart. He's not a murderer, you assure yourself; there's something too laddish and fragile about him. Through the baggy jeans, which have slipped to the top of the groin, revealing the elastic of his underwear, poke pointy kneecaps, pulling the material around his narrow thighs.

You come toward him, and embarrassment floods the amber eyes. "Not yet," he whispers, as you encircle his wrist with your hand (a thumb and forefinger nearly do it) and lead him gently to the bedroom, where the wooden scarecrow unfolds into something smooth and serpentine, weaving through your legs like multiple silk scarves, pinning you to the bed and covering your skin with bold, plush kisses, then revealing something enormous and hard, almost thicker than his thigh, you find yourself thinking as you grasp it.

Later, a sense of disorientation begins to flood the apartment as he sprawls in his underwear in the same easy chair, his lip rebuttoned, his eyes distant and avoiding yours. You suggest going out to dinner, but he shakes his head; restaurants frighten him. You suggest taking a walk; after all, he's never seen New York; but he sheds his shorts and strolls to the bedroom, into which you follow, and it begins to spin, becomes an ocean of moans. The lip unbuttons into a flaming cavity, the long legs coax you into magnificent positions. That night, he holds you like you're growing from him, and when dawn breaks, his mouth again begins stoking you into gasps that feel beyond your control, grunts of ecstasy that leave you embarrassed.

Later—is it that afternoon or the next?—he is still there, silent and naked on the couch, then sitting on the chair in front of a soundless television, avoiding your eyes. You try to keep busy, fool with the computer, decide to wash dishes; then, struck by the futility of everything, come back to be near him.

Time is beginning to simplify; the sessions on the damp and rumpled sheets are multiplying. To friends who call, you seem strangely distant. You turn down invitations, lying next to him before the soundless television instead. Your shoulders are relaxing like never before, your belly and buttocks letting go.

You realize you are beginning to lose count of the days; is it three or four days since he arrived? All this is invaded by his silence, as if you were living in an aquarium, a watery prison. You are beginning to feel desperately unhappy, empty. You can sense his increasing remoteness; his face seems to become more and more expressionless except during sex. You think of pulling a scene. But you know he won't answer.

How many days later is it? A week, ten, twelve, sixteen days? Your bills are scattered on the table unpaid. Bathroom towels lie on the floor in a wet heap. The small of your back aches. You walk with a limp. On the chair is a scrap of paper with bus times written on it. Down the hall, he is stuffing his wrinkled clothes into a backpack and lifting the battered skateboard. You can't believe you are grabbing his hand, trying to make him put down the skateboard, pushing him back onto the bed. "But you wouldn't talk to me, you wouldn't look at me. Why? Why?" you hear yourself say.

For the first time, he gazes straight into your eyes. "That's why I can leave now," he says almost tenderly.

"Were you using me?" you implore, but he's gone already.

A Libertine

AS I LOOK BACK over the last thirty years, my very active sex life forms an endless line of faces, some masked by forgetfulness or darkness (probably because they happened in the dark, with faces that were never revealed), and some still phosphorescent and palpable, still able to fill me with longing or distress. But one early episode stands out as if it were yesterday, despite the fact that it happened when I was barely eighteen, and probably for its failure. The question in my mind is why I let it happen.

He was an older man in my eyes, but as I look back on it, I can still see youthful forearms and smooth skin poking from a pink Izod alligator shirt, as well as a full head of hair. So what seemed old to me at the time must have been barely grazing thirty back then. I also remember a soldierly rigidity and two parenthetical lines beginning to harden around a rather compressed mouth, under mild, blue, too-youthful eyes. Chino pants and the kind of loafers I associated with golfing or lawyers on Saturdays.

He didn't particularly appeal to me. Even then, I was more comfortable with the wiry, skinny anger of the barely legal and still bored by the prudish judgments of riper male resentment, always associated with the father. Then why did his clipped voice, which commanded me to follow him at a distance of a few steps behind, with my hands clasped behind my back, make me fall into step like a junior prisoner?

He had a small apartment in a part of Manhattan that I considered a boring place to live—the East 30s. It was in a middle-class high-rise, filled with a few nondescript pieces of furniture, like a corporate apartment for those just passing through, everything suggesting an absence of aesthetics, a sparse, drab isolation, and a lonely, perhaps even mean-spirited, life. The closet door in his apartment was open, and I could see that the closet was empty. But in those days, there was always a flash of pleasure in entering the space of someone else's deprivation, exploding their alienation for a few sperm-filled moments with the power of your body. Such pleasure was increased by his vulnerable eyes, now burning with a kind of destructive excitement. His look was meant to turn me into a robot: put me into what I later heard called a "fugue state" by a psychoanalyst friend, a level of stylized emotion that makes you act like a hypnotized automaton. It's a state in which crimes are committed and risks taken, and its pleasure lies in dehumanization.

I was to remove all of my clothes and stand at attention, he said, the idea being, I suppose, that nakedness in the presence of a fully clothed body is humiliating; and to be honest, following that order did compress a breathless charge around my body, as if the air had congealed and all arrows of desire were pointed at me. But—unfortunately, I thought—his sadism had the limitations of the typical male, learned in horseplay or on the sports field, all square angles and barked orders, none of the minute, exquisite sensuality some of us associate with S&M and those pointed arabesques of irony and teasing torture.

I was only to become an animal, a dog, chase rolled-up balls of paper on my hands and knees, my discomfort increased by knees striking the cheap parquet, my balls swinging between my legs; and if I returned a tossed ball between my teeth by the time he counted to five, I'd be petted and allowed to press my lips against his thighs; if I failed—and I did as he counted faster and faster—I'd receive a series of whacks of an ever-increasing intensity on the butt, always more carefully aimed at the spot where the scrotum joins the flesh over the prostate.

Big deal, I remember thinking; but now that he was standing in his underwear, I took some comfort in the rocky feel of his muscular thighs, made more appealing by the short amount of time he allowed me contact with them.

Even so, the routine tired quickly, threatening his dignity. So he opened a dresser drawer and removed a noose, the straight end of which he tied firmly around a coat hook attached to the top of the closet door.

Why did I feel no fear, only a dull, suspended excitement, the way a ten-year-old does when he holds his breath, wondering if it will make him faint? It was the touching bid for intimacy in the eyes of the man's curt face. For what is the most riveting moment of a horror film? When the murderer looks at his prey with imploring, childish eyes, a disheveled request for compassion. So, knowing that what was to follow would be the only thing coming closer to the feeling of love, I obeyed, standing on tiptoe against the door as he slipped the noose around my neck and gently explained that lowering my feet would make the noose choke me. I had to keep my balance so that my neck remained high enough to keep the noose slack, or I was a goner.

If someone had been able to ask me at that moment how I could have consented to such a position, the true answer would have been that I knew the man would save me if I slipped. And this certain intuition raised my estimation of him in the context of this contrived situation, put me in his hands, and even filled me with a mild tenderness.

I hadn't counted on the blindfold, a handkerchief pulled tightly around the eyes and tied in back. Perhaps not so surprisingly, the total darkness produced a blissful abandon. Obviously, I was still at an age where abnegating all responsibility conversely recalled the security of the family nest I hadn't vacated so long ago. If only I could regain such blind trust again, now that I'm in my later years and assume, as I always did then, that whoever's driving just won't have an accident, that whatever drug I share with a friend will lead to pleasure and not the emergency room. The flexibility and complacency of youth can't be re-conjured once the caution and consciousness of age inevitably set in. Back then, however, it was still with me.

This is why I stood balanced on strong toes, playfully testing now and then how much the rope would chafe my neck if I lowered those toes a little, tasting the silence in the room as a kind of anticipation of something wonderful to come, a surprise, an enlarging, imagining his eyes on mine and the proud pleasure of possession with which I must be filling them.

The majestic silence was marred by noises, small scurrying sounds like a rodent's. I considered whether the man was coming toward me with a knife, or fingers spread and held in an open circle to strangle me. However, that care was assuaged by the thought of how cheaply made these modern buildings were and how thin the plasterboard walls were. This was certainly no man who wanted to be embarrassed by a scandal. Everything about him was too middle-class. But then, there could be the very quick effect of chloroform…

By scrunching my nose firmly in, I was able to make the blindfold slip down past my brow ridges; and by turning my eyes severely to the right, I made out the sight of him crouching at the heap of my clothes on the floor, going through the pockets, then removing a cheap little address book in which I had the habit of scrawling the numbers of friends. I had almost nothing but that to steal—nothing else but a couple of dollars. Still, the gesture annoyed me, and that's why I squealed out, "I want to stop."

Immediately my prudent partner padded over to the doorway and unhooked the noose from the door hook. He didn't have to tell me my words had broken the spell of our intimacy and that our game was over. The eyes had resumed their scolded, youthful, prudish look, like those of a little child told too soon that recess is over. To my questions, he explained that he had gone through my pockets for the thrill of complete control over me, as a way of violating my privacy.

Such an admission made me feel small. I had so few secrets to hide.

And this is how building intimacy became bad sex, reduced to a shoddy game between two grown-up boys in a building for insurance agents or flight attendants. And that is why I quickly left an apartment and a man who probably had very little of a life of his own and hadn't even received much of mine. Next time, I'll try to be nicer.

The Worst Place in New York

THE WORST PLACE IN NEW YORK is the surface of my bed, an area of 3,922 square inches bought by caring parents to support my lately overfed body in comfort and offer it a feeling of security that may extend my life by warding off illnesses caused by stress or fatigue. But this mattress positioned in an East Village building of poorly renovated apartments on a noisy street is the locus of certain activities of various degrees of comfort and risk and now supports my body next to one of considerably greater density due to its much younger age and many street brawls, its seasonal stints on an Alaskan fishing boat, its past as a transient avoiding arrest warrants, and its subsequent terms of prison.

A feature of the body that shifts the surface of the mattress out of the zone of security intended by my parents into a zone of chaos and possible danger like that of the busy street outside is the flat, tense chest. It would feature inflated pectorals if the body had been developed in a safe gym requiring a steep subscription but has instead been hardened by all that fighting and flight and work. Most of the power is seated in the back and stomach and forearms and wrists and thighs and hands (instead of the chest and shoulders) due to hauling, shoveling, punching, running, and kicking, as well, I surmise, as the tension of buried anger smoldering in every gesture and hunching the muscles into coils of potential threat.

This is not to say that the scarred, tattooed body that lies on this bed after its most recent incarceration for assaulting a Grand Central commuter who struggled against its theft of her purse is not capable of striking gestures of affection, or even elegant tenderness. Actually, gestures of sensuality would be more apt a word: impulses of the moment with no follow-up, commitment, or sense of contradiction were they to lead to other impulses, such as illegal appropriations of property or bursts of uncontrollable temper.

The possibility of this surface transformed from a place of rest and protected sleep to one of pleasure and risk and danger to become the worst place in New York seems somewhat likely considering the personal history brewing not very far below the sensual surface of this caressing, stroking, occasionally kissing, very dense body next to mine. He portrays himself as reborn and recovered thanks to months in a drug treatment program in which he was placed after serving this most recent prison sentence. Yet there is a hollow quality to his claims of new respectability touted by his starched, white short-sleeved shirt, his loose, pressed chinos, and those improbable loafers that looked so out of place in the East Village bar where we met. Under the shell of this wholesome image, I imagine, are deep chasms of hopelessness, promiscuous anger, black cynicism expressed in desperate ways. There are hints that he still looks at life in the same way as he did before his supposed recovery, which merely dumped him from the drug treatment center into a new bout of homelessness, though not yet long enough to wrinkle the wholesome white shirt and chino pants.

That shell of decency was removed long ago, as his temptingly dense flesh is spread out on this space of the mattress. But now the lean, strong hands covered with callouses and scarred cartilage on the knuckles are already gripping my shoulder, while the powerful arm with its homemade tattoos has my neck in something between an armlock and an embrace. The insolent, scratchy voice is already barking its boasts, commands, and interpreting as law what is happening on the television near the bed, while mocking my weak comments or crowing about plans for success in the rainbow, drug-free future, mentioning some of the objects in the room with a touch of angry envy, as he lolls against me and stares at my black cat, which seems to represent to him a consciousness he cannot master. It stays seated like a black sphinx, throwing back his gaze. And he's not the type who'll let anything humiliate him. Perhaps amplified by a substance he took in my bathroom, his teeth are grinding so hard that I can hear the vibrations in my own skull. It always happened that a child, a girlfriend, a prison guard behaved in exactly the same way, he's explaining. But he won't let an animal get away with it. Because on that Caribbean island when he was eleven before the death of his mother, he was forced to apprentice at a slaughterhouse. So that initial revulsion and tenderness and shame at lives cut short moment after moment soon changed into a sense of mastery. And now it's essential that he let the cat know who's boss. I have to use all my soothing, accommodating craft to lure him into forgetting that black cat. So I boost his ego, trivialize the incident, and build him up, becoming ever more diplomatic, admittedly finding my nerve in my swoon over the miracle of such a hard, alert, young body dropped onto the surface of this bed like a time bomb ticking and coiling toward an unknown moment of detonation.

But his sharp, hurt laugh is beginning to sound like something cracking. It's ready to go off in an irrational flash: the prelude to the subjugation of one male by another, on this electrified surface over which menace radiates in exhilarating waves.

To take my mind off it, I study the scar on his forehead which he has told me came from a foster father. When he was thirteen, he took a dollar bill from the man's pants pocket. Rage gushed from the foster father's eyes and contorted, drunken mouth as he lifted a sewing machine and hurled it at the boy. The spindle dented his forehead and slammed the back of his head against the peeling plaster board beneath the velveteen print of Martin Luther King. The impact of the collision affected a nerve in his face, which partly explains the frequent grinding of teeth and the lopsided smile curtailed by that grimace, I suppose. The extra cartilage on his hands must be from the bare-knuckled boxing he practiced one summer at the age of fourteen to win money to buy heroin. If he was knocked out, the small audience in the vacant lot bought him a bag to pay for the entertainment, and if he knocked out his opponent, he also got a share of the bets on him so he could buy more of the drug. This explains the slightly chipped front tooth, points to the blunt scars on his shins from tripping and falling on car parts in that lot after taking his shot of heroin and collapsing.

In order to win his bouts, he had to picture what happened when he was six and his father came in with noisy, humid breath, leaning over the mattress where he and his mother were sleeping, using superhuman strength to yank up the edge of the mattress until it was standing on its side as he and his mother rolled out of the warm, safe space, and her bony body thudded against his on the chilly pine floor. He had to crawl away as his father grabbed her by the ankle and dragged her across the floor toward the stove against which he knotted her head over and over until blood matted her long, dark gleaming hair. She'd always had such beautiful hair.

I really should not think about this. The more I look for reasons for the river of violence flowing below the voice, the more apt I am to provoke it. He pushes START on the remote control of the VCR. The Asian woman on the screen is being wrapped ever tighter with the silk cord, the legs spread-eagled at a wider and wider angle. The hairs covering her vagina seem improbably straight and stiff and long. Her eyes roll upward in their sockets, and her head thrusts back as she gnaws on the strand of hair in her mouth while fingers pry apart the lips of her vagina.

It would be most sensible to surrender to this force field he has created on the mattress surface slipping so far from the influence of my parents who bought it. Farther and farther away we seem to float. Or perhaps it is they who are receding like a camera image in reverse zoom. My best chance for safety is to believe implicitly in what is happening and accept his inflated claims, paranoid suspicions, ravenous mastery, tattoo, scars, chipped tooth, accusing empty eyes, bulging thighs, rapacious fleshy lips, steely back, deep sculpted armpit hollow.

Now his teeth are biting playfully but too roughly into my neck, the broad thumb and forefinger gripping my nipple in too firm a pinch, the heavy-as-marble thigh pinning mine under it, the mattress surface spinning in space as surrender makes my nipple melt into the stinging pressure and my neck into the bite as his full weight begins to crush me.

So that I must breathe in and out in synch, can only breathe in when the terrific breath breathes out or when the probing, insolent tongue in my mouth lets me come up for air. While the hands grip my temples with such tearing force that I'm sure they are leaving marks, and the body shifts to push my head against the wall as his penis rends my throat in two like a stake thrust into rotting wood and I gaze up at the shoulders bulging as if they were about to rip a tree root from the earth. Ripping me by my roots from the everyday boundary of the mattress surface into a rushing world where whores must pay or die and where our father is God and enemy.

In fact, the surface of this mattress feels open and flowing now. Lying next to me is a naked muscular man wearing a condom. The tip is flooded with semen. A sullen, humiliated look troubles his eyes. Light footsteps are heard through the ceiling in the apartment above. He leaps to his feet, pounding belligerently on the wall because people have no respect, then he is back down on the mattress surface again to light a cigarette as if nothing had happened.

But something has happened to me. I have become so relaxed, transparent, open, that the expression floating to my face immediately informs him of everything that I am thinking. The porno film is finished, and the TV program is back on. He explains what is happening in it, but he can see by my face that it is not so. My lack of submission annoys him, but it is obvious from the bored tolerance in his face that he is not surprised this has happened. He takes another drag from the cigarette, and when he exhales it, he farts and laughs. But the laugh is at his expense, his vulgarity, and I roll aside.

The surface of the mattress is reconstituting. It really is a quality mattress. Strongly stitched and reinforced, buttons sewn at predictable intervals, firm and regular, with a lifetime guarantee, it's the kind of mattress that might be a godsend for someone having to work in the morning.

He is getting dressed. Putting back on the same socks, which betray a faint odor, picking up the pressed pants that had been carefully draped against a chair, putting on the starched shirt, which looks slightly limper than it did before. The cat comes back to perch at the foot of the bed. As he takes the money I have removed from the desk drawer, his eyes focus on the floor. In looking for his belt, he has to walk around the perimeter of the wide mattress, which I have settled back on, the TV remote in one hand, waiting until he walks out and the door clicks shut.

To leave me alone on this strangely spacious surface, in the rank odor of sweat on the damp sheets, a stale silence clothing the hollow sound of the TV, life returns to its meaninglessness, and the surface of the mattress expands its boundaries against the living world, gets infinitely wider and more barren, horribly bright and stale, surrounded by darkness, and in its isolation becomes the emptiest, most cursed place in all of New York.

Myra

AS THE YEARS PASSED, my contempt for myself settled into a kind of grudging acceptance. Slowly, I began to realize that my sexual desires were settling into a definite pattern that was far different from the norm. As long as I could, I clung desperately to the hope that I was merely going through a stage, that this would all transform itself into a normal sexual routine. Two incidents that occurred very close to each other put an end to this and changed my mind about ever having a normal sex life.

I had taken a tremendous effort to force myself to begin dating girls, but after I began, I found it could easily be limited to the sisterly friendships I was used to, coupled with a few friendly kisses in the dark. To my surprise, I soon became very popular with all the girls, although the boys still distrusted me and thought that I was a pansy. We were at the age when boredom and impatience with the status of a minor hits the children of the middle-class, and they begin to experiment with drinking and wild parties, in imitation of their parents. Most of us were only playing around. There would be secret beer parties on a Saturday night, out on some lonely stretch of road, followed by making out in the back seat of someone's car, never anything more.

There was one girl named Myra, however, who had established a reputation for herself that stretched far beyond the imaginings of anyone else her age. She was already dating college boys, and rumor had it that she had screwed five of them one night in a shack behind her father's house. For some half-defined reason, I was fascinated by her, and I did my best to attract her attention. There was something about her aggressive, impulsive manner that drew me to her.

She was a fairly good-looking girl. Her effete, nicely sculpted face and black eyes were complimented by a turned-up Anglican nose. Her unusually curly black hair was always kept cropped very close to her head, and her face floated gracefully atop her slender swan's neck. Her figure was strangely husky but not fat, and she usually concealed its curves with a cape or smock made out of some outlandish material. The most outstanding thing about her was the amount of beer she could consume. At sixteen, she was already an alcoholic. After a few drinks, she could take on any man, although without alcohol, she was strangely withdrawn from all sexual activity.

Myra's position in our school was extremely precarious. The girls hated her, and the boys held her up to the contemptuous dictates of the double standard. She was a good fuck, they said. None of this seemed to bother her. She moved as fast and as straight as a bullet, reaching her mark and then moving on to another without regret or shame. Often she was the aggressive one, swooping down on her sexual prey and forcing him into submission. In effect, from a conventional point of view, she was extremely masculine, and this may have been one of the reasons I was so attracted to her.

When she began to notice my interest, she held me at bay for a long time, as if sensing that it would be impossible to handle me the way she handled the others. Eventually, she took me on as kind of a traveling companion in her ventures. We would go to a bar where they would serve us without any hassle and get loaded on beer. Then she would get louder and more outrageous until she had attracted some eager beaver to our table whom she would crush with the weight and superiority of her wit and then would drag back to the notorious shack behind her father's house.

Usually, I did my best to attach myself to other friends in the bar as soon as her eye began to wander, but one night was different from all the others. We were both especially drunk, and Myra was in especially good form that night, laying us all flat with her vulgar, sweeping wise-cracks between enormous slugs of beer. Her purse, which she had fashioned out of an old tobacco pouch, lay carelessly on the table before her, money and keys spilling out of the top, and she kept dipping into it to pull out bills for a round of beer or for the jukebox.

She shoved a wad into my hand. "Buy us a round, baby, and play K-2 again, will you? That's my favorite, old K-2," she said to everybody. It's 'Klondike Kate,' wailed out by old Louis Armstrong's horn. "Here, put in another quarter and play it three times."

When I got back with the drinks, she had a small fellow next to her by the collar. She was giving him one of her Mae West routines.

"Ya shouldda seen me up north a coupla months ago, babycakes. I was doin' the old soft shoe to 'Klondike Kate'—right on top of the bar. Had everybody in the place tossin' quarters at m'feet." He blinked and tried to smile politely while she took another sip of beer.

"Let me see," she said, tapping a quarter on the table in time to the music, "think I ended up on the corner of Main and Broad at four in the morning that night—stark naked." I laughed, but her companion colored and made an embarrassed effort to smile.

"Old Colt 45 will do it every time," she added.

I knew that most of the rip-rap she laid on people in these places was merely composed for the occasion. Shock appeal was her main strat-egy of conquest. This time, however, she had tried it on the wrong person.

He stood up and cleared his throat. "Well-uh-I have to go to the men's room for a minute."

"I certainly hope they let you in," she called after him as he stumbled toward the john.

Soon we found ourselves alone with each other and closing time drawing near. She looked at me with that mixture of drunkenness and deliberateness that I had seen her use toward other boys but never toward me. "There is absolutely no reason why you can't come back to the shack with me," she said.

I started to protest, but she silenced me. "I know. You've never screwed a girl before. But just don't worry about a thing."

"But—"

"Stop," she slurred drunkenly. "I don't want to hear another word about it." She placed her hand on the small of my back and slipped her fingers a little past the belt. It did not arouse me, but the feeling was kind of pleasant.

"I'm really inexperienced," I said.

"Don't you worry about a thing," she cooed. "Not a thing." And she began to rub my back with a soothing circular motion.

As soon as we got back to the shack, she pulled out a couple of beers from a hiding place and tossed one to me. Then she flopped down on the bed next to me and propped herself against the wall. I sat rigidly on the edge of the bed, a little drunk but still very uncomfortable.

"Why don't you relax?" she said.

I took a fast swig of beer. "I am."

With a sigh, she reached over to a little phonograph by the bed and put on a raunchy blues tune. We sat there silently for a few minutes, listening to the scratchy wail of some broken-hearted lover.

"How can you do-oo-oo this to me," he sang.

Finally, she slapped herself on the side of her head with her hand and sat bolt upright. "Ugh! Will you tell me why I was trying to make that creep tonight? Jesus Christ, he couldn't have been more than four feet tall. I almost dropped my beer when he stood up."

"I think you scared the life out of him," I said, laughing.

"Couldn't handle me," she said drunkenly. "Too much for him."

"Probably still hiding in the men's room."

"Christ, you'd be surprised the number of guys that are scared of a woman. Just plain scared! Reminds me of that joke about the guy whose mother was a prude and told him that women had teeth down there to keep him from fooling around."

I didn't want to tell her that I thought she did her best to try to scare them away. "You're quite enough to handle," I said.

"Yeah, big girl like me. I guess it's the peasant stock. You know. Strong bones, good teeth."

"Well, you'll meet your match someday," I said doubtfully. Then I thought to myself, what does she think sex is, a wrestling match?

We were silent again until she said, "Well, aren't you going to kiss me?"

I put my arm around her and pressed my lips lightly to hers, but she grabbed hold of me and, jamming her body tightly against mine, thrust her tongue deep into my mouth. I felt my prick stir against my pants. I rolled over on top of her, pressing it against her thighs. As I began to hump her, she started to moan and thrust her hips upward against my crotch until I thought I was going to come right in my pants. I put my hand over her breast and cupped it through the material of her sweater.

"Oh, baby," she moaned, "you're too good to go gay."

I rolled off her and jerked to a sitting position. "What did you just say?"

"I said you were too good to go gay," she answered, tugging me back toward her.

But I held myself back and took her chin between my thumb and forefinger, steadying her drunken head. "What do you mean by that?"

"Forget it. Just come down to me, will you?"

"No. I want to know what you mean by that."

She sighed wearily. "Oh, nothing. Can't we just forget it?"

"No!"

"Well, I simply meant that there would be a lot of girls missing a lot of good stuff when you—"

I gritted my teeth and turned red with rage. "What makes you think I'm gay?"

"Oh, God, Paul. I'm not stupid. Didn't you think I knew you were? Why did you think I never tried to fuck you before? But don't worry about that. I've made it with gay guys before. You may be surprised—"

"I'm not gay!" I shouted at her. "I'm not!"

"Fine," she answered, yawning. "I don't care whether you are or not. Kiss me, would you?" She pulled me to her, and I pressed my lips to hers again, but the hard-on was gone and with it the excitement I had felt just a moment before. I ground my body against hers and tried to push the evil words from my mind and the feeling back into my cock, but it was no use. I could feel it pressed soft and flaccid against my thigh.

Myra did not seem to notice the change. She wrapped her arms around me and began to slip a hand down the back of my pants, lost in the heat of her own passion. I did my best to get into the act, humping my body against hers and taking her lower lip between my teeth. Soon, I could feel my prick beginning to stir again.

She pushed me off and sat up. With one pull, she ripped her sweater off over her head and unfastened her bra. I was flabbergasted by the sight of her body. Her belly was covered with a cloud of black hair like a boy's that came together in a dark line and extended to the navel. There was even a light shadow of black between her breasts.

Noticing my surprise, she gazed boldly at me and said laughingly, "Yeah, this really turned the fags on one summer in Provincetown. Take off your shirt."

Modestly, I obeyed her, and when I had finished, she wrapped her arms around my stomach and began covering my chest with hungry kisses. "Not a hair on you," she said. "You're as slender as a woman."

She unbuttoned the belt of my pants and stretched open my underwear with her hands, burying her lips and teeth in my pubic hair. Then she took out my cock and began playing with it, using her hands and lips. It swelled to her touch, blossoming out into an erect and pulsing member, arousing her ardor more and more, until she grabbed hold of my pants and ripped them all the way off my legs. I was completely naked now, and I leaned back onto the bed, letting her cradle my body in her grasp like a child while she kissed and tongued it all over.

Eventually, it dawned on me that I must act the part of the man. I sat up and pushed her over onto her back. I began kissing her passionately, kneading her breasts with my hand and caressing her stomach until I gained the courage and the desire to slip my hand lightly between her legs. She was wearing slacks made out of a thin, silky material, and I could feel the hot dampness of her mound against my palm. It was the first time I had ever touched a woman in this secret spot. I stroked the area hesitantly with my curious fingers, puzzling to the warm, sticky feeling that seemed to have seeped through the material of the pants.

Unfortunately, Myra's experience made her impatient, so that she reached down to my hand and pressed it more tightly against her crotch. Then she grabbed her slacks by the elastic waistband and ripped them down to her knees. I was shocked by the wealth of hair that brushed against my hand, and when I opened my eyes to look, I saw that the hair of her belly continued and thickened until it became a dense curly bush between her legs. A lighter growth covered her thighs to the point where she had shaved it off just above the knees. The thighs themselves were unusually thick and firm without being fat, so that her body gave the appearance of some strange hermaphrodite with a female's vagina and the hairy legs of an athlete.

She lay back again, but the shock of discovering her body, coupled with the abrupt aggressiveness of her manner of lovemaking had squelched my desire. She reached down between my legs to feel for my cock, found it limp, and said sarcastically, "Well, I guess a fag's a fag."

"It's your fault," I said. "You're not passive enough. You never lie back and let anybody do anything to you. How do you expect anybody to—"

"Shut up. The other guys didn't have any trouble."

Impotent rage swelled to my temples. I slapped her hard.

"You little fairy," she sneered, and reaching over to the beer can, she poured a stream of the cold liquid over my head.

I slumped against the wall, feeling the alcohol sting my eyes and trickle chillingly down the back of my neck. I thought I was going to begin to sob.

"Sorry, Paul," she offered. "You know how drunk I get. We never should have come back here in the first place."

I looked at her through the blurred mixture of tears and booze that filled my eyes. She lay sprawled naked on the bed, a little disturbed about the whole situation but still sipping leisurely at the beer. Her body was kind of appealing when you took it all in—full, healthy pink breasts and a very narrow waist.

"You should have known better," I said blankly. Then I pulled on my clothes and walked out.

I must have walked about a block until I realized I was stuck on the outskirts of the city with no money. It was two in the morning. Just as I was beginning to despair about getting back before sunrise, a rickety panel truck came bouncing slowly by, washing me in a flood of head-lights. I ran to the side of the road and thrust out my thumb, surprised to see it pull over and slow to a stop a few yards ahead. When I reached it, the door clicked open and a voice called from the interior of the driver's cabin, "Hop in, son!"

I started to climb into the front seat, but the haggard face of a farmer met me at the window. "Not here," he said. "Git in th' back with Seth." So I stepped back down and walked to the back door of the truck. The double doors were open just a crack, but I pried them open a little more with my thumb and peered inside.

Crouched in the darkness at the other end of the truck was a hulkish figure. He was bending over the dim light of a kerosene stove on which I could hear something sizzling. As he looked up at me, the light hit his face, revealing a toothless man in overalls, with a shock of unkempt hair shooting straight upward from his forehead.

"Wull, climb in, buckaroo," he said.

I hesitated. The thickness of his voice had startled me for a moment. I thought he might be drunk, but when he spoke again, I realized it was just a habitual way of slurring his speech.

"Git in here, fella. We ain't got th' hol day."

"Are you going into downtown?"

"Yep. Hop in, wull ya!"

I climbed into the truck and settled myself opposite him so the kerosene stove was between us. He was frying potatoes in an iron pan into which he kept slicing pieces of onion. Bits of flying grease sparkled in the blue light of the burner. Finally, he pulled the stuff off the stove and dumped it into a tin dish.

"Have some!"

I shook my head.

He shoved some of the hot pieces gingerly into his mouth with his fingers. Then he pulled away a canvas flap revealing a square opening that connected our compartment with the driver's. "Here y'ar, Bob," he said, holding the plate so the driver could cram a few handfuls into his mouth. When the driver had finished, he retracted the plate and let the flap fall back into place. Then he began to eat hungrily from the remains.

"Me an' m' brother's been drivin' straight since Schenectady," he said, "and 'fore that we didn't get no sleep neither. You been goin' long?"

"No, I was just coming back from right where you picked me up."

He pulled out a packet of Bugler's and began to roll a cigarette. "Smoke?"

I shook my head. Soon the blue flame of the kerosene stove began to splutter, and he shut it off. Only his cigarette remained, illuminating his face each time he took a drag on it, then diminishing to a red point of light in the pitch blackness. I watched it move back and forth in the darkness, clutching the metal paneling on the wall of the truck to steady myself from its lurching. Soon I was able to force some conversation from my tightened throat.

"Are you from Schenectady?"

"No, me and Bob's from Illinois. We was just comin' out here to see our sister. Been all over th' country, me 'n Bob, in this little pickup here." He patted the side of the truck affectionately.

"How old are ya', young feller? 'Bout fifteen, I bet?"

"No, I'm almost eighteen."

"Y'are? Didn't look that old when I saw ya hop into th' truck. Let me see here."

He took out a match and struck it on the side of the truck, holding it in front of my face as it flared up. "Not a trace of down on ya," he said.

I blushed and wished that he would blow the match out, but he held it to the wick of a kerosene lantern instead. It blazed up to fill the interior of the truck with a wan yellow illumination. I was sitting next to some crumpled blankets and an old denim jacket bunched up to create a pillow.

"Do you live in this truck?" I asked.

"More or less." He crushed out his cigarette and began to roll another. Livin' like this is okay when you're a young chicken, but y' begin ta get tired of it as y' get older. Bones begin t' ache. I just can't believe yer as old as ya say ya are, son. When I was yer age I was out on m'own already. Ran away from home at th' age of thirteen."

"Really?"

"Sure."

"Well, I'll probably be leaving soon, too."

He was silent. The truck began to lurch over a rough area of road, and the swaying kerosene lantern created an eerie shadow play of shifting images on the canvas walls. Finally, he raised his eyes from his cigarette and looked up at me. The smoke curved in thin wisps about his face.

"You sure are a good-lookin' fella. Fool around wi' th' girls much yet?"

"Yes," I answered quickly, "I was just coming back from my girlfriend's tonight."

He grinned slyly at me. "Get much from her?"

"Oh, I do all right."

"Wull, I'm glad somebody does. Me and m' brother been lookin' for a piece of ass clear all the way from Schenectady."

"Yer damn tootin'," called the driver through the canvas flap. I had not known that he could hear us.

"And we's about damn near ready to give up!" added Seth.

"Say son," he said, pausing, "you wouldn't know where we could pick up on sumpin' tonight, would ya? You're from this town."

"What exactly are you looking for?" As soon as the words were out of my mouth, I wondered why I had said them instead of just giving a plain no for an answer. "I really don't know any places you could go," I added.

"Me 'n Bob ain't particular," he said. "We're so damn horny, we could take anything on right now."

He waited for a reaction, and perceiving none, he continued. "Hey, no kidding, kid. Sometimes ya can want a piece of pussy as much as ya can need a glass of water in the desert. Look what I got here."

He pulled out a rumpled magazine and tilted it against the flame of the kerosene lamp. It was open to a full-page color photograph of a naked woman, squatting on a red cushion and cupping enormous breasts in her hands. Her lips and fingernails were painted the same vivid red.

"Some hot cookie, huh?" he said, pointing to her rubbery voluptuousness. "Like them knockers?" It must have been a very old magazine for her hair was in the style of the forties, long with a crown of curls in the front. Her stomach was sucked tensely in.

"Well… ain't that sumpin', or ain't it?"

"Oh, its all right."

"All right? All right!?" he burst into a hearty laughter. "Come over to the light and take a look-see, young fella. Don't be shy!"

"Oh, that's okay, I…"

"C'mon!"

He tossed the magazine to me, and I moved over to the light with it. It was full of similar photographs, flaccid sex kittens on shagged rugs or in padded bedrooms. As I sat facing him, thumbing through the magazine on my lap, he began to talk incessantly in a kind of soothing, chanting plaint. "Not a bad piece of ass, huh?… Wouldn't ya like t' put your paws on those tits?… Could use some pussy myself right now… Sure like to dip my peter in that honey pot…" Then there was silence, filled only by the sound of his shortened breathing, and finally, "Could ya use some ass yourself, son, I bet?", and he placed his hand on my kneecap. "C'mon… let's jerk each other off, boy. We ain't got nothin' better… C'mon…"

I made no move toward him, but neither did I move away. I simply let my legs fall apart and my back slump against the wall of the truck. He cupped my crotch with his hand and began to squeeze it through the material of my pants.

"Put your hand on me," he directed quietly.

He reached for my wrist, but I shook my head and put both my hands behind my back, thrusting my loins farther outward and apart. This seemed to increase his arousal even more.

"Yer' cruel…" he breathed heavily. You young-uns are all cruel…" And he bent down and stuck his head between my legs, butting my aroused member with his face through the material of my pants.

"I'm gonna take it out 'n suck it," he moaned upward at me. "L'me at that young cock o' yours."

His own words seemed to arouse him, and he was searching for their effect upon me. Finally, he unfastened my belt and began to work on the button of my pants, but I was wearing thick corduroy, so he had a hard time with it at first. In his excitement, he began grabbing at my hard cock against the material like a hungry dog. When he got my pants open, he yanked them down to the top of my thighs with my undershorts. I pressed my legs together and watched my cock jump up between them, proud of the slender grace of my thigh's naked smoothness, my slim brown loins.

My penis slid into his slippery mouth, sucked inward by a glove of flesh that was a perfect fit. It slid inside until his teeth pressed lightly around the root, crunching on the dry pubic hair that surrounded it. It was the first time I had ever felt a man's mouth on my penis. Soon, his hand moved down to my balls and lifted them from the place where they stuck hot and moist to my thigh. He pulled them away from my burning loins and cupped them in the palm of his hand, squeezing them expertly, while his sliding mouth sucked up and down on my slippery cock.

My cock felt so very tall and smooth as his mouth traced its length, back and forth from the sensitive, twitching tip to the wide, throbbing root, butting against the membrane of his throat; then he would slide out again to the tip in a dizzying caress. It was as if there was nothing so swift and slippery as his mouth, which slid up and down the length of my sensitive cock.

But he would have more of me. He would have it all. He placed the palm of his hand on my stomach and pushed me backward so I was slumped against the floor of the truck with my head and shoulders pressing against the wall. Then he pulled my pants all the way down to my socks. I could watch him bending over me, see his eyes gleam red in the lamplight as his tongue traced the length of my legs from the top of the thigh all the way down to the ankle. I lay slumped against the wall of the truck, my legs spread in a comfortable V, watching him watch me. I saw him pant over the sight of my long spread legs with my cock bursting rigidly between them. It was glistening from the saliva of his mouth. Next, he began to move his tongue along the inside of one leg, starting just above the knee, and taking his time until he reached the top of my thigh, where he let his tongue slide deftly in and out of the crevices created by my hanging balls, tasting the pleasure of my burning flesh where it hid nestled against itself in soft folds.

He wanted to taste all of me and savor it bit by bit, saving my cock for last, so he began to explore the very inside of my thighs with his darting tongue, seeking out the most secret places of my crotch. He explored the flesh behind my balls, where the root of my cock was buried. He sought with his tongue-tip the crease of flesh that separated by thigh from my groin. Or he pulled my legs apart with his hands and moved deep into the recesses of my thighs, way down where the anus begins to show itself and the hair, which I'd once examined by bending over a hand mirror, thinned to a few boyish strands matted against the pink, tender flesh. These few strands of hair he would take in his mouth, threading them through his teeth as his lips played with the tender button of my anus, and his tongue washed the outer edges of my asshole in hungry licks. All of this I pictured in my mind's eye, like a third person, while I was yet a part of it, too.

My own hand moved to my cock in an effort to hold back the waves of pleasure creeping into it, threatening to make me come. Unable to resist, I began to jerk it vigorously with my hand. My eyes rolled back into my head as the shadows of the lurching truck played over them, creating a zany pattern of shifting red and black.

Suddenly, he yanked his head away from me and grabbed hold of my arm, stopping my jerking movements. "Save it… save it," he panted. "Ya gotta save some fer Bob."

The truck veered and lurched to a stop, throwing me against the wall, but he grabbed hold of my naked thigh to steady me. I had no idea what they were planning. Indeed, I was almost oblivious to the whole thing since I had been ready to explode at the moment he pulled my hand away. I lay against the wall of the truck, panting with confusion and arousal, my cock twitching in the thwarted effort of its release. My body felt as if an electric current had moved through it, and the cold in the truck was beginning to send shivers through my bare legs. I raised my head to see Bob, the man who had been driving, vaulting into the back of the truck and approaching us, hesitantly. He looked younger than the man who had been blowing me. He was tall and gaunt, with narrow shoulders. He had a small round head balanced on a long neck.

"Will ya' blow me, young feller?" he asked, quickly swallowing.

I shook my head tensely and crouched back against the wall of the truck, my hands on my genitals.

"He won't do nothin' back, Bob," said Seth.

"That ain't fair, kid. You gotta finish us off too," said Bob. He spoke rapidly and nervously. Then he moved abruptly toward me, but I pulled my legs to my chest and lowered my head between my knees.

"You're gonna do me," he said. "L'me in there."

"No, leave me alone."

"Leave him," said Seth. He seemed exasperated by the bluntness of his brother's approach. "He don't have t' do nothin' he don't wanna do."

Finally, Seth began rummaging for the girlie magazine and tossed it to me. "Here," he said. "Thumb through this and git yerself all hot 'n bothered again."

The ridiculousness of his gesture stunned me. I almost felt like bursting into laughter. I looked halfway up at him and shook my head, but since he had already tossed the magazine to me, I opened it on my lap and pretended to thumb through it. They stood there above me like two fools, waiting for me to get aroused.

Finally, Bob said, "Is she givin' ya th' old stiff peter yet?"

I shook my head.

They waited a little longer, shuffling impatiently. Then Bob squatted next to me and put his hand on my prick. He began to stroke it until he could feel it begin to stiffen. He took me by the arm and guided me to a standing position while Seth stood watching. As I hung passively before him, my hands at my sides like a little child being undressed by his father, he lifted my jacket away from my chest, motioning me to take it off.

I removed it, and he slipped his hand under my T-shirt and let it rest on my stomach. Then he lifted my T-shirt to the armpits, and bending to my navel, inserted his hard tongue into it. It sent a faint jolt of pleasure down into my bladder. He moved his head upward, sucked my nipple tightly between his pursed lips, and further upward, until his mouth was buried in my armpit, sucking greedily at the hair there. Then he encircled my ribs with his fingers and slid his hands up and down the length of my naked chest. He tugged impatiently at my undershirt, which had been rolled into a thin band above my armpits. I pulled it up over my head and let my hands fall to my sides, picturing myself standing there nude with my pants in a heap around my ankles. The thought of my own nakedness aroused me, and I put my hand to my cock, rubbing it.

"Now he's gettin' there," I heard Seth say. He moved closer to me and grabbed my cock in his fist. He began jerking me slowly while Bob moved backward and studied my body. "Oh… its nice… it's nice," he crooned.

Bob was now in back of me, running a lingering hand gently down my spine, pausing at the base where my buttocks swelled upward, creating a soft secret cleft, then moving downward into the furrow of my crack with one finger. Finally, he moved his hand under my ass and between my legs so he could clutch at my balls. The pressure of his hand became firmer, more insistent, so that for a moment I felt as if he was going to boost me off the floor by the crotch.

Seth was moving rapidly and expertly. My cock slid in and out of his throat with a delicious pressure. Bob spread the cheeks of my ass apart and burrowed against the back of my thighs until his mouth could reach my balls, which he sucked greedily. I stood above them, tottering over the two working heads wedged between my legs, rocking back and forth on my heels. Seth was sucking my cock with a plunging movement that caused his forehead to butt against the lower part of my stomach.

Finally Bob, who had been working on me from the rear, stood up and said to his brother, "L'me have a go at that cock."

I hated the feeling of Seth's departing mouth. It left my cock pointing stiffly into the open air, cold with the evaporating saliva of the mouth that had sucked it. But Bob dropped to his knees in front of me and took my cock in his mouth. It was a firmer, rougher pressure than Seth's. He milked it vigorously to the very root. Seth edged his head next to him and fastened his mouth on my balls, but there was not really enough room for him down there, so he stood up and began to suck at my nipple while his hands encircled me and clutched pieces of my buttocks. Still unsatisfied, he dropped to his knees in back of me and pressed his face against my ass.

For the first time in my life, I felt the tingling pleasure of a warm tongue sliding down my asshole's crack, gently separating the sticky cleft of my cheeks. Then he stretched the cheeks apart with his hands and plunged his tongue into the hole, washing the muscle edges of my rectum in a circular motion. He moved his hand to my wet ass and slid a finger in.

"L'me put my cock in there."

I shook my head, tensing the muscles of my ass around his finger. "No, I can't."

Bob continued to suck my ass for a while as his brother worked on my cock. Then Seth stood up and began to remove his clothing. He moved with a clumsy deliberateness, as if he were getting ready for bed, slowly removing his pants and placing them folded in the corner of the truck, then his shirt. I was amazed at the body that blossomed out from the neck of that haggard face. His face was deeply lined and furrowed, unshaven, atop a thick, sunburnt neck that stopped abruptly at his broad shoulders; but the rest of his body was strangely white, muscular, and graceful. He stepped out of his baggy pants like a naked prince from the rags of a beggar. He was hairless, except for a light blond down on his legs. The muscles of his thighs bulged powerfully, tapering gracefully at the knees. From the back, his buttocks swelled into firm, curving ovals. His large, dark cock surged out of the shocking whiteness of his groin.

He padded over to me and placed his hand on my cock again. Then he began to jerk himself off, moving his hand to his mouth and then back to his cock now and then in order to keep it shining with saliva. I watched his body despite myself, and when he was near enough, I grabbed his aroused member with one hand. I closed my eyes and slid it all the way up his cock until I could pinch the warm, soft balls that hung below. How strange it felt to feel the fleshy balls of another male! To cup them in my hands. I began to play with his balls while he jerked his cock. Bob fell to his knees and began to suck me. The back of my thighs began to twitch with my growing pleasure. Then I could feel my balls begin to swell and pump with the load they were about to discharge as I poised on the vibrating brink of orgasm. I grabbed at the naked man's balls with my hand in a last attempt to imprint their feeling on my consciousness. My shoulders strained backward as I thrust into Bob's mouth. Back and forth my pelvis jerked with a motion of its own, hurling me against the head of the kneeling man until I collapsed against him and spurted into his mouth.

When he had emptied me, Bob pulled away and moved over on his knees to his brother. Fastening his lips to the cock of Seth's well-built body, clutching the hard, white buttocks in his hands, he finished him off against the wall of the truck and gulped down his load on top of mine.

My senses returned to me as I watched the two brothers working together, and before the kneeling man had stood up, I was already half-dressed. Bob looked at me with glazed eyes.

"Please. Take me home right away," I said.

Bob took a step toward me. "Wait a minute," he said, "don't get dressed."

"No!" I pulled my shirt over my head and backed against the wall like a frightened deer. "I want to go home. Please."

Bob took another step toward me, but his brother, still standing stark naked, stopped him. "Let th' kid be, Bob. Can't ya see he's had enough? Now you jest git back in th' cabin and drive."

Bob gave a shrug of disgust and started to get dressed. He climbed out of the back of the truck. In a moment, it lurched violently forward, throwing us both against the wall. My cheek brushed against his bare back for a second. I felt his ass press against my crotch.

"Ooooops. Sorry, kid."

He moved to the other end of the truck and pulled his pants on. Soon the white body was swallowed up by the rags he had been wearing, the baggy pants, the oil-stained work shirt. He looked like a decrepit Okie again with his unshaven face and his thick, corded neck. Still, occasionally I caught a patch of white at the ankle or the base of the neck, a glimmer of the handsomeness concealed in the depths of those used rags.

I curled up in one corner and rested the side of my head on my arm. He rummaged aimlessly about the truck, a kind of embarrassed restlessness in his movements. Finally, he pulled the girlie magazine out from a heap of junk and began to thumb through it. Not a word was spoken until they dropped me off in the center of town.

It must have been about four in the morning by then. I walked through the deserted downtown area of the city, listening to the sound of my own footsteps and watching the mercury vapor light of the new street lamps bounce off the aluminum poles of parking meters. The whole thing had a kind of crushing rigidity about it. A kind of flat opaqueness like fake moonlight. I wondered why they had gotten rid of the old yellow lights in exchange for these glaring monsters.

I looked down at my wrist. The flesh looked grayish green in the strange light, covered with maroon blotches. I shoved it deep into the pocket of my jacket and began to walk faster, but I could not escape the click-clack of my shoes on the pavement. The weird lights stretched on for blocks, and, for lack of anything better to do, I was forced to pass over the hysterical events of the evening in my mind.

With a kind of paralyzing inevitability, the meaning of one minor incident in particular kept thrusting itself into my frightened heart. I could not avoid it. The memory of the vagabond's blossoming whiteness, the hard, naked body that had crept out of those rags—and I had touched him! I had reached out to touch his cock of my own free will!

The memory of this single action was enough to convince me that I had chosen. My path was set, and the consequences were inescapable now. But it was what I wanted. I was what I was.

When I got home, I tiptoed into the house and, throwing off all my clothes, dove into a hot shower. When I emerged, nothing had changed. I climbed into bed realizing I would not awaken in the morning without the knowledge of that night's experiences ingrained deep within me. I knew I would carry it with me for the rest of my life.

The Puerto Rican

THE PUERTO RICAN BOY was tall and muscled, but his face with its prominent cheekbones had something vulnerable about it. It was one of those faces you don't miss in a dark hole of a bar like this, because the color of the skin and the fixity of his large eyes seemed to detach from the crowd of people like something phosphorescent. Yes, it was a face surging from another dimension, slightly incandescent with suffering. It was, to tell the truth, a brutal face, and at the same time, it was a masochistic-looking face, like that of a saint.

For more than an hour I'd been studying him in his red tank top, his enormous shoulders expanding each time he bent over the pool table. He was obviously aware of my gaze, but he did not look back a single time. Instead, he performed a ballet intended specifically for me, which consisted of steps and turns that were perfectly executed between the bar and the pool table, as well as different methods of bending over the table, accompanied by extensions of his long and muscled arms each time he struck a ball with the cue stick.

After a while, I went to the men's room and was startled to see a couple doing cocaine. One was a man of around forty, and the other was a hustler of about twenty. In front of the urinal, the hustler had taken out his hard prick, and the man was bending over it. With great speed and precision, the man tipped out a line of cocaine along the length of the hard dick, and then consumed it with a single snort.

Only seconds later, the Puerto Rican came in. He gave no sign of wanting to talk with me, although I would have spoken to him regardless, but I was somewhat discombobulated by the scene I'd just witnessed, and before I could find my voice, the Puerto Rican had already pissed and left.

I followed him to the bar, where the two of us took our respective places. He started another game of pool, and I began to watch him exactly as I had before. Soon I became convinced that he wanted to speak to me as much as I to him but that there was some barrier preventing it. Like the bodies of two lovers who have been separated, our bodies took on a look of deprivation. He was still avoiding my gaze, but it was becoming obvious that he was more and more irritated by the fact that I wasn't coming up to him. His body betrayed tiny spasms of nervousness that seemed to stem from his impatience about our drama. As for me, I was just as frustrated by the situation, but something was holding me back, and I remained incapable of coming over to him.

Slowly, several others were beginning to notice our game, and they began to study us. The fact that they were intensified our excitement, and the Puerto Rican, who was wearing rather tight trousers, began to get an erection; but aside from that, there was no change in his behavior. He kept playing pool without looking at me.

When the situation was nearly unbearable, I decided to order him a drink. I gave the waiter specific orders. The Puerto Rican could have whatever he wanted. The price wasn't important, and as the waiter served it, he was to indicate discreetly that it was from me.

The waiter did exactly as I asked. I watched as he handed a very expensive drink to the Puerto-Rican. I think it was an Ice Tea, the kind composed of several liquors. The Puerto Rican took hold of the glass and raised it in the air. For the first time, he looked at me with a some-what flirtatious smile.

At that moment, all the lights went on. Two cops came rushing into the bar. At first, I thought it had something to do with the couple I'd seen in the men's room taking cocaine, but the cops had stopped on either side of the Puerto Rican. Rapidly, they slipped a pair of handcuffs on him. Then they led him roughly from the bar while everyone watched. The bar fell completely silent, as the luminous, paling and im-passive face of the Puerto Rican, looking more and more handsome, framed by the two cops and their smug expressions, moved farther and farther away from his expensive drink.

The Romanian Boy

EVEN WITH HIS FEATURES pinched by anxiety and the flesh under his large, dark eyes swollen by late nights, he was still handsome, more beautiful than a waxed wooden sculpture, his face framed by long, black hair shiny as velvet. Tell and thin, he was sprawled on damp sheets in a hotel room in Bucharest, his sinuous arms crossed over his naked chest, his long, pale fingers clasping his elbows, and his large, semi-hard penis curved across a slender thigh.

He was angry, he grumbled, but perhaps the right word is that he was humiliated, having given his ass to this hairy older man lying next to him and now propped on one elbow with a smug expression his face. He swore this was the first time in his life he'd tried such extreme sex. But for the gentleman, the mystery stemmed not from the act, but from its savagery, the fact that no matter how much he increased the pressure with a finger, two fingers, and even three or four to penetrate the young man, followed by his member, the young man had continued to say, "Harder, I can't feel it."

In a kind voice with just a touch of irony, the man asked him how he could withstand this ordeal of being stuffed if it was really his first time having anal sex. Imperturbably—but with an expression of anger that caused him to turn away from the man and offer only the side of his strong, corded neck—the young man answered that he'd tried the same thing with his own fingers and even with a broomstick several times, and that he was content to verify that doing it with a man had added absolutely nothing to the experience.

In reaction to these words that the man figured were untrue, a wave of tenderness took him over, making him caress the smooth shoulder of the boy and tell him there was no reason they couldn't enjoy a warm friendship without sex if the boy was that troubled by such an element. "In the future, my only desire is to caress you like a friend, a brother," he'd said, becoming aware of the specious pretentiousness of his words immediately after having pronounced them. And the boy had muttered, "I've already heard the same shallow promises from girls."

The two of them—the young man from Bucharest and the man from New York—had met two months earlier, on an internet site where the boy was working as a "model." For three American dollars a minute, you could "chat" with these models over video conferencing, asking them to take off their clothes and assume any pose you wished. Of the several hundred models who worked on the site, most came from Eastern Europe, and the man had been fascinated by the Romanian boy, who did not at all possess the face of a cynical, worn-out prostitute. It is true that his face was often paled by fatigue, and from time to time his eyes turned into pits drowned in malicious gloom, but his features betrayed a delicate sensitivity and anxiety that only exists in countries where dreams are born in the eternal games between East and West, but where the flow of history is a poisoned river in which any fantasy of ethical politics disappeared long ago.

What is more, the proportions of boy's face came from another age in which the Western rules of classical proportion hadn't developed, supplanted as they were by an Eastern esthetic, almost like an Orthodox icon. It was a long, perfect oval through which appeared the bones of his skeleton, complemented by Asian eyes and a full, generous, and suggestive mouth. During their time together, the boy enjoyed striking antique poses of masculinity from another era, like gestures the man imagined could be traced to the male harem of a sultan. Perhaps this notion wasn't quite as improbable as it sounded given that the entire Balkan peninsula had once been under Ottoman suzerainty that had lasted several hundred years.

In order to persuade the young man to meet him when he went to Bucharest on business, the American had squandered a great deal of money on video conferencing on that website and had demanded nothing more than conversation from the boy. During one of these sessions, he'd been surprised to learn the boy wasn't at home. Because he was too poor to buy his own computer or subscribe to an internet plan, he was working with a couple hundred others in a cyberstore, where the greedy management kept the majority of the money he made. The work was dangerous, too, since this type of labor was considered pornographic, and those indulging in it could be arrested. Even worse, the boy was nearly homeless. He slept with two other "models" in the same bed in a shabby hotel. His only telephone was a cell that could receive calls but couldn't make them. His dream, he had confessed several times during sessions, was to buy his own computer, quit this humiliating job, and study programming. But that was an impossible dream; even after ten years of the life he was currently living, he'd never have enough money to accomplish his goals.

The American was so shaken by the account of this pitiable life during these very expensive video conferencing sessions that he'd offered to give the boy a secondhand laptop as soon as he arrived in Bucharest. But on the day he did arrive, as soon as he walked into his room at a luxury hotel, he'd noticed that it offered wi-fi. Because he wanted to send his New York friends daily accounts of this exotic trip and this fascinating boy, he'd decided to keep the laptop for the two weeks of his trip and give it to the boy on the day he left.

A few moments later, he'd called the boy and arranged to meet him in the street. He was thrilled by the idea of seeing his online buddy in flesh and blood, and when he did, the boy was even more handsome than he'd looked on screen. He invited the boy to dinner at an elegant restaurant in spite of the hesitancy and protestations of the latter due to the way he was dressed. Afterward, both had returned to the man's hotel room. He showed the laptop to the boy, who displayed his prowess with such machines as he examined it. Then the man explained to him that he would need it during his stay, but it would belong to the boy when he left.

Once the man had ordered a bottle of champagne for the room, he'd realized he was afraid to touch the boy, and he'd asked permission a bit shyly. The boy had said yes, but from the moment he'd begun to embrace him, all the boy kept saying was "harder."

After this strange sexual escapade and the conversation that had followed, the boy left without a word. As the days passed, every time the man tried to telephone him, the boy would say, "I can't see you."

More frustrated and angered each day, the man finally decided to call one more time. "I think I understand your feelings about our encounter," he said. "It made you feel dirty. But it's time to forget all that. There's no reason why we can't have fun together like friends and nothing more."

"All right," the boy answered in a cold voice, "but I still can't see you today, I'm too busy earning a living."

"Call me," insisted the man, forgetting that the Romanian's phone could only receive calls. "I'll be waiting." However, by the end of his stay in Bucharest, the boy hadn't called.

Tortured by feelings he couldn't analyze, the man tried to call the boy just before leaving. "Why"? he simply asked, perhaps a bit too dramatically when the boy answered. "Why'd you abandon me?"

The boy laughed coarsely. "You think I was embarrassed by what we did? Well, that isn't the case. I wanted to do it, and my only reason was because I wanted your laptop."

The man was struck dumb at first, but then he managed to say, "I told you that you could have the laptop, and you didn't need to have sex with me for that. Come over now and take it."

"No!" answered the boy curtly and hung up.

PSEUDO NOIR

The Old Switcheroo

THE DOGS ARE YAPPING at my heels & Trixi's nursing a bit finger when somebody scratches at the door. Thinking it's the manager who handed us our walking papers this afternoon come to see if we've put the mutts in the cages, I pay it no mind so I can put all my talents to chewing out my wife while figuring how to get out of town before those bounced checks catch up with us. My wife in name only, I mean: being married gives me & Trixi that added tinge of respectability & makes sharing a hotel, running a dog act, or chatting up a nervous widow seem a little less slippery to those deadheads with nothing to do but think up shaming names.

Grabbing at the little terrier ripping up her kimono on the bed, Trixi turns on the waterworks; she begins blaming me for getting us into the whole mess: 3 bounces passed in Philadelphia to buy this menagerie, after which it takes more than a month just to find out neither 1 of us can get them to jump through a hoop. & when we finally get our act together & find a club in Miami, Trixi gets her finger bit, the animals go running into the house & the manager gives us the 86. But the dogs are howling at the door now & Trix says you better open in case the lady in the audience who got her dress ruined has called the police.

The woman in black pinstripe & hair like a torch walking into the room shuts up the mutts with 1 snap of her fingers. She pats Ruby the welsh terrier on the head & holds out a skeleton hand decorated with 1 of the biggest pinky rings I've ever seen.

Countess something-or-other, she says, I've come to extend my apologies for ruining your act. I'd just lighted a cigarette & the flame must have frightened the pooches.

Matter of fact, I had noticed those pinstripes in the front row of tables & wondered whether maybe she was working undercover for the spca. But any airhead can tell our Countess is no mere mutt advocate. She's watching Trixi spill out of her kimono like a melon judge at a county fair. Trixi pulls her belt a little tighter so the goods spill out even more. 1 bat of her eyelashes leads to another & the Countess happens to mention she'll be leaving for the island this weekend—which strikes me as kind of fishy since everybody knows it's about to fall to the junta.

True. You see, it has always been my dream to visit the island, explains the lady. This may be her only chance. In fact, the very last scheduled flight leaves early tomorrow. & would we care to join her?

The Countess tosses out more small talk when the phone starts ringing to the tune of the 4-figure bounces, inspiring me to give Trixi the sign to rev up the eyelash motor to maximum.

Of course, you'll have to dispose of the canines, the Countess yawns, spacing her conversation to fall in between the rings.

That's no problem, I say, just as the Ruby the Welsh reads my mind & burrows under Trixi's kimono. Don't hurt 'em, she blurts. I'm kind of gettin' used to the little creatures.

Countess marches over to the terrier & picks it up in 1 claw. The pooches will go to my place, she announces. My staff will take excellent care of them. How happy they will be to see you when we get back! She jerks the little mutt to her breast.

You're almost too nice! gasps Trixi. Picking up 1 of her fake pearl earrings, she winces as she tries to shove the thing into a partly closed-over ear piercing. Countess whips out a mirror from her safari bag & holds it up for her. Then you'll be ready at dawn?

I got no big towel, complains Trix. Think the 1 at the hotel will be big enough for the beach?

Tempest in a teapot, scoffs the Countess. We'll buy you 1 there—with your initials on it.

You really shouldn't, you know, answers Trixi in a breathy voice she picked up from a marilyn monroe movie, looking in the mirror & rubbing lipstick off a tooth with 1 knuckle.

Bags packed & 2 hrs sleep under our belts, Trixi & me meet Countess What's-Her-Face at the deserted airport. Trixi's showing it off in her new orange & white polka-dot pants & the Countess is clutching the safari bag that falls open for a sec, revealing a fat roll of currency & an american express card caught in the prongs of a fancy hairbrush. Me, I got nothing—except maybe the knack of bringing 2 people together at the right time & riding it as far as it'll take me.

Before we know it, Trixi's caught the scent of the duty-free shop & is banging on the gate for the clerk to open up.

We don't open for another 15 minutes, sneers the bleary-eyed worker.

I don't care, whines Trixi, cause I gotta have those earrings for the beach. She's pointing in the window to a pair of genuine fake gold ones shaped like conch shells.

The Countess sticks her scratchers into the bag & pulls out a 10-spot, sticks it through the gate. Give the lady what she wants, she says.

Geez, Countess, says Trix all breathy, that was really nice a ya, & then she sneezes right on a little kid standing under her with his nose pressed against the duty free window. His mom takes 1 look at our crew

& yanks the kid out from under her. Cover your mouth! I hiss between clenched teeth. Then I smile apologetically at the Countess.

What about a car? says Trixi. Seems to me we should get 1 to drive around the island & bone up on the points of historical interest.

Just as long as I do the driving, I warn.

I can handle a wheel, argues Trixi.

This ain't no slot machine, honey. The only wheel you ever been behind's the 1 in a casino.

I do know how, insists Trix.

Then let's see your license.

I ain't got one. They took it away. But that don't mean I can't drive!

What it means, I say, is that we'll be spending the weekend in the local monkeyhouse.

You wish to visit the zoo? No problem, says the Countess, with a vacant look on her face. I guess it's 'cause she's not a native speaker.

Everything's swell when the charter takes off. It means these bounces can't follow us, is the only thought I'm thinking. The Countess has gotten a little green. Poor woman, says Trix. Should I ask the girl for a alka seltzer?

It's not serious, the Countess mumbles.

Ain't she brave, Perdido? Trixi twirls her genuine gold-plate conch shell in her ear & flashes her pearlies. Right than I know what kinda weekend it's gonna be.

Not me nor Trixi's ready for the sight of dripping palm leaves & wet sand when our cucaracha express bumps onto the runway & the door creaks open. Suddenly the place is like a steam bath. The beehive of the woman sitting in front of us begins sinking. Oh, Jeez, guys, says Trix, it's rainin!

Not to worry, the Countess assures us with a green smile.

I begin wondering if she thinks she can order new weather with that american express card of hers.

When we come down the ramp, the air is thicker than a poached egg. The Countess has got her handkerchief pressed to her mouth. Everybody seems to be staring at Trixi's orange and white polka dots like they can't understand where she got something even they threw out 10 years ago. & I'm just thinking it's probably good for them. Maybe it'll change their idea about America being so hoity-toity.

By the time we get to the hotel, you can't tell whether it's raining or the air has become 1 big raindrop, & I'm hoping it's possible to breathe something that's almost pure water. The hotel is a 4-story job overlooking the beach with an outdoor feed station for the local drugstore cowboys. Things really do look like a remake of suddenly last summer, 'cept I can't tell which ones are playing sebastian & which liz taylor. The native boys are all lined up in a row watching the 2 dames & kind of glancing at me funny like maybe I got something they want—but there's also a row of flour sacks from new york looking fish-eyes at the boys. Right away Trix begins to take issue. This is crazy, she says, We gotta stay here? They don't like women, that 1 looks like he's gonna kill me.

Put a lid on it, Trix, I snap. That's no way to greet the natives. I tell the Countess to hand her piece of plastic to the broad behind the counter & get us up to our rooms quick before the knives start slippin' outta the monokinis. But the rooms aren't ready so we go to looking for chow & I spot a restaurant.

I'm hungry, says Trix, redundant as always, & she begins asking the Countess to translate all everything on the menu. The Countess recommends they start with the fresh pineapple juice, but the yokel brings 'em 2 pieces of pineapple instead, then plops down 3 plates of ravioli.

We ordered pineapple juice, says the Countess.

You won't get it as juice, says the waiter, not on this island. Fresh pineapple means fruit, not juice.

The Countess smiles past the guy's head & puts a piece of the stuff between her teeth. She chews it up real slow & swallows it. Utterly tasteless, is her verdict. & who ever thought of bringing pineapple at the beginning of the meal.

People eat melon first, I tell her. She acts like she doesn't hear me. The girls are hot & thirsty & are sampling the local water. I'm turning h20 down & wondering if Countess's got any paregoric in that bag of hers.

When we get back to the hotel, the crowd of whales & domestic sardines is getting thicker, & the whales are beginning to flash some green. My room still isn't ready, so we all pile onto the girls' bed & try to get some shuteye. I flip on the muzak speaker. A lawrence welk meringue pipes into the room. Things are just starting to get hazy when the phone rings. Trixi picks it up. Wrong number, she tells us, somethin' about a bad credit card. Suddenly the countess pulls the phone away from Trixi & goes into a tirade in the native tongue. Then she hangs up & smiles.

No problem, she says, 1 big mistake. Simply that the bank did not yet receive the payment I sent before we left. 1 big mixup that will straighten itself out all by itself.

In my day you paid cash, I can't help sayin', but Countess is already lying back & putting her sleep shade back on. I try to give Trixi a sign, but she's already got her face buried in a pillow.

They tell me my room's ready, & the girls decide to take it because it's bigger. They leave me lying on the bed with the smell of the Countess 4711 cologne on the pillow. As soon as I'm alone, I begin to see what the setup is: Trixi & the Countess in 1 room with the bucks; me here penniless listening to latin muzak, a phony credit card floating around. I start wondering if the local slammer is air-conditioned before I drift off into slumberland.

It's happy hour at the meat rack. Business must be better than usual because of the rain. Nobody expected it this time of year, according to the bartender. Trixi & the Countess are sampling a tropical brew, & I'm sticking with red-eye & lemon peel—no ice, straight up—the local water makes me nervous. The dames are staring into the air so their eyes won't meet nobody's & talking under their breaths. These people are awful, says the Countess.

Can't take the intensity, says Trixi.

I notice the busboy's acting kinda strange. I don't hear any music, but every few minutes he sets down his tray & starts palpitating to a '45 that must be playing in his head. He's got a mad look of joy in his eyes, & each time he sees somebody he knows he makes bleating noises. It's then I realize the busboy's deaf & more or less dumb.

Then he starts grinning at me.

There's a church with a silver altar, says the Countess. A young man was killed on that spot in the 17th century when he was thrown from a horse. It's in the old city, where I'm told there's also a decent restaurant. What say we go?

There's no need to hunt up umbrellas. The air's so wet, our clothes drink it up like a cotton ball. So we pile onto a bus & ride it to the end of the line.

Dusk is settling over the old city. The wet palm trees look black & shiny like oil. Gentle-looking people are leaning on their elbows over filagree railings & making a point of looking past us. Nobody has glass windows, just shutters made of wooden slats.

Me & the broads start walking up the street that winds along the bay & gets higher & higher. Under us are pink & green & orange shoeboxes. We can see kids hanging out the narrow windows & people standing in the streets drinking beer. Tin can music floats. Get out your ermines, girls, looks like a big night. But the Countess is staring down into those slums with a hard look in her eyes. It's almost like she recognizes the scene from someplace before.

That's when the strangest thing happens. A handful of locals watch us walk by & their eyes light up. Before I know it, they're following close behind, singing some kind of song that sounds religious, & all of them got Trixi fixed in their stare. I'd even wager their faces look transformed, as if they've seen a vision or a ghost, a ghost they were hoping to see. 1 of them catches up & grabs Trixi's hand, kisses it.

Trixi freaks & pulls her hand away. Countess, what th' hell do they want from me? The Countess says something in the native language that sounds threatening. All of 'em scatter.

What in hell happened? asks Trixi.

Mistaken identity, answers the Countess, but she still has that hard look in her eyes.

We never do find the church. Instead, Trixi spots a dive where they give you a coconut hacked open with a machete & a straw to suck up the juice. Trixi starts whining, & the Countess buys her 1. Countess buys me another red-eye—no ice.

When dinner's over, I sniff out the local night spots with the girls close at my heels. We find an outdoor bar with a blender & a view of the bay, & I push the Countess into giving the bartender the 3rd degree about the places where a fella can get his pipes cleaned.

Turns out I coulda asked the bartender myself. She's actually a California girl with a lot of miles on her back & the tattoos all over her arm to prove it. She takes 1 look at me & says, The boys who work on the cruise ships come in here Friday & Saturday—Italian, English, Belgian. They hang around for a few stiff ones & then hightail it over to a place on Calle de Luna.

Why don't you take off without us, says Trixi, you'd probably have a much better time. Isn't that right, Countess?

The Countess is too well-bred to get rid of me like that. You amuse us, she says, but we don't want to be an albatross around your neck.

Don't worry, Countess, I never been 1 to stay too long at the party, but I kinda forgot my mad money tonight. If you could slip me a fin or 2, I'd be gone faster than you can say piña colada. The Countess digs into her roll & sticks a C-note in my hand. No further encouragement needed. It's asta la vista time.

Calle de Luna lives up to its name. All the stucco looks white & silvery, & under the moon the whores are stepping over the drunks in the street. A guy behind the door takes a peek at me from a little window & buzzes me right in. Then he conjures 5 out of me & pushes me through a moth-eaten curtain into the bar, revealing the 2 people sitting in it. I take a whiff of the place & decide I'd better use my other 5 to flag a cab down.

It's just my luck to get a driver who's a fan of the old regime. According to him, in those days you could buy anything in the city with american cash & still have enough left over to thank him with a stiff tip for finding it for you.

Be careful about wandering around alone, he warns. The world's been taken over by extremists who think it's a sin to make a living or have a little fun. By the way he adds, if I'm interested there're still a few places left where a fellow can get his pipes cleaned.

We glide past lit-up rexall drugstores & pizza joints without any customers. Our hotel's the only lit-up place with a pink neon sign saying ROOFTOP ORCHESTRA. I know what it'll be like to sleep under that: last year's hits are making the whole building vibrate.

The dames are huddled alone at the bar, snug as 2 bugs in a rug. The Countess has lost her blasé look & is hot in discussion with Trixi, who's got a serious frown on her pretty face. Hey, professor. I tap Trix on the shoulder & she smiles up at me, says, the Countess was just tellin' me about her education. She was brought up in a french convent school, real strict & classy.

Hey, Countess, I didn't know you went to refinishing school.

The Countess throws me a stiff grin.

She really thinks I should be a translator, says Trix, & work at the united nations. Countess's got an in there.

Before I know it the 2 of them are whispering in each other's ear & making me feel like a 5th wheel again. So I go back up to the room, but just as I expected, it's like being inside a big heartbeat. I ring up the desk to find out when the patient's due to kick: 3:30 am would be early… So I turn up the muzak loud as it goes & flip the lights off. Just as I'm about to conk out, I hear gunshots from far away. Where'll I get the most sleep, I wonder—here or in the clinker when the junta takes over or the Countess's american express card fizzles? With that question in mind, I fall out.

The phone rings & it's my adored wife.

Jesus, she says, have you heard what's happenin'? The Countess was listenin' to the radio & the junta's been executin' lefties right & left, I mean left & right—oh jesus, I just looked out the window, & it's still rainin'.

You & me got to talk, Trix. We got to settle a few things 'bout the Countess. I slip into a pair of clamdiggers & my only shoes—wingtips—to go knock on the lovebirds' cage door. Trixi opens & walks to the mirror to slip into her bra. What's buggin' you, Perdido?

I can't take another night in this meat cooler, Trix, & I'm willing to bet it's driving Countess crazy, too. The Countess's got class. When she's trying to get some shuteye, she don't need a snare drum lullaby. &

between that & you lyin' next her, I'm sure she ain't getting a wink. I'd say it's worth our while keeping the Countess happy, wouldn't you?

Trixi pulls her babyface into a tough frown.

Button me up, she says, while you button your lip. Watch the safety pin!

I grab hold of Trixi's pants & slip in a safety pin where the button should be. Meanwhile she lays into me:

Maybe the Countess don't want no sleep while she's lyin' next to me. Ever consider that? Anyway, it's none-a your business.

As for changing hotels, Trix claims the Countess's got friends on the island whom we have not had the pleasure of meeting yet, & they want her to stay here.

As a matter of fact, Trix recommends, maybe I should use that C-note the Countess gave me last night to dig up a ticket back to Miami before the season's over & the last divorcée has taken her charter back to Des Moines. If the Countess is going to deliver, it won't happen with me hanging around.

In point of fact, she goes on, the Countess's meal ticket may not be as mink-lined as we thought it was. Seems the desk called up again to say her american express card was no good. Countess says it's cause they're tight on credit here now, which is why they make such a big deal about keeping the books straight day to day. When the government falls to the junta & quashes all the commies, the dollar will be worth a fortune on the black market, the Countess just happened to mention in passing. Seeing how this is saturday & monday's memorial day, she gave 'em a story about a swiss bank not getting a check from ny. Ouch! Watch that pin! & no, she doesn't know whether the Countess's line checks out, but the Countess is kind of interesting & it's worth getting to know her better & what's more the Countess has got enough green stuff for a while—that is, if she only has to spend it on 2 people.

She grabs hold of a blue blouse with white polka dots to put on. Countess is kind of fond of me, she adds. Hey, wait, Perdido! Where you going?

A vague sun is puffing up the clouds like a water blister, & a few of the tykes on day duty are running on the beach scooping out heel marks in the wet sand. Countess is nowhere in sight.

I think I'll break that C-note for a ham & eggs 'cause I'm sticking around. Trixi's not exactly subtle when she thinks she's onto a good thing.

A couple of the juniors are lolling on the coke machine as if they've been left over from the night before. 1 kind of gives me the sullen eye before he puts his shoulder blades between me & my view of the rest of the cowboys. The deaf mute is dancing his rag & tray from table to table. Every time he passes me, he eyes me like I was his long-lost daddy finally come to claim him at the orphanage.

It's almost out of nowhere that the angel appears. Mutey runs up & throws his arms around him. It's the handsomest man I ever saw, & I can't help gawking at him. He tosses his head back to get the hair out of his large, liquid eyes & grins. Then he gives the deaf-mute a good squeeze & hands him a lollipop with a face on it. It makes mutey howl with pleasure & the handsome guy's perfect eyes—cold before—light up.

Countess shows up, from a walk on the beach, she says, & sits down next to me. She begins shedding some light on the conversations going on around us.

The worst possible cliché. If you could hear what they're saying, you'd be… She pauses. Maybe you'd be fascinated. The naïveté & provincialism are—overwhelming.

I flip my yolk onto my toast wedge & keep my eye looking into my coffee. By the way, Cuntess—I catch myself, it was just a slip of the tongue—I mean Countess—where'd you say you hailed from? Maybe you said madrid? Or maybe you said nothing?

Our civilization is centuries old is her non-answer.

It's all bucks, Countess, & I'm sure you know the song. When ya got it, everybody thinks you're the livin' end, but when you ain't—well, I'm sure you heard that Bessie Smith song about nobody loving you when you're down & out. Bringing me to a little question about that gold-edged piece 'a plastic of yours.

The Cuntess—did I say that again? I meant Countess—grabs my toast wedge & flips my 1 & only yolk into her mouth. With great care she chews it all up before gulping it down.

It seems the bank has made a mixup with—

What a pity, I cut her off. Praise the lord that Trixi remembered to bring her checkbook. Of course, it ain't no good, but on a little island like this with ties to uncle sam, who's gonna check till after memorial day & that's an important detail. Right? That Trixi, dizzy as a bee who's been swimmin' through the belladonna. She figured she'd lose those checks & gave 'em to me to hold. If we keep movin' & don't spend more than a hundred in any hotel, that credit card will keep being our alladin's lamp, don't you think? But just in case there's any objection, we'll get Trixi to sign 1 of those checks with her name printed on it that I got here right in my pocket. I mean, it's not like I'm suggesting' you spend any of that thick wad of cash I happened to glimpse in your safari bag…

You don't know what you're talking about, she answers.

Wait just a sec, Countess. It isn't like I dragged you here without nothin' to entertain ya.

Trixi comes skipping over the flagstones to our table. She's wearing her basic orange & white polka-dot number with a blue & white polka-dot blouse & stinking of the Countess's 4711. The seventh graders are blowing the hair outta their eyes to take a better gander at her.

Jeez, says Trixi, I'm famished.

The Countess's eyes seem to light up. How about a nice american breakfast, ham & eggs?

Oh, no, demurs Trixi, not when I'm travelin'. I want a continental breakfast, you know, crepes & a mimosa & everything.

That ain't a continental breakfast, continental is just bread & coffee, I correct.

Shut up, says Trix, you never been to the continent.

I hope he ain't givin' ya trouble, Countess, cause if he is—

Just then a minor typhoon comes up & sends my paper plate flying with what's left of the ham & egg.

Ha, ha, laughs Trixi, & suddenly it's like a pail of water landed on our heads. We start running for shelter while all the local boys do is pull combs out of their pockets & run 'em through their wet hair.

Jesus Christ, & I thought we could get a car & go sightseeing & all, says Trixi. We can't see anything in this rain.

The Countess grabs an empty paper plate & puts it over her hairdo. No matter. You go back to the room, & I'll get some things to amuse you at the drugstore. She trudges bravely out into the rain with shoe leather squeaking, leaving me & Trix under a lean-to watching the local gentry do tricks with their hair. The mute kid has pulled off his shirt & is dancing from table to table in the rain, throwing up his arms & tilting back his head to catch the rain in his open mouth.

He's sweet, says Trixi. Why don't you give him a chance? Hell, Perdido, you don't always wanna be alone.

Aw, I dunno Trix, a kid with a handicap like that can be lots a trouble.

What's trouble, says Trixi, when you're in love, & she puts her head on my shoulder. Jeez I'm confused.

*

Me, Trix, & the Countess all pile into their big queen-sized bed. The Countess has brought Trix some candy bars & about a dozen comics. Strangely, the Countess has got the giggles & thinks maybe they've piped some kind of laughing gas into the room with the muzak. We all drift off into shadowland.

Get dressed , girls, it's all you can eat at La Concha down the boulevard.

Oh boy, says Trix, & rolls off the bed, jumps into her red dress with all the white squiggles on it. How do I look? All that candy don't show on me yet, does it? Gracious Lord, where'd I put that safety pin?

In a couple more minutes, the Countess is got up in a new pair of black pinstripe trousers & black turtleneck, & she's got her jacket balanced on her shoulders like otto preminger or do I mean von stroheim?

We find the Concha Hotel & head for the dining room, which is shaped like a giant conch shell. Every table except ours is for 2 in the corner. Every girl's got on a white dress, & every guy's wearing a golf shirt. Every girl's taking a bite out of her swordfish & chewing it with her mouth closed, her eyes giving her sugar daddy the ice queen routine.

Ever notice how these couples never say a word to each other while they're eatin', says Trix. It's downright creepy.

Say, garçon, says I to the senior in the sailor outfit & yachting cap, when ya get through swabbin' the deck we'd appreciate a few plates over here. Sailor boy comes over with some saucers & we head for the buffet table. If you want a little advice, I tell Trixi, don't waste your time on the pickled beets & red bean salad. Go straight for the good stuff. After ya come up here for the tenth time, they tend to call the house detective.

Aw, don't worry, says Trix, my belly's killin' me from all those baby ruths. Jezuz, what's this! & she lets what looks like a leprechaun's legs drop onto her plate.

Those are frogs legs, says the Countess. Can you imagine the idiocy of including frogs legs in a seafood dinner?

Well, I thought frogs like to get wet, says Trixi.

Around dessert, the Countess digs into her safari bag, scoops a handful of nickels out, & tips them into Trixi's hands.

Which ones look lucky? asks Trixi, pointing to a row of slot machines the colored lights on top. Stay away from the one's that just rang, go for the sleepers, I instruct.

Trixi starts tossing nickels into the slot & yanking the handle while the countess stands at attention nearby, & I edge my way over to the blackjack table, fingering the roll of twenties in my pocket from the Countess's broken C-note. When I look up, the Countess's eyes are drilling holes in me.

Don't, she warns. We aren't made of money. I'm in the mood for some music. Let's go! she barks, startling both Trixi & me. She grabs my arm, & the 3 of us leave the casino.

There's a junior vegas extravaganza going on in the lounge, & the same couples who kept a tight lip during dinner are going through the motions of a rumba.

Hey, Countess, says Trixi, what if you & me was to dance together?

I speak not from any shame, sighs the Countess wearily, but why challenge them? We'll find a more appropriate setting.

We do find 1 of those places with the windows blacked up & a strip of black leather curtain in front of the door. There's a sign says GIRLS, GIRLS, GIRLS! plastered across the front, & the countess tells the dame behind the bar to give us 2 vodka & soda + a red-eye for me.

A tiny señorita is sitting at the bar with a guy with a fat arm who looks like an insurance-fraud dick. Little missy's sitting on the bar stool, but her head don't even quite reach to the edge of the bar. Her great big saucer eyes look me over right through the crook in her date's arm.

Little missy hops off the bar stool & disappears into the ladies' room. A few minutes later, she comes out in a bikini & flicks some stage lights on. She puts a few coins in the jukebox & begins a slow grind.

Her hips aren't any wider than the space between my ears, but she can move them 'round the world without losing control of the wheel. She bends over & holds onto the back of a chair so her mini-butt is sticking over the stage.

Sweet little thing, sighs Trixi. Don't forget to slip her 5 when we leave.

Just as my 2 ladies are starting to dance together & things are starting to feel cozy, I begin thinking about making my exit like the night before. We're walking back toward the hotel on the boardwalk when I catch the scent of blood. I can hear bongo drums coming from the dive across the street, & there's a sign says MEMBERS ONLY over the door.

Ladies, I tell the 2 of 'em, that gentlemen's club across the street is where I'd like to apply for membership. Why don't you wait for me here during the interview? If you don't hear any screams in about 5 minutes, you can be on your way.

When I get to the top of the stairs, a little grilled trapdoor opens up. Gentlemen only, says the local yokel. You're with those ladies outside, no?

I'm about to give him the line, That was no lady… but instead I come back with, & what do you take me for? The door swings open & I find myself in the same situation as the night before. Only 1 customer, sitting at the bar.

This time the music's turned up loud enough to shatter safety glass, but the kid dancing on the bar doesn't seem to mind & nor do I mind him. He gets down on his knees & starts shakin' it in the face of the lone customer.

I don't know what kept me there for 2 hours. Something told me I couldn't go back to the hotel without a different feeling between my legs. So I plunked myself down on a stool & waited for some others to show up. That was when something miles high in ladies' clothes came in with a chaperone. Since I'd been to beauty school to study being a hairdresser, I could tell her blond ponytail was what we call a fall. It must have measured a couple yards, caused it reached all the way to her rump. Gladiator girl sat down at the bar & pulled some dollar bills out of her bra with her jumbo-sized hands, then stuffed the money into the dancin' kid's monokini. The trouble started when a half-asleep kid in back of her reached over & tugged on the ponytail. She jumped off her stool & put her hands on her hips. Don't you ever pull my hair, she began shouting in bassa profundo, don't you ever ever, & in the dim light it looked like she tore at a hunk of his hair real hard. Like it? Nobody likes it! she bellowed. Don't touch the hair!

Gladiator girl sat down with her chest heaving, & I thought how somebody should tell her to always get mad, cause that's how her jugs looked the most real—when they were moving up & down 'stead of just sitting there while the rest of her was moving. This way you really knew they were attached rather than her brother's athletic socks wadded up.

The kid who'd yanked her hair went & sat down across the room & I started scoping him out. He had snaky slim hips & bony little elbows poking out of his short sleeves like matchsticks, & great big eyes that never looked at you even when they were staring you straight in the face.

He was a little dragonfly kind of teen. Somebody watching me look at him might have found it kind of funny the way I was giving him the eye—a big hunk of flesh like me—while he swayed to the music like a pigeon feather in a down draft. They might a wondered why he looked down at the floor when he walked by me & let 1 matchstick wrist slip against my fly, while letting my arm snake 'round his waist, until he was lolling on my chest like a bunch of water lilies on a pond & I could taste those cold white teeth I saw a moment ago floating in the dim light.

I'm a romantic, you see.

Crumble up a shiny old kimono & drop it on a bed, toss a few handfuls of platinum hair on it. Mix it up with a bunch of blankets & pillows & throw in 2 plump alabaster arms. That's Trixi in the morning.

Now pull the head up & kiss last night's brandy off that sleepy pout. Roll her over as you pull up the shade with your other arm & yank. That's how you get Trixi up in the morning. You'll know why anybody that's ever known her ended up calling her sugar, & you'll understand why the Countess ain't made a peep about not being comfortable ever since we came to the island.

Holding her gentle like a piece of cotton candy you don't want to crush kinda makes things seem worthwhile regardless of the situation. But when you let go of her, the sad thing will stumble out of your arms & use the wall to help herself to the bathroom, that kimono trailing off those snow drifts for shoulders. You let your arms fall to your sides & your hand reaches for the door as you pull yourself together, put some snap in your voice, & tell her: Trix, move ass & get dressed. See ya outside.

Outside, the Countess is sitting at what's become the usual table, her eyes shiny as brand new silver quarters, her neck straight as a gun barrel, her fingers playing with her napkin.

Top 'o the mornin' to you, Countess, what's that wet look in your peepers?

I didn't bargain for this, says the Countess.

Had your fill of papayas?

I'm so confused.

Funny thing, Trixi was just saying the very same thing th' other day.

Countess screws up her lids over her melting orbs like 2 steel clamps squeezing 'em dry & says, I of all people had no idea this would happen to me.

Well, Countess, Trix's like flash paper. It don't take much for her to light up. Get too close & you'll catch fire. Not that I'm belittlin' your appeal, but I been present at plenty of her bonfires, & the flare-ups don't last too long, kind like a flash in the pan, if you'll excuse the cliché. 'Specially when the other person takes hold a the torch. Now, it's sad to say, but the best way to hold on to her is to make her think you don't give a hoot. At any rate, I think a change of scenery would do us all some good. What say we get us some wheels at the local try-harder & head into the interior, maybe we can leave this steam bath behind.

Right, says the Countess. But first we have to go into the old city. Trixi wants to go souvenir hunting.

About an hour later, Trix comes bouncing toward our breakfast table looking fresh as an ear of august corn. We goin' shoppin' today, Countess? I saw a couple really cute pieces at the souvenir shop. There's this ashtray that's shaped just like a banana.

Not 'fore we all eat, I say.

Trixi has the waiter line up six little paper cups on her tray.

What's that for? I ask.

Coffee. I got shoppin' to do.

Trix, if you swallow all that we're gonna tie a rope to you & make you run next to the car.

The Countess gives a big american laugh like I never seen her do before & says, drink up, little bee. I'll go to the desk & check us out. She gets up from the table & disappears. Might have to pay cash, though.

Trix takes a big gulp of coffee. We rentin' a car after we go shoppin', I hope? Oh boy. I been studyin' the map. All we gotta do is head south on this big highway 4… what was it? oh yeah, 409, & at the bottom of the island, they got this incredible lagoon that lights up at night. You see there's these teeny creatures in the water with built-in headlights, & every time you stir 'em up they flip the switch, kind of like fireflies but better—

Can the chatter for a minute, Trix. I wanna know what kinda line you been force-feeding the Countess as of late.

Trix sticks her chin up in the air. Whatever may you be talking about? she intones. I ain't feedin' the Countess no line, Perdido. We're gettin' along just fine.

Now, Trixi, I says, nobody could hope you & the Countess would get along more than me. I got what you'd call a vested interest in the whole deal. But you been in the entertainment business a long time & you know the golden rule; never let things get too sticky with a good client.

Trixi slams down her cup & the brown stuff splatters over her wrist. I don't like your innuendo, she says. & you got it wrong on both counts. The Countess isn't lookin' for entertainment. Couple night sa pleasure don't sit right with her. She wasn't brought up that way, but there's no use tryin' to explain it to you. & as for what's happening 'tween me & the Countess—that's 'tween me & her. You better get that straight right away. Trix starts shaking, & finally she crumbles into tears.

Oh, Perdido, I'm so confused. What's happenin' I don't know. Countess is a wonderful person. I never thought I could feel this way 'bout a woman before. I don' wanna go back to the states, I wanna stay here forever.

Just then the deaf mute who's been wiping tables does a crazy pirouette, throws up his rag in the air, & plops himself down at our table.

He reaches out & touches Trixi real gentle on the hair. He's grinning at me, but his eyes are pleading.

The Countess comes striding back. The deaf mute jumps up & skips away. Trixi pulls herself together & wipes her eyes before the Countess has a chance to see what's been happening.

Feeling a little jumpy, I maneuver the back of our brand new impala toward the curb. From inside a tiled hallway, a kid is staring at me through a filagree iron gate. Above his head a big ceiling fan next to a rickety staircase seems to just make it around. The kid doesn't blink. Maybe he's making sure I don't leave a scratch on his daddy's car parked in front of the building.

Countess & Trixi are curled into the corner of the backseat with big blank smiles on their faces. Turn around & look, will you! I shout, surprising myself by my own nervous mood. Countess turns around & cranes her head to guide me into the spot.

I climb out of the car. Then they climb out. There's a hush around the 2 of them, an invisible circle that says do not enter. & sometimes their happiness makes you paw at the glass like a dog with his tongue hanging out.

The Countess leads us up the steps of a church & peeks inside, hoping to see that famous silver altar, but we got the wrong church. She spots an old lady selling little relics & begins blabbing to her in the native tongue. The lady hands something to her & she slips the old broad a few bucks.

Lemme see, Countess, what you got? says Trixi. The Countess keeps both hands cupped together & opens them a crack. Trixi peeks inside. Jeez, says, Trixi, a rosary that glows in the dark! Countess pours the beads into her hand. Wow.

She grabs my head & shoves it down for me to take a look. Lying on a bed of green beads & a cross that glows in the dark is a shadowy jesus, his head thrown back & his arms thrown apart looking all off center, making me think of the deaf-mute for some reason.

Can I keep it?

Countess nods.

Once we slide into a pew in the church, Trixi pulls out the rosary & starts swinging it like a strand of pearls in a B show. Trix, I snap, will you cut it out! A rosary ain't no joke to these people!

The Countess pulls the beads gently from Trixi hands. Let me show you how you say the rosary, my dear. Her long, slender fingers slide over the beads, stopping at each station of the cross. It takes a long time, explains the Countess, & she tells Trixi the prayer that has to be repeated for every bead.

But what do you say it for? asks Trix.

Penance, says the Countess. After you have made your confession to the priest.

Neither of them have noticed the pair of knees on the rough stone floor, peeking out of the curtain over the little cubicle in the wall. Or the black hem of the priest's robe in the cubicle next to it. Or the sobbing that comes leaking out of the cubicle in little waves.

My mother, says the Countess, goes several times a week. But I went for the last time after I heard the rustling of the priest's robe.

What're you talking about?

A vow of chastity, says the Countess, has been an assumption of the priesthood for centuries. But as you can imagine, it's very hard to keep. When a priest asks a young girl or a woman very detailed questions about a venal sin, you'll sometimes hear a rustling of his robe. It's not difficult to imagine what he's doing with his hands at that moment. All girls giggle about it, but I had never heard it until that time in confession.

Aren't all men alike, Trixi opines, even the ones who don't wear pants.

Perhaps that is why there are many women who never reach satisfaction without a fantasy involving a priest, instructs the Countess. As she talks, the rosary keeps sliding through her fingers. Trixi's eyes get big & round like a sucker at a carny show. Countess pours the rosary back into her hand.

Let's get outta here, I tell 'em.

We slide out of the pew. Trixi's still got her hands cupped together like a little steeple so she can stare at the rosary through a crack.

We cut through a side street & see a place that looks like a barbershop—only it's marked tattoos. Let's take a peek, I suggest. I got a yen for a lily or maybe a naked lady on the bicep.

One of the native boys is sitting in the torture chair with his shirt stripped to his waist. He's got his chin stuck out, & the rest of his face is set in a nonchalant expression while the artist digs in with a needle that makes a sound like a dentist's drill.

In between the anchors & hibiscuses on the wall to choose from there are crowns of thorns, jesus faces, & variations of the virgin he'll prick into any part of your body you say. & in a book that looks real old, he's got pictures of his famous clients, some without any clothes on to show the full extent of his work. There's a bald guy has had a crown of thorns drawn on his head & a pretty little lady with all the stations of the cross etched onto her body without a patch of white skin left. Each of her shins are little masterpieces, too, glowing visions of the virgin with her arms spread at her sides, which must make it look like mary's comin' at you when the lady takes a step.

Well, what about it, Perdido? says Trixi. Want us to tie you down?

The artist looks up from his buzzing needle & grins, showing his silver teeth. But the kid he's working on keeps his face set like a sawdust dummy.

C'mon says Trixi. I'll go get a bottle of rum, you can pick a picture out & get tanked. When you come to, you'll have 1 of them beauties on your arm.

Aw, Trix, I ain't that committed yet.

That's the problem with you, says Trixi, you ain't committed to nothin'. & she steps by me & out into the street. She's got that rosary in her hand & is craning her head up to the sky.

The farther we go up the mountain, the more we leave that steam bath behind. The air begins getting thinner & dryer, & finally the sun comes out. Trixi's up on her knees with her head hanging out the window & her hair flopping in the wind like spaniel ears. The Countess's got us tuned to a nice pachanga station.

Ow, says, Trixi, got any gum? My ears are popping.

Swallow, says the Countess.

I bear down on the gas, & our jalopy crawls up the mountain. Then we follow the signs to a little dirt road & an inn built around an old mineral springs. I can smell it already—kind of sulfury.

The Countess balances her jacket on her shoulders & goes to chat up the clerk. Then she tosses us some keys so we can take our bags to our rooms. I'll be up in a little while, she tells us.

The wooden rafters in the girls' room are higher than the Roxy balcony, & 1 wall is all windows looking out on a swimming pool.

Quite a setup, says I.

Oh, Perdido, it's beautiful. If only we could stay here forever.

That's just it, Trixi. We all gotta go home sometime. I wish you'd keep that in mind while you're givin' your pitch to the Countess.

She's not listening to me. She's looking out the windows watching the little green lizards jumping off the wall of the inn. 1 of them has made its way inside & scutters across her foot.

Swank, opines Trixi. She slides open 1 of the big windows, & perfumes come through the screen like christmas at the macy's cosmetic counter. Past the pool, I can see flowers popping out of vines. Somewhere a cockatoo cackles.

Trixi's unpacking her little things & hanging them up, smoothing them out with her hand, trying to make them look good for the Countess, I guess. When she pulls off a stocking in front of the windows, the sun lights it up, & I can see the trees through it. As she walks back & forth to the closet, the sun flames up in the little curls around her plump face. It's hard to see past her with all that sun, but through the window, I can still make out a dark figure standing near the pool, with a jacket balanced on its shoulders. Too much glare to know for sure if it's the Countess, but whether or not it is, it's standing in conversation with another figure—looks like a man—and he's standing with his back turned to me.

Trixi doesn't notice, having turned away from the windows. You gonna go upstairs to your room to take a nap, or do you wanna rest here with me? she asks in a soft voice. Her white body sinks onto the bed, & she holds out her arms. I drop down next to her, touch her cheek. Trixi, I says, you & me still gotta talk—but suddenly the whole thing touches me & I let go. Her body feels like a smooth, cool egg. I put my head on her titties & fall asleep.

When I wake up, twilight has snuck into the room like some kind of powder & my face is swimming in drool on Trixi's titty. I must have slept with my mouth open. She's still fast asleep. As I get up slowly, I see that the Countess is there, tall & straight in a chair that faces the bed.

Countess, says I.

Shh, says the Countess, you'll wake her.

This isn't what it looks like, I whisper.

How peaceful she seems, says the Countess under her breath. Then she gazes into my eyes, keeps her voice low. I know what you're thinking. What you fear. What started out as a rather shoddy shakedown has backfired. You're afraid you'll be left without any cake.

Oh, Countess, that ain't necessary to say.

Hush! You consider this little lady very useful to you, don't you? & no wonder. I understand you perfectly. I'm prepared to set your mind at ease.

The Countess reaches into her jacket pocket & pulls out a bankroll, hands it to me.

I can't take all this. Well, maybe half of it.

Count it.

Holy willikers, there's 5 g here!

I want to buy her, says the Countess, her eyes brimming with tears. I want to buy the little lady from you.

But I don't own Trix.

Let's just say your partnership with her is over. No more setups.

Well, jeez, shouldn't Trix be in on this? After all, she's the one—

Listen to me, says the Countess. When we get back to the old city, you're to disappear. As simple as that. I'll do all the explaining. She takes the money out of her hand & drops it back in her bag. Think about it, she says.

Trix gives a sigh, & her peepers fall open. She yawns & stretches. Oh, I dreamed we were all in 1 great big egg together, Countess, me, you, Perdido. It was sticky, but all you had to do is lie there & float. Whew, it is kinda sticky in here, isn't it?

Me, Countess & Trixi decide to head for the mineral springs near the inn. Since it's nearly dark, we have to kind of feel our way along the dirt path. The air's full of crickets that sound like ticker tape. Every time a lizard hops off a tree, it gives me a little start. Trixi looks up into the branches of those trees that look like black webs in the twilight air & shudders. They're covered with some kind of cocoons.

Look at all of 'em!

Some of them have even grown off the trees & are hanging from the telephone wires, like rows of sleeping bats.

The clerk at the desk said the american company which owned the grounds has moved out because of the political situation, says the Countess. They must have stopped spraying.

Some kind of caterpillar disease, says I.

On the telephone wires? wonders Trixi. She tells the Countess about a movie she saw: things from outer space that leave pods that take over people's bodies so they can make replicas without feelings out of them. Imagine somebody takin' away your feelings, she says. I wouldn't wanna go on.

Well, I dunno, I counter in a mumble, I ain't so sure I wouldn't like that.

In the darkness the Countess's face looks flat like as a paper bill with 2 zeroes on it.

Look out! gasps Trix, & she pushes me right into a patch of brambles.

You almost squashed that little fella!

I pull a pricker out of my shin. Trix, it was only a bullfrog.

Only? What's a matter with you, Perdido? She lets out a big sigh. Sometimes I ask myself who I been hangin' out with all these years.

You tell me, I answer, real careful.

Trix is wearing her rosary like a necklace. All I can make out in the darkness are its glowing beads & the Countess's 2 round white eyes.

Maybe you should give it some thought, I add.

Give what?

'Bout who you been hangin' out with… Trix doesn't answer. Maybe you're tired a hangin' out with me, I go on, real cool. I can see the 2 white eyes floating in the dark narrowing.

Perdido, what're you talkin' 'bout? says Trix.

Nothin', really.

The stars are out & the night is chattering. The leaves look black, but the cocoons are glowing dull gray among them. Trixi's hair looks like a white flame floating in the dark. We come to the sulfur baths, a series of pits in the cliff by the side of the path. The stairs up to them are made out of boulders covered with slippery moss. Using our hands to keep from falling, we edge our way toward the sound of splashing & voices speaking low in the language of the island.

Steam is rising from the sulfur pits into the already humid air. The moon hasn't risen yet, & above the pool, the trees with their cocoons have made a canopy to shut out the stars. The few bathers we can still make out in the diminishing light are dark blurs against the walls of steam. As soon as they become aware of us, the voices & splashing suddenly stop. We can feel them listening, trying to figure out who we are.

Tourists, says the Countess. You'd think they'd prefer the pool at the inn. They're afraid of us. She's calling her husband & children & they're going to leave.

The splashing starts again. A little kid cries & his mother hushes him. I can just make out some people edging their way down the stairs. There's the snap of twigs & then silence.

Well, I guess we got the place to ourselves, I observe.

I didn't mean to kick 'em out, says Trix.

A bullfrog croaks.

It's safer for us this way, says the Countess. You don't know who we'd run into here in the dark.

And dark it is, pitch black, in fact.

Let me lean on you, Perdido. Trix starts peeling off her duds. I light a match so she can see what she's doing. The Countess is already in the raw, her jacket still balanced on her bare shoulders. She takes a few steps through the wall of steam & disappears. In a few moments we hear a splash. I'm way over here, she calls out from the farthest sulfury pool.

I go next through the steam & lower myself in to the pool nearest me. It feels good, I gotta say. Hey, c'mon in, Trix. I can just make her out climbing in next to me. Pipe the new fish, I joke.

The bullfrog croaks again, & I think about the 5 g's when suddenly Trixi goes into a dither.

Help, Perdido! Big clouds of steam are billowing into the air. Help, somethin's got me!

What's the matter, Trix?

Perdido, please help me!

You okay, Trix?

No, help!

I freeze & stay rooted to the spot. I've never been much of a hero. Laughter laces the black air like saxophone notes.

Perdido, help!

Still I don't move, feeling like a cad, trying to peer through the wall of steam. I think I can make out the rosary, then Trixi's silhouette with the hair flattened. I can hear the Countess panting as she threads through the water, searching for Trixi. Trixi, are you all right? Where are you? she gasps.

Jesus, Perdido, why didn't you come in after me?

Well, I dunno, Trix, that wouldn't a been too smart, really.

Oh my god! Trixi's rosary bounces up into the air as she struggles against a shadow in back of her. You lug, she shouts. Didn't you get the message? Get outta here! Who the hell are you?

She's answered by another peal of silver laughter.

You scared the livin' daylights outta me!

A soft male voice purrs in the native tongue.

He was embarrassed, answers the Countess. You were in the men's pool.

Well how in a month a Monday's was I supposed to know that?

The voice purrs again. He's afraid you swallowed too much water, explains the Countess. It can make you sick.

Somethin' wasn't quite right 'bout the way he bumped into me, Trixi goes on. In the pitch darkness I can hear her & the Countess slipping back into their duds.

What are we waitin' for? Trixi rags. Let's get th' hell outta here!

As we start down the stairs, I can just make out that the figure has popped away from the steam. In a moment he's caught up to us. I can even feel his silver laugh falling onto my neck. The purring talk starts again.

Tell him to get packin', Countess, whines Tricki. Her breathing is getting quicker & shorter.

He wants to accompany us as far as the hotel, translates the Countess in a dull voice, to make up for frightening you.

We don't need his help! Trixi complains.

The purring shadow is so close behind us that once or twice something soft brushes against the tops of my thighs. His purr arcs into the air, like the edge of a canoe panel skimming water.

He's glad there's no moon, says the Countess. All his clothes are in his car.

At least I woulda seen him first if there was a moon, says Trixi.

Mixed with the smell of the leaves & flowers around us is just the hint of good tobacco coming from the figure's breath.

Dinner, at the inn, says the Countess.

Huh?

He's inviting us to dinner at the inn.

Tell him we got other plans.

The voice dips into a cooing sound.

Eight o'clock, says the Countess, sounding strangely nervous.

Countess! The guy's a masher. Tell him no!

Do as I ask, this 1 time, whispers the Countess.

In my room, I scrape the lizards off my pant legs before peeling off, turning on the shower, & diving in. I begin wondering again about the Countess's bankroll, now that she's been willing to part with a piece of it. Was that money she first held out to me really just a dream? A picture of the 5 g's pops into my head, then the Countess's face with its 2 burning eyes flat & smooth as a piece of paper. Was that her I saw standing by the pool before Trixi & me took our nap? If it was, who was she talking to? It's gotta be some kinda hype. Who would pay 5 grand just to get their hooks into my wife? An uneasy feeling creeps over me & settles in my stomach. Maybe I been underestimatin' Trix all these years.

He's waiting in the dining room wearing a dinner jacket with a bottle of bubbly in an ice bucket, hair soft as velvet falling over tan satin skin & lips like ripe fruit twisted into a grin. He's a young guy, pretty young at least. But then my head fills with that old refrain: where have I seen that face before?

He jumps smoothly to his feet & pulls the chairs away from the table for both ladies, then grabs my hand & flashes a row of ivories. The where-have-I-seen-him bulb gets brighter.

Angel, says the kid.

Huh?

That's his name, says the Countess. Pronounced in English. With a dash of his hand, he draws a little halo over his head. Swell.

Trix stares down at the floor to keep from making eye contact with him. The kid pantomimes eating movements & smacks his lips, explains something to the Countess in his language. Seems he's already picked out our spread in advance. Not local food—for us. He's taken the liberty, he explains, because he knows the ropes.

The Countess nods gravely, & his eyes take on a weird sparkle. It's like they're drilling holes in her. Where've I seen that...

Dinner's the best food we've had on the island, & the kid makes it a point of letting us almost finish eating before he digs in. He's the life of the party without takin' over the party. He knows when to talk, when to shut up. Where've I seen it before?

Trix is watching him through her lashes, her eyes fixing on the perfectly starched cuffs, big, shiny links, & manicured nails. She narrows her eyes at the sparkling soft lips. The Countess's face is set in a deadpan, & the tone in which she responds to the questions he asks in his language seems equally dead. Maybe she thinks she's too good for him. But the voice keeps up its purring nonetheless, charm oozing from every syllable. What are they saying? The Countess's answers seem to be getting shorter, but that only makes the guy more animated. The Countess smiles nervously as the guy's purrs lengthen & slide across the table like spiders. Then she starts to stutter, turns beet red, then dead white. She casts her eyes to the ground.

He's puttin' the make on the Countess, hisses Trixi. I can tell. Countess, what's he sayin'? The Countess looks up at Trixi with panicked eyes.

The smoothie! I knew it the minute I bumped into him. You just tell him you got all the company you need! Don't bother t' be polite.

The Countess doesn't answer.

Well, tell him! She looks him right in the eye. Listen, Angel face, she says. NO GO. Understand? TAKE WALK!

The look he gives back is cold & sweet.

Countess! whines Trix. Will ya tell him!

The Countess keeps starting at the ground.

Trixi's eyes brim up. Countess, why're you doin' this t' me? I can't take it any longer. She gets up & runs out of the dining room.

The Countess jerks, as if about to stand up & follow her, but it's like she's glued to the spot. The guy's look has pinned her down like a needle pushed through a butterfly. Once more his laugh spills out like a silver ribbon. He croons something to the Countess in the native tongue.

Angel would like to go to the swimming pool with you, says the Countess in a shaky voice. Then she gets up like a robot & marches out.

Angel's stunning face twists into another grin. What say? he voices in English.

The teeth in the hatchet-lean face seem cut from the same moonlight that falls over the pool from the newly risen moon.

I been trailing you for 2 days, Mr. Perdido. Don't you recognize me from the hotel or the bar?

The deaf-mute & his lollipop explode in my head. I see the guy that was hugging him, but I don't mention it, keep cool.

For someone couldn't spit a word of English you must've found some phrase book.

Oh, I went to school in the states, says the kid, gazing up at the moon. From the look in those big, gleaming eyes, you'd guess he was thinking of buying it. The thought occurs to me: obviously, he was playing the no-speak-english act 'cause he had words for the Countess he didn't want me & Trixi to understand.

You sure fooled me with your act.

I'm not the only 1 fooling you, says the kid. Maybe you won't mind my asking, Mr. Perdido, why a shark like you with all your experience would let a two-bit con artist take advantage—

Hold on, sonny.

Don't get me wrong, I admire you. You could even say we're cut from the same mold.

2 gingerbread cookies, huh?

Well, I learned my ropes in the old city, says the kid. The 1 where all the men look like ladies & the kids dance on the bar?

Really? Rough.

Got to the states sort of like you got here. American tourists were a lot more generous then. I was only 13. But I never felt like I belonged in the states. I always planned to come back here. After I did, I kinda felt resentful of everybody, if you know what I mean? Especially the ones had made me eat it raw when I should have been on pablum.

Sure, kid, I read ya.

I figured I'd kinda get back at 'em, I guess. All the vultures that had taken it out of me for a couple a bucks or half a warm bed for a night. & that's why I was wondering why a pro like you, who's obviously spent more years at it than me—getting back at 'em, I mean—would let your wife get involved in this Monopoly game.

Trixi?

Sure, says the kid. The Countess—what she's calling herself now— is one dangerous character.

You must be makin' some kind of mistake, kid. Why, the Countess—

The Countess, snorts the kid, & the silver laugh falls out of his mouth again. She's about as genuine as her so-called Swiss bank. It'd be more correct to call her Betsy Ross, that being her name. Born right here on the island, daughter of the richest american planter who was killed by his workers when he beat 1 of them to a pulp.

Where do you get your information?

My father worked on that plantation. Field hand. The planter had a daughter—name of Betsey, as I said. When she grew up, she embezzled a lot of money from her own pop. Ran away to the states & his whole operation folded. Daddy went bankrupt & shot himself.

An american tragedy, says I sarcastically. Who got you to run after her? I'm not expecting the full answer.

The kid doesn't say anything. & If you ask me, there's something fishy about his whole story. I been around. It's obvious he's leaving out some key details, but that doesn't stop him from going on.

I'd be willin' to bet our so-called Countess has been pulling the wool over your wife's eyes too.

That laugh again, a laugh I'm beginning not to like because it sounds mocking.

Hey, what are you, some kind of private investigator?

The kid just stares at me in a way I don't feel comfortable explaining.

Back at my hotel room, the kid starts peeling the lizards off his argyles, tossing them out the window 1 at a time.

Quite a place, he says, glancing 'round. People who live here on the island don't usually get a chance to see something like this.

We might as well make the most of it, I tell him—while it lasts.

You might as well.

I mean we.

Hot in here, got a fresh handkerchief? he says. I like to feel comfortable, Mr. Perdido. It makes my job easier.

What's that job again, private dick? This time he shakes his head. Gimme a glass of water, will you? he says. Funny how the water here makes the tourists sick but doesn't hurt us at all. Let's get back to the question. What'd you say brought you to the island, Mr. Perdido? He flashes that cold grin yet again.

I went 'cause Trixi went. I've always kinda hung out with Trixi.

To pick up her scraps? Doesn't sound like much of a job.

Maybe not for you, dick tracy, but I got a knack for being the middleman. & despite what you might think, Trixi's not a bad egg.

The kid's mocking eyes stop me cold with their glassy look. He begins to peel down & I head to the head for his glass of water. When I come back, he's in the raw, lying face down on top of the bed, arms spread out like wings, back & buns striped by the moonlight through the venetian blinds.

'Bout time, he says, I almost fell asleep.

I sink down next to him.

The Countess was in possession of a big wad of cash, he says, and do you think it's still around?

Rather than answering, I keep mum.

Morning finds the kid more fresh-faced than ever. He's obviously 1 of those kids wakes up feelin' at home in any bed 'cause he'll never be in any bed he calls his own. He doesn't bother to get dressed pronto. Instead, he sits up on the edge of the bed & says, Got a rag?

I toss him a dirty undershirt. He grabs his patent leather shoes, spits on 'em, & begins wiping off last night's dust. He checks out his halo in the reflection on the shoe & grins, then lets the shoe drop back down again, stretching his arms up over his head. Feel like a swim before I take care of the Countess, Mr. Perdido? You wouldn't happen to have an extra pair of trunks, would you?

Sure, kid, got a pair you'd look great in.

The kid yawns & stretches out his hand for 'em.

Sure, kid, I think to myself, take your time. Maybe it'll give me enough time to figure out your game.

The pool has broken my reflection into little bits. The kid is lying poolside next to it, staring into the sun. His body doesn't shatter like my reflection in the water. In the sun, he looks welded into 1 bright, solid piece, seamless as steel.

I ordered a couple drinks for us, the kids says, but the waiter never came back out with them. With the americans about to leave, you can't get service any more. The old style of waiter has disappeared. It's almost like they broke the mold.

Maybe they knew what they were doing by discontinuing that model, I tell him.

I don't know, says Angel. I seen some pretty sad lemons put back into service. My brother, for instance. He was born deaf & he can't speak.

I remember those eyes, the rag & tray, the bleating.

You wouldn't think they'd take something like that off the shelf & put him into action, now would you, Perdido? His words seem bitter, like drops of black oil hitting those white bedsheets we were lying on.

Seems like a nice kid, I say.

You mean, compared to his brother? The words fall from the mouth like more black & bitter oily drops.

Both of you seem swell to me.

He raises his head & moves it out of the sun to look me over. I'm sure you don't wanna put Trixi in danger, he says.

I told you I had nothin' to do with those two and their great love affair.

& I believe you.

Trixi's not got a thing to do with anything shady, either.

He turns over. These trunks are elegant, Mr. Perdido. You got lotsa style.

Takes 1 to know 1, kid.

Guess it takes 2 to make a good pair of trunks worth wearing, Mr. Perdido.

You fill 'em out swell all by yourself, kid.

He rolls over again & stretches back his arms. It's gonna be no fun when the americans leave, he says. They probably won't even let in american tourists for a while. I sure did have a good time last night.

You sure gave me a good time last night, kid.

Angel lets out a sigh & turns back onto his stomach. He presses his cheek against the side of the pool & dangles his arm to let his hand poke into my reflection. You know, he says, I happen to know that the Countess was walking around with 50 thou in cash, but I wonder if she's blown it all already. All I know is if the people that money is intended for don't get it—hey, rub some oil on my back, would you?—they'll settle for a little blood.

The kid stretches under my rub, hand still dangling in my reflection, which changed shape all by itself when I knelt down with the oil. You know, he says, I've already alerted the police & they're on their way to pick up the 2 broads. It sure would be great if you & me could get hold of your wife before the cops come—not to mention that cash the Countess may still have. Think you could get into their room with some excuse?

But what about Trixi?

Like I said, if the people that hired the Countess don't get that money back they'll want blood from somebody, says the kid. Keep rubbing that oil in, Perdido. He falls into a snooze.

The door & all the windows in the Countess's & Trixi's room are shut, but even before I can put my hand on the knob the door flies open. Countess squeezes out, shutting the door quick behind her.

You look white as a ghost, Countess.

Perdido, have you given some thought to our conversation?

Beg pardon?

The money. There's been a change in plans. I want you to leave now. Or you may stay here. I really don't care. In any case, Trixi & I are leaving.

Hold on a minute, Countess.

Haven't you heard? There's fighting going on in the old city.

Kid me not.

We can't go back there.

Where's Trixi?

Asleep.

I'd really like to speak to her.

There isn't time.

She'll wanna say goodbye, won't she?

She shoves the bankroll of 5g's into my hand & her body stiffens. You've been talking to that fabricator, haven't you? Well, he doesn't have the whole story. Don't believe him.

Do tell.

You've never been very concerned with politics, I'd wager to think, observes the Countess. After all, you're an american.

Yeah, Countess, politics's never been my thing, but must be different for you, since you're a local.

I don't deny it. But your new friend's a communist. If you're planning on hooking up with him, you don't know what you're getting into.

Just let me tell my wife toodle-oo, I say.

Goodbye from both of us, says the Countess, & slams the door shut.

A miniature breeze is shaking the leaves outside the screen of my room. They look like gold coins. The sound of weeping comes faintly through from the room below. I give my wingtips a dust, slip out of my trunks into my clothes, & throw my 2 other shirts into my bag. As I start for the door, I notice Angel's dinner jacket lying on the floor. He'll have to come back here & change. Might as well leave my bag here for the time being.

I peek out the window toward the pool. Angel is still lying there, on his stomach now, looking like a tipped-over Oscar. I push the blind slats shut. Pull out the roll again & count the 5 g's.

It's not a dream. But what about the 50 grand Angel mentioned? Must have been referring to that roll I glimpsed inside the Countess's safari bag at the airport. Angel wants to get his mitts on it, that's for sure. Of course, I could give him a glimpse of the 5g's & tell him that's all she had left. Or I could even take off on my own. Maybe they all deserve to be left high & dry. Nah, I've never been a solo act & I just can't do that to Trixi. I guess. Maybe I'll check out the happy couple again. I take out the 5g & cut it into 2 halves, put 1 in my pocket & the other in my bag.

The weeping gets louder as I near the girls' room. A muffled voice leaks through the door.

I ain't goin'!

Then I've got to go without you, snaps the Countess's voice.

Don't say that to me. You couldn't mean it.

Then get dressed!

Can't I even talk to him?

There's no time!

Trixi's sob bursts through the walls.

Stop that!

Why won't you tell me what's goin' on? Where's Perdido, I want Perdido, she whimpers.

Get away from that door!

Please, Countess.

Open it & were through.

I drum a few taps on the door.

Shhh! I hear somebody.

The door opens a crack, enough to glimpse 1 swollen eye.

Top 'o the mornin' to you, Countess. I'm back.

Get out of here, will you?

You'd think after all that stormy weather we've been havin' & what a perfect sunny day we got now, you'd be out here dryin' off at the pool with Angel & me.

I'm in no mood for sunbathing.

I'm a fool for telling you, but seems Angel don't care which 1 a ya gets nabbed. Long as it's somebody. In fact, folks he works for won't let him go home till he's collared you—and the money you're holdin'. Be a sport, Countess. Trixi don't deserve this situation. Don't make Trix pay for what you done.

The Countess's face colors, & her eyes avoid mine.

Tell Trixi I'm out here waiting, I say. I'll be at the pool. If I were you, I'd take off now—alone. Junior has called the cops.

The door creaks shut.

Angel is just waking up when I get back to the pool. He cranes his neck to get a gander at his back. Why didn't you wake me up, Perdido? My tan's uneven.

We'll have plenty a time to divvy up sunbeams, kid. I just settled a little score with the Countess.

You mean you got the money?

Let's just say your services are no longer needed.

Whoopee. Perdido, you & I were cut from the same die.

Made for each other, huh?

They don't make 'em like us any more.

Yeah. Now why don't you go upstairs & slip into your duds, but before you do, I got a few questions to ask.

Where'd you put it? The cash.

When you go up to the room, check out my bag. Little present in there for you.

Sure thing! The kid hops to his feet & starts to head swift for the stairway.

Maybe it's not as much as you were expecting, I call out.

Angel stops dead in his tracks.

What's going on, Perdido?

You don't think it's time we leveled with each other?

Angel walks back to me. You first.

Well, the crux of the story is that I can't leave Trixi. Don't care what happens to the Countess, but I don't want Trixi a part of it. Okay? The

Countess laid 5 grand on me. Your half's in the bag up there. Take it & do what you want with the Countess, but Trixi & I don't want no more to do with it.

Wait a minute, says Angel. I was hoping not to get you involved in all of this, but I think the time has come for the real story.

Why don't you start out by telling me all about being a commie?

He nods. Good place as any to start, but let me go back to the room to get something first.

Sure kid. Business first. When you're up there & opening my suitcase, could you find the alka seltzer? I keep gettin' a bad taste in my mouth.

Angel nods & heads for the stairs.

There ain't a breeze around. I got my hat on. My picture in the pool is smooth as glass. I take my shoes off, roll up my pant legs, & sit down & stick my feet in the water. There's that reflection again shattering into a thousand pieces. Slowly the pieces come together until it's good as new. Reluctant as I am, I drag myself to a standing position & stride back to the inn, scratch on Trixi's & the Countess's door once more.

Silence.

I put my mouth to within a smidgen of it. Trixi, I call, we gotta get outta here. Open up.

Nothing.

I creep back toward the pool. When I get there, I can see the door creaking open, the Countess peering left & right. Bag in hand, she makes a run for the car, hops in with her bag, & slams the door shut. Trixi comes out next & climbs into the other side.

Well, I guess she's made her decision. The motor turns over & they peel off down the road. Hey, that was our car. What am I supposed to do?

The sun is bright as a new silver dollar. Too bad we had to arrive in the rain. I loosen my tie & pop my top button open. A dragonfly lights on my hand, & I let it sit there until I hear footsteps coming from the inn. I don't have to turn around to figure it's Angel finally come back from my room. Hope he isn't too disappointed with the sum he ended up getting.

& then it dawns on me. The cops haven't come, & Angel hasn't jumped into his car & started chasing theirs. There has to be another game going on, & nobody has taken the trouble to clue me in. The thought gives me a sinking feeling in my stomach. What about the rest of the money the Countess had? Did Angel get his hands on it? Wish somebody would bring me that alka seltzer.

A tiny breeze comes up, & my reflection blurs over. Another reflection joins it. Angel is sitting next to me.

I believe you called me a communist, Mr. Perdido.

If the shoe fits. But don't take it wrong, kid.

I got something to show you. He's holding a photograph in 1 hand, sticks it under my nose.

Why you got a picture of Trixi?

Take a closer look, Mr. Perdido, seems a lot like her, doesn't it?

On second look, it's somebody damn sure resembles her, close to being a dead ringer, except that this 1 has a wild, determined look in her eyes, eyes, mouth, entire expression fixed on a prize, a look Trixi's never really had.

She's my sister, says Angel. I mean, my half-sister. I know you don't know much about the political situation here.

Hmm, the Countess was just saying the very same thing. I know the island's in trouble, Angel, if that's what you mean. & my heart goes out to you, I suppose. Where's Trixi?

I'm a lot more involved in the situation than I let on, Perdido.

I figured something didn't click. For 1 thing, you haven't even gone off after the 2 broads. Is it because you already managed to get hold of all the money?

Don't be too mad at me. There was a lot I couldn't say. In fact, most of it was me trying to rev you up to get your wife out of this mess. but now that those 2 have taken off, you're the 1 whose help I'm going to need even more. This island is about to fall, Mr. Perdido. The communists, who coalesced from the people who work the plantations, & the junta, a bunch of brutes fighting for a military dictatorship, are about to decide the fate of this place. I'm just trying to keep it from falling to the junta.

I don't get it, kid. What I got to do with it?

I'll explain, but we got to get going.

I said I didn't want to be involved.

You will when you know the whole story. That is, if you care at all about your wife.

Angel hustles me back to the room & tells me to pack pronto. He hurries me to the car, & we squeal out of there on 2 wheels.

The kid's an ace driver.

You already told at least 1 lie, I observe out loud. You're no private eye, are you, kid?

Angel shakes his head as we careen around a curve. I'm a revolutionary, you could say. I want the communist insurgents to win, & I'm doing everything in my power to make that happen.

Like I said, it's all Greek to me.

I told you I was the son of a field hand—and that's the truth—but I only said that because of my mother. I'm the illegitimate son of that planter. Countess is my half-sister, too—technically. His only legitimate child. That american bastard who owned the plantation wasn't satisfied beating his field hands to within an inch of their lives. He took liberties with their wives too, which is how I came into the world. The sonofa-bitch just couldn't keep it in his pants, & my half-sister, the 1 in the picture I showed you, was illegitimate too, sired by him with an american actress. Both of them were too worried about his reputation with the ruling class on this island & the big shots in Hollywood to admit it. Nei-ther of them acknowledged her, & she grew up with my field-worker family. Our so-called Countess, his only legitimate child, is a thieving chip off the old block—her dad—& when she took off for the states absconding with his money, there was nothing left for him to do but off himself.

Trash begets trash, I suppose. But why would you care, kid? You haven't drawn too appetizing a picture of the deceased.

I wouldn't, 'cept our ersatz Countess outdid him by a long shot.

Where'd she get that wad of green I spied in her safari bag?

It's money she's collected in the states for the junta, I'd expect, to buy arms.

You're joshing!

No, unfortunately. Countess wants her pop's plantation back. & she wants a lot more than that. She's been working with the junta, & she's got it into her head that when the island falls—to the junta, she hopes—as the legitimate daughter of the most powerful planter on the island, she'll claim the right to be the head of the new government. Especially if she can first get that war chest she's collected in the states into their hands.

Wait a minute, what's that mean for Trixi?

The answer to that is why we're in a hurry, Mr. Perdido, but there may still be a chance to save her.

Save her?... I start thinking of that pic of Trixi's lookalike, when it dawns on me. You're talking about the old *switcheroo*? I blurt out.

Bingo. I knew you had a head on your shoulders. How'd you guess?

Switcheroo's 1 of the oldest cons in the book. The problem's finding the lookalikes, but I seen it done with twins.

My half-sister, Trixi's uncanny double, is just as committed to the cause as me, if not more so. She's been leading the communist insurgents ever since this drama started.

Got it, kid. & Trixi looks just like her so…

Bingo, again. Countess is buying some time while she hunts down Trixi's lookalike, my sister. & if she finds her, she's planning to interrogate her. By torture. & then eliminate her.

But what about Trixi?

She needs Trixi in order to buy time. As soon as she saw her in Florida, she realized how valuable she could be. I'm pretty sure she plans on making a double delivery. First, she intends to dump her dead body somewhere the insurgents will find her, to make them think their leader is dead. Meanwhile she's planning to use the extra time to deliver the war chest to the junta and keep my sister alive, probably tied up in that hotel room, just long enough to interrogate her.

Step on it, kid.

The city is crawling with the junta, & it seems like the entire remaining population has locked themselves away to avoid it. Angel has a hard time making it back to our hotel. It's only his expert knowledge of back streets & side alleys that gets us there, but when we arrive, it looks like the hotel has shut down. There's only 1 employee left at the outdoor watering hole, & that's Angel's deaf-mute half-brother, who seems to have been expecting us. He looks scared to death.

Where are the girls? I scream at him, as if the volume of my voice is gonna vanquish his deafness & inability to read lips in any language. Angel waves me silent & fixes his bruvver in the eye. Like some Catskill comic, with the outstretched index finger of each hand, he traces the va-va-voom outline of a cartoon jayne mansfield, then lifts & spreads his arms with his palms pointing up & a confused look on his face as a way of saying, where is she?

The deaf-mute ain't no dummy & immediately starts playing charades, using his own private sign language. First, he uses 2 fingers to pantomime walking on the palm of his other hand. Then he points toward a staircase & starts poking the air in that direction.

Come on, says Angel, but as we start up the stairs, mutey runs over & grabs his bruvver's arm, trying to pull him back. He thinks it's too dangerous, explains Angel, shaking him off.

Angel & me start up 2 stairs at a time. We choose sides of the deserted hallway & begin creeping down it & pressing an ear to every door. Halfway along, Angel points to 1 of them.

Hey, Perdido, he whispers. I think I heard something. He knocks gently on the door but nobody answers.

Taking a couple steps back, he scrunches down like a lineman & collides against the door. When the cheap lock snaps, it flies open. Trixi's on the bed, but she's not moving. She's got on a new outfit too: army fatigues & a beret à la che guevara.

Is she dead?

Angel shakes his head. It was her snoring made me find the room, he explains.

A weird sentiment takes me over. After all these years hearing those snores while I was trying to get some shuteye, trying to push Trixi on her side, which never got rid of the nuisance, gratitude for those snores is filling me with relief. I go over & start shaking her by the shoulders. Wake up, sleeping beauty, it's time to take a powder.

I can't wake her up, Angel.

She's been drugged. Hoist her up & throw her over your shoulder.

Having read about those mothers who suddenly find the strength to lift an entire volkswagen when 1 of their kids is trapped underneath, I try to summon the same powers. But every time I get Trixi's limp carcass halfway off the bed, she slips out of my arms again.

Angel pushes me aside. He picks Trixi up like he's truly a volkswagen mother & balances her on his shoulders.

Let's go, I say.

Not until I find out what happened to my sister, is his answer.

When we get back to the stairway, Angel tells me to help carry her. He goes first, 1 ankle in each hand. I bring up the rear, holding each of the wrists. Halfway down, we're greeted by the sight of the deaf-mute, & he's having a hell of a time. He & the Countess are locked in mortal combat on the stairs as he struggles to wrest the gun away from her. Trixi's drugged double, dressed just like her, has been temporarily discarded. She's lying face down on the concrete floor of the patio.

That's when Angel lets go of Trixi's ankles, & I keep hold of her wrists to keep her from sliding down the stairs. Angel lands a punch squarely on the Countess's nose. Countess goes tumbling backward & hits her head on the patio floor. She ends up in slumberland next to our own private la Pasionaria, leader of the communist insurgents, Trixi's doppelgänger, & sister of Angel the brave.

I think this kid is beginning to grow on me. While the Countess is out, Angel & me carry Trixi & Angel's sister back to his car.

How we got the mother of the resistance back to her supporters in the jungle outside the city is a matter of history. Why I was willing to let the best-looking man I've ever met slip out of my hands & go back to his revolutionary cell is a matter of… Well, to tell you the truth, I don't know what it's a matter of, but I suspect Trixi had something to do with it.

I can hear her now, dragging her mules across the pavement toward the pool at this motel we're staying at in Fort Lauderdale.

She sniffles, then plops down next t' me & sticks her feet in. She's still wearing her kimono.

Countess left, she says.

Hey, kid, wicked luck.

After I told her I'd go anywhere with her.

No kidding.

She played me for a sucker, Per-deed. I—I was even gonna leave you, but I guess it got complicated, 'cause I can't remember every single thing that went down.

She clears her nose & begins pullin' the tangles outta her hair. Jeez, Perdido, I'm a mess. You—you ain't mad at me for almost leavin' you, are ya?

Naw. I figured it was up to you.

Figured? Then you knew about it? You — you weren't plannin' on lettin' me go was you?

Are you jokin'? It never crossed my mind.

What we gonna do now, Perdido? Trix digs into her kimono & pulls out a few crumpled bills. What you got in your pockets? she says.

Oh, I still got most a that C-note the Countess gave me for the return ticket. Stroke a luck that those friends of Angel were willing to get us back to the states by sea plane. But I'm afraid I had to surrender that 2 & a half grand of which I was once in possession back to those revolutionaries.

That's it, huh? Nothin' up in your room?

Oh, I doubt there's much up there anymore, says I, pokin' at my reflection with my toe.

Tell you what, says Trix, I'll get dressed, & then we'll head out & buy ourselves a thick, juicy steak with these bills I just dug up & put our heads together about what to do tomorrow.

She hops up. Startin' now it's gonna be your turn, Perdido. We're gonna find you the handsomest boy you ever saw.

I dunno, Trix, my back's gettin' to me. Maybe I'm getting' too old for that kinda thing. Or maybe it's just the heels in these dime store shoes I been wearing…

Trixi isn't listening. She's fingering the rosary around her neck under her kimono.

You know, Trix, maybe I been underestimatin' you all these years…

No, you ain't. Her eyes mist up.

Maybe. I mean if somebody pretending to be a real countess could ask you to—

Pretendin'? What you mean? She stops playing with her rosary & squints at me.

Nothin'. Just a slip a th' tongue. Close your kimono, Trix, there could be people watchin'.

Recommendations for the Mass Production of Teenagers

It is completely feasible to specifically design an animal for hamburger. —Bob Rust in *Successful Farming*, October 1977

Part I

IT WOULD END with a curious charge: alienation of affection. And it happened early one morning after three a.m., as he trudged up the street, not wearing his clerical collar. To the pimps, prostitutes, and dealers collected in front of the bus terminal and all along the avenue, he could have been any potential customer. This certainly wasn't the first time they'd seen a balding, middle-aged man in a black raincoat and scuffed shoes—who looked like a salesman on the road from another town— plodding through the flotsam and jetsam of the city's red-light district. So, nobody was surprised when the morose-looking man stopped to talk to a glassy-eyed, hollow-cheeked teenager, whose matchstick, tattooed arms poked from the rolled sleeves of his grimy sweatshirt.

The speeded-up kid had the lean, ravenous look of a wolf. He sucked in his cheeks, tossed the man a look, and began to walk beside him. For the boy, this was a familiar scenario. He could almost guess what the mark would say next. What he didn't suspect was that the seemingly casual words coming from the hangdog face of the man were careful… strategic… And that he'd rehearsed this conversation a hundred times. Slowly the man's easy, receptive manner began to forge a link, while the boy remained unaware of the merciful trap that had been laid for him…

The strategy put beads of perspiration on the lined forehead of the man, who was known as Father Bob. His lips grew moist. He saw the kid's kiddishness and wolfish depravity with a kind of hopeless wonder. He felt the familiar surge of being in close touch, shoulder to shoulder, with evil…

DETECTIVE PERDIDO'S REGULATIONS clicked across the tiles to the edge of the pool, toward a body covered with a beach towel patterned with yellow smiley faces. In the center of the pattern, over the abdomen of the body, was the slogan *HAVE A NICE DAY*. The detective pressed his lips into a line. In one fast move, he folded the towel down to reveal a face, a scar-edged patchwork of skins of various hues and various features, awkwardly welded together. The detective grimaced in disgust. "What a lousy sew job."

The body, on the other hand—now visible to the waist—was smooth and athletic, a perfect specimen of teenage manhood. Earlier that day, a family had identified it as belonging to a certain William George Champion, of South Pasadena. The body of Champion—who, coincidentally with his name, was the winner of the regional high school decathlon—had been missing since the day his severed head had been found on Bailey Road, or Lover's Lane.

Perdido unfurled the towel still farther. This was definitely the splendid body of Champion. He remembered it from the photographs.

For several months, there had been a series of murders in the Pasadena area, linked only by the similarity that each corpse had been found with some part of the body missing: a nose, two ears, a mouth, chin, or eyeballs neatly severed and removed. Unfortunately, the face by the side of the pool had been put together too haphazardly to determine whether it contained any of the missing features. Detective Perdido covered up the body gingerly.

"That him?" called out Miguel, his rookie assistant. Watery-eyed and nervous, the wraithlike kid sat at the edge of the pool in bathing trunks, hoping to catch a quick dip after they went through the formalities with the body. He still had his Weejuns on, and to avoid looking at the corpse, he kept his head lowered and picked the lint off his black socks.

"Looks like it to me," said Perdido.

Both Perdido and the rookie were glad it was. The strange apparition now lying lifeless by the pool had been terrorizing schoolyards and drive-ins for weeks with sudden and violent appearances. Because its superhuman strength seemed equaled only by its animal rage, astonished bystanders had done nothing to stop it. Understandably, there had been a sigh of relief throughout Pasadena when the discovery of the corpse was reported. But the fact that no one had come forward to claim credit for destroying the beast left Detective Perdido feeling uneasy.

It was possible, the detective thought, that the killer of the beast and whoever had created him were the same person. Choosing his words carefully, he began to sketch the probable psychological makeup of this Frankenstein for the benefit of his rookie. Perdido's words pulled Miguel's attention away from his socks and sent goose bumps traveling up his bare legs.

The detective reasoned that the deranged creator of this living collage was probably, to all appearances, your run-of-the-mill middle-ager. A man in a black raincoat. Although trauma kept him from reconstructing his own childhood except in the most fragmented and spasmodic of fashions, undoubtedly he was obsessed by a fervent desire to relive it as he thought it should have been. This impossible dream had led him to the grotesque mistake now spread out at their feet.

To elaborate on his theory, Detective Perdido began to cite a certain Statute 444, which set limits on the weight of a minor's testimony. The value of a minor's statements could never be taken as incriminating in the legal sense. Such testimony was almost considered a kind of hearsay, about which the original speaker could never be contacted. Thus, in the most legitimate of contexts, the true thoughts of minors were, for all practical purposes, unavailable. There were even certain recorded cases in which parents who had the vanity to take a child's remarks at face value were judged guilty of neglect or abuse.

"Haven't you ever noticed how everybody over the hill thinks he wasted his youth?" the detective reminded his rookie. "'If only I had it to do over again,' they all moan.

"Too late, of course. Some of 'em have babies. Run the kid through the obstacle course called life and get off by watching. It's perfectly legal. Too bad, though, that like I said, children's thoughts are unobtainable to anyone that's reached majority. So, this jerk, this butcher who did this, tries to make his own kid, but one he can get a handle on. And because he wants him to be just like other kids instead of like his deranged self—what parent wouldn't—he took the parts from all these average teenagers. Have a good look!" He stripped the towel all the way off the corpse.

Miguel used the sweat on his palms to smooth the sides of his hair. Then he swallowed hard and forced himself to look up at the corpse. A stream of vomit began pouring out of his mouth into the turquoise water and all over his bathing trunks.

TEENAGER. Any fully developed nonadult, a concept that barely predates the Renaissance, during which licensed domination of these subjects was first asserted. The implantation of rational thoughts into them then became a laudable occupation, and specific instructions for this process were treated extensively by late medieval and early Renaissance prescriptive writers.

Aquinas was perhaps the first to assert this belief in the context of Christian terminology by affirming that irrationality in these subjects was a sign that God had made them specifically for civilized society as a whole—meaning Christianized humans—to instruct or implant. Although they never replaced the pre-Christian symbolical sacrificial vessel of the kid or lamb, imagery involving their being pierced by lances or consumed by fire slowly found its way into liturgical representations.

Despite, or perhaps as a result of, the upheavals of the Industrial Revolution, the tendency to regard them as incapable of self-determination was strengthened, culminating in several minor philosophers of the Cartesian school being the first to conceive of them as mechanistic. Put simply, they maintained that a lack of sophisticated language and thinking skills thereby made them "machines."

Freud and Darwin were the first to point out, however, that rationality is by far not the strongest measure by which to judge the functioning of any entity. Nevertheless, these discoveries did little to further the acceptance of irrationality in humans as a whole but served only to increase the teenage burden of liability for it.

Ownership of. Western law has always regarded the fully developed nonadult as highly invested property, thus affording a high degree of protection. Both local and national laws specify they be provided with certain standard comforts, such as food and ventilation, yet conditions that may occur during the actual experiments that can be performed on them are not necessarily foreseen by regulations. Although there are established procedures for many of these experiments, subjects are officially, if not in reality, denied pain-releasing drugs during their administration.

It will become increasingly interesting to track developmental changes in these procedures as the demand for teenagers with predictably designed parameters becomes more urgent in a world of shrinking resources and exploding, promiscuous infrastructures.

AT THE MOTEL ROOM. Detective Perdido helped Miguel out of his soiled bathing trunks. "I don't feel like going swimming anymore," said the rookie, collapsing onto the bed.

"I understand, kid."

Since they were on duty, the detective kept up a businesslike tone with his protégé. He cleared his throat and stationed himself at the tiny desk in the room, pushed the Bible—still a fixture in hotels and motels—aside, and began going through some photos of corpses from the morgue with deliberate concentration.

The naked rookie struggled to a standing position and lumbered dizzily to the shower. As water pelted his thin body, nausea at seeing the corpse began to fade. He began to enjoy the feeling of heat penetrating his muscles. But as his eyes followed the rivulets trickling down his skin, a familiar anxiety resurfaced. Whenever he was undressed and looked down, he hated being reminded that his thing was darker than the rest of his body.

Miguel had little comparative data from which to judge the contrast. Found near a dump on the outskirts of Bogota as a baby and brought to Pasadena where he had spent his childhood sometimes with foster parents and sometimes in group homes, he had lived most of his formative years with Caucasians. The cocoa-colored thing in his hand seemed alien to the rest of his body, which had a more golden hue. He didn't know which of his theories about this discrepancy in body parts bothered him the most. Either he was the product of a dramatically mixed marriage, some kind of genetic defect that showed itself as he matured (he hadn't noticed much of a color contrast until a few years ago), or else certain manipulations of the organ had poisoned it. The color was indicative of a kind of cirrhosis of the penis.

Now, as the thing, which seemed to have a will of its own, grew turgid, he wrestled with the idea of consulting a doctor. He began to finger a pimple, plumped up by the hot water, on his shoulder, to take his mind off the quandary. When it popped, his mind was able to move on to other things.

Miguel had let his mentor, the incomparable Detective Perdido, pull strings so that he could skip three months of training and become the detective's assistant. It was a lucky break, but the rookie hadn't bargained for the long hours, routine investigations, and panicky moments of climactic discovery. Today had been the acid test. His neck had been frying in the hot sun all morning as they went to filling stations, drive-ins, and malls, covering the area where the creature had last been seen. Then the call about the stiff had come in. They'd had to table lunch and rush over with the siren on.

As they neared the motel, the rookie's heart had lain like a lump in his throat. Here it came: his first stiff. There was supposed to be something so creepy about this one. Kids not much younger than he being used as patches to make the thing. And a rumor that whoever was doing it pumped his victims up with chemicals first. They'd start acting weird, run away from home, never come back, or get discovered with parts of their bodies missing.

Miguel climbed out of the shower to check out his reflection in the mirror while he dried himself. This time he was careful to keep his eyes off the thing. Using his nails to arrange the few hairs in the middle of his chest into a vee, he sucked in his stomach and flexed the pec nearer the mirror.

Yuk. Nothing turned out how you thought it would. For the past six years, all he had dreamed about was being a detective like Mr. Perdido. They'd met when Detective Perdido was first assigned to the runaway unit of the Pasadena Police Department. Miguel had been caught trying to jump the Rhythm Rush train at the amusement park after running away from his group home. As soon as the detective discovered him in juvenile detention, the fate of the two was sealed. Something about the eyes, was the way Perdido explained it.

So, after the case was over and Miguel had been returned to his apathetic foster workers, Perdido showed up at the group home with some stock car racing tickets. The other kids were green with envy. Then came Saturday boxing and the roller derby and a wilderness survival weekend and Sundays at the pistol practice range. Perdido, whose career had never allowed him to marry, became a regular. Over ice cream, he'd relive some of his more intrepid exploits for his "godson." Finally, the detective began to ask him if he wanted to trade these vicarious kicks for some real action. Miguel decided to join the force.

Miguel slipped back into his briefs, chinos, and short-sleeved white shirt, then began the complicated process of styling his hair. Meanwhile, his mentor was still at the desk, resolutely shuffling through photos of victims, looking for features that might match the thing at the pool. A half smile crossed the detective's lips as he thought of his rookie's childish reaction to the stiff. But the boy was climbing back into the saddle. He could hear him sprucing up in the bathroom. The public guardian had to admit that he was more than a little proud of his own talents as a mentor. Miguel was a throwaway kid from a group home. He would have had the dimmest prospects for making it on the force.

Perdido looked down at the photo in his hand of the recently deceased William George Champion. Now here, on the other hand, was a boy who, to all appearances, should have had the brightest future of all.

WHO WAS WILLIAM GEORGE CHAMPION, and how exactly did he fall into the clutches of the maker of the collage monster? The answer to that question is buried in the distant past.

Champion was Pasadena's most prized junior athlete, the son of a respected businessman known as King Champion. His mother, Beatrice Champion, was a well-liked Pasadena TV talk show hostess.

Trim and golden as an ear of new corn, Champion Junior had known only triumph as a teenager. He was the kind of letter man parents held up as an example to wayward children. "Why can't you be more like William George Champion?" was a question heard repeatedly in the game rooms of many homes in Pasadena.

Unknown even to Champion himself was a psychic flaw that would later seal his fate. It had been inculcated some fifteen and a half years ago, when Champion's mother, Beatrice, returned from the hospital after rhinoplasty. Her decision to remake her nose had been influenced by her highly rated afternoon talk show along with the tiniest drop of her own vanity.

As she stared into the mirror at her bandaged nose and swollen, blackened eyes, Beatrice's heart began to beat anxiously. It had never occurred to her that she would have to go through this interim period of disfigurement while the surgery healed and set. What bothered her most of all was the idea of her three-month-old infant, William George, being subjected to the monstrous sight. Having had a talk show guest who explained that bonds between parent and early infant are first established by the "reassuring and tender expression on the face of the mother," Beatrice was deeply worried about her son's conceptualization of her face. Her fears about traumatizing him led her to the memory of a cotton sock.[1]

---

[1] Unorthodox conjugal practices are sometimes at the basis of the most successful marriages. In the early years of their marriage, Beatrice Champion and her husband, King, peppered their intimacies with marital aids they'd read about in obscure magazines. As an example, they played a "seeing-eye" game in which Beatrice sometimes spent an entire weekend deprived of her sight with the use of various decorative blindfolds and led from couch to table by her husband, whose caresses came at

To Beatrice, it seemed in the best interests of healthy child rearing to create a substitute face temporarily for the tender infant until the swelling had deflated and the nose had healed. It was an image that she then spent hours forging, basing it upon the advice of the best books on child rearing she could find in the library, and using paint, inks, cosmetics, and color photographs of herself. For approximately two weeks, little Champion was treated to a facsimile of his mother's features, frozen in an expression she considered being the most receptive and nurturing for a young infant. In short, the development of Champion Junior's self was indelibly marked by this "static" episode in which there were no mobile clues to distinguish among the times when Mommy was pleased or not pleased, ready to come forth with the food, or to abandon, etc.[2]

We come now to Champion's golden-haired teenagehood, the talk of Pasadena, but in some ways merely a graven image, a mirroring of Mommy's synthetic expression, forever fixed in the same monotonous, nurturing mode. Such a history of stunted ego formation makes it no surprise, then, that the lithe-limbed youngster was easy prey for the dissector of Pasadena.

We can imagine him after school on the day it happened, soaring through the air at the track field as was his wont, each tapered, bronzed leg flung rhythmically in front of the other. Then later, in the locker room, his slender waist creased by a spankingly white towel, William George is gazing intently into the mirror, but perhaps a bit "too blankly, wondering who he could be, arranging his still damp locks into a study of insouciance and wishing something magical would happen to him.

---

unpredictable moments. This soon developed into a kind of fond foreplay in which King covered her entire face with a cotton stocking fastened at the neck, upon which he drew or pasted new features, referring to her in childish tones as his "Kewpie doll."

[2] The well-meaning Beatrice unfortunately had little familiarity with object-relations theory, which demonstrates how dependent the preverbal child is upon its mother's changing expressions. Even the tiniest infant intently studies a mother's facial gestures in an attempt to build a composite personality from their transformations.

Meanwhile a car is creeping up to the gymnasium. With book bag slung over one shoulder, Champion leaves the gymnasium and sprints toward home, raising clouds of dust around his coltish ankles. His mind is empty and unformed, like a still pool waiting for the concentric rings of a dropped pebble. The car approaches like a dark phantom, slows down… Whether a hypodermic syringe darts suddenly from a sleeve after the boy is drawn into the car by an appeal through a tinted windshield to his yearning for self-discovery, or whether he is later proffered a sugared drink laced with a deranging chemical, no one knows, but something has been loosed behind the mask, something darker and more uncontrollable. Something like an animal.

PSYCHIATRIC EVALUATION

Patient: Wm. G. Champion

Date: November 5,19-

Source of Referral: Patient was referred by ER, where he was examined yesterday evening.

Presenting Problem: Family complained of extreme irritability, aggression, irrational behavior, etc.

Patient is a healthy-looking teenager of sixteen, Caucasian, dressed in an immaculate, tapered T-shirt and tight blue jeans, brought to me by his terrified and exhausted parents, who had first noticed a mood swing on Sunday evening, November 4, at about six p.m. Later that evening, his mother and sister had brought him to the emergency room, where he was denied admission to hospital by examiner who found no PCP or other known hallucinogens in his urine and who referred him to me for the following morning.

On first entering my office, body language indicated a highly disturbed state. I mean to say that movement through space was little more than a series of writhings, fist clenchings, and shoulder hunchings in the manner of the late actor James Dean—a near convulsive expression of defiance, fear, and rage.

Uncertain how to approach an adolescent in such an exaggerated emotional state and fearing for my safety, I thought it best to remain as silent as possible during the initial part of the interview. I shrugged off all accusations of a delusional nature and all of his explosions of temper with mute empathy. Finally, toward the end of the first half hour, I managed to extricate a story whose climax would have made a less seasoned professional withdraw in shudders.

It happened yesterday evening when the boy was sent home from the hospital and presented to his father, who was unaware of the mood change, having returned home late from a ribbon-cutting ceremony for a new branch of his chain of stores, Golden Champion Gear. Once apprised of the situation by mother and daughter, the father expressed categorical disbelief and accused the mother of being overprotective, demanding that the boy be brought before him that instant. Upon seeing the boy in his obviously agitated state, the father suddenly became outraged and categorically refused to hug him after this was suggested, and then repeatedly and tearfully requested, by the mother.

The boy admits then feeling an irresistible urge to show his invulnerability to any intervention—well-meaning or not—on the part of his father. He savagely challenged his father to hit him, which was forthcoming in the area of the face. He prodded him to repeat the cuffs on the face, which grew in intensity until the boy's mouth and nose were streaming blood.

Surfacing as if from a trance, the father was filled with horror at the sight of his own handiwork. He fled to the bathroom with the son at his heels, who in smug, dry-eyed silence, watched his father leaning against the sink and weeping.

The father then went to bed without further discussion, sometime after which the boy rose from his own bed, took his father's hunting rifle, cocked it, and went into his parents' bedroom. How much time had elapsed between the beating and this action is unclear. But at present. the boy seems to have no sense of any connection between the two incidents. Apparently, he held the barrel of the gun for what he suspects was over an hour against his father's sleeping head, until his mother awoke to the scene and begged him in a whisper to hand her the gun. According to the mother (whom I interviewed afterward), the boy then folded up like a released spring and seemed to lapse into a kind of trance-like state. He was taken back to his bed.

Little more was noted during this first interview, aside from certain physical symptoms that undoubtedly have psychosomatic parameters.

For example, the boy complained repeatedly of foot cramps, claiming these were so severe and prolonged and caused such a pronounced downward curvature of the foot that he sometimes had to walk on the tips of his toes, toe walking being an experience he then claimed, paradoxically, to enjoy.

HEY I CAN'T WALK on the soles of my feet anymore, I can only walk on my toes,[3] they feel springy and heavy at the same time. Hey my toes are stepping out of the house all by themselves into the backyard. Help, that barking and growling, all of them whirling around me, making me deaf. Look at the teeth on that one!

Wow there are points of teeth at my crotch and hot breath on my belly. GO AHEAD, EAT ME. I want you to. That Big One standing at the edge of trees, pretending not to look at me, must be the leader. What a snout, it looks enormous and that bloody smell coming from it. It kills me the way that little one leaps up and begins nipping at the edge of Big One's lips, prying his jaws apart with her nose, and now she has her whole head in his mouth. She's gurgling down something coming up from Big One's throat. All the little ones, too, they're crowded around Big One, except nobody seems to care about this old hunter, standing over me with his teeth clamped in my ear. AM I YOUR SWEETIE, OLD MAN? That smell sliding out of your mouth, old guy, it smells so yummy that I want to lick some of it. Those others yelping around us, they won't hurt me, will they? You want me with you, seems to me.

We're running wild, from smell to smell. I love it, I can learn to know the smells we want right away. But now it's getting more mixed, there're all kinds of other yukky smells that are not so good. Something twisted keeps us going, though, you just have to! Those guards that stay at the flanks keep ripping at you! Big One up there in front with Her isn't even paying a damn bit of attention to where we're going, he's too into Her and keeps up that zigzagging around Her. I wish he'd let go of her smell. It isn't right where he's taking us, these smells getting more and more mixed up, but I can't stop, I'm just too excited. Big One's chest's so pumped up, maybe he's mad and wants to eat us. He keeps whirling around and lunging at die one behind him and suddenly the whole line has to pull back squealing surprised.

That mind-blowing smell emerging from all the rest! It's so sweet, it's almost unbearable and now it's turning into a sound that's earsplitting, as if Big One is laughing at us, making fun of us so we'll throw ourselves against the boards, rip 'em away. Who cares if the wire cuts right through our gums. Our mouths are being

---

[3] Unlike humans and bears, who walk on their soles, canines can only walk on their toes.

bandaged by feathers, the kind that feel good tickling the back of your throat, making you want to throw up, feed the young ones—soft, exploding skin and crackling bones, blood spurting out everywhere. I never thought it would keep going like this. Now I can feel it wanting to rise back up out of my throat. But I want to keep it down, I don't want to give any away to the little ones, it feels so randy—GOD! WHAT WAS THAT? Something yanking me back, an invisible sharp pull and then that horrible searing stinging and then blackness.

FERAL DOGS TIED TO COOP SLAYINGS

South Pasadena—Last night, the third of incidents involving the slaying of farm animals occurred in the Pasadena area between midnight and one a.m., off Sawyer Road at a small chicken coop kept by residents of the Twain Trailer Park. A resident, who identified himself as Phil Android, a breeder, said that he became suspicious when he heard high-pitched wails, screeches, and snarls coming from the area where the coop is. The next morning, it appeared that the coop had been forcibly entered. Some of the sixteen hens had been removed or had escaped into the nearby woods while others lay slain not far from the coop.

What is important about this particular incident is that it provides contradictory evidence to previous theories about the animal killings that have occurred these past three months in the Pasadena area. In all of these cases, human involvement had been assumed. The county examiner's office has suggested that anxiety over the serial disappearance of teenagers in the area may have fueled suspicions that the animal murders were the work of a deranged individual. But on close inspection of the coop, an ASPCA investigator discovered teeth marks on many of the boards. It seems that the boards were ripped off their frames by animals of the canine family. Despite the fact that a canine capable of wrenching the boards out of their frames would have had to have had a jawbone and dentition of superior strength, like a wolf's, wolves and coyotes have been extinct in the Pasadena area, as in most of the West, for over sixty years. Nevertheless, it is now assumed by the ASPCA and the county examiner that some type of canines, probably feral dogs, are responsible for the recent chain of farm animal killings.

"THINK ABOUT IT," said the detective. "How many of the thoughts that you had at four do you remember? And if you did, would they mean two cents to you? It seems to me that the twist to this particular case lies somewhere in that gray area."

It is nearing midnight in Pasadena, but the sleuths' day is far from over. They're still sitting in the motel where the body was found, going over and over fragments, trying to piece them together.

"But didn't you tell me," said Miguel, "if I got your earlier explanation of Statute 444 right, that minors got no real thoughts?"

"Oh, they've got 'em, Miguel. They get 'em from their parent or guardian."[4]

"Jeez." The rookie nods dimly.

"I'm convinced," the detective goes on, "that whoever is doing this is specifically interested in the big crossover, when thoughts are passed to you without your knowing it. But let's get back to the evidence. We got a lead here, come in this morning, but it could be a dead end. A kid who allegedly was abducted and given the drug and then escaped. We got the guy he was accusing, who is some kind of ghetto priest, but we'll probably have to let him go on his own recog while the case is pending. And the kid has gone loony. He's under observation."

Perdido reached into his briefcase to take out the file, which had just been sent over from headquarters.

---

[4] The voiding of conflictual strain and other troubling psychic material by transference across generations is a social projection of our instinct for species preservation. For those who find themselves entering adulthood with uncharted anxieties or a lack of original purpose, a repository for this debilitating existential burden must be created. Thus, individuals who could drift aimlessly into vagrancy or violence are furnished with an agenda that will carry them through their most potentially dangerous years: it is the production of inheritors. Inheritors themselves are generally unconscious of their roles as objects of transference during the time that they serve as implantation units for the defense mechanisms of the previous generation. And by the time they discover their legacy, there is little alternative but to pass it down the line. Grandparenthood accordingly represents the most blissful of conditions for any individual anxious to reconstitute repressed conflicts and anxieties in a relocated space, assembly line style. In this case, the burden has been shunted so far ahead into time and space that only an unfettered and miraculous gratefulness is felt toward the new, largely unknown bearer, finding expression in the phenomenon of "spoiling."

In the victim's own words:

I was minding my business trotting along Old Mill Pond Road, just watching my shoes raise clouds of dust in front of me. Or maybe I was listening to the cuffs of my corduroys whoosh against each other. Or was I noticing the smell of the new vinyl book bag my mom had given me? School and practice were over, and anticipating what might lie ahead for the evening filled me with excitement. I began to skip. Suddenly a car horn blared, there was the screech of brakes, and I narrowly missed getting my toes squashed by the big black treads of a car tire. When I looked up, I saw the red, angry face of a man[5] cut in two by sunlight hitting his tinted windshield. Since the man I am referring to looked very angry, I hurried to do what I felt was expected of me.

I darted around the front of the car to the open window of the driver's seat.[6] My lowered eyes rested on his forearm, which lay on the edge of the car door. This part of a man's body, with its sparse hair, is only less disgusting to me than sprouts of hair in the ears and nostrils. I wanted to avoid this sight and immediately looked up, but only to be startled by something in the eyes. Although they were the overexerted yet determined eyes of their kind—riddled by the desire for achievement—there was something jewel-like, or unmanlike, about them. Something very much like my own.[7]

I don't remember his exact words.[8] I only know I wanted to make up for my foolishness. So when he asked me how to get into town, which was still eight miles away and involved a series of detours around Old Mill Pond because the bridge had collapsed, I eagerly began to supply him with the information (I've always been super

---

[5] "My definition of a man is somebody who doesn't look like me, a boy," the complainant would later explain. "For instance, men often have extra skin on their face that tends to hang down from their jaw. Also, a man is not tougher than somebody like me, as is generally claimed, but softer, or flabbier, with his drooping, wrinkled eyes, thick hands (maybe there is a stale smell thinly disguised by mouthwash and shaving lotion coming from somewhere). Everything to do with me is skin stretched tightly over bones. I never huff and puff, and it never seems I'm hurrying. No, there is very little about me that resembles a man."

[6] Apparently to apologize to the driver without having to squint into the sun.

[7] Complainant later clarified this remark by explaining: "For some would say that I am a puppet with hard, unchanging eyes made of glass and a face made of the smoothest wood, whereas others call me a boy."

[8] The exact nature of these utterances can only be imagined.

at giving directions). But he impatiently waved me still, announcing he could never keep such a mishmash straight, and I should show him on the map. He told me to climb into the front seat. After he had spread out a large map that covered both our laps, his blunt, hair-sprouting finger began to trace a meandering path through an area I could not place. He began speaking in a singsong voice; I only realized later he was pronouncing a series of non sequiturs, phrases used to ask and give directions, to orient oneself on a map and discuss it with others.[9] Under the map, he let the back of his hand, which was bent so that the knuckles protruded, sink more and more emphatically against my thigh, until he slid the hand along the corduroy, then turned it over and clasped my thing through the material.[10] Although the car had seemed of average size stopped on the road, the interior now looked enormous, amazingly spacious; the windshield was a blinding pool of light, and the thick, mahogany-rimmed dials of the radio gleamed like the finest silver. When he had unzipped my fly and slipped his fingers under my underwear to take hold of my thing, he placed his other hand under my chin and inserted the tip of his thumb between my lips. And then, without a word, he turned away and began driving.

We seemed to drive for hours, and as we did, the sun gradually sank until there was darkness. I had no idea where we were going, and the landscape seemed more and more unfamiliar. It was as if we had left my neighborhood, the town, the country—I won't say "the world." But soon the roadside was filled with the shadows of foliage I had never seen before: tall, thick, gnarled trees with stubbed, wisp-covered branches, all pointing upward. And then I think there were strange square cactuses with enormous bulbous leaves. Finally, he pulled into a long, graveled driveway he said led to his home, and in the darkness, I saw many gables. Two enormous Dobermans came bounding toward the car, barking. He opened the door, and they leapt in and began to lick his face. They ignored me.

The man's house was all glass, silver, and Lucite. There was very little fabric, and when there was a need for it—for instance, the couches, bed sheets, or towels—

---

[9] Complainant later remembered that this action caused him to glance around the car and notice the upholstery was especially luxurious; it was made of the richest leather and the carpets were of the thickest pile.

it was always a spotless white. This is your new home, he said. It would be impossible for you to leave this place, because if you try, you will only walk into mirrors or bang your head against panes of glass. You will remain naked because you have no need for clothes. When you clean yourself, you will imagine your body is made of an almost grainless wood, as white as birchwood. Now you exist only to experience pleasure, and any thoughts you have will be as transparent as the prisms in this chandelier above your head. The idea of being a prisoner here left me no regret for my parents, but I did think I might miss my grandparents.

After I had undressed and he had touched my body everywhere, he led me to an enormous white marble table that seemed balanced on a pedestal of glass. And I saw his hands move through the rainbow-studded air to pour a few drops of crystal liquid onto a plate that seemed to be made of silver; then the glistening drops flowed together into a gleaming, pearlescent shape into which he slid the edge of a shiny knife, which sent flashes through the air that lit up parts of his face and his cold, steel-like blue eyes. Suddenly, the knife soared through the air, and his head tilted back. I could see his large, dark, moist nostrils, and the thudding of blood through a cord in his neck, which suddenly looked very powerful as the liquid slipped into his nose and disappeared. Now you take some, he said, and as the drops rolled along the cutting edge of the knife toward its tip and the knife flashed toward me, I was afraid it was going to slice my eyes, but the blade slid flat against my nose and the cold liquid was sucked into my nostril as I inhaled, making the whitest light in the world burst through me until I exploded into a million tiny pieces that...

INSPECTOR PERDIDO THREW DOWN the report in disgust. "I think we've heard enough of this tripe."

"Jesus," said his rookie assistant, "that kid really knows how to tell a story. My knees got wobbly."

"Even a rookie cop should be able to tell that kid's lying," snapped Perdido drill-sergeant style. "This reads like it came straight outta Sing Sing—the writing program! The whole thing's like a molester's fantasy, the kind of people this kid is used to pleasing!"

"You mean that isn't what happened?" blurted out the rookie incredulously.

"I would doubt it," said the detective in a sinister voice. "Here's my version. This sounds more like it to me."

I ran away from my fucking asshole of a father because he was always getting drunk and beating up on the old lady. I thought I'd have to walk to town, and then be able to hitchhike to the city by morning, when along comes this fruit in a fancy car, making eyes at me through the open window. "Hello, young man," he lisps, "Do you need a ride?" I get in, and right away he's got his hands all over me. Normally I would have smashed his face and taken whatever was in his wallet for doing that, but I really wanted to get out of town before my old man sobered up enough to call the cops on me, So I tell this faggot, listen, not now, I mean, why don't we go to the city and get a room there or something and really have a good time, but we better not try anything here because I'm underage, and the people in this town know me. Well, it was the wrong thing to say because immediately this guy starts worrying about the law, wants me to get out of the car, so I put his hand over my dick, and when he feels how big it is, he says okay, okay, then let's go to the city. So, in the city he stops at a grocery store and buys two six-packs, and we pop 'em open and start drinking. I'm kind of high, and the fruit is getting sauced, and then he gets this bright idea: hey, we don't have to waste money on a room. I know a place we can drive where there is nobody around, and I think, shit, where the fuck am I going to sleep if he takes off? So I say okay, but then you got to pay me, and the faggot says you never said anything about money before. Both of us are making such a hell of a lot of noise that a cop comes up to the car and sticks his flashlight in. And I figure, if they're gonna send me back to that asshole father of mine for a beating because this faggot was too cheap to pay for a room, then let him take some of the consequences…

What I remember is I was all filled up with feathers and blood gurgling in my belly, my nose full of that wild singing smell and sharp yelping in my ears, when something pulls me backward into pain and blackness. And when I wake up, the pain thing is still waiting there for me! I had to do everything it said. Like I would be leaping forward into the bright air, thinking that it's gone, when suddenly the hot pain would rip through me. It began at my neck, then made my legs go stiff.

Or I'd be lying in the sun minding my own business, letting it bake me so I felt like part of the ground, and suddenly something yanks me up to a standing position, it drags me across the grass to another place, maybe to some hay that smells like urine. The creaking of metal, I had to stay there until I felt the yank again. The worse part was when there was a smell that I got into, it went inside me so it seemed like a sound and told me what to do. I'd let it run me forward toward the next smell, and then suddenly the horrible pain again, ripping me away from it, fighting to be stronger than the smell and winning.

By the time this clenched fist was held out for me to lick, I was trained and ready to do anything, bowing down to the salty taste of the hairless skin and licking it to show that I would follow it and live under it, rubbing against the thigh because I'd begun to realize who was the master of my pain. And then just one time, right before the pain came, I happened to turn around to try to see who—or what—did it. I saw a man in a black raincoat holding out a steel rod attached to a wire, moving it toward my neck. He was wearing a collar too. No, not that kind. I think it was a clerical collar.

Part II

THE GHOST-PLAGUED TELEVISION crackled with static, making the commentator's voice seem two-dimensional.

"The story you are about to see may not be a reality in your city. But thousands of miles away, it is daily fare for the many children who must live it…"

The scene dissolved to a tropical setting, palm trees in still air over a litter-strewn street. Beneath one of the trees, a heap of dirty cardboard began to stir.

"Here is Pepe, age twelve, waking up under his piece of cardboard. He's had to fight off the other boys huddled against him for warmth all night to keep them from stealing it. He's searching his pocket for his tiny pebble of crack, or freebase, and his tinfoil pipe. It will help to wake him up and stave off the usual morning hunger. He'll be stashing it away quickly before the police come by for the daily sweep…

"Pepe and his friends are on their way to a garbage dump near the city limits, where nonbiodegradable fragments—bottle caps, razor blades, and plastic bags—can be salvaged from the decomposing organic garbage. If enough of these scraps can be found, he might be able to trade them for a few pennies worth of food at the market…

"It has not been a very profitable day at the dump. And, unfortunately, weeks of wading in the compost heap have infected Pepe's legs. Further contact with the enzymes is painful, obviously, and tends to inflame the sores…

"This is Pepe's friend, eleven-year-old Tito. He is showing Pepe his new clothes and the silver lighter they will use to smoke the crack they will share. Tito is explaining that he has met a rich Belgian tourist who likes to buy him presents. Maybe Pepe would like to meet him too…"

Insomniacs who watched these events dramatized on a late-night television show rushed to their checkbooks with sighs of relief when the appeal to support the faraway mission came on. The program had been especially heartrending, since it purported to use as actors the actual children to whom these events had occurred.

Checks written out, lights were turned off with the reassuring feeling that one's own children would never be subjected to a similar horror. God willing, they would always be protected by loving parents and grandparents, right-minded teachers, or charismatic law enforcers. In this city, children were neither a useful product for the work force, nor a drain on the economy, but a luxury, something to be cultivated into masterpieces of which the creator could be proud.

Things looked different in a seedier part of town, where a balding, disheveled priest watched the broadcast on a flophouse TV. He was a man who knew this tale well, a man who had spent the greater part of his life in the thick of it.

Father Bob wasn't a bad man, but perhaps one who expected too much from this world below. He was a man who equated the act of putting innocent flesh to its ordinary trials and tribulations with subjecting it directly to the gaping jaws of evil. And try as he might to resist, he always found himself succumbing to the temptation of face-to-face confrontations with the process.

His eyes left the television to rest on the bony figure passed out on the bed. Through the window curtains lying dead in the stale air, blue neon from the sign outside the window illuminated the blunt young face. Father Bob had a vision of snowy wings framing the surly mouth and dark-circled eyes. Then he remembered that the boy's name was, ironically, Angel.

In boys like Angel the priest took the opportunity to uncover many layers of his own psyche. He realized that he had always wondered, for example, why those with the least interest in the future—teenagers—were assigned to be its harbingers—a fate they claimed to revile but later embraced. Father Bob also wondered why full consciousness of their own secret longings and elastic physicalities was denied certain individuals by terrified others who insisted they serve as epitomes of purity and ineffectuality. In short, Father Bob was an idealist who yearned to free teenagehood from its enslavement; rescue it from its prefabricated, labeled state; return to it its Edenic vitality. But all his efforts had only succeeded in drawing out animality and violence.

The priest woke Angel up.

He stretched. As a street person, he knew how to enjoy the luxury of a real mattress, but ingrained caution made him stop in the middle of his relaxed movement when he felt Father Bob's eyes resting on him. Jerking to a sitting position, Angel lit a cigarette and began watching the story of the abandoned children on the snowy television screen. "I gotta go," he mumbled.

"But you've hardly rested," said Father Bob. "And I haven't even told you about the club."

"What club?" said the boy.

Father Bob averted his eyes and did not answer. He had spent years studying the insecurities of people like his listener and knew all about their need to belong. Their fear of being ostracized could lead them into hierarchies that they would not question. What is more, their yearning for an identity gave them a special attraction to the aura of the secret society, especially if it involved handshakes, passwords, ceremonies, and the like.

"First, I have to know I can trust you," said Father Bob. "The club's a secret."

The boy nonchalantly took a puff on the cigarette and blew smoke rings into the air. His face lapsed into an affectation of apathy, but Father Bob thought he saw a spark of interest beneath the wolfish street cynicism. "I won't tell nobody," the boy said. "Has it got something to do with boosting electronic equipment or something?"

"Much more exciting," said Father Bob, trailing one finger through the dust on the night table.

The boy's eyes grew wider. "You mean pushing?"

"No," said the priest. "More powerful."

"Pimping?"

"No. Mind control."

"What is that supposed to be?" The boy started to get up.

"It takes a while to understand," said Father Bob, gently forcing him back down as he produced a ring from his pocket. He held it up into the flashing blue neon. "Do you like this?"

"Yeah, it's really fresh," said Angel, reaching to touch the silver wolf carving on it. "Can I have it?"

"It's part of the initiation ceremony," said the priest, "for the club. We all have rings like this." Raising his other hand into the neon light, he showed the boy the ring on his finger, identical to the first.

Angel took the first ring and began turning it over in his fingers. "What's this club about?"

"Tell me about your parents," countered Father Bob in a casual tone.

Angel looked away, stared at the fuzz on the television screen now that the station had gone off the air. "Lasts I heard about her, she was with her sister in South Pasadena. Him, I don't know where he is. I hope I never run into him 'cause I'll kick his ass if I do."

"What does any parent really know about his children?" said Father Bob with a sigh.

The boy's ears pricked up.

"Parents are the last people to know what's best for you," the priest went on.

"You're telling me?" said Angel with a glint of appreciation in his eyes.

"Teachers, too," said the priest. "Don't listen to them."

"Hey," said Angel enthusiastically, "what is this club, anyway? You haven't told me yet. Are you the leader, kind of like the don? What do you deal in?"

"Souls," said the priest.

"*Souls?*" Since Father Bob was not wearing his clerical collar, the boy burst out laughing. He slapped one thigh, and the mattress creaked. "Souls! Are you some kind of religious nut?" He tried to stand up.

"Wait!" Father Bob's voice was stern now. "By souls I mean an entire mentality, not some outdated hocus-pocus. I'm talking about consciousness here, everything that's been stuffed into your head since you were old enough to see and hear." He leapt up, shut the window, turned off the television. "I want to show you something. See that ring you're still holding? Open it up. The top part opens."

Angel bent over the ring and tugged on the silver wolf. It fell open with a tiny ping, and immediately Father Bob held a saucer under it. Drops of a crystalline liquid fell onto the saucer.

Father Bob scooped the drops onto the edge of a knife, then quickly held the knife close to the boy's nose. "Smell," he said. Immediately the boy's eyelids closed. His head lolled sideways.

Grim anticipation coiled in Father Bob's belly. What better frame of mind for the preparation of instruction was there than one in which the subject was hypnotically open to influence? For influence can only enter the mind as a drop of water will enter a moist sponge.[10]

As the boy's head dipped backward one more time, Father Bob gently pulled him to a standing position. He began to drag the limp body, which slumped against him, through a kind of foxtrot, humming "Fascination." Then the boy suddenly straightened and began leading, jerkily, on the tips of his toes. Movement through space became more stylized, extended into writhings. Now he hunched his shoulders and pulled back

---

[10] Ignatius Loyola, *Spiritual Exercises*

his loins in spasm; his arms were flung up and back as if nailed there. A stony look transfixed the eyes.

An intensely pure tenderness welled up inside Father Bob as he swept the boy to the bed. The youngster lay stiff and arched on it, without moving. Perhaps, hoped the priest, he had him in a pure state now, and this time the subject would not lapse into animality.

Slowly and methodically, he began his implantation.

A hope for saving other runaways from a similar fate rested on a new technology just purchased by the Pasadena Police Department. It is called "computer aging." Designed according to the latest research in aging factors, it involves feeding an image of the lost child from a photograph into a computer with graphic capabilities. The image can then be systematically "aged" with input from environmental factors, to produce a picture of the child as he or she might look at the current time.

When the Bureau of Missing Persons in Pasadena acquired the device, it already had been tested extensively by the Atlanta Police Department. What is more, a less complex model was being employed by psychotherapists who worked with the bereft parents of long-term runaways. Many of these people were still plagued by the image of a beloved face frozen in time, even though the face may have long ago evolved into that of an unimaginable individual. Now, before them on a color CRT, a gracefully matured image of their little boy or girl materialized—sturdier chinned and longer nosed, but perhaps with the same vulnerable expression in the eyes and the same unconscious expression in the parted lips. The patient then engaged in imaginary dialogue with the screen as one step in the wrenching process of disinvolvement.

Most recently, computer aging is being put to wider applications. It was mass-marketed as a program for home computers, and those fearful of the ravages of time upon their looks hoped to use the program to second guess the aging process. But for this it proved unnecessarily demoralizing.

Now it is rapidly taking hold as an educational tool. In some of our nation's more prestigious academic institutions, a child entering school for the first time receives an image of himself upon successful graduation, with proper weight and height gains, intellectual achievement, and character maturations printed out below. A duplicate is sent home to parents, and the image is used by teachers for instructional modeling of the development of the child.

Nine p.m. In their bungalow in the Pasadena hills, Perdido and his rookie were getting ready to climb into their twin beds. For the past few moments, the detective had been congratulating himself for his perseverance, which led to his matchup of six photos of teenage corpses with the face of the corpse at the pool. Only the chin of the body at the pool, which seemed to belong to a Caucasian, did not match the Negroid skin tones of the corpse on which that particular feature was missing.

Miguel was pulling on shorty pajamas. He turned down the covers and hopped into bed. Tonight he was filled with silent admiration for the patient sleuthing talents of his mentor. Maybe being a rookie was not half that bad after all. He settled into his pillow and was overtaken suddenly by a sense of having a personal stake in this case. He could almost feel it pressing in around him with an enchanting yet dangerous intimacy. He gazed at his mentor for reassurance, but the sight of Detective Perdido in yellow pajamas turning down his covers mysteriously accelerated the nervous, intimate feeling. Pushing against the sheets with his toes, he realized they had been pulled in too tightly. He suppressed an impulse to ask Mr. Perdido to get up and loosen them, even though memories of being "tucked in" by the detective did not reach far into the past. He hopped out of bed and loosened the hospital corners himself.

"Got ants in your pants?"

"I hate to be constrained, Mr. Perdido, maybe 'cause when's I was little, this foster mom I had for a while was always putting me in one of those harnesses—you know, the kind with a strap attached so you can't run too far."

"A mom's got a lot invested in a kid," mused Perdido.

Because tomorrow would probably prove as grueling as today had been, neither detective nor rookie were anxious for their usual ritual of lights-out immediately, barracks style. Instead, Perdido opened a copy of a favorite book, *Adventures of Huckleberry Finn*. He began to read it aloud, after reminding Miguel that this was the story of the very first American runaway. But after a while it was obvious to each that the thoughts of the other kept returning to the case.

"Are nigger chins less dark than the rest of their faces?" Perdido asked.

"How should I know?"

"I thought all Colombians were supposed to be part Negro."

Miguel considered the truth of the supposition in light of his alien appendage, but sleep mercifully took hold of him. He drifted into a dream about his onetime foster mother, Georgia, a model, and her sister, Betty, a photographer.

"You lift his legs over his head while I wipe. Yuk! I should have done this an hour ago."

(All flipping upside down. Leg things flying away from me.)

'Now, help me turn him, will you, Betty? Fiddlesticks, he's going to need a bath after all. Will you get that tub again? And fill it up halfway. Stick your elbow in."

(Jiggles.) The pink tube growing.

"Ain't we cute. Stop touching that nasty thing. C'mon, let's see a smile now. Let Aunt Betty give you a kiss."[11]

(Jiggling.)

"Okay. Up we go and in we go."

Help. (Bleeding or melting.)

"C'mon, angel, the water's not going to bite you. Stop whimpering."

Help.

"Betty, hold the edge of this tub."

Draining away.

"There now. Everybody likes a bath."

Push back again. Here we go. (Melting again.)

"Dam. He's peeing. He's too full of liquids. Hand me that Q-Tip."

Here it comes, mouth.

"Don't grab at it! Stop biting it! Oh! you're splashing me! Bad, bad, li'l boy."

That stick so loud? Should swallow it.

"Stop it! Do you hear me! That's a good fella. Now, just a little shampoo. Look, isn't he adorable, Betty! Get the camera. This one's not to be missed. Let's give him the duck. Hurry, before he starts splashing again."

(Stabbed.)

"Okay, only one more shot. I think the flash frightened him."

(Stabbed.)

---

[11] The curious phenomenon of slobber kissing (coinage: U. Molinaro) has served as a point of juncture whereby procreatively inactive members of the extended family become tangentially engaged in the libidinal thrust of generation. Certain zones of a minor's body are designated as the legitimate field for slobber kissing. In most contexts, these include the cheeks, neck, and top of the head, but rarely the lips; whereas in settings where partial undress is considered normal—such as the beach— the arms, chest, abdomen, and, in the case of very young children, even the bottom are included. Although the sudden and sometimes unexpected assault of wet lips on most of these areas would be considered prosecutable or at least a public embarrassment when the object is an adult; individuals who have not attained majority often have extensive experience as the object of slobber kissing, intimate familiarity with the smell of Aunt Heidi's White Shoulders or Uncle Morton's gum disease being the rule rather than the exception. During the period of slobber kissing, the above-named zones become communal property of the extended family, thereby being put at the service of those individuals not fortunate enough to have created their own generational transference units (see footnote 4, page 143), e.g., maiden aunts, bachelor uncles, unmarried sisters, widows and widowers). In rare cases, the odors and other sensations experienced by the object during slobber kissing become cathected and take on libidinal associations that influence one's adult search for mates.

"That flash really did frighten him. You're not angry at me, are you, cuddles?"[12]

The rookie awoke, blinking perplexedly at the sun streaming into the room through the blinds. What was the meaning of his strange dream? Did it hold a clue to the case of the curse on the teenagers of Pasadena?

There wasn't much time to think about that. It had to be after five a.m. already. Miguel could hear the slap of Detective Perdido's razor against the strop and smell his shaving soap. The sensations filled him with a sense of helpless excitement. Once more, for reasons he couldn't express, he felt the case all around him, daring him to reach out to its solution, which Miguel imagined as a kind of soft underbelly that seemed alternately poisonous and yielding.

Heart beating rapidly, he hopped out of the twin bed and glanced around the blue room, letting his eyes rest on Mr. Perdido's gleaming regulations parked heel against heel beneath the blue and yellow curtains with their rodeo motif. The detective's worn badge case lay open on top of the dresser, next to Miguel's new one.

Miguel picked up his badge and walked to the mirror with it. Still in his shorties, he practiced whipping the case out and flipping it open. Then he began his precise routine of dressing, tucking his button-down shirt into his high-pulled Jockey briefs for a smoother fit, and adjusting the waistband of his black chinos so that the crease passed right to the top of his shoes.

---

[12] Fully repressed by Miguel was the fact that the sisters sometimes amused each other at home by setting up and shooting novelty poses, which they occasionally offered for sale. When Betty sees the coil of clothesline lying on the table near the tub, she just can't resist. Sneaking up on Georgia from behind, she throws her expertly to the floor. Georgia's legs go kicking into the air, but before she has time to right herself, Betty gets astride her. "Yahoo! Get along, little horsie!" Working expertly against Georgia's kicking, gartered legs, she begins to bind her. Several turns of rope around wrists and waist are enough to lash them tightly together. Her stockinged thighs are bound together just above the knees and just below them, as are her ankles and delicate little feet. Finally, Betty takes a smaller length of rope and attempts to tie Georgia's neck to her heels, but Georgia can slip out of it by pressing her feet together. So, Betty gets an extension cord to tie the neck and feet. When she has finished, Georgia is ingeniously bound from throat to insteps. Betty delightedly shoots the pose at various interesting angles keeping in mind the enthusiasms of a few faithful customers.

Fifteen minutes later and too nervous to eat, he sat inhaling the scent of the detective's Old Spice over bacon and eggs in their breakfast nook. Perdido handed him a photograph of a twelve-year-old boy.

"Routine work," said the detective through tightened lips, "but important. Hightail it over to Missing Persons and run this through the computer ager. The kid disappeared four years ago, and I want to see if his could have been the chin on that thing we saw yesterday by the pool. Throw a little more down on the cheeks, tighten up the jaw." He tossed Miguel a small key. "This'll get you into the computer room."

Detective Perdido stayed seated in the breakfast nook until he heard Miguel start his car and pull out of the driveway. Then he rose and gently parted the curtains. He watched the car snake down the curving road toward downtown Pasadena.

Sending the boy on assignment always filled him with a tingly feeling. It was like the mixture of pride and trepidation a kid feels when he sets a windup toy on the floor for the first time, points it in the optimum direction, and lets go.

The thought of a windup toy always reminded him of the first one he had as a kid. It was an acrobat in a silver leotard that did somersaults when you wound it up. He could see the toy leaping high above the faded rag rug all the way up onto the edge of a bed. The woman lying on the bed fumbled to remove her satin sleep mask when she felt the toy land on her. She sat up and squinted into the afternoon light. It illuminated her platinum finger curls, making them look almost transparent.

As if it were happening again, Perdido felt the surge of joy that came whenever Mom finally woke up. She would always send him to the medicine cabinet over the sink in their trailer for her "medicine," after which he was allowed to play and make noise. Sometimes this didn't happen until the sun was setting, so Perdido spent the day sitting next to the bed and fantasizing that Mom was a sleeping beauty waiting for a prince to revive her.

Then, finally, she'd get out of bed, drink the magic potion he'd brought her, glance at a picture of a man in tights and waxed mustache standing near a trapeze—who was supposed to be Perdido's father—and go behind the screen in their trailer. She'd emerge from it all dressed up in a spangled bathing suit and fishnet stockings, her platinum hair studded with rhinestone pins.

Mom had a dog act, and mother and son followed a traveling carnival in their little trailer. Perdido had loved the mutts; he could almost feel their wet noses nuzzling his ankles.

But he'd had enough of reminiscing. He'd lost an hour already, and he had a case out there to solve. Slipping his badge into his pocket, he walked briskly to his own car and headed for headquarters. He wanted to take another look at the file on that priest.

By the time he got there, the file was gone.

AT MISSING PERSONS, Miguel had gingerly made his way down the half-lit hallway, overly conscious of the squeak of his rubber soles on the tiled floor. Missing Persons wouldn't be open for another hour, and he could see through the glass window that the computer room was dark. He tried to create a mental picture of the room, searching his mind for the location of the light switch. Ever since he'd been a little kid, he'd hated stumbling around in the dark, looking for the lights.

He took out the key Detective Perdido had given him and inserted it, but before he could turn it, the door swung open with a creaking sound. Someone had broken the lock.

Miguel stuck a hand into the darkness and began feeling along the wall for the switch. He kept his eyes on an eerie shaft of green light that shot from the shadowy forms of electronic equipment. Finally, he felt the switch, and the overhead fluorescent lights fluttered on.

The green glow had been coming from the dials of the computer ager. Whoever had last used it had left it on. Miguel could hear a high-pitched whine coming from the machine. The green light indicated that whoever had been using it had forgotten to remove their diskette.

Miguel pushed the eject button and nothing happened. He tried to turn the machine off, but the on/off button didn't work either.

The rookie felt his palms sweating again, and a cramp retracted his scrotum. Would the detective think he'd botched a routine job? Who had been there before him and broken in? Nervously, he peered inside the slot to see if he could spot a jam. Then, using the key to the office, he gently picked at the diskette, which suddenly came popping out.

Looking back on the episode, Miguel wondered why he had decided to put the diskette back into the machine and see what was on it. At the time, he thought he was just being thorough, like Detective Perdido would have been. Or maybe he wanted to put the finger on whoever had broken into the place and left the machine in such a state. The diskette made a whirring sound, and the rookie pressed "Initial Image."

A balding, middle-aged man's face came on the screen. The dark, watery eyes seemed to belie the vulnerable, pouting expression of the mouth. Miguel pressed the plus button and nothing happened. Sliding his finger to the right, he pressed minus. The machine clicked and moaned. The face disappeared from the screen and returned, looking more youthful. The eyes were brighter, and the jowls hung less loosely at the jawline. Now Miguel understood why the machine had jammed. Somebody had been trying to make the ager go *backward*. He pressed the minus button again. The machine moaned once more, eclipsing the image and replacing it with the same face, even younger. Now more hair sprouted at the crown of the head, and the eyes seemed to challenge. He pressed minus again, and this time the eyes had softened. They were larger looking. Thick, shiny curls framed the face, whose fuller lips rested in a shy, almost guilty pout. Paradoxically, it was not until this teenage image came on the screen that Miguel realized where he had seen the first adult face before. There was something about the teenage image that evoked the man better than his present picture. It was the priest who had been brought in for questioning.

AN HOUR LATER, Miguel sat trembling in the Hyundai, holding the photo of the missing boy Perdido had given him for the computer ager. He'd been so overwhelmed by his identification of the priest that he'd forgotten to put the photo on the machine. Instead, he'd dashed over to headquarters and surreptitiously grabbed the file on Father Bob. He was determined to interview Father Bob alone, despite what he knew Perdido would say about sober craft and good sleuthing judgment. If the interview did lead to something, he wouldn't be in for anything but praise.

Miguel looked down at the photo of the twelve-year-old once more and shuddered. The sloe-eyed, rosy-cheeked kid had been missing for four years and was probably dead. It counted as one more child sacrifice. If the boy's disappearance had anything to do with this case, he owed it to this kid and to kids like him to take a few risks. This had become a children's crusade.[13]

Before long, Miguel had left Pasadena and its suburbs. Gradually the roadside was filled with the shadows of foliage he had never seen before, and he felt as if he had left the neighborhood, the town, and even the country.

The strange landscape seemed to take him into another plane. His usually sweaty palms and the butterflies in his stomach were replaced by a floating feeling. It was as if he were traveling vertically, higher or deeper, instead of driving straight ahead. As he drove, images of his life alternated with details from the case. He saw himself worriedly fingering his member in the shower, then gazing into turquoise water that suddenly became filled with vomit; he was watching with excited envy how the intrepid Detective Perdido bullied a shady motel owner for

---

[13] **Children's Crusade**—one manifestation of a popular pietist movement, beginning in the second decade of the thirteenth century. The movement is thought to have been fueled by an impulse of the rural lower echelon to burst the bonds of clerical and noble hegemony. In addition to thirty thousand children, numerous shepherds, tradesmen, and other rural poor took part in the movement, which at times resembled a pillaging rampage. Some of the child participants met an unexpected fate. They were, allegedly, sold into slavery or concubinage upon reaching the coast of North Africa.

information, then kicking and screaming as Georgia lowered him into a tub; finally, he imagined himself as a newborn infant wailing with hunger in a dark house in a strange country, above which floated the face of the priest as a teenager, an almost sacrificial tenderness in his sad eyes. Somehow this puzzle fit together, but how? It was an insane patchwork, like the Frankenstein-like corpse that had been lying by the pool.

It was getting dark already. The trees had become smudges in the sky. Miguel was turning up a long, graveled driveway. The sight of the black, sharply pointed gables of the house made his head swim pleasurably. His mind almost blank, he left the car, flanked by the two Dobermans that had suddenly appeared at his side. He entered the house without knocking. Light stung his eyes from every direction. It was as if the black-and-white tile floor was spinning, carrying him sensually down one Lucite-and-silver corridor and then another. Finally he was standing before the priest, who looked as he had in the first age-reduced image, an attractive man in his early thirties, with clear eyes and a full head of hair. He was wearing a kimono bathrobe, the kinda bachelor would wear.

"It would be impossible for you to leave this place," the priest began to intone in a hypnotic voice like a fortune-teller in a TV movie Miguel had once seen. "You now exist only to experience pleasure, and any thoughts you have will be as transparent as the prisms in this chandelier above your head."

"Cut the crap!" barked the rookie, struggling to regain control of himself and making an effort to reproduce Perdido's hard-boiled tone. "Just tell me one thing. What's a priest doing in a groovy bachelor pad like this?"

"Everything exists in conflict with something else. All teenagers know that," answered the priest in a tone of great gravity. "'Freedom without responsibility'; 'Protect me but keep your distance'; 'Save me but let me struggle!'"

"Why'd you foul up that computer ager?"

"I thought, foolishly," answered the priest with a sentimental sniffle, "about traveling back and starting over again to understand it better. But I got stuck like this."

"Then Detective Perdido was right. It was you who tried to build the perfect teenager."

"When that didn't work, I thought the answer lay in nature," said the priest, gesturing grandly around him.

For the first time, Miguel noticed they weren't alone. A low-pitched growling came from the edges of the room. Draped on the Lucite-and-white furniture and slouched in comers were some of the boys whose pictures he'd seen at Missing Persons. But they looked different now. The hair on their heads and eyebrows had thickened, their jawlines had narrowed into snouts, and they stood balanced on the tips of their toes. Miguel recognized the boy whose picture he had, but sharp teeth now protruded from his mouth, and his eyes were narrowed into suspicious slits. He hissed half consciously at Miguel, then leaned back drowsily against the glass wall.

"They all became animals," the priest went on. "I couldn't implant anything."

Miguel's hands fluttered to his pocket in search of his badge. He flipped it out and displayed it to the priest. "I'm taking you in!"

"Forgive me for disobeying you," said the priest. "Though I have little belief in the authority of your profession, I have the deepest respect for the prerogatives unjustly denied your age group."

Suddenly the pack of boys sprang snarlingly into action. Miguel was surrounded. They began to drive him down a flight of stairs to the basement.

COULD IT BE that the owner of this Lucite-and-glass house, this jailor of wereboys, was also the possessor of a mysterious laboratory, a place where chemical—and alchemical—miracles were performed? The possibility had never occurred to the rookie. He'd overlooked a crucial clue: the strange crystalline liquid that seemed to alter mind and body.

Surrounded by a kind of vicious, sensual guard made up of the fanged wereboys, Miguel stood gawking at bubbling beakers and alembics in Father Bob's basement laboratory. A viscous, whitish substance dribbled from the spout of one alembic into a graduated cylinder.

Coming out from the tangle of test tubes and piping, the priest held up two gels, quivering in their beakers. "In one beaker are the child's thoughts, and in the other is his flesh," he explained.

Apparently the first gel consisted of nervous tissue in which were imprinted adolescent thoughts, longings, and dreams, a task that had taken Father Bob the entire previous week. The other vial, which had a plasmatic, almost iridescent cast, contained the raw material of young flesh, a purified tensor for thoughts and longings.

"This method is far superior to the last two," said the priest. "Piecing together stereotypically wholesome body parts or trying to purify the teenage mind were both grave errors, I now realize. No amount of hacking, sewing, or dosing could ever have brought me the results I'm looking for."

The priest poured the two gels into a crucible. They did not mix, but each time they bumped together, they trembled. He picked up a graduated cylinder full of white stuff.

"All that remains is the union of the two gels by the addition of a few drops of the binding catalyst—which is a kind of parent in a jar—to create the invincible culture," he explained.

The wide-eyed rookie remained rooted in place.

The priest raised the cylinder and measured two drops into the crucible. The gels became turgid, entwining in a spiral that caused the crucible to rattle. A striated glow pervaded the substance, flickering between gray, rose, and brown, as if in search of the elusive tones of flesh. Miguel wondered what orthopedic object would emerge from the humors, what fragmented body. Would it have the motor skills of a newborn? Or the fully coordinated grace of another Champion?[14]

An intact yet ghostlike image of a teenager streamed from the mouth of the crucible and hovered above it. The priest curiously extended a hand, but to his chagrin, his arm passed right through it. Flickering in and out of vision, the image began to speak.

"O evil, deluded man. Give up your tacky experiments and let me rest for eternity. An unholy pact doomed me to insubstantiality. But your wacky potions and spells called me back into a half existence. Take heed, for you are once again on the brink of a stupid criminal mistake."

Swirling as if made of water, the image continued.

"Poison did this to me. I began my life just like you did. Fragments of a body—arms, hands, eyes—seemed mysteriously to supply my every need. You know the scenario. When I awoke, food was there to satisfy my hunger. When I felt like burping, there was a hand patting my back. I grew accustomed to the service, then terrified of losing it. How could I have guessed that they'd put something in the food?

"So, almost before I knew it, my nights became a purgatory. I was racked by run-of-the-mill, uncontrollable longings. Bitter thoughts of revenge against Mummy and Daddy stung me as well. My deranged mind told me that in the name of protection, I was being humored, deceived, intimidated, cajoled, and betrayed. But I kept on swallowing more because I was polluted. My hunger and the food that had been forced on me had become identical.

---

[14] Probably the latter if Father Bob's theoretical basis for his experiment concurred with the ideas of French historian Philippe Aries, who maintained that the children of medieval Europe were indistinguishable from adults in every important way, being regarded merely as adults in miniature (Philippe Aries, *Centuries of Childhood*, translated from the French by R. Baldick, 1962, Jonathan Cape).

"Above all I somehow knew that I was never to reveal the cause of my night tortures to those very beings who might have implanted them. So, I kept changing the sheets and Mummy never knew. The masquerade continued, and my punishment increased. The greatest burden was the feeling that I was now charged with all that was desirable and that at the same time its fruition was forbidden. To rev myself up even more, I would fantasize my fragmentation in the future into the plane of power that had instigated all this suffering. I dreamed of being just like Dad.

"Finally, abuse broke the vicious round. My jailers, who were seized with longing, committed the ultimate transgression. At night when my pains were raging, they appeared before me in unfragmented form. The effect of this was horrible. As soon as the fragments assumed a definite shape, I became a cannibal and was simultaneously tormented by the image of my own body laid out on a table for culinary purposes. To avoid that fate, I attempted suicide. I was punished for this by being forced to assume the form in which you now see me."

Miguel, and even the wereboys, listened transfixed, their mouths hanging open and their eyes wide as saucers. Father Bob was staring at the image with a tragic, almost exalted fascination. Then a cleft appeared, a kind of slit that, opening ever wider, threatened to make the image disappear. It was the only weapon of this passive, powerless entity, a vortex opening wider and wider. As if in a wind tunnel, Miguel felt himself being sucked toward it. "Help me!" he shrieked to Father Bob, his hair blowing about his ears. "I'll do anything you say!"

But Father Bob had been pulled off his feet and turned topsy-turvy. First his feet and then the rest of his body were sucked into the orifice.

The image loomed like a rubbery doughnut. It slithered out of the crucible and turned into a pool on the floor.

Miguel saw that the wereboys had fallen back into their trance. A shudder passed over him at the sight of their hollow eyes, which stared perplexedly at what had become a pool of plasma on the floor. He drew back with a sigh of relief as he heard Detective Perdido and a squadron of police barreling down the stairs. What had ever made him think he wanted to become a cop?

EVENING FALLS ONCE MORE in Pasadena, but one unlike any other in the past few months. It is a special night for the city's mothers and fathers, the first in many months when dads can confidently toss car keys to children or send them off in their pajamas into the dark streets to slumber parties. The case of the curse on the teenagers of Pasadena has been solved.

In their quaint home in the hills of Pasadena, Detective Perdido is once more getting ready to turn in for the night. Since today is Wednesday, he does forty brisk sit-ups and push-ups in the living room before changing into his pajamas. Then he sprints breathlessly into the bedroom and finds his rookie, who is to be awarded for his bravery by being raised to the rank of officer tomorrow, standing over a suitcase.

"Goin' somewhere?"

"I didn't have the nerve to tell you, Mr. Perdido. But I figured, well, that maybe it was time I lived on my own, don't you think? I'll be moving into the Mark Twain Trailer Park with a roommate tonight. Name's Android. He's a breeder, and I was wondering if I should look into the field."

Tight-lipped, the detective turns his back on the rookie and marches deliberately into the bathroom. As the boy continues to pack, he can hear him gargling with mouthwash. The detective comes out with a bright smile pasted on his face.

"How's about a kiss?"

"Huh?"

"I said, how about a kiss goodbye… Officer."

Miguel hops over his suitcase, plunges into the policeman's arms, and rests there in safety, just for a moment.

Recovered Memory

_ YOUR LIMBS FEEL ALMOST like they're floating, your eyelids, heavy…

_ Go ahead…

_ … His eyes.

_ Staring at me…

_ Just his eyes?

_ I don't like them because they're too… open. They're pretending to care about me.

_ That bothers you?

_ Because…

_ Do you feel you don't deserve it?

_ Yes—I mean—no, I deserve it, it's just I don't trust those eyes.

_ Because you don't think he cares about you, really.

_ He does. I mean, I think so. But as far as I'm concerned, caring about, or for… somebody… has to be self-serving…

_ …

_ … in a way…

_ And who is *he?*

_ …

_ Go deeper... The voice speaking from you is none of your concern. You don't need to help it at all because it knows exactly what to say... Because you're so sure of yourself, and the rest of the world doesn't need you right now... It can take care of itself... So relax... and go deeper—

_ But I don't know why those eyes scare me so much.

_ You don't have to know... The voice that's been speaking knows... all about it... Doesn't even need to say what it is as you go deeper... into a delicious state of relaxation... while the world takes care of itself. And it becomes clearer that you will go into this delicious state any time you feel the fear of being... adored... cared for... and your arm floats upward as if it's weightless, while you decide why being adored is a fearful feeling... If you really have decided that it's a feeling that's best dealt with by being afraid... As you rest in this delicious state of relaxation deciding if distrust... and fear... are really the best way to deal with the eyes caring for you, even adoring you...

_ But what about the eyes?

_ Stare straight into them. Go ahead. Look!

Blue eyes with flecks of silver. Much older than those of the one who's afraid of them. But open. Vulnerable. Too vulnerable for the age and weight of a man pushing forty-five and 195. Eyes in an aging, moisturized face. Secretly knowing how well it can playact vulnerability or innocence or risk-taking, and other youthful attitudes that are beginning to look out of place on his sagging features.

Honest eyes.

That's what he'd say even now, lumbering down the almost deserted city street, sending out his careful youthful earnestness to an imaginary public, his overly fixed eyes scanning the street as if it wasn't deserted, about to lose its whole identity just like he is.

The street that used to be the main drag of the red-light district; but now it's in transition; he can remember better times when this street was a menu of easy pleasures and scary appetites, can see the way the bar on this street used to be as the memory leaks out in small details showing:

a young woman with deep-set circled eyes calling attention to the skull beneath the skin, rearing her head into the red light of the bar the way it used to be, rubbing below the red into a dirty pink blouse, sliding her fingers inside its shadows, rubbing red and pink, over and over, robotically, below the red light. It seems as if she's been doing it forever. She speeds up whenever anybody glances in her direction even accidentally, increasing the pressure and urgency of her stroke when one of the older guys actually talks to her as she asks him for a drink, fixing him in her eyes with rubbing, rubbing…

This is the bar that got all the rejects. They call it the Last Resort. Hidden from a teeming street near an alley where the streetlamp keeps getting busted by the same boy, over and over. A place for whores in dirty pastel colors, taking a break from the street, rubbing, in case somebody would look. Stony-faced shirtless male hustlers in summer, with liverish nipples sculpted from adolescent skin, their pinpoint pupils fleeing the 5 p.m. light, looking for an early trick for the by-the-hour hotel around the corner. Working class gays coming in from long unskilled day jobs just for a nip. That homeless man with the purple bruises nodding out at the table. The Hasid like a hallucination furtively stopping in over and over to peer at the whores of both sexes, turning round and round on his swiveling barstool before dashing out again. In the john before the small mirror with its greasy thumbprint whorls, people scoring drugs and lumbering out into the alley to do them in and out. In, out. In and out.

But the bar's gone now. The alley sealed by a larger structure. The whole street almost deserted. Everything closes so much earlier nowadays. The new souvenir shop with its plastic replica of deco-era landmarks and its unlit neon has already been shut behind its gate. And next to it is a theme restaurant formaldehyding memories of Tin Pan Alley. These days, except for the glassy, reminiscing flame in the man's blue-gray eyes, it might not have existed. If it wasn't mushrooming into full intensity in his head in the sudden flash of the image of that Puerto Rican lap dancer as she hops down from the black wooden stage in the cramped bar, among the cracked red barstools near the torn red banquette and the grime-covered ceiling fan, to grind against a client, around whose suited shoulders her arms hang loosely so she can fan out bills like a hand of cards behind his head to count her take so far. He remembered it so clearly, could see it. Her tight, ergonomic body in g-string making the same repeating gyrating motion. The bullet of her head with its full mouth like a lead seal and the slick black cloche wig bobbing up and down… Later… she is standing alone like an abandoned toy, making the same arabesques to blackness, robotic gyrations…

He remembers waking up the next day with that horrible hangover, the clattering image of that dancer spilling out of the bright sunlight through his pounding head like a noisy row of dominoes set in motion. The only antidote was to double the usual dose of the benzodiazepine tranquilizer, until it began to lather over the hammering image with the white suds of tranquilized sleep, wrapping it in gauze like a mummy, so he could go back to the dank bar that very afternoon raging in full summer daylight and watch the same lap dancer taking a break, holding a Tequila Sunrise, talking to her brother—it had to be her brother—with the same smooth shell of a face branded by lips that seemed asleep in mourning, his burly shoulders tapering to a scarred naked abdomen under his open vest.

There was something about the downward cast of both necks, the convex lids of both eyes, that hinted of historical despair. And from the long pale arms of brother and sister dropped grimy hands balled into fists like tear drops. As he watched them standing together, he thought what it would be like to lie next to both—her and him—to feel each ultimate rejection.

He's what's known as a "summer john," a teacher during the year, a habitué of dark places during summer. Both lives are neatly compartmentalized, except that the increasing chaos of each succeeding summer is making getting it together for fall more and more difficult. And the anticipation of summer as the school year's predictable seasons wear on is getting more and more urgent, which is a bad sign. He is, in fact, a vastly popular teacher, a survivor of the city public school system who identifies so strongly with adolescent turmoil and has lived so long with emotional ambiguity that students are drawn to him. He's a soulmate rather than an authority figure, even a romantic image for some.

Other teachers' classrooms have been torn apart by gang violence. His room is where truces are made and controversial problems worked out. There are people in prison who've mentioned him as the one cool person at one moment in their stalled lives. There are practicing sexual minorities who've fantasized him as confidante. There are painters and writers who now think of him as the first person to notice they had something. Faculty and administration regard him with suspicion and even hostility, a wild-eyed threat to order at the worst times.

But in the street, he has another kind of status. He's a type. Too intense a gaze… Not bad looking, badly dressed, too casually for narrowed sharp-shooting street-survivor eyes. Too opaque to them and a boring enigma. Why wouldn't a man with a regular salary want cleaner sneakers or sharper pants? They, who are used to shouting at the world about every little thing they've won, ask. Is he too crazy to do something about it, or smart enough to mock their own concerns about it, which is worse. So they approach him as a mark and a john, ironically, with contempt, but with hesitation… avoiding the eyes.

_ Are you still looking at those eyes, Buddy?

_ … Yes. But there's no face. They look like somebody cut them out of a magazine and pasted them on the wall. It's weird. There isn't any face around them.

_ Where is this wall?

_ In a bar. With black walls. It's one I used to go to a long, long time ago.

_ How long ago?

_ Yes, it's real dark and crowded inside. Only red lights.

_ How old are you in this bar?

_ Fourteen.

_ How do you feel being there, Buddy?

_ Great. I feel great. So many people are looking at me. So many people want me.

_ Does it feel good to feel eyes on you…?

_ Well…

_ Are you looking at the eyes?

_ Like I said, they're looking at me.

_ How do the eyes make you feel?

_ I don't feel anything. They don't bother me at all.

_ The one with the eyes? Can you see his face now?

_ Yes. It's his face the very first time I saw him.

_ How does he make you feel?

_ I guess I liked his face… for a john.

_ And how is he looking at you?

_ He seemed fascinated…

_ The eyes?

_ They see… through me.

_ Penetrating?

_ … right to what's good about me.

_ What a nice feeling it is to be understood…

_ You're never understood… in this situation. If you go into it wanting to be, it'll end in disaster.

_ You don't trust the eyes?

_ They're creepy. I don't like them at all.

_ Always?

_ This time they're not… but they're still scary. He's staring at me. He's looking right into me.

He's seeing what he thinks is a girl in the shadows. Lovely blond hair, almost fluorescent in the dank shadows. It looks like a child. Hiding next to the torn red banquette on the other side of the jukebox in this mostly Hispanic and Black bar, where the few white people are mostly johns. Peering at him.

Not a girl. But a boy. A delicate face. Impossibly large eyes, generous lips. The tank top hanging off the bony chest. Wrists like matchsticks. What on earth? What's he doing here, a child here in this place?

It was on that summer afternoon in the bar, when he went directly from his bed where he'd slept all afternoon thanks to the merciful benzodiazepines and passed in an instant from the blinding sunlight of the street into the dark bar. First, after his eyes had adjusted, he'd seen the brother and sister—the body doubles—and then, in the corner, the fluorescent blond curls had caught his eyes, so out of place here. And then, perhaps because at first he'd thought it was a girl, he found himself staring at that angelic face—with its almost too large eyes—and that fragile body, like a young girl's. In fact, maybe it was a very young girl, without even any breasts yet. No matter how long he stared, he couldn't tell for sure. He couldn't tell, really.

Actually, he was caught by the enormous amber eyes. Were they the eyes of a frightened deer? A lion cub's eyes? Ferociously scared and proud. Casting loneliness and mastery into the dark of the bar. Defiant eyes, so vulnerable. So, he glued his eyes to them. This time he went beyond his usual conscious projection of the candid and the kind. He boldly poured his middle-aged soul into his eyes, and they catapulted into the other's.

Which—if he wants to be honest to himself—wasn't all that unusual for him. At that moment, he wasn't thinking what it meant, with his long summer histories of adolescent women, who were all prostitutes. He hadn't been thinking what it meant to have been wandering into this bar lately, instead of the one up the street where he used to go, which was hard-core female prostitution. The fact that this one was mixed was a realization he diluted by his theory of body doubles: for every male he looked at here, he tried to locate or remember an equivalent female body. He was merely doing genealogy.

And then again, the last few summers had been characterized by such anonymity. The bodies were mock-ups of youth into which he vomited all his tenderness and need. Girlish junkies with wispy, dirty blonde hair approaching transparency. Bony arms dangling over his shoulders, or even left passively by their sides and pressed into the rumpled sheets like baseball bats placed next to their thin bodies, while he felt himself hovering above them, barely feeling their heat through the walls of the condom. Feeling instead their fragility and disdain, which excited him. Hoping to cradle their abjectness but realizing how little he had to lose if they rejected him. How can you really be rejected by a street prostitute? Shifts others might consider major would actually be negligible to him, a slight narrowing of the pelvis to young male proportions, a bend in the wire of the form, a hardening of a few muscles. Were their brothers really so different an experience? Maybe some of them hadn't always been girls.

What hid in the corner of the bar was different, fading into the vague light like dirty water around the impossibly large yellowish eyes, mouth pouting defiantly as if after a reprimand—wet, gleaming lips, face unbelievably broad and heart-shaped, sweeping up to the vast dome of the forehead; but especially the pale, cavernous eyes.

And now he felt himself walking toward him, forgetting all social embarrassment or fears of legal repercussion—sleepwalking into the swallowing stare. And talking everywhere but inside the strange desire gripping him everywhere, because he'd had lots of practice at such sublimation. As a teacher. For how far were care and concern from desire? The desire to love. To which this young person seemed to respond.

_ I'm staring back at him now. Right back.

_ How does that make you feel?

_ Ballsy.

_ And now… and now?

_ I'm looking at his open mouth as he speaks. Gold, and a tooth missing. Hey, well, it's not the most appetizing mouth. But I gotta do what I gotta do. I have to do my job.

_ Which is?

_ Hustling.

_ I want you to go deeper, Buddy. Stay with the conscious memory of that moment. You're comfortable now, safe. It's something that happened long ago in the remote past. Let that memory, the unappetizing mouth, float in your mind like so many particles of dust in the air, insignificant, like those cut-off eyes on the wall… Now maybe a voice inside you will tell you why you are inside this bar, looking at this man, at his eyes, at his mouth…

_ I feel… tears…

_ Go ahead and let them come up. They can't hurt you, because the past no longer exists.

_ … like I'm gonna cry.

_ Let the voice inside you feel the tears, Buddy. Does the man want you to cry?

_ No… no… he doesn't! But… somehow he knows I'm about to. Oh, I don't want him to see me!

_ Why?

_ He'll take advantage of it. No, I won't cry. I didn't. I just… hovered there. You always wait for the mark to speak first.

_ The *mark?*

_ The john.

_ What's he saying, Buddy?

_ He's making a bad joke. Telling me he thought school was still in session, so what am I doing here. Ha… He says maybe I shouldn't be in here and that maybe he shouldn't be either…

_ And you're—

_ Trying to glue the eyes to mine, 'cause I don't want them to look down at my hands.

_ Can you see your hands, Buddy?

_ I can see my hands in the back of my mind, but I'm not looking at them. Cause then the john's going to look. He'll know that I live outside, that I'm sleeping in the street. They're more than dirty… cracking, dried up, what happens when you sleep outside… but I don't want to go back to the street tonight.

Sturdy legs, probably creamy, clad in bargain camouflage pants, and that limp, yellow tank top, shoulder blades poking out, sculpting the egg-white skin into meringue wings. A breastbone carved from soapstone.

He drinks in the child's diffidence like water for an animal dying of thirst. His eyes part the shadows that enfold the boy, wishing he could become those shadows. He strains to know the bar, the street outside, the police, the summer heat exactly as the boy would know them. It's a talent he developed in his classroom, a way of focusing that resembles a trance in which he turns into the listener as he explains the siege of Troy to him, the Holocaust, exactly the way an adolescent would conceive it.

Meanwhile he watches the boy—always watches. The boy is concocting a story he guesses might raise his status in the man's eyes. He's obviously used this story before about really being eighteen and knowing he looks younger, his mother dying that spring and his never having had a father… All of which sounds appealing and tragic to most ears, wins him sympathy, and helps clear away anxieties about jailbait.

The boy goes on about the supposed aunt he lives with. Who means well but expects him to go to work right away. Though he was planning on going to college instead. Which is why he has to get some cash together easy and quick.

Until the man with the caring eyes gently asks him, how did Mom die? And under the phosphorescent blond hair, the camel eyes get wider and more vacant as he loses himself in his delicious wish-lie about a motorcycle accident: a silver motorcycle. He likes the idea of a mother on a silver motorcycle. Barely old enough to be a parent. The fact that people sometimes thought they were brother and sister tickles his fancy, too. Himself as his mom, barely grown up and irresponsible, sizzling with unlimited energy and taking big risks; after all, she used to be a go-go dancer! And… dancing more some place else after work until early morning on ecstasy, in tooled boots among gay men who might be fashion stylists, in her cream satin rodeo shirt trimmed in silver thread, a silk kerchief in colors of rose and yellow trailing from her pale neck, black satin pants tailored like jeans… As blue neon caresses her blond hair at a disco, he also imagines her empty smile, blank eyes, a look he mimics for the man. After which she climbs upon her silver bike—reflected in a gleaming black puddle by harsh lamplight—and the tires spin the puddle into broken mirror shards as she's tossed high into the air to land on the pavement with a bone-crushing thud.

Why should the man worry about the truth of the story? Especially when he can see the enormous taupe pools mutating to clear ginger— the boy's eyes—transforming into vials of fantasy. What difference, then, the catalyst for such a mutation? All that interests him is seeing the boy sacrifice himself to the trance he has produced for himself probably by lying… In return, the man's flesh composes around a grateful availability to the boy, in the way that a talented guidance counselor, priest, or veterinarian places his physicality in harmless, reassuring availability before a skittish client.

The boy doesn't fall for it right away. He's seen comforters become predatory, stony, or contemptuous. If that's going to happen, he just wants the money. So, he lets his body ignite unavailably, mocking those middle-aged flames farther along the continuum of time, already dimming and guaranteed to pale next to his.

The man stiffens the privilege of his older authority. His eyes gently but sarcastically show how much more he knows, can buy, protect. And the boy succumbs.

They're out on the street. Blue dusk caresses their profiles and separates them in outline. A man and a boy. Never having touched before and then, by accident, the bare wrist of the boy grazing the man's sleeve… the man staying casual. There are cops, concerned adults everywhere. His arm shoots up into the salmon-colored sodium vapor lamplight. It's easy to get a taxi with all of them having just dropped off passengers for the theater.

It's dark inside the cab. Even dark enough to swallow the boy's enormous eyes, so the man can't see him thinking about his real mother, who's old enough to be his grandmother and puffy and cloying that last time he saw her—a little past sixty now—if she's alive, thinks the boy, collapsing out of fantasy.

There's only this brief time to sink into real memories before leaving them amputated and isolated with the usual scars thickening around them. He already knows enough about prostitution to realize he must drink up this darkness to relax so he can burst into a white flame later, ignite the fantasy paid for when flesh is pressing against his. Sensitive as the man might be, he couldn't stand to understand what the boy feels these interim moments, the poignant sense of luxury at merely having been given this little respite between performances. Farther and farther into the dark recesses of the cab his mind retreats into a self the man won't ever know. The most the man will ever glimpse of this real identity is dreamy silence, a stopped automaton tired of projecting fantasy but caught in light that isn't quite dark enough.

"Don't know why I'm going home with you," says the man.

"Want me to get out of the cab?"

"This is the first time I ever did something like this."

"You never paid a hustler?"

"I've been with lots of hustlers... girls."

"So what the fuck you doing with me? Do I remind you of a girl?"

The boy does remind him of a girl. He knows what he is doing. All the girl junkies turn him on because they aren't... female. The dope turned their hormones off and made them neuter. He doesn't particularly want to be reminded of being a man most of the time, which tends to make him feel like a failure. His story is typical. He wants pale bodies beneath his. The skin needs to seem so poreless that if it were moist, it would be like the skin of a snail. He can't even see the boy in the darkness of the taxi or doesn't want to. Funny how he never realized how good he is at compartmentalizing certain things, like work with the kids at school. He doesn't even think of them as boys or girls. Just empty capsules waiting to be injected with compassion. If anybody seems human to him, they do. Wanting to fill them up is greedy, he knows down deep. But there he always is, caring and empty, ready to pour his thirst into what they're suffering.

Does this boy remind him of a girl? He doesn't remind him of anything, he's sorry to think. He doesn't want to be reminded of anything, he must admit. The boy reminds him of a big gap in himself.

Time is distorted now. A very short stretch seems like it lasts forever. Or perhaps it's the opposite. Time passes without our realizing it.

_ You've been quiet for a very long time, Buddy. You're in a deep trance, very relaxed. Do you want to go even deeper? Or do you want to remain where you are? Or "wake up," even?

_ *(Don't know. It's so dark in the stairwell of this building. First the taxi was dark, but now… the bulb is out in his hallway. It's almost pitch black, so he has to help me up the one flight of stairs from behind. He could have walked upstairs in front of me and let me hold his hand or the hem of his shirt, but instead he stayed behind me, slipped his fingers under my belt to steer me upstairs so I won't bump into anything. Like being lifted…)*

_ Want to tell me what's happening?

_ *(Steering me down a huge black hallway with the fingers still pushed under my belt, my cheek colliding softly with a metal door, but he still won't let go of the belt. His other hand jangles the keys and the door falls open, pushing me into the apartment until I'm at the opposite wall, with him sandwiched against me.)*

_ Buddy! I want you to describe what's happening.

_ Nothing. It really is nothing *(just darkness and his body pressing into mine so I can't tell the difference between them, his thing a little up in my fatigues from behind. He won't let go of the belt. I don't really care, but I won't admit it, an old guy's body pressing into mine, his thing pushing up the material over my crotch.)*

_ Do you want to wake up, Buddy? I'm going to count to three and—

"You should let me fuck you. I mean, you chose a guy."

"Usually, I'm the one who does the fucking," answered the man. But maybe there is no answer, just black, his arms floating up way above his head, feeling light but bare as they fall against a cold wall; arms up high, like when the cops bust you up against the wall and search you. The man's hands fumbling with a belt buckle, kind of clumsy hands.

_ My pants must've come down, 'cause my ass is damp, and I can feel the cold air conditioner air stinging it and his hand searching for something, but I just won't let him.

_ Did he… force you?

_ No. I swung around, I said, "I don't do that." (*and suddenly his hands are all over me like butterflies, cool and dry, pulling up the tank top, holding my fatigues down with his foot so that I can step out of them, and his pants and shirt are off, I can feel his body against me kind of soft and hairy, the hair was a little like a punishment*).

_ Buddy?… Can you answer me? You probably should wake up now, slowly. Can you hear me?

_ Hmm, hmm.

_ There's nothing to worry about.

_ (*I know there's nothing to worry about. There usually is, but not now. The feel of the clean sheets for once in such a long time, the safe locked door and the pillow… There sure isn't anything to worry about. And his hands on me, not greedy… more like gentle. Going all over me, I don't mind. Putting my hand on his dick that feels thick and rubbery… Old guys aren't very sensitive, it always feels a little rubbery. But here in the dark… with the walls shutting out the street, and a clean smell in his place, I pull the guy against me… I pull the feeling of falling asleep round me like a warm blanket…*)

His sleep is too deep for dreams. The relative safety and comfort, the caressing kindness of the schoolteacher, can't exterminate a memory hardened into a mean core. This memory of being eleven years old is the prime reason for being here next to the man tonight. He was perched uncertainly in the front seat of a canoe on a big moonlit lake.

To him the endless expanse of black water looks thick as oil. It is ready to swallow him up. He isn't a very good swimmer, and his hairless, skinny, white legs in their orange surfer trunks begin trembling as the canoe teeters. He's scared. But he wouldn't tell Rory, his older brother, who is sitting straight-backed behind him, black coarse hair sticking from thighs and shins. Rory's paddle precisely pierces the water, breaking its black skin (*like a hypodermic needle*, Buddy thinks), then it quickly rotates to make a J-stroke. It plunges the canoe forward like a snake goes through sand, militant resentment sparking from each prick of the paddle. Buddy can feel it attacking his spine like electricity. That performance-paddling is really just an angry display of Rory's own talents, a mockery of Buddy's lack of them. Worse still, it is yet another embarrassing appeal on Rory's part to bond. His need and anger leaking out under the pitiless black sky, revealed by grimaces of white teeth under moonlight.

The spine of the canoe cutting black water. The day flipping through Buddy's mind: his shirtless brother dragging him into the room for a surprise for his birthday. From under the bed comes a white cake box.

But instead of the butter cream cake that Buddy loves, the top flips open to reveal gleaming steel:

a Bowie knife, a dagger, a bayonet, an entire collection.

The stiff brotherly arm thrown around Buddy's shoulders wilts as Buddy turns away and denies any interest in collecting knives or learning knife mastery. He is looking instead at the single blue vein running down Rory's hard, pale fifteen-year-old abdomen. Buddy doesn't want to look at it. It's almost as if the vein were pulsing with rage at Buddy's finicky rebuff.

He's thinking of the time their father sent them out into the field to play catch, figuring it was a thing brothers might do. Smack, smack went the ball against the leather. With each smack, the vein on Rory's hard abdomen, always naked in summer, seemed to puff, as if from swollen pride. Dad wants you to be normal, he kept repeating, accenting the word *normal* with a half-smile on his face. *Dad wants you to be normal.*

Now Buddy is handling his own paddle even more awkwardly, while Rory hisses mocking corrections. Buddy tries to pay attention to all the orders but can't, not when he feels so frozen and so afraid of Rory's eyes. He fumbles. The paddle drops into the water, and as he bends to snatch it out, he almost overturns the canoe. Rory lurches to the other side to ballast the weight, and the canoe rocks dangerously. How Buddy wishes he hadn't gone canoe riding in the first place, but Momma was already asleep, Dad wouldn't stop them, and Rory literally dragged him off the porch to the edge of the black lake, barking orders to lift one end of the canoe and wade in. The horrible feel of cold water stinging Buddy's ankles.

Farther and farther out into the lake hurtles the canoe, fast enough to make the wake hiss against its spine. Buddy's lips are compressed with fatigue. He thinks of the obstinate presence of his brother in the house, like a black thing standing between him and his parents. *Momma really doesn't care for Rory*, it seems to him. *She really doesn't,* he was thinking today, to take his mind off Rory teasingly tracing light figure eights along his neck with the tip of the dagger, while Buddy stood stock still, afraid to move. Are you sure you don't like knives? Rory kept asking, while Buddy held his breath, the veins popping from his forehead, which had gone scarlet. I like 'em, Buddy finally managed to force out, though the point stayed pressed against the skin, and Rory's knuckles grew pale around the handle. Finally, he moved the dagger back and Buddy took a long breath. Sit down, Rory ordered, his face growing vulnerable and needy, then jumping into desperate beaming delight at his brother's sudden change of heart, as if it had come willingly, his hands eagerly removing all the knives from the box to lay them out at precise intervals on the bed.

Check out the Bowie. *Whack!* An issue of *Popular Mechanics* tossed onto the bed started curling into ribbons, slashed by the amazingly razor-sharp Bowie. *Pfoofff!* The point of the bayonet whizzed through the thickness of the magazine, pinning it to the mattress. Breathless from his own mastery, Rory looked at Buddy with sullen eyes. Really what did you mean, you didn't like knives?

A sudden swerve of the canoe that is almost a right angle. Grasping the boat's edge, Buddy can literally feel Rory gloating again at his own prowess. We're going to a secret place, he announces. It's one that Buddy has never seen before. He has no idea where he is. An inlet concealed by poplar branches that Rory makes Buddy pull aside. Then they are in a narrow lagoon, which has a slight stagnant odor. Clumps of squat raspberry bushes line each side, like sullen, blurry stains in the dark air. Get out! Rory orders.

Buddy hesitates, then hops out reluctantly, feeling green slime creep between his toes. As he does, he sees the canoe shoot backward and Rory paddling out of the lagoon. Hitch a ride home! he screams, laughing manically. But Buddy dives forward and grabs the edge of the canoe. Rory stands and tries to rap Buddy's knuckles with the paddle, flipping the canoe, which tumbles him into the water. The overturned canoe bobbing, bobbing… That's all. No Rory. Until wan-colored rage rears up, wet hair plastered to a head over darker lips curling with hatred. Buddy backs up, but the slippery green slime sends him falling back. Underwater, he feels his head bang against the slime-covered rock. Then the foot pressing on his head, pinning it down. His fluttering fingers sliding like minnows over his brother's hairy leg, trying to loosen the foot. *This is the moment that will mean everything,* he hears himself thinking, as he feels the sinewy, hairy calf sliding through his panicked fingers until the thoughts leak sweetly away from him like black ink.

Embraced by strong arms. Miraculously lifted like a baby in strong arms out of the blackness. Surrendering to the arms, swooning into them as they hoist him up into the air against a hard chest, holding him tighter than he ever remembers being held, cupping his limp body against the dark pressure of a groin, backing him toward the bank and lowering him into the slippery mud, under the hem of a clump of bushes.

Too exhausted to resist the caress of the brotherly hands moving over him, happy for it, breath coming in big fascinated gulps, gasping in the new blur of air and mud while rough hands stray to his trunks and coax them off to make cold air cauterize every place between his legs, and stroking, stroking hands mold his thighs open. At first, he has no idea what is causing the strange pierce of pain.

He wakes up to it, and it doesn't stop.

_ Buddy, what's happening? What's happening?

_ Those eyes aren't the same any more. They changed back. Jumped right out of the face again and glued themselves to the wall. Now they look just like all the others. I hate those eyes.

_ Whose eyes were they, Buddy? Do they belong to the man who raped you? Are they the eyes of the man they found dead?

_ They're only eyes in a dream. I just got to figure out when the dream stops and the real thing begins. I don't know, I swear to you I don't know.

I Murdered My Sim

MR. STEVE JOBS
iPhone Department
APPLE Computer Inc
1 Infinite Loop
Cupertino, CA 95014

Re: Why I murdered my Sim

Dear Steve:

Yes, I killed him—in cold blood. But believe it or not, violent games with hand-to-hand combat or bombing bridges don't pull my chain. When you made all that hoopla over the new *The Sims 3* app for the iPhone, I thought you were finally thinking of a game for me. Instead of getting beaten to a pulp by a Popeye-armed jarhead, I was going to get immersed in psychology.

I admit I've always been a mega-*yente*, Steve, so I couldn't wait to stick my nose into the business of my Sim and his rockin' community. But what really caused me to cough up the $9.99 was the promise of creating my own personal monster. As *The Sims 3* website cajoled, if I wanted to, I could make my Sim "evil, artistic, insane," or even "a romantic kleptomaniac." This made a thrill course through me. Maybe I'd never be lonely again!

I had lots of plans for my Slenda-Sim avatar. I'd start by giving him a Hedi Slimane look circa 2002 and put a couple of tapered shirts over his flat-as-a-pancake chest. I'd let him have longish locks he'd be continually blowing away from his blue eyes. I'd noticed in the ads that all SIMS in bathing suits were completely hairless. I just couldn't wait to put mine through his paces.

But Steve, don't you think the way you change the gender or race of a Sim is, um, rather unusual? You click on what looks like two dice, which leap onto the figure's crotch area, transforming his or her sex or race instantly. Even at the start, society—or maybe the iPhone's pixel gradations?—imposed its inequities. There are three shades of Caucasian but only one for a person of color!

I did have the pleasure of personally dressing and styling my little dude. The closest I could get to that sideways lock of Hedi-hair was a kind of modified shag, one side of which obscured half an eyebrow. Maybe there'd be some strong winds; I knew I'd never pucker those lips any other way.

Things got worse when it came to clothing the torso. I picked through an uninspired baseball jacket, hooded sweatshirt, cardigan, camouflage T-shirt and a couple of dangerously tight sports jackets that were a long way from achieving the Thom Browne effect.

As for shoes: sandals, flip-flops, Crocs(!), sneakers, square-toes, dress numbers with a Macy's feel, silver-toed disco boots, and a lavender leather creation with cutout designs. Get the picture?

It spells s-u-b-u-r-b-s.

Well, I guess I was in an impish mood, because I chose those lavender leather shoes to go with pale pink pants. Too bad nobody got the joke. It had become abundantly clear that my Sim couldn't be anything else but a bottomy wuss. Maybe it would be fun to push him around.

By the time I got through dealing with furnishings, I decided never to go shopping in this town again. I wanted better stores. Or maybe I wanted to sneak with a loaded Uzi into the home of the graphic artist responsible for all this stuff and wait patiently for him in the dark.

Although my Sim seemed awfully phlegmatic, I was still hoping to make him the town philanderer. If that didn't lift my spirits, I could always "put him to sleep." Supposedly, you could starve them to death, make them collapse from lack of sleep, or maybe even burst their bladder by keeping them away from the bathroom.

Heartened, I skipped (or rather, made my Sim skip) to town. It was a boring little burg, but I hadn't come to see the sights. What I *had* come for was in the form of a college-aged guy named Johnny with blond hair and a swimmer's build. He was standing on a dock on the water, so I had my Sim hightail it over.

What happened next is at the crux of what I don't like about *The Sims 3* for iPhone, Steve. To win, you're supposed to get all civic-minded. Polite chatter, a generous nature and good hygiene all get you rewarded—just like in fucking real life.

Well, you can image Johnny's chagrin when I had my Sim break through all the bullshit and just try to grab him. Johnny pushed my Sim away, but all he could manage to say was, "Wooo, dargy dar!" Meanwhile, a couple of talk balloons showed images of fish, a toilet, and other unrelated imagery. I guess they haven't worked out the bugs yet.

Suddenly a note informed me that Johnny was "beginning to dislike your Sim." So me and my Sim followed the little blond number to his place. I won't go into much more detail about what happened, except to say that Johnny must have gone to court and gotten a restraining order. My Sim changed fast from "disliked" to "enemy" to "nemesis." And all this just because my guy wanted a little nooky? The last time they met, Johnny stayed outside his own house until my Sim left. Maybe the green mist floating off my Sim had something to do with it. I later found out it meant he had body odor.

Around that time is when I decided to murder the little nothing. You wouldn't believe how hard it is. Keeping him awake and unfed did make him pass out once, but the sucker had the luck to fall onto a bed.

I don't think it was Johnny who killed my Sim. It was something as pedestrian as starving to death or not being able to take a leak. The next screen showed a shadowy graveyard, with some kid looking at my Sim's gravestone. By now I wanted another notch on my belt, so I could call myself a serial killer.

I started the game again. You can imagine how astonished I was to see the glowing emerald icon that had always indicated my Sim's presence.

Out of curiosity, I tapped it. I ended up back in my Sim's tacky apartment, watching him doubled over, clutching his stomach in hunger. He'd risen from the dead! I was immediately told that he had to pee, shower (with his underwear on, of course), eat, sleep. What was I, some kind of unpaid nursemaid?

This time I decided to go for broke. With a flick of my thumb, I cut off the juice. The screen went black. There had to be some way to get rid of him for good—short of tossing my phone. But maybe there wasn't. A Sim's nervous system is all electric. Everybody knows you can't remove an iPhone's battery.

TIME-WORN TALES

Pinocchio

for Angel A.

THERE ARE THOSE BOYS-TO-MEN whose slightened look seems built in, permanent. Are they beautiful through the sheer fact that they've been thwarted? With lithe, curtailed limbs and a taste for shiny, tailored clothes, they resemble jockeys. But when their heart-shaped faces are pinched by too many sleepless nights on the street, their wiry bodies take on a shrunken look. It is then one realizes that their delectable slightness may be the result of early drug use or their mother's own libidinal activities during pregnancy.

Such a creature was Pinocchio, marked by inheritance to serve pleasure. His only known biological parent—his mom—was a homeless rape victim, caught in a park and taken against a tree. The foster parent who'd tried to raise him before he ran away was an old Jewish bookbinder who'd been thrown out of a Soho loft to make room for an artist cum investor.

Playland, a video arcade of jingling games and digitized grunts and groans, became the truant place where Pinocchio and his runaway friends passed the time and plied their wares. With the good nature of those people who have no attention span, Pinocchio attracted his fair share of admirers. He wore silky tank tops over miniature muscles with gleaming gold jewelry on his satiny patina, against which the daddies never tired polishing their voracious, slippery tongues. He also had a rakish grin. But his unreliability earned him some enemies that resulted in a growing number of gouges and nicks on his splintery rib cage. Needle marks and knife blades then marred the polished blandness of Pinocchio's underdeveloped looks. As times grew bad, his oversized pants slipped halfway down his nonexistent buttocks while his big, sallow elbow joints poked from his ripped sweatshirt.

One day the most nearsighted and bloated of Old Fags came into Playland to beg. His dried-out pate was pitifully plastered over a greasy forehead. "Take pity on a man who has wasted his years and come back with me to my little Bowery room for a pittance," begged he.

Pinocchio's pinpoint eyes sparkled with the fun of having caused such a sweet, needy reaction. "I'll go anywhere with you for a slice of pizza piping hot and a new, smooth twenty-dollar bill," he said brightly. "Anywhere at all."

The Old Fag waddled discreetly to the door ahead of the giggly puppet. This was because a passing policeman could have been very disturbed at the sight of such an obvious couple leaving the palace of pleasure together.

Out on the street, Pinocchio's ebullient impatience made him skip in circles around the lumbering john. They made their way toward the subway past Pinocchio's cronies, runaways and petty thieves lounging against the grimy walls of the avenue. The thought that he had the power to throw some happiness unconcernedly the old whale's way made Pinocchio sparkle with celebration. He flashed gallant grins at the filmy Coke-bottle lenses of the trick but from time to time also sneaked mischievous glances to his lounging buddies, who all snickered at the sight of such an old bag of moldy jelly wheezing along next to the clattering legs of a young, brave marionette.

The Old Fag's room was just as decrepit as he was. Next to a lumpy mattress was a scratched desk and some tattered notebooks. And next to the notebooks was an old-fashioned ballpoint with a barrel made not of plastic but of some kind of metal.

Pinocchio gave a cursory glance at an open page of one of notebooks. Although he could not read very well, he was able to make out the title, which was, "How a Puppet Became a Real Boy." Writers, who were often failures, made Pinocchio bored and uneasy. Like a leaf, he floated away from the drudgeful writing and onto the mattress, surprised even his negligible weight made the springs creak. His pointed face with its hard little lines still held its rakish smile, for he feared not the greasy touch of the failure's lips on his little wooden knob. It had long ago become permanently stiff and practically insensitive, so used was he to poking it into slots that would yield some advantage.

Pinocchio fixed his eyes out the window on a fleecy white cloud scudding across the blue sky. He was sweetly oblivious to the drool leaking over his hard little thighs. That whimsical generosity that he had been born with made him hope the Old Fag was experiencing pleasure. But then the trick did the one thing Pinocchio couldn't tolerate. With the nubs of his blunt, ink-stained fingers he began to fiddle with Pinocchio's hinges.

"Hold off, just a minute," said Pinocchio, pulling back the head of the trick with his own splintery little fingers. "Those are not rust-proof hinges. As you can see, they are built in to protect them from the rain. I told you I did just about everything, but that's one thing I won't. I can't stand to be handled at my knees, ankles, wrists, or other movement places. It gives me a creepy feeling as if somebody were messing with my insides."

He who had seemed humble and needy before now became overbearing and greedy. With his much greater weight, he attempted to bend poor Pinocchio's legs over his shoulders so that he could lick the metal hinges that attached his thighs to his buttocks. But all the hinges in Pinocchio's body slammed straight with the force of a rat trap and the tips of the man's fingers, as well as the tip of his tongue, were nearly severed.

The man sat up and pressed his throbbing fingertip against a forearm, and his bleeding tongue tip against compressed lips. The puppet had paled with rage and was almost the color of unfinished pine. "You've made a big mistake," said the Old Fag, talking like someone balancing a hot potato in his mouth. "Though I wasn't devoid of desire, I was also well meaning. You're a sad wooden thing who never really gets to be genuine. Consequently, you are doomed to repeat the same mistakes for the rest of your life. But by opening yourself to your own feelings and treating others with the tenderness for which you so secretly long, you might one day become a real boy!"

"I'm realer than you'll ever be!" shouted Pinocchio. As soon as his lie had crossed his lips, his little nose, which up until then had resembled a smooth wooden button, grew and grew. It became so big it could only have been the nose of some rare creature, an anteater perhaps, until finally it was so long that it reached halfway across the room. And it was perfectly cylindrical, like a Ninja chuck. Whereupon Pinocchio, panicking, began to whirl about, and his long wooden nose struck the Old Fag a rude blow in the temple.

The man's eyes bugged out, and he slid off the bed in a slump. And when he did, Pinocchio's face, which had grown harder than mahogany, glared with triumph.

"I was lying," he crowed, "for I've never been real and see no sense in ever being that way. Real people must die, but wood is already dead and, if it's well kept, will last practically forever."

As soon as he told the truth, Pinocchio's nose shrank back to normal. But it is likely the man did not have the chance to hear his words or see the nose shrink because he had already died. Pinocchio looked quickly around the room, realizing no one could stop him from stealing. There wasn't much, however, not even a shade on the window. He wondered if he should take the notebook with the writing entitled, "How a Puppet Became a Real Boy." He stared at the scratches on the page, but they just gave him a headache. And besides, it must have been a very boring story. What self-respecting puppet would ever want to become real?

As for money, in the man's clothes and in his drawers was not even the twenty dollars he had promised, so Pinocchio grabbed the old ballpoint. He had suddenly thought that its metal barrel might make a good crack pipe. Off he skipped on his merry way, unscrewing the barrel of the pen and tooting on it in triumph, for though he had gained little from the encounter, he had his nose back, and that was something to be happy about.

It wasn't long before the rumor spread throughout Playland that the police were looking for a notched, nicked, nasty puppet, last seen with a derelict whose carcass had been found rotting in a dismal Bowery hotel. Pinocchio almost went mad with worry. He couldn't go back to Playland because they were sure to look for him there.

Before long, he came to a large structure with a vast open mouth. It looked like a giant fish—a whale with its baleens bared for feeding. And indeed, hundreds of commuters, some who looked almost as important as minnows and others who seemed as insignificant as microscopic particles of plankton, were inhaled through these openings, while others seemed to be vomited out. This great fish's hunger seemed insatiable, for the eating and vomiting was continual. Pinocchio soon learned that the giant fish was really a building known as the Port Authority Bus Terminal, and it contained all manner of men and beasts in its bowels.

Some remained in it forever because they couldn't find their way out. No one, reasoned Pinocchio, will discover me here, for the stew of creatures is just too thick and perplexing. I'll lose myself on the staircases and in the restrooms.

So, Pinocchio let himself be sucked through the huge mouthlike entrance and buffeted about by the streaming crowds, and it was a pleasurable feeling. But since he was a puppet of seasoned wood, he always kept one predatory eye open. One day, as he stood at the urinal pretending to pee with his little wooden knob, he was struck by an image of wealth in the opposite mirror. It was a tall, elegant person in a dark suit, holding a briefcase. The person's skin had a heavenly or deathly bluish cast, and what was even stranger was that his hair was blue, too. And from its eyes, which seemed glazed, floated a kind look of renunciation.

Pinocchio didn't know it, but this was the Blue Fairy. The Blue Fairy had been lithe and attractive just a few months before and had loved every kind of pleasure—dinner parties and clubs, sex and leather. Then a spell had begun to transform him into an unwell, emaciated man. But his ravaged body had a look of purity. In fact, it seemed worn and polished down into simple, elongated curves, much like Pinocchio's.

Pinocchio was very attracted to the Blue Fairy and very excited to be standing next to him. Without looking down at Pinocchio's thing, the Blue Fairy glanced at him and smiled sweetly. He wore a suit of such a perfect cut that Pinocchio was sure he must have lots of money.

Actually, the Blue Fairy was just as taken by the little puppet whose little wooden knob stuck straight out toward the urinal but from which no liquid streamed. How wonderful, thought he to himself, to be made of wood and never have to worry about getting sick. And should you be reduced to splinters or even used as kindling, I bet it wouldn't hurt at all. For by then everything hurt the Blue Fairy. His legs ached dully and sometimes felt like they were made of wood, and his feet always felt like hot, streaming sand or a swarm of angry bees, and when he moved his jaw, it felt creaky as if it were set on broken hinges.

Before long Pinocchio sat in the Blue Fairy's penthouse and learned that he had been a stockbroker and still had a large bank account and very good disability and medical insurance. Weeks after that day, Pinocchio was still sitting there. He passed the time watching all kinds of cable stations on the big stereo TV. But sometimes he grew tired of this, and his dry eyes ached because no one had given him lids and he could not close them no matter how tired he was. He even smashed the TV once, but the Blue Fairy shrugged it off as a tantrum and bought another. At other times, Pinocchio filled the big sunken tub in the bathroom with gallons of water and lots of bubbles. Then he would float on top of the water without sinking, just like a piece of wood, staring—unblinkingly, of course—at the ceiling.

As tired as Pinocchio became of the cable TV and the big tub, he stayed inside because he was afraid the police would be looking for him. The Blue Fairy, who didn't feel that well, began staying in more and more, too. Occasionally, the Blue Fairy asked Pinocchio to get on the bed. Then the Blue Fairy would slowly remove the clothes from his own emaciated body with its polished blue vellum skin. Pinocchio would wriggle out of his tiny undershorts. The Blue Fairy's bony pelvis would clink against Pinocchio's beveled wooden hips. Their heads would bump lightly against each other and sound like someone knocking on the door, and the experience would really be quite pleasant.

Blank, insensible surfaces often long for decoration, which is probably the reason why Pinocchio soon began to yearn for a gold tooth. He had always fancied one to set off the oaklike sheen of his little heart-shaped face and its surly wooden mouth. He wanted it right in front, where everyone could see it. Unfortunately, the Blue Fairy thought Pinocchio was already hard and durable and shiny enough, and as he got sicker, he was beginning to wish for something softer and more enveloping so he refused to get Pinocchio the tooth. This led to terrible fights that exhausted the Blue Fairy and left Pinocchio pouting for days.

Then, one day, the Blue Fairy went out. As soon as Pinocchio heard the key turn in the lock, he leapt from the couch and began rifling through the Blue Fairy's drawer. And since he thought the Blue Fairy would be very angry this time and would never forgive him, he took all the money he could find.

He ran to a jewelry store run by Chinese people in Times Square. In the window gleamed a gold cap with a small diamond embedded in the center. The gold was very yellow, and the diamond shone brighter than a mirror. Pinocchio almost chipped his nose as he pressed closer to see and the nose bumped against the glass. He pointed to the cap, and the Chinese man motioned him into the store. When Pinocchio had given the man half of his money, the man took a large file and began shaving Pinocchio's upper front tooth away.

Pinocchio's mouth filled with sawdust, and he was afraid he would choke to death. Finally, the man held up a mirror to show that there was a little wooden stub where Pinocchio's front tooth had been. Then the man took the gold cap with the diamond and slid it over the stump and clamped it tight by twisting it with a large pair of pliers that sent sparks flashing through Pinocchio's brain.

The next few days were a blur of pleasure as Pinocchio paraded through his old haunts with the gold tooth always showing. He even went back to Playland. No one, he thought, would identify him as the bad puppet now that he had the new tooth. The gold tooth was so spectacular that it made him look like a real person. And he was sure people would pay much more to be with someone they thought was a real boy, a realization that made him chuckle about his bright future.

In a few days, the rest of the money was gone. Pinocchio still had the gold tooth, but his clothes were beginning to look rumpled. What was even more distressing was the fact that he had been trapped in the rain for a whole day. His shins and forearms were beginning to feel stiff, probably because of warping. The next day a whole gang of giant rats from the subway who had watched Pinocchio boast about his gold tooth and wanted it chased him down the Up escalator at Port Authority. The little puppet with the warped shins stumbled and went rolling down the metal stairs with a crash. His head struck the railing, and the tooth popped out. One of the rats snatched it up, and off they scrambled.

From then on, Pinocchio looked like a little puppet with a dizzy smile and a dark gap in his mouth. He never grew any bigger. Everyone knew he was a puppet, stick-limbed as he had become. What's more, his warped shins and forearms made him move in a jerky way some found charming but others thought was a bit pitiful and robotic. Now and then he remembered the manuscript the man in the Bowery had been writing and wondered what it might be like to be a real boy. But he thought of the possibility less and less. Thus, little Pinocchio found his calling early in life. Even as he neared twenty-eight, he was still stuck mimicking the charm of the wobbly-headed playmate, easily influenced yet unpredictable, accommodating yet wooden.

If this story has made you a bit squeamish, recall that those born in misfortune and toughened by hard luck endure with little complaint levels of suffering that to us are unimaginable. Theirs is the blank smile of constant hardship, unmitigated by others' pity and destined to repetition. Some become entertainers, because little wooden faces branded with sparkling eyes and buttery-looking lips have been marketed as playthings through the ages. For a surprisingly long time, their noses and other defiant appendages merely grow longer and stronger the more that they are abused.

Stations of the Cross

THE PRIEST AWOKE with a feeling of uneasiness. From far away, last night's occurrence winged toward him on the tones of a ringing phone. But he brushed it aside. Who could be calling? A satin-skinned boniness, whom he liked to call his spiritual son, had the new number. But the boy was passed out, at peace beside him on the sheetless mattress. Who else? Dazed as he was, he tried to remember exactly when he had changed the number. It was when the calls got out of hand. When the plug was put back in the wall, rings would rattle the phone, and when the receiver was lifted, curses and threats pierced the eardrum.

The priest pulled himself from the bed and faced the arid day through a funnel of dizziness, light sifting through olive trees into the window. For a few seconds, he convulsed into the customary sobs, the overwhelming plight of the human condition. His mind soared past a brief vision of agony in a garden, the snowy dome of a forehead with drops of sweat turning to blood. He saw a phone ripped out of a brown-skinned hand, then relaxed with a yawn into the familiar feel of his eternal damnation. From the open doorway to the other room came the waxy smell of dates and the stench of the old man asleep in his cane chair. His rosary would be sprawled obscenely across the floor, no doubt.

The priest stumbled to the bathroom—saw the rosary on the floor just as he'd imagined. The old man had, of course, dropped it. Curled up in a corner was the younger brother of the one now lying in the bed. Last night he had wept softly, but now he slept, his blackened feet pulled up against his thin thighs. He looked in better health than his brother, the priest remarked, and he'd be an attractive lad someday.

Numbly he cuffed aside a spasm of shame at these thoughts, leaned his great bulk against the sink, and nearly drank water from it as he had when a child. Then he remembered the water was impure. He decided to go out. He would get some of the old man's change to buy bottled water and fish. Today he would borrow the old man's clerical collar once more, also—and take one of the crucifixes for good luck. He'd do it before the old man woke up and realized he was trapped in his chair for the rest of the morning, with only one or another of the brothers who might happen to feel like helping.

Thus, he moved spiritedly back toward the bedroom, his mind divided between telescoping shame and a pulsing anticipation of roaming the streets—perhaps with this boy or that—got up in clerical garb, for all the world to see.

But the sight of the wiry, satin-skinned body sepulchered in shadow on the soiled mattress temporarily drove the thought from his mind. It reminded him of last night's tortuous dialogue. How had it all begun? He had been explaining to this sullen, street-surviving child, who apathetically sat smoking on the bed, how well he understood the indignities and exploitations suffered by children. Why he knew them well. He had portrayed in imagery, for his benefit, a young friend succumbing to these deprivations in a deplorable manner, years ago, in another land. The boy had been someone of breathtaking charm and beauty. The priest explained how he had tried everything in his power to elevate the child's situation, how his obsession to help seemed only to plunge the lad into further misfortune.

But his companion did not seem to be listening. The bored, heavy-lidded youth kept pulling on his cigarette, his potential for learning still glowing so fixedly before the p r i e s t, but still so unrealized. For instruction was the deed that the priest desired to do most of all.

So, he had gone on with his story, mournfully describing how the long-ago boy, at barely seventeen, had been sent to the purgatory of prison. And during this incarceration, the priest spent every waking hour on his knees praying, but to no avail. He found himself stumbling into the blackest, deepest despair. To make matters worse, he soon learned that this trod-upon flower had fallen ill. No one could say whether his fever and increasing intestinal pains were the result of the abuse of older prisoners, and no one was to guess that the infirmary would prove more diabolical than the cell.

Soon the other prisoners in the sick ward recovered and were released, and all that remained was the frail, though still magnetic, youth. His gleeful nurses and orderlies, all members of a different race than their tearful charge, expressed their delight in being able to devote all their time to his case. But it was their serial penetration that caused the boy's peritonitis and sent him on an agonizing journey to his maker.

Thus did the priest reach the climax of his account to his young interlocutor—a climax, he explained, that was meant to be instructive. But he had not accounted for the bottomless apathy of the present object of his affections. He was stunned by the boy's absence of reaction, which may have stemmed partly from the fact that he happened to come from those peoples who play culprits in this tale of incarcerated woe. His only response to the story was to find in it an explanation for his passionate cultivation by the priest: at least you're getting back for what they did to your boy, he suggested.

Getting back? Had the priest heard right? The idea was so monstrous and such a perversion of intention, that for a moment he gazed at his sullen companion with genuine distaste. To cradle a soiled vessel in tender arms, to recover it the caresses its own mother had denied it—getting back? Certainly, the boy had to understand and appreciate someday, given time and prayer....

An image of wood weighing an already scourged shoulder was eclipsed by darkness, as the priest noticed that the boy seemed hardly concerned with the discussion. The conversation had not touched him at all. Already he nonchalantly held a small square of paper curled in his fingers into which he tipped the mouth of a jar filled with tobacco, shavings of hashish, and free-based cocaine. Whenever the lad made up his mind to flee feeling and sense, there was nothing anyone could do. In fact, he rarely bothered to eat these days, so taken was he by his cursed, damning drugs.

Grim anticipation coiled in the priest's belly. As much as he loathed drugs that stole intelligence, skewed emotions, and could even kill, so was he well aware of sudden swoops of grace, opportunity. Perhaps the child was too thickheaded and stubborn to listen to reason—to what the priest in his confessions was trying to implant; then reason had to be forced upon him. And what better state of mind for this could there be than one in which the subject was hypnotically open to influence? Influence can only enter the mind as a drop of water will enter a moist sponge. So saturated with self-loathing at this reasoning was the priest that he made up his mind for a swift solution: he would take the drug, too.

Gazing at the human hand whose shape mirrors that of the one nailed to wood, but which was attached to his own body, the priest had seen himself reach for the smoking concoction rolled in paper, take it from the young, brown-skinned hand, and inhale it deeply. Was there any use in going over what happened next?

Perhaps not. The priest shrugged wearily, resting his eyes on the boy's sprawled form, struck by ever-brighter pebbles of light from the window. He heard the old man moan from the next room, trying to call out, but too weak. Well, today he could wait until the priest was good and ready.

Then the tones of the phone lashed out again. It was strange that the boy did not wake up and lunge to answer it as he usually did. Instead the priest stumbled to it, determined once and for all to rip the cord from the wall permanently; but he fell and moved on his knees to pick up the receiver.

There was silence at the other end of the line, and the caller hung up with a sharp click. The priest heard this sound with a delicious irony; it was like the sting of a whip. Then he remembered last night's call, when the boy had gotten to the phone before he had. Someone—the boy or his brother—had plugged it back in.

One of the tormentors was calling—one of the boy's perverters or whores. Although the boy had been warned over and over never to give the number out, callers had become legion. There was always an excuse. Either the crude voice supposedly had work for the boy, or the female voice was a cousin with news of his mother. Until finally, a single voice returned again and again. It haunted the priest constantly. It was a nameless voice that the boy denied knowing each time. He wanted to make the priest believe it was many people. And the voice rapidly changed from distant politeness to cooing irony to acid threats.

The caller coveted the boy. The priest even had reason to suspect he was a pimp, that the boy worked for him when he could get out. And then there was the jewelry, the watch, that had suddenly disappeared from the house. Could it be that the boy was stealing from them and funneling it to the voice on the line? It was an idea that filled the Father with helpless rage. Didn't the boy have everything he needed right here: food, shelter, understanding? He had to get him away from the phone, rip it out of his hand, pin the slender body against the wall.

Once released from the priest's arms, the child said nothing to defend himself. Passively he marched back to the bed as if he agreed with his accuser. He lit a cigarette. The priest looked on, fascinated through the merciful buffer of the drugs.

The boy got up and started pacing. Then movement through space extended into writhings, he clenched his fists and hunched his shoulders; suddenly the arms were flung apart and backward as if nailed there, and a stony look transfixed the eyes, as the boy halted inches from the priest, staring in a convulsed manner into the face of that one who would dare seek imprint in his psyche.

The priest's arm swept out and the gaunt face became a vibrating blur. When the priest was finished, he was filled with horror at the sight of his own handiwork. The pouting mouth and aquiline nose were obliterated in a sea of blood, an eye had become gleamingly raw. The priest fled to the bathroom and wrung his hands, gazing into the mirror with disbelief and self-loathing. Then through the door he watched the boy lurch to the bed and fold like a released spring.

Now was the time to move, he realized. For at this moment and at this moment only would the will of the shattered boy be open to what was most vulnerable in the priest himself. An intensely pure tenderness welled up inside him and swept him to the bed, where the youngster lay, wings folded in a swoon.

And the rest must be left in shadow. For duty calls. The moans of the awakened octogenarian—a priest who once guided him as well as caring for a large parish—fill the air. He'll give the old man a pill before he goes out.

With brisk purposefulness, he goes to the other room to choose the black garment and white collar and to get the barbiturates. He stoops gently to pat the tousled head of the little brother upon which he imagines a peculiar crown.

But the vial of pills is nowhere to be found. And as the priest searches for them, the older brother opens a swollen eye, uncurls fingers tinted red by a handful of sleeping pills, and receives each flat, thin lozenge on an outstretched tongue.

She

(with thanks to H. Rider Haggard)

MY NAME IS AYESHA or she-who-waits, and I used to be very powerful. These tits you see are real, models for the very first drinking cup used by man. I was around before all of them, honey. Isis, Kali, Helen of Troy, Miss Thing. When things took a turn for the worse, I did what I had to do. I took the stroll on the Deuce and worked a peep show. But when I tried to boost a stereo from a regular john, he blew the whistle on me. They took me to Central Booking where I lay chained on the floor in my underwear, next to Angel, a pimp arrested for promoting prostitution of a minor.

As soon as Angel saw my tits, he swore to find me again at Rikers. The uncovering of my breasts is a sacred act pertaining to my cult, and he who would gaze upon them is mine forever. But fate is fickle. Angel went to the regular wing while people like me with tits went into protective custody.

Twice two years did I wait. And twice two thousand more would I wait again for him. I who lived among the dead. And I made all the dead my subjects with a metal mop wringer I used to bust skulls.

And in my cell, which I called my tomb, or my boudoir, or my urn, or my clam, others came to see me on their bellies because they had heard that a beautiful creature who was seldom seen but who was reported to have power over all things living or dead could stand between them and a cigarette, a sandwich, or another hour alive. For I call myself she-who-waits, but they had to call me she-who-must-be-obeyed.

And in the second of the twice two years, I couldn't take it anymore. I mean, Mary, could you? And I went to the warden, who sat in a room filled with pictures of love scenes and executions and tortures, and unveiled my face, and folded my arms over my tits, and said, In this temple and slaughterhouse, which are one, will you not grant me the right to be with my beloved? I can't transfer you because you would be a threat to the other prisoners, answered the warden. You would incite them to sexual misconduct. And I answered, Why would I steal milk when I have a cow? And the warden told me that because I was not natural, I would have to remain in protective custody. So I went back to my boudoir, and when I was at lunch took a blunt knife and cut the bleach out of my hair. And I went back to the warden and said, Will you deny me the right to see my beloved? And he said, You are still unnatural! So I went back to my cell and wiped the shoe polish I used for mascara and eye shadow off and when I was at the infirmary borrowed the scissors and cut off my fingernails. But the warden said. You are still unnatural. So I ripped open my shirt and held out my tits and said to the warden, Will you have me cut off these too? And when he saw this, the warden said, Transfer granted.

So, the next day I was brought to my beloved's wing where I saw things most terrible. I saw a man's eye poked out for asking for a cigarette. I saw another man's cell set on fire because he made others wait for the phone. And I saw two men who fought over a third as the third hacked at his wrist with a piece of glass for fear of being left defenseless by his protector.

I saw a lion fight a crocodile and win, and the lion was my Angel, to whom I said, You are my chosen. I have waited for you from the beginning. And I washed his socks and cleaned his cell. I became his female, whereas the others had to come to us for everything and no one could touch me because I was protected. And to prove it, I took a knife and carved into the shower wall, AYESHA AND ANGEL RULE C-76 WITH TITS OF STEEL AND FISTS OF IRON. And even the corrections officers believed because they feared a riot.

Yet even when you are divine, you are still the subject of a stronger power. You could just as well try to make these walls melt away as to sway this passion from its natural course. Then blame me not for wanting Samson, the new inmate, whose fists were harder than Angel's and whose gaze was more ferocious. I am she who took a knife and went into the cell of Samson while he was sleeping and veiled his eyes and cut him and left before his eyes could be unveiled so that he could not see who had done it. And when he came rushing out with eyes that saw blood, I am she who whispered: Angel did it.

And Angel, being too weak to fight Samson, went into his cell to take the sheet from his bed and tear it to strips and hang himself. And I was sorry for what had happened. I wrung my hands and pulled my hair and clawed my face but could not raise him from the dead. And after Angel, there was Samson. And after Samson, there was Apollo, and then Mohammed and Lance and Jesus and Attila, and after him another, and then another and another.

But I am she-who-waits. I am still endless and always there. While all the others must live a spell, and then they die not knowing there is no such thing as death. Not understanding that there is only change.

The Sea

FOR ME THE SEA represents death, codeine, orgasm. I mean this quite literally. From my earliest years, the sea was something dangerous, enticing me to nonbeing. How many times have I stood on a parapet, dock or ship and gazed down at the flat, swirling surface of the water, wanting to pierce its gray skin, feel penetrated by it in every pore? I stood too near the sea, which made my mother nervous. How many times have I lain floating in the sparkling darkness on some opiate and thought I was floating in the sea? Unfortunately, the sea is also a metaphor for losing control, which has happened to me again and again. And one time, many years ago, in Deauville, I swam far out into the ocean, with a soldier, who told me to kick off my bathing suit, which produced a giddy, groundless feeling. Later, we fucked over the footbath in his concrete changing room. At the time, I believed that the sea washes away the danger, germs, and actions repeated in or near it. However, the problem is that the sea is uncontrollable. You can't make it stop washing. Ten years ago, on Fire Island, in the wake of a hurricane, the sea became a moving wall with me trapped in it, a whirlpool of punishing gravel, until it finally spit me onto shore gasping and coughing, with a bloody gouge on my foot. I still have the scar.

THE SACRED ART OF BREEDING

A Visit from Mom

LAST NIGHT, WHEN I HAD SEX with a suspected murderer. It was in the Carter Hotel, or maybe the Rio or the Fulton. About six this morning, actually.

Was it in the Carter, or was it the Fulton? I forget which one. It's the one that lets you pay with a credit card. After which you must convince the second party to leave when you do. Or else the signed credit slip at the desk will have the time added to it until he decides to check out. This is a situation that might be called awkward—isn't it?—when the second party is homeless and when, if you stay, you won't get any sleep yourself… no… you probably wouldn't.

I had come from Port Authority where I had taken Mom to make sure she got on the airport bus safely. I wanted to make certain. There are a lot of troublemakers hanging around Port Authority. Mom was in New York for a regional conference of the United Jewish Appeal. Since her conference was near the Algonquin, I had told her to meet me there for a drink. From there, I knew it would be easy to get a cab to Port Authority, a few blocks away. Mom is beginning to have a little trouble getting around, and the streets were icy.

Everyone knows Port Authority is an unofficial shelter for the homeless. The terminal is not far from the *Times* building on Forty-third

Street, opposite which is a place where drag queens wearing gowns and pantsuits go to use the bathroom or perfume themselves at the bar. But today, as it was barely six p.m., only a poor queen named Missy was sitting at the bar. Missy was dressed down in a muddy old turtleneck. The bar was stifling, but I kept my coat on. It was the one I'd bought on sale at Barney's that I knew Mom would approve of. I was also wearing the sweater she had sent me for Hanukkah.

I remember thinking how pretty Mom still looks with her soft white hair, sparkling blue eyes, and lots of rouge. Yet what a relief it is to get her safely onto the airport bus and know she's on her way home. I guess it's a relief, although after she's gone, I always miss seeing her. Over sherry and peanuts, Mom had told me about her work with the less fortunate aged, the Meals on Wheels program she helps organize in our hometown, the parties for senior citizens, the craft afternoons at the center. Mom had also been to Lord & Taylor that day to look for knitwear for Aunt Heidi. I chided her for sallying out over the icy sidewalks, but I didn't make a big deal out of it, because I figure Mom's sense of independence is the most important thing she has left.

I must have been in the bar at least an hour when the bouncer came in with his brother. The brother looked like he had been in jail. He had a jail body. It's a thickness of certain parts coming from constant, unsupervised exercise of those parts, I suppose. Nor was his goatee, or the tattoos that said AVENGER and BABY LOVE, any evidence to the contrary, especially since the tattoos looked like they'd been drawn with a razor blade, after which shoe polish is carefully rubbed in the wound. The bouncer took his seat by the door, while his brother went to sit on a stool by the bathroom. It was the brother's job to keep an eye on the head.

Mom is having a little trouble getting around these days. I guess it's osteoporosis. But otherwise, she is clear as a bell and just as energetic as ever. She and I have always been as close as anyone could be. Whenever

I had a secret, an adolescent worry about not being popular or sports-minded enough—when I thought I would die if I didn't tell somebody—there was Mom, eager to lend an ear. I always told her. And I still do, almost always. Yet there are now certain things I just would not say to Mom, because I figure that being close to the end—her own mortality—is enough for her to worry about. It's time I took care of my problems myself.

Yet by the second sherry, Mom's irrepressible concern rose to the surface. She said that she had had enough of talking about herself and wanted to know all about what was going on in my life. What about the job in school production at the textbook company? Was I happy there and did I think there was some kind of future?

Although I myself have never been in prison, I feel that my great sociability, cheerful openness, and keen, observant behavior have informed me about the experience. Having been in jail must be, I've always thought, a powerful psychic marker. I will admit that there is something about a person who has been in jail that attracts me. Which is not to say I take the experience at all lightly—I doubt that I would survive it. But how does someone who has been in jail speak to his wife or child when he is pleased or displeased by her or his behavior? How does somebody who has been in jail make love with somebody else? What would he be thinking about to get excited? Having been in prison leaves its imprint on a person's body, which becomes vigilant and tense like a coil. Yet a person who has been in jail seems somewhat resigned; his body speaks of great patience. Take the bouncer's brother, with his strong-looking wrists, stubby, scarred hands, sullen face, and tattoos reading ON THE EDGE, AVENGER, etc., running up one bulging arm. As he perched on the stool, he held a wooden club, one eye constantly on the bathroom door, though there was still no one in the bar except myself and Missy. No, he could wait all night for somebody to try to use the bathroom for the wrong purpose, the hand was waiting on the club.

Exactly what did I do between this time and six in the morning? What could I have been doing in all that time? I keep wondering. I put Mom on the bus for her plane, which was supposed to leave at eight-thirty… so I must have put her on the bus near seven; I must have sat with her in Port Authority until a little after seven. Which means I didn't get to the bar until after seven. I guess it is a relief that she's gone, though I do kind of miss her. But there are so many things that could happen to her in this dangerous city. Also, I start to resent her prying too much into my business. I now remember that as we sat waiting for the bus, she brought up the job business again. She said she knew from experience, from the days when she and Dad were both working to make enough money to give the children a nice home and a good education, that by a certain age—my age, she added pointedly, looking at me with her piercing, uncompromising blue eyes—a person has to make a real commitment to a job, instead of just camping out there, if he wants to get somewhere.

I decided that there was no sense in complaining to Mom about the job. No sense in trying to explain that mechanically shifting papers from one desk to another, keeping logs and making lists, writing memos, was far from anything a real human could make a commitment to. I didn't want Mom to know that I hated working there, even felt humiliated by it sometimes. What sense would it have made to tell her that? To make her worry about my future as she sat in the dismal departures area of Newark airport waiting for a plane that would take her back to desolate upstate? So all I said was that the job was just a way of making money. Clear and simple. I didn't like it or dislike it and that was good enough for me.

Now I remember. I didn't stay in the bar the whole time. Instead I left to go eat—hadn't the bartender said it was nine thirty shortly before?—across the street to get some lamb from the Greek. It was surprisingly good lamb, and I ate a very gelatinous rice pudding. As I ate, through the window I could see a few queens making their way across the ice to the bar. Their heels looked so skinny and high that I was afraid one of them would slip and fall. It was so cold out, but even so, a lot of them were dressed to the nines. Why not go back to the bar? I thought.

Why not go back to the bar?

As we sat in Port Authority, the conversation had somehow turned to Mom's will and her worries that I would not handle the money she had "slaved for" in any reasonable way. It is my opinion that Mom should really think about enjoying the money herself while she still can. Instead of worrying about how I am going to use it. In the first place, she has nothing to worry about, and in the next place, if she wants to put restrictions on it from beyond the grave, then she shouldn't be leaving her precious money to me at all.

"Who knows? Your father and I could use it all up in a nursing home if we got sick," Mom suggested.

Seeing the queens slide across the ice to the bar had made me want to go back in. If Mom wanted to put restrictions on me from beyond the grave, that was fine, but tonight I didn't want to think about it. Inside the bar I recognized another queen, a very tall Latin in a leopard-print sheath, pantomiming the song that was playing to a tubby businessman. Missy was propped in a corner. Her face looked anesthetized into a Mona Lisa smile. The very strong wrists of the bouncer's brother were still resting on the club in his lap as he sat perched near the head. It was as if the wrists were on display; I remember that I kept looking at them. Finally I spoke to him. "What's up?"

"I'm working, man," he answered.

The bouncer's brother started to talk. He was from the Bronx, but he was trying to get a place to stay in Manhattan. And yes, he had been in jail, a year and a half, or maybe six months, ago—but it was a strange story that he guessed most people wouldn't believe. It seems that he had been arrested on suspicion of killing his twin brother. They had been smoking crack all day (something he used to do but didn't do anymore, he added)—and when one of the "rocks" from one of the vials seemed to have disappeared, he began thinking that his twin was holding out on him, after which he started to turn the room upside down. (In fact, it had happened at the Carter, or was it the Fulton?) He turned over the mattress and looked under tables, crawled on his hands and knees across the carpet looking for the rock, until he was overcome with anger at his twin, whom he thought he had caught a glimpse of in the mirror laughing at him; so he went to his brother's clothes—both of them were naked at the time because it was summer and there was no air-conditioning—he went to the clothes and looked in all the pockets, he even tore the cuffs of the pants apart, but still didn't find the rock, so he decided to send his brother out to get more. Neither of them had any money. "That don't matter to me," he growled, feeling as if he were about to snap, "You go out there and you find another bottle 'cause you been holding out on me." And since he was four minutes older than his brother, the brother obeyed.

The rest is somewhat unclear, but the gist of it seems to be that his twin happened to go to a bodega on Ninth Avenue looking for crack just when there was a drug war going on; supposedly mistaken for a backup man, he was shot. After which somebody—who is now in hiding, but at the time was staying in a room next door at the hotel—testified that he had heard the twins arguing shortly before the murder…

I feel really bad about the way Mom said goodbye. With the talk about the will the last topic we spoke of. I didn't want Mom to know how much I hated that job, or that I was planning on leaving it. So I held it in. Mom must have been out for blood, though, because the more I would try to shift the subject to something uncontroversial, the more adamantly she returned to what she surmised might be my problems. Then suddenly she said, "You drink too much."

To be perfectly honest, I had been to an AA meeting just the night before. I have never had a blackout or hurt myself or anything like that, but I was worried about the amount of time I was wasting getting drunk. The AA meeting only seemed to increase my anxiety. Their never fully acknowledged portrayal of drinking as a world entered by excess, a world that was ruled tyrannically by drink, in which you could never hope for any control except by self-exile; the idea that you had to go through a door to another world that was just as uncontrollable as the first, but that was more conventional, and structured in a way that made your survival more likely; the idea that you had to endure life knowing that this door between the two worlds was always there, yet never opening it again… seemed to transform living into a continual struggle against the temptation for self-annihilation.

I wanted to live as if there were one world, not two.

It was time for Mom to get on the bus. I assured her that I wasn't drinking too much, but this did not seem to allay her fears entirely. Instead, she began to talk about diaper days. There was a startling contrast between me and my older brother, she said, who had suffered greatly because of hyperactivity and its effect on the nerves of others, while I had been a practically troubleless toddler who never complained and always smiled and laughed, who spoke in complete sentences by the age of one and a half; these sentences often incorporated the word *please*. But then, by adolescence, the two brothers seemed mysteriously to change places: The older brother abruptly settles down and starts doing what he is supposed to. He enters medical school. Now the younger brother begins "… sowing wild oats. I guess your brother had already gotten it out of his system."

I actually didn't go to the bar right after I left Port Authority. It occurs to me that I went to the peep show at Show World. There was a film in my booth called *Bigger the Better* with a scene in a classroom in which the teacher asks one student to stay after class because his marks are not up to par. They end up making it, during which the student, who has an inhumanly large cock, fucks the teacher in the ass on top of a desk.

As I kissed Mom goodbye at the bus, I took a good look at what she was wearing. She was wearing a lovely suit of pink wool, and her shoes were cream, very fashionable. Mom refused to wear "old-lady" shoes even if they might be more practical at this point. She was holding a cream-colored purse and her suede briefcase that I assumed was full of papers having to do with the United Jewish Appeal. "Take care of yourself, honey," she said.

It wasn't the strenuousness of Mom's occasional visits to New York that worried me, but her lifestyle in the wintry land of upstate New York with my aging father. Both of them still drove despite his considerable loss of eyesight and her hearing problem. Her reflexes were obviously much slower than they had been in her prime, and although the area was far from congested, compared to this city, I was constantly picturing the sudden swerve of a car at a lonely intersection, literally feeling the brittle fragility of their old bones at the impact of the accident. What, the thought had sometimes occurred to me, despite my efforts to repress it, would I do if one of them were injured and totally incapacitated, yet lingered for years? How would I manage to care for them? How much, I thought with a guilty swallow, was I depending on the security of my inheritance? Anyway, neither of them understood or approved of what they thought of as my lifestyle. Something told me that any inheritance would have severe restrictions placed on it in an effort to control my life—after their death—according to a plan of their choosing.

During the recitation of the bouncer's brother, who had been arrested for the murder of his twin brother, his broad wrists stayed displayed on the club, unmoving. He told me that, in actuality, he was working two jobs this evening. He had to watch the bathroom to keep the crack-heads from going in and to keep the drag queens from turning tricks in there. But if I was looking for a good time, he would be glad to get somebody else to take over for him. I went into the john and counted the bills in my pocket, realizing that—not counting whatever might be in the envelope Mom had slipped into my hand as her lips brushed mine before stepping onto the bus—I had only thirty dollars. Taking Mom's envelope out of my pocket, I opened it, glancing at the front of the card on which were written the words *To My Son*. Inside it was fifty dollars. The bouncer's brother had said he wanted sixty, and I was planning to use my credit card for the hotel room. I left the bathroom and nodded to the bouncer's brother, who went to speak to the bartender.

The bouncer's brother is called Mike. I was disturbed by the fact that Mike left the bar wearing only his T-shirt. "I'll pick up my coat in a minute," he assured me cryptically. Then, as soon as I had paid for the room, he took a long, mumbling look at the number on the key and handed it back to me. "Wait for me up there and I'll be back."

How, I wondered, as I stood in the room still wearing my coat, had I ended up waiting on the fourteenth floor of a hotel—it was the Rio, I think—for someone who had been accused of murdering his brother? The setup was beginning to seem more and more obvious to me. He knew the room number. After he went back, supposedly to get his coat, he would return with a friend, who would wait somewhere on this floor. At the right moment, perhaps with the aid of a weapon to keep me still, Mike would leap up and let his friend in. The two of them would roll me.

Mom and Dad's golden, or fiftieth, anniversary a couple of years ago was our most successful family affair in years. My brother Joe and I had planned it, though it had begun as his idea. For our celebration, we chose an inn by the lake where the whole family had spent countless summers when we were children. "Don't get us anything extravagant," Mom had cautioned. "We won't live long enough to enjoy it." Joe and I hadn't listened. Together we bought Mom a gold watchband and Dad a high-tech snowblower for the driveway. Unfortunately, I had been short of money at the time and had to work out an agreement with Joe where I paid for only a quarter of it. Dinner at the inn had taken on the form of a joyous tribute to the longevity of my parents' relationship. And all of Mom's and Dad's oldest friends were there. Our cousins even came all the way from California. It occurred to me that Mom and Dad had always acted on their concern for me by being intensely practical on my birthdays, Bar Mitzvah, and graduation, never getting me anything that was likely to be damaged by childish carelessness—no matter how much I begged for it.

There was a knock on the door of the hotel room, but I stood rooted. Finally, Mike began calling me through a crack in the door. "Hey, will you open up, it's me."

Trembling, I moved to the door and opened it slightly. Mike pushed it against me so that I stumbled backwards, and he walked in. Then he closed the door and locked it.

"What's a matter with you?" he asked, staring at my still-coated figure. "You hiding a gun there or something?" Mike started to undress until he was down to his underwear. His body was an unstable column of muscles beginning at his shoulders and lats and tapering only at his shins and feet. One nipple was sliced diagonally by a six-inch scar. The name Mickey had been hand-tattooed above his waist. "Well, go ahead," he said. "Peel down."

Only because I noticed that Mike placed all of his clothes on a table, out of reach of the bed, did I hesitantly begin to remove my coat. For I knew that if he had been hiding a weapon, he would have kept the clothes within reach of the bed. I took off my shoes. Mike, in his black briefs, stood watching. Was I imagining that one ear seemed to be cocked toward the door?

Mike got onto the bed and motioned me to him. In my white briefs, I padded to the edge of the bed and sat down. "Relax, man, would you," he muttered. I lay down next to him and he raised one hand and tweaked my nipple. Then he said, "This may have to cost you."

In fact, the aforementioned lake at which our family had summered often returned in dreams. For my birthday, which is in July, Mom would bake the kind of layered butter frosting cake you rarely see anymore, and Dad would make hot dogs and hamburgers on the grill. Aunt Heidi always came out for the day on Greyhound, and in her bag was a present for me. Two rules were waived for the day: I was allowed to take the boat as far away as I wanted, and I could stay up as long as I liked. Understandably, my memories of those days have the scent of adventure, sun-spangled water followed by endless nights shot with stars.

"Relax, man, would you. I mean, you got to pay more depending on what you want to do." Mike leapt to a standing position on the bed and pulled down the black briefs. With his back to me, and legs straddling mine, he bent forward and spread his cheeks. "How's this? Look at that hole. Isn't it something?" He began to gyrate.

As soon as I had slipped on the rubber that I got out of my wallet, Mike began to twist his ass onto my cock. He straddled me and began to rock back and forth so that the bed shook and my cock slid in and out. Clenching his teeth, he mumbled, "That's right, man, it belongs to you. Treat it right and you'll own it." Then, having soon been directed to "shoot that cream deep inside," I hastened toward an orgasm, after which Mike raised himself deftly from my phallus.

"I'm hungry," Mike said.

"What's this you said about it costing me?"

Mike's body stiffened as his eyes got that look of someone about to begin a complicated tale. "You don't know who you're with," he began. "You don't know who you've got right here in this room." Mike went on to detail his identity. According to him, he was closely connected to the bar owners—too closely for comfort, he added. As a matter of fact, one of them, after whom the bar took its name, had been watching our every move and had instructed Mike to leave his jacket as collateral before we walked together to the hotel. Mike had been very hesitant to go with me at all, "seeing that these guys tend to think they own somebody and I am kind of their boy." But they had generously given their permission. Go with the guy and give him a good time, they had counseled when he came back for the coat. But make sure he makes it worth your while. Now what would Mike do, he wanted me to tell him, if he came back to the bar with his ass full of grease and didn't have all the money— the one hundred and fifty dollars—they were expecting? What is more, it would be foolish for me to suppose that they couldn't find out where anybody lived.

Dipping my hand into my pants pocket, I pulled out all the cash I had. Mom's card flipped out, too, and floated down to the floor. "Hey!" Mike said, bending toward the card, "is it your birthday?"

I knelt quickly and snatched the card away, bending it in half as I stuffed it back in my pocket.

"Don't touch that!" I snapped.

Mike and I began to get dressed, but he was stewing. "There's only eighty dollars here," he hissed. "What the fuck do you expect me to say when I get back?"

"I told you, that's all I have."

But Mike was not to be daunted. Crawling around the carpet, he began cursing, accusing me of taking his socks. When he stood up, his face was livid and his entire muscular body was trembling. "All right, keep the damn socks," he spat, "if you're that kind of pervert, but you gotta pay for 'em!" He pulled his Adidases on over bare feet, grabbed me roughly by the Hanukkah sweater, and forced me toward the door. "C'mon, man, you must have a bankcard in that wallet. We're going to a cash machine!" As we left the room, I noticed dirty white socks sticking out from under the bed.

Planes move so incredibly faster than real time, and by now, six a.m.., Mom would have gotten home long ago and been asleep, with Dad, her husband, for several hours. I do hope she got home safely and that there was no trouble at the airport.

Family Romance

"TAKE THAT STUFF AGAIN and you have a good chance of dying in the process, clear and simple," he said. He put my chart back in the folder. That's all there was to say. An irregularity had been found in my EKG, due, the doctor suspected, to cocaine. Cocaine having been taken in the most powerful way possible: inhaled in a gaseous state, reaching the cells of the brain in less than ten seconds, causing an almost instantaneous jump in blood pressure. One muscle of the heart had been overexercised, and that put pressure on the other parts, as I understood it. My heart wasn't normal.

I was in our wood-paneled den watching the news, listening to a report about an athlete who had probably died from an overdose. It seems his wife had called an ambulance when he started going into convulsions. By the time they got him to the hospital, it was too late. If it hadn't been for this news, I probably would not have been thinking at that moment of the doctor's visit. Especially since I wasn't alone. My adopted son was sitting on the bed, puffing on a cigarette; my wife standing in the door frame, hand on hip.

We'd just finished a painful conversation about my son moving back in here, and he was against the idea. My wife was for it and was using money as a pivotal issue. But my son maintained that since he is eighteen, the decision should be entirely up to him. What's more, he hadn't lived in this house for four years. His leaving had been my wife's idea, not mine. But it also had been my wife's idea to adopt a child.

We'd been trying to have a baby for almost six years when we adopted him. We'd been through everything available at the time, including a doubtful surgical procedure, but nothing worked. Then came adoption agencies with decade-long waiting lists. So we put an advertisement in the *Pennysaver*. It was composed by my wife and went something like this:

Couple with love to spare
would like to share it with a
healthy white baby.
Generous reward.
We are a stable family.

I argued that the word *white* was too blatantly racist. We'd just wait and see when we met the people, I suggested. Then we could always say yes or no. But my wife was adamant that the word stay in. As her trim hands sliced carrots and celery for a roast, she passionately began defending the word *white,* claiming that the baby had to resemble as much as possible something that could have come from her. She had to feel, in fact, that it was hers. This would be the only compensation for our inability to make ourselves live on through succeeding generations. Our failure was made even worse, she contended, flinging the roast abruptly into the oven, by the fact that she was an only child, the end of her line.

I gave in. And late one night we had our first response. He was a man on the telephone known only as Sloane. He knew where he could get us a white baby, if we wanted one. But a white one would cost a lot. Was he the father of the baby? I asked. The idea must have seemed absurd to him, as he scoffed, far from it. Then he designated a place on the highway about a mile from a shopping mall in another suburb where we were to meet him if we were really interested.

My wife was at the mirror, yanking her short reddish hair into a ponytail. Her eyes welled with desperation when I protested the wisdom of dealing with such a character as Sloane. My hesitation made her furious. Why was she being put in such a position, she demanded to know, when all she wanted was an ordinary baby? There was nothing unusual about her ambition. Women a hundred times more unremarkable than herself were granted the wish without the slightest hesitation. Why should she be denied? She made up her mind to meet Sloane whether I went with her or not, slipped into duck shoes (it was raining), and stormed out to the Honda.

She careened into the driveway about an hour later, her pert face pale and fervent, her eyes burning. It was all settled. They'd agreed on a price. She'd given him some cash already. Apprehensively, I questioned her about Sloane but could discover little. Of course, I'd been right, she said haltingly. He was probably a very dangerous man. Those eyes, those eyes, she kept repeating. As for his sources for adoption, they had to be criminal. It would be best to have as little to do with him as possible. Just get it over with fast. The child would be delivered the very next evening.

That night in bed, she pulled me toward her. To be honest, she didn't have much information about our child, she whispered in my ear. Only that it was guaranteed white and healthy. The necessary papers would be delivered with it too.

Her precipitous determination was fate, like a pregnancy. It was like something happening inside one for which two had to share the responsibility. Strangely enough, over the misgivings, the news that I was about to become a father made me feel proud, almost powerful.

We spent the whole of the next day driving to outlets that sold strollers and playpens. My wife said that we were going to have a boy.

We furnished the guest room in our ranch-style house with a crib, blue polka-dot curtains, and some toys.

It was midnight, and still no one had come. Are you sure you gave him the right address? I asked my wife timidly.

One would think so, was the curt reply. Then she grimly began to change into her nightgown.

We were awakened by the crunch of car tires on gravel in the driveway, followed by a heavy thud. Headlights flooded the window as a car screeched away. My wife and I ran out in our nightclothes to see what looked like a bag of laundry lying on the lawn near the rosebushes. The bag was moving. When I untied it, a boy of about eight crawled out.

My wife brought him into the house and began to examine him. She clasped his forehead to her breast to see if he had a fever and checked his teeth. His hair was matted and his nails looked dirty, so she led him to the tub.

I stood in the doorway to the bathroom, watching the soapy washcloth slide over his soft-looking body. He didn't look exactly white, more likely Hispanic, as he was somewhat coffee-colored. He had large, liquid black eyes, a full, slightly drooling mouth, and a flat nose.

It's not a baby, I pointed out, not daring to mention the race thing as well. He needs a mommy and daddy, my wife retorted.

Of course, the crib, the stroller, and the playpen had to be gotten rid of. We bought a bed for him. My wife spent a large part of the next year sleeping near or on it. It was because of what had happened to him in the past. He was afraid to be alone at night, she said.

What first struck me about my adopted son was that he didn't seem to know very many words. If he had a native language other than English, I never discovered what it was. "Mine," he would say with a frown, grabbing a piece of steak right off the fork at the barbecue, then dropping it in the grass with a howl because it was too hot. Or he would sit with his back to me in front of the television, barking over and over, "Change! Change!" until I got up and flipped the dial.

My wife pieced together a story for him. It was gleaned from their nights together and from the books on child abuse that she had begun to lap up. He was likely to have come from a Central or South American country where he'd led a wretched existence as a throwaway, she said. To survive, he may have resorted to stealing or worse practices. He could have spent his day wading through industrial dumps in search of machine parts to sell on the street. Such dumps were known to contain caustic chemicals, which could explain the strange discolorations—perfectly even reddish bands, like slave bracelets—around each of his ankles.

It was clear that he would require special patience and attention. We talked about his need to feel loved, accepted. But there was something about him. He didn't really seem like a kid. I felt it, for example, when I snapped his picture as he hung from a jungle gym or put on a pom-pom-festooned hat at a birthday party. I could see him—unlike other kids his age—turning to get a good angle, coming on to the camera.

What is more, having a child hadn't strengthened our marriage at all. It was as if my wife were in a trance whose circle was closed to me. Motherhood for her was a bliss bordering on the manic. Things that had bothered her before couldn't touch her now. The child was more important.

When I suggested to my wife that her absorption in our son was unhealthy, obsessive, she countered by accusing me of a lack of sensitivity for the boy that was based on a character disorder. I was borderline, she said. I had never really felt anything. I was cold, and I always withdrew from everybody. As an example, she cited our sex life. What had before been passionate, involved sex, spiced by a desperate desire to create human life (before time ran out), had become routine and faceless. I'd stopped taking the challenge. There was no more commitment on my part, only a dull desire to get off. And how could I disagree? I'd sunk into a kind of apathy that I don't really think of as my life anymore.

My waistline sagged, and I was getting out of breath on stairs. I had no real friends. My work wasn't going well at all. I'd gone freelance to give myself a more flexible schedule, with the excuse that I'd be able to spend more quality time at home. But I did nothing with the extra time. I became a fanatic sports spectator, bellowing with rage if anyone dared to place a hand on the dial. I felt regarded as no more than a fixture in my own home, an out-of-date piece of furniture gathering dust in front of the television. And my son was already thirteen.

He looked different. Maybe it was his hairstyle, identical to boys' his age in the neighborhood, that made him look more Caucasian; still, I could have sworn that his skin looked less brown, his nose and lips less blunt. His English was casual and colloquial now. It sounded fake, as far as I was concerned. I couldn't shake the feeling that he was playing at being average. For example, he made a point of pretending an utter lack of anxiety about the future. "We'll just handle that one when it comes around" was one of his bland remarks, ostensibly put forth to soothe too-neurotic me when I expressed a worry that couldn't have been all that unreasonable. Then he'd go out to play hockey. I'd sit home and watch hockey on television, pop open another can of beer. Or maybe he'd gone to the science club or the debate team or the karate studio.

My wife had hung awards and trophies for these activities on the wood paneling of the den, where I sat in front of the TV set. There was a plaque with a big, gold-painted plastic test tube. He'd gotten it for being third runner-up at a science fair. Then there was a laminated report card for a semester in which he had scored a B+ average, and a framed photo of him smashing a board with his foot at a junior-level karate exhibition. Surrounding me at various points in the room were other paraphernalia: a computer that had a chess program, an Andre the Giant wrestling video, a Yamaha electric piano, and a punching bag on a wire pole.

His own room was his own world. There was a camouflage-print tent pitched over the bed, a can of Sterno on the dresser, next to an empty, encrusted cage once inhabited by a now defunct iguana. Interspersed with rock posters and bicycle parts were implements for survival in the jungle: a hide skinner, some snakebite suction cups, and an army-green compass.

One day while he was at school, my eyes were drawn to the corner of a yellow envelope sticking from his top dresser drawer. For some reason I took it out and opened it. It was stuffed with scraps of paper torn from a loose-leaf notebook, a kind of scrawled diary.

"Saw Sloane again today. So cool. He had on fatigues."

"Sloane got his nipple pierced today."

"Did crack with Sloane again. Bare-assed."

From the bottom of the envelope tumbled a glass tube fitted with a screen, then a handful of evil-looking little vials painted in camouflage colors. They were vials of crack.

I stood holding the stuff in the palm of my hand, staring at it. Sloane? Could it be the same Sloane? The one from the very beginning? The idea was absurd, since my son had been only eight. Then maybe my wife too. But I couldn't force my wife's image into the picture. Instead, I imagined assignations between Sloane and my adopted son, the crack and naked bodies, defiant laughter. The room they were in. Big reconnaissance boots near the bed.

At dinner that evening, while shoveling in fish sticks and coleslaw, my son offered my wife a garbled account of his favorite TV series. It was apparently about a mutant Robin Hood whose headquarters were in the New York sewers. My wife feigned interest in the account while she kept reloading his plate, now and then injecting a mild remark designed to instruct without being critical of his sensibility. He was wearing his cream-white karate outfit with the loose half-sleeves. His hands and skin were still delicate like a girl's, but his forearms and shoulders were wiry and more mature-looking. In my mind the sight of him at the table—stuffing fish sticks into his mouth followed by hasty gulps of Slice soda, rocking his chair back and forth on two legs—alternated like a flip book with images of him with Sloane in a rented room somewhere. One of Sloane's nipples was pierced.

My wife was undressing for bed near her tulle-trimmed night table. I took one of the little vials and the pipe into our pink bathroom. To get the pieces of crack out of it, you had to pry the cap off with your teeth. Under the bathroom light, the little chunks looked slightly translucent. I tasted one of them with the tip of my tongue. It was bitter. The pipe was nothing but a glass tube, smudged with carbon, into which a piece of screen had been shoved about half an inch down from one end.

To light the crack without it rolling out of the glass tube you had to tilt your head back so that the nugget rested against the screen. As you inhaled, it sputtered and began to melt, sticking to the screen, or trickling down the sides of the tube. The white smoke streaming through the glass tube tasted cooling but poisonous, like airplane glue, and the sight of it being so instantaneously connected to the mental feel of getting high was disorienting. It went to the brain almost immediately, producing a pumped-up, cartwheeling high. A rough-and-ready excitement was everywhere. It flowed into my limbs and groin. It made me want to take things into my own hands.

I hid the pipe and the vials in the toilet paper roll, hurried back to the bedroom, and watched my wife at the mirror in her bathrobe, putting cream on her face. Her breasts drooped slightly against the pink-quilted material. Her small mouth pursed as she massaged a drop of cream into her lightly freckled skin with a circular motion. I felt as if I were seeing her for the first time.

I came up from behind, trembling, slipping my hands under the bathrobe and into her nightgown. The warmth of her skin set me moaning immediately. My hands squeezed her breasts and my fingertips wandered over her nipples. She began moaning, too, and stood, turning to kiss me. My tongue, which was slightly numb from the crack, plunged into her mouth. I pulled up her bathrobe and nightgown and cupped her ass cheeks, parting them as one finger sought the crevice.

Sunday breakfast. My wife in her quilted robe hums as she cooks pancakes and bacon. My son eats his favorite cereal, Honey Smacks, while I sip coffee and browse through the paper. As I switch sections, my boy comes up with the kinds of remarks you'd expect from someone his age and generation. ("I'm not into war and all that shit, like one country over another. But, you know, I really respect the flag. So many people died for it and shit. And they were so young, they didn't even know what they were doing.") Smiling, my wife and I nod to encourage his investigative thinking. She stacks pancakes on each of our plates and bends to kiss me. My son drowns his in syrup, before spearing a few pieces, and then pops up, announcing that he is leaving to play soccer. Give 'em hell! I shout, and have a nice day! My wife stoops to wave prankishly over the edge of the kitchen shutters as he gallops across the driveway.

I'd really like to know if his nipple is pierced too. He is always barricading himself in the bathroom for long periods of time. Sometimes he leaves an open jar of cold cream behind, next to the pimple medicine.

Several times a week, after my crack ritual with one of the vials in the bathroom, and after my wife and I have had exhaustive sex and she has fallen into a sated sleep, I lie, sit, or kneel near her naked body, constantly changing position for a better view, because the drug is still circulating in my brain. I watch her nipple rise into a strip of light and then slant sideways as she inhales, or I stoop close to her armpits to catch the scent. My hands search nervously over my own body—which is getting thinner—caressing it as my throat constricts in continual dry swallows. On my belly between her open legs with my cock pressed against the sheet, I take in the whole cunt, its moist folds. If she is on her stomach, I imagine slave bracelets on her ankles, like the red discolorations on my son's legs. Then I could part her legs to fasten each ankle to a side of the bed, start licking the backs of her knees, and slide my tongue up to the warm crevice.

The idea of my tongue buried in her as she begins to convulse is riddled into the flow of thoughts by the crack, as if by a jackhammer. I'm getting hard again. My hand moves between my legs. I'd love to have sex, but I know she is spent and wouldn't want me to wake her. She might suspect something. So I begin to jerk off, more and more furiously.

"Sloane, Sloane, Sloane…" I hear myself mumble repeatedly with rising titillation, keeping my eyes glued to her body. Finally, having spasmed and shot for the second time, I wipe the semen off with the sheet and fall to her side once again. I'm still racing from the crack, maybe my mind is playing tricks on me. I consider whether my son is in bed or out of the house with Sloane, whom he may meet while we are asleep. They go to the city to after-hours clubs that are open all night, where anyone of any age or any sexual persuasion can be found. And there is every kind of drug imaginable. The walls are painted black and have red light sconces. Blond wigs border black skin, silver and gold lamé frame cleavages or are used as codpieces, there are overdressed whores and bored sophisticates, half-naked transsexuals and gowned transvestites, gangsters and child prostitutes, drug dealers, punks, and gigolos. Sloane standing there is a broad back in the dark as a shaft of light catches hairs on the knuckles of one massive hand gripping the shoulder of my boy, who is in his karate outfit. The two bodies are swallowed up by the throng of bodies and pop out again over and over. Until the thought of the live body lying next to me starts me panting once more and I stroke my flaccid penis. I may not be able to come this time or even get an erection, but I keep going on and on with limbs flashing limbs, until my cock is swollen and abraded to the point of bleeding.

My son is in the den putting together a model airplane. I'm not in there. I don't watch television much anymore. My wife is napping. Silence in the house. I'm studying my nipple in the bathroom mirror. It's flat and extended, not very much to grab on to, really. What exactly would it be like to pierce it? Is an anesthetic used? I take a needle from my wife's sewing basket, grab the tip of a nipple and stretch it outward, place the point against the skin. Would I ever have the courage to run it through, Sloane? Would I be able to stand the pain, Sloane?

My wife has come tearing into the kitchen in her tennis outfit, clutching the envelope with my son's diary. Will you take a look at this, she spits. She is furious, at wit's end. Our boy isn't who we think he is, he's been pulling the wool over our eyes. She keeps pacing in circles as I pretend to read the scraps of paper for the first time. Something has to be done, she says.

She confronts him when he comes home. I keep my eyes lowered. He must know that I've known for weeks, ever since the crack disappeared.

As indulgent as my wife is with the boy, she now becomes adamant, unyielding. She chooses the medical approach. He has a drug problem that demands immediate treatment. My son disagrees with her, referring to the scraps of paper as exercises in creative writing. He accuses her of spying and barricades himself in his room.

Finally, my wife slips a note with an ultimatum under his locked door. Get help, it begs, or get out. But he's barely fourteen, I point out. My wife silences me. There are places for boys his age that can handle problems like his. That night she explains "tough love" to me and cites certain magazine articles. Her ultimatum is merely meant to shock him into taking responsibility for his life. What will happen next is that he'll think it over and come around by morning. Then we can take him to see the right professionals.

But the next morning, he and some of his clothes, including the karate outfit, are gone. An hour later we are presenting the situation to a silver-haired detective, who seems to be searching my eyes, studying my slightly unsteady hands. He wrinkles his brow and slides a thumb over his square chin, assuring us that our son's leaving is a bluff, the proverbial running away from home. When he gets cold and hungry, he'll be back and ready to listen. With deliberate strokes the detective writes down the telephone number of a good drug treatment program and hands it to me.

My wife tries to remain firm in her belief that she did not behave unreasonably. The facade begins to wilt when a week passes and there is still no sign of our boy. That night in bed, I decide to test her. I merely pronounce one word: Sloane. Her eyes compose a puzzled look, but do I see them moistening at the corners? Then she buries her face in a pillow and twists away.

I have read that the use of cocaine or crack creates a pleasure circuit in the brain. The memory of the pleasure is so intense, unfading, that you crave the substance regularly. Now that my supply is gone, I have to find other sources. I certainly don't want to get to know my suppliers, but dealing with them isn't as difficult as I thought it would be. A quick drive past a certain corner in a nearby city where our Hyundai has become recognizable: I hand the money out the window and a handful of the little vials are tossed in. One of these times I'm seized by the feeling of having glimpsed my son, a familiar sleeve protruding from the entrance to a doorway.

The little vials keep sex athletic. Yet, as they accumulate, its strategies become more predictable, its plots a little repetitive. There are some strenuous lurches on either side as each of us competes to get off before the other loses interest. The fact that my naked body now looks paler and paltrier has caused concerned remarks about my health on the part of my wife on more than one occasion.

And there is still no sign of our boy. As I imagine it, he's living with Sloane. I haven't shared this conjecture with my wife, who has become too inaccessible. Where I saw need before, even if it was somewhat defended, I now see brittle resolve. She has decided to begin working full-time to take her mind off our son. Each morning after breakfast she leaves dressed in her fabric-blend skirt and blouse with a bow. She calls her job a position in human resources, or personnel, but from her description it sounds more like police work to me. It is her task to screen prospective employees, and she's become expert at spying out character defects that could keep someone from "working out."

When the deeper, less familiar voice on the phone identifies itself, we are beside ourselves with joy. He's had a change of mind. In fact, right now he's at a New Age rehabilitation center just over the state line. Can we see him? Of course, we can.

The place looks like an old factory, the small-time kind that used to make Christmas ornaments or prosthetic devices. There are plenty of smiling faces and firm handshakes. We spot him coming toward us in the patient's uniform, which resembles the karate outfit, a kind of cotton pajama with a loosely belted top. And he's large now, bordering on the obese—something I find myself noticing with a smug yet embarrassed irony. His first words to both of us are, "I'm sorry," spoken in a concertedly earnest tone.

It's a progressive organization. When he was first brought in by an unidentified man, their policy was to let him stay, even though the fake name, age, and address he gave didn't check out. Now he's ready to handle contact with us again. But treatment must go on. He'll come and visit on weekends.

I'm in front of the TV watching a hockey game while my son sits at a table working on his journal. Since it is the weekend, my wife is home, baking two pies, one for dinner and one for my son to take back to the program. I can hear his pen gliding rapidly across the paper. It's kind of like having a son who is in a religious order and has come to visit. Careful and considerate. All remarks deeply thought out—well in advance.

When he leaves to wash for dinner, I spring up and leaf quickly through the journal.

"I had to surrender to a higher power. It was the only way."

"I admitted that I lost all control. And it felt super. I'm ready to live and love again now."

"Problem: is the one I love brave enough to take me on?"

After dinner he cornered me in the den, confidently repeated how happy he was that we were reunited, then sat me down across from him knee to knee. "I sense a certain uneasiness in you, Dad. Sure, I understand totally after the changes I put you and Mom through. Like I said, I'm really sorry about that. I want you to know that, like, whatever else you might happen to be dealing with right now, I've been there. It's okay that you're not willing to share yet. Nobody can help you but yourself, not even God, and not until you're ready."

And I wasn't ready to "face it" for several more months, until I had an episode walking up the stairs. I suddenly ran out of gas, couldn't catch my breath, and collapsed with chest pains. As I fell backward, clutching at air, I wailed out for help. No one came, and when I finally saw a face hovering above me, I croaked, "Where were you?"

"Meditating," my son answered. "I guess I didn't hear you."

The next face floating above me was the hospital doctor's, who had come to chide me for ruining a perfectly good heart.

In the meantime, my wife and my son have achieved a reconciliation and a new beginning. She's been promoted at work—a good thing, seeing as I'll be in no shape to support the family for a while.

Since my son is rehabilitated, my wife wants him to move back in the house and finish high school. She'll even consider taking him in as a boarder if he wants. He can get a part-time job and contribute some money as rent. They want to know my opinion.

Ask Sloane, I feel like saying as my eyes dart to the bathroom, thinking of the toilet paper roll where I stowed another rock of crack in case I feel like smoking tonight one more time.

I really can't make up my mind.

WHEN CRACK WAS KING

A Happy Automaton

I

I WAS TREADING WATER in New York City when I hooked up with Custard the black albino, by way of Oklahoma, in Times Square. For two years I'd been combing hustler bars near Forty-second Street. I'd slowly dumped a career, taken up my savings, found a room in a hotel, and dropped out of a circle of well-meaning friends. Now I wandered this small maze around Eighth Avenue where no one knew my last name.

I'd seen him—Custard aka Rambo (see tattoo on left arm)—a few times before, I suppose. Those hollow cheeks, pinholed saucer eyes, scruffy goatee were far from unusual in the places we frequented. What set Custard apart from the others, besides the fact that he was an albino, was a kind of violent yearning or dread coating every word or action. I was soon to learn that it could take control of the tender, wiry body.

But I'm getting ahead of myself. It isn't just that the chain of events is tangled in my mind, it's the fact that the beginning seems hidden and ongoing at every moment. For example, eight, maybe nine, years ago. A time of normal, banal, unrestrained pleasure seeking. Talk of a new illness that is probably sexually transmitted races through the grapevine. I am lying in bed alone, with a fever that undulates and a splitting head-ache. It marks the moment when I decide that I am being invaded by a deadly virus. No sense in trying to corroborate it medically or to stem its tide by a change in behavior. The sickness growing inside me has a slow will of its own.

And years before this watershed, there is a hallway in an Art Deco building. Orange light from new fifties fixtures illuminates the camel-hair cap that matches my towheaded older brother's little overcoat. He is eleven. He has come to pick me up at the optometrist, and a sudden surge of brotherly sentiment makes him put his arm over my shoulder. The gesture makes my skin crawl. Later my brother will become sadistic to animals and other children, but especially to me. I am convinced that it is all based on my repulsion of that single gesture in the hallway near the optometrist's office.

A fatal outcome of both these incidents lies far in the future—last year, in fact. His name is Sphinx. Aliases Shadow, Joey. He has a way of calling forth new tricks by arching his eyebrows quizzically. His liquid, encircled eyes remind me of a Velazquez painting. According to his story, he has no memory of his real parents. He was taken away from them while still a baby and sent upstate to a foster home. There on the farm, the Sphinx quickly became little more than one more pair of hands. On the day of his sixteenth birthday, he told the old farmer who had raised him that he wanted out. He planned to go back to New York and find his half-sister. The old man thought it was a dumb idea. Go, if you want to, he sighed. So Sphinx left, and it was obvious they would never see each other again.

This is the probably true story he tells me the night of our first meeting under seven thousand watts of fluorescent light in Times Square's McDonald's. I am listening carefully, frozen over coffee, watching the shreds of lettuce spill over his blackened fingers. In this shadowless light his face is as blunt as a feline's, the snout almost as foreshortened.

I am walking into a dim bar perhaps a couple of days later. The person called Sphinx is sitting up front, hands in pockets, face in a deadpan. His eyebrows trigger up, and his eyes fix mine in the mirror. I buy him a drink. His fingers tremble as he takes the glass from my hand. The fingers of his other hand drum impatiently on the bar while a foot taps incessantly. He keeps talking. Whenever he pauses, his teeth begin to grind.

About a year and a half after he came to New York he got sent back upstate to a correctional facility. Maybe it was just a question of hanging out with the wrong people. There was a friend of his who had a gun. They kept talking about what it would be like to have a lot of money…

"Over here's the methadone clinic, Sphinx. There's this doctor works here gets paid once a month, on a Wednesday. He's a black dude, see. During lunch this doc will always cash his paycheck over there across the street, then go back on the job till four. Then he comes back out, walks to that blue Mustang over there…"

Sphinx is telling the doctor—a trim black man in his forties—to unlock the door of the blue car. Both he and his friend are grinning as if they have just run into a pal. Under the friend's jacket the gun remains jammed against the doctor's back.

Sphinx is lying on top of the doctor on the floor in the backseat of the car. The friend is watching outside with the gun. Sphinx finds the wallet against the man's ass, ties him up. They run.

What happens to the three or four thousand they get this way? How long will they have to enjoy it before getting caught? Sphinx's big eyes blink, not registering one word of my question. He lights a cigarette and suggests we take a walk. He leads me down a dark path of broken street lamps toward Tenth Avenue. Passing a park, he hops over a railing into bushes and unzips his fly, motioning me over.

The next night he says, Want to get high?

We go back to my hotel, I give him twenty dollars, and he leaves to get the smoke. Lying on the bed, I let my eyes float to the wavy lines of the TV. Hard to believe that giving into uncertainty can make anxiety retreat. Then only repetition is left to be dealt with.

He is taking out a glass tube. Fitting one end with a wire screen. Then he opens one of the two tiny plastic vials. "Where's the reefer?" I ask.

"Reefer? This is crack, man. You got a lighter?"

Sphinx scowls at me when I tell him I don't, but he digs out a book of matches. Having never smoked crack, I watch him.

He does it by taking one of the "rocks" out of the little vial and putting it in the end of the glass tube, against the wire screen. As the crack is heated it melts, turning to smoke, and it actually does make a crackling sound. Then you heat the sides of the tube to turn the melted part to more smoke.

His pouting lips suck the glass stem. He takes a long pull and holds it, then lets the white smoke stream out. It smells like plastic. He takes a second pull and puts the stem down to cool. He jumps up suddenly, runs his hand through the hair on his neck, goes to the door to check the lock, sneaks back to see if the pipe is cool, hops to the window to peek out of it.

When the stem has cooled, he holds it shakily to my lips, tells me to pull slowly. He puts a match to the other end, and the white smoke begins to stream into my throat. It feels burning and numbing at the same time, like dry ice. As the smoke enters my lungs, my heart starts pounding almost instantaneously. It is a strange sensation because the tangible smoke is so immediately connected to the racing feeling of getting high.

After I take a second drag, he gets up again. He strips off his tank top. Lanky arms and chest. With shaking hands, he begins to caress his crotch through the black jeans. Suddenly he lunges at me, and I collapse backward onto the bed. Our mouths fasten together as he unbuttons my shirt, kneads my chest, his hands streaming with sweat. Bulky and wide-hipped as I am, my body fits into the lithe puzzle of his—hard, bony, covered with scars and scratches. We struggle for control over one another, stopping every few moments to light the pipe, inhale the smoke, and exhale it into each other's mouths.

When I wake up, he is gone. I have a rapid pulse, short shallow breathing, aching muscles, raw nipples. This will be followed, surprisingly enough, by weeks of intense well-being. Someone has pulled out a stop. Pounds begin to melt, and daily routines, like dressing myself or styling my hair, become effortless, creative, for the first time. Yet I deny that I am becoming a "crack-head." The "crack attacks," as Sphinx begins to call them, are few and far between, less than four or five a month.

… I'm going to rape you. Are you ready? It will be the only "man rape" in the whole history of crime. Let me get those hands behind your back and pin you to this couch here. You're not going to get away. Now I'm going to rip off your clothes and rape you.

He certainly plays along, laughing with delight as I pin his arms behind his back. And he is still laughing, but derisively, when I look up from our entwined bodies into the grim eyes of our parents. Heart pounding with embarrassment, I leap off my brother, run down the hall into my room.

Now they know.

There is the creak of the bathroom door and animated whispers from my father; laconic, bemused answers from my brother: Just don't encourage it, that's all… I'm not… We're really worried about him.

And years later I would not be exaggerating to maintain that this is one of the lenses through which weeks with Sphinx will slip by. Weeks that have a semblance of days without incident. I mean to say they have a seeming reasonableness. I may make a quip about chaos or out of nowhere admit the importance of being organized. At that moment, someone who knew me intimately would be able to see something peel off and drop away…

From time to time, friends come to see me and Sphinx, though *friend* means something else out here. People know that I have money, but they also have to respect me because I have protection. Supposedly my boyfriend is taking care of that. *Boyfriend?* Then do we love each other? Perhaps. Sentiment, jealousy, and resentment are all extended states of mind in another, more familiar story. In that story they stretch consciousness out like pulled taffy into a narrative. Out here where I am now, the same feelings exist as spells, only for the moment and in a relation of discontinuity…

Sphinx is nonetheless worried about my state of mind. I'd sent him out to score get-high and he'd come back with a single vial. We opened it and found that it contained only tiny chunks of macadamia. "Shit," I heard him mumble, "ripped off by fucking Freddy."

I knew whom he meant. Freddy is a spittle-lipped Polish boy who dresses in fatigues and shaves his head. Sphinx went out to look for him but came back empty-handed.

According to Sphinx, weeks will pass before what I will tell about is supposed to have happened. We're sitting at the bar when I realize that Freddy is sitting at a table across the room eating a bowl of chili. I can feel myself leaping to my feet, pointing an accusing finger at him. "Hello, Mr. Rip-off!" I am shouting across the room for all to hear. "Sell any macadamia nuts today?"

There is silence in the bar as everyone turns to watch, Freddy's jaw freezing as he asks if I am referring to him.

"Who else?" I spit.

Freddy's body is convulsed by trembling as mine is inflated with a sense of omnipotence. As the tip of his tongue darts over his lips, he seems to lunge toward me while men on either side hold him by the arms. One is shakily trying to calm him. "Forget it, Freddy boy."

Freddy's big knuckles are growing pale on the edge of the bar stool, but I have not gone back to my seat. The Sphinx, my protector, has become ashen. As awed whispers begin to erase the silence, he leads me out. I've never seen him look so upset before.

"I can't believe how dumbass you are!"

"What do you mean? He's the one who ripped us off, isn't he? I mean I know it wasn't you holding out on me."

"Sure it was him. But that was a month ago and nobody around here remembers anything. Even I forgot about it."

"Fuck it. He's a cocksucker."

"Listen, Bruce. About a year ago I used to carry around this piece. It made me feel good. Like I used to play with the idea in my mind, if anybody looked at me funny I'd just take it out and blow 'em away."

"I don't give two fucks. I don't get ripped off!"

"Listen, Bruce. You got five dollars so I can get something to eat?"

"Sure, Sphinx, sure."

And a week later, had he really forgotten? When I mentioned the incident, the eyebrows flew into their quizzical arch, and the mouth went slack. It was the dull, wry look of a gentleman.

"Well, I'm going home," I told him. His face remained without expression.

"I mean just for a couple of days. My mother has cancer."

I flew upstate the next morning. Some of her hair had fallen out from the chemotherapy, but her eyes were aglow with the abstract idea of having a son home.

We sat in one of the more expensive local restaurants with Dad, eating canned asparagus tips under hollandaise. Mom began a conversation. "See him?"

She meant a middle-aged man who was sitting across from a pregnant woman. He looked bottom-heavy too. His thinning hair was neatly clipped in back, but his sideburns were long and fanned. For some reason he reminded me of a lawyer during the Nixon administration.

"Yes, I see him."

Mom nodded toward my black leather jacket. "See him, see you."

"What's that supposed to mean?"

"I know his mother. You're about the same age."

"Okay."

"Look how decently dressed he is. How neat his collar is." Suddenly Mom's sad eyes leapt desperately into mine, mascaraed lashes trembling. "Couldn't you try to look more like him?"

"No, I couldn't."

"Why not? I know it isn't living in New York that made you change because I've been around too. People are basically the same wherever they live. But he's sitting with his wife, isn't he? And you're sitting with your sick old parents. Wouldn't you like to be sitting where he is?"

"I don't think that would be too appropriate, Mom."

"And why not?"

"Just because."

"Because why?"

"Because I am middle-aged like him, and college-educated too. But I'm also a cocaine-using homosexual living on the fringes of crime with a nineteen-year-old ex-offender hustler. Now you tell me. Is where that guy's sitting really appropriate for me?"

Dad piped up. "Clown. Eat your asparagus."

It is probably in the very same frame of mind that I see myself standing in her garden without my shirt, looking at her enormous roses. "I was just admiring the flowers you planted," I hear myself say.

"Well, you got quite a bum, son."

"I did not, Mom."

"You sure did. Oh, my God. What's that on your arm? It's not AIDS, is it?"

"What are you talking about?"

"Good God, it's worse than AIDS. Does my son have a tattoo? Why, Bruce, why?"

"Because I like tattoos."

"You *like* them?"

"They're romantic."

"I'd hate to be the girl you go out with."

"I mean like literary romantic."

"Literary? My son the writer. He writes all over his arm, disfigures his body. Won't they love that at the Pulitzer committee."

"Did it ever occur to you that some people could find a tattoo on a man's arm sexy?"

"Sure. I know what kind of people you're talking about. I know more than you think I do. You wouldn't think, would you, that your old mother would know anything about that. But I'm going to let you in on a little secret, Son. I got something to show you on my left buttock. Excuse me for hiking up my dress and pulling down these panty hose. Go ahead. Look."

"Oh, my God, you've got a tattoo!"

"That's right. Now come close. Don't be afraid. I want you to read it."

"'The door you open to cross my threshold of pain… pain?' I don't get it, Ma."

"I'm talking about ass fucking."

Bathed in sweat, I come to in the middle of the dream abruptly, to the sound of a slamming door. Sphinx has walked in with a girl of about fifteen. He says her name is Oklahoma. She has unbaked white skin, bluish-circled eyes, and stringy, dirty-blond hair.

"I was wondering, Bruce, if Oklahoma can stay here tonight since she's got no place to stay."

"All right."

Sphinx packs up the crack pipe for us. He hands it to Oklahoma, who takes a drag and begins to rap. Apparently she really has come from Oklahoma. She claims to have forgotten her real name. She remembers her arrival in New York at Port Authority in search of her boyfriend, about a month ago, where she immediately looked for a pay phone to call a shelter that asked no questions for a bed.

The number she dialed was called by many runaways. But a pimp had been able to have the calls rerouted to his own number. (A week later the ruse would be found out and reported on the evening news.) He told Oklahoma where to wait for him so he could take her to the shelter. She ended up in a hotel, where she was raped after being injected with heroin.

The pimp must have misjudged the dose because she fell into a coma. When she came to alone in the hotel, she had a vivid memory of the incident, but no recollection of her own name.

As we get high, Sphinx and Oklahoma start to kiss. He will cradle her in his arms, lavish her with caresses, lull her into believing in him. The maneuvers are far different from any he has ever tried on me during our acquaintance and lovemaking. The two get naked and climb into the bed next to me. At some point I must have fallen back asleep.

Cathy!

I awake with a start, the name ringing in my ears. Oklahoma has claimed to have discovered her real name! We are all naked in bed together. Rolling away from Sphinx, Oklahoma Cathy curls up against me. "I owe you," she sighs.

"For what?"

The Sphinx's naked body doubles up with laughter. "You don't remember, man?"

How many nights later do I come to again, feeling like the wrong thread ripped out of a fabric by the weaver, the room dark but light streaming from the open bathroom door? Squinting into it, I think I see

Oklahoma Cathy's naked silhouette. Then a male body coming out of the bathroom. He glances at the bed and leaves.

"Where's the Sphinx?" I manage to call out. My mouth and throat are so coated that I can hardly speak.

"He went out. Now go back to sleep."

But when I wake up this time, I am even less than a single thread in a vast, empty grid. The sheet feels wet and grimy, caked to my thigh. A more emaciated Oklahoma Cathy in halter, short-shorts, and a different hairdo is smiling down at me. I open my cracked lips to try to speak, but a pattern of needles shooting across my face prevents me. Running my fingers over the skin around my mouth, I feel the tiny lesions.

"Don't touch," says Cathy. "They're goin' away."

"What happened?"

"You just had one toke too many. One moment you were on a roll, you helped me figure out what my real name was. Then bingo: out like a light. Do you remember yesterday? You came to then, had us laughing all night long doing imitations of your folks before you passed out again. All them sores popped up when you were sleeping, what are they, herpes, right, Custard?"

Bare-chested under his leather jacket, his face serious and pale under a tight yellow natural, Custard, aka Rambo, comes to sit at the edge of the bed. His saucer eyes keep getting lost in shadow. With a bruised-knuckled hand he touches my face lightly. "That's right, bro. Herpes. They ain't nothin' to worry about. I had a case of 'em in jail when I got knocked on the head. They'll be goin' away before you know it."

"What's he doing here? Where's Sphinx?"

"Don't talk about Sphinx," says Oklahoma Cathy. "Don't you remember how he went away soon as you got sick? And he took your bank card with him, I think."

"I want to talk to the Sphinx."

"You seen the Sphinx around?" Cathy asks Custard with a nonchalant sigh.

"Lasts I seen him was with Shorty," says Custard.

How can there be theft in a thieves' world, where possession is a parody? To whom do even our bodies belong, when self-possession exists only in the instant and when possession is only pursued for pleasure? At the bar. Shorty raises his tiny claw, which is missing part of the thumb. "Yeah, I seen Sphinx. I got something to show you." With a flourish he whips off his little baseball cap and sets it on the bar next to his Southern Comfort. Then he lowers his head to show me a four-inch bald spot with stitches.

"Tell Sphinx thanks for me, will you?"

"Sphinx? Come on," I say. "He didn't do that to you."

"No, bro, you're right. He didn't," squeaks Shorty. "But the Sphinx sent a friend. The Sphinx sent him."

"I don't believe you."

"I was coming out of the Marriott with this john, a senator always gives me ninety. They seen me walking out there with him. The friend beaned me with a lead pipe and Sphinx comes for the ninety."

"Like shit he did. I'm going to ask the Sphinx."

Shorty pulls the cap on quick again. "No, don't! It'll only cause trouble. I don't want them coming at me again." "Okay, Shorty, don't worry. But who's this friend of Sphinx's?"

"I don't know him, pop, but I seen this dude before. He's a what-you-call-it. . . albino."

A dizzy spell dips me backward, and my face falls into a shaft of light for a moment. Shorty sees the sores.

"Yo, how come you got weird sores all over your face?" He peers up at me curiously, while my mouth remains sealed. I am only a thread in this amorphous, shifting tapestry. I live to perpetuate the laws of the world.

II

THERE IS NO PAUSE to put down the briefcase or take off his suit jacket. "Something's wrong," he says. "Something's wrong," says Dad again. Instinctively he goes toward the hall where the thermostat is located. Then he backtracks, goes to the kitchen and gets a flashlight. "What's wrong in this house," I hear him mumble again as he snaps on the flashlight and beams it at the thermostat. Then he bends close. Like a jeweler working through an eyepiece, he squints and trains one eye on the dial. He shifts the dial less than a millimeter. "Somebody's been fooling around with this," he says.

"Isn't it set for seventy-six?" I ask. "That's how you always have the air-conditioning. I remember it was put on seventy-six."

"It's not set for seventy-six," he says.

I am drawn to the thermostat. I peer at it over his shoulder. "It's set for seventy-six," I say.

"Ah ha," he snorts, "so you think so. But if it is left like that, it'll keep going until it gets seventy-four. The idea is to put it *here*." He shifts the dial to seventy-seven, but it really isn't seventy-seven, either. It is an infinitesimal space below the mark for seventy-seven, a position so precise that no one can find it but him.

"*There*," he mumbles, moving the flashlight closer. "There!" Suddenly he whips around with uncharacteristic abruptness. "I know your mother couldn't have done this because she's too sick to get out of bed. But you, you don't understand. You're wasting energy. Were you hot in here? You're crazy, it's not hot in here. Do you think it was hot in here, something is wrong with you if you think it is hot in here, go ask your mother, because it was seventy-six!"

"I—I'm not hot in here," I answer.

"Good," he sighs. "I'm glad you're here, son. Your mother is so sick, and she's glad to see you. Stay for a week, why don't you."

"I won't be able to, Dad."

"I understand."

Though Custard's hands and feet are peeling from eczema, the rest of his body looks smooth and yellow, like custard. He is sitting on the edge of the bed in his underwear. He's got my shaving mirror and is trimming the edges of his sparse blond goatee. He is trying to convince me to buy some crack so that he and I can get high. His girlfriend, Oklahoma Cathy, went out about three hours ago to try to turn a trick, and there is still no sign of her.

I am unwilling to buy crack, as Custard well knows. I was out for five days the last time I smoked. I must have gone into convulsions or something. And then the herpes. Herpes is a bad sign, I explain, it has to do with the immune system. Besides, money is running low.

Custard puts the mirror down so he can rest a hand on my leg. He explains masterfully, with a smile, why I am mistaken. Did he tell me about getting the herpes all over his ass in jail after a fight? And now he's A-okay. It depends on how pure what you smoke is. None of that stuff made with ammonia. That's poison. I know where to get some pure shit. Just lay twenty or thirty on me, I'll be back.

When he gets back, he takes out the new glass stem and jams the screen tightly into it. Gallantly puts the first rock in for me. Begins to tell me about him and Oklahoma Cathy, before taking his pull. She's been his woman since she was thirteen. Then he had to leave her in Oklahoma to go West with his brother.

In his underwear again, the smoke streaming out of him, Custard struts back and forth across the carpet as the words spill out. Life is a fuckup. I fucked up my hands in Death Valley, working in a borax mine. It gets into your skin and burns cracks into it. Saw people crushed by falling slabs of borax. Me and this little Mexican cunt living in a trailer near the mine. You know those pincers on poles they use to get the cans down in grocery stores? We tightened one up. Caught rattlesnakes with it and cut off their heads and tails, chicken-fried 'em.

Reggae on the radio. Custard is talking politics. Those Jews, man, who think they can let a land go then come back to claim it, kick everybody out. And that fucking Reagan, who thinks all people have to be like him, somebody should teach that asshole a lesson and blow him away. What about poor people who don't got ranches in Santa Barbara?

Station changed. Custard is dancing. Doing an R-and-B stroll. Singing along with the words as he mimes with his hands. We used to do this in jail.

Stops. Eyes go far away. Mouth tightens into a grimace. That's right, man, I was in Sing Sing. The saucer eyes get even bigger and the pinholes look tinier. Fucking two and a half years because I had a happy trigger finger. I'm fucking not going back to that fucking place, man. I made up my mind about that. I want to get a job, go back to school.

Anger begins to flood Custard's pink, blank-eyed face. Is it jail or a job? Cathy? The mines? Does it matter?

"Tell me what's happening to you."

"I don't know, Poppa. I feel funny. I feel like I could take somebody's head and smash it, you know what I mean?"

"Of—course—I—know—what—you—mean." It's hard to speak with the crack building up in my head, inflating spaces between each word. I pull the eczemaed hands into mine, massage them. Feel the once broken, ill set bones.

"There."

"That's right. Poppa," says Custard. "It feels good, don't stop."

"I'll take care of it for you."

"Harder, I can't feel it."

"I'm massaging your hands as hard as I can, Custard."

"It feels good."

Violence shuddering through his muscle-addled spine, he has sprawled facedown on the bed, legs kicking. "Fucking goddamn, it's not fair. Massage my legs harder, bro."

"I can't take it all away from you, Custard."

"You can, Poppa, you can."

He kicks off the shorts, struggling for breath, cursing threateningly. My hands are aching from the effort of massaging his buttocks. "I can't feel it," he says.

"Yes, you can, baby." He has turned on his back now, is holding up a hard-on and trying to push my face down on it. But I am refusing to suck it without a rubber. So my hands, trembling from crack and limp from fatigue, manage to rip open the package and fit one on him. The wave breaks soon in one gigantic convulsion that takes us with it, legs closing around my neck in a scissors lock, ferocious pumping…

He leaps to his knees on the bed. Rips the rubber off and holds it up to the light from the television. His face is streaming sweat. His hollow eyes triumphant, exultant.

"Look! Look! How many sperm! A million? A billion? Enough to start a whole nation!" He ties a knot in the end of the rubber and throws it in my face. "Put it in the sperm bank!"

A few days later, as his head is resting on my thigh, the telephone rings for the first time. Custard wanted a telephone. Of course, it's not Oklahoma Cathy calling. She's been gone more than a week since that day she went out to find a trick. She would have no idea that there is now a phone in the room. I pick up the receiver.

"Hello?"

"Hello, little brother."

"How did you get my number?"

"There are ways, when you work for the government in Washington."

"But I'm not listed."

"I told you, there are ways, that's all."

"So why are you calling?"

"I want to know how my little brother is."

"Fine."

"Are you? I doubt that. I doubt that you're fine."

"Do you now."

"Yes. And I thought I would just try to call you now because even though it's two p.m. on a Thursday, well—I didn't expect you to be at work, no, I didn't expect you to be working."

"What business is it of yours?"

"Well, as it turns out, brother, it is very much my business. What you are doing with your valuable time is very much my business, some people might say."

"Those people are wrong."

"Are they? Well, I don't know if they are. Because I think it would be very much my business how you spend your time when you will be living off the money our parents slaved for. And I am out here trying to support a family."

"Your fucking family doesn't concern me, big brother. Nor am I interested in what you think of the way I spend my time. And as for that money our parents slaved for, I am not living off that precious money but on my own savings, for your information."

"Well, it's a whole new ball game now, kiddo."

"What do you mean?"

"I mean that Mom is dead and for some perverse reason she has left you a rather substantial trust which both Dad and I intend to oppose to the bitter end."

"Mom is dead?"

"That's right, kiddo. Be talking to you."

"Rub my ass harder, man... Give me that stem."

"How's that?"

"It's all right. Keep rubbing it… Yo, Bruce, when you first saw me, did you think I was white?"

"I don't really think about what color people are, Custard."

The pale-eyed, pink skull-face looks at me with annoyed contempt. "You mean you didn't think about was I white or black?"

"I just didn't think. Could I have some of that pipe?"

"Wait a minute."

"Jesus, Custard, you're hogging it all for yourself. Give me some of that."

"Open your mouth one more time and I'll let you have this."

"Give me that pipe."

"Don't get me mad, man."

"What would happen if I did?"

"You ever been worked over before getting cornholed, Bruce? Kind of opens you up first. Happens all the time in jail. Keep rubbing my back, rub my shoulders for me."

"I don't like violence, Custard."

"Nobody does, Poppa, but sometimes it's necessary."

"When would that be?"

"Keep acting wiseass and you'll find out."

"Maybe I just will, maybe I'd like to find out."

"You know I wouldn't hurt you, Daddy, long as you keep looking out for me."

"Hmm, hmm."

"Feels good, don't stop."

"Who do you think I am, your wife or something?"

"That's right, baby. Why don't you put on Cathy's panties and walk around for me, like a real wife."

"Very funny."

"And don't talk back to me, neither. I hate a white female talks back to me."

"Whatever you say, darling."

"Keep rubbing my legs like that. Give me that pipe. Cmon, put on Cathy's panties for me, would you?"

"I'd feel silly."

"No you wouldn't. Now put on some lipstick."

Way back when… We're back at the beginning again, when the stakes were not so high. Life was a banquet then. People who were around in those days would know what I mean. Our libidos found a free, expansive structure. You know the rest. I'm talking ten, twenty years ago, before pleasure got detoured into dread. You had sex or got high when you wanted to and tried not to give it much conscious value. You wanted to be directed but thought about it as something that was just happening to you… So let's get high again, baby. This time it's me saying it. Custard's been out like a light since he got back at five. Why won't he wake up? The moving job must be taking a lot out of him. Too bad we need the money. Cathy has disappeared. I'm stone broke and any money from the will is years away. So c'mon, baby, wake up. I want to get high.

I walk over to the pile of clothes on the floor and pick up the industrial stapler lying next to it. The thing weighs more than an anvil and spits one-and-a-half-inch staples. Custard says he uses it to put together wooden packing boxes.

Get up, baby. You don't even look like you're breathing. Playfully I aim the gun at his ass and start to pull back the trigger. He flips around and jerks to a sitting position. "Chill, bro, I need my rest, man."

"And we're going to rest, baby. We'll get high while we rest."

"Why don't you go out and get it?"

"You know I'm no good at that, Custard. You always get the good stuff."

With a grudging sigh he puts on his jeans, his work shoes, and his leather jacket, takes twenty out from under the rug, slams the door.

I lie back with a sigh. It is almost a sigh of luxury. For the first time I am… But how to explain the luxury of a life virtually without choices? It is an automatic life and I am a happy automaton.

Then why must the following happen?

Custard comes back and tosses two crack vials on the bed. I pop one open and dump it into the stem. I light, I pull, there is no crackling sound. Tipping a rock from the stem into my hand, I taste it. Macadamia nut.

"Who sold you this?"

"The Sphinx," says Custard. His tone is hollow, almost dead. No clue whether he is telling the truth.

The Sphinx?

It is not the Sphinx, or Custard, or even myself pulling me off the bed, putting my clothes on. I slip the stapler under my coat. It is not my mother, my father, or my brother who brought this pain, this suffering, this betrayal down on me.

Sphinx is easy enough to spot, weaving in front of the crack house on Ninth Avenue, wobbly-kneed high, his hand jerking from the back of his neck to his pants, then back again. Those familiar old eyes. As I come toward him the eyebrows arch quizzically, just as they did that long-ago day in the mirror. But this time my hand has a plan: to fly out and cover his face and slam it against the wall of the building. Starting at the Adam's apple, the other hand begins punching its neat row of staples all the way down to the navel.

King of the High Con

by Edgar Mercado and Bruce Benderson

THERE'S THIS GUY CALLED Sweettooth, better known as Stingray, gangster of gangsters, thug of thugs. And he was going out with Sparky, his girl that broke out on him. The bitch started playing virgin on his ass. What comes down after is for me to tell, cause my name happens to be Sweettooth, the King of the Long Con.

I went on a mission to find my female and get some *crica* again, but it turned out she was hiding out with Diamond Sue and Sugar Fly. Sugar Fly's a rotten down member of my crew. The three of them were over there on the South Side on Hughes Street, 'tween South Fifth and Sixth. Sugar Fly broke down the door and they went in.

Now South Fifth ain't our territory, they got rival crew out there. But before it was light, I'm over in front the crackhouse conversating to this banjee wearing his colors.

"Yo man, where my woman at, you know, the one what broke out with the Latin King?"

"She ain't nothing to you, bro."

"Just tell me where they at."

"Upstairs in his crib, man—him, his female and another girl."

"That girl happens to be my female, bro."

"Up in the last, man. They got the door barricaded, I sure hope you are his homeboy."

The door was jammed just like he said, and Diamond Sue wasn't about opening it no way. She wanted me to talk through a crack. I had to spit out my lungs hard for hope Sugar Fly'd hear and come to the rescue. Finally I just busted my ass in. Sugar Fly was there all right, cleaning out his gun. He had a wise-ass grin on his face. Diamond Sue was standing at the door popping out pregnant.

"What's up, Diamonda, you got a muffin in the oven. And you, you fucking crazy outlaw, you cleaning out your barrel but you ain't cleaned your oversized jeans yet."

"No, I still got my ninety-year-old socks and my hundred-and-two-year-old pants on."

"So I'm telling you homeboy that I come here to see Sparky and knock some sense in her head."

Sugar Fly hopped off his bench to hold me back, while Diamond Sue started to disrespect me.

"She ain't here. She don't want to see you anyway, Stingray!"

"But I'm telling you both, I can hear her breathing behind that bathroom door!"

And I grabbed hold of a chair, I busted the lock right off that nigga.

After Sparky come out from behind the shower curtain, she wouldn't look up from the ground. Finally she asked me what do you want.

"Want? I want you, baby. What could I have done so wrong that you don't want nothing to do with me? How could you ever forget about all those nights we chilled out together? Before you go walking off like that, before you go making me feel like everything's my fault, making my friends laugh at me like if I fucked up with a female, throwing my life into turmoil, making my whole fucking existence like it ain't worth a turd, just tell me: what I did to you to get treated like this? You got to answer now cause I can't take it another minute."

"It ain't you. I just got to think. I got my own problems, you see."

"Baby, whatever is wrong with you, whatever is going wrong with me, whatever is going wrong with us… I wish we could settle it here and now."

"I joined the beauty school over on Forty-ninth in Manhattan. Before the year is out, I'll be a cosmetologist working in a salon."

"I'm so proud of you momma! You got to tell me all about that. Let's go over in the other room, you know, you got a TV over there?"

I took Sparky in my arms and squeezed her tight, and we went into the other room. That was all it took. I fucked her again and gave her a couple days of that before I told her she got to leave. Me and Sugar Fly and Diamond Sue started living there.

We were having a great time in there. I used to go out to make money, to the park, and I'd come back home after I see Yvette my real woman and my kid over there in the alphabet projects in Manhattan. One day I walk in the apartment from breaking night, there was a kid in there. So I asks him, who are you, man?

"My name the Snapback."

"Why they tag you that for?"

"Cause no matter how wasted I is, I always will snap back."

And he starts showing me these freaky hip hop moves, like snapping his hands inside out and shit.

"What's your game, Snapback? What kind of joshing do you do?"

"Hey, I do everything, I do anything."

"And do you got any money on you?"

No, he says. Fuck, I'm thinking. I better tell Sugar Fly about letting broke motherfuckers come up here.

So we started going about getting high. Sugar Fly had stashed some rockets behind a loose brick in the wall when he thought I was sleeping. And then we said let's play cards. We got to talking about the people we know from the Deuce which is all but shut down now. It turns out this little guy he was in the Nine-and-a-Half crew like twelve years ago, and you know I was in the Crazy Bishops. And night comes along, and I ask him how swift are you, bro, you want to make some money with me tonight?

So that night—a freezing cold night—we went to get paid over to Central Park and waited under a bridge. And Juan and Jose was with us too. Our asses were almost frozed off before this white dude comes by in these Timberlanes, and his girlfriend had a purse too.

C'mon let's go get paid, Juan says, or turn to ice and get busted. And I says don't you think it's a little too soon, and Juan says c'mon Jose, let's break out.

So Snapback is creeping way up ahead in front of the dude and his girl, and Juan and Jose and, well, me are far enough but not too far behind. Snapback turns around quick like he forgot something and bumps into them just when Jose grabs the girl. Juan is choking the guy when I start going in his pockets.

"Don't say a word. We'll stab you right here, you fucking white bastard."

"Please please, don't hurt him."

"Shut up, bitch. Let's fucking empty out your purse too."

We took his wallet, watch, and everything and whatever she had in her purse, her jewelry. Then we told him to take off the Timberlanes. He tried to argue about that so I dropped him. He hit his head or something when he fell.

Now we had some money. I told Snapback, c'mon I want to show you a way to make more. We're going over to this bar near the Deuce where these johns go. And Snapback he thought I was going to let one of the faggots suck my dick, but I rightened him quick on that. No Snapback Man, I am not about that.

Inside the bar there was this homo name of Charlie who always wears this wack red wig. I told Snapback watch this, man, faggots are easy to shake down.

"How's my man, buy me a drink?"

You just talk to him for a while as you kind of rub your dick.

"I been working out, can you see the difference?"

It's good if you can think of Janet Jackson and get a hard-on going.

"I'm into this school for auto mechanics now, Charlie. I'm doing pretty good at it. And I been looking after my mother, I got a job so I can pay the doctor and shit…"

Then you can ask him for five or ten. You just say it like he owes it to you.

"Yo, let me have a few bucks will you so I can get something to eat. C'mon, man."

Shit, you do that four, five times and you got thirty, forty dollars in one hour.

Back at the crib in Brooklyn, Diamond Sue was all hectic paranoid upset cause she had a problem with the super-lady who was saying Diamond Sue put a curse on her. The rice was hard and the beans would burn. Seems like everything was going wrong since Diamond Sue moved in there. The super-lady's daughter kept coming up here to hang out with Diamond Sue and she would come home high. Then the super-lady would feel a puff on her face in the bed at night so she went to the botanica and bought a candle to hex Diamond Sue.

Me and Diamond Sue got this game going telling everybody we brother and sister. So I went down there to talk to them. What's this your wife wanting to beat up on my little sister who's pregnant? I said to the super-man. And before the faggot can answer, his slut comes running out the kitchen screaming that bitch upstairs, she don't even belong here. Look, you skanky bitch, I told her back, ain't nobody gonna hit her when she's pregnant. You fight her after she has the baby. For now you come and fight me. I'll fuck you up and anybody in your family. Her husband didn't like that, so I had to waste him. And their daughter was there, and she looked like she was enjoying the whole thing.

"Please don't hit my father no more."

"For you baby, I'll do anything. But tell your pop not to get loud if he can't back his words up."

Everything was squash from there. But we never really got over. We was always talking about how can we get back at them. The super's daughter kept coming upstairs to hang out with Diamond Sue and get high. She was a cute little dark-skinned thing, nice little butt, little young titties. Seems like I was always in the house walking around in my underwears when she was up there.

So one day I was like doing this Eddie Murphy thing for her and Diamond Sue and had them laughing, I told the girl I got to take a shower. You want to come in here with me? Well, what for? I told her to get inside and locked the door. I got a secret I want to tell you, really, listen. I put my mouth to her ear.

Next thing you know I started fingering her. I had her up against the bathroom sink. You're hurting me. Diamond Sue kept banging on the door and saying what's going on in there. So then I took the girl's hand and put it on my cock and told her to play with it for a while. I had her drawers down and my pants was dropped. I sat her up there on the sink and started to put my cock in her and she was crying. I guess it hurt her a little. She must have been a virgin, she started bleeding a little bit. The next thing you know the front door started banging.

"Somebody told me my little girl was up here."

"Hey, I don't know where she at. She came up here and she left."

The girl tries to open the door. Unh, unh mamita, wait a minute, don't make no noise. I have to come. So I finished and I came, and then we came out of the bathroom. The girl was crying.

I had this uncle help me get a job breaking boxes in a factory, so I started going to the apartment less and less. One day I hear Diamond Sue had her baby so I stopped over there in the middle of the night. The weeks went by, I don't know, I kept breaking up these boxes and got too tired to go out and get money. But one day I got this call from Sugar Fly at my uncle's saying I feel like killing myself.

Over to the building Diamond Sue and Sugar Fly was sitting outside with the baby. I could see his eyes all glittery from far away and she was crying too.

"We lost the apartment. We lost the baby."

"What's that, the baby? You know what I am, you know by heart and by god I am the baby's godfather, what's wrong with the baby?"

Well the baby was dead. The baby got something they call crib death, they laid her down and she stopped breathing sometime. I felt like ripping out my own heart.

But I'm an outlaw, and if it's one thing I know life can't be brought back with tears. I said, let's go get some Olde English, let's go hang out, let's go smoke a rock somewheres.

And that's just what we did, after we went and turned the baby in.

Suicide Ecstasy

IT WAS A CASE of extortion, a kind of love at first sight here in this electric-blue bedroom in the South Bronx, not far from "Dark Park" where the drugs are sold. The broad-shouldered youth with a part razored into his close-cropped hair stood with his lean belly pressed against the TV screen. He was slitting open a cigar with a knife blade. Between his buttocks and the wall, on a narrow bed, I sat perched and stiff, trying to avoid creaking the mattress by making the slightest move. In fact, I had strict orders not to bat an eyelash.

The boy's long, scarred hands worked swiftly. He peeled the outside leaf off the cigar and sprinkled marijuana into it. Then he pulled the cap off a bottle of crack with his teeth, tipped out the rocks, crushed them with the edge of a water glass, and added them to the marijuana. He moistened the joint with the blunt end of a pink tongue and winked at me.

Don't make a move, he warned, I wouldn't want Grandma to hear the creaking and come in to see what's up. He chuckled, then took a long drag of the joint and quickly shoved it into my mouth. Pull on it, he managed to croak out over still held breath, and I did.

Within seconds the partnership of the two drugs began to gallop through me. It was a pumped-up, exaggerated, yet meditative high. The boy was talking pell-mell, going over the evening's happenings. Most of all he couldn't get over the balls I had shown; I'd taken being the only white man on the streets of the South Bronx at three in the morning in ride, even when dudes in front of the bodega where we bought the cigars began to heckle me. Nor had I been stymied by "Dark Park" with its busted street lamps, where we went to pick up the weed; or the crack house, a semi-abandoned building guarded by an unchained pit bull and a homeboy with an iron pipe.

The boy took another draw on the joint, then tugged at his crotch through his pants, making a rhyme about his back being strong and his rod being long. Bending close to my face, he grinningly described turned-on sexual possibilities to come, provided we stayed stealthy and managed not to wake up his grandmother. His grandma was, in fact, a very light sleeper who'd require an alibi from us if she happened to decide to check out the room.

The crack in my brain was jolted into sharp relief by the marijuana as I tried to think up an alibi. Voice catching, I heard myself begin to suggest one or two. But the boy was laughing through his clenched teeth. He said she'd never believe I was a teacher or counselor from a school he used to go to, and nobody would believe I was an uncle of a girl he was going out with.

His black eyes narrowed contemptuously as he took another drag of the joint. As its red ember was reflected in them, a panic tinged with irony about my presence seemed to sweep over him; Grandma began to multiply into a host of potential intruders: a jailbird cousin, stepfathers, homeboys who hated faggots, a drug dealer. Now he was suggesting that I try to hide my leather coat under a pillow while there was still time.

Pulling my coat around me, I got ready to spring to my feet. But the boy's eyes locked with mine, forbidding me to move. Even the slightest shift might make the bed creak. Suddenly his leering panic exploded into rage. What made me think I had any excuse to be up here, anyway, he demanded, as his hand flew between my knees to find something under the mattress. Not until I heard a click did I realize it was a gun being held against my head.

At moments like this it's not a question of your whole life passing before you. What happens, rather, is a pulling back, a widening of perspective. For the first time you begin to see how seemingly unrelated events fit together. You take a second look at yourself hurtling along Forty-seventh Street and then down Madison, on the way to discuss what is known as "the product" at the office of a textbook publisher. But there is another motive for my making haste. I am trying to keep up with the person walking in front of me.

The person in question is no one I know. He is just the back of someone's head, the brim of a Kangol hat, a swell of buttocks and calves under Adidas pants. Feasibly he's a messenger or a janitor in one of the Madison Avenue buildings. But as he strides across the intersection, I break into a clumsy trot, closing up the space between my overweight body and his. People might be staring at me, I dimly realize. I must have a fixed look on my face.

It is conceivable from the easy swing of his broad shoulders, corded neck, thick wrists, and cocky, alienated stride that his life has perpetually deviated from mine. I can see him as a sinewy child in the backyard of a building in the Bronx throwing a ball against a crumbling wall. Over and over he throws the ball. The mental image beneath his clenched brow is to throw it so hard that it shatters. This never happens, and the wrist gets thicker and stronger.

As he strides into an office building and I hurry into mine, the image discharges. His real world fades… and the world takes over, contained by polished marble and revolving doors.

Fluorescent lights poach my eyes. Seated around the circular table of a conference room are casualties from a recent publishing holocaust. In the past year the company has been merged, relocated, sold, restructured, resold… cut back. Two of its survivors, a corporate good soldier with a Third Reich handshake, and an old, tic-laden company mouse, greet me enthusiastically. A Chanel-suited project editor smiles icily over narrowed eyes.

I have come to present a written creation, my sixth-grade science feature called "Betting on the Biosphere." We will also be looking at the accompanying three-color art.

I can hear my voice grow hollow as I read the text aloud and slides of the visuals are projected on a wall. The project editor seems fixated on one visual. It is a full-page picture of Smokey the Bear scolding a bunch of careless campers near a Winnebago. She is insisting that Smokey is too teddy bearish and wants him redrawn as more virile and authoritarian. She also demands broad, benign smiles on all the scolded campers.

The Smokey controversy sweeps spiritedly around the table as my mind drifts back to the street, and the wrist I imagined getting thicker throwing the ball. But now the editor is demanding my opinion and the corporate soldier is urging me to come forth. If Smokey is a daddy who carries a big stick, I hear myself say, he should know how to use it. Confusion flashes into the eyes of the corporate soldier, but he wipes it away with a quick nod and clearing of the throat. Then it's settled, he says.

I am standing at a urinal on the same floor as the conference room, watching someone in one of the stalls in the mirror. All that are showing are burgundy jeans pushed down over hightops with perfectly flat, white, half-inch laces. Yet the hightops have an authority and intimacy that nothing else in my field of vision seems to have.

The hightops and burgundy jeans are strong clues as to what the rest of this person might look like. I mean only in the sense that he is probably brown-skinned or black, while his hair, if nappy rather than shiny and straight, could possibly be clipped into a precise shape that only kinky hair can hold. Perhaps he wears a favorite emblem, too, a Playboy Bunny silhouette on a hat, or on the socks, which are now concealed by the burgundy jeans.

Unable to pee, I remain at the urinal, hoping that he will stand up and come out. But he seems settled in. Though my stillness and the sound of my breathing may be making my fixation obvious, I cannot tear my eyes from the mirror or stop the images and dialogue from trickling forth. He is bounding into a cramped apartment, ignoring the *bendicio* from his wrinkled, yellow-skinned grandmother, or wolfing down a plate of *pasteles* and a Budweiser in front of a wrestling match on TV. Later he is playfully hoisting high a faceless, dark-skinned adolescent girl, whose laughter rings forth as her peg-panted legs scuff against his hard thighs and belly.

Piss gushes forth, so I can zip up quickly and walk out, making a forced effort for each footstep to sound casual. Back at the conference room, the new Smokey is being passed around the table. He's kind of a mild-looking, middle-aged weight-lifter bear.

I'm tilting through a landscape of wind-tumbled newspaper and exhaust fumes, my eyes wearily scanning the street for the bank. At this time, shortly before three, it is bound to be a pilgrimage to pettiness and anxiety, a dead wait in a nearly unmoving line. Panty hose and running shoes, Connecticut-student hair and knapsacks, ties and Adam's apples are all caught in stopped time. As I stand waiting, my desperation surges into a teary blur, until my eyes come to rest on an anomaly. His is a hurt image. His oak-trunk neck is covered with gold chains that hold enormous initials, devil's tails, and a crucifix. His massive brown arms are bare and scarred, and a stain on one of them looks like auto grease. There is a part etched into his close-cropped hair. Sparks of defeat seem to shoot impudently from his every point of contact with the bank, as if a hunter-gatherer had suddenly appeared in a leafless landscape meant only to annihilate him.

Unlike the rest of us, this particular customer seems to have accepted the fact that life is an endless game of waiting. He is oblivious to, or contemptuous of, this line's tortures. Biceps stained with grease, he has probably just come from the garage where he works—no... most likely he doesn't have a regular job, he got the stain working a one-day Manpower job in the garment district unloading trucks, and when he leaves the bank, he will probably have to give the money to the child-mother of his baby (formerly seen hoisted in pegged pants against his belly). Then they'll fuck and he'll tell her, "I've got to go do some more business, mamita." "See you later, Juan," she will answer.

No—not Juan, probably Raoul. And when Raoul leaves the home of the mother of his child in the Bronx, he will turn left toward the poolroom instead of turning right toward the subway, as his wife thinks. His friends Tony and Carlos are already at the poolroom shooting a game; they live in a nearby hotel. Both are wearing leather bombers with fur collars because they make good money running supplies to the neighborhood crack house.

Tony and Carlos are probably itching to go make more money tonight and are trying to convince him—bare-biceped Raoul—to go on a crack run with them. But Raoul is hesitant and keeps nervously touching a fingertip to his razor part as they shoot pool. He is trying to stay away from the crack and having a hard time at it. He's only been back at his grandmother's about six months now, after a two-and-a-half-year stint in a church-sponsored rehabilitation center for adolescents in Kansas. Raoul chose the institution over prison, when the judge in Family Court gave in to his tearful, rosary-clutching grandmother, who pleaded that her grandson, arrested for armed robbery to support a crack habit, at least be given a chance to learn to know God.

The watery-haired teller is explaining to me that instant credit on my check is being denied due to a delay in the transfer of funds between my Super Now, Musclemarket, and Flexifund accounts. Although I am insisting that there is more than enough in the three accounts to cover the check, he is impatiently waving me in the direction of an assistant officer, who is sitting at the computer terminal covertly gabbing into a phone.

Raoul is likely to have spent the first several weeks at the center endlessly and mindlessly pumping iron. Weight lifting and the meals put muscles back on his crack-emaciated body while mandatory religious instruction went in one ear and out the other.

Then a certain Father Kilrory took an interest in him. Kilrory was a practitioner of a New Age theology he had begun to develop in the sixties. It taught the shaky believer to internalize the idea of God as something personal and individual that each carried within himself. "Each one teach one" and "To each his own" were two cornerstones of this simple humanist theology, which is bolstered by nightly discussion groups and Sunday night Quaker-style prayer meetings.

By the time of Raoul's release from the institution he would have given anything to remain longer. But this was denied, so he begged Father Kilrory to recommend continued therapy for him back in New York. To this the father responded that only one kind of therapy would now be necessary, the instant therapy of baptism. One month after his return to New York, Raoul, no longer a minor, chose to have himself instructed and baptized and found a full-time job breaking boxes in a factory.

The pearly nails of the assistant officer click with blasé familiarity over the computer keys, her other hand holding the phone as she chats with someone named Adele about a recent cruise to an island where the ocean liner was met by natives in hollow tree-trunk canoes who sold souvenirs made out of iguana hide. Peeking at the computer screen, she muffles the phone receiver ceremoniously, informing me that the system is down. In response I throw a frantic expression into my eyes. She extracts a quartz crystal from her drawer and places it in the palm of my hand. Hold this and concentrate on the energy, she explains, the system will be back up in no time. With a masterful half smile she returns to her phone conversation, describing a complex reducing salon on the luxury liner.

One month after his baptism he is arrested. He is stopped at Thirty-fourth and Sixth for jumping a turnstile on the PATH train. But unbeknownst to him, a major cleanup of the subways, focusing on homeless people of color, is in progress. Unwilling to get saddled with a fine when he has almost saved enough money for a church outing to Atlantic City, Raoul jokingly gives Ronald Reagan as his name to the officer and says his address is the White House. For this he is written up as homeless, possibly unbalanced, and resisting arrest. He is taken to the Midtown South precinct for a computer check, but the computers are down.

By morning the precinct's bullpen is filled to standing room only. Because of the overload, he is not removed from the cell for thirty-six more hours and doesn't receive any food in the interim. Unfortunately the fact that the computer was down when he was brought in means that his name has never been entered. No one has any idea what he was arrested for and, out of a better solution, he is sent over to Central Booking. At Central Booking the overload is such that charges are being retroactively thought up for those few for whom no report can be found. Raoul is charged with vagrancy and resisting arrest and taken to a cell in the courthouse. Here he dozes off for a few moments while another inmate slips off his sneakers and puts a tattered, smaller pair back on his feet.

It is not until three days later that he is brought before a judge. Weary of the constant influx from the cleanup, the judge listlessly sentences him to ten days at Rikers Island. Raoul is brought to cell block C-76 that morning, his heels hanging over the backs of his too small sneakers. To his surprise, it is hard to distinguish between inmates and guards. They seem to be on familiar terms with one another, and some of the inmates are highly favored over others.

A guard comes into the ward to do a count, and one inmate jokingly calls out random numbers to distract him. The guard flies into a rage and starts to beat the inmate savagely. Suddenly two other prisoners jump into the melee. But instead of fighting the guard, they are enthusiastically beating and kicking the other prisoner.

Cowering against the wall in his too-small sneakers, Raoul clams up, puts a blank look on his face; later he mentions the incident to another prisoner, careful to use a nonchalant tone. The man explains that the guard and the prisoners who beat up the other inmate had been smoking crack together.

The next morning Raoul is in the showers when he recognizes the voices of the inmates who had fought on the side of the guard. As he walks out, one playfully encircles his neck and refers to him in Spanish feminine diminutives. Raoul suggests he go shit on the cunt of his mother, and the other prisoner's fist flies toward his face. Raoul falls. All he remembers then is a folding chair being slammed across his ass and back over and over again.

Heart pounding, I am wandering aimlessly down Madison toward Forty-second, and then west, with my hard-won money, dramatically ruing my meaningless day and boring work responsibilities. The story of my life is one of severe deprivation: my mind posing on cathexis points that bring me into contact with other human beings only for a moment; a brown wrist or biceps, a pair of hightops, the edge of a Kangol hat. It is apparent that the vitality and tragedy of others will always be closed off to me most of the time; yet it is too late to keep back this insane flood of words and images. On and on I clumsily trudge, lost in hopeless, yearning bitterness. On and on I trudge, toward Eighth Avenue.

In less than an hour after his return from Rikers, he got hold of a crack pipe. After the last ten days it seemed the most logical, the smartest thing to do. His reconciliation with the drug was like meeting the father all over again. And what had been driven out returned tyrannically, determined to take a more tenacious hold.

Within a month Raoul began to find it difficult to get to his job in the morning to break boxes at the factory. When he did show up, he sometimes had to spend the greater part of the day nursing his nerves on large quantities of milk. Church outings to Atlantic City were forgotten; he sold his blue sheepskin coat one Saturday at four in the morning, and after he was ripped off twice in "Dark Park," he got hold of a gun.

He leans down to take his shot at the pool table, wondering if Tony and Carlos's offer to run some stuff with them might not be a good idea. But since doing so would force him to admit his snowballing involvement with crack, he decides to get money tonight some other way.

He thinks of a hustler bar near Times Square where he once went with a friend. The friend had promised that it was a place to find easy money. All you had to do was let one of the faggots who went there suck your dick, and sometimes you could make him so scared of you that even that wasn't necessary. His friend hadn't been wrong. Raoul met a faggot in a toupee who took him to a hotel where you could rent by the hour. The guy gave him twenty-five dollars for a blow job that took about ten minutes. He'd been polite and come up with the money immediately, and even when Raoul sarcastically referred to him as female, he didn't seem to mind.

But this evening the bar was not very crowded. Even if it had been, the man perched in a comer would have been likely to stand out. He looked out of place here, maybe because—though far from a young man—he had a childish, bewildered look on his face. Something about him made Raoul feel he should speak to him, and as they spoke, the man stared with a strange intensity that seemed to hang on Raoul's every word. When you thought about it, the man really didn't seem to be listening to what you said but was fascinated by the way you said it, the words you used, or the way you pronounced them. It was almost as if the guy was getting off without paying, and Raoul started to resent the whole situation.

Still the man persisted, and soon Raoul became impressed by a kind of desperate respectfulness he felt coming from him. He found himself telling a little about his life in the Bronx at his grandmother's, and the man asked him whether he thought they would ever see each other again—and if they did, whether he could ever visit his neighborhood with him.

The boy seized on an improbable scheme. He would get the guy up to the neighborhood tonight, and then get money for drugs out of him once they were up there. A white guy up there alone was certainly not going to make too big a fuss.

But during the long taxi ride to the Bronx their rapport grew. The man seemed strangely eager, even when the boy began to mention drugs. It was obvious that the guy had never been in a neighborhood like this, much less in "Dark Park" or a crack house. The evening was turning into an adventure and Raoul was becoming an enthusiastic teacher; what was more, the guy seemed quite willing to shell out money for drugs, cigars, and even a six-pack. When the man suggested they go somewhere to get high together and then have sex, the boy found himself acquiescing. There was something approving about the stranger that made it all seem okay.

He saw himself tiptoeing up the stairs of his grandmother's building with the white guy behind him. As he unlocked the door, he realized the absurdity of what he was doing. What if his grandmother woke up, or what if the guy turned out to be a narc? As soon as they were squeezed into his tiny bedroom, the image of the guy sitting on the bed in his leather coat looked wrong to him. There was something about the eyes, like they were pleading with him and hitting on him at the same time.

He tried to forget about it and rolled the crack and reefer into a joint. Then they shared it and the boy felt himself going through changes. One minute the white guy looked like an angel. Like a teacher or the father. The next minute there was something creepy, almost slimy, about him.

The boy tried to make it all right by talking, but it was as if the man were devouring every word. Soon there would be nothing left, and he was going to drown. In an effort to gain control he tried to make the guy lose confidence. He said there'd be people coming in, that it was too dangerous to have sex, that he'd have to give him money, anyway. But seeing the man get frightened only began to fill him with rage.

"Who do you think you are you can come up here and spy on me," the boy blurted out. "You're the kind thinks you can take whatever you want in the world. I've seen people like you all my life and you should have a stake put through your heart. You'd cut out the heart of your own grandmother 'cause you ain't got one of your own. You're bugging out on the way us people are living and taking notes on me. It's a sin to have you in this house, and I swear on the soul of my grandmother, I'm going to shoot you dead before she finds out you were ever here."

Raoul pulled the gun out from under the mattress and held it to the man's head. Then he clicked back the trigger.

"To each his own…" said the man suddenly, sounding exactly like the father. And Raoul's thumb froze. The image of him faded. The bank and the conference room and my life's petty details came back into focus. And desire, which is the feeling of being alive, drooped back into namelessness.

The New York Rage

IT WAS 1990, BUT it felt like the future. I'd been careful for a long time, avoiding the sharing of bodily fluids, testing myself regularly to prove to myself that I was not infected and was thus presentable to others on several essential levels. But Aunt Heidi was seriously ill. I hadn't been to see her for over a year, despite the fact that we lived in the same city.

Could it have been my debt to Aunt Heidi that plunged me into the black car with the number 17-9 decaled on its tinted vent window? Normally I would have hesitated—at least if I hadn't been waiting so long. Two licensed Yellow Cabs had stopped as I stood hunched in the cold drizzle. They'd flicked on off-duty lights and sped away when they heard I was going all the way to Castle Hill Avenue, the Bronx.

It was with a mindless sense of release of the type often experienced in this city that I perched gingerly on the leather seat, kept balance with one hand on the hang strap, and peered through the darkness at the sleeve of a camouflage jacket to suggest, "Twenty dollars?"

The car lurched forward and barreled onto FDR Drive. "Not that a few bucks matter one way or another," a drone bounced sulkily off the vinyl ceiling. "It's the kind of person, you know, makes the difference.

I'm perfectly able to toss the wrong element bodily out of the car and into the gutter, where he belongs."

No meter, of course. No hack license. The price for the ride, like the driver's credibility, was negotiable. And his remarks were only the kind one got used to hearing in the city.

Cab driving had been a solid bread-and-butter profession some years ago, the life's work of family men whose greatest risk was lower-back syndrome and who harangued you with basketball scores. Now it was becoming less lucrative, more and more dangerous. The job was filled by increasing numbers of transients who rented licensed cabs for the day, and by unlicensed "gypsy" drivers who snatched up trade left by those cabbies who shunned burned-out neighborhoods.

We plunged ahead over the Willis Avenue Bridge through darkness and rain, as I sank back into the plush headrest, gazing into the green digital on the dashboard and trying to justify my long-term neglect of Aunt Heidi, bedridden in the Bronx.

Part of it, I assured myself, was the difficulty and expense of getting there. I could have taken the 6 train all the way up to Morrison Avenue, then chanced the streets for a bus or a cab. But reading about the still-at-large Uzi sniper who had operated indiscriminately from the 6 a couple of months ago had taken away all my gumption.

Aunt Heidi languished in a still safe enclave surrounded by a veritable war zone. And if a nephew who repeatedly tested negative and had a bearable job as a word processor in a law firm felt he had something at stake, it was understandable that my visits had grown less frequent.

"We certainly don't want another Vietnam here."

The interjection had come from the cabdriver. He was in the midst of an involved holding-forth on the state of the nation, to which I had paid only marginal attention. It had begun, I was vaguely aware, with a cranky baiting of the "wimpy" Carter administration as the beginning of the end, then spanned erratically into an apotheosis of the eighties under

Reagan, and finally bridged—manically, I thought—into one's options should there ever be a military takeover in this country.

I'd floated away again then, perhaps inspired by his monologue, but more probably as a defense against his discharge of negativity, into vague speculations on some fundamental changes going on in this country. For a long time, it had seemed to me that everything was falling into the same modality. It no longer mattered whether you were middle-class, working-class, or part of the lumpen proletariat. Everyone had become contaminated by the same limp images.

Despite the fact that the media vampirized underclass physicality and dynamism, ripping off tropical colors, African music, exterminator spices, and the passionate fatality of boxing, that same energy remained a target for our projected fears; it was still a threat to the social order.

Even underclass people had become yearningly fixated on the bland, dreaming of over-aping the washed-out yuppie elegance of a Virginia Slims or accessorized *GQ* man.

"It's a dumb colored person's cliché of a rich white person. White piano, lots of Scotch, mink blanket on a king-size bed."

The driver was relating the plot of a movie he had resented. It was impossible to tell at which point it had suddenly synched with my thoughts. His gripe centered around the fact that the director was black, whereas the movie was a comedy about a rich white couple in a divorce suit fighting over possession of a co-op. I can't remember the rest.

Trapping my eyes in the rearview mirror as if sensing in them some doubt as to his qualifications as a film critic, he added suddenly, "I've got a Ph.D., you know, and I'm a member of Mensa."

Automatically, I complimented him. I infused my tone with the proper measure of enthusiasm, meanwhile wondering why his identity was so threatened that he needed these exaggerated labels to feel he could discuss a movie.

I strained to catch a look. This was the kind of person, I suspected, who would have gone to great lengths to disguise origins. All who claimed Mensa, which is supposed to be an elite organization for people of high IQ, were that way.

In the darkness I could see only the stiff collar of his camouflage jacket, yanked high, and the khaki back band of a paramilitary cap. No clue as to whom I was dealing with.

It didn't matter. In America everyone had the same identity: deprived—our only durable legacy being, in fact, that of the immigrant. It had always amused me to consider that in most veins ran the blood of someone who at one time or another had seen some form of hardship, learned to identify it solely as economic, and vowed never to be lacking again regardless of the cost.

We were barreling along Bruckner Boulevard. Through the rain I could see the silhouettes of the projects. "Motherfucking public housing. It's nothing but a drug supermarket now," the driver muttered. "I wouldn't take any fare there. Get a gun put to my head."

As he spoke, I imagined those apartments filling up with larger and larger phantom families as the wrecking balls of the future reshaped the city into one monotonous skyline. But he kept gesticulating impatiently through the window at the sleazy landscape, comparing it to the Bronx of years ago, when he grew up. And the hand looked orthopedic, due, in all probability, to the sleek and molded effect of a shiny black leather glove that gleamed in the darkness. Drugs, he kept repeating, waving the gloved hand, were destroying the country. Like subversive politics and mind-robbing cults, they had not, he assured me, been born on these shores.

The eyes that had fixed mine in the rearview mirror suddenly locked, this time sure of penetrating my reserve to discover the worst. The effect was all the more eerie as the eyes seemed to be surrounded by blackness. I couldn't make out the color of skin in the mirror or even the outlines of a face structure, and though I subtly strained forward, the black field remained impenetrable.

In that nervous way New Yorkers have of venting their frustrations and real opinions under the guise of agreeing with someone who has the potential to be threatening, I pushed back my thoughts with difficulty to discuss his new topic noncommittally: a raid on a cult that had been accused of drug use and infant abuse. "You'd expect some kids to be attracted to cults," I carped blandly. "They offer a certainty and a sense of belonging they can't find at home."

Many cults, I well knew without saying, were desperate attempts to forge identities that could not be co-opted. And for this reason they had elements that were destructive, purposely unjust, and illogical. As I chatted, my mind began running through a profile of a black cult I had read about. It was known as the Five Percent Nation, but the New York City police dubbed it no more than a cooperative of street gangs, responsible for some violent crimes in New York, including the murder of a Jewish storekeeper and his wife in Harlem.

Developed and propagated in prisons during the seventies as one way of promoting Islamic culture, the Five Percenters drew their name from the assertion that eighty-five percent of humanity was poor and uneducated and exploited in serfdom by a controlling ten percent. The remaining five percent were Muslims and their children—in other words, Five Percenters.

As a basic social unit, the Five Percenters had created a family system that was supposed to parallel the laws of the universe and was centered around male ascendancy and polygamy. All Muslim men were known as "suns," their one or more female life partners as "earths," and their children as "stars." Earths were denied the use of birth control because one of their primary functions was the production of offspring that would enlarge and strengthen the movement. Their male children were turned over to suns at the age of seven for Islamic instruction, but females stayed with their mother until they were old enough to be given in wed-lock to a sun.

The cabdriver's banal remarks had eaten away at me. I found myself irresistibly meeting the challenge of his narrowed eyes in the mirror. The eyes had become increasingly symbolic—or should I say iconic?—for me. They had begun to represent the eyes of all the ventriloquists' dummies whose bandwagon support of the status quo prolonged everything that was wrong in this world. At the same time, a lenient voice argued that he was no different from anyone else.

A tense silence filled the cab. Then the persistent beeps of my pager rang out.

"What's that, your beeper?" the driver asked suspiciously. As we listened, the beeps tolled their galvanizing call.

With an uncontrollable thrill, I realized that it was time to stop thinking of myself as an ineffectual word processor on his way to the Bronx to see a debilitated aunt. The time had come to start thinking of myself in terms of my second, secret occupation.

I soundlessly pulled a camouflage headnet made of Spandex mesh, with eyeholes, from my jacket pocket and slipped it over my head. I clicked a button in a device that looked like a pen, released a Ninja dagger, and held its point against the neck of the driver.

"Do not lose control of the road, and do not look back," I directed in an emotionless tone, watching his black-gloved hands tighten around the steering wheel. "This vehicle is being commandeered. Take the Prospect Avenue exit."

He did as I said, silently, while I struggled to keep my excitement from avalanching into vigilantism. It was unwise, but less and less could I now repress my repulsion at his simpleminded condemnation of crime and immigrants, his petty cabdriver's political rantings. It was, of course, these shortsighted, egotistical views of law and order that had perpetuated and polarized the increasingly dangerous world we lived in. No wonder that I found it hard to suppress an image of the knife I held plunging into flesh until all the hot air rushed out of this windbag once and for all.

But I had to stay in control, there were people counting on me. So I fired off a pell-mell series of directions that took us into the heart of the South Bronx, past the Fort Apache precinct, and onto a block that had nearly been reduced to rubble. Here, I knew, there would be little chance of drug dealers or muggers bothering to interfere with what I intended to do.

We had stopped across from a dismal park, and I could feel him trembling under the knife point. Applying a little more pressure, I said, under my breath and through clenched teeth, "Open the door."

"Wait, buddy, listen," he answered tremblingly. "What you going to do?" Stiffly he strained to glance at me but did as I said and unlatched the door. For the first time I saw his face, which was, to my surprise, that of the jowly father of grown-up children, the spitting image of the kind of old-time cabdriver I had imagined being almost extinct.

In less than a second, my left hand had applied the tip of a stun stick to his face, and as a spark illuminated the cab for an instant, his skin seemed to stretch back to allow his eyes to bulge. Then he fell backward, his weight swinging the door open until he slipped out of the car onto the curb.

I had to act quickly. The time during which a person remains incapacitated by a stun stick varies depending upon age and the relative health of the nervous system. Before he had barely hit the curb, I had leapt out of the backseat, over his body, and behind the wheel.

What the Five Percenters had failed to realize is that avoiding affixation of enslaving identities is as easy as you dare. The best way to evade co-option is by trading in your old identity for a new start, which I had already done on several occasions.

Real as my bland and insignificant identity as a balding word processor may have been, in the sense of the hours it took and the ways in which I depended upon it for income, all of it was overlaid upon a specious core and thus essentially free of official regulation. In 1984,1 had begun studying literature that taught one step by step how to change at will one's birth certificate, driver's license, passport, or Social Security number. I was perfectly capable of adding university degrees, military awards, or clerical titles to my name as well.

By being discriminating enough to answer the correct ads in magazines available to anyone on newsstands, I had gradually acquired expertise in certain skills: unarmed defensive tactics, roadblock evasion, nomadic living, resistance of interrogation techniques. I had acquainted myself with tactics of minor sabotage and demolition. Through these home courses had also come the contacts who had involved me in my present line of moonlighting.

In offices, hospitals, and schools, under Hathaway shirts and Laura Ashley dresses, these contacts of mostly a certain age were, to my astonishment, everywhere. Some had begun honing their skills as far back as the sixties with the appearance of the infamous *Survivalist Cookbook*, a how-to potpourri on grass-roots electronics, surveillance machines, bugs, drugs, scramblers, and other subversive devices and methods. Others had played a part in 1971, in the birth of the newsletters of The Youth International Party Line, which had disseminated diagrams of the laughingly simple "black box" for making free long-distance calls.

Then the age of computers had begun to interlace us all in its great matrix of information control, and old subversives were eclipsed by a new generation of apolitical intelligence amateurs. These computer and phone company "phreakers," "phrackers," and "hackers," for the pure fun of it, trashed through phone company refuse bins to confiscate old directories containing diagrams and codes, flanked an attack upon "autoverification"—the telephone company's greatest secret that allows anyone to eavesdrop on any other two parties—and uncovered all the police, highway patrol, federal agent, and military codes used in this country, including those for jailbreak, major disaster activation, kidnapping, "notify news media to respond," Civil Air Patrol intelligence, the Coast Guard, passenger air-traffic control, power utilities, and aeronautical telephones.

This great net of illicit intelligence spread over two generations. But it was skewed in contradictory ideological directions. In fact, by the late eighties, some of the best disrupters of information security of a few years ago were now enjoying weighty salaries working for corporations in the security field. Nevertheless, in these times choked with infrastructure, which ideological side of the fence you were on no longer mattered. What did matter was the fact that there were educated people on both the left, right, and in the middle, in our banks, government offices, schools, commodities exchanges, communications fields, and welfare agencies with a legacy, however hidden, of discontent, rebellion, and subversion.

I sped through the darkness toward Manhattan, listening to the sound of my beeper going off a second time, indicating the urgency of the summons. I felt my heart open wide to take in the city. My window was cracked, and my face, from which I had removed the headnet, was bathed in the acrid air and pelted by raindrops. How much a part of this vast city I felt at that moment. I was large, as large as it was—as fatal, as erupting, and as durable. With an exultant heart I bore down harder on the gas pedal. The car bounced across potholes on FDR Drive. The motherfucker could at least have put better shocks on his car, I remember cackling.

At the east end of a block of Thirty-ninth Street in Manhattan, I crouched low in the seat, studying the front entrance to a bar at a distance of about three hundred feet. What night was it? Thursday? The usual collection of cars: cranked-up Hondas with speakers in the back window from the 150s and Broadway, a limousine or two, a jeep. A couple of whores and a crack-head leaning against one of them.

I zeroed in on the actions of the black, husky hooker in stretch pants and a sweater, her red wig wilted by the rain. From her wild gestures, I could tell she was in a heated argument with a shrunken crack-head, a white guy with a hawk's face, who stood his ground falteringly.

From the inside zippered pocket of my vest I slipped the earphones, snapping them to the sound detector, which I pulled from my jacket pocket. The device can amplify sound five thousand times, having been developed to enable hunters to hear animals at a distance of miles. Now prison guards were using it to eavesdrop on inmates. It leapt easily up the deserted block, and under the amplified sound of the rain, it brought all their words back to me.

"I'll fuck you up, sweetheart. I'm a ho, I'm a prostitute. I'm a drug dealer. You know that. I'll stab you right here, you white faggot."

"Suzie, wait, okay? I tell you I didn't house that stuff. The dude had a weapon."

"You're beamin' on that pipe out here all night, right? You been runnin' through some crazy money. Now what you telling me *he ripped me off!* Go back in that hotel and come back with my scotty. Or give me my money. I'll waste you sky-high and send you to the Klingons!"

"I'll get killed if I go back up there!"

"Shit, I'll go up there myself! I'll bust every door down till I find somebody tell me what happened to that money."

Scotty, I knew, was a word for crack. She'd sent him into the hotel to cop some and he'd come back empty-handed. Now she was threatening to go up there.

I leapt out of the car, dashed up the block and past them into the bar.

Saigon Ruby's Circle Bar is a cavernous hole tricked out in grimy red velvet and beaded curtains. Within the center of the circular bar is a fountain with plastic tropical plants lit by colored lights. Spreading outward is another circular level with pool tables, then more levels fading into the darkness.

It was, in several senses, a place of levels. From the waist up, the people milling about the room looked like any other midtown "down" crowd, with its mix of whores, dealers, johns, users, and cruisers. One could spot a tooth or a finger missing here or there, an Eighth Avenue Korean wig, a leather bomber among the olive-drab jackets worn by Vietnam vets stooped gloomily over beers at the bar.

But I knew from experience that if the eye moved subtly to another level, below the waist, to track hands—a world, or rather an oiled system of passes and exchanges, would open up. On this level everything had a purpose, was a piece of a jigsaw puzzle being fit together, as a hand dropped a vial into another palming a crumpled bill, or strayed toward a fly to trace a teasing path along the zipper. Gold chains caught the light for a second before sliding into pockets and purses; and hormone ampules, which were of use to transvestites and had been smuggled from German clinics, were dropped into silicone-filled bodices.

Buzzers behind the bar controlled access to the rest rooms, a small ballroom, and finally to rooms in the adjoining hotel. The hotel itself was a towering edifice with a public entrance on the next street, a place where hoodwinked Midwestern and European tourists, as well as happy-hour prostitutes and their tricks, rented budget rooms. But few were aware of this entrance from the bar, leading to rooms reserved for special operations.

It was here that I had made my contacts and begun my moonlighting career as a kind of domestic mercenary. For it was here that a variety of malcontents, from the left or the right, political or apolitical, operated. And in one room lay my charge, whom I had been called in to protect, and who was, as far as certain people were concerned, the final hope of all avengers, the cutter of that great reflexive knot that our society had tied. In other words, our Destroying Angel.

I shouldered my way through the sullen crowd to the bar, behind which How, Ruby Saigon's Vietnamese manager, supreme sellout and human clearinghouse, stood. In his black undertaker's suit, with his clandestine fingers always pushing or refusing to push a buzzer button, he managed to seem all-knowing and knowing nothing at the same time. He was gazing impassively into the face of an angry customer, an adolescent B-boy wearing dollar-sign jewelry.

"I said buzz me in, man! I gotta pee!" The boy wanted to smoke crack or a joint in the john.

How smiled at him with serene, blank sadism. "Oh, no. Sorry. Toilets out of order tonight."

How's eyes shifted away from the boy. He looked at me and then directed his gaze to the street.

"I know," I said under my breath. "I heard her threatening to go up there. Does she know the rooms?"

"Used to work for Yolanda," How answered with a suspenseful yet smug half smile. He was referring to the madam who had been booted from the rooms with her girls when we took over.

"Then she knows how to get to those rooms from the front entrance?"

How nodded gravely; then a mischievous twinkle flickered through his eyes.

I swept away from the bar and past the pool tables. How's timing was perfect. As my hand touched the door to the ballroom, the buzzer sounded and it clicked open. I ran through the darkened room with its broken chandeliers to another level, where a second door miraculously buzzed and clicked as soon as I touched it.

I was trotting down the dingy corridor of the special rooms in the orange light. It was nearly too late. At one end I heard the hooker screaming with rage, pounding on a door.

"Open up! I can see that light in there. I'll tear you up, you mother-fucker. I want my money back!"

Wild for crack, she began to throw her body against the door over and over again. Her breasts bounced and the curls in her wig shook. Just as I reached her, the door gave way, and she fell stumbling into the room.

Catching sight of the secret, she was galvanized. He faced her head-on. His enormous body was propped against the far wall, to which he had been manacled, his columnar legs spread out on the floor in a vee. Somehow he had managed to spit out the gag, even though his neck was held flush against the wall by a steel collar.

The hooker stood stock-still in her tracks. Her mouth drooped open in amazement. She gazed into the brazenly derisive and handsome face. "Shit…" she managed to say.

A glob of spit, inhumanly large, shot from his mouth and hit her in the face. Before she could react, I removed the blackjack from my pocket and struck her head. Her wig tumbled off and dangled from a hairpin. Then she collapsed, and the thunderous laughter of my Leviathan bellowed forth, while I knelt to bind her wrists and ankles with elastic cuffs.

The floor kept shaking with his peals of laughter. They took hold of my body and lifted me on currents of excitement. In the harsh light he seemed unbelievably large, electric, and Frankenstein-like. I looked giddily at the gag, which lay spit out on the dirty rug. Dare I try to insert it back into the howling mouth? I'd probably lose a few fingers if I did. And so, as his chains clattered with round after round of maniacal laughter, I came as reverentially close as I dared and stood there, bathing in the chilling sense of intimacy and solidarity that I felt.

I let myself be penetrated and liberated by the nihilistic aura coming from the man dubbed public enemy number one, the most incorrigible criminal in the entire correctional system. He was the avowed committer of over three thousand violent crimes, a ready attacker of his prosecutors, guards, defenders, and fellow inmates alike, a living mockery of the justice process.

Now that he had escaped from prison, sought solace with my contacts, and temporarily been contained here, he would soon be unchained, provided with every manner of weapon, and set loose on a mission to resolve the contradictions of the city. Military headquarters, hospitals, schools, and government offices would be burgled one after the other, merely to give him access.

I felt the city around me, simple and solved, for a moment unconflicted. I left him then, stopping at the bar to get someone who would put the gag back in his mouth with a metal pole and then take care of the hooker.

The thought of visiting Aunt Heidi's scrubbed and simple apartment, with its polyester cafe curtains and wall-to-wall carpets, seemed suddenly appealing. I went out to the street, where the rain had stopped. A hardworking Haitian with a real hack license and a gold-capped grin immediately pulled his cab over. He was desperate for a fare, no matter the destination.

Pretending to Say No

I'M NOT SHITTING YOU, man, and why should I be? She came, she came to our house! No, really, the buzzer rings and I tell myself, I'm not answering that shit cause if somebody wants to see me they call first. I only answer that bell when I know who it is! But the bell keeps ringing and ringing and Tito, that's my uncle, trying to sleep, says, Answer the fucking bell and tell them if they touches it one more time I'm going to blow 'em away! Me in my drawers yet. Who's going to run downstairs five flights to give 'em that message? So I press the buzzer, listen for the door and shouts, You got the wrong place whoever you fucking are, stop leaning on that bell unless you want to get blown away! Let me in, a white-lady voice calls up the stairwell, It's me, Nancy Reagan.

No shit, man. It was the President's wife coming to see us. So I ask Tito, Quick, you know Nancy Reagan? 'Cause since he got involved with those Colombians and started to deal the crack he has contact with some very swift people. They got limousines and everything. And he half asleep saying, Sure, I used to fuck her but her ass was too tight. No, I says, the President's wife.

Yes, it's the President's wife, comes the white-lady voice right at the door this time, Would you please open up for a minute? And my uncle, hearing it too, sits right up in the bed: I gonna knock that damn fool head right off those shoulders if you brought that white drag queen up here, what's her name. No, I says, I didn't tell no drag queen to come up here! I didn't bring no drag queen up here except maybe once. And it was Tito got me to know them, always running crack for him to this bar near the Deuce, and some of those queens, really, listen, if you was standing right next to one of them you might think she was real.

So I walk real quiet to the door, on tippytoes, and take a good look through the peephole. It's a white lady for sure, it ain't no drag queen. For one thing, this one's too old, and real skinny. She's not wearing no coat, and she's got a red dress on. What you want? I call through the door. I just want to come in for a moment, she says and sticks her hand in her purse, pulls out bills and waves them at the peephole. She got money, I tell my uncle. Oh shit, says he, some white bitch coming in the middle of the night to buy crack. But don't let her in now, say I ain't got none. Come back tomorrow, I call through the door. Please, she says. We ain't got nothing, lady, go away.

Then she starts banging on the door real loud, louder than Mr. T. can hit a door, so my uncle gets really pissed and telling China Sue his Chinese chick that he in bed with, Mama, you roll yourself up in this quilt here, and cover your head, okay? 'cause I going to open the door, and he went and got the shotgun. Okay, he goes, Now when I give the sign, you throw the door open, one, two, three, go! He aims the gun and I throw open the door. Wait! goes the white lady, don't do it! I come as a friend. I ain't going to shoot you if you moves your ass out this building now, lady, I ain't got no scotty and I don't want no trouble from the super. Hear me, please, for a second, says she. Who sent you here? says Tito. I just rang any bell. What you doing that for? I need help . . . Now wait a minute, lady, if I let you in, what you going to do? I'll even pay you. She waves the bills at us again, and the top one at least, well that's a twenty. Tito keeps the gun on her but motions with his shoulder. Get in here and put the money on the table.

Nancy Reagan gives a sigh of relief, comes in and puts the money on the table. Tito picks it up. Now what else you got in that purse? Give it here. Oh there's no need for that, she says, your kindness will be rewarded. I've just come from Odyssey House. Do you know what that is? The drug program? I says. Nancy Reagan smiles and at that moment I know it's her.

So I tell Tito, Yo, man, this ain't no crack head, this be Nancy Reagan. Tito looks at her close and says, C'mon, man, I told you before if you be bringing those drag queens here from the Deuce you got to tell me first. You can't trust a drag queen, they into stealing and acting like some kind of grand lady, that's what they are all about. Now you got to go 'cause I don't want my nephew hanging out with drag queens.

Yo, man, this ain't a drag queen, you be making a big mistake.

Tito takes another look at her and then he calls Suzy. Tito trusts her about some things. So China Sue comes out and Tito says, Suzy, this a drag queen? Oh my god, Suzy goes, and runs back to the bedroom and puts a sheet on.

So Tito puts down the gun and he kind of bows to her and says, How you doin', Nancy Reagan?

Not so well, says she, since you ask. Maybe you happened to watch TV tonight? Yeah, I did, says Tito, what that got to do with it? Well, says Nancy, didn't you notice what happened to me? Oh, I saw it, pipes up Sue, coming back with the sheet wrapped around her. You were at the drug program and you put your arm around this little black kid and he told the TV audience how he used to take angel dust and how much you helped him? Nancy Reagan listens real careful to every word China Sue says, and then looks her straight in the eye and says, Is that *all* you saw?

Yes, Mrs. Reagan, you were wonderful, oh, and then you said that this was only one of many young lives that had almost been ruined by the insanity of drugs. But tell me, dear, Nancy says, was it all in closeup? I don't know. Well, would anybody happen to have a needle? Nancy says. Tito's mouth drops open, my eyes bug out. And a little bit of thread? Nancy goes on. You see when the reporters left and I went into the ladies' room, I bent down to fix my hose and saw that the hem of my dress had come undone. In front. And here we were supposed to go right on to a midnight supper to discuss the fund-raiser and I was stuck in the ladies' room with a sagging hem. So I went out another entrance hoping to find somebody who could help me fix the thing before I had to face another reporter. I was so terribly embarrassed, I just couldn't go back, and when I realized there wasn't anywhere to find a needle and thread this time of night, I panicked and began ringing doorbells and now I'm at wit's end…

She keeps going on like that while she parks her ass right at our kitchen table and puts her purse down so I can take a good look at it. Genuine alligator. Well, I says to myself, too bad I didn't noticed that before, Nancy Reagan, when I was trying to figure was you shitting us.

So I go over to her, and real polite and everything says, You want a Bud? I'd love one, says Nancy. Well give her a glass, barks Tito. A glass will not be necessary, Nancy tells him.

Don't you worry, goes China Sue, I can fix that hem for you pronto. Tito, you got any thread? It'll have to be scarlet, says Nancy, or at least a magenta. She puts her hand to her ears to see if both earrings is still there and takes a swallow of beer.

Tito starts running all over the place, opening drawers, cursing, and slamming 'em shut, looking for thread. And I am wishing I'd cleaned up like he wanted me to before China Sue come over so's the place wouldn't look so bad.

Nancy Reagan takes a good look around, checks the place out. Well, look at you, I keep thinking. Here's the First Lady of our country, but she ain't wearing no diamonds or Gucci and not even one gold chain. Shit, if I had her money I'd be wearing ten gold chains and mink-lined Adidas.

So where are your parents this evening? she asks. Oh, they's out, I answer quick. Out to dinner. And will they be back soon? Nancy says, looking at the lipstick on her beer can and covering it up with her hand. Carlos ain't got no parents, Suzy pipes up. Everybody has parents, Nancy sasses back. So Suzy wraps the sheet over her head and ranks, Well he don't, what you think a that? and Nancy stares up at the wall.

What about him, anyway? I says to my uncle, talking about my father. He dead or what? He ain't dead, he in jail, says Tito. You know that. And what does your father do? Nancy goes on, like Tito didn't say nothing. Construction, I tell her. But I lives with my uncle. Uncle here don't mind my staying here long's I clean up before he brings girls over. And I do all the laundry for the both of us too.

Well how about your little sister, says Nancy, can't she help out too? You mean Suzy? That ain't a sister. Can't you see she Chinese? She's Tito's wife. Carlos, shut your mouth! Suzy hollers, laughing. They ain't married and shit, I goes on, she's just his woman. And how old a woman *is* she? is Nancy's next dig. Fourteen, I says. But I'm eighteen. I got ID. You want to see it? I get up to get the proof I bought at Playland, but Nancy starts waving me down.

Now don't you start giving me that kind of questioning shit in my own house, First Lady, Tito says, trying to sound polite. I wouldn't do it if I was in yours. Nancy pulls a mean face at him and grabs for the alligator purse, she opens it up. I'm really glad to have met all of you, she tells us in a sweet ho-voice. Did you find the thread? If I did I would a told you, says Tito, getting pissed. That's strange, she says in a voice gone all cold, that you don't have any, and she keeps looking through that purse. Come to think of it they said on television something about her having a gun in there.

Fiddlesticks! she says all of a sudden. Don't tell me I forgot that beeper? Now how am I ever going to get in touch with Jim? She snaps the purse shut loud and Suzy jumps and starts laughing again. The two of them acting so spooky, it's starting to scare the daylights out of me.

Who's this Jim? Tito'd like to know. We don't want no Jim up here. Jim's my bodyguard, and he's a perfectly lovely fellow, Nancy tells him. Yeah? You got a bodyguard? I says. She just gives me a look like don't put me on, dude. Shit, I goes on, I bet he gots some fresh weapons, I mean since you rule the country he can get his hands on just about anything. We don't rule the country, Nancy says, and starts looking bullets at me. Hold on a minute, I says to myself, and if she do got a gun in there? So I tell her how sorry I am about opening the door in my drawers. I really didn't know you was deciding to come and see us. And anyway, we got plenty of beer, why don't I put a little music on. That's sweet of you, she thanks me, and this time it's that same hooker's voice. Go ahead and do what you usually do.

So I put something mellow on. It's got a good beat. And before I know it I start relaxing and forget all about that we got the First Lady sitting right here. Tito and Suzy are maxing too. Come here, baby, he tells the Chinee. They snuggle up and bug out on each other, 'cause to tell the truth they was very high when they went to bed. Suzy got these problems in her pussy, she went to the hospital twice but they didn't do nothing. They said it was some kind of miscarriage and they sent her home stuffed up with Kotex but still bleeding. That was yesterday, I think, and since it hurt so much Tito give her all the crack she wants, he even put a little bit in her pussy. It was more than the hospital would do.

Finally I says, Nancy, you comfortable? I can call you that, right? Oh yes, she says, and I'm comfortable, but Ron must be worried. You mean the President, I says. No, she says, I mean Ron, Jr., my son. He was with me tonight. Then damn right, I agree with her. Like if I thought some drug addict at Odyssey House was to fuck with my mother or my sister I would be getting my gun already, they would not be alive today. You must care a lot about your mother and sister, she says. Yeah, I'm a family man. You want to see a picture of my baby girl? You mean a picture of your girlfriend? she says. No, I says, my little baby girl, she's a cute little thing. But weren't you just telling me about your girlfriends? says Nancy. I didn't tell you about no girlfriends, I says. Tito the only one brings girls up here, that why I got to clean the house up for him. I don't trust fooling around with no girls anymore. You never know who they been with. They all sick.

Sick? asks Nancy, and she starts playing with that hem again. Well, I says, I know this girl lost all her weight. They says she got the AIDS. Had these terrible headaches in the hospital. They wanted to cut her head open but she wouldn't let them. She left in the middle of the night 'cause they said they wouldn't let her out.

The First Lady lets go of that hem. The poor girl! she starts shouting at me. Yo, wait a minute, I tells her. I know rich people got delicate stomachs. But it ain't my fault. Me and my uncle are helping her out all the time. Anytime she wants to get high, we get her some dope 'cause we be willing to protect this dude that supplies it.

Oh, but this is terrible, terrible, says Nancy, like a little chick all of a sudden instead of an old lady. This is so terrible that I can't believe what you're saying is true. You are giving heroin to an AIDS victim. Well, yeah, I says, we are doing what we can because we are good people. We try to help out when we can. If I have my facts straight, she lays on me, drug abuse can give that awful disease to people. No shit, I says, you mean we're making her get more sick?

Just a minute, Tito interrupts, and he lets go of China Sue. Every time we get her high she thanks us and telling us how much better she is feeling. But that's only temporary, Nancy shoots back, you're killing her. We won't do it no more, Suzy promises. But the First Lady has already got a whole different look on her face, a bright idea. Write a letter to me, at the White House. A letter? says Tito. Well I ain't going to sign it. We're going to make certain this young girl gets help, says

Nancy, that's all. You mean you got something that will make her feel better? I says. And she nods. It's all the lady will tell us and it sounds mysterious. Probably something only she can get hold of.

So I am worrying how am I going to write this letter when the worst thing happens. Because the doorbell starts to ring again. I keep making like it's not, but whoever it is is leaning on it like the First Lady did before. And the more it rings the madder Tito is getting. Until finally he starts calling out my name: Carlos, c'mere! And I go over and he shouts in my ear, Go downstairs and get rid of you-know-who!

That's when I realize I still got just my shorts on and run into the bedroom red as a beet. I start pulling on my pants quick so I can get down there and get rid of her before she gets inside the building— 'cause I know who it be! But I know it's too late too, 'cause, someways, she is always getting in this building. I can hear those heels, then her calling through the door, Carlos, Carlos honey, open up!

Don't you answer that fucking door! Tito hisses at me, but she hears him and shouts back, What's a matter, you got a girl in there?

So Nancy grabs her purse quick and stands up. What's going on? she says loud, which is what we didn't need. All you ever do is lie to me! comes through the door, and Wait till I get my hands on you! Oh, says Nancy, even louder, Look at the trouble I'm causing after you were so nice. Young lady! Don't worry, I am not his girlfriend, I'm Nancy Reagan!

Bitch! comes the answer through the door, I'm Diana Ross! So Nancy gets right up and opens the door and says. You see? I'm not his girlfriend.

Well, it's this black queen comes up here sometimes. Calls herself Chaka Con, like the singer. She gives Nancy the onceover and can't believe her eyes. Honey, that drag is so convincing! But do you really want to look that old? Connie, shut up, says China Sue, this *is* the First Lady. Hmm, hmm, says Con, looks like the Last Lady to me.

Connie comes over to sit on my lap. Whatever got into me, thinking you was cheating on me. I take back everything I said.

Chaka, you got to leave, Tito tells her. I just finished saying to Carlos that he got to ask me first before he bring a drag queen up here. But instead of getting up, Connie gets mad. No queens, huh. Then what she doing here?

Connie, I tells her, this is Nancy Reagan for real. Okay, says Connie, it's a big world out there, and anybody can be anything they want. Nancy Reagan's got class and I can see somebody wanting to do her drag, if they can afford it. I ain't complaining. Now I'm black so I want to be Chaka or Sheila E., but if I was white, I'd probably want to do Farrah Fawcett or somebody.

What you want here tonight? growls Tito. Okay, I'll get to the point. I come to get a ten but I only got five and I can bring the rest to you tomorrow. I don't sell that stuff no more, says Tito. What's a matter with you, says Connie, you know you can trust me. I really want to get high, baby. I'll make it worth your while. Both a you.

Chaka Con licks her lips and looks at Tito, then at me.

Me and Tito try to give the First Lady a look like what is this queen talking about, but Nancy has turned into some kind of statue. Maybe she has slipped a Valium. Chaka starts looking her up and down. What you doing here, honey? I ripped my dress, says Nancy. This isn't the girl you were telling me about, is it? Oh no, First Lady, I swears, this one don't take no dope.

Chaka Con takes in Nancy's purse. Oooh, look at that! It's just like the one Nancy was carrying on TV tonight. Where'd you get it and how you know she was gonna have it tonight? You come here to cop, girl? Why else would a white queen with an expensive purse come all the way down here? Come on, honey, share with your sisters, I'll give you five and you give me a rock.

So all of a sudden Nancy gets this look in her eyes like something dawned on her. No, that ain't it either, how can I explain it? It's like maybe that is happening somewhere in her head but then she deciding to show that to us. And slow like a statue with a motor in it she turns to me and says, *So that's what's going on.*

Tito hops up fast. After all this is the President's wife. You going to believe any nigger drag queen come in here out of the street, Mrs. Reagan? he says.

The Con hops up too. Wait a minute, dudes, what is going on here? I demand to know! Who is this queen and why is she making everybody so jumpy?

Chaka Con, says China Sue, I am trying to tell you! This is the First Lady! She come here to get her hem sewn.

So Chaka walks right up to the First Lady and looks into her face. And then she takes a good look at the hands and the shoe size too, and says, Holy Shit, you're her! And she grabs hold the First Lady's hand, says, Mrs. Reagan, I didn't know, will you ever forgive me? I have admired you for such a long time. All my girlfriends love you.

It's perfectly all right, says the First Lady. I know you didn't know.

Chaka Con grabs a mirror out of her purse, checks herself out fast and throws it back in. Have you, have you known these folks long? she asks. We just met tonight, Nancy tells her. Umm, excuse me for asking, but in that purse, would you happen to have a needle and thread? No, honey, I mean Mrs. Reagan, I don't, says Connie like some kind of lady, I do all my sewing at home. In fact I am known as quite a seamstress. If you like, I will send my address to the White House and you can drop by for alterations anytime you please.

But Nancy gets a deep-freeze look in her eyes again, I never seen such a hard look, and gives a long sigh that everybody can hear, before she says, How kind of you to offer. Now who expected her to say that after that look and that sigh? But I need help now, she goes on, and drops her head and covers up her face with her hands. You can hear a pin drop.

Suzy is looking down at her feet, 'cause she don't want to see the First Lady that way. Me, I keep quiet. Finally Chaka says, Listen, now buck up, lady, c'mon now, I mean you are the First Lady, you ain't supposed to be crying like that over one silly little hem. Now cut it out, will you. You got responsibilities.

It's easy for you to say, Nancy whimpers, you don't know what it's like. Nobody does. So Chaka Con gets up and puts her hand on the First Lady's shoulder. Mrs. Reagan, Mrs. Reagan child, you stop that crying now. And the First Lady says, Well, we have feelings too.

Can I ask you something? Chaka says. You want me to get that needle and thread for you? Same color as the dress you're wearing? That would be ever so kind of you, the First Lady mumbles through her fingers.

Then don't you worry, Mrs. Reagan, croons Connie, but—uh, well there ain't no stores open now, oh I mean I could get you some black thread—the First Lady shivers a little when she says this to her—but to match your color, well I'm going to have to go all the way up to 128th Street, to a friend's a mine…

Nancy looks up. Then you'd better hurry. Do you need cab fare? Well, the cab costs a lot, I hate to ask you for that, child, says Chaka Con. But already Nancy is opening that purse and all of us kind of leaning over to peek inside.

How much do you need? says Nancy.

How much do I need? How much do I need? says Chaka. Mrs. Reagan, I got lots of needs. See this wig? See these shoes, see this dress? Well, the wig costs money, the shoes costs money, and the dress costs money. You know how it is, don't you. I been looking for a job. I sure hope 1 find one tomorrow. Because, you know, I'm not like those other niggers out there. How I look, the kind of image I have, well, that's important to me. I can't stand people don't take care a themselves. People who let themselves go and ain't got no respect for themselves. They make me sick, you know what I mean? They lying in their own shit, they expect other people to carry the load for them and then's they don't appreciate it when's they do! And I don't want to be one of those people. I mean it's hard for all of us, ain't it? All I need is just a little head start, things is bad now but all I need is just a little push to get me going 'cause I got plans. And once I get going nothing can stop me. What you got in that purse there, anyways?

Nancy shuts that purse fast. You—you got a weapon in there? Connie says, and she looks up at Tito and swallows. Don't believe everything you read in the papers, Nancy sneers. I didn't mean nothing by that, Mrs. Reagan. Now listen, you want me to get that needle and thread for you?

The First Lady's eyes kind of go dim. I suppose so, she says. Well, gimme a hundred dollars, says Con.

Nancy starts to freeze up again but makes a big effort. She looks real hard at Chaka Con and she starts to blink a whole lot. I pay it back to you, says Chaka. So Nancy goes back in that purse and takes out two fifty-dollar bills, hands 'em to the Con. Tito, Chaka says, can I talk to you for a minute? But what about the thread? Nancy says. Oh I'm going right out, child, lickety-split.

Chaka gets up and gallops into the bathroom.

So now me and Suzy are sitting there alone with the First Lady, and Suzy is just looking down at her feet and finally says, I got to get a drink of water, and trots away too. And I'm left there staring at Nancy so after a minute I says excuse me too and go in the bathroom too. And Tito is just now lighting up that pipe and Chaka Con got it stuck between her lips. But when she sees all these folks and only one little rock in there, she says, C'mon, load it up, I want a king-size toke.

So we begin to get high, and 'cause Tito has really packed that pipe up, after two tokes my head is rushing like you wouldn't believe. So when we hear Nancy banging on that door, we look at each other and bursts out laughing. But finally Tito says, Well we got to go out there. And ones of us got to go find that thread for her. And that'll be you, right, Chaka Con? And Connie looks at him and says, Unh, unh, baby. I'm the one got us this money to pay for all this shit, I ain't going nowhere. So Tito says, Carlos, you got to go and find that thread. And I tell him, I'm too stoned. So we decide that we going to tell her that Chaka just remembered that friend she thought she had on 128th Street ain't there no more, she made a big mistake. And if she asks us for the money back, we only give her twenty because she owes us the rest for letting her chill out here. 'Cause wouldn't the kind of hotel that she would go to cost even more?

So we go out there together and tell the First Lady just how it has to be. And everybody is waiting for her to get shit-faced mad and call that bodyguard to come back here. You can imagine how surprised we are then when Nancy don't get mad at all. She just sits there, with that alligator purse in her skinny lap and her knobby hands folded on top of it. Life has its slaps in the face, she says, I'd be the first to admit that. So Tito tells her no hard feelings but some folks don't find it so easy to get by. And Nancy answers him back, I've seen more than you can probably imagine. And Suzy says to her, But First Lady, I thought you was living in some kind of wonder dream. And Nancy Reagan looks her straight in the eye and says, Well, the dream I am living, that fairy-tale dream that I wake up to each morning, in which I am lying next to the kindest, bravest, and most understanding—and I suppose the most powerful— man in the world, well that dream came true for me but I had to work for it. Lord knows I worked to make that dream come true. And looking around me at you, I see these bright, young shining faces. Sure they have suffered a lot already, but they still are alive and burning and aching with the desire to have the things they should have.

And then she says, Do you know what? I've got a funny feeling. Call it an intuition, but you and you and you and you, you'll have that dream someday. And that's why it is such a joy to look into your eager young eyes and see the power to make it happen...

Well, I didn't hear the rest of what Mrs. Reagan was saying, 'cause suddenly my head started to float. It was like—well it was like we are always going to movies me and Tito and my friends. It's all we ever do side from getting high. Now here comes the part where the basketball player kid who up to now is the underdog meets some older person making him realize that he can make it too. It's the part we all like the best, but we never knew nobody who was going to do that in real life. I mean somebody who could really say that to us. So it was a great high. And suddenly that nervous skinny old lady sitting there got changed into some kind of holy lady. Or a queen. Yeah, that's it, a queen holding out this wand, and each time she points it at somebody everything goes all right. You gonna be rich now. Or maybe that's not it. But it is like you going to be rich and have everything you want.

But the most bugged-out thing of all, that's when I look over and see Connie and she's crying. I can hardly hear her but she is saying that, O, Nancy, you came to visit us and we done treated you horrible, girl, we showed you no respect, you know what I be doing with that money you gave me already, I—

Hush! says Nancy. There is no need. I don't need the thread anymore because the experience I have had here is a million times more fulfilling than any press conference or TV camera. I will go back to Odyssey House and tell them about this experience. Nancy stands up and it's like a ray of sun shining on us, and she says, Would you mind if I used your bathroom?

So Nancy gets up and goes to the bathroom. And we keep sitting there saying nothing. I look at Tito, and China Sue, and Chaka Con, and I see changed people. Nobody can talk.

Then we start to hear it. I guess I was the first one. Plop plop plop. And I realize I can hear the First Lady. And Tito looks up and so does Chaka Con and China Sue, and we look into each other's eyes, and finally I says it, because I know that's what we all thinking. Wouldn't it be fresh if we could get a look at the First Lady taking a dump?

So one by one we all get up and tiptoe toward the bathroom door to peer through the crack, to watch the First Lady drop her load. She's got her dress all bunched up and held out in front of her, and the panty hose are just kind of shoved down at her ankles. I don't know but I expected the First Lady to roll them panty hose down. And then she reaches for the paper—and if you thought about it—well wouldn't the First Lady take just a few squares at a time and put them on top of each other all neat so that the edges matched? Well this one just grabbed the end of the roll and yanked. But then something else happened, and I don't know if I want to tell you about it. But okay, I will, and what happened then was, instead of lifting the edge of her ass off the seat and wiping, the First Lady stood up. And when she did, it knocked us all on our ass, because the biggest cock you've ever seen flipped out the top those panty hose.

Well at first it was like a punch in the gut. I mean, being stoned and all, we couldn't get over it—that the First Lady wasn't no lady. But finally Chaka Con gets enough breath and says, Child, child, child, you mothafucka, you pulled the wool over our eyes. And the First Lady yanked up the panty hose and pulled off her wig and came out laughing, big, loud, low laughs, laughs I heard before. And Tito, who can hardly get his breath neither, manages to cuff me on the head, gasping, You fool, didn't I tell you it was a drag queen. And then still laughing, everybody goes to punch Brand X, 'cause that's who it was. This drag queen

Brenda from the Deuce. They call her Brenda X or Brand X most the time. And Tito still gasping, I knew it all along, and Brand X laughing and laughing and saying, Like hell you did, and going to grab that crack pipe, saying, Give me that shit, 'cause I am the one who paid for it. And Suzy laughing and saying, No you wasn't, it was Nancy Reagan. And where'd you get that kind of money, girl, Chaka Con is saying. You wouldn't believe the sick trick from Washington, says Brand X, gave me five hundred to put on this drag so he could pretend he was fucking Nancy Reagan. And then the pipe starts going around and our heads fill up with smoke and the First Lady shrinks away, right back to TV size.

Casio Like the Keyboard

CALL ME CASIO. Like the keyboard, man. I used to play in a band. Check out the wrist. Digital, bro. I ain't going to settle for less. You says you want to see the neighborhood? Well, ain't nobody knows it better than Casio here. This is my territory. I ain't never got less than three bitches working for me at a time. I'm the king of bitches, poppa. But you got to lay the jack on old Casio in advance if you want to see that.

Let me take you down the Deuce here. That's what we calls Forty-Second Street. It ain't what it used to be. Eight, nine years ago, it was jumping. I could do this block in ten minutes. Take the stroll and put enough in my pockets for the day. I jump the train in the Bronx cause my pockets was empty. Come up these same stairs with hope in my heart. Let's count the steps between here and that peepshow. One... two... three, four... five and six... seven. In the door and down the stairs. Into Faggotland. Don't let me down now, Moby Dick. Find me a faggot has twelve quarters and two five spots. Sound of the quarters slipping into the slot. Watching me a straight movie, you better believe. This dude needs chocha to get off.

You see, old Casio knowing how to play this scene by timing it. Minute I flip my dick out, I raise my digital to my face. If it's a good cocksucker, I can shoot the first load in three minutes flat. If it's a slow gummer or a nipper or wants to give my balls a physical, he got five minutes to cover the map. Fifty-eight, fifty-nine, sixty… Over the finish line with a heavy load gets me ten. Taking these stairs two by two. I got money in my pocket and not a whole lot of time to waste. If traffic ain't bad, we take it like this by the diagonal. Two, four, six, eight… we will not procrastinate. Fourteen, twelve, ten and eight… got no time to masturbate.

You got to pay to get in this movie. Putting down five leaves me three, being the faggot gave me eight not ten at the peepshow. Five down but fifteen to come if the action be happening downstairs in the head. What they got in the head you want to know? All kinds of action. I got a homeboy that owes me, fencing shit he boosted from the tourists. Or maybe I got a couple friends holed up in the stalls smoking a doobie. They can do me five or ten till I get paid.

But look at that, bro. This must be my lucky day. That fucked-up pair a burgundy jeans showing under the door of the stall got to be that rank-ass from downtown. The motherfucker's smoking scotty sure as the fuzz on his little sister's *crica*.

Open the door of that stall, faggot! What I tell you 'bout smokin' crack in there. I'm the manager of this theater now, you know. Lemme see that stem! A rock, just like I thought! What you got in them pockets, *nino*? You better pass me some jack or I'm going to make *pasteles* out of you. What you saying you ain't carrying no money today? Step over here so I can turn you inside out. Look at this, a razor blade? Well, I didn't know you was Rambo. Excuse me if I just house your weapon too. Mean to say that all you got but a dollar? Next time you see me, you better not forget that you owe me!

Let's go upstairs cause my uncle likely be waiting for me. He's a john likes to lay on the floor of the movies sucking ten little piggies. Yeah it tickles, but I'm a man, and I know how to hold my laugh back. One time a Chinese karate come on. I got overexcited and kicked Uncle by accident. But he ain't here today, and I already paid for the movie. Now I'm five out. With the three left from the faggot and one from the punk, I got just four. We got to hop over to the Port Authority before the day shift changes.

I know so many people over here I call this the "Mansion." There are plenty of motherfuckers, but the ones I call family stop by from time to time. Over here be one of my homeboys.

Yo, man, lemme talk to you? Step up, don't be shy. You know Ricky got a finger missing, the one with the tattoo say "Scorpio." No, not the Scorpio always wears the earring, the one with the frizzy fade. I ain't talking about the faggot with the fade, man, that be Jose.

You seen the motherfucker here at the Mansion? Don't walk away like that, you seen him up the stairs? Well, I want you to tell him something from Casio. It be three days ago I hooked his 'ho up with a john, and he ain't gave me nothing. Seem to me he been playing me ever since he moved into the Mansion. Now put your eye here and bust this. I got a razor blade sitting on my tongue, which is why I sound funny. I run into that *maricon* acting the way he is last night, I going to cut him.

Girl, what you doin' here so early? Didn't I tell you to wait for me at the crib? What you trying to say I didn't leave no money for the baby? I'm out here all day trying to make enough to get by and you come to tell me that. Get over here, I want to take a good look at you. Your nose be running, your face is all covered with sweat. What you mean you having the flu these past few? Two days ago when I stopped by, there wasn't not a thing fucked up about you. You tell me you knocked up I going to kill you and your baby. I been wearing a goddam bag every time we fucked. Don't think about looking to me about this one.

You sick, ain't you. Step away from me or I'm going to knock you out. You ain't gonna catch me having a junky for a female. I don't care you only sniffed twice last week, you ain't got no flu, and it ain't no baby making you shake like that.

Step off, I told you. You ain't getting nothing from me. Get your hand away from my pants cause you ain't gonna find nothing in there. Now stop sobbing like that, you know how it makes me feel when you cry. All right, take all a these three. I'm giving you all the loot I got.

What, baby? You know I ain't holding out on you. I know you needing at least another two to get off. Don't worry, momma, you can always count on Casio. Just go up those stairs there and ask for a dude with a fade called Ricky. Homeboy owes me five for hooking up his female with a john. Go straight up there now. I don't want you doing no 'ho stroll. Don't look at nobody. Just keep looking down.

Shit. One fucking dollar and the law be around with their dogs already. What time is it? Midnight? This ain't my day, but the day ain't over yet. Come to think of it I got those rocks I housed from the punk. We'll go around the corner to 41st and see what we can do with them. Sad to say, but these bums would sell their last piece of cardboard for a toke. Wouldn't you know it'd be raining? Well, let's make the best of it and press our asses to the building.

Jumbos! Rocks! A buck for a toke! Step right up, I ain't got all day. Yeah, you can have a toke, but first slip me a dollar. Hold on, old man, you're going to swallow the stem and end up shitting glass. Yeah, it's packed, I just slamdunked two rocks in there a minute ago. I give you one draw and I guarantee it be smoking the whole time.

Who's next now! Looks like the rain washed them all into the sewer. Don't mind if I take one toke myself, I got nothing better to do.

Word, that first hit goes right to your *cojones*. Every time I taste that shit I get horny. I should go back to the Mansion and look for my female. Naw. She probably be nodding out by now. Yo, you remember the look on the face of that piece of bootie at the movies? He was bugging when I pulled him out of the stall and told him to empty his pockets. Come to think of it the *pendejo* got a sweet ass I wouldn't mind tasting. I should break him in over at the hustler bar on 46th. He liable to bring in a lot a money.

Wonder if I should go look for him now… Naw… He's probably on the bus back to Jersey… This rain starting to come down heavy now…

C'mon man, be my faggot and buy me a drink on 46th? I got a dollar, all you got to throw in is two. C'mon, man, haul ass, would you? Don't be acting like we got all day.

Apollo's Curse

HE YAWNED AND PEERED through the orange mercury vapor street light, as the departed wave of Dilaudid dropped him on his ass again. Carly was across the street. The transvestite stopped at the curb and yanked up her top to bare her breasts, grabbed them and squeezed them. She looked good from a distance. Glancing quickly both ways, she pulled down her miniskirt, keeping her cock pressed between her legs, and mimed a pussy dance just for him. Apollo mimed cheers and applause.

It was only for a split second that a collapsed version of what had happened maybe two months—a year?—ago flared up in his brain. He'd been her boyfriend then. Kind of.

But, well, then one night he needed… something… from her purse—all right, it was fix money—and when she found out, she came looking for him on the Deuce. He'd had the bad luck of talking to another queen when she found him.

"Carly, *really* I woulda asked you."

"I'll fucking cut you, you son of a bitch," she said, reaching into her purse.

"No. Come on now, put that shit away. There's cops around."

Carly's big hand, with its inch-long fingernails, whipped the gleaming blade from side to side. First it slashed open his shirt, then some long cuts across his chest. She kept reaching for his face, but he fended her off; let her cut his forearm instead.

Winded, she let the knife drop to her side, her eyes streaming with tears, running the mascara. *Her* wispy hair had come undone and was plastered to her face with sweat.

It wasn't so much being cut by a queen in public, but the sight of her with her hair undone and the ugly drops of sweat on her forehead that curled his fingers into a hard fist. He smashed her face, knocking a tooth out.

"Is this guy giving you trouble, little lady?"

"Yes officer, he tried to rape me." Her head was bowed, her hand clasping her bloody mouth. She was sobbing.

"Against the wall! Put your arms up!"

"Can't you see it's a guy, officer! That's no lady!"

"Shut up!"

The cop found his works and a bag right away, so he was shipped bleeding like a pig to Rikers, and waited three months without bail.

Some of the guys had put ads in gay papers about being lonely and needing a gay they could write to and call collect. Then you were supposed to write about your big dick until the guy cracked. You'd talk about all the things that would happen when you got out and then hit him up for money and cigarettes. For some of the guys, the relationships turned into long-term ones. It was ripe for fantasy. The person on the outside starting to do all kinds of favors, calling relatives for them, sending them cigarettes, books, commissary money. Occasionally, the locked-up one getting strung out so that the other's generosity took on strange. impossible significations, sexual identity stretching like a rubber band.

It was just his luck to get one who wanted to be a "nice guy" more than anything else.

"Don't write me sexual letters. Let's be honest with each other." A series of "spiritual" letters passed between them discussing third world liberation, sexual politics, the prison system. The guy complimenting his intelligence. Sensitive talk about relationships and the meaning of friendship.

"May, upon the arrival of this letter, it find you in the best of health…"

Apollo always began each letter cursing the fact that his perpetual damning and desperate need always had to rear its ugly head again. "I sincerely hope that you…"

"Please forgive my asking but…"

"Hope you are well and by the way could you…"

"I'm sorry we got to know each other under such bad circumstances for me but if you could…"

This time it was worse. When you're alone in your cell after lights out, anguish might settle in. The loneliness seems limitless. You're tempted to think that this guy could… Later it will seem absurd.

Nightmares of torture and sadism, witchcraft being performed on and by him. He felt, as he sat bolt upright in bed in the middle of the night, that it was only fair to warn his pen pal with whom he was dealing. "I've got to admit to you right off the bat that I'm not a very trusting person. I hate to say it but I'm full of bitterness and rage."

The admissions backfired. "I'll *take* the chance… I can handle it" were the guy's responses. An avalanche of feelings welled up. An irresistible *need* to believe that the guy really might understand everything. Ferocious hate about the better possibility that he would not. He wrestled with it, pushed it away.

"Dear Comrade…

It was too late. The mark had marked him. There were sweet moments, his weakest, when he sank into the dream of a friend and protector who was taking care *of* everything. A kind of Frankenstein patchwork of a buddy-brother with a strange, scary, erotic aspect. It intoxicated him like nerve gas. Coming down from it was worse than withdrawal from dope. The sense of injustice riddled him and made him feel murderous.

"This will be our last letter. For both our sakes, I think it better we stop communicating. I'll never be able to make you happy—

But the guy kept writing. Was he the con artist of the century? It had almost lulled Apollo into what seemed like a passive, infantile state. A desperate, intolerable need leaking with sexuality. It felt like incest. There he was daydreaming lying in his arms like some kind of woman. He'd turn into jail pussy if he wasn't careful.

Then on Christmas, came the pair of Nikes he'd been asking for. And with it, a letter that set his teeth on edge. "This should prove to you that I'm really thinking about you in the best possible way."

And what exactly was that supposed to mean? A man who needs shoes on his feet like anyone else having to bow down and kiss the feet of the one who provides them? He wrote a grateful-sounding letter, but he had the gnawing sense that every word of it stoked the guy's ego.

A month later the guy came to visit. Apollo had saved the expensive sneakers for when he got out and never thought of wearing them. Not thinking that the guy would not understand the communal nature of prison, he borrowed new sneakers from buddies to dress up for him. Traded a pack of cigarettes for a haircut, got a pressed shirt and even some stolen cologne. He cleaned his teeth.

Sitting in the courtyard, a sinking feeling as he tried to imagine what he would do when he got out to please his benefactor, the guy's hairy arms, his school-teacher-like clothes. He pushed it out of his mind, courageously promising himself not to let his friend down.

The guy was starting at his sneakers.

"I thought you said you desperately needed sneakers."

"I did. I borrowed these from somebody."

The guy gave him a doubtful, lacerating look. It made him feel lucky to be locked up, because all he wanted to do was slash up the guy's face and hurl the sneakers against the wounds. Everything he'd suspected had come true in one overwhelming wave. By accepting the sneakers he had branded himself a user, coated himself with slime. And all of it had been ordained by the other person, who was always in the right.

But for the guy, it had obviously been no big deal. He kept up the sweetish letters, spelling out high ideals, forging his high-class image. Apollo's emotions, like hot coals, put all his strength into playing along, waiting for the chance to strike.

The guy's letters and calls had a plaintive element now, because his father was dying. Apollo mimed the right sentiments, said he was there for him, until the guy wrote that his father had finally passed away. Then Apollo went right to work.

"May upon the arrival of this letter, it find you in the best of health… I've got to admit what I think of you… You're a sad, lonely gay guy who likes to fantasize that he can control other people's feelings… I felt sorry for you and appreciated what you did for me. I was willing to make some sacrifices for you when I got out—sacrifices, if you know what I mean…"

Gleefully, but with gritted teeth, he took his punishment as cigarettes, commissary money, books, and promises of lodging stopped abruptly. The rejection was exhilarating, as the reins fell back into his hands, the bitterness reinstated its protective bulwarks and life became simple again.

So simple that here he stood, in the spot he had been hundreds of times, a couple blocks from Jilly's bar, without any money and a gnawing yen to get high, a citizen of the world of dope following its laws…

Counterfeit John

"THAT'S THE BEST WAY to get the sucker—put eye drops in his drink. Can't remember nothing and starts walking bad. Shitting in his pants before he gets to the corner. You just follow him at a distance, wait your chance…"

Miss Wonderful's hand tightened around the small plastic bottle. "Visine'll do it?," she said, You ain't shitting me, Fierce One? If so, I'd be snappin' mad."

"Baby, read my lips. The Love Bandit don't lie. I'm into crowd control. Now bus it, 'fore the john leaves."

Fierce One raised a blunt finger to test the tightness of his gold cap and tapped the queen on the ass toward the john, a clear-eyed slob in a suit and tie. She tucked the Visine bottle between her silicone titties and slinked forward, nervously smoothing her blonde wig curls against her dark-skinned forehead. The john had a worried mouth, which put her off a bit.

I was the john. Or at least I was pretending to be, and I'd been near enough to hear and see every detail without it occurring to them that I could. My brother Buddy had been missing for two months. Our father's will was waiting to be distributed, save for the signature of my absent brother; and this bar, called The Crib, was a good place to start looking.

"Looking for a good time?" Miss Wonderful had squeezed up to the bar, next to me close enough to smell her cold cream and feel her lanky thigh, her bony knees pinning one of my thighs between them.

"Like a drink?" I said.

"Oh, but let me." Her fingers snaked along my pant leg, then plunged into the pocket, burrowing for cash. "I found the family jewels, honey, but no bucks."

So I took my wallet out of my other pocket.

"Doubles?" she asked, testing her luck, and at the word, Ethel Girl, the mop-headed bartender, came running with a bottle of vodka from the B shelf, her lips parted to reveal a rotten-toothed smile.

Miss Wonderful pressed fingers to her mouth while she waited for Ethel Girl to stop pouring and for me to pick up my glass. Then she picked up her own and managed to hook her arm through mine. We raised our drinks in a toast—Latin style—arms linked and eyes glued to each other.

"Out of town?" she asked, letting a shiver pass through her body. She jerked her naked shoulders to jiggle her cleavage, which moved as one piece below prominent collarbones. The curls of her wheat-colored wig bobbed up and down.

"Yeah," I said.

"Welcome to the big city," she whispered into my ear, slipping an index finger under my belt and tugging me closer. "But couldn't you buy me some Newports, darlin'?" Feigning shame at her own boldness, she covered her mouth again, averting her face but watching me obliquely.

With my back to Miss Wonderful I made for the cigarette machine, affecting a limp I thought suited a vulnerable john—all the while imagining Miss Wonderful reaching into her cleavage for the Visine bottle and raising it to her teeth to unscrew the cap, then spraying a strong stream of liquid into my vodka. I knew that when I got back both she and Fierce One—the gold-toothed giant with scarred arms—would be watching for the moment when I raised the glass to my lips. And that was why I caused the ruckus, accusing the chest-high bangee boy next to us, the one with a fake gold chain slung over a caved-in crackhead chest, of rifling my jacket for a wallet, until his anger and paranoia got the best of him, and his teeth gleamed with spit and his breath came in pants between his furious protestations, and the bouncer came running and Miss Wonderful and I moved to a quieter corner—during which I switched our drinks.

Miss Wonderful, white sash stained with vomit, dark bony legs hugged to her chest, rocked back and forth on the edge of her hotel bed, her eyes and nose running, alternately shaking and falling into erratic, expansive Elizabethan riffs from the effects of the Visine. Floating in and out of rap, she was telling me as much as she knew about my brother, mixed with bursts of perplexed hilarity or frightened gasps for breath. And she was telling me more than I would have gotten out of her if I hadn't sprung part 2 of my plan. As soon as we'd gotten to the hotel room, I'd pulled out the fake badge I had ready and had told her I was an undercover cop.

The diarrhea was over, and though the Visine had had the effect of pulling everything liquid out of her, it had also sent her nervous system racing, like an overdose of not-so-good speed. She didn't want to be left alone either, terrified as she was of the strange chemical feelings, this bad trip, and probably assuming that the mistake had been hers—she'd just picked up the wrong glass after the fourth double vodka I'd bought her. Her ladylike inflections were punctuated with specks of downhome South and con jargon, her speech jump-cutting from one memory to the next, getting lost in rhymes, her body perking up and falling back like a Yo-Yo.

"I'm talkin' without thinking, doll or Officer. A white dude, huh? A writer? La. On the avenue? Ah. Or did you say the street? Might have been—la—in front of Jimmy's, hmm? Jimmy, wow, like what a big Greek!

"Say the writer took a powder? Well… He didn't inform me. Seems strange him not confidin' to his Mis' Wonderful. For that the truth, baby, every night of the week!

"La, la lemme see… Told me that she… oh don't scold me, officer, if I says she when I mean he… was always scribblin' somethin' on a teared-off beer label, to jot down some kinda story, that swelled head. In a hustler bar, yet?—claimin' to be writin' 'bout the brain dead. Buggin' near the front to catch the neon for light. So's you say it's a morgue where that high-class hamburger be chillin' tonight?

"You ain't never said he got offed? Then I'm the one who made a mistake. Now don't get excited if you please. Nobody said the man is dead! Just one of Miss Wonderful's strategies, tryin' to find out what he means to you. Am I right to suspect he's more than a case? You got a vested interest. Sorry then that I said dead, it's my way of rummagin' in your head.

"Seems to me he was hooked up with some kinda boy. Toy. Now I'm not dissin' this mother. But if you ask me that so-called writin' fool was a meter for trouble. The man you invesigatin' was quite a slummer!

"Now that rent boy of which I speak? Girl's name tattooed on the back-a each finger—always tweakin' at his *pinga*. Playboy bunny thing scratched onto the shoulder over here? With a knife and a little ink of course… Lord, how coarse!…

"Strange fancies that butch queen writer… He'd grab the bad ones 'fore they was eighty-sixed. Come back for more, but then they'd be in the slammer! Even had his butt kicked a number a times. But always went for the same numbers!

"That boy which he was seen with was a wide-lapped mother! Plenty a space from thigh to 'nother. Ha! And what he got hangin' 'tween them thighs? Well, Miss Wonderful might have inside info on that affair. But that's a different story… Hey!… what you lookin' at, Officer. La, watch them eyes!

"I seen 'em conversatin' 'bout 2 a.m. Wide-lap was playin' the writer for broke. La, was gonna reach into his pockets and then, la, buy himself a toke? The writer was playin' hoodlum priest. Thinkin' about his wanger but wearin' a clerical collar. If Father Bruce Ritter hadn't a been sent upstate for greasin' them Covenant House kids, you might a thought you was starin' him in the face! The writer's drag was a double game. Or maybe triple more like it. He wants to play with the homeboy's head. Steal some shit for his novel and then wind up in bed. He also wants to be Sister Goody-Goody, be sure that the homeboy is tucked in fine with a goose-down quilt and some milk and honey.

"No, Officer, I said 'honey,' t'was your fine ears heard the word as 'money.'

"But street-trash ain't about to buy that line. All he wants is a tokin' dime. 'Daddy, I'm hungry,' I heard him say. 'They gots the bests fried chickens, it won't take but 1 minute. But since my belly's real empty it'll cost us a 10. Slip me a 10-spot. I'll be back in 10.'

"Seems butch queen the writer was hip to that. Too many times he's seen his green palmed by something with them frozen eyes, walk like a robot out of his vision. Smoke it up like it was so much nothin'. Never to return until the next day. And skinnier. Apologizin', and askin' for more bread!

"'Listen fella,' says the writer, 'I made a decision! If you want chicken, I'm going with you. That way I can make sure some bird ends up in your gullet.'

"'Word, Mr. Writer. Don't you trust me? Like I said, I'll be right back. Just palm me the 10, don't let nobody see it. You know how jealous these homeboys get. They see a full wallet, their plans get large. And while I'm gulping the chow, I won't be here to watch your back.

"But Daddy the writer, he jes' wouldn't give it up. He wanted it his way. He knew wh'a was up. 'Course the homeboy knew what log lights the fire. He took holda that worm through his pants right in front a my eyes. Pulled all the writer's thoughts out a his gray matter and dumped them in his pants to start that fire.

"Still Mr. Writer kept his dignity. Sister Goody-Goody can't buy no kids crack. They supposed to do a commercial about how that shit is wack. 'I'll go with you,' he said, 'and buy that chicken.' So Homeboy tried his final ploy. He said, 'I'm fessin' up papi, it ain't no chicken gonna bring me joy.' Then he used one a the writer's words. He tells him, "Don't get *judgmental.* If I smoke rocks, I can still stay gentle. You see this shit's an aphrodisiac. To eat your dick, I need some crack!'

"'Your brain has cells that hold all your pleasure,' said the writer gettin' serious. He knew it was his duty. As an educated queen, he was a great repackager. Puttin' the street trash in shiny new wrappers.

"'Each cell has a gate,' he went on gravely. 'If something feels good a key unlocks it. Chemicals come pouring into all your pleasure circuits. You'll feel good and not into robbin'. Maybe you'll get a job or maybe you'll go shoppin.'

"'But if you keep forcing that lock off those gates by big tokes, you'll break the hinges. The gates fall off, it feels good for a while. If your grandmother dies, all you do is smile. Then the feel-good's used up and the gates are broken! You'll feel like you been arrested even if you got a token!'

"'Word,' said the homeboy, 'I'm kinda converted. You mean that shit I was doin' was hurtin' my mind? I only get high every other day. You sure them gates can't take a little rattlin'?'

"'Not only that,' said the Kindly Writer. 'I'm thinking of the ticker 'neath that beautiful chest. At every inhale it gets larger and larger... Not to mention the fluid filling them lungs, till they drip and droop like two used condoms.'

"Now here's the point where the plot gets seedy. Officer, you got mileage with the sick and the needy. Lots of it, right? So what was goin' down in the homeboy's thoughts? Did he give two fucks 'bout them smoked-out lungs? Would he save his brain and heart from the likes of scotty? Would he stop suckin' on the devil's dick cause some bald white guy with glasses gave out free health classes? Excuse my bird if I get philosophical, but the hustler's life is strictly topical. If the john drops a cue for a homeboy-lost, he'll put on that hat faster 'n you can say jumbo rocks and pour out a story of tough luck like a trooper—all 'bout no mami nor papi payin' the rent, group homes in jersey, ruses 'n' abuses. If he got his GED when he was upstate, including some brainwash from the Five Percenters, he might spice the story with some political jive, 'specially if his interlocutor's skin is ivory.

"As a man in blue you seen it before, the way people get off through others' woe, the missionary man with a collar a sadist gettin' kicks by helpin' and hearin' slaves holler. This white trick writer was not an exception, an appetite for pain outdid the one for dick, it was all he could do to keep from scribblin' down the words poppin' from the homeboy's mouth. The pair was so hot the whole bar stopped to listen, and from that duet came a transformation, the homeboy'd startin' to believe his own words. Which ain't unusual for the homeboy mind. From moment to moment they go with the flow, to get convincing they con themselves. But their commitment only lasts a second, livin' with time in the now is their bit a heaven…

"So their rap turned into the social worker's dream. I swear on the grave of my whore of a mother, who took her last breath down the street, yeah, Mami was one 'o the whores on this beat…

"Huh? No really, Officer, you might a touched her with your billy club… Now don't react like that, that wasn't no snub.

"But here's the story that the homeboy spit up. And even the other con artists stopped and ate it… Like I said, the bar fell silent wanting to know if homeboy really was changing or joshin' the writer for some change.

"'If you want the truth, I wanna start nourishin' myself right now on that chicken,' says the homeboy. 'With your help, daddy, I can lick all this shit. I'm supposin' I'll come up with a thousand warrants, so we'll start from scratch. If you really down for my rehabilitation and gonna talk to the law, find me a head shrink so I ain't sad, pay for cookin' classes and make me a chef, 'tween our two careers life'll be def. But don't be thinkin' there ain't no reward for you in all this shit, *papi chulo*. Rest of my life I'm gonna walk on your arm like l'il brother, and clean the john every day, be polite with your mother, and as for hustlin', that jive won't be necessitating no more, 'cause for your flatscreen TV I'll be an all-day whore. I'll keep that kitchen a yours full a mofungo, you'll be my buddy at Great Adventure, ain't' nothin' gonna wrong go.'

"The writer's eyes was glowin' like some vampire. "Scuse me,' he says and starts his scribbling, tearin' beer label after label that he filed in his pockets.

"Meanwhile that boy kept up his babblin', pourin' out some honest-to-goodness tea, everybody in the bar knew he meant it, even me. This wasn't no con, no it was a genuine rehabilitation. And when Miss Goody-Two-Shoes came to that realization, slow as her white brain was in grabbing the realness of the street, she stopped scribbling fast and dropped her rod. In the Ivy League collar the adam's apple starts to bob.

"See, he'd been conning herself with all them missionary notions, that shit was pure fiction, just some white man's diction. Behind them coke-bottle glasses he saw what was up, he'd conned some poor hustler into thinkin' he was pop. He didn't want no pup like that, he wanted his bad boys to keep their mean, disappoint him tragically, he was a crisis queen.

"And when the homeboy sees it in his eyes, rage at bein' conned smoked up like some cock-fight yodel. The rest you probably got in your files. The writer freaks and skedaddles to the street, homeboy tails him, resultin' in dead meat. That's right, I'm back to that theory. It's just my hunch, and you should know I'm sorry.

"And as for the boy he was claimin' to help, he made him a con for the rest his life. And I bet Miss Goody-Two-Shoes made the papers when she became a stiff. I bet some galley slave in a midtown tower is typing up them beer labels into a book, so that all the armchair white readers can have a safe look. And maybe them pages memorialized the homeboy, will gave him some clout with the cons up river, and that's the way the writer in the end was a giver. I swear to you on my wigs and crotch suppressor, I told the whole truth like you was my confessor."

The Other Maria

THE PHONE RANG. Without beginning with "hello," the voice said, "Listen, your brother's in trouble."

"Who is this?" I'd inquired into the phone that first time.

"Jesus."

"Funny. Now who is this?"

"Jesus! You know, like Hay-sooz. Your brother said once call you if he ever got in trouble."

"In trouble? Who are you?"

"I'm kinda… his roomie! He ain't here no more. He don't come home, he ain't paid in six weeks, they're going to kick me out."

According to him, my brother had disappeared over a month ago, leaving all his possessions.

"Even his toothbrush, a change of underwear?" I wanted some sign telling me whether the trip had been foreseen, perhaps a short trip had turned into a long one.

"What 'ya mean, man. I ain't wearing his underwear! I don't know. Wait a minute!" I heard the phone thud into a pillow. Then he was back.

"Nah. His toothbrush's still there, th' 'lectric thing."

"My brother never said he had a roommate."

"I told you. I'm like his—nephew! Somebody got to pay for this place, they gonna house all his possessions you know. You're a lawyer, maybe? You can do something about the situation?"

I scribbled down the address and set out. It was only a couple blocks west, not far from Ninth Avenue. No lock on the door in this hotel. When I knocked, it squealed open to reveal that Jesus character lying on crumpled bedsheets, dressed in Adidas pants and a T-shirt. His plump lips cushioned dangerous-looking white horse teeth and were ringed by a wispy black goatee. The nearly empty room with its single bed was lit only by grimy light from an alley window.

Jesus brought a finger tattooed with the letter "M" to the corner of an eye to pull away a sleep grain. Nothing at all stirred in those shiny black eyes. But his mouth kept moving—yawning and then drooping into a sulk. In fact, no matter what was happening or what he was saying, those eyes and the rest of the face stayed anesthetized, while the mouth could do anything—spread long and thin into a terse, ironic homeboy smirk or spring into a boyish oval of good-natured laughter or purse into a hooker's come-on. He reached behind his propped pillow and pulled out a comb, which he ran through slender strips of licorice hair, trained back werewolf style. Eyes fixed on me, he yanked the hem of his cut-off undershirt toward his blue Adidas pants to cover his belly.

"I just woke up. Got a cigarette?"

I shook my head, and he studied me for a moment, the mouth tightening into a smirk at my rumpled suit slightly stained with Miss Wonderful's emissions. He climbed to a standing position, suddenly looking much larger and more muscled, and did a few shoulder circles to loosen up. Then he kneeled and began sifting through an overflowing ashtray on the floor. "His brother, huh?"

"Yes."

"You ain't nothing like him." He picked up a few ash-streaked butts and lined them end to end. "Now take me, and my brother. Like two peas in a pod," he said, sticking the longest butt in the corner of his mouth. "Everything happens to me or him is like it's happening to the same person. Like a piece of my heart out there!" He struck a match as emphasis, turned, and tipped back against the wall. "'Cept I think I got a bigger *bicho…*"

"A what?"

"Dick!" The dead eyes alighted on mine. He lit the butt a lighter lying next to the ashtray, sat back against the wall and exhaled a large, fragile *0.*

"So when was the last time you say you saw my brother?" I asked.

Jesus's mouth tensed into the homeboy look. He tilted his head back and let the eyes swallow me. "Seems like you don't care about your brother so much."

I shrugged.

"You saw him when the last time, your brother?"

I didn't answer.

"Maybe all white people's that way." The eyes fell to his crotch again. "They're slick. I couldn't tell mos' the time what your brother was think-ing."

"Neither could I, Jesus."

"*Hav—sooss,*" he corrected. "I'm kinda his godson!"

"Listen. How do you know my brother?"

"Met him at this place The Crib. Ever heard of it?"

I shook my head, deciding to lie. Jesus took another drag. The *0* started to come out and then was pulverized by a chortle, followed by a volley of coughing.

"You okay?"

Still coughing, he nodded. "I come up to him, shit, you won't believe this. I come up to him and say, 'You don't look like a faggot.'"

He had, he claimed, been adopted by my brother shortly before his disappearance but could produce no legal proof beyond a scribbled note in my brother's handwriting that said:

GOING OUT FOR A FEW. KEEP YOUR EYE ON THE PLACE AND DON'T LET ANYONE UP. I KNOW I CAN TRUST YOU. TREAT IT LIKE YOU'RE PART OF THE FAMILY.

He gestured around the nearly empty room, which I noticed for the first time had a broken chair and a television whose aerial was wrapped in foil. "They're gonna put me and all our things on the street if he don't come back soon. I'm like his nephew, you know? Somebody got to pay for this place, or they're gonna house all his possessions. You're supposed to be some kind of lawyer, ain't you? You can't do something about it?"

"You already said all that."

He dropped flat back on the bed, eyes to the ceiling. "You checked out The Crib?"

"Told you I didn't know that place."

"The homeboy network—makin' mo' money with no money," he snickered.

"Remember exactly when you met my brother there?"

"Yeah. It was like a Monday. Just some of the night people and a few a' the queens."

He sat up and tipped eagerly onto his knees. I'm pointin' at this queen, Maria, and I'm askin' Shorty, 'Is this the other Maria?'"

"Who's Shorty?"

"My older brother. T'ree years. Yeah, we alls us look alike. Like my uncle? I look like him too. 'Cept I got a bigger *bicho*."

I studied his hands, which had never stopped moving, either to smoke or just to twist in intermittent angles and circles, like a belly dancer's to a half-murmured song, or they moved to his pants to pick a piece of lint off them, or fluttered before his eyes in a kind of private cartoon show. For me, it was a strange rhetorical style.

"Wait a minute," he said, "I just remembered. Saw him one more time before he disappeared. Talking t'dat queen Miss Won'erful over in front th' bus station. And she wuz makin' stoopid dollah's las' night. Really fineass."

I strained to distinguish the last word. "Finance," "finest," or "fine ass"? I couldn't decide.

He began humming, staring at his own hand motions. They looked like break dance moves now. *"Pullin' 'em in 'fore dey have a doubt…"* he sang to himself as his mind wandered back to Miss Wonderful. "Say, wanna stick around for a while? You got me over a barrel, you know. I'm about to get homeless, unless you decide to pitch in. Why don't you come sit here on the bed with me, poppy, let's keep it in th' family. Come on." He was moving toward the TV. "I'll put Jerry Springer on."

THE REFORMERS

They Had Stories Then

THERE'S A MUSTY REEK to old books that is more enervating than the odor of most rot. Their smell resembles that of aging writers, whose crotchety faces have the embittered flatness of a dried-up page. Back when the page ruled in America, bookstores were poorly heated spaces floating with dust mites. In these colorless places, the word was sovereign. Images were banished as they were from the Hebrew temple.

In those hallowed times when I was very young, the Anglo-Saxon writers I respected tended to be slovenly or wilted. They wallowed overweight in coffee and dressing gown all day and night like Auden; grew elfin, wizened, and virginal in funny hats like Marianne Moore; or took on the vampiric elegance of an Edith Sitwell. Libidinal as the act of writing may be, the page is stagnant. On its surface thoughts congeal and set forever. Neither will words jump off the page at the viewer like the surface of a painting.

Writing is dust in its most desiccated and tenacious form. It won't wash off, and the writer is coated with it until the moment of death. This sterile filth is the only stuff that writing produces, and for that reason some have called it priceless.

In our new age of light, representation admits its insubstantiality. Words on a computer are just a temporary blockage of light on a neutral ground. What looks like permanent patterns of darkness disappears with a single gesture, giving way to light. No matter how long the words stay on the screen, there's no encrustation but only something reversible and expendable.

Today in America, the old eccentric bookstores of the past are all but gone. Thousands of watts illuminate the Barnes & Noble super-chains. These facsimiles of something Anglo-Saxon and mahogany are astoundingly alike and endlessly reproducible. Titles and book covers flash into appearance and slide into obscurity with the speed of light. The most astounding thing about the stores is how clean they are. Their shelves are scrupulously wiped like the counters of a supermarket, as if the inorganic objects being sold there were actually fresh produce or recently butchered meat destined to spoil in time.

The atmosphere is reflected in the faces of the bookstore's scrubbed clerks. Bland, impassive, and distracted, in their identifying smocks, they robotically stack shelves or give programmed answers to customer queries as time ticks and they dream of being elsewhere.

There is, however, the new method of soft sale. Every word of every book is offered up free to anyone who has the time to sit on the comfortable couches or at the convenient desks, creating a facsimile of the old neighborhood bookstore where regular customers could browse endlessly or even stay to read. What is being sold now are objects; to leave the store with a book rather than merely the words on its pages, a person must pay. Since words can now exist electronically, they are a less solid product. The book itself, on the other hand, is as valuable as furniture.

Last week, an old midwestern writer nearing eighty who came to New York four decades ago in a blaze of publicity over his ground-breaking novel of sex and the working class hauled himself through the revolving doors of a Barnes & Noble bookstore with fear and loathing.

No one seemed to recognize him but me. He squinted with contempt at the huge posters branded with writers' faces. It was obvious that he had an instant aversion to this retail store masquerading as a T-shirt-selling library. But perhaps he'd heard that a colleague's book recently released and unaffordable could here be read for free in relative peace and quiet. Though the library had yet to stock the book, he could find it on these shelves, so he splurged on an espresso, and settled not far from where I was sitting, next to a cluster of stone-washed denimed students flipping through Gen X magazines.

A stench rose from his dull black suit and graying shirt, like a heraldic cloud. His neighbors noticed it immediately. They scanned the area with wrinkled noses that finally pointed toward him. Some shifted farther away. One got up to move to another table.

His knobby, arthritic fingers were blotched with typewriter ribbon ink, the old kind that must be threaded by hand. This must have made him seem even more repulsive to the young onlookers, who darted glances at him stooping over the book, his shoulders rounded like an old tailor's, touching a thumb to his open lips from time to time to wet it for page-turning.

The smell wafted inexhaustibly into the air. What exactly was it? Like old leather left out in the rain? Newspapers accumulating in a basement for centuries? Something depleted and almost bonelike, yet still defiantly musky.

The prophet of the poor, now nearly destitute himself, kept reading. Pleading glances shot from outraged customers to passing clerks. The clerks were fluttering at the loss of what to do. Who'd ever thought that an indigent person would invade a store whose requirement is literacy? It's true it happens at the library, but they aren't selling anything there. The idea of such a store as this was too unique and new for the indigent population to have discovered so soon. More of him would mean the death of the entire concept and its shared assumptions of cleanliness, purpose, and income.

And finally, a red-faced clerk marched up to him. The old writer, deeply absorbed in his text—because his ability to become absorbed had grown more intense with years of practice—didn't notice. The clerk chose to see this as an affront, which gave him the courage to speak up harshly.

"Sir! Can I help you with anything?"

I wanted to call out, "This is a famous writer!", but something forced me to hold my tongue.

As if from a dream, the old man looked up at him in bleary-eyed confusion and shook his head.

All eyes were on the clerk, who decided to push the issue. "This isn't a library," he said. "Do you intend to shop here?"

With somnambulant authority the old man slowly scanned the room. Magazine browsers colored guiltily, and some even pressed their hands over their reading. The old man fixed the clerk squarely in his gaze.

"There is some possibility," he answered. "Have you inquired of the others?"

The stymied red-faced clerk could only lurch away. Frozen faces dipped back into their magazines. The old man took a tiny sip of espresso and a weak smile crinkled his face. I tried to return it, but he avoided my eyes.

Perhaps he was thinking of his great, groundbreaking novel, which some had called subversive at the time. It was, in a way, a prediction of today's vast legion of homeless, foretelling a massive, odorous, and libidinous underclass clogging the streets, bus stations, highways, and libraries. But he had never thought of this. No. He had never thought of the invasion of the bookstores. At the time, he couldn't have known they would bloat into supermarkets.

He closed the book and rubbed one hand slowly through the other. His face softened and grew wan. Quite probably, so many years and so many pages had passed that fantasies and words had interwoven. His thoughts and his writing were of a piece. His predictions were his reality whether they had come to pass or not.

I watched him carefully, trying to intuit the thoughts running through his head. Perhaps he saw the unwashed bodies of his novel accumulating at the store entrance, a dense cloud waiting to stain and to inform. He saw the startled clerks, the lawsuits, the collapse of another class bastion, the outraged letters to newspapers. In the heady perfume of this near future, he settled back with a satisfied grin.

Around him, the white, matte walls under bright spots seemed to leak, oozing something black and scabrous, like ink, dribbling in calligraphic patterns all the way to the floor.

Why Oh Why, My Brother?

I'M BEGGING YOU for an answer:

...why *no one has ever been able to describe the meaning of the post-Stonewall-coined phrase "gay culture" without being accused of stereotyping....*

...why *a lot of gay men who insist on their right to the sacraments and legal benefits of marriage indulge in promiscuous sex...*

...why *married men who indulge infrequently in homosexual activity are accused of being "really gay" and never "really straight"...*

...why *men who indulge infrequently in heterosexual experiences but more often in homosexual experiences are called "gay," rather than, for example, "really straight"...*

...why *the most educated and well-off homosexuals often say they are "queer" whereas those less well-off commonly refer to themselves as "gay"...*

...why *those who vehemently deny that gays are different from others also insist on the necessity of their own books, magazines, and clubs...*

…why *most of today's theorists or activists fail to understand that a certain depth of need or disorganization makes a person stick it in anyone or let anyone at all stick it in…*

…why *bisexuality in prison, on the street, and throughout the Third World do not resemble the philosophical bisexuality of our contemporary post-feminist, post-Freudian enlightenment…*

… why *HIV became a powerful force in the mainstreaming of homosexuality and escalated its absorption into the culture at large…*

…why *homosexuals don't admit that their subgroup can never be permanently exterminated because it doesn't depend upon biological laws of succession so that a generation of gay children don't need gay mothers or fathers to come back into existence…*

…why *the Stonewall, remembered by those old enough as the wildest and most libidinal bar in New York, has been recast as a shadowy, dour environment for oppression…*

…why *no one discusses the fact that promiscuity is actually a powerful method of penetrating age and class barriers…*

…why *people don't understand that there are sexual impulses too fragmented to base an entire sociological identity upon…*

…why *some gay studies classes claim that the writing of William Burroughs is a positive endorsement of gay life, which is equivalent to saying that Sade's writings are an endorsement of affectionate sex…*

…why *academics have invented distanced cynical terms like "performance" or "transgression" to conceive of outsider cultures…*

…why *university departments stress the danger of applying cultural stereotypes and defining someone by their race but keep promoting ethnic studies…*

…why *"multicultural" committees are composed of people who all tend to come from the same economic background…*

…why *most academics have ceased to believe in historical precedence and in history as continuous and connected…*

…why *minorities who want assimilation have recast subversive elements of society—like homosexuals, ghetto inhabitants, or alcoholics—as normal people who participate at least mentally in wholesome middle-class life but are in need of protection or help…*

…why *small, educated segments of every subculture claim that everyone has the right to determine how he is named in society and then go about choosing names for everyone …*

…why *the word "people" became a code word for "middle-class people"…*

…why *anyone doesn't mention that American Blacks are frequently from Protestant backgrounds whereas—since Max Weber's* The Protestant Ethic and the Spirit of Capitalism—*the analysis of Protestant (i.e., Puritan) culture has provided a key descriptor for American identity in general…*

…why *it's considered indecent to suggest that ethnic cultures have in a similar way been shaped, or even transformed, by economic factors…*

…why *theorists of identity politics have admitted the poor into their dialectics primarily as bashers, batterers, sex objects who don't understand their oppression, or macho closet cases*…

…why *we no longer allow open discussions of "the culture of poverty"*…

…why *we tearfully sanctify the neediness of urban minority groups at the same time vilifying individual members of them who indulge in crime as a remedy*…

…why *those taught to respect the poor and empathize with their life are refused use of the same vocabulary the poor themselves employ to describe it*…

…why *it is now considered a slight to a poor person's integrity to say that he's a member of the lower classes*…

…why *there's an unspoken agreement among people of the media that everyone shares the same values and that those who transgress them have become inexplicably evil*…

…why *those shaped by educations that emphasized identity politics so often seek the approval of politicians, family members, corporations, or the clergy*…

…why *the disorganization and unrestrained energies of poor urban neighborhoods that inspired bohemian artists of the past began to frighten artists starting with the arrival of the first American generation from the suburbs, popularly called hippies*…

…why *today's undergrounds produced less of an avant-garde—in literature, art, or fashion—than late nineteenth century European café culture or even the 60s cultures of self-gratification*…

…why *the number of white men from affluent families who want to be photographers increased exponentially during the last ten years…*

…why *emerging artists spend more energy on self-promotion and networking than on making art…*

…why *the difference between publicity and art has suddenly collapsed…*

…why *it was decided that our plays, films, novels, and plastic arts aren't really mirrors of our soul but prisons of manufactured significations…*

…why *people in their twenties who say they want to be photographers and then receive a monthly check from their understanding parents to supplement their rent often never become photographers…*

…why *the meaning of the word hipster changed from someone close in lifestyle to Black urban jazz cultures to a young professional who goes out in a spirit of opportunistic alienation seeking weekend pleasures in all-white clubs…*

…why *urban hipsters once fascinated by the energy of the poor decided to form block associations and neighborhood police committees…*

…why *our familiarity with any counterculture is directly proportional to its absorption into the mainstream, during which it ceases to be a counterculture…*

…why *August Everding said that whoever "marries the zeitgeist will be a widower soon"…*

…why *fashionable people often don't know the actual name of the cultural or historical icon their appearance is aping…*

...why *pornography has become the last allowable expression of bourgeois transgressive consciousness*...

...why *hippies of the 1960s didn't realize that their colorful return to nature owed much to the German* Volkisch *movements, which had already been proven to be key inspirations for German National Socialism*...

...why *the permissive climate of the seventies, which was the result of a massive cultural upheaval accentuating pleasure, quickly began to seem anticlimactic*...

...why *travel no longer feels like a radical departure from anywhere*...

...why *no one seems to notice that the twenty-first century's virtual space has copied physical space of the past more than we imagined it would*...

...why *so few seem to notice that we are not moving toward a watertight Orwellian 1984 but toward a Gibsonian future of virtual rapists, unintentional data leaks, schoolboyish terrorist attacks, and chaotic mumblings in virtual superspace—not into an information vault but an information sieve*...

...why *it's common for us to see ourselves becoming what we reject*...

...why *we begin to resemble our parents once those parents have been so exhausted by our rebellions that they are nearing death*...

...why *it's considered normal if someone from the current generation chooses to live with Baby Boomer parents when he is past the age of 25*...

...why *Baby Boomer parents with liberal mores who encouraged children to bring lovers home to sleep with have produced adult individuals who are prudish, judgmental, and passive*...

…why *Baby Boomers past their prime refer to anyone under 35 as "only a child"*…

…why *those who condemn inter-generational pairings because the young person does not have the "option to choose" never admit that these young people lack the same option when it comes to living with their parents*…

…why *the difference between protection and confinement has become obscured in discussions of the raising and education of children*…

…why *a law passed by the U.S. Congress in 1980 stated: "Children have a right to family, not to independence"*…

…why *licensed psychologists and psychotherapists stopped admitting that the sexual power of children covertly provides the principal mandate for their control and protection*…

…why *child beauty pageants sprang up in the most militant anti-pedophile states of the U.S. with the harshest laws*…

…why *it's common for older homosexuals who are still living to portray adolescent encounters with older men in the big cities as treasured memories of sexual awakening*…

…why *the same population of adolescent boys who tended to crow about seducing a female teacher now maintain it means they have been molested*…

…why *campaigns against child abuse are concurrent with the new use of the term "boy" in gay culture*…

...why *homosexuals ceased valuing their orientation for its implicit subversion of the daily life of the family*...

...why *no one will point to the moment when academic and intellectual labeling begin to embalm what they described*...

Take My Advice

TAKE MY ADVICE. What an obnoxious imperative! Never once as a young man did I listen to it. Advice coming from mouths fighting gum disease and brains fighting regret? In other words, from a different physiological reality. Take my advice? And trade my resilience, energy, thirst for adventure, and inability to imagine death for your fragility, fatigue, need for security, and nearness to the grave? Never!

Yet the advice-givers were right 9 times out of 10. Sex with strangers is mucho risky, drugs can destroy brain cells, friends can become users, an artist's career is a gamble full of frustrations, old age sucks without money. But maybe old age just sucks.

No, I didn't take their advice and… I think I have been lucky. I've slalomed through the heady experiments of sex and the heartbreaks of love and the bitterness of lost friendships, and the toxic experiments of drug-taking and the bohemia of no money to pull from them a rich fantasy life, and perhaps even some hyper-awareness of the Other. And maybe my excursions into the libidinal realities of other ages, races, and classes, mostly by fucking, has all been narcissistic, but it makes stunning copy! It has made me a better writer, perhaps a more compassionate writer. And yes, I could have died.

P. is twenty and already has a completed novel and a music CD under his belt. He told me that he has to become famous—soon—because he lacks interpersonal skills, and getting attention that way is the only way to feel that he exists. Take my advice, P. (*Did I say that?*) If success is what you're looking for, get an M.B.A. But if you want pleasure, then think of your art as play. Art is the radical decision to enjoy yourself at all costs. And serious pleasure, despite what they tell you, can engender meaning, creativity. Which doesn't mean that an artist doesn't work his ass off. It only means that in striving to rework the world according to one's fantasies, for the purpose of pleasure, beauty, and the kink-filled shock of having stumbled upon original meaning, the need for fame should play a minuscule part.

So take my advice. Just don't blame me if you fuck up.

Time-Warped Vision

IN MY DAY, you inscribed your invitations on heavy wax tablets and strapped them to the back of a half-naked slave, who ran a marathon through forests and across deserts to place your missive at the feet of the powerful or deserving. Now, you send invisible electronic impulses through doubtful labyrinths paved with attention deficit disorder. You can't even choose the thickness of your linen paper or indicate a degree of intimacy by "sir," or "my love." It takes only a tiny typo in an address to keep a message from reaching a best friend, while those unintended, or even unimagined, end up as perplexed but apathetic recipients. Call this a scatter-shot approach done in the dark, like the primitive biological strategies that drove evolution, the trajectory of a thousand sperm sprayed at some remote target never actually seen, and which few are destined to attain. But should this invitation reach you the intended, consider it engraved and scented.

Hosting Made Easy

IN THIS COUNTRY, rules surrounding hosting lack stringency. If this were ancient Japan, an untold number of etiquettes for host and guest would be codified. I'd know how to serve beverages holding my arm at a certain angle or incline my head for small talk. Over here, too many transactions are confined to the nuclear family. Hosting and guesting for those outside it can be highly improvisational. I have consequently endeavored to detail my own host/guest etiquette. Maybe it will overlap with your *Weltanschauung*.

How are sleeping arrangements determined?

Even a ninety-year-old's severe arthritis isn't sufficient reason for giving up your own room's creature comforts. When it comes to deciding who will be more comfortable, the answer is simple: you. Verbal etiquette specifies that the guest is pre-eminent ("Sleep as long as you like." "I'm giving you the crocheted quilt Aunt Heidi made because you deserve it.") The reality, tacitly accepted by any guest, is that he or she is a second-class citizen—absolutely unworthy of the largest towel, quietest room, or down. Guests will accept these measures uncomplainingly as long as none of them are verbalized.

I was the victim of a violation of the host as master just last week. Unhappy with her musty, flattened pillow, a remnant of my childhood bedding, my guest invaded my bedroom and snatched one of the four quality down pillows I like to be surrounded by while sleeping. Well reared in taboos of verbal expression regarding hospitality, I waited for her to go out to correct and chastise the offense by reclaiming my pillow and hiding her original. Upon returning, my guest lacked the courage to refer to her lapse in breeding, but in a small, chastened voice asked me what had happened to "my pillow." "The exterminator promised all those bedbugs had been taken care of," I answered in a sweet, concerned voice. "I thought I saw a couple of eggs on the pillow."

Are you responsible for your guests' meals?

A notorious filmmaker, who will remain unidentified, availed himself of my hospitality for several days. Around Happy Hour, he returned holding a twenty-five-cent individual bag of corn chips and a single beer. Looking pointedly at his meager booty I casually mentioned, "Wouldn't have minded a bit of that myself." "I'm Scottish," was his laconic explanation, before taking the spoils into his bedroom and consuming them alone.

I did not want to indulge in an offensive complaint to my guest a second time; even if, that very morning, he'd indulged in a kingly breakfast of my provisions. But I feared that the rank odor of his frying four pieces of bacon was in danger of encouraging my eviction.

The next morning, I bought a Kryptonite lock and a thick length of steel chain, fastening them tightly around the girth of the refrigerator. He returned that evening with an unrefrigerated six-pack, probably hoping to make up for his previous infraction, and immediately realized he'd be drinking warm beer that evening. It was easy to explain away the chain & lock by mentioning that in-home robberies had sharply risen.

Are there any polite measures you can take if your guest disturbs you by rising too early?

A couple from my hometown have an eighteen-year-old son, Bobby, coming to the city for college. Would I be kind enough to put him up for a mere two months? Having seen him only as a toddler, I was startled by Bobby's lithe figure and sculpted features. Each morning at 6 a.m., he caused a racket in the bathroom. I uncomplainingly and graciously bided my time until the weekend, when there'd be no reason for him to rise that early. Bobby countered with the remark that habit would likely dictate it be the same.

Claiming a chronic ailment that required an inordinate amount of bed time, I suggested we "put our heads together" for the problem. Unversed as he was in non-familial social experiences, I brought him easily to a solution: on weekends he could share my bed for an intimate view of exactly when I woke up and wait until then to start his morning ablutions.

I think I neglected to tell him that I do not own pajamas.

A Hero

THE NEIGHBOR ABOVE my San Francisco apartment was a monster. I could hear him through the floor boards reducing his ashen, submissive wife to tears or doling out "tough love" to his ten-year-old son. When I played music above a whisper, his broom handle inevitably began its military rat-a-tat-tat on the floor. Everybody in the building detested him. His calls for law and order at block meetings and his Republican car stickers made us think we'd found our own personal Mussolini.

Then came the big fire that reduced the top floor to charcoal. As all of us stood trembling on the street, our detested neighbor defied the firemen and bounded up five flights. He rescued two kittens and a Chihuahua. The tyrant had become a hero.

On September 12, a day after the attack on the World Trade Center, I turned on the television and saw a face I no longer recognized. In all honesty, it took me over sixty seconds to identify it as the face of Rudolph Giuliani. Gone, at least temporarily, were the undertaker's rictus, pursed lips, and flinty eyes. In their place was a pale, benevolent face cleansed by fear. It reminded me a little of those saint's faces in early Renaissance paintings, which are smooth and clear as shields.

The face might have been caused by the fact that Giuliani had been crying in the last forty-eight hours, or working tirelessly to set up offices at the Armory and coordinate police and rescue work. Or maybe this really was the face of a man who had discovered a new compassion and openness. Over the weeks that followed, some of my most hard-liner anti-Giuliani friends would begin to hem and haw. Maybe the guy who'd reduced welfare benefits, sold off the hospitals, suburbanized Times Square, and gotten lax on police brutality wasn't so bad after all.

The only other time I'd seen the mayor's face so transformed by an event was when he was diagnosed with prostate cancer in mid-2000. This was soon after he'd released the sealed juvenile records of Patrick Dorismond, a Black man who'd been shot and killed by New York undercover officers and whose murder was being protested by the Black community. Giuliani had had the records dug up to prove that Dorismond was "no altar boy," as he put it. In the midst of radiation treatment and an impending divorce, the mayor sheepishly apologized to Dorismond's mother for his rash statements, going so far as to say, "When you're faced with your own mortality… some things happen to you… I find myself feeling a tremendous amount of compassion and feeling for people who are in the kind of situation that I'm in." But Rudy, unlike Dorismond, wasn't dead.

I've written three books about New York's underclass. At readings and panels, there was often a certain kind of person who'd start heckling me. In a rage, he'd demand to know why I, an educated, middle-class person, wrote about the urban poor. I had to be either romanticizing them or exploiting them, he'd say. Curiously, these objectors were inevitably from working-class backgrounds. They'd struggled to better their situation, and they were phobic about anything to do with the class beneath the one they'd come from—the underclass—which could have ended up swallowing them forever. They were angry and defensive about those who, unlike them, hadn't managed to pull themselves out of the muck.

According to biographer Wayne Barrett, Giuliani's father was a thug who made his living partly by working as a violent "muscle" for a debt collector. In 1934, when Giuliani's father and another man were arrested for holding up a milkman at gunpoint, the father was sentenced to five years at Sing Sing. Until this was revealed, no one had ever mentioned Giuliani's father's criminal background. His only comment about his father had been that he was a janitor and Brooklyn barkeep and that he'd instilled in him a reverence for hard work.

Giuliani, then, is one of these self-made miracles. In his past are threatening memories of violence and corruption. I'd imagine he's done everything he could to push them away. This may be at the root of his stunning and vigorous opposition to crime. He has even accomplished the impossible: getting the mob out of the Fulton Fish Market and the San Gennaro Street fair.

It's natural, isn't it? A man whose father may have disillusioned him by his own corruption would either be corrupt himself or want to fight bad behavior with an obsessive thoroughness. Perhaps this impulse provided the rigor Giuliani needed for his campaign against quality-of-life crimes. His theory was that getting people for small offences would round them up, or demoralize them enough, to keep them from committing large ones. And it worked. In the mid-1990s, New York saw an unprecedented decrease in violent crimes. It also saw an increase of 135 percent in complaints against the police for illegal searches.

However, although he never said as much, Giuliani's quality-of-life campaign wasn't just an effort to get rid of crime. It was also an imposition of an aesthetic, an effort to rid Manhattan of its distressing, embarrassing underclass. Squeegee workers—those people who forced you to let them clean your windshield—weren't dangerous. But they were some of the first to go. The vendors of *Street News*, a paper about the homeless, also got driven out of business. Rudy sent them on their way with a kind of Marie-Antoinette-Nancy-Reagan-style advice: just "go and get a regular job." Work is ennobling, he preached, without much attention to their mental health profiles or shelter addresses. Rudy just couldn't stand the sight of them. Perhaps they were too reminiscent of the past.

Low-income people haven't been the only ones affected by Giuliani's "Lysol" mentality. During the Brooklyn Museum controversy and the renovation of Times Square, culture mavens and porn enthusiasts saw their lives radically changed. However, in both instances, Giuliani, I think, was less concerned about indecency than he was about marginal identities, which stimulated his phobias about the culture of poverty and the disenfranchised. When Black British artist Chris Ofili's Madonna portrait was exhibited at the Brooklyn Museum, Giuliani illegally tried to strip the institution of hundreds of thousands in funding. He objected to the use of elephant dung and vaginas torn from porn magazines to portray the Virgin as an African fertility figure. However, few discussed the cultural bias in his condemnation. No one seemed to ask any ethnic Africans what they thought of the ancient connection between the Madonna and the fertility goddesses. Giuliani wasn't defending religion, or he would have looked more carefully at the religion of other ethnicities. He was more worried about those minority viewpoints that interfered with the decent, middle-class mentality to which he, as a working-class boy, had always aspired.

Likewise, the closing of many of Times Square's porn shops wasn't just the end of dirty old men and low-income real estate, it was the removal of the threatening Other. Thousands of go-go dancers, homeboys, South Bronx video game players, hustlers, trans people, and street bums who'd frequented the area for decades had to clear out. No attempt was made to offer them some alternative activities in the area, because such people can't exist in Giuliani's landscape. A different class of "decent" people moved in. Morality, economics, and cultural bias were eternally and inextricably entangled in the mayor's maneuvers. And he moved nimbly from one to the other.

From the beginning of his tenure as mayor, Giuliani has known only one mode of behavior: red alert. Whether it was something as simple as squeegee workers or as serious as the welfare budget, he attacked the problem like a commando. His handling of crime, the economy, and "decency" issues have been quick, sure, and impatient. It's no surprise that such a personality was of invaluable service to us during the days after the World Trade Center attack, because he's always conducted himself as if he were at war. But did we need a Green Beret mayor full time?

Was the mayor tough when it came to terrorism? You bet. Way back in 1997, he lambasted the Immigration and Naturalization Service for letting alleged bomb-maker Gazi Ibrahim Abu Mezer apply for asylum in April 1997. A few months later, Mezer and another man were captured during a raid on their Park Slope apartment, just hours away from pulling off a suicide bombing at a New York subway station. In 1998, when Clinton began bombing alleged terrorist sites in Afghanistan and the Sudan, Rudy and police commissioner Howard Safir had the city on high-alert.

Nevertheless, there may be a fine line between a strong stand against terrorism and a dangerous jingoism. Rudy's response to the Arab world seems more connected to a fetish for law and order—perhaps in reaction to his father's lawlessness—than to any deep interest in the Islamic terrorist controversy. In 1995, he went so far as to boot Arafat from a concert at Lincoln Center that was a celebration of the U.N.'s 50th anniversary. Was this a political statement or a performance?

As a mayor, Rudy's involvement in international issues sometimes seems a little out of place, almost compulsive. Perhaps his most quixotic and inflammatory outbursts happened when he decided to visit Israel in

1996 to show his support for the country after a bus suicide bombing. After a ride on the bus line that had been bombed, he was confronted by a Long Island Jewish couple, Ibrahim and Hanadi Younan, whose relative had died in a March 3 bombing. When the couple told him that they were upset because he talked more about fighting than promoting peace, he impudently accused them of "making speeches."

Rudy's Arafat baiting should not be confused, however, with any special consideration for the problems of Jews. In 1995, he warmly welcomed Irene Pivetti, the speaker of Italy's Chamber of Deputies, who had praised Mussolini's actions and suggested the Jews were persecuted over the centuries because they were just too involved in their "identity as a racial, religious, and cultural minority." I wasn't at all surprised by Rudy's warm welcome to Pivetti. I know that he's a deeply emotional man, not a man with consistent ideas. How could he resist Pivetti's fascist sensibility, since Fascism is an attempt to eliminate the abject feelings produced in us by the disenfranchised? Pivetti must have appealed to Rudy a great deal.

Obviously, it's important for all of us to understand our reactions to Giuliani as he waves goodbye. And those of us who are literate, educated, and liberal may even have been seduced by him. When it comes to issues that don't involve class or needy minorities, such as abortion or gays, he's proven himself a friend of the Left. He's supported both the right to choose and gay rights. This doesn't, however, eliminate the fact that Giuliani has exorcised his own ambivalence about poverty, crime, and the disenfranchised by turning it into a fairy tale fight between Good and Evil. Issues of class and ethnicity are his bugaboo. He's built a false morality out of them. Like the Taliban, and like my San Francisco neighbor, he's quite sure of his values and ideas. He thinks he knows who the enemy is. And this indeed made him a resolute actor, even a hero, during an immediate crisis—the World Trade Center attack.

Yet over the long haul his sense of justice has been deeply limited by his emotions; his perception of the Other is stunted.

An Anarchiste de droite

J.-K. HUYSMANS, AUTHOR of the book that started the Decadent movement in France near the end of the nineteenth century, claimed to reject the intellectual tyranny that was a legacy of the Age of Reason and to hate parliamentary democracy, which he saw as no more than easily influenceable mob rule. He was in favor of a deeper aesthetic and a more radical metaphysical search. He saw right through the artifices of perspective in painting, so lauded as an earmark of the Renaissance's new "realism," and preferred the flat perspectives of Asian and medieval painting.

I'd go so far as to say that he believed culture had begun a downhill course at the end of the Middle Ages, which were a last period of profound spirituality with a visceral connection to the elemental currents of human existence. He preferred the late-Age Latin poets to the celebrated Classical ones, scoffed at the artificial fantasies of a return to nature promoted by the Romantics, hated the conforming qualities of cosmopolitism (the equivalent of today's global capitalist culture) and yearned for the lost pageantry of hierarchy.

As far as he was concerned, industrialism, popular culture, modern technology, economic liberalism, and anything else that separated Man from his fundamental nature as a soul in agony were all specious. But most interesting of all, he was in a way the first Walt Disney, the first master of "CGI effects" in literature. Having trained under Zola as a Naturalist, he'd developed the linguistic skills to describe anything in "living color"—in sensory detail à la Dickens. Why, he thought, shouldn't the same full-color techniques, the same illusory concoctions meant to trick people into thinking they are witnessing real life, or documentary, be used to bring alive scenes in which, for example, the most masochistic Catholic saint drowned in deluges of pus flowing from her abdomen, or the medieval monster in search of alchemy, Gilles de Rais, disemboweled kidnapped children (he describes this in his Satanic novel, *Là-bas,* which means "Down There," as in Hell)?

Zola and Dickens developed expertise in depicting the *abject* in three dimensions, hoping to use it as a kind of socialist tool to complain about current economic conditions and poverty. Huysmans ran off with the same linguistic skills and used them to describe religious visions, Christ on the cross, or hellish hallucinations. In a weird way, he invented Hollywood. He's part of an entire group of artists of that period who also contributed to the high-jacking of naturalist description as a transporting experience, a vehicle for fantasy. Just, for example, listen to Ravel, and you'll realize immediately that he could have been writing music to accompany movies if he had lived in a more recent era.

The re-routing of naturalistic techniques in all the disciplines of the time are at the basis of all the "entertainment" that makes up the phenomenon that Debord tried to sum up as "the Spectacle." Advertising, the evening news, and movies are merely this corruption of Zola's and Dickens' original attempts to serve up grimy reality for the purpose of reform. Little did they know they would be adopted to the service of entertainment.

A Closet Catholic

TIRED OF PLAYING my own confessor, I began to experiment with the mentality of Catholicism, wondering if its libidinal opportunities were any less curtailed than those of our Puritan heritage. In cultures where the Protestant mentality dominates, one never participates fully in one's own sins due to an emphasis on self-reliance, which comes down to carrying one's confessor on one's back, as if it were a stunted, judgmental Siamese twin, constantly interpreting, punishing, and curtailing each act at the very moment it is executed. Protestant values favor the questionable virtues of forthrightness and immediacy, which makes us confess to sins at the moment we commit them, rather than displacing confession into the future, where it is less likely to interfere with each moment's sensory possibilities and each moment's good manners. Inversely, Catholic cultures—and more particularly, their Latin incarnations—offer complicated loopholes for pleasure, stringent as their official prohibition of libido may be.

Finding Catholicism sexy, sensual, or even sensory today is very much at odds with the liberal definition of freedom of appetite. Catholicism has been identified as a principal villain in the war against birth control, promiscuity, homosexuality, and other aspects of sexual indulgence. However, such official policies only describe the surface, neglecting to admit the conditions of arousal that support good orgasms. In many cases, arousal depends upon those barriers set up to prevent or defame it. That's what made the Italian sex comedy films of the sixties and seventies so enticing.

Catholic sensibility makes it as plausible to indulge in sin as it is to denounce sin thoroughly during the moment of confession. This necessitates a complicated relationship between surface and depth. Rituals, images, forms of courtesy, fashions, furnishings, and other surface elements serve a social function by maintaining the status quo and leave one's inner life personal, original, inviolable, and quite different from what shows. The Catholic sensibility values politeness as well as a romantic sense of individualism. Its outer shell serves as a safe, acceptable screen for sensual projections and as a bulwark against the id-ridden turmoil trapped underneath.

Protestant sensibility, on the other hand, calls for an impeccable match between the surface and what's underneath. Any contradiction between the two levels is considered dishonest. Hence, the startling sight of a Dutch town at night with the parlor windows brightly lit and no curtains to conceal one from one's neighbors. And the equally startling image (at least to a Protestant) of a sumptuous villa owned by an Italian Communist devoted to a revolution of the working class.

Free-thinkers consider the northern European Protestant countries—Holland, Denmark, and Germany—to be models of sexual liberation, places where legal prostitution, homosexual rights, and early age of consent give the appearance of an evolved, even futuristic progressivism. Their liberal sex laws are based on a rational demystification of the sexual act and sexual desire. According to this pragmatic ideology, all that is to be feared from the sex act are those aspects that can be quantified—venereal disease, incidences of rape or bias. These problems are considered controllable by laws and public health policies, and one would think that such methods would create a sexual paradise; but whenever I visit these countries, I have the feeling that categorizing sex as an act that can be apprehended by reason becomes a kind of reductionism that isolates sex's primitive libidinal components and ends up as a kind of repression.

The submission of sexual desire to the rational are what sexual liberation or gender liberation movements, such as feminism and gay lib, offer. Consequently, such movements have generated much more interest in the United States, England, and the Germanic countries, where Protestant sensibility dominates, than they have in the Catholic countries. In France, despite essential ideals of democracy and equality, the mysticism of desire, its rituals and obfuscations, are of utmost importance. French arousal depends traditionally upon the romanticized or the abject. In my hundreds of visits to French saunas, parks, bedrooms, or pissoirs in the seventies and eighties, I observed French eroticism gathered at two intense sexual poles, with very little continuum in between. These were (1) the tender and the precious, full of caresses and endearments, and (2) the brutal and macho, full of conquest and contempt. In France, I found none of the intermediary athleticism of American sex, the endless round of soiling and clean-up I experienced in German sex, or the arch class-aware sex I experienced with the British.

Several years ago, I was hired by the French magazine *Actuel* to write a long article on the sexual underground of San Francisco. For the part on the new female bisexual community, I described a woman-run sex shop, specializing in dildoes and vibrators. It had been described to me as a bastion of liberated feminist sexuality, a pornographic space that had managed to escape both the exploitation of the sex industry and the guilt-ridden judgments of Puritanism. In fact, I experienced the place as sex subject to rationality and to public health measures. Instead of the harsh lights, packaged porno, and sullen male clerks characteristic of the traditional American sex shop, I found a clean, airy, but far from erotic, atmosphere—a cross between a conservative lingerie shop and a progressive birth control clinic. The saleswomen seemed cool and intellectual and were devoted to public information. With great efficiency, they patiently explained the features of each sex device to mostly female but some male clients who had come to be fitted for a dildo, harness, or vibrator. There was a forbidding plethora of bondage toys and erotic books and videos as well, but they seemed strangely out of place without the venal smell of cheap disinfectant or raincoated men lurking in corners. In fact, despite the bright lights and open technical talk, there was a clinical tenseness that bordered on the grim in Good Vibrations' attempts to take the subversion and inequality out of sex.

This store was in strange contrast to another liberated space for dealing with sex that I visited in Paris. I had come to this city in 1995 at the invitation of a publicist when my novel was published in French. I was to be filmed visiting a swingers club called Chez Denise with a talk show host known for his decadent forays into the seamy side of Parisian night life. Chez Denise was essentially a disco, but it had private rooms where one could have sex and swap mates as well as women who worked for the establishment by wandering across the dance floor, masturbating some of the men through open zippers.

What startled me about Chez Denise were the relaxed grins on everyone's faces; it felt more like being at an office Christmas party than at an X-rated sex club. Chez Denise was a discreet bourgeois hangout, but this does not mean that it was also tense or furtive. Indeed, Denise herself, pouring me a glass of Veuve Clicquot, described the atmosphere of her club as "la fête."

I consider Denise's cheerful leers another example of the Catholic capacity to suspend judgment during the duration of the pleasure experience, regardless of how it might have to be judged later. Her establishment was in strict contrast to the Times Square places I was used to, where sexual transgression was acted out as sordid and even morbid. However, Denise's atmosphere of bourgeois frivolity ended at her doorstep. When the video of me and my talk show host dancing with sex workers was shown for an informal grouping of my publishers' employees, faces clotted with chagrin, and the Catholic recrimination about loose morals took over. Everyone was embarrassed for me. In the Catholic tradition of displacement, visiting the club had been a light-hearted celebration, but viewing what I had done with others later was a dreary inquisition.

This illuminated another cultural aspect of the charm of Denise's club for *les partouzes* (swingers): the Catholic genius for compartmentalization. Because of the changing significations of sex in the Catholic mind, it can easily adapt to a variety of social spheres, including business. Nonchalance about the connection of business and sex was more visible before the Americanization of Europe, when bordellos dotted every major French city. Paradoxically, these pre-war "maisons de tolérance" helped maintain the conservatism of France's Catholic cultural institutions by the mechanism of compartmentalization. They kept promiscuity away from the family circle and other legitimate social spheres and subjected it to legal and political sanctions. This wasn't, however, like the current Dutch organization of sex in the public sphere, which concerns itself with making sex healthy, publicly surveyed, and demystified. French bordellos were thought of as maison closes, conveniently hiding perversity and unsanctioned behavior. Such a situation made the maison close an authentic underground experience in which individual experimentation—and imagination—as a result, played a large part. One proof of this is the large body of literature dealing with the world of the maisons closes and their prostitutes. The over-illuminated world of the Dutch sex industry, on the other hand, has rarely led to works of the imagination.

L'Etoile Bleue, a bordello in the old part of Tours, isn't, of course, what it used to be. Its ground floor dance hall, behind which soldiers, farmers, or the bourgeois once picked their girls through a one-way mirror, now houses the Junior Chamber of Commerce. And the apartments on the floors above, which I visited about eight years ago, were rented to two respectable young women, a hard-working single mother and a professional singer. Like every maison close in France, this place went out of business in 1946 when a new law closed all the cathouses. It forced the prostitutes who lived full-time in them—with miserable salaries and under the watchful eye of the police—into the streets. The closing of the bordellos, spear-headed by social reformer Marthe Richard was, in part, a symbolic gesture, for during the Occupation these establishments had been pressed into service to the Germans and had become associated with the taint of collaboration.

Inside and outside L'Etoile Bleue, architecture and memories persist. Each business day, the Junior Chamber of Commerce's secretary nonchalantly types her communications under an erotic fresco, painted during the bordello's prime years in the late 1930s. It shows a farm girl with hoisted skirt, pressed against a wine vat, about to be mounted from the rear. In the apartment above, the single mother told me she sometimes envisions her normal-looking laundry room the way it used to be, when it served as a jail cell for misbehaving prostitutes; once she came home rather late, and as she opened the building door, an aged local standing in the street, who remembered the old days, jibed, "Bonjour, salope ("Hello, slut")."

Jean-Paul Veyssière, Tours's rare book purveyor, was born next door to L'Etoile Bleue just three years after its closing. He and his childhood friends got their sex education playing inside the building in front of erotic murals or leafing through the pornographic photos still left in some of the rooms. When a puritanical mayor tried to bulldoze the building, Veyssière and three others dug up ex-prostitutes, former clients, and even the son of the laundry man, who offered a historical account of being pressed into the standard client's delousing before he was allowed to climb the stairs to deliver clean sheets. Veyssière and his preservationist colleagues organized a petition among locals that literally stopped the bulldozer at the door.

Today the building stands intact, its art-moderne-inspired facade of red and blue mosaic looking garish and disjointedly mystical on the rue du Champ de Mars. Some of the tension between the kitsch and the occult throughout this building comes from the repeated five-point-star motif on the doorway, on the iron banister and elsewhere, suggesting hidden or forbidden codes. Though clientele and prostitutes have been banished, evocations of past functions remain: the vivid blue and red doorway has a pentagonal peephole covered by a grill, through which the management could scrutinize prospective clients. Inside, the vaguely chic ballroom with its golden-and-beige mosaic floor rests undisturbed beneath the clumsy star-shaped chandelier. Its walls feature a stylish mural of a twentieth-century naked Diana cavorting ambiguously with her hounds as well as an X-rated fresco of nymphs and satyrs. All of this pink festivity is undercut by the one-way mirror offering a view of this room from the smaller room behind it. Forethought and salesmanship were actually essential to the seemingly abandoned pleasures of this building. Secret surveillance always cast its calculating glance on the naughty pink, blue, and red decor of this palace of love.

In the Catholic model, the same sex act is good at one moment and bad at another. Contrarily, the attempt to control sex over time, so that it always has the same value, as in the liberated Protestant model, can reach absurd and ironic proportions. Often such control accomplishes the opposite of what it sets out to do. This is illustrated by the comparison of two sex-obsessed writers from different cultures: French novelist Pierre Guyotat, who writes within a Catholic context, and American feminist essayist Andrea Dworkin, who writes within the context of Puritan America.

Pierre Guyotat has been called the last "poète maudit" in France, that country's last "accursed poet." He first came to prominence in France in 1967 with his novel *Tomb for 500,000 Soldiers*, a minimalist recant of lurid sexual and violent atrocities during the French Algerian War. His next book *Eden, Eden, Eden*, made up of endless, uninterrupted descriptions of sexual brutalities, some involving children, was censored by the French government for eleven years. A later book, *Prostitution*, is a homosexual collage of Arabic, French, German, and Black "deviant language," or, to use one of the author's terms, a "linguistic minority." All the elements have been welded by elliptical spellings and phonetic distortions into a flow of glutinous consistency. They contain triple and even quadruple puns on often obscene words.

Guyotat sees his books not as sexual but as political and writerly. His texts are a flaunting of sex as power in the voices of the powerless. And rather than a prudent levitation of the indicated minorities to a respectability they are assumed to deserve, as would happen in a Protestant-inspired text, the literate writer is mercilessly sacrificed to their appetites. However, complete license in Guyotat works to deaden sexual excitation. In this sense, his texts are moral, an attempt to drive home the point of the dulled inhumanity inherent in monotonous sexual exploitation by making the reader actually experience it.

Andrea Dworkin claims to accomplish what Guyotat really does. Her book *Pornography: Men Possessing Women* is a dense and feminist political tract on pornography as power that strangely complements Guyotat's texts. Part of her writing, like Guyotat's, is an endless drone of repetitive sexuality, which she says is calculated to arouse our disgust and stimulate our understanding of all pornography as oppressive to women. Her book is also a minimalist text, constructed from only two major devices that follow each other repeatedly. Device 1 recounts the plots of pornographic books and films in lurid detail or gives detailed staccato descriptions of pornographic photography. Device 2 provides an exhaustive, narrow political analysis of the pornographic description coming before, using the same monotonous, relentless style that was used to recount the pornography. In another culture, the obsessive rhythms of this text, in which the material being attacked and the attack itself are spit out with the same driving beat, would cause the book to be looked upon as a monumentally perverse achievement, such as that of Guyotat's texts, which are both an indictment and a celebration of sexual repetition. But whereas Guyotat's texts may be cathartic, Dworkin's are constructed like aversion therapy. One is aroused by the detailed pornography, then brutally sermonized into numbness about its evils. Just below the simple wavelike pattern of the text, one feels a frantic, repetitive affirmation in the very denial of those unspeakable acts the author feels compelled to contemplate. The book numbs like highly charged pornography—repetitive, ceaseless fantasies and memories of abuse playing at suicidal volume.

Dworkin's and Guyotat's texts are typically Western in that they depend upon the tension between pleasure's affirmation and a disgust about pleasure. This simple dichotomy between sex and guilt about sex may not exist in the East. A two-month stay in Japan in the late seventies led me to review Ruth Benedict's *The Chrysanthemum and the Sword*, which is a sociological survey and analysis of the basic components of traditional Japanese culture. Her book makes a distinction between shame, which is fear of others' reprobation for an act; and guilt, which is an internalized sense of wrong-doing. Shame is superego: a feeling of what one's parents, leaders, or communities might think or do if they knew. Guilt is more deeply internalized superego, a feeling of wrong-doing even when one is alone and without reference to outsiders.

Benedict felt that the Japanese have shame but not guilt, and my sexual experiences seemed to confirm her hypothesis. Well-bred

Japanese young men whom I cruised in subways or on the street colored with embarrassment as they gave in to their attraction and finally made contact. One would have thought they were wracked with guilt about sex or about homosexuality. But once we were inside with the screens drawn, many displayed an easy sexual openness that contrasted with their public behavior in a way that would have classified them as schizophrenic to the uncomprehending Westerner. Never in my life have I seen such unfettered appetite, such relaxed orality. Libidinal controls in Japan were public only. They had to do with behaving inappropriately and losing face. But they were not internalized restraints, like those of Judeo-Christian guilt.

A word remains to be said about the relationship between sex and art. Although sexual energy may be a component of art, art cannot participate fully in committed eroticism. Art can be arousing, but beyond a certain point it acts to impede the transporting process of sex away from self-consciousness. Attempts to aestheticize pornography almost always interfere with the animalistic build-up of eroticism. Again, this is not to say that some art can't be sexy but only to say that "artistic sex" is inhibited sex. The Protestant mentality of self-consciousness and self-confession concerning the libidinal act is proof, in my opinion, that one can't think about anything else but pleasure while pleasure is happening. One can instead, and perhaps should, portray and analyze the act later, at the writing table or in the confessional.

Perhaps, again, a Catholic model for the equation between sex and art is what's needed. In fact, the exaggerated sensual imagery of some good Catholic writing, such as J.-K. Huysmans hagiography, *Saint Lydwine of Schiedam*, has the same annihilating drive as good pornography. So overwhelmed is the reader by the fantastic visions (or were they hallucinations?) of this early fifteenth century Dutch Saint as described by Huysmans, so fatal and perverse are her illnesses and sufferings, that the most cynical nonbeliever is carried away in a sensory torrent that suspends thought in favor of fantasy.

If trade-offs are necessary, I am, then, in favor of the Catholic model. This harkens back to the old European idea of specialization and service. Forsaking American self-reliance, I'm calling for the establishment of professional services that displace one's activities in time and space: going to a hairdresser to do one's hair, a restaurant for one's meals, a sex worker for one's conjugal problems, and a confessor to hear one's sins. Why should we assume we must take care of everything ourselves? To this old-fashioned idea of service, I append a more contemporary attitude that is currently sweeping though our culture. And that is the idea of credit. Why pay for any enjoyment at the time of its partaking when we can always pay an albeit steeper price later?

Weird Trips

The Grandstander

THE SMART-ASS MEMBERS of a literary society who invited me to Kyoto were just what I'd expected through the bias of my age: guys too young to remember sitting on a GI's lap for a stick of gum but still well into the dotage of their forties, fifties, and sixties. They were the Japanese equivalent of our Baby Boomers, I suppose; but their fantasies about American literature reminded me of a strain of sad sack wannabes I knew in the New York literary world, still convinced that hard-drinking Beats and their punch-happy Abstract Expressionist buddies were the apotheosis of contemporary art. What's more, these Japanese lit freaks seemed completely unaware not only of more recent trends, like chick lit, minority literature or twenty-first-century minimalism, but even seemed not to know that the Swinging Sixties had actually happened; and my ignorance of their postwar cultural history kept me from deciding whether they'd experienced anything similar. Geezer that I was, I was still operating with the same playbook I'd been impressed by in my twenties: anthropologist Ruth Benedict's *The Chrysanthemum and the Sword*, penned in 1946 at the behest of the U.S. Office of War Information wanting to fortify their grip on the occupation of Japan, but stymied by what they termed "contradictions" in the so-called inscrutable Japanese mind. In her book, Benedict had claimed that these recent enemies were inhibited by an excess of shame while being completely free of Judeo-Christian guilt. A trip to Japan in the 1970s, where I fucked my way through the bars of Kyoto, Kobe and Tokyo, had merely defended that thesis for me because I'd stumbled across a never-ending trail of male tail who were into Americans but more uptight than the worst of the WASP prudes I knew in the States. They could barely look me in the eye in clubs and bars. In fact, one bar in Kyoto was still operating under an ancient tradition of discretion. You had to accomplish your cruising with the bartender as intermediary by informing him of your interest in a lad, and—should he deem it appropriate—he would make everyone sitting around the bar change seats in order to put you next to your heart's desire. Shortly after, when clothes were shed and shades pulled, all the abashed companions I'd managed to lure back to my hotel room metamorphosed into red-blooded studs with unrestrained libidos, eager to spread the length of lean, silky thighs to offer my face the porcupine tickle of their coarse, shiny, straight-as-a-needle pubic hair. I'd even discovered proof of a bisexual propensity in some Japanese circles after spending an evening in Kyoto with an aging queen who invited me to a Yakuza bar in the hills, which was frequented by tattooed-back gangsters confident enough about their masculinity to keep from minding being blown by a homo for a few drinks or a couple bills, just like those many homeboys I'd sucked off in New York's old Times Square in exchange for buying diapers for a real or imaginary newborn. But I digress…

These Nipponese aficionados of American writing had chosen one of my stories for their anthology of "bohemian" literature. They were, apparently, not scandalized by descriptions of drug dealers, male hustlers, transsexual call girls, and other spirited Times Square lowlife. Even so, the fact that my text was abundant with street slang made me wonder whether they had actually realized the world I'd described was homocentric. Confusion was possible, since the story was a genderfuck banquet of shemales and straight rent boys who rather than their birth names bore such street tags as "Izod" or "Cosmetica" that didn't make clear what was hanging—or missing—between their legs. I would, however, describe the process of being published in Japanese as rather a blank experience mysteriously devoid of social signals. There was no way for me to decode the emotions behind the few words I'd received in a message bearing their society's letterhead, which—typographical errors and misspellings aside—read something like, "Respected Author, We admirers of the narration of Otherness requesting the honor to reprinting your masterful with title, 'Miss Wonderful Squeezing Apollo in Times Square.' We are Japanese who revere American Beats, which include of course strange tales of sexuality and think you continued in that awesome tradition." The letter already included a check, which should really be termed an honorarium: $50.

I hate to admit it, but that sum was enough to make me apathetic about whether the translator or any of my future Japanese readers had a clue as to what was going down. The gracious offer was signed, "Ishikawa Hiroshi, Translator from the American." It's true that he'd gotten the title wrong. The story was actually called "Miss Wonderful Puts the Squeeze on Apollo in Times Square." But, whatever. Even that certainly wasn't enough reason to turn down a round-trip ticket worth thousands that they offered me after the magazine came out. Poverty encourages an artist to abandon his standards. If they wanted "bohemian," I was planning on giving it to them.

I imagine the fact that my speech would be in English was what stoked my chipper willingness. I was going to push the "bohemian" envelope without any regard to tender sensibilities and have a ball acting out—as my seventh-grade teacher once termed it—the kind of thing that, if unpunished, always supplied me with kicks. The question of what kind of individual gets a kick out of saying shocking things to people who can't understand him may be perplexing. I suppose you'd have to be this narcissistic and think of yourself as your best audience to understand it. I might not go as far as Bukowski, who'd once drunkenly whipped it out right on French television, pissing all over the set of the program *Apostrophe*, but even so… Taste be damned.

A week later, their trembling, admirative translator met me in a bar to supply me with a copy of an earlier issue of their magazine in Japanese and confirmed his virtual absence of English. His conversation was limited to "very happy," "please," "cheers" and, curiously, "don't ask." Someone had obviously taught him that the last, imperative remark was a polite but convenient way to avoid saying anything that made him uncomfortable but had left him unaware that it was usually voiced with a look of comic irony. His "don't ask" was accompanied by a polite, content smile and nod, as if he were saying, "be glad to." Despite these impediments, he somehow managed to communicate his pedigree to me: he was the grandnephew of a Japanese scientist of the same surname who'd invented "the fishbone diagram."

One thing became clear: I was their token rump ranger. They may not have understood the class parameters sketched by my story, but they were definitely aware of its sexual orientation. As a matter of fact, they were expecting me to hold forth about "LGBT writing" in Kyoto, obviously having picked up the multicultural p.c. bug from some academic. The only other remarks my translator managed to stammer out during our drink together had something to do with his notion of literary theory, but this seemed to be as intelligible as those disturbingly empty English phrases I'd been startled to see on some teenage Japanese clothing: sweatshirts and book bags emblazoned with unsettling word combinations like "Precise Dwarf Bravery" or "Clock Over Here." Or one of my favorites:

"It is the event of ancient times. There was grandmother."

In my admirers' magazine, whose title my companion confidently translated as *American Hipster Going Down on Pavement*, contributors' names also appeared in English characters. I could therefore verify that this book-lovers' society had expertly mined the population of under-financed East Village writers in search of Bohemian styles. I recognized almost every name, which provided me all the more reason for distinguishing myself not only from such a list but from those literary fans I considered foolish enough to be interested in them—my upcoming audience, in other words. With this in mind, I vowed to make a spectacle of myself, a form of behavior I suspected these guys themselves definitely weren't capable of.

Two months later, my Japanese hosts, two affable middle-aged men who were members of the society, picked me up at the Kansai Airport in a brand-new Honda and presented me with a wrapped welcoming gift, which turned out to be a very tasteful Baccarat crystal ashtray. They did their best to chat with me during the ninety-minute trip to my lodgings in Kyoto.

Something I'd assumed I'd get was a large, Western-style hotel, the kind that had been so convenient decades ago in Tokyo, not only for its comfort and central location (back then all the street names on maps and signs were in Japanese characters, and the city was hard to navigate) but because ramrod-straight attendants in marvelously detailed bellboy drag would avert their eyes every time I swept past them with a trick half my age, at a frequency that eventually reached three times a day—one after lunch, one for cocktail hour and a sleepover. The rooms had been clean and quiet, welcoming save for the initial experience of lowering your ass to the toilet seat and feeling nothing under it, just a onetime shock produced by the discovery that most Japanese thrones are only three quarters as high as the American model. Either the book-lovers' society was on a severe budget, or they'd figured I'd prefer a more authentic dwelling, because our Honda pulled up to Reiko-San's guesthouse, a dirt-cheap hostel with tatami-mat floors and paper shoji screens for walls.

I'd experienced a similar sleeping environment during the long-ago trip on a budget. Knowingly, I shed my shoes at the entrance and promptly sought out Reiko-San, a plump, crabby old lady still wearing the worn *yukata* she must have slipped into that morning. Out of sheer necessity I dug through my brain for a term I'd learned in a Japanese phrase book so many moons ago to insist politely she upgrade me to a *koshitsu,* or "private room." Doubtlessly having had her fill of clueless Americans with loopy requests, Reiko-San defiantly led me to a large, yawningly empty room and irritably pointed downward at a tatami mat. That would be my *koshitsu,* I divined—my very own tatami mat in a room that could sleep fifty.

After unpacking and re-admiring my new crystal ashtray, which I set on a table under a *No Smoking* sign I imagined hadn't been there or anywhere else the year of my last visit, I grabbed my GPS and went on foot to check out Ryoan-ji Temple, which I was hoping hadn't changed in any significant way. Not that I expected a Zen temple dating to 1450 to be Disney-renovated like New York's South Street Seaport. Dorothy, this wasn't Kansas anymore. Indeed, its bewildering yet fascinating garden of fifteen rocks on raked whorls of polished river pebbles had remained perfectly intact, designed so that no matter what angle you viewed this garden from, one rock (which one it was changed) always disappeared. From the moment I'd glimpsed it, I'd decided it was a perfect model of the human psyche, which I conceive as a perversely engineered rubber blob rather than as any kind of fixed classical geometrical structure. In all my human relations, I might become convinced I'd learned to know one protrusion currently offering itself to the outside world; but every time I reached out to it with the anticipation of ending the loneliness, my touch seemed enough to make that bulge disappear. It would dive inward toward its invisible, inaccessible and probably shifting center to give rise to various other salient features I could have sworn either weren't there or had not been noticed before.

In my experience, such are the results of attempting to understand another brain, or at least they describe every love relationship in which I've become embroiled. It would take time to realize how well the Japanese deal with such metamorphoses of the ectoplasm known as the human psyche until I began to divine that the still surface of their faces could only be a kind of frankness acknowledging the impossibility of communicating the infinite amebic mutations of truth and emotion.

But how I do go on. There were new creatures thronging the sidewalks of Kyoto, making it look like the population had quadrupled. It took me awhile to realize that most of these pedestrians, the majority with compressed lips I interpreted as sour moods, were tourists from China. Few seemed pleased about being here. I may have misinterpreted their discreet expressions, but at least they were decorously silent, which can't be said of their fellow Germans, French, or Americans, who were letting it all hang out right there on the street or in public transportation, filling the air with lackluster cacophony—every one of them boobs—convinced as they were that no one else understood their language. Jetlag set in as I returned to Reiko-San's on a crowded bus held captive by the dialogue of an American couple separated by four rows of seats and loudly discussing rectal-fissure surgery, which the husband found absolutely unnecessary and the wife thought urgently essential as soon as they got back to the States. This soundtrack reduced gracious old Kyoto sliding by through my window to a kind of blue-screen effect.

It was already time for bed at Reiko-San's, forcing me to zigzag my way among several dozen prone bodies and precariously straddle others until I reached my inviolate tatami mat, now sporting a decent-looking futon and fluffy *kakebuton* (quilt). Lying there on my back I could divine other sensory phenomena, such as hiking-boot-marinated feet, stale trail mix, unpacked soiled laundry and… well, what exactly was that furry smell that made me think of sex?

The very next evening, the eternally re-twisted balloon sculpture called human experience pushed out a new bulge, daring me to grab it. A breathtakingly gorgeous college-age kid in leather pants, who introduced himself in decent English and signaled me to climb onto the back of his *Blade Runner*-style Suzuki motorcycle, drove me to the event at which I was to give my talk. Was this perhaps another gift like the Baccarat crystal ashtray? I knew it wasn't. Just the burdened son of a bossy literature enthusiast who'd given his kid orders to pick me up.

I was only going to be here for four days, and my first had already been eaten up by my trip from Kansai Airport, my tourist outing and jetlag. My last day in Kyoto was likely to be wasted up packing, the requisite farewells, and the long drive back to the airport, even though my return flight didn't leave until early evening. That left almost no time to explore Kyoto's bar scene or to see if any of my formerly purchased Yakuza paramours (or, more likely, their sons) still had their lair in the hills. As far as getting my jollies in, this ride was probably the only possible opportunity; so I encircled the slender waist of the body straddled in front of me a bit too tightly and surreptitiously buried my nose in the wind-swept Beatle-cut hair. As we sped through the streets, something between my legs the boy could probably feel began to stir, but I was banking on him being too polite and embarrassed to make any reference to it. I did, however, add a note to my mental task list: "Find out if the #me-too movement has reached Japan."

I thanked my handsome transporter as he dropped me at an enormous building with skewed concrete panels that made it look like a ripped-apart cubist version of Brutalist architecture—the Kyoto International Conference Center—and he sped away from me without a glance. The man at the desk directed me to one of what turned out to be hundreds of meeting rooms, where I was treated to my first sight of my audience, something that rudely filled me with an unanticipated feeling of respect, which quickly mutated to fear. Many were gathered around a refreshment table, elegantly draped with red velvet cloth and holding a row of gleaming bottles of Suntory whiskey. Behind these was a generous array of tempting finger food—nori-maki rolls with center bouquets I later found out featured shitake mushrooms, generous skewers of chicken yakitori with scallions and a regal arrangement of lacquered boxes with rice balls of various hues, probably accomplished by the addition of cod roe, seaweed flakes, red Shiso leaf powder or other colorful spices or tiny bits. There were even some versions of Indonesian satay lamb, pork and beef.

I had, in fact, forgotten to eat that entire day, but I barely had time to fill a plate before I was hit by the shock of a closer view of my audience. There were probably more than two hundred male guests milling about. Their appearances were more than enough to finish pricking the bubble of my former scornful huffiness. The Swiftian satirical superiority I'd previously relished was eclipsed and suddenly seemed deplorably racist and ungenerous. It wasn't the sheer number of book lovers but their sartorial style—a careful and imaginative homage to Western literary prestige, I suddenly realized. In my stained sneakers, ripped jeans and baggy T-shirt I shamefully took in a man with handsome features and a trim figure wearing a velvet waistcoat and loosely knotted satin butterfly tie, *au Baudelaire*. Another sported the heavy tweeds of the Bloomsbury Group, and a third an oversized flowing shirt and lengthy chiffon scarf, clearly referencing the *style négligé* of the old Latin Quarter. That's when I also noticed there was indeed at least one woman present. Whether her black wool cape, three-cornered felt hat, and enameled brooch were referenced to an adulterous Anaïs Nin or spinsterish Marianne Moore was hard to say, but what I'd been hiding from myself was becoming obvious. My callous attitude had been mostly a defense to mask the stage fright I've always battled on occasions of public presentations.

Suddenly I no longer wanted to "pull a Bukowski" and pelt these disciples of the written word with slang-ridden jibes of disdain or belittle their admiration as cultural naivety. They'd done their homework, so to speak, and had even shown the good taste of demurring from their own literary tradition to salute mine. What if some *did* speak good English, unlike my translator? Nauseating panic slithered through my belly and turned my attention back to the Suntory, which now seemed of much more importance than the food. It wasn't as if this would be the first time I'd taken a drink to smooth out my nerves before walking in front of a crowd. In fact, my custom had always been to slip into the lavatory for a few snorts from my flask just before I appeared at any lectern. Tragically, that flask to which I'm referring had been chucked into a TSA bin a day ago as I boarded my plane. The realization panicked me, and in the space of seconds I'd grabbed an unopened bottle of Suntory and hightailed it to the restroom—before a single book lover caught sight of me, I hoped.

If only I'd behaved like a human being and settled for a drink or two at most, standing at the table while I chatted in my most decorous version of a visiting author and sipping at a whiskey—neat. For one thing, it might have clued me in to their level of English proficiency. For another, it wouldn't have gotten me pie-eyed. But instead—in shame and with cowardice—I tremblingly stood inside a locked toilet stall chugging at the bottle of expensive booze.

Luckily, the broken voice of my translator croaking out my name curtailed my progress toward alcohol poisoning. Balancing the Suntory bottle on the toilet seat (I certainly wasn't going to put it on the floor and have him catch a glimpse of it.), I came out of the stall miming the zipping of my fly while he offered a tiny, nervous bow. "Ah, Bruce Mr.! Looking at all the places for you. Thinking of he not here!" After a pause he judiciously added, "Don't ask, please," and formed his customary smile.

My sheer act of will suppressed the swimming vertigo in my brain and let me produce a casual smile. "Think I wasn't coming, huh?" I don't think he understood my tepid jibe or perhaps found it too embarrassing to acknowledge. "You are coming," he merely urged, pushing open the door of the lavatory and pointing empathically outward.

My audience, silently seated in rows of folding chairs that seemed to go on to infinity, crushed me like a single anvil. From the lectern, I peered out into the sea of expressionless faces that looked identical— until deep shame at such a clichéd impression in an Asian country drew a veil aside and showed their many particularities. The truth was, I couldn't decide whether their features were displaying timid respect or patient boredom. Certainly no one was smiling. The cues I usually depended upon when speaking were probably going to be absent from this talk. I wouldn't be able to pause after I noticed one of my lines producing the shadow of a smile and then to try to goad it into laughter; or sweep into a climactic tone if a change in their breathing patterns signaled excitement and intense absorption. Instead I'd be afloat in a mirror sea with no signifiers, having to navigate without the slightest clue as to which way the wind was blowing.

The liquor had produced a comforting blur. Inappropriate as it seemed, since I now had no opportunity for on-the-fly rhetorical strategies, I was left with the old discourse I'd imagined before I started feeling chastened and foolish for thinking that way. It would be like reciting a speech from the past to which I no longer had any relation, but there was still a good chance nobody would realize they were watching a Charlie McCarthy rendition. In certain high-anxiety situations, you always think things make more of a difference than they do. I'd let myself be carried along by my old-drunken-comic-does-umpteenth-performance-of-tired-routine. Maybe nobody would realize that the puppet master controlling my lips was a genie in a bottle of Suntory sitting on a toilet seat in the men's room.

"To speak to you about LGBT writing, I'm going to have to talk about gay ass-fucking, my friends."

You could hear a pin drop. All I saw in my line of vision were dozens of unchanged masks. I had to take this as a go-ahead.

"Let me make one thing clear. You guys invited me here to tell you something about 'LGBT,' or 'gay,' literature. And what does that mean, exactly, seeing that—contrary to what some deluded gay activists are now claiming—the only thing gay now refers to is what you do with your dick and mouth and asshole. Otherwise, we guys who fuck asses and burp sperm eat the same foods you do, and our sphincters work the same as yours. We just know how to relax them when we want to."

There had to be a laugh. Or at least some reddening faces here and there. But there weren't. Even so, I made the false gesture of gazing out over the crowd with a prankster's twinkle in my eye.

"I know you'll disagree and point to the host of 'gay' magazines, films, books; but as the need for an aggressive radical gay politics decreased, it became all too clear that everything we thought we were was just our reaction to a disapproving society and the oppressed underground subculture we created to protect ourselves from it—I'm talking about the whole Oscar Wilde routine. The more gay rights were won, the more that limp-wristed shit dropped away, until someday, talking about gay culture will make no more sense than if we were talking about 'heterosexual' culture. Get what I'm saying?"

I didn't think they did.

"I know you've read the Beats and understand very well that you can't separate their artistic output from the substances they imbibed. May I remind you of the adage that you're only supposed to write about what you know? You don't have to explain to me that you straight dudes know bars because you go to them to get drunk or watch soccer on TV or sing karaoke and sometimes even to talk about books. But I should explain that the same wasn't true of us. We went mostly to get our asses worked over. Maybe you don't know that we even sucked cock right there in some bars. A good share of them had porn playing right up on the TV screen to heat up the action.

There are even still a few drinking holes where we whip each other or lick each other's boots."

No echo, which was giving me exactly what I'd bargained for. My irreverent words were disappearing immediately into the endless crush of still faces—like a stream rushing into an ocean you couldn't see. Prickles of paranoia sparked through me. Maybe they did understand what I was saying and were letting me speak into this funnel of emptiness just to teach me a lesson. Ironically, it was exactly how I'd concocted the experience beforehand in my mind. What had never occurred to me then was that I'd have no proof whether they didn't understand or whether it was the very opposite and the joke was on me. They certainly were polite enough for that kind of one-upmanship. I'd always felt pretty much the same way about all taciturn people. Was what kept them silent timidity and humility or anger and passive aggression— or both at the same time? I'd come to the conclusion that shy people fell on a kind of continuum and that for some, it was a double-edged sword. What torturous ambiguity. I'd never been comfortable or trusting faced with the case of too few words. Through the throbbing Suntory haze, the impenetrable faces hovered in the containment of their secrets.

"Although some of these places do still exist in a more vanilla version, the last hot gay bar in New York disappeared in the late 90s right after Mayor Giuliani announced he had prostate cancer. While he was peeing radioactive pellets, his Gestapo was closing all the good hustler bars and backrooms and take-it-off shows and chasing every decent transvestite hooker from Times Square. So what I tell you will have to be about something that mostly isn't around any more. What's left to write about when it comes to 'gay?' Not a fucking thing, boys. Sorry that you invited me to come 8,000 miles even though, for quite a while now, there hasn't been anything interesting to say about the endless throng of white faggots with gym bodies and shaved balls dancing on E to mindless house music. Consequently, to speak to you about gay

writing at all, I'm going to have return to the ghetto of the past; and since you've made the choice of inviting an ancient codger like me to hold forth, it'll be fairly easy."

I was flailing like a trout out of water in a no-fishing zone as I came to the meat of my discourse.

"You may be familiar with some of that classic dick-chasing literature from the fifties, intrepid book lovers. I'm sure you consider William Burroughs as one of your boys, but I hope you also know that he wrote early about the search for dick in his groundbreaking novel Queer. *Just a few years after that, John Rechy portrayed a hot, alienated hustler cruising the streets, bars and beds of Times Square and the rest of the country in* City of Night. *I think we're getting to a theory here. When cock sucking and ass fucking were illegal, writers who couldn't get enough dick put themselves through all kinds of risks and dangers in an underground culture that had its own rules. So what they wrote about was pretty inspired. Those were the days when gay bars could get raided. But when they didn't, they had good Mafia management that created a place where libido could run wild."*

Complimenting the Mafia? Surely, just that one word could accomplish the impossible—raising just a single eyebrow. I looked around with a specious expression of challenge.

"I said MAFIA. Well, all I'm saying is don't believe the hype, dudes. Don't buy the revisionist story claiming the spaces run by the Mob, like the infamous Stonewall, were oppressive places where sad homosexuals hid from police oppression and where Mafia bosses exploited their desperation. Any illegal bar run by the Sicilians always had the hottest, most inspiring atmosphere. I'm sure you agree that excitement, risk, and underground activity are what makes the best writing. The Mafia may have created a lot of heartache in our cities, but we owe them a debt for having created such good illicit bars at the basis of a lot of good American literature!"

Finally, I was on a roll.

"As for me, I probably wouldn't have written a decent word if I hadn't discovered Times Square and the hot Puerto Rican hustlers who came down from the South Bronx to frequent its mostly Mafia-owned bars. You see, the other ingredient of good literature is class 'penetration.' Pardon my double entendre. But if you sit on your ass

all day writing stories about infidelity at the local university, you'll end up like the poet of the American suburbs, John Updike. Updike wrote for retired insurance salesmen, biology professors, and alcoholic housewives. Oh shit…"

Had I awkwardly stepped on the toes of anybody who happened to be in those walks of life? That wasn't the kind of provocation I was trying for.

"I mean Updike was one of those tight-assed Americans who are part of our non-exportable 'folk' culture. The motherfucker actually thought he could uncover some poetry in suburban life. Can you imagine, Mary? (By the way, we real fags used to call everybody 'Mary.') Now where was I? I'm saying that those who write about encounters with other classes, other worlds have found the secret of exciting narratives. All the tensions of class encounter make for some fucking good prose. In fact, that's one element of noir, *if you think about it—a kind of nondangerous field trip into a lowdown subculture."*

I wasn't too drunk to realize from experience I was suddenly treading on thin ice. After having been invited to France a few years before to hold forth about *noir* literature, which is a genre a certain kind of French male can't get enough of, I'd put my foot in my mouth claiming that those who liked it were suffering from "homosexual panic" and needed to wallow in that threatening environment in which the protagonist is never married or in a stable relationship with a woman, all of whom are portrayed as treacherous castrators or blowsy former femmes fatales. It had to be related to insecurities about their dick size, I'd suggested. That last item was really something I shouldn't have added, because all the male-bonded fetishists of crime and betrayal—all those fans of Hammett, Chandler, or Thompson—began booing me off the stage. Tonight I forced myself to put the brakes on and changed the line of thought.

"Getting back to those fabulous Times Square bars, guys, the first and most famous I ever went to was called The Haymarket. Go ahead and write it down if you're some kind of scholar looking for gems of research about LBGT writing. I

doubt you'll ever hear it again from those jokers who claim to be specialists in the genre. The Haymarket was a sprawling former Blarney Stone on Eighth Avenue in Times Square with cheap drinks, a long-ass bar counter, booths you could sit in, and a big pool table. In those days, a lot of the hustlers were poor white kids. Since the minimum drinking was eighteen (rather than twenty-one) during those more enlightened days, there was some very young tail in there. The place was pulsing with testosterone and horny old men willing to spend the $20 on some teenage flesh. All around The Haymarket were a lot of rundown hotels that rented rooms by the hour.

"A typical hustler's day was like this: he yanks himself out of some trick's bed around six p.m. and goes to the local deli to buy a bologna sandwich. Then he heads over to The Haymarket to play some pool and wait for a trick to start ogling his ass. Pool playing is great for hustling. All the bending and arm extending really show off the goods to the prospective customer. But I should add that just because an ass was on display didn't mean it was available. Most of the rent boys at The Haymarket thought of themselves as straight and would only play the active role. So the ass display was often kind of a bait-and-switch operation.

"Once the hustler scored a twenty-dollar trick, if he was a junky, as many were, he'd lay out five of it for a bag of heroin. Then he'd stagger back to the Haymarket and start searching for another trick. Around three a.m. he probably had enough extra cash to go party. So he and his buddies would rent a room in one of the shitty hotels and do up some more dope.

"One of the best books about that scene was written by a talented sicko named Paul Rogers. It's a novel called Saul's Book, *which tells the story of an angelic but fucked-up Puerto Rican hustler-junkie and his Jewish john-daddy who quotes Shakespeare and forges checks. When the book was published around 1980, it won a prestigious literary prize called the Pushcart. Everybody thought that Paul Rogers was a social worker who had learned about that sleazy world of hustlers through his altruistic profession. It turned out, however, that he was just like his character Saul. He was a drug addict and con man with a taste for young trade. The love of his life— a fucked-up white kid with a learning disability and a drug habit—eventually*

bludgeoned him to death to get a fix. And Rogers was dead before he could even write a second novel.

"Another very gifted writer was linked to The Haymarket scene. His name was Alan Bowne, and he wrote the play Forty Deuce. *"Forty Deuce" means Forty-Second Street in the lingo. The play got rave reviews on off-Broadway and was one of the first starring roles of a twenty-year-old Kevin Bacon. Later Paul Morrissey, of Warhol fame, made a magnificent movie of* Forty Deuce, *but the film was never released.* Forty Deuce *is a comedy of sorts and tells the story of a group of hustlers who end up with the corpse of a twelve-year-old boy in the bed of the hotel room they use to turn tricks. They plot to pin the death on a very bourgeois john played by Orson Bean, by slipping him angel dust. But there's a happy ending to the story.*

"When I came to Times Square, Burroughs, John Rechy, Paul Rogers, and Alan Bowne had already paved the way for me and the books I would write about it. But let me make one thing clear. I didn't start hanging out in Times Square because I wanted to write about it. I guess only a journalist would do that. Those guys are used to picking a subject that will make them a few bucks whether they're inspired by it or not. They end up having to take notes and use tape recorders. But as I said, I didn't go to Times Square to write. I went there cause I wanted to fuck straight guys. As I already mentioned, most of the hustlers in Times Square were straight. At this point, the majority were Puerto Rican. And they were always short of cash. Getting their dick sucked was a lot easier for some of them than robbery or drug dealing. I wish more of you straights were like that. All they had to do was whip it out and stand there while some very experienced cocksucker gave them an ace blow job. It's true that some of them with fancy drug habits had to learn to suck dick themselves, but in general their performance wasn't very inspired.

"I hope you Japanese readers can understand this concept. For a straight Latin or North African or other Mediterranean type sticking your cock in a guy's mouth or ass isn't considered 'gay.' The only thing that makes you a faggot is if you yourself take it up the wazoo. Okay, some of them did, but they were high. You could take advantage of that, but then there was a chance that when they woke up the next morning, they'd stab you.

"Keep in mind that I came to Times Square in the early 80s, just as the AIDS crisis was exploding. Let me tell you, I was really fucked up about that. I spent a lot of time examining pimples in the mirror, or staring down my throat with a flashlight. There was no test for AIDS at the time, and I was obsessed and terrified about the idea of maybe having it. But in Times Square, hundreds of homeboys lived with death on a daily basis. They had fathers who'd overdosed, mothers who'd died of cirrhosis, and stints in prison that had subjected them to every kind of abuse. They weren't walking around examining every pimple. Instead they were out there looking for money or a good time. In comparison to me, they seemed to be living their lives with what fate gave them.

"Getting to know those homeboys gave me back my courage and a sense of proportion. I stopped worrying about AIDS and started thinking about living. And live, I did. O'Neal's, on 48th Street, was the bar that took the place of the defunct Haymarket. It was a two-room affair with a little garden at the back. The manager was a handsome, laid-back Greek named Alex. Murphy, a big bearded guy who looked like a Hell's Angel, and who'd been the bouncer at the old Stonewall, was at the door. Later somebody said he was a police informer. Now Murphy's gone. He died of AIDS. Some of my best memories come from hanging out in O'Neal's in the mid80s. South Bronx hustlers, doctors and fashion designers, runaway kids, drag queens, drug dealers and the homeless all frequented the place. Around 1986, crack hit the streets. People were puffing on glass pipes (known as devil's dicks) in the garden at O'Neal's. There was a lot of brawling. One guy got gutted by a knife. I'll never forget the day this one gigantic hustler got mad cause he lost a pool game. He picked up one end of the pool table and overturned it. It went crashing through the glass window.

"It was in O'Neal's that I first became fascinated by the speech and minds of street people. Sure, I liked sucking their dicks, caressing their tattoos made in jail, kissing their scars and sleeping with them in my arms. But I was also trying to figure out what gave them their courage and coolness, what wisdom they had that none of us educated folks could ever master. After a while, I found myself imitating the way they talked, and that was when I began writing stories about them. Luckily, I was no *idiot. I never lost sight of the fact that I came from a middle-class background and could never think entirely like they did. So when I wrote fiction about Times Square, I was always careful to include some middle-class characters. I wrote about the colli-sions—sometimes absurd and sometimes tragic—between the classes. I thought I was writing comedies of manner.*

"One other place where I got my inspiration was Sally's. It was a tranny hooker bar on 43ʳᵈ Street near 8ᵗʰ Avenue. After it burned down, Sally, the sometimes-transvestite owner, moved his operations to the Carter Hotel. The majority of the 'girls' in Sally's weren't weekend ladies. They lived full time as females and were in various stages of the transformation. All of them had tits, but a lot of them hadn't cut their dicks off yet. Most of them were professional lip-synchers and could do Whit-ney, Barbra or Sade as well as those original singers could do themselves."

Bingo. I was convinced I'd seen a flicker of recognition pass through some eyes right after the name *Whitney*. Praise be, we'd been on the same page for a second. But there was no sense in pressing my luck. It was time to gallop toward an ending.

As I was about to launch into it, something unnerved me. My eyes had strayed to the refreshment table, to check whether there was any food left, I suppose, since I was dying of hunger. The food was still there, but as my glance took in the row of Suntory bottles next to it, the arrangement began to look hallucinatory. I shifted my feet and tilted my head, first in one direction and then the other, but those bottles of am-ber liquid were no longer in a straight line. The explanation for this was simple. Obviously, after some had been picked up to pour from, they hadn't been put down as meticulously. Or had they? Because somehow, they'd taken on the composition of the rocks at Ryoan-ji. Every time I changed my viewing angle, one, and only one, disappeared. I don't know how long I stopped in stunned contemplation of this phenomenon. I may have even left the lectern to get closer to the table and seek out other lines of sight, but when I came out of my fugue state, I realized I had finally caused a reaction in my audience since most faces seemed to radiate concern.

"Sorry," I said, but before I could resume my talk, a man in the front row stood and retrieved one of the bottles and a glass. He walked to the lectern and held them out to me. Apparently, the assumption was that I was desperate for a drink. What other explanation could they have thought of? I shook my head and went on.

'Getting back to those bars, there was a fairly heavy chemical trade going on by then. Not just the black market in hormones from Europe, but also crack, dope, and weed. At Sally's, too. It was at the latter that I learned about a sex change from Philadelphia who worked for a doctor and would come up to New York with a shipment of loose silicone a couple times a year. She'd set up shop on somebody's kitchen table, and the trannies would pay her for silicone shots to round out their asses, thighs, cheeks or other body parts. It wasn't the healthiest thing they could do. Loose silicone sends the body into emergency drive. After an injection, some of the girls would have to lay up for a day or two until the fever and pain subsided.

'I can't say that the girls of Sally's were overly into me. I wasn't a tranny chaser, nor was I nelly enough to be one of their 'daughters.' Can you guess why I kept hanging out there? I was into the trannies' boyfriends. Transsexuals and transvestites attract the most masculine men that exist. Think about it. Not only do they have to be heterosexual enough to dig a woman, they also have to be macho enough to control a man. The problem was, most of the trannies' boyfriends weren't into somebody like me, who looked too much like a dude. There was, however, one notable exception. They called him Izod, after the shirt.

'Izod was a light-skinned Puerto Rican with a beautiful pompadour, slightly Asian eyes, and massive shoulders. He pretty much had his rhythms down to a science. He'd get a tranny and a john to support him at the same time. With the money he'd develop a major crack habit. Sooner or later, the habit would land him in jail. Then he'd cool out, gain weight, and come back to the street. Well, I was smitten with him. Crack habit and all, I did everything in my power to get Izod to move in with me. When he finally said yes, I met him at a bar where he left all his bags with

me. All he needed was $40 from me to pay a dealer in the hotel across the street. Otherwise, they were going to waste his ass. I gave Izod the forty and waited with his bags for him to come back from that hotel. Only problem was, he never did. Once he paid the $40 back, the dealer treated him to a few free tokes. Before he knew it, he'd smoked enough scotty to become the dealer's slave again. I saw him on the corner about three days later. He was dealing, too.

"Both Sally, the club owner, and Izod were big inspirations. Composites of both appear in one of my novels... Jeeze, I feel like I've been up here forever. Uh—any questions?"

I really hadn't thought up much of an ending. To improvise a certain structure, I would have had to follow their reactions as signposts. What I still wonder is why I didn't just quit while I had the chance. Instead I felt compelled to offer the following coda:

"That's about it, friends, except you guys should be proud of yourselves. The U.S. doesn't hold a candle to what a white faggot can find in this country. True, I was here decades ago, for only two months, but I've never felt so successful anywhere else—what with my being tall, husky, blue-eyed, and hairy, especially hairy, all of which the homos over here seemed wild for. Or at least maybe they did then because some were old enough to remember their childhood experiences with Americans during the Occupation. Regardless of the reason, I never sucked so much cock or sunk into so many smooth buns. All that shiny, stiff, straight-as-a-rod pubic hair tickling my face was something, too. In those days the bars in the Shinjuku district were almost as good as those in old Times Square. I'd walk into them and everybody would start pulling at the hair on my chest and arms, and uh..."

For the first time I made out my translator, who was standing at the back of the room. His polite smile hadn't faded, but he was making a horizontal sweeping motion with his hand, as in... time to go, buddy. All I did was speed up.

"Okay. Any questions? Didn't think so. Oh, and if any of you hot, straight Japanese guys are going to be stopping by New York and feeling horny, get my email

address from your magazine. I have some great straight porno and a full liquor cabinet. All you have to do is lie back and I'll take care of the rest—"

That was the moment when I tore away from the lectern without transition and made a clumsy bow. Then I hightailed it toward the refreshment table in a void of silence, as my listeners were undoubtedly taking in the fact that the talk was suddenly over. Regret flooded my capillaries to the polite but far-from-overwhelming patter of their applause. I imagined a menacing gulf between me and them, some of whom were already heading toward the exit to go home while others had stood and wandered into small groups to whisper to one another. Nobody was looking in my direction.

I attacked the food, most of which wasn't warm anymore. Obviously, that part of the evening was supposed to be over, but this was probably my last opportunity to eat. Flipping piece after piece with a pair of chopsticks onto a small plate, I accumulated a miniature mountain of stuff, then began maneuvering it to my mouth as quickly as I could. As I ravenously chewed my third rice ball, I began wondering how I was supposed to get back. Then I heard a polite-sounding, possibly familiar voice coming from behind. I swung round. The speaker trained his eyes on mine as it dawned on me who it was: the motorcycle kid.

"You came to take me back? Sorry, didn't mean to keep you waiting, I was just so hungry!"

The gleaming eyes kept their focus on my face. The mouth was smiling. "I never really left. Only had to lock up bike and just missed very beginning of talk. Sorry for that."

"You were *here?*" My eyes shot downward in dismay, and one hand squeezed the back of my neck in anguish.

"Yes, in the back, last row. Difficult to notice us from so far away, probably."

To clarify who *us* were, he casually draped an arm around a pleasant-looking youth standing next to him. "Daiki, my boyfriend." The boy extended a hand, but I couldn't muster the will to reach out and take it. Mine was trembling and drenched in sweat. The kid Daiki had gussied up for the occasion like some of the others I'd noticed earlier. He was affecting a beatnik literary look, down to the horizontally striped French sailing shirt and shadow of a goatee. Or maybe it was just a look currently in fashion among these young people. The thought that at least one audience member—a sweet-featured, affable motorcycle boy—had to have understood some of my talk sent humiliation for my reckless misbehavior coursing through me. But wait—what had he just said?

"Your… what? Listen, I was just doing one of my tired routines. I don't really think that—"

"*Ukeru!*" interrupted another, treble-pitched voice with startling volume. "So funny!" the same voice enthusiastically translated. It belonged to the lady poetess I'd noticed earlier, the middle-ager in the outfit I'd thought was referencing Anaïs Nin or Marianne Moore. Moore, obviously. She'd been standing a little apart from the two boys, and my anxiety had created a kind of tunnel vision. Moreover, she wasn't a she. It was another young guy in drag.

Next to him was the fourth member of their group, an older, non-Asian guy—a Westerner. He looked like he was in his forties and was wearing a conservative navy blue blazer with a speckled ascot and pressed gray wool pants out of which peeked two Gucci loafers. From what I could tell, he was examining me with a glowering expression; or at least, he was the only one in the group who was neither smiling nor chuckling about my talk. I averted my eyes quickly.

"I didn't mean to—"

"Bruce," interrupted the motorcycle lad. "Please I may call you by your name given?"

"Uh, yeah. Given name. Sure." I nodded timidly.

"Hoping you come now to little party at our apartment. Not at all far from Reiko-San. Walking distance."

The two boys lived in a studio apartment on the sixth floor of a ramshackle high-rise, the kind of temporary living space you'd expect for two college-aged kids. It was just a studio with a kitchen area at one end featuring a half-sized refrigerator and a hotplate. Taped to the wall, a couple of rock-star posters and an art reproduction—Dubuffet, I think—unless I'm confusing it with memories of my own college years. A futon served as couch-bed. I was perched on it, shoeless with my outstretched legs running along the floor. The position was torture on my butt.

The other three—goatteed Daiki, Marianne Moore, and the *gaijin*—had promised to meet us here by car, while my trusty bike boy—whose name turned out to be Nobuo—had invited me to climb on his motorcycle behind him once more. For this return trip, I was a paragon of good manners—a bit ironic seeing how aggressively I'd behaved with him earlier when I'd never imagined he could be gay. But that acting out appeared defensive and insecure to me now. I felt shame.

I hadn't misheard the word *boyfriend*. Daiki and Nobuo went to the same college and had chosen it partly to remain together. Daiki was majoring in sociology, and Nobuo was studying American literature. They told me they'd been intimate (surreptitiously at first and later more blatantly) since the age of fifteen. As for "Marianne Moore," I don't think he understood much English; and the only thing I could glean from him was his requesting that I call him "Doris"—a camp gesture, I assumed, since he didn't look like a full-time transvestite. "Like Doris Lessing," he had politely added with a smile.

Stan, the much older, conservatively dressed *gaijin*, was Nobuo's former professor in American literature and originally from Missouri. I imagined it was partly his sexual orientation that tied him to these much younger friends. It was a charitable assumption on my part, since the real story was probably that he was just into much younger guys, something he never gave me the chance to verify. Stan wasn't the type to reveal personal details to someone he'd just met.

Once the boys had heated up our sake with a small pan of water on the hotplate, they brought it over with some little cups on a small lacquer tray and served Stan and me first. Stan had plopped down next to me on the futon. "Doris Lessing" was stationed at the other end of the studio going through CDs, alternating Japanese House with American jazz for our pleasure. He'd removed the three-cornered Marianne Moore hat, revealing a rather handsome masculine profile and a plush, sensitive-looking mouth.

Stan did tell me he was in his seventeenth year in Japan. He seemed to radiate the uninviting mood of being stranded and resenting it—that is, when he wasn't pretentiously posturing about his special status as an in-the-know ex-pat. The latter, of course, made him disdainful of his own natal culture, which he claimed he could "see through" because of his more "international perspective." I'd encountered jaundiced men-without-a-country types like him in Prague and Paris, people who'd come and never left, now beginning to feel they didn't want to be there. Like them, he was piqued at his adopted country for never fully making him feel he belonged but felt too changed to go back to America. Unsurprisingly, he spoke fluent Japanese and only that language when relating to the three others. This more or less cut me out of all their conversations. Since he was the only other person besides me with a high level of English, he not only used it with me for long periods but kept it at a sophisticated level, successfully dividing our get-together into two. I knew he was making me his hostage, so I couldn't escape the punishment he would eventually inflict; but there was also another, contrary impulse motivating Mr. Been-There-Done-That. Like the typical ex-pat, he was yearning for a bit of temporary camaraderie with a countryman to stem his sense of isolation. I was under pressure to feed him a few scraps of that homemade apple pie.

"Makes no difference how long you stay here, you know, or how perfectly you can speak their language! You're just not part of the family," he carped.

"Must be hard," I dutifully commented.

"It works the opposite way, too. Nobody ever expects you can speak Japanese and treats you like a language retard—even if you show them that you can. So you finally end up surrendering and *giving* that impression. The longer you stay here, the more you feel you're not a part of their culture, and the more you project your sense of separateness, so why should anybody ever expect you can speak Japanese?"

I nodded understandably and didn't tell him that he was aggravating the problem tonight by not sticking to slow and simple English so that all of us would be on the same page. Stan lowered his voice conspiratorially and narrowed his eyes into a cunning expression. "That may also be their Achilles heel. Ever thought of that? The kind of exclusion they force on you can turn you into an undercover agent."

"Way to go, John le Carré," I weakly quipped. As soon as I said it, I realized he possibly could be working undercover—for the CIA or something—so I lowered my voice like his. "I mean, unless you really *are* a spy."

"Ha! You don't know the half of it, buddy. 'Spying,' as you dubbed it, is often the *only* way to figure out what's going on over here."

"I know. I couldn't make heads or tails out of what they were thinking tonight. Usually when I give a talk, I can feel the audience's reactions."

Stan leaned closer to me, and I thought I detected a crazed look in his eyes, but it might have only been the flicker of the candle Nobuo had lit and placed on the sake tray near our feet. He and Daiki were opposite us on the floor, their backs against the wall, and Nobuo had his arm around his partner again. Now they had leaned forward and looked like they were straining to understand our conversation.

"Do you realize how much power there is in a face of passivity?" asked Stan. "The only name for it in our country is 'poker face.' That's quite insufficient for the many varieties of subtle communication on these shores. Call it the genius of Japanese discretion or whatever you want. For us, they're so cultivated beyond imagination that all we usually see is a mask of mild good intention—even when they're at the height of being *entertained*."

"Now that's a strange word to use. *Entertained?* Are you saying they found my talk entertaining?"

I could have sworn his eyes shifted covertly to the two boys for a moment as if he were checking to make sure they weren't understanding. It was like he was going to impart some classified information to me that he didn't want to share with them. "Double agent, my friend, double agent. I was listening in before you arrived, when they were all milling around the drink table and, of course, not saying a word to me. They never talk to me. Eavesdropping is easy when they all take one look at you and assume you understand bullocks."

I was beginning to believe this guy really was in the CIA. "They were really looking forward to the *entertainment*," he added, using the word again.

"What's with that damn word?" What I really meant to say was, Why do you keep using that word with such ghoulish irony scrunching up your face?

"Don't you tell me you didn't know you were there for their amusement, buddy. Come on. Or you wouldn't have pulled that outrageous routine of yours."

"Yeah, well…"

"Ha! Ha! I'll tell you what entertainment is. Being entertained is watching a foreigner make a damn fool of himself when all of you are too cultivated ever to act out like him. Being entertained is making him think he's being given complete freedom. It's being superior enough to slip under *your* radar! For laughs. You, my friend, had all the freedom you'd ever want. The freedom to make a total ass of yourself!"

He had gotten me pissed; at the same time, a sense of shame was rising in my gut again. "Who are you talking about, me or you?" I countered. "Because I'd say you're making a pretty good ass of yourself right now." I tried to stand up, but he placed a firm hand on my arm.

"Wait a minute."

The tense, lost look on both Nobuo and Daiki's faces told me they had no idea what he was saying. Their expressions didn't look that different from most of the audience earlier in the evening. Did Stan's bullshit about my listeners being secretly in the know hold any water at all? Or was he just baiting me and punishing me because of his own paranoia?

"Think of it in reverse," said Stan in a friendlier—or perhaps faux friendlier—tone. "Imagine if we invited them to come over and speak with the expectation that they'd satisfy every cliché we know about 'the Orient,' that we invited them over expecting to be entertained by a 'Cho-Cho-san' or 'Charlie Chan' routine, let's say. You see, these rather regal people are so good at taking their pleasure that you'd never be able to find out if their expression of low-key good humor is because they're particularly benevolent or because they can't understand a word you're saying or because they understand every single word but are experts at hiding the fact that they're howling inside with laughter! Because you yourself can't interpret the subtle variations of expression on their faces, which all of them can!"

"Enough!" I said sharply. Nobuo and Daiki flinched and watched more anxiously. But Stan let out the most horrifying bellow, laughter that sounded maniacally ill intentioned.

"You just can't beat class, buddy, you can't—especially if you're an American. Don't even try." Before I could react, he'd leapt to his feet. "Gotta take off. I teach early tomorrow. *Arigato gozaimashita,*" he thanked the boys. *"Arigato."* He glanced at me one last time—"Remember, bud, *double agent*"—and walked out, but not before an attentive Doris Lessing began blasting a recording of Chita Rivera singing "Hey, Big Spender!" as exit music that sent the four of us into a gale of laughter.

Nobuo refilled the glass of hot sake I'd been drinking and gazed at me with the hint of a twinkle in his soft eyes. "What the fuck was that?" I asked.

"Trying to think of American word for Stan," he answered in a soothing tone. He looked at Daiki. "Ah! I remember now. *YUCKY!* Correct?" There was another bout of laughter among all four of us.

"*Obnoxious* might be a better word," I suggested. "This a friend of yours?"

"Not like America here," said Nobuo. "It is just… sticking together. No big gay groups like you, so we must pay acknowledgement to our brother. Better that way."

"Oh, come on!" I protested rather irritably. "I was here ages ago, and even then there were gay people in every city I went to. Kyoto, Osaka, Kobe, Tokyo, even the town of Arima in the mountains. It almost seemed like there were more homos in the Shinjuku district than in all of New York. Nobody seemed to pay it any mind at all. You mean to say the gay community has become so thinned out, you have to band together with any moron who shares your tendencies? What happened? Was it AIDS?"

Daiki shook his head. "Hard to explain. Yes, you are correct. Many gays and no mention, more so in earlier years. This was the problem. No community. We try now to come together, maybe even have politics, like the Western way."

"Who needs that if you can do what you want?" I said cynically.

"Loneliness," answered Nobuo.

Daiki nodded in agreement. "You like movies, yes? Japanese movies?" he asked.

"Sure."

"Then maybe you saw movie called *Gohatto*."

"Maybe. Did it also have an English title?"

"*Taboo*. Last movie of Oshima. But not a very good translation for title in my opinion. *Gohatto* strange word. It is paradox, really. *Taboo*, yes, correct. But I prefer *unlicensed*. Sounding more pleasurable."

"Hmm… I might have seen that film. Tell me more."

"You know something about pre-modern gay in Japan? No law against it, but no law for it, too. Because…" He looked at a loss to put the information further into English.

"No strong connection between gender and sex," continued Nobuo. "Everything tradition, tradition, maybe like ancient Greece, especially among upper class, among samurai. It was not the same as freedom, as you think it. Very strong codes controlling everything. Called *nanshoku*, male erotic. Code never saying to be gay is wrong but saying such love only possible between older man and young boys. When the boy old enough to cut off part of hair that decorates forehead, he reveal his face of man and become no longer object of sexual desire. So no taboo about love between males but many taboos and rules to follow inside of love code. Nothing hidden. No, that is not correct. Nothing hidden, but much thought to be mysterious. You know, you cannot separate old-style Japanese homosexuality and *mono no aware*."

"What's that?"

"That means 'sharp noticing of small, changing things,' 'beautiful heartbreak of things leaving,' without person ever understanding completely this impermanence."

"Sad beauty of fleeting nature of all things," called out Doris Lessing from his deejay station.

"There are beautiful books from old times that speak of homosexuality in this manner. There is especially one in the seventeenth century by Saikaku Ihara." Nobuo used the traditional manner of giving the surname first. "Called *The Great Mirror of Male Love*."

"Is that what this film *Taboo* is about?"

Both boys nodded. "Samurai love," said Daiki. "In Kyoto, 1860s. It is happening Late Tokugawa period right before the fall of feudal Shogunate, soon being replaced by our imperialist Emperor. Story of the Shinsengumi militia that want to stop rebellions against shoguns. A militia living close to edge of honorable death at all times, very violent, disciplined."

"Sounds like Yukio Mishima's Shield Society," I said. I'd read a lot of Mishima, and I understood a little about the way both his sexuality and his aesthetics were intertwined with extreme right-wing militarism, so extreme it had ended with his ritual suicide. "The romance of fascism."

Nobuo chuckled. "So correct. Story of right-wing love. Among samurai, or militia, you can also find many woman-haters, known as *onna-girai*."

"Not all *onna-girai*," called out Doris Lessing, objecting from his station at the CD player. "Many are *shojin-zuki* too!"

"Doris saying many did not hate women. Many were bisexuals with taste for boys."

Doris nodded with a justified expression.

"Anyway, *Gohatto* is story of most beautiful, cold, brave Japanese boy who joins militia and makes many men love him," Nobuo went on. "And there is much bloodshed."

"The idea that homosexuality is a perversion, a mental illness or something. You got that from us, too, didn't you?"

Nobuo nodded. "Yes. With Meiji period, as Japan opens to Western influences, becoming more 'scientific'—in eyes of the West. Suddenly we have Japanese Krafft-Ebing people telling us we are perverts."

"Okay, then why did I find gay sex so available when I came here?"

Nobuo shrugged. "Even West cannot change us completely, you know. Too many centuries in which male love and guilt gone separate ways. Shame yes, but only if social codes are broken. So maybe some Japanese thinking like Westerners have decided that gay people are sick, perverted. But they also think, 'How does that change my life, my world?' As long as gay remains impenetrable to them, they don't care what we do. Anyway, all that is changing. First, they must see us and understand when AIDS come to visit in 1980s. Much information in newspapers. And then, by 1990s, there is even groups of gay liberation here. Western influence very big, almost like second Meiji."

"Speaking of gay liberation," I said, "what did you really think of my talk?" I knew what I had just said was actually kind of a non sequitur.

Nobuo grinned. "For us, very funny. Not same funny for you as for us."

"Oh, in other words, Stan was right. People were laughing at me rather than with me."

"Repeat please," said Daiki. I repeated the words much more slowly.

Both boys shook their head. "No, no. Stan is crazy," said Nobuo. "*Funny* for us more like exotic. You tell us about years of life as 'pervert.' Showing how people told to feel guilty, to feel ashamed, will rebel in colorful ways. Maybe ways not in best interest. You tell us about ghetto. Your words touch us in many ways. I cannot explain everything. You have much wit, and that is big tool to fight suffering."

"But what about all the others?" I insisted. "They must have found it offensive, or shamefully funny?"

Nobuo looked at me disapprovingly for the first time and almost spoke through his teeth. "Do you really think Japanese people that simple? There are many reactions, I am certain. I could understand many faces of listeners, but you I know see nothing. Some not understanding. Some understanding some part and like or did not like. Some very amused like us, impressed by richness of old American subculture. How could you even think for a moment Stan spoke true, that everybody is laughing at you? I know you are confused because for you our faces look impenetrable."

It was the second time he had used the word *impenetrable,* and the same word had already come to my mind several times during this trip. "Yes, I have a hard time reading Japanese faces," I admitted.

Daiki's eyes lit up. "Do you know that Western sociologists, psychologists claiming that humans have six emotions, each basic emotion having own set of face muscles?"

I remembered he was a sociology student. "No, never heard of that."

"One more example of Western hegemony," he said. "Not so untrue that Westerners must rely on six basic expressions. Sadness, happy, fear, angry, disgust—and my favorite, surprise. Each emotion need own set of facial muscles working to produce. This is what Western people see, even in science experiments called cluster analysis. So they think this is human nature. Darwin was thinking so, too."

"Isn't it?"

His lips curled into a slight smile of irony, or at least I thought they did. "Not for us," he said. "Six expressions are Western expressions, not human expressions, not universal. You know how computers now can read all dimensions of face, just like first Apple phone with this talent?"

"Facial recognition," I said.

"Using facial recognition of many dimensions so many surprising things. Six Western expressions may not be same as basic East Asian expressions. For example, maybe shame is part of East Asian list. Maybe respect, too. Also, you and me using different muscles to show intensity of emotion. Asians using eyes more for this, while Westerners using whole face."

"That's incredible," I said. "All our facial contortions must make us look like cartoons."

It was true, I realized, because both boys lowered their eyes for a moment to nod with mild embarrassment. "Yes, for us, rubber face," shyly confessed Nobuo.

I laughed, which gave them permission to laugh, too. "Well, for us, your faces sometimes look like masks," I dared to say.

"Study eyes," instructed Nobuo. "Look for eyes. You will see someday. You cannot see them yet."

"Big problem of Stan," added Daiki. "He speaking perfect Japanese, even most complicated expressions of politeness, rare for a *gaijin*. But such strong American accent. Stan not speaking Japanese language of body. He think he is ignored, but he is ignoring them. With his eyes. He only listens, does not look."

I was certain the boys knew I also translated French literature for a living. What they probably didn't know was that, when I spoke, my French accent outdid Zsa Zsa Gabor's in English. The thought brought to mind a faraway, treasured memory of Ursule Molinaro, a much older writer and translator, now deceased, who had been a close friend and something of a mentor. She had successfully undergone a complete metamorphosis from French fiction writer to American writer a few years after migrating to New York from Paris to work for the United Nations. Ursule spoke a total of six languages fluently and had no accent in any. One day, frustrated and somewhat disgusted with my heavy accent, she asked, "When you're in France and touch a wall, what do you feel? Do you feel a wall and then in your mind translate it into its French word, *mur*? Or do you actually and immediately feel *un mur*. Well, when the day comes that you feel *un mur*, your American accent will disappear. All you have to do is link your sensory faculties to your language skills."

Obviously, complete communication always involved the sensory. I studied Nobuo, realizing how exquisitely handsome he was with his silky skin, gleaming and expressive almond eyes and strong, graceful, mobile neck. An impulse to tell him so rose in me, but I restrained it. Instead I said, "There's the issue of discretion. Japanese people are so much more restrained—or should I say, polite—than we are."

Nobuo shook his head. "Not discreet. Humble. If they do not say, it is because they do not think they can speak truth. This is again spirit of *mono no aware*, noticing of everything changing forever. If you want to show your respect, cannot ignore this, or you—what is term?—sell short. Offering opinion too soon means you sell people short."

I thought of that rubbery, amebic blob, my metaphor for the human psyche, and realized that for me the problem lay in the fact that such a condition of impermanence made me anxious, aroused fears of abandonment inculcated since my childhood. I wanted to stick a pin in the fluttering butterfly of all my relationships until they became still and definable, something that risked destroying them.

When another moment or so had passed, Daiki offered to walk me to Reiko-San's, which was only ten minutes away. It was after midnight on a Friday, and Kyoto seemed entirely undone. I heard rowdy laughter as men tumbled out of bars. One in a business suit was perched on the roof of a car with his buddies surrounding it, goading him with catcalls that I, of course, couldn't understand. Everyone seemed very drunk. Reading my mind, Daiki said, "This doesn't count, you know."

What he meant, he explained, was that there were certain hours, at least for men, in the Japanese day when stringent codes of behavior were temporarily suspended. It was somewhat like that recess from reality in France, which they referred to as *cinq à sept* (five p.m. to seven p.m.), a lacuna in the day where infidelities or other transgressions could occur without really changing things. In Japan, if an inebriated person misbehaved—like the drunken man I'd seen in Tokyo some thirty years ago plunging his hand into a goldfish bowl on a bar counter and trying to grab one of the animals—if a man peed in the middle of the street or knocked down a parking sign like a rowdy frat boy, the time of night and the factor of his inebriation could temporarily excuse him from his duties as a citizen, father, husband, or worker. Even if he was arrested but apologized to the police the next morning, using alcohol as his alibi, he had a chance of being released without charges, as long as his sober state paid acknowledgment to the proper values of Japanese life. However much this was true, there had been infractions of the behavioral code in Japan—errors that might have seemed like unimportant details to us—of such heavy traditional import that they'd required the honorable act of *seppuku*. Such extreme measures may have been rare today, but that didn't mean honor and shame were any less important.

I thanked Daiki at the entrance to Reiko-San's and asked him to assure me he'd tell Nobuo what a great time I'd had. "Oh, almost forgetting," he said. "You must dine tomorrow evening at home of president of literature society."

There went the one chance left for bar-hopping, I thought.

"Name of president Nishimura Fumio," Daiki informed me. As was traditional in Japan, he as well had pronounced the man's surname first. "They will bring you at nineteen hour," he added, meaning seven p.m.

"Nishimura? Isn't that Nobuo's last name, too?"

"Father of Nobuo," said Daiki, with a mysterious smile and a brisk goodnight bow, whereupon he left me at the entrance.

I stripped down to my underwear and shimmied under my *kakebuton*. A constantly shifting kaleidoscope of that evening's events swept past my shut eyelids. But as I spiraled into half-sleep, I began thinking of Nobuo's take on discretion. It required a kind of containment I knew I didn't possess. If holding back, tact—having a private life, in other words—were at the root of respecting others, in the Japanese context, I was the most contemptuous of human beings. I was an open book and a confessor, someone who couldn't keep a secret, could keep very few of any thoughts inside. It was fear of being alone that turned my words into a desperate glue, gushing out incessantly in hopes of attachment to my listener. When there were none available to hear me, I had to write my words down. Anything but the well of loneliness caused by silence. The hardest thing in the world for me was just to shut up. Obviously, subtle facial signals, the artful use of eyes, were beyond me. Certainly, I could never become Japanese.

The Nishimuras lived in an upscale faux-Modernist high-rise that had probably been erected at the very height of the Japanese economic miracle, referred to as the "Golden Sixties." The end of the Cold War had all but stopped this impetus by the nineties, even though the country remains one of the world's principle economic powers to this very day. Everything about the lobby spoke of this nouveau riche trajectory, down to the installation of artificial orchids and mid-century furniture knock-offs. However, once I had entered apartment 1006, the world changed to a distinctly Japanese environment, starting with the *genkan*, a small entryway just inside the front door, where I knew I was to shed my shoes and my coat. Before taking off those shoes, I faced the rest of the house, so that I could step out of them directly onto the raised, adjoining tatami mat floor of the living room, without my cleanly socked feet being soiled by the *genkan*, which, whether it was or not, was considered to be inferior in quality of hygiene.

I'd learned all these niceties during my first trip to Japan, so I was also equipped with an *omiyage* I was hoping was appropriate: a gift for my hosts, like the proverbial bottle of wine or bouquet often brought to American or European dinner invitations. Mine was a small jug of genuine Vermont maple syrup, as well as some maple candies shaped like leaves from the same source. I'd planned on bringing them with me to my talk and giving them to whomever had been responsible for my trip to Kyoto, but jetlag and the rapid succession of events had made me forget completely. Now, I planned to put them to good use.

I even remembered the proper way to present my *omiyage* to Nishimura-san, who was waiting for me just beyond the *genkan*. Instead of handing it to him with one hand, I clasped either side of the small package with each hand and made a slight bow as I held it out to him. Nor did I omit the requisite humble putdown of my gift by calling it "only a trifle." As I did, I rather exulted at the thought that my behavior tonight was in complete contradiction to the inappropriately ballsy behavior I thought I'd exhibited the previous evening at my talk. A small, perverse wave of rebellion had risen its ugly head again, and I remember hoping rather maliciously that the new me would confuse my host.

That thought evaporated when I straightened from my mini bow and took in Nishimura-san's appearance. He turned out to be the first person I'd noticed at my talk, the attractive slender man dressed like Baudelaire in a velvet waistcoat and satin tie; but tonight he was impeccably dressed in tan-and-gray Ralph Lauren casual, enough to put the rather flashy East Village look I'd concocted—ironically retro, flared striped trousers and a black motorcycle jacket—to shame and turn it into my second sartorial humiliation of this trip.

I suspected he was in his late forties, and he was very well preserved, with a healthy complexion and what was probably a genuine Rolex. A thought about the American homily of shoes making the man flashed through my mind as I realized judging someone by his footwear would be impossible in the context of invitations to a Japanese home, since everybody would be in socks and/or slippers. The apartment was intriguing, indicative of an imaginative and creative mind while remaining appropriately minimal. Aside from the tatami mat floor, the spacious room had *shoji* screen walls and some low lacquer tables, along with a few useful and aesthetically pleasing pieces of Western furniture, including some state-of-the-art LED lamps with what looked like hand-blown glass shades and an electric blue velvet couch upon which was seated an attractive woman in complete traditional garb. Upon seeing me, she rose immediately and smilingly bowed, and her husband presented here as his wife, Eriko. As she straightened, I took in her features, which were uncannily similar to Nobuo's. She had the same rather far-apart almond eyes, wide forehead, full, slightly pouting lips and delicate skin; and although her neck certainly had none of the sturdy athleticism of Nobuo's, it was almost as long and gracefully set above relaxed slender shoulders. Her husband's face was noticeably more angular than his son's, an effect perhaps partly caused by higher cheekbones and a more masculine square jaw, but he had Nobuo's full, soft, shiny hair, set off to best effect by an expensive haircut. It was obvious where Nobuo had gotten his good looks.

It was only after the introduction to Eriko that I realized I'd arrived late after asking the driver they'd sent me to wait because I hadn't been finished dressing. Perhaps I'd thrown off the timing of our dinner, because almost immediately, Nishimura-san led me to the dining alcove, which featured a long, low, narrow, polished table. To my relief, it was set above a rectangular depression in the floor, a couple of feet deep and surrounded by flat cushions. This allowed sitting on the cushions the traditional way—on your heels, with your legs folded under you—or using the cushioned edge as a kind of bench, allowing you to put your feet at the bottom of the depression, which brought you to the same approximate height as your hosts. I don't think I could have made it through the evening sitting on my heels with my legs folded, which always cut off my circulation.

Although the table was practically bare when we sat down, it soon became obvious by the placement of plates, glasses, cups, chopsticks and other ware that only two people would be seated at the table. Starting with cocktails, Eriko silently disappeared into thin air and reappeared repeatedly as an equally silent, gracefully gliding ghost bearing the proper drinks, foodstuffs, and condiments. Everything about her manner suggested humility and retraction, which raised my feminist hackles, until I studied her eyes more closely during each appearance from the kitchen as I'd been instructed to by Nobuo and saw that they seemed to be shining with excitement. Was it dignity, a simmering pride, a kind of satisfaction with her own prowess? Nevertheless, I had not been raised to approve of such exclusion. "Why can't your wife sit down with us?" I asked Nishimura-san.

"You are not hungry?" he answered with a note of irony in his tone.

"Yes—but. Couldn't one of us help her? Or can't we wait until everything is on the table and then she can sit down with us?"

"That would be impossible, because meal has many courses," he explained. "But I understand, and I will be honest and tell you that… Actually, we are trying to make impression. This is not way of eating for every evening. In fact, sometimes I am cooking. So maybe we were wrong to decide that you enjoy a traditional experience. Maybe Eriko should not have decided to wear traditional costume for you."

I felt ashamed. "No, no, please, I really enjoy it. I'm just eager to get to know your wife."

He smiled indulgently. "I saw you watch Eriko as she is serving us food. That was not a way to get to know her? I am pulling your little leg, Bruce-san. I mean, I am pulling your leg a little. I know many Americans are concerned with women's rights at this time. But truth is, both Eriko and I, we are like a modern Western couple. Now that Nobuo is grown, Eriko and I, we both work. She earning as much money as me as university researcher. I am *sarariman*…" He chuckled. "I suppose she is *sarariman*, too." This was the Japanese way of pronouncing "salary man," and I knew that it had a different meaning than it did for us. For one thing, most Japanese people worked with the assurance that their job had lifetime security, just like the old gold-watch-for-retirement days in the U.S. Not only that, but most of them didn't see their jobs as albatrosses they wanted off their neck as soon as possible. They put all their effort into achieving excellence at work. They were as dedicated as artists to their calling.

"Except—" Fumio started to add.

"Except what?"

"Except our intimate relationship still follows old code."

"In what way, if I may ask?"

"Oh… You know." He sighed a bit wearily. "I don't think I will ever understand Westerners all the way. Here you are, still calling me Nishimura-san, like saying Mr. Nishimura, instead of my given name, Fumio. And you are doing that even though I say Bruce-san since you walked in door. And then… Well, and then, still calling me Nishimura-san, you say I must tell you about the most intimate part of my life."

He was right, of course, but not right enough to inhibit my aggressively indiscreet curiosity. "All right, Fumio-san, what's so 'traditional' about your intimacy with your wife?"

"Just because… Eriko is wishing above all that I receive my pleasure."

"Oh, you mean unlike those women who have to have an orgasm every single time, even after you've come or haven't had one yourself? The ones who say you should be manipulating their clit while you fuck them?" I said crassly. I'd only had one whiskey, but obviously the cocktail was already beginning to talk. Then, realizing that his wife had appeared and was refilling our sake cups, I stopped short, leaned forward and said in a comically nervous whisper, "Uh, listen, does your wife speak English?"

Fumio-San burst into amused laughter. "No. Don't worry, you got away with it."

"So, uh, is that what you meant?"

"Yes, and more."

"More what?"

"It goes even further than that. Please, try this marinated octopus. You will find it is not too acidic."

I'd stepped in shit again, obviously. Shot my alcoholic mouth off. I tried to change the subject. "I never thanked you for sending your son to take me to my talk. Very thoughtful of you. Did he tell you he invited me to a little party he'd organized afterward?"

I could have sworn that Fumio-san blushed through his rather swarthy skin, but he managed to force out, "Oh really, didn't know." I'd chosen the wrong tack again.

"Yeah. And he's studying American literature. Must have gotten a taste for it from you."

At the mention of "literature," Fumio lightened up. "I've been meaning to talk to you about that. Excuse me." With his chopsticks he deftly brought a single rice grain to his lips, and I remembered another element of Japanese etiquette. You were supposed to finish every kernel of rice in your bowl, even the last. Although I was comfortable using chopsticks, I doubted I'd ever be able to pull off such a feat.

Fumio swallowed the rice grain, took another sip of sake and went on. "I cannot in honesty tell you about your talk because I understand so little of it. I have so few trouble speaking English. I must travel for my drug company half the year, and I am always speaking English. But sitting and listening to English, out of one's own context, very difficult for me. Still, parts were very impressive. Entertaining."

I couldn't believe he'd used that word, but I decided to take it in a context that differed from the way Stan had used it.

"I read very much Western literature," he said. "This I can do. In French, as well. Although long hours as *sarariman* make that difficult. In fact, every name you say familiar to me. Alan Bowne. I have bootleg videotape of his *Forty Deuce.* "

"Really? That's hard to get even in America."

"I also have old videotape of *Short Eyes,*" he added proudly, referring to the filmed version of the play about a child molester in prison, written by the junky genius and ex-con Miguel Pinero, who had first composed and staged the play while he himself was in prison. I was amazed, and the more he said, the more my former assessment of the magazine's literary enthusiasts was belied and belittled, the more superficial and prejudiced I appeared in my own eyes.

"Are you aware," he said, "of strong connection between Western writing from late nineteenth century and early twentieth century to that of Japanese writers? Goes in both directions. You know, Marguerite Yourcenar writing about Mishima. Certain Japanese writers seeing Artaud as aesthetic guide. And Mishima, well, early Mishima, it could not exist without the French Decadents. Mishima owe much to Huysmans, Baudelaire, even Comte de Lautréamont. Much entering of Japan from West during Meiji period."

"I've read a lot of Mishima," I said, "and I was aware of the French decadent influences, but I actually once taught the book *Sun and Steel* to a class of gifted college students, and I know he rejected that entire world view once he discovered the martial arts."

"True," said Fumio-san. "I like to think of Mishima like medieval French monster Gilles de Rais, who try to be alchemist. I am sure you know that Gilles de Rais wanting to turn lead into gold, and somehow this becomes located on physical plane and he is accused of disemboweling little boys."

I looked at him in puzzlement. In the space of ten minutes he had covered every borderline tendency in Western literature: decadence, insanity, pedophilia, a serial killer. Was this guy trying to tell me something? Did I want to know what it was?

"Okay, so in *Sun and Steel,* which is all about failing to find transcendence by burning the midnight oil and laboring over sensual texts with a weakening, pale body and then realizing he could locate the same tragic aesthetic more successfully in the blinding glare of the sun and the destructive sharpness of steel and the military brutality of his muscles, are you saying you see a desire to become an alchemist. Is that what you mean?"

"Exactly."

"Hmm. I think I see what you mean. I mean *Sun and Steel* is really about Mishima's loss of faith in metaphor, in the symbolic and the intellectual, and his hope that he could make it real by bringing it to the physical plane. So in a way, he didn't want to turn lead into gold, but gold into lead, at least from my point of view."

"Very possible," said Fumio-san.

"Since you did bring all these writers up, I might as well mention an anxiety I had. I mean, it wasn't exactly an anxiety, but I was assuming that you guys, almost all of whom are probably married and heterosexual—I'm talking about the guys in your book lovers' society—I was betting they didn't have much of a taste for descriptions of gay sex but thought that the whole LGBT thing was a politically correct element your magazine had to cover. Consequently, I pushed the envelope rather brutally when I gave my speech. I guess I kind of rubbed it in their faces."

"And you enjoyed?"

I didn't really know how to answer that question.

"Japanese people very different from Westerner about sexuality, and homosexuality, too. What is more, there is still great tradition for respecting age here, Bruce-San. Even in domain of sexuality. Good place for you to retire, maybe," he added with a twinkle in his eyes.

And suddenly, the twinkle seemed almost as if it had been some signal, for at that very moment, his wife materialized and said something that astonished me. Since she'd addressed me in Japanese, Fumio had to translate, and what she had said was: "Bruce, you are very drunk."

"I beg your pardon!"

Fumio waved a hand intended to be calming. "Please, she is only worried about you getting home. Now is too late to call car service. We think it best that you stay here tonight. I will make sure you leave in the morning when I go to work because I know you must pack for flight."

"Oh no, I—"

His wife addressed me with another remark, and I wondered if it was just as pointed. "What did she say?"

"She say you cannot leave."

"What, I'm being held prisoner here?"

Fumio-San laughed again—exuberantly. "No, no. She has concern. I agree with her. Will you do me the great pleasure to stay here tonight? We will make sure you are comfortable, that you enjoy."

Partly because I realized I'd be on my own if I left, I gave in to them. Fumio-San made a gesture with his hand, and his wife swiftly disappeared.

"She prepares the bedroom," he said with a smile. "Why not enjoy more sake as we wait." Before I had answered, he had refilled my cup. "So, we drink to each other," he chanted, raising his cup to his lips and waiting for me to do the same. It was a moment in which I wished I had followed Nobuo's advice again and studied the eyes of my interlocutor more carefully.

"I must prepare for good night," he informed me. "My wife will take you to correct place." He stood, bowed gracefully and left me sitting at the table.

Moments later, Eriko returned holding some towels and smilingly managed to say in English, "You will please follow me?"

She led me to a small study, but there was no bed, or even couch. She pointed to a slender wrought-iron staircase spiraling up into an opening in the ceiling, and I realized they must be living in at least a semi-duplex. Eriko handed me the towels and was gone. When I'd climbed the stairs, I discovered they led to a single door, set into a wall that, by architectural necessity, ran along an oblique line. From the room, I heard music, a kind of lazy R&B "Quiet Storm." My god, I thought, they've even chosen my music to fall asleep by.

The door was narrow and didn't fully open because of the impediment of the staircase railing, and I had to turn partly sideways to squeeze through it. It opened onto a compact but comfortable-looking Western-style bedroom with wall-to-wall carpeting and, in the center, a four-poster bed. The angle imposed on my entrance had concealed half of a shapely leg, which I'd soon discover was invitingly parted from the other. From his position on the bed, a naked Fumio-san smiled up at me.

It never occurred to me at that moment, but the next morning at the hostel, as I packed for the airport, strange and variable emotions would pass through me, ranging from a feeling of having been humiliated to that warm wave that comes over you from the mere fact of having received a gift, while turning a Baccarat crystal ashtray over and over in your hands.

To refresh a long-ago memory of two months spent in Japan, I availed myself of information on the Internet. Here are some of the brief articles I perused.

"*Gohatto*, or the End of Oshima Nagisa?" By Andrew Grossman. *Bright Lights Film Journal.* July 1, 2000.
http://brightlightsfilm.com/gohatto-end-oshima-nagisa/#footnote_10_16201

"Japan's Queer Cultures" by Mark J. McLelland. University of Wollongong, markmc@uow.edu.au. In Theodore and Victoria Bestor (eds), *The Routledge Handbook of Japanese Culture and Society*, Routledge, New York, 2011, 140-149.
http://ro.uow.edu.au/cgi/viewcontent.cgi?article=1277&context=artspapers

"Japan's Gay History" by Sunagawa Hideki, translated from the Japanese by Mark McLelland. This article originally appeared in Fushimi Noriaki (ed.) *Dōseiai nyūmon* [*Introduction to homosexuality*], Tokyo: Potto shuppan, 2003, under the title '*Nihon no gei no rekishi*', pp. 44-47.
http://intersections.anu.edu.au/issue12/sunagawa.html

"Facial Expressions are Not Universal." Patrimundia's Indiu-Uni, Archeologie et Antrholpologie, University of Glasgow.
http://www.archeolog-home.com/pages/content/facial-expressions-of-emotion-are-not-universal.html

"Facial expressions of emotion are not culturally universal" by Rachael E. Jack, Oliver G. B. Garrod, Hui Yu, Roberto Caldara and Philippe G. Schyns PNAS 2012 May, 109 (19) 7241-7244. Edited by James L. McClelland, Stanford University, Stanford, CA.

https://doi.org/10.1073/pnas.1200155109
http://www.pnas.org/content/109/19/7241

"Japanese Etiquette: How to Be a Polite House Guest" by Maile Proctor. September 16, 2015.
https://takelessons.com/blog/japanese-etiquette-z05

"Invited to a Japanese home?" by Marina Villar. *Taiken Japan.*
https://taiken.co/single/invited-to-a-japanese-home

Varian Studies, Volume Three: A Varian Symposium. Edited by Leonardo de Arrizabalaga y Prado. Cambridge Scholars Publishing, 2017, Newcastle upon Tyne, NY.
https://www.google.com/books/edition/Varian_Studies_Volume_Three/2jI9DwAAQBAJ

Return to San Francisco

IN 1994, I LEFT judgmental, high-stress New York with a tense neck and aching temples, hoping the gusty vagueness of northern California would ease my deadline-oriented mind. A French magazine was sending me to take a deep look at the counterculture of sunny San Francisco, a city that stood as a strange hyphen in my life and in my writing career. Twenty years earlier, from 1969 to 1974, I'd lived a bohemian existence there, stranded on public assistance and virtually without contact with the conventional workaday world.

From today's perspective, my life had been one of strange contradictions, a way of getting by that seems completely marginal now. It was a total rebellion against not only the work ethic but also current conventions regarding success, fulfillment, and security. My goals were personal and pleasure-oriented and had nothing to do with accumulating money, obtaining material objects, or winning respect and attention from the society around me. At the time, I was part of an entire, extensive subculture—still largely undocumented—that felt exactly the way I did. We thought the outside world was a rapidly dimming nightmare, fueled by concerns about money, security, and power, ready to be overturned by a coming libidinal revolution. As we awaited this event, we firmly believed that we already had the right to construct our own private paradises. We cultivated the art of living as an endless span of free time, full of infinite choices for leisure, promising any kind of fulfillment and requiring not the slightest effort.

Filling the cheap, sprawling Victorian homes of San Francisco with throngs of friends, we called our living spaces "communes" and forsook privacy and luxury for a festive, privileged poverty, open to both adults and children. Forsaking marriage, we chose promiscuity and celebrative group sexuality. All that remained was to find a means to pay for all of this; so we devised ways to trick the government—which financed widespread social service programs at the time—into providing us with a subsistence living. Every day, we purified our blood with macrobiotics and ginseng root but poisoned it with hallucinogens and cheap California wine. Our wardrobes came from both genders (it was not at all unusual to see a bearded young man in a woman's blouse or housedress), and our hair went uncut for years or was styled in the bathroom by a scissors-wielding friend.

With all the free time of my unemployed life, I spent hours a day in San Francisco pursuing intellectual pleasures, learning French from bilingual editions of Rimbaud and Baudelaire, without any connection to a university or school, or writing stories and prose poems to entertain myself and my friends, without the slightest thought of publishing them. It turned out to be a marvelous accidental education. While other young writers were developing within the strictures of competition and the pressure to succeed, I rambled through the terrain of literature, language, and the arts, pausing unpressured when anything enticed me, acquiring knowledge without the slightest goal in mind. I still remember this time as my golden period of creativity, in which I regarded poetry, film, music, and the plastic arts as no different from the pleasures of the body. If I at all merit the title of an original writer today, it's because of this unfettered, festive education, free of any worries about the future or any need for recognition.

All of this transpired twenty years before my second visit to San Francisco, in 1994. In 1974, I'd left San Francisco for New York, begun salaried work for a public arts program, and started to devote myself quite seriously to a freelance writing career. I left San Francisco because I'd become distressed by the static nature of so much freedom. I'd begun to think that life was boring and meaningless and wanted a taste of a world in which survival was a more pressing issue. But because of the leisure time of the previous five years, I arrived in New York with my writing talents finely honed. A mere few months later, the atmosphere of competition and ambition in New York had infected me. I was writing just as much, but, suddenly, being published had taken on an urgent importance.

When the offer came from the magazine to revisit my old romping grounds, I jumped at it because I hadn't set foot in San Francisco in twenty years. The friends who'd remained still spoke of it as sustaining a unique, perhaps non-exportable alternative life, whose closest European counterpart might have been Amsterdam (but is currently, in 2007, Berlin). According to my friends, invented styles—from experiments with sex and gender to New Age spiritualities—were still more visible in San Francisco than any place in America. I had to take their word for it, because little information about these phenomena had reached the mainstream press. Did the City of Love still hold any part of my lost past?

Like Europeans, but to a lesser degree, American East Coasters are inexorably subjected to the pressures of history. The Ivy League universities, banking empires, and government centers of the East Coast, many aspects and traditions of which were imported from Europe, tie that region to the foundations of America. Power networks established several generations ago still hold sway over East Coast cities, and many can be traced back to America's illustrious first settlers; speech and manners are established and exigent.

The West Coast, on the other hand, has come to represent the ideals of old America. It's a place where new immigrants can develop without judgment and assimilate with relative freedom. To create an atmosphere where this can take place, the West Coast has managed to erase all the sharp particularities of its cultural types. The Catholics of southern European stock seem to have lost most of the gutsy emotionality prevalent in the countries of their origins. Among their Jews, there seems a lack of the irony and sarcasm that distinguishes them in the major cities of the East Coast. The only minority ethnicity that seems salient is composed of members of the Latino population, who have had a foothold in the region since its earliest days.

The first people I wanted to see in San Francisco were my friends Cara and Sal, who had somehow managed to survive the fade-out of sixties counterculture and were shining even brighter in 1994. At fifty, they still lived in an immense, semi-converted garage, bursting with mystical and hallucinogenic images and blessed by constantly changing pagan altars to celebrate the solstices and equinoxes. Whole fields of demon faces, Buddhas, and Mexican death heads—most of which were made of plastic or cheap, painted wood—grimaced from the shadows. Sal, with his long, ash-white dreadlocks, wore a sarong and a happi coat. Cara wore striped silk pants and a turquoise tunic.

The air in this dense atmosphere was infused with multiple incense sticks and marijuana. In the past few years, both Cara and Sal had dedicated even their bodies to the overflow of psychedelic imagery that filled their home and minds by commissioning huge, complicated tattoos. Cara's partly shaven skull was decorated with a large blue spider. An immense tattoo of a red and blue bird fanned over one shoulder. Sal's thigh was a dense tapestry of Indian gods. And on his shin was a portrait of his deceased Mexican and Filipino parents as Mexican death heads in a kind of macabre wedding portrait.

After several hookah bowls of marijuana, Sal led me to their ramshackle '62, Volkswagen so that we could drive up Haight Street, the center of 1960s hippie culture. Cara's dark eyes shot strange sparks of jubilation as she talked about the tattoo she planned to get on her ribcage in a couple of days. She described the pain of tattooing as building slowly, a worsening burn, especially if the work was over a protruding bone. Yet both she and Sal claimed the pain was a focusing meditation, a kind of exorcism that left permanent holy stigmata on their bodies.

Both Cara and Sal were interested in death imagery. They attended San Francisco festivities for the Day of the Dead every year on November 1 and 2. Though the threat of AIDS may permeate the current alternative cultures of the city, the San Francisco counterculture has always sought a cheerful, spiritual relationship with the Grim Reaper. When my friend of thirty years would die shortly after from AIDS in San Francisco, his room would be full of cartoon skulls, skeletons, and other, mostly lighthearted but still occult images of death. Death has always appeared in this city as a fellow celebrant, sometimes glorified by the established Church of Satan in San Francisco, whose High Priest had been the occultist Anton LaVey. I was to meet disciples of LaVey near the end of my visit and learn about their theories of sensuality, power, evil, and race.

Fifty years ago, San Francisco was a city with a strong working-class flavor and powerful left-wing trade unions. It was a magnet for famous rebels, dropouts, and cultists of the American postwar period. Marginal artists, poets attracted by the cultures of China and Japan, fugitives from the law, renegade psychologists and Satanists came to the area. None of them had much money. Aside from New York, this was the city where the Beat movement established its strongest roots. The writers Lawrence Ferlinghetti, Jack Kerouac, Michael McClure, Gary Snyder,

Kenneth Rexroth, and Diane di Prima all made their reputations and found their inspiration here.

In 1994, however, the city's counterculture was already significantly changed. It was, as well, different from when I had lived there, for many underground types had full-time jobs. Counterculture had become a lifestyle deeply rooted in the American white leisure class and was playing a part in the gentrification of San Francisco real estate. A neighborhood known as the Fillmore, which was poor and black when I lived in San Francisco, had been mostly repopulated by the overflow of a new generation of white Haight-Ashbury hedonists, who paid high rents with professional jobs but still hunted for drugs, wallowed in the new cafés, or danced themselves into oblivion in raves that lasted all weekend. According to my friends, some of them still showed up at clubs looking like Indian gods, grasping mosaic canes, caressing their own hair, holding out drugs, laughing mockingly, or jangling cheap bracelets on their blue, red, or bone-colored arms. These days, a significant part of the culture of San Francisco served as a safety net for the middle-class rebel, who could enjoy a counterculture lifestyle in relative tranquility without really threatening the mainstream and while perhaps helping real-estate values rise.

Cara, Sal, and I got out of the car feeling very stoned and walked through a head shop cluttered with hookahs and hash pipes, "Free Marijuana" car stickers, and posters of Jimi Hendrix, Jefferson Airplane, and Bobby Seale. Imagery of the sixties, from civil disobedience to Eastern transcendence, glared from every corner, yet the salesgirl, with her short, bleached hair and black T-shirt, had a Courtney Love, post-punk look. This store hadn't survived from the past; it was merely a nostalgic reconstruction of it, for only in the last three or four years had the "Love generation" returned to the Haight. Haight Street had become an emporium selling the old Haight. Bill Belmont, producer of Fantasy Records and manager of the Grateful Dead, had reissued all the old band recordings; and the Fillmore—the legendary concert hall that once hosted The Doors, Janis Joplin, and Bob Dylan—had reopened. It functioned as a strange placebo for certain people, for, in the face of a growing emphasis on cultural identity, the white, liberal majority had found itself identity-less. And pagan rites, trance music, distinguishing tattoos, and small eccentric communities were just what some of them had been looking for.

As the hookah bowls carried out their climax, Cara and Sal's lifelong surrender to sensuality began to overwhelm me. I'd thought I'd completely outgrown the indulgent, provincial playfulness of the Haight-Ashbury ghetto. But suddenly I felt my defenses dropping, and I lost my objectivity. Endorphins were flowing, and my stiff neck relaxed to the torrent of psychedelic images, trance music, and vivid chatter pouring through me. Eager for new sensations and new pleasures, I left Cara and Sal to plunge into the world of the Radical Fairies, a neo-pagan group of mostly male, mostly white homosexuals who'd inaugurated their vision around 1978 with a mystical gathering in the Arizona desert.

The Radical Fairies were in part the brainchild of eighty-two-year-old activist Harry Hay, who'd founded the Mattachine Society—the first homosexual American organization—in 1950. Hay's vision had been of the sissy as shaman, in touch with a transcendent androgyny that gave such a person special access to the worlds of Nature and the supernatural, with a potential to heal the divisions of the social body and point toward a universal community of mankind. In other words, Hay saw the homosexual as a kind of "Magickal Faerie," who'd had a special spiritual leadership role in many previous cultures. The striving for acceptance and membership among the larger social body that he saw among the new politicized homosexuals distressed him greatly, and, in protest, he'd helped found the Radical Fairies, whose politics and mysticism are indistinguishable from each other and who live lives of deeply felt androgyny, revolutionary consciousness, and free sexuality.

A precursor of radical fairyism had developed in the early 70s when I lived in San Francisco. Two communes, the Cockettes and the Angels of Light, had spontaneously developed out of members of the Kalifower Commune into a performance group that exhibited proto-Radical Fairy attitudes and ideas along with pop culture parody. They raided the thrift shops of poor neighborhoods to find dresses, veiled hats, high heels, and jewelry from the 1930s and 1940s and created comic hermaphroditic personae that shocked and delighted a wide audience of supporters. Half terrorist transvestites and half performance group artists, they held Hollywood extravaganzas in a Chinese movie theater after midnight and in parks. They wore slinky, transparent Jean Harlow dresses and glued glitter or sequins to their beards as well as their penises, which poked through holes they had cut in the dresses. They mimed polymorphous sex or staged primitive Busby Berkeley musical numbers in front of baroque scenery, wearing coconut-shell bras and grass skirts, while a stoned audience that included me howled and screamed. They eventually became so well known the New York media began to promote them. Truman Capote, Gore Vidal, and other notables finally flew to San Francisco to attend their performances. But when they were brought to New York to appear on Broadway, Manhattan's professional theater community reacted with contempt, and they flopped.

I wondered what the Radical Fairies would be like in 1994, with high rents, the politicization of homosexuality, and increased gay bashing added to their environment. How, especially, would their emphasis on free sexuality be affected by the AIDS epidemic that was ravaging San Francisco?

Twenty-two-year-old Billie Jack was small-boned and petite—elfin—a graceful boy-man with a dyed fluorescent orange beard and orange hair. Although he met me at the door wearing a woman's emerald green pullover and an Indian-print skirt, there was nothing ludicrous or even particularly feminine about him, perhaps partly because he also wore large, lace-up Doc Marten boots. He exuded a sweet, meditative calm that was both palpable and profound—the monklike manner of someone who has made a major, irrevocable lifetime commitment. These qualities, coupled with his gentle speech and hallucinatory orange beard and hair, literally made me higher, as if I were in the presence of some mystical, fairytale vision. But what interested me even more about the luminous presence of Billie Jack was his intimate portrayal of his life as an HIV-positive person. He had discovered he was positive at the age of nineteen.

Billie was born in Iowa, one of eleven children in a strict Presbyterian family. He described his childhood and early adolescence as one of repression and sexual guilt, with the burning desire to escape his Midwestern environment. He had fled to Los Angeles at eighteen to become an actor and had begun a life characterized by a vengeful, rebellious emphasis on sexual pleasure. He had made several gay porno films but didn't blame them for his HIV status. Instead, he said it was compromising choices in general in his avid search for an erotic identity that made him take the chances that led to infection.

We were sitting in Billie Jack's room, on the mattress on the floor covered with a boy's quilt from the 60s, a pattern of smiley faces and peace signs. Billie lived in fairly cramped quarters with his family, a serene twenty-three-year-old woman of black and white parentage named Allegra and her two children, eight years and seventeen months, the older of whom was born when she was fifteen. Billie's room was a pastel landscape of tinsel, crayon drawings, and an altar that wouldn't have been out of place in a corner of Cara and Sal's converted garage. The altar took up the entire larger closet of the room, and in it he had hung bundles of white sage from the San Gabriel Mountains, which he used as smudge sticks to purify the atmosphere, just as Cara did before her parties. On his altar were things he had collected from the land when he felt the closest to his spirituality, such as a gourd and a phallic-looking rock from the beach.

Billie had just come back from Wolf Creek, Oregon, from one of the established communes of the Radical Fairies. There he did mushrooms with the Radical Fairies and "connected with the earth." They had celebrated the Celtic Beltane rite for May Day, which included a maypole dance and group safer-sex orgies. During this ritual, he had come to the conclusion that the HIV virus caused a heightened sense of life because it created a stronger sense of mortality. His HIV-positive condition had led him to a profound new spirituality because he had learned to "channel demons and release anger."

Perhaps I should have realized how the Radical Fairies would process the AIDS crisis. They would incorporate pain, illness, and mortality into their naturalist, cosmic view of the world. As we lay on Billie's bed, he stuck out his tongue to show me the long, steel barbell that ran through it. Shortly before New Year's, his tongue had been pierced at a ritual. The next few days there was swelling and an increase in pain. But Billie saw the pain as a positive focal point. He'd had a lot of trouble focusing his thoughts before, and now he was able to. He said he had used the entire healing process as a meditation.

I've always been amused by Californians' tendency toward hokeyness and the over-dramatic statement. When I had seen a filmed sequence of a rite at Anton LaVey's San Francisco Church of Satan, the Hollywood hamminess of the details prevented me from appreciating its spiritual aspects. The robes worn by the mostly big-breasted female initiates seemed to be made of polyester, and their hairstyles seemed more appropriate for the movie *Barbarella* than they did for any church, no matter how diabolical. But on the seventh day of this return visit, I was more open to the idea of authentic ritual, real paganism, and black magic. I knew California was a haven for fanatical, mostly white cults, as if the West Coast were some last-ditch attempt on the part of

Caucasians to drum up some salient, hard-edged group identity. After a week back in the San Francisco counterculture, I was still searching for strong medicine, and I realized people whose lifestyle couldn't be justified by easy political theorizing or even a general laid-back attitude might be hard to find. As it turns out, I found what I was looking for in the persons of Danielle Willis and Violet, a couple, who, for better or worse, led what seemed an irrevocable lifestyle.

I first got Danielle Willis's name from the writer Dennis Cooper, when I asked him to list some women in San Francisco who were pro-sex and sexually empowered. For years Danielle had been working as a dancer at a porno theater, and the world of the night was the one with which she identified the most. She'd also written a book called *Dogs in Lingerie*, which contained some of the best writing about "abject sexuality" I'd come across. One story, especially, in which she took the role of a vampire in a freak show whorehouse who gave dangerous head, but who fell in love with a dying mermaid, had aroused my admiration. We fixed a date late in the afternoon of the next day, and she promised to show up with her boyfriend, Violet, whom some people had already described to me as a "half man/half woman," but about whom I knew little else.

From the moment Danielle and Violet smiled at me over our table at a Vietnamese restaurant, I knew I was dealing with people who believed in the radical gesture. From the parted lips in Danielle's white pancake-makeup face and Violet's velvety white one poked vampiric canines. They were permanent, steel-reinforced porcelain caps, which a Harley-Davidson-loving dentist had installed in their mouths, and they were 100 percent functional. The physiognomies, clothing, and tastes of both Danielle and Violet were in perfect harmony with their fangs: both were tall, attractive, sinuous, and waxen, with long, raven-colored hair. They shared a penchant for velvet coats and cuffs with ruffles as well as Death Rock music.

What is more, they were vampires.

Both Danielle and Violet, who sometimes dressed as a transvestite, were fascinated by the erotic and mystical connotations of human blood. Violet claimed to have a license as a phlebotomist, and when friends needed to go to the doctor's for a blood test, they sometimes took him along, because of his adeptness with needles. He had a large collection of syringes, tubing, and needles, which he used regularly to draw out his own blood and the blood of Danielle. Together with one other woman, the two participated in blood feasts. All three of them were HIV negative, although Danielle didn't set much stock in the absolute truth of medical tests.

For Danielle and Violet, blood drinking was a sexual and spiritual rite that symbolized their dedication to sensuality, the intimacy of their relationship, and their identification with the animal world, especially that of wolves. Although both claimed to be Satanists, they didn't worship Satan as their god but only saw Satanism as the precept of being for oneself and learning how to exert one's will over the outside world to get what one wanted—a kind of enlightened self-interest.

Danielle said she liked the way blood tasted and claimed that it gave her "a psychological high." Violet agreed with her: "When you're fucking, it's great to seize your lover by the neck and ram a needle into her vein. I love the idea of reaching the very inside of one's love."

Both Danielle and. Violet claimed a friendship with Anton LaVey, the Satanist, who, then in his sixties, was something of a mentor for them. Like LaVey, they were moved by archetypes of power and will, and both expressed great interest in what they referred to as the "archetypical Satanic images of the Nazis." Although these images were attractive to them for their mystical, and not political, significance, there was a certain amount of racial theorizing in the Church of Satan, at least as Zeena LaVey, Anton's daughter, practiced it.

At the time I learned about her, Zeena LaVey claimed to have dedicated her life to fighting "Judeo-Christian hysteria." Since then, I've been told she currently lives in Germany and devotes part of her time to debunking the many lies her Satanist father perpetrated about his own biography. Zeena LaVey is an articulate writer. At times her sharp, literate utterances seem sadistically trenchant. However, they also smack of race fantasy, a base desire for a cleansed racial identity. As co-director of the Werewolf Order, Zeena LaVey was engaged in a thirteen-year ritual to revive atavism for the coming millennium. According to her, the North American land mass was a "cursed area" because it had killed off the descendants of the land's original tribe, who were currently seeking vengeance by hexing alien races and creeds. She saw her spiritual soil as existing in Europe, where the German myths spoke of a vanished but altogether epic, atavistic life.

Since LaVey is of western European descent, she claimed her chemistry was most sensitive to the western European tradition. She subscribed to ancient Germanic magic traditions and predicted the end of the world and the beginning of a new Satanic era. She viewed the Germanic magic tradition as a broad spectrum that stretched from Faustian black magic to Paracelsus and included the runes and the Rosicrucians. She saw the German National Socialist leadership, which claimed inspiration from the Germanic myths, as having been motivated by diverse currents and unified only in its search for a European mythos that was not "an imported Eastern slave cult."

LaVey's ideas about blood and Satanism were much more formulated than Danielle's and Violet's seemed to be, and her references to race myths probably would not have aroused their interest to a high degree. Nevertheless, the meeting of Danielle and Violet was a culmination of a growing conflict for me. On the one hand, San Francisco had seemed to be the very opposite of categorizing, pigeonholing New York, where race, profession, class, and income are prime markers. But on the other hand, as the days passed, I had the increasing sense of being locked in a ghetto of uniform race and class that would have been impossible in crowded New York, where dramatic, though brief, encounters on the street immediately brought home the verbal, gestural, and dress style of the ghetto. In the New York art world and counterculture, the "blood" origins of thought and lifestyle were hopelessly "contaminated" (multicultural). For although the bohemian East Village style of New York was white-dominated, it was geographically permeated by the neighborhood's other cultural styles, especially Puerto Rican and other Caribbean cultures.

San Francisco seemed different, less cosmopolitan. The European orientation of the Radical Fairies mythology, the consumerist hedonism of the neo-hippies, and the race mythology of Zeena LaVey spoke to me of an identity that was potentially alienating to other races and classes. Now I was beginning to wonder: Were the experimental personae, mystical adaptations, and alternative medical practices of the people I had met made possible only because they had been grouped together according to common background, race, and education? What would happen, I wondered, if the urban ghetto floodgates were opened, and Americans who cared only about the next fifty cents or the next rock of crack were added to the mix?

The next afternoon, I trudged up the stairs of Danielle and Violet's home with my magazine's photographer. Although Danielle and Violet had offered to draw out my blood as a gesture of camaraderie before we photographed them, I had demurred. But to be honest, I had a certain thirst for theirs, as if it held the answer to all my perplexing questions. Was San Francisco, with its counterculture of shifting identities, kaleidoscopic mysticism, and sensual delights a place of freedom or the preparation for a new cult of white tribalism, yet another co-option of nature by the Caucasian horde? Would hedonism lead us to a pansexual world of peaceful tribes or to a blood feast?

Violet had wrapped a belt around Danielle's waxen biceps and was drawing blood into a huge syringe. She was naked from the waist up and serenely watched her blood flow through the tubing. When Violet was finished, Danielle sat in a chair under some meat hooks that hung from the ceiling and arched backward. The blood from the syringe raised above her by Violet began to trickle onto her face. She licked at it hungrily. When her lips and breasts were covered with blood rivulets, she stood and Violet stripped off his velvet jacket and ruffled shirt. His lean, hairless body looked like pulled tallow. His fang-parted lips dove to her chest and hungrily lapped the spilt blood—rivers of liberty and appetite in the bold San Francisco sun.

I flew back to New York with my copious notes the next morning. My San Francisco experiences had been intriguing but confusing, mostly because the culture I had once been a part of had taken directions I never would have predicted. The atmosphere of paradisiacal hedonism I had so supported now seemed clotted and a bit tortured, undercut by darker, more desperate quests for pleasure and meaning. I understood more profoundly why I had left this city. In the end, my project of ultimate personal freedom had been a failure. It wasn't just the fact that one had to face economic realities down the line. It had something to do with the limits of individual imagination and desire. It seemed quite obvious to me now that if I had continued to pursue a life free of any defining context, I might have lapsed into banality and repetition.

Then, suddenly, I thought of all the confining strictures to which I'd subjected myself in New York: breadwinning and the opinions of publishers, sarcastic friends and the judgments of the media, goals, deadlines, and competitive colleagues. Well, maybe San Francisco wouldn't be a bad place to visit now and then, after all.

No matter, because from what I have read, and from the reports of my few friends still living in San Francisco, the city is no longer very "pagan." Six-bedroom Victorian homes, which we rented for about

$230 a month, now go for several thousand, making the casual formation of unemployed groups of friends nearly impossible. Those without money form burgeoning ghettoes of poverty and danger that the middle-class residents of the city assiduously avoids. Counterculture types from my era have moved away died, or "reformed."

Liberal as the city is, San Francisco is now completely infused with a work ethic, making it little different from the rest of America. This, I think, makes my tales of a largely undocumented experimental period even more important. Let's pack these notes away now, hoping some faraway generation will once again appreciate their value.

Lost in Bucharest

BUCHAREST, WHERE I'M SHACKED UP for ten disorienting days in the crumbling Hotel Bulevard with the love of my life, a Romanian, is part *Blade Runner* and part Boulevard Haussmann. It's a sign that—at least in the East—the city as we knew it still exists, with all its chaos, decay, and unpredictable energies.

Let's start with our gigantic circular room in the 1878 Hotel Bulevard, a ghost building with a pink rococo marble restaurant where the only dinner guests are myself and my partner, and where the only company in the cherub-encrusted bar is its four Cher-lookalike prostitutes. Our room, by the way, is gigantic; we have three terraces, but we just can't seem to get the chain hanging from the ceiling in the bathroom to flush the toilet. The hallways are cavernous and unlit, like the set of *Last Year at Marienbad* after thirty years of cobwebs. We meet no one, and no one sees us as we move dreamlike through our own private post-Communist Alphaville. Add the soft-core sex broadcasts that are a staple of Romanian television, and you could say we were living in a private sensual paradise, if only somebody would pick up the garbage.

Now, if you're brave enough, step onto the street with us, among the sundry wild dogs and even wilder homeless children, who have a way of surrounding you like the last reel of *Suddenly Last Summer.* Wipe the grime off your brow (it must be the low-grade gasoline) and look up at a disjointed skyline of nineteenth century palaces; Communist futurist strongholds; dank, pious and tiny seventeenth century Orthodox churches; and Soviet-style housing projects caving into an adjoining building like Bangkok-style leaning towers of Pisa. Everything looks pieced together by Crazy Glue, fighting for space, and contradicting everything else, like structures on a baroque wedding cake made by a chef on LSD and left to gather dust in Miss Havisham's house. This doesn't mean you should be afraid to traverse the roads and alleys that seem to thread signless among these buildings, sometimes ending in mud paths, where the eerie light from a gothic window in streets that are almost pitch black at night illuminates the camouflage uniform of a member of the army, who work here in conjunction with the police to maintain order.

No, don't ask the nice policeman directions. The cops don't know, the army doesn't now. No one respects them. In fact, my Romanian partner made me cross the street on the opposite corner, just to avoid walking by them. Find your way around alone, instead, for outside of petty pickpockets and rather aggressive pimps, crime is at the zero level.

You'll find, oh lost, disoriented, entranced tourist, that the ramshackle cabs are no ticket to information either, since ninety percent of the drivers don't know where they're going and end up charging you three times what it is supposed to cost. But think of the wonderlands you may end up in by accident, such as the time our cab driver drove us into a mudslide, and we crawled out of the cab only to find ourselves in front of a large, red turn-of-the-century house, that should have belonged to *Psycho*'s Mrs. Bates. When we entered, a woman in a revealing red cocktail dress asked us whether we preferred the smoking room (we weren't sure what substance she was were referring to), the "bath lounge" or Purgatorio, a room in the basement with chairs decorated alternately with red devils' horns and white angel haloes. We found, to our astonishment, that the establishment, which calls itself Opium, is owned by the renowned Romanian actress Ioana Craciunescu, whose much younger partner, director Bogdan Voicu, is working with her to create theater entertainments for the special few. There are, for instance, performances weekly in the bath-salon, a bordello-red room featuring an immense gold bathtub. And in the Purgatorio, a new trend of stand-up comedy in English has begun, because, according to Manager Mada-lin Guruianu, Romanian stand-up is just a series of jokes about our private parts. Next door, in the yellow opium room, there are eery pan-tomimes among the oriental cushions… But enough said. If you can find it, go see for yourself.

In general, our treks through Bucharest took us nowhere, for in this half ruined, half-rising city, there are no tangible encounters, only moods, as in a kind of post-nuclear Venice. The fact that there are few cash machines means that you are likely to find yourself penniless for a night or two, which only adds to the potent, fateful charm of this wounded, poetic city.

Bucharest is a tender experience that is only enhanced by its ultra-Latin population, whose language is the closest living one to ancient Latin but who have spent an eternity hemmed in by harsh Slavic realities, which only adds more vulnerability to their often dark, tear-dropped-eyed faces. No matter that I haven't yet found the fabled queens who frequent the park in front of the Opera. No matter that I can't even get the desk clerk to tell me the hotel's telephone number. Bucharest is, for my partner and me, a kind of paradise, a place where you can get lost. A place where there is really no way to define where you are or who you are. A place, in short, without your Visa card.

Convalescence

DRUG ADDICT AND ALCOHOLIC, I was fresh out of several years in the worst, most derelict bars imaginable, determined once and for all to put an end to my downward spiral. Because my favorite addiction had been crack, I knew even the most insignificant word or image could start the chain of associations going—an energy synapse series with a conductive will of its own.

"Smoke," "match," "rock," the sight of an unbent wire hanger like the one I had habitually used to dig out my glass pipe, a certain odor, or an inkling of police presence on the street suddenly took on a kind of fetishized eroticism, bringing me back to the past where the close air of a sealed-off room, the isolation of out-of-date jazz and occasional voice-overs from a TV left carelessly on all contributed to the heightened atmosphere of onanism.

Crack pipe in hand, I had seen time telescope into a jagged series of arousals and climaxes, as I lay enfolded within an endless and ecstatic state of orgasmic disintegration. Continual masturbation, aided at times by a videotape or an underclass prostitute, but often spurred purely by a cascading imagination, was fueled by frequent inhalations from the pipe. And only when the last rock had melted into smoke did the crawling, searching nightmare for more of the life substance descend upon me with all its horror. Then consciousness was compacted into a ghoul-ish struggle, as each gesture became fraught with imminent failure, and life slipped through my fingers like sand through the hand of a skeleton.

As time went on, even continual inhalations could not delay the en-croachment of time. An ever-blacker tide of dying was swallowing me up with maddening slowness. It wasn't long before I subjected myself to recovery. I was aware that the public testimonies and self-accounting of the recovery process owed much to Luther; but, off-putting as such a thought was, I was determined to undergo this contemporary form of conversion. I swallowed my distaste and gave myself up to the repetitive spiritual biographies designed to break down defenses and make me sur-render to the recovery community.

Within a year, I felt confident enough to return to normal life. I had planned to take up again the profession of scholar, which I'd abandoned for almost a decade in favor of my addictions. Fortunately, I'd chanced upon an unusual opportunity. A disabled French scholar whose name had meant a great deal to me in my youthful academic days had placed a small ad in a journal asking for a temporary assistant. He was a spe-cialist in a *fin-de-siècle* writer known for his decadent excesses and for a later zealous conversion to conservative Catholicism. Within a week my letter had been answered, and arrangements were made for my voyage to the French Alps, where the scholar was now living in a sanitarium.

It was in the mountains, fifty miles from Grenoble, that the scholar had been sent for a lengthy, perhaps terminal, convalescence. The tumor that had shrunk him to skeletal proportions had not responded to treat-ment, and the disease had spread to the rest of his body. Wracked by toothaches and migraines, the famous scholar of the infamous late nine-teenth century yellow-book writer found himself following in the footsteps to Calvary of the very man who had been the object of his lifetime of study. For that man had himself spent his last years in excru-ciating pain while living near a monastery as its oblate.

However, this mirroring process between the writer and his scholar might have been called the last cycle in a series, considering that the late nineteenth century writer who was the subject of my employers-to-be study had himself emulated medieval sages, among them the formidable alchemist and monster Gilles de Rais, who had not only once fought beside Joan of Arc but had also been accused of a series of child murders.

After writing his treatise on Gilles de Rais, the *fin-de-siècle* writer had undergone an intense religious conversion in hopes of avoiding the bestial urges that had come with too much familiarity of Gilles de Rais's bloodthirsty practices.

Curiously, even the writer's pious impulses had taken on a sumptuous tinge that could have been described as decadent or lurid. Only those saints whose sacrifices could imply an insatiable masochism seemed capable of inspiring his imagination to devotion. As in the work of the late medieval artist Mattheus Grunewald, whose paintings never ceased to fascinate the convert, the drama of fall and redemption merely promised more vicious scenarios.

He went so far as to devote an entire book to the late medieval Dutch saint Lydwine of Schiedam, whose flesh had rotted to the bone and whose loins had been the home of enormous tapeworms—although the fluids she exuded smelled like cinnamon. To make matters worse, while in the prime of his talents, the now religious writer suffered unbearable pain in the region of the mouth and eventually discovered he was suffering from terminal cancer of the palate. Thus did the writer, and, almost a century later, his most devoted scholar, whom I was about to meet, suffer very similar fates.

With a pounding heart, I swerved through the mute landscape of rock, grass, and patches of snow up a peak close to Mont Blanc, whose razor silhouette could actually be glimpsed from time to time through the crabapple trees. A wind seemed to explode their blossoms from the branches, spraying them against my windshield. The exhilaration I felt for the first time since my addiction reawakened my hope that I had not broken all libidinous ties to the world but could once again vigorously partake in the pleasures of sensuality.

Soon I reached the mountain peak and the sanitarium, housed in a former monastery and currently staffed by nuns. As I was shown to a small white cell with a cot, washbasin and writing desk, instructed to appear at meals promptly, and handed a schedule of events that included prayer and meditation, the sinking realization came upon me that being a visitor of the sick, I would be expected to enter their austere code.

Here, illnesses of all persuasions, from tuberculosis to AIDS, were reduced, if not in theory, at least in sensibility, to the same context of original sin, and no one questioned the sick person's duty—or right— to the correct, nearly silent life of the terminally ill Catholic. The kinds of discussions that tend to establish hierarchies in a community weren't considered meaningful here, as all had been reduced to the identical final stage.

Within this sobering atmosphere, I was brought to the professor, an emaciated old man with wispy, transparent hair and an inflamed, peeling face. Pulling himself up from a carved wooden chair by means of a walker, he extended a limp hand. He was, he said, anxious to take a ride down the mountain up which I had just come, and without so much as another word, struggled from the room, signaling me to follow.

We were intercepted by one of the nuns, who, in cautionary tones, reminded him that the obligatory luncheon was about to be served and went so far as to lead us away from the outside doors and into the dining room. She barely was able to look into the professor's face, seeming to find some kind of unholy terror in the sight of his emaciation.

At the rows of white-clothed tables sat patients and guests in a co-coon of decrepitude and discretion. Our frugal meal consisted of a tolerable red wine, a soup that was only a thin, unsalted root purée, some steamed fish, and macaroni covered with a bechamel that I declined. The plates were brought by waiters in black trousers and white jackets, whose crisp service seemed yet another kind of discipline for both patient and staff. Opposite me sat a woman whose sight had been affected by a tumor, and her daughter, a teenager whose blank expression didn't mask her frustration in being helpless to do something for her mother. Having been told I was an American, the mother released a small cascade of good English, after which we began to eat in silence. The professor took a spoonful of the soup, seemed not to be able to swallow it, and gave up. I brought the gruel to my lips, hyperconscious of the sound of my spoon touching its plate. Slowly it became obvious to me, as if I were observing from afar, that an entire other commentary overlaid this banal ritual, designed to produce a mute and anguished reconciliation with a landscape oblivious to human suffering in its immutable materiality. But my gradual surrender to this commentary was suddenly broken by a plaintive voice that sliced through my reverie with a feeling of absurdity.

"… the crust is sheer delight, and the gratin really like no other. It seems the cows feeding on mountain grass get more magnesium than in the other parts of the region, giving all their dairy products, and especially this marvelous cheese, a certain aftertaste."

It was the woman with the tumor again, and her gloomy attempt at small talk, again in English, merely reminded us that even the strict but sensual etiquette of French table conversation could not conceal our awareness of the fact that, in this place, the spirit was being gradually coaxed to loosen its grip on the body. Even her teenage daughter compressed her lips and colored, and the rest of my meal was passed in pure silence.

When we were finally allowed to begin our afternoon drive, my employer was bundled into his Scottish shawl and pushed toward the exit in a wooden wheelchair. We moved briskly across the polished floor of the dim corridor, broken at regular lengths by squares of harsh light coming through window panes in wooden doors, which reminded me in a melancholy way of those in prewar elementary school classrooms.

When we burst into an even harsher blaze of sun coming through the glass doors leading outside, the professor's voice broke out into a raspy drone.

"I hope you don't mind beginning immediately. When we come back tonight, you will find a large canvas sheath on my dresser containing a manuscript with which I would like you to become familiar. There's an enormous amount of work waiting for you."

The width of the corridor made it impossible to walk beside the wheelchair, and I continued some distance behind, hoping my silence was enough to signal my acquiescence.

When we finally were outside, the nun who'd been pushing the wheelchair so speedily left us, in a manner that suggested she was quite familiar with the procedure. Immediately she was replaced by a scruffy local of about thirteen who jumped abruptly onto our path. He had a flattened, feline snout and a big impudent smile that would have looked like a leer on an older person.

"I hope you won't mind including my little friend in our downward jaunt!" said the professor, whose words sounded like an incantation. Immediately the boy grabbed the wheelchair with dirty, callused hands and trotted toward the parking lot with it.

At the car, the boy lifted the frail professor out of the wheelchair and into his wiry arms. There was a wolfish gleam of content in the professor's eyes as he gazed with happy familiarity at the boy, who seemed, surprisingly enough, to return the look—if a bit impishly. The boy placed him on the front seat and hopped into the back without a word. I snatched a quick, rather peeved look at his lanky frame as I climbed into the driver's seat. I took in his thick, peltish black hair and his flawless skin, which was so pale that the circles under his mean-looking almond-shaped eyes looked bluish. His famished cheeks formed two shadows over a gleaming, impudent mouth and a tiny pink tongue that nervously kept it lubricated.

I wondered if he were a peasant from farther down the mountain. The stains on his rolled-cuff woolens had to be mud or manure; and those tiny pinprick scratches on his neck and forearms were probably from fieldwork.

The air became heavier and the light denser as I steered the car down the spiraling mountain road, waiting for my employer to broach the subject of work. As I rounded each curve, he swayed slightly, one raw red claw weakly gripping the dashboard.

At the moment it seemed as if everything were about to gel irrevocably into frozen silence, he ventured a comment, "Spring has come late this year," and then lapsed again into autism, staring passively at the brilliant, glittering landscape rushing by, almost as if he were aware that his suffering both welded him to unstoppable outpourings of nature and at the same time forbid him any real enjoyment of it.

I myself was suddenly filled with a longing to bond with the exploding blossoms and chilly cascades of water reverberating on stone, whose cathectic vitality released yearnings again for hyper-stimulation, recalling countless nights in which a glass stem streaming with plasticine smoke turned every cell of my body into pure process. How I longed for that shortcut to dilation. After all, I too was recovering.

Strangely enough, we were passing a cafe named Le Relais, a word that can refer to a relay race or a truck stop, but also implies refreshment or renewal, based on the assumption we are living in a reality riveted by relentless beginnings. I backed up until the car was in front of the cafe, thinking we are continually casting off the rotting built up by time and going back to the point we were before hunger, thirst and fatigue reminded us of our diminishing. It was as if we were constantly hoping to go nowhere.

Would the professor mind wasting a few moments for a drink? I asked timidly. We could sit on the terrace and talk about the research he wanted me to help him with.

He climbed painfully from the car with the boy's help, testily warning me, "You cannot trust their aperitifs here. Too much stem and leaf, not enough fruit." We sat at an outdoor table under the sinking sun where we ordered those aperitifs, and where I was sure he would begin to discuss our project. Our small terrace was situated on an esplanade cut into the slope of the mountain, near a torrent, and a harsh light pierced us obliquely, as if nailing us and our tables and chairs to their shadows.

"That's the mountains for you," complained the professor. "The sun shines through the thin air, and it's utterly scalding. You pass into the shade, and the cold lashes through you like a knife."

I brought up the subject of the manuscripts yet again, but the professor interrupted me with a nearly phobic insistency. "Nobody seems to recall that his most extravagant flights of inspiration were the result of his dangerous liaisons with lowlifes!" he said about the writer we would be researching. "No one remembers how he broke his ties with the suffocating world of the ever fatter, more banal bourgeoisie."

Piped through the chasm of stone in which we were seated, his words mixed with the rush of water in the torrent and took on a giddy, brittle intensity that pulverized my attention into anxiety. Now he was talking about food, a kind of leek cooked in bouillon flavored with cognac, which he'd always wanted to try. The more he veered from what I considered our main subject, the more perplexed, distressed and suspicious about the professor's mental health I became. And yet I felt strangely identified with his careening words, which made me remember how crack-inspired thoughts used to rattle through my own head.

Despite my evident discomfort, his chatter rushed monotonously from him like the torrent, endlessly spattering me with staccato insistency, his head darting about like a bird and his eyes fixing from time to time on the boy. I doubted the boy could understand a word he was saying, even though he grinned back brazen and glassy-eyed, until the professor stopped speaking and devoured him with tragic, plaintive eyes.

"He's a local," said the professor, flashing a knowing look at me that I couldn't interpret, while the boy bit at the dirty nail of one hand and peered at us from the edge of his glass of watered-down white wine. "In fact, he's something of a casualty." Suddenly the boy resolutely and noisily sucked the rest of the wine down. The professor moved his eyes away from him and focused on the snow-capped peak of Mont Blanc in the distance, touched by the setting sun.

"Speaking of snow," he blurted out, "are you a devotee of *oeuf à la neige?*"

"It's kind of a meringue floating in a sauce anglaise, isn't it?" I answered rather tersely, perhaps betraying my annoyance for the first time. "But I wish we could talk about the research I'll be helping you with." I really didn't want to hear another word about *oeuf à la neige*. It was especially disgusting to see someone that ill waxing on with culinary greed.

For a moment his eyes refocused, and he asked me how comfortable I was with the colloquial, non-literary French of that period but again veered abruptly into a wistful description of the boy's Alpine dialect, which resembled what they spoke just over the border in Italy, on the other side of Mont Blanc, where most of the names ended in -az and where one could visit the city of Aosta, a name that is a corruption of Augustus, as in Caesar.

I listened tensely, trying to deny to myself that his sudden swerves of context were symptoms of a mental deterioration, as my eyes anxiously swept past the other tables in an effort to avoid his darting gaze.

"Have you ever heard it?" he asked.

"Heard what?"

"That dialect."

For the first time I noticed a woman sitting at a nearby table, her eyes cast to her feet, and I remembered this was a mountain of more than one sanitarium, including one for the mentally ill. Her eyebrows had been redrawn on her face, and she was wearing a turban, perhaps to conceal a hairless cranium. Behind her was a red-faced old man wearing a wool cap, most likely an employee in one of the sanitariums, and farther toward the edge of the esplanade and downing a pastis was someone I had seen at our luncheon. He was very thin and about sixteen and also had the hairless pate of a chemotherapy patient.

"They're from the sanitariums," said the professor, catching my gaze with a kind of eerie satisfaction.

"You mean they let them drink?"

The professor did not bother to respond, and in this I thought I detected a note of contempt for my remark. I avoided looking at his apéritif. Then I heard myself insisting that we leave, that we had better go back up the peak before the sun set. With a shrug, the professor pushed himself to an unsteady standing position and took the boy's arm with his claw of a hand.

By the time I had started the car, some of my annoyance had subsided. In an attempt to establish some context of conversation between myself and the professor, I said, "They're rather severe up there at the sanitarium, aren't they? They run the place like a convent. Have you gotten to know any of the other… guests?"

"One woman who has a blood disease," the professor replied flatly. "We took a chair to the mountain peak once. She keeps her distance now. I'm sure she's told some of the other patients what I have."

The tone astonished me. It was cautious, almost conspiratorial, with a hint of a boast. I turned onto the road a bit rudely, and the professor was jerked forward; the frail, raw hand was again extended to grasp the dashboard. The boy in the backseat tumbled sideways and let out a rude, boisterous laugh. The anxiety that had invaded me before returned and made me increase my speed. We passed one village after another at each small plateau, with cars parked around its single cafe. I found myself wondering if I knew anything at all about the professor's illness beyond a couple of facts, and from what he'd just said about another patient keeping her distance, I had a fleeting, irrational fear that it could be contagious, but I couldn't believe a French sanitarium would allow close contact with such a patient.

"You must stop this driving," said the professor suddenly. "It's making me ill." And indeed he did seem to have a new pallor underneath the red, peeling skin.

I parked in front of the next cafe and went around to the other side to help the professor from the car. There was a woman outside, her face and forearm a patchwork of scars, in the act of mailing a postcard. From inside the cafe came raucous music, boisterous voices. Thinking that the inside would be unacceptable for the professor due to noise and foul air, I suggested we go back to the car and sit in it with the windows rolled own, but his energy seemed to have returned all of a sudden. He took my wrist and pulled me forward, and the boy followed us, as if participating in a game.

It was a tawdry, boisterous cafe, with workers in caps and woolens sprawled along the zinc counter overloaded with pastis or beer, as well as some local teenagers arguing by a pinball machine and some blowzy women who may have been prostitutes and moved back and forth between the bar and some of the tables to cajole a few sullen-looking men who sat drinking alone. I maneuvered the professor to a table as far away from the music and hubbub as possible. "Where did all these drunks come from?" I said irritably.

"They're from the sanatorium mostly," replied the professor with the same eerie satisfaction.

This time I didn't say, "You mean they let them drink?"

Perhaps oiled by the cognac he himself had ordered, the professor began to talk about our work. He said the reason he had asked me if I was familiar with the vernacular of that period is because we'd be working on a handwritten manuscript from Lyon—one of a kind—that did not rely upon literary language. "You'll need a bit of courage to face it," said the professor, a trace of irony compressing the corners of his mouth. "It was secretly culled, I suspect, by our author from a certain cult hiding in the slopes of Lyon, which was, as you must know, the mystical center of France. And it was found among his possessions after his death, thought to have been destroyed—but no."

"Did he use it to research his great novel of the lower depths?" I asked.

The professor shook his head and, as he had established a precedent to do, ignored my wondering glance. "Those slopes above the rivers of Lyon," he went on, "were notorious for sheltering brigands, fugitives, and especially enemies of the church. And what is described in these pages… Well, not even the successor to the Prophet Eugene Vintras, the formidable Abbe Boullan, who successfully applied poultices of excreta to psychic wounds and compelled nuns to drink their urine for their own protection, ever spoke of the practices discussed in these pages."

"Were they that horrendous?" I asked.

"Well, they certainly were the most brutal antidote for that ever fatter, more banal middle class I believe I mentioned."

"Messieurs, please."

The man standing before our table was squat and florid with powerful arms, in his sixties. He had a scar on his weathered neck.

"You're from the sanitarium, aren't you? Would it trouble you to take me with you back to the top? Impossible, since we are going down the mountain, not up," I wanted to say, although I had every intention of going back up as soon as we left the cafe. But I caught the cautionary look in the professor's eyes, which I interpreted as the solidarity of the sick, and felt obliged to say, "But it's getting late, isn't it? Yes, come with us. We should all be heading back."

The man fixed me in his frank gaze. "You'll be leaving now, or will you give this old timer a moment for another pastis?"

"Have your pastis, friend," said the professor in a voice suddenly gracious and relaxed, before I could say anything. "We don't mind waiting."

The drinker grinned, showing inflamed gums, and offered the three of us to join him, but we refused. Promising not to be a moment, the man mounted a barstool, ordering a pastis for himself as well as for a certain Marie, a middle-aged woman exploding with curls and clasping a Pekinese to her swollen bosom. As they downed their glasses, she chucked her florid companion's cheek and entertained him with mock sobs at the thought of his leaving so soon.

Was it my recent experiences with recovery that so soured my reaction to the sight of a sick man downing a pastis while indulged by a local prostitute, until finally I heard myself say sulkily to the professor, "Take a look around you, we are in a pub of ill people. That woman is wearing a wig, and that one carousing with that man over there is just a Frankenstein of scars."

"Well," answered the professor, and I thought I again detected a note of contempt, "perhaps you don't understand how boring and monotonous death can be."

When our passenger re-approached moments later, he was weaving dangerously. He stumbled after us to the car and sat next to the boy in the backseat. However, I had not made more than two or three hairpin turns up the mountain toward the sanitarium before the professor complained of my driving again and commanded me to stop. He was getting nauseous, he said, and couldn't bear the to-and-fro of the curves without resting. As for our new passenger, he had fallen into a noisy snooze, his head tilted back against the seat behind us.

As we sat in the car by the side of the road, I noticed the sky darkening. In fact, it would be night in another half hour. A tense silence seemed to have crept with the darkness into the car. As it did, I thought I heard the breathing of the professor deepen into relief. The boy began to hum a mindless tune to himself. The drunken local woke up and gazed around in confusion. Some intuition seized him. With a look close to panic, he quickly thanked us and said he preferred to walk the rest of the way, opened the car door and nearly leapt out, then staggered up the road.

The boy went back to the humming of his mindless tune. Over and over its empty little intervals spilled into the darkness. And with each degree of darkness, the tune got slower and more deliberate.

Then a flashlight pierced the trees. A fist rapped on the window next to the professor's face. I bent over him to wind the window down, and a middle-aged man poked his head into the car.

"Has your car broken down?"

He was porcine and ruddy, and in the darkness, above his turtleneck, floated a fat neck and a falsely solicitous smile. I couldn't help thinking of the "ever fatter, more banal middle class" the professor had grumbled about. "Have you had a breakdown?" he asked again.

The boy lunged forward from the backseat and grabbed him by the head, managing to roll up the window to wedge it within the frame. The professor sank his teeth in above the turtleneck. The neck struggled and dug against the window's edge, but the boy kept it jammed in place. Tremblingly the old man drank his fill, while the stranger's face changed from coagulated red to ashen gray.

The professor fell back against the seat and smiled beatifically. His mouth was crimson and dripping. "So many things that were known have been forgotten," he said, as if explaining. His ancient face convulsed into a rictus of laughter, which shook his body with such force that I was afraid his ribs would snap. The effort had to have been too much for him, because it was cut off suddenly. His head fell to his chest and his body crumbled against the car door as if he were unconscious—or dead.

Blood trickled like rivers of liberty and appetite from the pallid neck attached to the lifeless head lodged in the window frame. The boy bent forward to take a drop of it onto the tip of his finger, brought it to his mouth, but stopped midway and sweetly extended it toward my face. His pointy tongue flicked back and forth seductively, from the wet hole of his gleaming mouth.

Mouth of the River

An excerpt from the novel *Pacific Agony*

I TURNED UP one of those steep inclines toward Stapler's ramshackle Victorian mansion in Astoria, Oregon, suddenly feeling quite happy to be in the oldest U.S. settlement in the entire West. The house, once gracious and stately, was in dire need of repair; it had become a dowdy old spinster, full of cobwebs and busted-spring furniture. Although it was unlocked, as if expecting visitors, it wasn't particularly welcoming with its thermostat set to sixty-two. The first thing I did was twirl the dial up to seventy-six. I could hear the old furnace groan as if in astonished protest, then burst into rumbling flames. Stapler had said he had no intention of coming out until the following weekend and had crisply requested I be sparing with the heat. But no one would know until the bill came. By then I'd be back in New York, I figured; let them take it out of my salary.

The next thing I headed for was the liquor cabinet. It was quite well stocked, to my delight. I poured myself a scotch and took a sip to swallow a morphine tablet, then headed for the sinking porch, which creaked under my feet. Since the house hadn't warmed up yet, I'd be no less comfortable in the damp and drizzle. It was noon, and the view in the encroaching fog revealed only the sharp edges of roofs, between which one could catch glimpses of the leaden water of the mouth of the river. However, in some areas of the sky, the droplet-saturated air caught the rays of a struggling sun and diffused them into a lustrous wash. This was reflected in the wet black asphalt to create a disorienting, mirror-like sensation, similar to the one achieved by staring directly into silver. Dimensions and directions get lost in the watery glare, and you plunge blinded into its metallic dispersal. With the help of the scotch and the morphine, I floated into this melancholy evanescence until a female voice startled me out of the watery feeling.

Claiming to have been sent by Stapler as a sort of local guide was an ancient, shriveled woman with elfin eyes and crudely cropped hair, who introduced herself as Delilah. Was I ready for a trip into the heart of Astoria? she wanted to know. But first, she said, eyeing the scotch, would I be willing to supply a little "fuel"?

I felt surprisingly profligate with the borrowed bottle, and I led the old witch inside to pour her a stiff one. As we entered, her wrinkled face burst into an expression of astonishment. Was I planning on opening a sauna? For her, the place was stifling! I compromised by turning the thermostat down to sixty-nine, and we settled into one of the broken-down couches in the high-ceilinged Victorian parlor. She clutched the glass of scotch with knobby, arthritic hands and toasted me with the Finnish expression, "Kippis!" Then she bottomed up faster than I could raise my glass to my lips.

A half hour later, we were in Delilah's strangely well-preserved Studebaker. I could hear her gasp and wheeze as she struggled with the clutch, but each time I looked at her with concern, she shook the glance off with hostility. Then the sun suddenly broke through the clouds, revealing one of the oldest faces I'd ever seen. Above a mass of deep wrinkles were two cataract-clouded blue eyes; and from them glimmered a silvery light, producing the same effect as the silver-tinged sky of Astoria I'd noticed earlier. Perhaps I imagined that the eyes seemed to be sizing me up; and her mouth, which was little more than a thin, rigid line, seemed to curl at the corners with a hint of perverse amusement.

"How... old are you, Delilah?" I heard myself blurting indecorously.

"A hundred and two," she barked. "Now put that behind your ears and cogitate on it!"

Delilah was part of the large community of people of Finnish extraction who still lived in Astoria, Oregon, many of whom had ancestors who'd been squashed by the government and the industrialists during the climax of the labor movement. She was, in fact, no real Delilah, but a Finnish immigrant, appropriately named Aamu, who'd come to work in a salmon cannery at the age of thirteen and had moonlighted more than eighty years ago in the offices of the Finnish Communist newspaper *Toveritar*, a publication with strong connections to the Wobblies, as well as other labor organizations and the Communist Party.

We were heading in Aamu's pickup for the docks because, as she explained, she had a very special surprise in store for me. Her great-grandson, Jukka, whom most people called Johnny, had just received his certificate as a bar pilot and would be guiding his first Japanese container ship under the Astoria Bridge. It was a lucrative, but potentially very dangerous, job. Hidden under the swirling waters of the river's enormous mouth were treacherous bars, which could act like sucking mouths that created huge, voracious swells. A good number of even experienced sailors had met their death there, riding one moment on the flat surface of the sea, which seemed as stable as a floor, and then suddenly swooning downward, with enormous walls of liquid rising up menacingly on either side. That's why a supply of highly trained local captains were needed in Astoria, to get the ships safely past the river mouth and take it upstream.

The thought of our upcoming adventure sent a thrill coursing down my spine, and I wondered, perhaps wildly, how such an experience could have been prepared for me. Was not the river, with its predictable downstream course, lined on either side by the punctilious settlements of commerce, the perfect objective correlative of the predictable, bland cultural tyranny I so deplored? And wasn't it just and natural that when it met the swirling id of the sea, a violent and ungovernable reaction should occur? But how, in a million years, could all of those who seemed to be shaping my trip out here realize that this represented the distillation of my imaginings, that I myself had been slipping downstream on a dull, predictable path of aging, only to find myself suddenly facing an inexplicable unmooring, dark, full of exciting, perhaps treacherous currents?

Aamu had parked the car a few blocks from the pilots' pier, to give me a better feeling of downtown, I assumed; and as we walked past the Maritime Museum on a neighboring wharf, I saw that the adjoining harbor, which was full of sailboats and recreational cruisers, had been invaded by a colony of enormous sea walruses. They were sprawled on the docks as if drugged, some belly up, morosely staring at the heavens. At the sound of our walking by, several of these tubby mammoths flipped to a standing position with surprising speed and charged along the dock toward us with raucous, rageful honks. Inebriated as we were, both Aamu and I broke into startled laughter, and together, our noise and the animals' seemed to shatter the moist air like glass.

With this feeling of libido and spontaneity rippling through me, I followed Aamu onto the small pilot boat, which immediately took off from the dock and headed toward the bridge. Three men were with us: the driver of the pilot boat, his assistant, and the river pilot. According to the usual procedure, Aamu's great-grandson Johnny, the bar pilot, had been driven out earlier beyond the bars to meet a container ship coming from Japan. He would navigate the freighter past the bars and under the bridge, whereupon we would meet him at the ship with the river pilot. It was the river pilot's job to relieve Johnny and then guide the ship a hundred miles along the river to Portland. Both bar pilot and river pilot had months of rigorous training under their belts. Only they, and not, for example, the Japanese captain of the freighter, knew every current, inlet, and shallow of the Columbia and its mouth, a necessity for getting safely from the ocean to Portland.

The light, euphoric feeling of release still dominated my body as we skipped across the waves toward a speck in the distance. Droplets of rain made glimmering, blurred patterns against the windshield of the boat; its pilot was in a merry mood as well, spouting river tales of past gales and sailor bloopers, flirting with Aamu, whom he'd known since he was a child, as if she were an attractive young filly, by peppering her with harmless, macho banter. Each time he turned to gaze out the water-spattered windshield, Aamu would make comic gestures of contempt in his direction, then swiftly slip a flask that she'd filled with Stapler's scotch from her purse, take a quick swig, and rapidly pass it to me.

Slowly, the ship we were heading for came into view, enlarging almost imperceptibly, until it finally revealed its full 900-foot length, the size of three city blocks. It was a faceless, windowless gray hulk, rising several stories above the level of the sea—like a monstrous steel anvil that had the miraculous ability to float on the surface of water. The closer we came, the more its menace increased, dwarfing our small pilot's craft to the proportions of a fly, making it clear that if just the wrong swell of water were to thrust us against it, it would take us out like a sledgehammer could shatter crystal. There it stood, almost motionless, as if glued to the ocean, a fragile rope ladder hanging from its wall of a side like a spider web.

"They must be carrying, say, about 4,000 Toyotas," said the driver of our boat with a slightly ironic gloat. "Looks pretty stable now, but when they get out to sea, they're so top heavy that they really roll."

The gray, floating mammoth sent a shiver of awe through me, not so much from the imminent danger of getting close to such massive bulk, but from the realization that every feature, aside from its utilitarian function, was designed to repulse. Faceless and sealed to the environment, its only purpose was to protect and transfer 6,000 tons of steel, plastic, and rubber; and inside this windowless prison, which moved at only twenty-two miles per hour at top speed, was a crew of about twelve or fifteen, who spent several, probably dismal months at sea. It was commerce at its ugliest and most oppressive; but this didn't mean that it, as well, couldn't be deceived and destroyed by the vortex at which nature met civilization. The thought of this afforded me a perverse pleasure.

Slowly, our small craft inched toward the hulk more and more slowly until we were side by side, almost touching. Then the river pilot bid us a cheery goodbye and hopped onto our deck. Seizing the rope ladder hanging from the container ship, he climbed up the side of the boat with the agility of a monkey. According to the driver of our boat, we now had to wait several minutes during which the bar pilot, finished with his task, presented the river pilot to the Japanese captain, and turned over direction of the freighter up the Columbia River to him. Then the bar pilot, who was Delilah's great-grandson Johnnie, would come back down the ladder, and we'd transport him back to shore.

Just as predicted, a body appeared at the top of the container ship's rope ladder. It moved even faster than the one that had gone up, because it was younger and slimmer. As it stepped from the bottom of the ladder onto our deck, I caught a glimpse of the oval face beneath the black wool cap. It was beaming with excitement, probably from his having accomplished his first journey past the bars by itself. It was a stirringly handsome face, strong and sculpted, with just a touch of Billy Budd vulnerability; or at least that's how I saw it in the trembling excitement of the moment. Then the shadow of a darker thrill passed through me as I studied the large, tempestuous blue eyes, which seemed to hold that same wild energy I'd been so startled and confused by earlier. My entire soul fell into those eyes, and my whole journey compressed in my mind into one wordless, insane, realization that I cannot describe.

There was, however, another surprise in store for me. Instead of pulling away, our boat hovered, still unmoving, inches away from the container ship.

"Aren't we going now?" I ventured.

The question was met with a tense silence.

By now Johnny, the bar pilot, had entered the boat. Was I imagining that he kept staring at me with a playful, teasing smile? Aamu spit out some cursory introductions, after which silence reigned again, while our boat stayed inexplicably in place and Johnny kept staring at me, almost challengingly, I thought. To avoid his glance, I studied his large, dry, but somehow sensitive-looking hands, letting my eye trail from them up his arms to the curves of his muscular shoulders. Then my gaze slid downward along his broad, flat chest, pausing irresistibly at his crotch to discover that the material of his pants was raised like a tent, signifying an erection.

Just a few moments later, another figure appeared at the top of the rope ladder and scrambled down to our deck even faster than Johnny had. He was dressed like the two pilots, in down jacket and work boots; but around his face he had tied a black bandana, which had been pulled up to the level of the top of his nose. As he hopped onto our deck, a second, almost identically dressed figure appeared at the top of the rope ladder; and it, too, scrambled down to our boat. Both of them were much smaller than Johnny, wiry and crouched, as if ready to leap up and bolt at any moment.

Immediately Aamu extracted her flask, and both strangers in bandanas took a gulp from it. Tension was as thick as a knife as we headed back to Astoria. No one had introduced me to the two extra passengers. The waves had risen, and we leapt swiftly over them like a weighted cork, but while the other passengers and I were tossed upward a bit each time we hit a wave, the two strangers remained in place, their knees spread, their feet planted firmly on the floor. They had still not removed their bandanas; and everyone in the boat seemed to avoid their and my glance, except for Aamu and her great-grandson, who seemed to be gazing at me with a gloating, almost jubilant expectation.

As soon as we got back to shore, the two extra passengers scrambled to the deck and hopped onto the dock, sprinting toward the street until they disappeared. It was as if they hadn't existed; the thickness of tension suddenly broke, and the driver of our boat resumed his corny, homey banter. Aamu began chattering in her croaky voice about celebrating her great-grandson's first successful run by taking him back to the Labor Temple and Café for a few more drinks. She commanded me to meet them there in an hour. "You just got to," she bid me severely.

"Delilah," I managed to croak out, "who were those other two men?"

She let out a raucous peal of laughter, as if my question were absurd, and Johnny turned away to gaze at the street. "You know," she said offhandedly, avoiding my eyes, "sailors used to have a ball when they finally got to port. It made up for all those dreary days at sea. Nowadays, with the terrorist threat and all, most of 'em are confined to the ship."

"But who were they?"

A note of exasperation crept into her voice. "Silly man from another land, there's still a lot of solidarity among people of the sea." And with that, she waved goodbye, but not until her great-grandson, to my astonishment, had given me a playful slap on the ass.

It was growing dark as I trudged back up the hill to Stapler's house. Now the setting sun had become powerful enough to inject strong shafts of rose through the watery sky, which seemed to writhe with the pleasure of it. Then the play of light deepened into a lid that weighed heavily on the city, congealing into a black viscosity that made it hard to see my feet below me.

The house, which I'd left set at seventy-two degrees, was toasty as I liked it; and as was my wont when I was indoors, I kicked off my shoes and stripped down to my underwear. My memory of what had just happened seemed to crawl over me like insects, or was it like the feeling of colliding with a spider web in the dark: invisible sticky strands that are impossible to remove and cling in places that are difficult to pinpoint? For the first time, a terrible sense of confinement began to close in, the feeling of becoming a pawn in someone else's diabolic game; and the fact that I seemed to be the last to know suddenly filled me with an impotent rage. But I certainly didn't plan to show up at the Labor Temple and Café; they could find another East Coast imbecile to use as their patsy.

I stalked back and forth in my underwear in the dark house, windmilling my arms at invisible fears, then hurried to my luggage to extract another tablet of morphine and threw open the door of the walnut cabinet of the bar, which struck the wall, chipping the plaster. Grabbing what was left of the scotch, I swilled it down, then doubled over coughing, letting the bottle crash to the floor.

It was in this tortured position that I noticed the seashell on the floor below the couch, and something metallic gleaming from it. The shell held a large key, the classic type that had been used over eighty years ago. That's when I realized I hadn't yet bothered to examine the house.

Muttering and with head bowed, I walked up the stairs in the dark until my forehead collided painfully against a door. At first the key didn't seem to fit; but after jiggling the handle and key at the same time, I felt the door give and pushed it open. Behind it was a narrow, very steep flight of more stairs, almost vertical, of a type I'd seen only in the cramped houses lining the canals of Amsterdam, leading to the attic. In my inebriated state of bewilderment and rage, it was all I could do to pull myself up them, sputtering for breath. At the top, I fumbled for a light switch and flipped it on, which illuminated only half of the immense space. Beneath the sloping walls of the attic was a single gigantic room, which looked almost like an army barracks, mostly because of the rows of about thirty cots that filled the center. The walls were lined with books; and stooping under the sloping sides of the roof to examine them, I began scanning the titles. Everything was impeccably arranged, in alphabetical order: from Bakunin, Bey, and Goldman to Debord and Zerzan; but pop marginals were there, as well, such as McVeigh and Manson. Stacks of clippings recounting attacks and arrests that went all the way back to the Symbian Liberation Army and the Panthers had been carefully paper-clipped together in folders.

At the farther end of the room, which was still plunged into gloom, was a large, white board on a wooden stand, blocking the triangular window, the kind of board used in kindergartens on which you could write with a felt-tip pen and then erase by wiping off. On it, in the semi-darkness, was a childishly rendered, multi-colored drawing. I stumbled toward the light switch on the opposite wall and flipped it on. A brass Revere chandelier, hanging precariously from the ceiling and outfitted with flame-shaped bulbs, illuminated the room with a wan glow. On the white board was a felt-tip map of the Oregon coast; it was obvious that it had been painstakingly but rather inaccurately copied and enlarged from a smaller map in a book, in an artless attempt to reproduce the many inlets and tiny peninsulas that jutted from the shore. Red dots had been used to indicate the cities, and blue lines depicted the highways connecting them.

It took me a moment to realize that the green line running north/south was a visual rendering of my itinerary. There it was, beginning at a little asterisk next to the city of Seattle, advancing down along the Washington and Oregon coasts to Portland, then dropping further down to Eugene and back up to Portland, zigzagging west to Astoria and then across the bridge to Washington State on toward Canada.

Through the numbness of alcohol and morphine, I stared dazedly at it, mouthing the strange words in brackets next to each stop on the itinerary:

1)   Pre-Assignment: New York—Background Investigation

2)   Seattle: Brush Contact With Target—Cold Approach

3)   Portland: Maintain Cover—Plant Drugs If Necessary

4)   Eugene: First Contact, with Cell—Begin Biographic Leverage

5)   Portland: Honey Trap (Use Raven for Co-option)

6)   Astoria: Employ Usual Stringer; Contact Is To Maintain Deep Cover; Some Disinformation Could Prove Helpful; Raven May Use Pressure

7)   Aberdeen: Continue Attempt at Re-Education

8)   Vancouver: Target Should Be Ready for Enlistment (Employ Multiple Ravens Again, If Necessary); If Recruitment Negative, Burn[1]

But why should anyone believe me? Why should I believe myself when I know my blood was saturated with more alcohol and morphine than even I was used to imbibing, when I found myself lying in my underwear among shards of glass from the broken scotch bottle in the middle of the downstairs living room floor the next morning, without any memory of getting back down there, if I had, indeed, ever gone up?

Moments later as I was loading the rest of Stapler's liquor supply into my duffle bag, I felt a large, rough hand with a strangely sensitive touch gently caressing the back of my neck with its big knuckles. Then the hand grasped my neck and turned me around, after which I saw enormous wild blue eyes staring into mine. They were, I decided, the eyes of Delilah/Aamu's great-grandson, Jukka, if you'll allow me to use his Finnish name, and they pulled me toward him with a strange

---

[1] Slang term for deliberate sacrificing of an intelligence agent, usually a newbie.

magnetism, until my lips were crushed against his, tasting the flavor of the licorice Snus he kept in his mouth between cheek and gums, then opening to the plunge of his tongue.

After we pulled away, the look on his face was in no way in accordance with the amorous gesture he'd just completed. His features were hardened into a blank, militaristic impassivity, and the blue eyes had dulled into the impenetrable color of tin. "I've received instructions," he said, "I don't believe his car can make it all the way to Vancouver, so you'll be leaving it here and riding with me in my Jeep for the rest of the itinerary."

Without answering, I took a step to the side so that I was in line with the open door behind him, through which the first truly sunny day of my visit glared; but he rapidly shifted his position, forming a barrier between me and that portal of freedom.

"Get your bag," he required in a flat, staccato voice that bordered on the sullen, then folded his arms over a puffy chest and stood blocking the door with legs astride. I'll never forget the image of his back-lit, unmoving, booted body, in its khaki green clothing, transformed into a two-dimensional dark silhouette by the constriction of my pupils to the harsh light outside the door. It changed everything around it into a fable, within which he became the central golem.

"You should have showed up at the Labor Temple and Café last night," was all he said. "We were expecting you." The severity of his tone was enough to make me follow wordlessly with my bag to the Jeep.

The Jeep rattled down the steep incline toward the water and then swerved left toward the bridge. Jukka had lapsed into a stony silence, which complemented my emerging sense of being held prisoner. He answered my few questions in monosyllables or short sentences, almost the way a superior briefs a petty officer. In such a situation, others might have been fixated on the possibilities for escaping, or at least be trying to unravel the web of manipulation that had put them in this perplexing position. But amazingly, my entire mind was occupied by the notions with which I'd arrived in this region and how artlessly "off" every impression was that I'd had.

This was all I thought about as we drove over the Astoria Bridge toward Washington State, not so very far above the steel-gray, thrashing waves of the mouth of the Columbia River below. It was a thrilling experience, almost like driving across the surface of the water itself, because of the relative thinness and astonishing length of this truss bridge. We were headed, Jukka informed me, for the eastern end of Grays Harbor, on the banks of the Chehalis and Wishkah Rivers, to pick up a "shipment" (human, I suspected) before continuing on to Vancouver; and as the spray stung my face through the open windows of the Jeep, I had the impression that I was finally understanding this region for the very first time. It was neither an Edenic natural paradise nor a smug, opportunist hub of commerce; but actually an accidental, brilliantly grotesque collision between the two. Again and again in the fine mist of sea and rain, huge stretches of forest and water would hypnotize me into a state of awed surrender, whether I saw the gloom-ridden, totalitarian majesty of a stand of old Douglas firs or waves slashing a desolate, pebbly shore; and then all this would be interrupted suddenly by the baldness of a clearcut hill or the sinister smoke-spewing stacks and tangled juggernaut of a power plant. Unlike the East, where, in many places, such sights had long ago tamed and supplanted nature, here the struggle aggressively raged in all its blatant and elemental vulgarity. Everything seemed accidental and random, and, at moments, I chastised myself for my naiveté in thinking I'd been assigned to an insipid territory that was energetically working in an orderly manner to spread the commodified North American dream. No, by some accident, I'd fallen upon another form of chaos—I, the critic who had always lauded the chaotic adventure of the Eastern urban scene. This was a place—I finally had to admit—of violence and struggle, a thrillingly ugly battle between the land and humans that produced a rich, stupefying sensory experience. Here there would never be a chance for genuine order; only the snarl of nature echoed by the discontent of the human condition—and all of it hiding under a featureless mask of progressivism because the people here were well aware that their struggle could never be completely expressed in words.

Having read a fair amount of literature about the next stop on my itinerary, I knew what to expect of Aberdeen, the small city at the eastern end of Grays Harbor: a drab southern Washington mill town not many miles from the other side of the Astoria bridge, population approximately 17,000, a good number of whom, after losing their jobs in the declining lumber industry, must have declined into alcoholism, which the surprising number of taverns and bars in the nearly deserted downtown area clearly confirmed.

Jukka parked the Jeep on the main street, informing me that we were about to "make our choices from the shipment." He led me into the only establishment in downtown Aberdeen that seemed to have any activity: a pool hall cum newsstand in which a collection of savage male adolescents, fated for dereliction and homelessness, loitered, playing pool, bumming cigarettes, and breaking into occasional scuffles until the proprietor, a pallid, middle-aged, blond woman with ringed eyes, bellowed at them over the sound of The Doors' "People Are Strange."

Never before, even in the ghettoes of the East, had I seen such ebullient desperation. Scraggly-haired and scrawny, jittery with rageful anxiety, the shoulders of their shirts and their cigarettes drenched by the rain outside, they marched up and down the length of the pool table, often hitting the ball with such force that it went flying off to hit a wall, an event that produced catcalls of perverse jubilation. Others stared glumly with slackened mouths at the "game" in process, calling out acidic insults every time someone missed a shot. The majority had the habit of rubbing their crotches during an idle moment, not in any gesture of sexuality but in the bored spirit of passing time evoked by a cat licking its fur. They were speed freaks, I assumed, but they were also casualties of a failing economy, more than likely to have been abused at home by working-class parents who were victims of the new service economy, wore sweatshirts calling for the frying of the spotted owl and spent the endless rainy season unemployed paging through copies of *Soldier of Fortune* magazine, which one of the youths sat perusing at that very moment.

Jukka picked several of them, drew them into a corner of the pool hall and whispered an inaudible proposition into their ears. I sat across the room studying them, interrupted regularly by one or another bumming a cigarette, until my pack was depleted, while I continued my meditation on my journey in a new demoralized way. Once again, I was seized by the impulse to escape the subversive activities of this outfit, which now seemed to have become increasingly apparent at each stage in the journey. Yes, I was through with my "research." There had to be a moment when Jukka would forget his vigilance.

Jukka's new recruits, he informed me, would meet us the following morning at the garish motel he'd chosen for us, with neon signs promising pleasures that ranged from waterbeds and mini-gyms to cable TV. It was less than a block from the local casino, and Jukka specified that it be booked in my name, traveling as he undoubtedly was undercover.

It was very early evening when we checked in, even too soon for dinner. Despite the orangey light of the bedside lamp, Jukka's perky features—which included a small, regular nose, dimpled chin, blue, enormously lidded eyes and pink, sinuous lips—suddenly took on an exhausted pallor. Then a strange gleam of compassion crept into his formerly opaque irises, and he gently motioned me to him on the bed. Quite rapidly, his entire face was contaminated by this new delicate emotion; he took my head in both enormous callused hands and stared into my face with a disturbing frankness. The words that followed astounded me, because despite their liberal use of euphemisms, they contained an uncanny awareness of my own mental processes. I seemed to be, he said, about to fail at the accomplishment of the project for which I'd been drafted. This, he had to admit, was causing him an uncustomary feeling of consternation; it was not often the case that he developed a sense of protectiveness about his "targets." It was, in fact, downright unprofessional of him; but the task he'd have to perform if I did not swiftly progress in my "re-education" was one he now dreaded.

Taking a different tack, he made some references to the prejudices with which I had arrived but said he wanted to make it clear that he was, in fact, quite impressed by my intelligence. However, I seemed to have a tendency for a certain kind of emotionality that the "drafters" hadn't considered. I wouldn't call the tone that followed "pleading," but the tiny tremor in his voice rather closely resembled it. All I had to do, he explained, was open myself to the struggle of the people of this region. Then his voice darkened, returning to its robotic frigidity, as he added, with a strange casualness, "Otherwise you're finished."

I suppose the gesture that came next was an attempt to color what he'd said as convincing, and I will not describe it in detail because none of this really has much relevance to my story. I won't dwell on every feature of his deliriously silken, wiry body, nor the two hard melons of his buttocks, which tightened into steel with each thrust into me as we lay together on the still made bed, because I doubt anyone would believe me, and because my state of confusion at the time would not make me a very reliable narrator. I will admit, however, that despite the swooning surrender necessary to accommodate such maneuvers, I did not lapse completely into the manipulated subject that was the intended goal because, shortly after he fell asleep, I crept to retrieve his olive khakis on the floor and gently extracted the key to the Jeep. Then, with no idea where it would take me, I sped up East Market Street and northwest on East 2nd, where I found myself in a lower-class residential neighborhood and a frustrating cul-de-sac. I threw the Jeep into park and sat anxiously staring through the dirty windshield at the eternal drizzle, wondering about the easiest way to find egress.

Those thoughts were quickly interrupted by the sight in my rearview mirror of an approaching taxi, quite far off, but driving much too fast for the transportation of a normal client. Fearing that it was indeed Jukka in the backseat of the cab, in search of me, I leapt out of the Jeep and looked around wildly. For lack of a better idea, I crept under the small overpass bridge at the end of the street, happy the drizzle had turned into an angry torrent and might keep anyone from spying me.

It was a low-slung bridge, and I had to stoop to keep from hitting my head as I scaled the small incline of bare dirt beneath it. Dizziness caused by the excesses of the night before, as well as a sudden rush of fear, suddenly overcame me. The rain was coming down in sheets, and I doubted I could make it back to the Jeep and attempt a belated getaway without falling in my suddenly enervated state.

Halfway up the bare dirt incline under the bridge, there was a depression in the earth. It was almost the exact shape and size of a mummy's coffin, with what could have been the outline of a human head at the top and a swelling in the curve halfway down to accommodate the arms. Just like a preserved, bandaged corpse, I lay down inside it; its curves fit almost perfectly around my prone body, and it was deep enough to shield me to some degree from the spray-laden wind, which came in gusts through the open spaces on either side and concealed me as well, I hoped, from any prying eyes.

From my position, I couldn't make out the person who jumped from the back of the cab through the sheets of rain, so I stayed pressed into the earth. But I supposed there was as good a chance as any that it could be Jukka.

Then I don't know what happened. The rain suddenly began to come down with such ferocity that all images and sounds beyond the underside of the bridge were cut off. With each gust of wind, sheets of it were flung at me under the bridge, and my body was bathed in its iciness. But for the first time, I blessed the rain, because I knew it was my only chance of remaining concealed. There even seemed to be something ritualistic about it, a strange, violent baptism toward which other experiences in this region had been leading.

As those in a panicked state of suspension are wont to do, I let my eyes move around in an attempt to distract myself from the eternity of these moments. If you thought about it, this really wasn't very different from the inside of a mummy's tomb. There were calligraphic scrawls on the walls that from this distance could have been thought of as cuneiform, and around the rear side, where the incline at its steepest met the bottom of the bridge, which I could see by straining my head backward with all my might, someone had left a trail of artificial flowers and leaves. One of the inscriptions was large enough to make out from my position. It said, "Thank you, Curt. All I knew I learned from you."

Who was Curt? And why did this place, punctuated by the continual hammering of rain and the hysterical gurgle of the river, with a view of broken pilings like stalactites in the water beyond, feel so sepulchral? I wrestled with the thought only for a few moments, before passing into unconsciousness.

Deep Springs: Blood and Brains in the California Desert

OUR 1963 CESSNA PLANE dips past the Inyo Mountains and into a desert valley the size of Manhattan. Spread out below is the crater of a salt lake; then slightly to the northeast, a small patch of brilliant green. The plane grazes that patch and taxies over a cattle guard, into a ranch. A very special kind of ranch. This is also the maverick college where I teach.

Deep Springs College, the only human settlement in this vast desert valley just east of the Sierras, is America's best-kept academic secret. It's a tiny, exclusive men's school with only twenty-six students that has produced diplomats, world-famous scholars and the writer William Vollmann; yet few people know where or what this college is.

At first sight, Deep Springs, which isn't on any map, looks just like those scattered cattle ranches popping very occasionally out of the desert on the route northwest from Las Vegas, about 200 miles away. Bewildered German tourists, down to their last drop of gas on the long haul to the next station in Bishop, California, might wander onto campus in search of fuel. They find themselves among alfalfa fields, several hundred head of grazing cattle, and a couple of field hands in faded

Carhartt jeans. Nothing about these field hands suggests they'll be cramming for a paper on Baudelaire, population biology, or Nabokov that very evening. In fact, some of the locals in Bishop, which is forty miles to the west, still believe Deep Springs could be a reform school masquerading as a college. Others suspect it's a cult.

Founded in 1917, Deep Springs is the brainchild of bachelor industrialist L.L. Nunn, a co-producer of the Niagara Falls hydroelectric project and creator of the first hydroelectric system in the far West. A photograph showing him in his heyday about eighty-five years ago, looking caped, puritanical, and a bit vampiric, looms over students in both the dining hall and main building. Nunn's abstruse, Emersonian theories of education are set forth for students in a booklet that describes the "moral nature of the universe" and "the spirit of the desert." He believed that both leadership and altruistic character had to be built in the wilderness among a select, tightly knit group of elite young men.

Each year, male students who score in the top one percent of the SATs receive a brochure inviting them to apply to Deep Springs. The college offers only a two-year program without a degree, but its academic standards are so high that both Harvard and Yale have agreed to accept all of its transfer credits. Since the student body is self-governing, they have the right to choose the freshman class as well as a constantly changing roster of professors. Self-governance by adolescents has led to jokes about the school being the setting for *Lord of the Flies*. And at times, as I've taught there, I've wondered if it is. But in many ways, Deep Springs seems more like a progressive monastery or even an old-fashioned Quaker community.

Those thirteen lucky students who are accepted each year, out of the hundred or so who apply, vow to forego girls, fraternities, alcohol, and urban or suburban life for two years of milking cows, moving irrigation lines, planting potatoes, cooking meals, riding horses, and herding and slaughtering cattle. These responsibilities are no joke. If students shirk them, the ranch could fail. Cattle might wander out into the highway. A cow's udder could burst. Everything, including meals and maintenance, is their responsibility. And if those assigned to the dining hall sleep late, there won't be any breakfast that morning. On top of that, students are often burdened with several hundred pages of challenging course reading a week, and they're graded for their participation in class.

Those are the harsh facts of this maverick ranch college, but its story is also an eccentric fairy tale full of folkloric characters. There is the vice-president of the college and ranch manager, Geoff Pope, a handsome mustachioed Montanan, who is the owner of the 1963 Cessna airplane that took me over the valley. Pope can ride, lasso, brand, manage ranch work, and fly a plane. Every week or so, he takes that plane up to check the whereabouts of cattle. He's also the one who chooses the student cowboy.

The student cowboy is the most glorious position at Deep Springs. His main responsibility is the herd of 280 cattle, including their branding and castration, but he's expected to sabbatical with the previous year's cowboy all the coming summer in grazing land 12,000 feet high in the mountains. There they stay without another soul, herding cattle, bathing in a stream and sleeping in a cabin, for weeks at a time. The student cowboy is chosen for his discipline and independence, but he's also likely to be quite a looker. He's not only the cattle herder, but a kind of symbol of the school, a "poster boy" for the "spirit of the desert."

The *eminence grise* of Deep Springs College is its sixty-two-year-old President Jack Newell, a former Deep Springer. Although the school is ostensibly run by students, his veto power can be absolute. Newell, who's been known to ride his motorcycle up treacherous mountain roads, has just managed a multimillion-dollar renovation of this tuition-free college, which exists entirely on private endowments. One day he left me gasping for air as he led me almost at a run on a hike up the sagebrush-covered hills. Then there is the stylish-looking school chef,

Tom Hudgens, who is a former employee of Berkeley's Chez Panisse. Hudgens trains student cooks in the sophisticated preparation of beef from the ranch cattle, custards from milk taken directly from the cows' udders and vegetables from the garden—for meals that are served three times a day.

Social relationships at Deep Springs speak loads about the peculiar situation of being a talented, overworked eighteen- or nineteen-year-old stuck without girls in the desert. Inevitably, these students bond with their peers on an intense level. Those who don't are all but lost—mentally exiled to the vast and empty desert where they have only their own consciousness to encounter. Bonding can occur during a yearly "Death March," an eighty-mile hike around the rim of the valley, which few ever finish. There is comradely nude swimming in the reservoir during the warm months, or an exhausting, mystical nude climb at night up shifting sand dunes. Occasionally, there have been bloody boxing matches staged to settle arguments. Friendships are passionate, almost familial. It's not rare, for example, while teaching, to look up and see one student stroking another's hair, or with his head on his shoulder. In the majority of cases, it's not a matter of sex, but of those intensely claustrophobic friendships that come from living and working in a desert community.

If this is the most highly unified community of any college in the United States, it also produces some of the most interesting individuals. Nietzschean philosophizing, hermit-like treks to the desert lasting several days, and lonely bouts of studying mold iconoclasts. Eccentric or original teachers, who are sometimes at odds with conventional academia, are invited for their material. I have taught at Deep Springs on two separate occasions, most notably a course called "Degeneracy, Bohemia, and the Urban Avant-Garde," which cast a harsh contrast to the bucolic environment and gave a few students nightmares.

This time, I became the advisor of a deeply emotional, private young poet. His work—which he showed only to me—popped out of him with astonishing speed. He devoured Whitman, Ginsburg, and other poets and brought forth beautifully crafted, sometimes terrifyingly visceral poems. Not every student has his particular talent, but all are fascinated by extreme performance. Addicted to service, adventure, and hard work, they've been known after Deep Springs to take jobs in Cambodia and Kosovo, to hitchhike to Alaska or work part-time as paramedics.

Their commitment is a perfect match to the self-challenging, almost masochistically macho values of the entire community. Students are encouraged to go off alone into the desert and face themselves, for a couple days at a time. As in biblical times, the desert is often a place of visions, or at least new ideas. Some come back inspired or even mesmerized. There are, as well, highly affecting practical rituals at this school that are quite controversial. They force students to develop positions about survival, compassion, and animal welfare. It must be kept in mind that a lot of the food eaten at this school has been killed with the students' own hands. Every couple of months a cow is slaughtered. I took part in a slaughter this year. After cutting the throat of a young bull, students pierced the back legs with meat hooks and hoisted it for skinning, disembowelment and quartering. That afternoon, before some of us had even had time to wash the blood off, the liver and heart were served for lunch.

If any group in America can ever be compared to Japan's ancient samurai culture, then this must be it. Are Deep Springers a prototype for a new kind of heroic male? They're soft-spoken intellectual warriors with their feet in the mud. And they've learned what it means to spill blood.

Goodnight, Manhattan

WHEN YOU HIT THAT GREAT BRICK wall that hopefully breaks through to Heaven, where will you be? My dear friend and mentor, novelist and linguist Ursule Molinaro, had her "brick wall" all planned out. A "graduate" of the Nazi-run prison of Fresnes in France for hiding a Jewish couple, she decided forever after to escape all institutions. Hospitals were at the top of that list. Making her future departure foolproof and pill-enabled didn't prevent her from imagining endings that could happen before her well-planned exit. Once I flagged down a New York taxi for the two of us. To the dangerous swerves of the clumsy cabbie she conjured the following: What would happen to us if we left this level together in the company of this gap-toothed Haitian chatting on a cell phone in his coconut-oil infused cab? Would it somehow entangle our afterlives with his? I don't know. What I do know is that it matters where you die because that's also where you've been living.

Such questions never concerned me until July 2 of my fortieth summer in Manhattan. That was the day in 2014 when a substance-fueled boyfriend with whom I had foolishly assumed I would spend the rest of my life peremptorily dumped me. Gazing back upon decades of sexual encounters numbering in the thousands, including eleven failed "love affairs," I asked that Peggy Lee question: "Is that all there is?"

I was sitting in my spacious East Village apartment when I faced that issue, among mostly mid-century furnishings and original art by friends. I gazed at the several books I'd published that had all finally found their way to the remainder table. My eye strayed to the oversized flat screen and my hard drive collections of over 2,000 films. I studied the walls cleverly painted in an array of Technicolor hues inspired by my favorite films.

No, I did not want to die here.

I was born and raised in the do-you-really-call-it-a-city of Syracuse, a land-bound enclave so median that it had become a national center for market research product-testing as I grew up. So brutal were the winters, that snow in May was no occasion for comment. So conservative was our upper-middle-class Republican neighborhood that children barely set foot on its manicured front lawns. Sidewalks that knew the footprints of anyone but the mailman were few. When the sun fell and the tastefully retro streetlamps blinked on, the empty lanes looked like footpaths in the tonier sections of Forest Lawn Cemetery.

I suppose I should admit that I'm even old enough to have graduated from my segregated high school before busing changed its population in the second half of the 60s. Our nearly-all-white-kid dress code was rigid. The principal stood in the hallways with a ruler to measure hemlines and sent any girl whose skirt was more than one inch above the knee home to change. First to don an olive army jacket, round-framed hippy glasses and a "Jewfro," I'd made a vow by junior year to escape my origins and dump my provincial upstate accent. By 1974, after a four-year hippy hiatus in San Francisco, I became a confirmed New Yorker.

In 2001, my brother and I inherited the family house after my mother's death at ninety-eight. I couldn't wait to turn it into cash. Bro' bought me out, and I used the money to get more notches on my belt of promiscuity throughout four countries in Western Europe. Then I came back to New York for another thirteen years. When 2014 hit and the brooding boyfriend coldly split, I suddenly realized how old I was. I also realized I had used up all the city had to offer. Was that why I found myself hoisting a giant Victorinox suitcase onto the racks of an unreliable Amtrak headed for Syracuse on October 14, 2014? Why was I bringing so much with me?

To say I stayed a long time is an understatement. It is now August 2015, and I'm still upstate. Roughing out one of the worst winters in history without a car, I figured the supermarket was a mere five-mile round-trip walk through snowdrifts and howling winds. I had a lot else to keep me busy, too. Six months previous, I'd been hired at a discount rate to translate an award-winning French biography of director Jean Renoir. The thing is 1,000 pages—for gawd's sake—and the type is small. After a couple of months of tackling it and cleaning out a ten-year collection of take-home hospital inhalers and those weird yellow circular hospital washbasins my parents had come home with in the last years of their lives, I set up a couple of old TVs from childhood with signal converters and rabbit ears. Then I settled into my routine of translating punctuated by twice-daily viewings of *Perry Mason* over the air on *ME-TV*. I rose early, and mornings were never wasted. The first hour, over a Keurig cup of coffee, I spent bawling and cursing my ex. (Still doing it, too.)

Only now have I fully realized what kept me in the town I'd made every effort to escape. In the first place, every street in big bad New York City still reminds me of the pitiless person who has destroyed my chances for love. I can't pass a McDonald's without remembering the sweltering day in June I waited two hours in front of its Delancey Street branch for him to come from Brooklyn and "discuss our relationship." Turns out he'd gotten arrested that day for an open can of beer on the street. I frantically called every hospital, as he was calling his best friend instead of me.

Knowing I wasn't at the top of the list even at Central Booking set the tone for that summer. It included the temporary loss of that parade of twenty-something, attractive, gay would-be writers who I'd thought were enthusiastically connecting me to the younger generation. They laughed at my jokes. However, the youth connection stopped abruptly last summer as they flocked to shares in Fire Island. Apparently, there wasn't room for me. My only consolation was being saved from having to appear in front of them in a bathing suit. I think you call what they are "fair-weather friends." My only companion that entire summer was Turner Classic Movies and my broken heart. TCM was comforting because of the childhood era it projected. Kind of like having Mommy and Daddy dug up and placed handily in the corner.

I could go on about the many things that disappoint aging gay men in the context of city life. Instead, I'd like to list some of the benefits of the provincial lifestyle. One trustworthy long-term friend whom I'd taken to the senior prom is still in Syracuse. In getting to know her again, I rediscovered something very exotic for a New Yorker. In friendships with the people of small cities, there *is* no complicated subtext. They actually mean what they say and do what they say they will. When my friend agrees to spend an evening together, there isn't the slightest chance in the world of getting a text saying she decided to go to a gallery opening instead. As for the rare friendly overtures from those I have met up here, I can be fairly certain they haven't researched me on Google first and aren't hoping I can connect them with a dealer or publisher.

The best aspect of all of provincial life, however, only showed itself with the spring thaw. It's the land, and the rich earth of which it is composed. One spring day, while sipping my Keurig and surveying my mother's sad, weed-overgrown peony-and-daffodil garden, a strange power overtook me. It sent me to the dust-laden garage in search of a hoe that hadn't been touched for more than a decade. As I dug into the moist earth, periodically checking arms and ankles for signs of deer ticks, a wonderful sense of reconnection to the world was born. The results of this revelation climaxed in July, with a burst of zinnias grown from seed, a newly planted Japanese maple, a hydrangea, and an indigo plant. Not in a million years could I have imagined wise-cracking, snarky, story-crafting, international me finding gentle ecstasy in working in a garden. But the best thing of all is that even if the care and love you lavish on the kingdom of flora does not reach its goal and the plants all disappoint you, they don't expect you to take it personally.

Old Europe

FOR SOME TIME I've been in love with Old Europe, though she treats me like a stupid, underage concubine. My American friends wonder what I can see in such a worn-out tart, her silly Cupid's bow drawn with lipstick over a slack mouth, her hackneyed prejudices, and skin cast in the pallor of a bad liver.

I adore sliding my tongue between her set of rotting teeth, caressing the permanent scars on her skin from decades of constraining corsets, inhaling the complex, fermented odor of her sighing breath. I also love her supple evasions when it comes to discussing her past, the way her eyes go blank when she thinks of all that trauma.

How invigorating and enduring she is, filling me, contradictorily, with new life. Her body is an abandoned palace full of cobwebs where all discoveries are tied to some sad, sumptuous sacrifice. Plunging into her is like sinking into tar, because my intricate, often mute Sphinx is lost even to herself.

In some strange way, she's a window into the secret of my own existence. If I gaze into her glassy gray eyes long enough and swim in their shadowy depths, a delicious terror of must invades me; a shrieking form of wisdom is communicated: the fact that I came out of blood and slaughter.

What could my experienced, melancholy mistress possibly want from me—she who has seen everything and already been disappointed by it? What story or attitude could I possibly append to her accumulated tragedies and volleys of black humor? I know she loves me for my hope and banal optimism, even if the creases at the corners of her mouth show she's waiting patiently for them to be crushed. My pealing laughter always startles her, and my fascination with the old, outmoded beliefs of her land, which she has taken the habit of discarding, fills her, I think, with a secret pride.

She also loves my brazen athleticism and pretends to be constantly amazed when I bring it to our love-making. My bouts of energy, ambition, endurance amuse her to no end, and perhaps only to flatter me, she claims to envy them. But behind her remarks, I sense the knowledge that all energy comes to naught as surely as our flesh locked in mad embraces is doing nothing more than struggling to a future of dust.

I suspect she's using me as a scapegoat for her own passivity, flaunting me in the face of her secret enemies, gloating at my infatuation, which she sees as a rejection of them. She's happy that I've come to quench my desire on her slack thighs spread sullenly in abandonment; yet I had to, having grown tired of the futile strivings of those on my level. Still, for her, I'm new energy to exploit, booty brought into the lap of someone too exhausted to continue hunting, who assumes the prerogative for devouring it of any respected elder. She takes hidden pleasure, I think, in dreaming of my inevitable doom, which will make us soul mates.

Supposedly weary of living, she's the most avaricious mistress I've ever encountered, and she's drowning in her own sensuality, which she constantly vaunts as exquisite taste, despite the fact of its vulgarity.

I have mostly known my love upon her couch of pleasure, draped in the finest silks of her legacy, brought from the East as spoils by her marauding ancestors, but now spotted by our reckless entwining. She doesn't seem to mind. She pretends contempt or boredom for all those ornate trappings, and utters a desperate, almost malicious laugh when I spill my seed on them.

Our love exists, it seems, only in the horizontal, as if she were frozen in the perpetual lolling of an odalisque. Those few times when I convince her to stand, her flesh spilling in great waves, I become suddenly aware of her colossal girth and great height, which make me feel diminished. With a sigh, she adorns herself in her precious jewelry that has been tarnished by time, and which she refuses to polish, maintaining that the encrustations give it character. Draped in her odorous, understated robes, she leads me to her favorite café, whose walls are stained a sick mustard by tobacco, and whose vaunted charm is a mystery to me. Spending little and staying for hours, she seems to have become a fixture of these surroundings, a perpetual condition. Even the reproachful eyes of the insolent *garçon* are a part of her pleasure. Here in the café, she accomplishes what she calls "soaking up the multitude," as if the humdrum chatter, exhausted eyes ringed by the care of work, stench of poverty, shoddy clothing, and general misery were a purifying bath for her.

Is my love a sacrificial lamb, or merely nostalgic for the lost rhythms of life, now festering only in the slums? Why does she insist upon the detours we take through the most despicable neighborhoods as we make our way back from the café and the effects of too much drink force her to lean on my arm? Does she enjoy the roiling misery around her, the tense desperation of passersby, and the thought of her indirect responsibility for the encroaching chaos? Does she hope her sauntering, indifferent, half-drunken walk will provoke an eruption that might take her life but will install a new reality? Sometimes I think so, but at other times I don't. This is probably only the vacuous stroll of a lady surveying her territory, counting the heads of her chattel as temporary distraction from her own emptiness, and mourning, in some perverse way, her distance from them. And so, soon she wearies of her promenade. In a tone dulled by too much of the same kind of disappointment, she begs me to take her home.

A similar cycle occurs on those rare occasions when we go to the opera. For these, she laces herself into her corset, slips into her finery, powders her décolleté, places drops of Jicky perfume in the hollows of her collarbone and, without removing her furs, takes her place in her box, from which she surveys the crowd with an affected air of tedium, reserving special glares of resentment for the generals and politicians beneath us, whom she paradoxically detests for carrying out her aspirations. But by the second act, her resentment has changed into an empty-headed coquetry, to the point at which she even casts flirtatious glances at the old windbags decorated in medals.

Such is the nature of my love, who seems both ruler and slave at the same time, contemptuous of her masters and her victims, yet perhaps secretly hoping to be extinguished by either, as if it were her inheritance. Used to servants, she has no qualms about employing her wiles to get others to accomplish the harsh necessities of life. In a shrill tone of protestation, she can provoke her supposed opponents to carry out her own hidden goals. Flattering her enemies, while goading those rasher than herself into punishing them, she remains guiltless in her own eyes, absurdly supposing such subterfuges go unremarked. Or perhaps she keeps her shame for them hidden beneath her haughty bearing and cloaked in sudden excesses of moral scolding.

What a coward Old Europe is. When it comes to confrontation, danger, she'd rather slither out of her moral positions or bargain like a usurer in the spirit of her Mediterranean legacy. These are qualities she likes to project upon others, and she'd be the first to accuse some outsider, rather than herself, of having them. But question her as I might, I cannot hold her to account. All she finally does is smile at me in her rotten-toothed, lazy way, which resembles a death rictus, and blame all of it cavalierly on her mixed blood, the Oriental infiltration of her genes. Language and rhetoric seem identical to her, and she slides between truth and falsehood with the nonchalance of the entitled.

It is due to her poor housekeeping, I am convinced, that our home is now crawling with all sorts of vermin, especially rats come on ships from the East. Yesterday, on one of her rare outings, she left me alone in the house, and during her absence, one of the creatures skulked from its lair behind a bookcase and confronted me head on. I'll admit I was mesmerized by its glistening, beady red eyes, its yellow, pointed incisors, and quivering, salivating mouth; but did I imagine the perplexity in its slightly cocked head, like a pet that has unwittingly chosen the wrong mistress? And there we stood, frozen, staring at one another for a moment: I, the overfed, pampered visitor, with little understanding of the beast's miserable past, and it, wily but defeated, torn between retreat and attack. Days later, when I found it lying dead at the threshold of our door, poisoned by some neighbor, I pointed it out to my love, who lifted her skirts and skittered gracefully past it. "Did you kill it yourself?" was all she wanted to know.

As I have already pointed out, my mistress is tall and large beyond imagining. She towers above normal figures. On those few times that we go out, such height is probably responsible for her remote stare, as if the bent-backed beings toiling or engaged in felonious acts beneath her gaze were ants whose features are hard to distinguish, and human misery were strangely exiled from her participation. But there are times when she unleashes a sudden gesture that plunges her into the fray, exhibiting pent-up power and drama that has until that moment been concealed.

Such was what happened on our most recent outing together. Weary of her café and the opera, bored by the predictability of her strolls through the usual neighborhoods, she pulled me farther and farther toward the city outskirts. Such a long excursion was highly uncharacteristic behavior for she who is so attached to her couch. Perhaps it was a desire to return some of the vigor she constantly claimed that I supplied her, or to compete with it. Or perhaps she missed her youthful jaunts into the Red Belt and Chapelle, decades ago, when she rubbed shoulders with bohemians and other disruptive types.

The nearer we approached, the harsher the red ring that lit up the horizon became, until it resembled a circle of blood and smoke that I imagined smelled like singed flesh stung my nostrils. I kept suggesting we turn back, first casually, in the low-key way she considered good taste to express such complaints, and then more vehemently, as fear for my safety overcame me. She laughed off my misgivings and unflinchingly pulled me onward. We swept past the homes of the idle, venal rich, who had reclaimed the city center so recently; then past the humbler dwellings of the middle-class, with their respect for work and talent; and finally, past the homes of the workers who had given up their efforts to change our system of production in favor of arriving late, leaving early and slowing down output. It was then that we began to glimpse the first Black Maria's lumbering in the same direction we were, with death in the hearts of their drivers.

We came upon an endless wall of flames that licked the heavens with tongues of rage. All right and wrong seemed lost in this conflagration; young and old, good and evil were indiscriminately consumed by the pure energy, which seemed determined to incinerate all of History. I thought of the red gleam in the eye of the rat, and I shuddered. The flames roared as they do at a smelting plant, turning even metal into vapor.

But my usually apathetic mistress had transformed into something flamboyant and coarse. And her size had grown even more gigantic, like some mammoth, mechanical Gargantua. I had never seen her standing in such a vulgar and competent way, with her skirts hiked up and her legs straddling the blaze, over which she loomed, the reflection of flames mottling her noble features and reddening her lips, her nostrils flared with determination, her mouth contorted in superhuman effort. Then she squatted, and from between her thighs emerged a thick stream, like a Niagara, which promptly quenched the fire.

Times Square Redux

Night

IN THE SUMMER OF 1993, humid nights closed in on Times Square like a cloth doused in ether. The heat threaded sluggishly through the narrow streets or hung mucoid on the wider avenues. Like debilitated birds perched on dirty window sills, air conditioners rattled from sucked heat. Buildings sweated, and the black street pavement looked sticky. Each night I walked the streets, glaring at the new skyscrapers rearing up like great barriers to the exhausted breezes. Whose idea was it to create these monuments to airlessness, I kept thinking? Who would want to block the fresh winds from the bay and lace them with these suffocating chemicals?

In the center of Times Square, a blaze of lights spits brilliant contempt on the masses creeping across the island where the cheap tickets are sold. Each car and taxi gleamed like a scarab deflecting the lurid rays of surveillance. The play of neon illuminated for a moment a surly jaw topped by an impudent mouth. I cruised it. Then it was gone, replaced by round hips in seam-splitting jeans and a mound of lightened, fly-away hair.

War against darkness is what Times Square is about, it occurred to me in those days. Glitter versus extinction. In a New York that wrenches apart and rebuilds in a dreadful parody of nature's cycles, Times Square was its overblown jungle orchid, each fifty-year cycle pushing from filth an exaggerated blossom left on the stalk to rot. Little did I know that a New Times Square was being born starting from that very moment. They'd talked about it for years. I didn't believe it could happen.

Times Square in 1991 was still a shabby monument to memory. Mildew, urine, and soot encrusted its faded deco glory. Its streets were a treacherous Styx over which nervous commuters gingerly wended their way to their suburban safe zones. Foreign tourists stepped from well-maintained theaters bewildered at the grimy chaos juxtaposed to their sixty-dollar spectacle. They picked their way across the crowded streets, giving wide berth to that hollow-eyed youth perched on the filthy staircase or that scrawny woman pacing the corner like a puppet. They scudded past panhandlers and kept their purses pressed to their stomachs.

Later, long after the theater-goers were gone, in the black night that smelled of tar, apparitions would materialize. Part of the royal court of Times Square would begin its sporadic stroll down Eighth Avenue. A door would slam to reveal an oversized image of a female. She was wearing a black vinyl dress cinched at the waist over mile-long, matchstick-thin legs. Stiff, ruffled petticoats pushed the skirt out like leathern flower petals. Near the shoulders, sleeves flared like the fins of an old Cadillac. The wig was a cascade of rust-colored curlicues.

Where was the apparition going? I remember wondering. And I followed it, as it disappeared and rematerialized in each pool of salmon light cast by the vapor lamps. With a clockwork gait, it swiveled onto a garish street that bathed it in a myriad of colored lights: neon from an exotic lingerie store, the blinking wattage of a sex shop, the harsh facade lights of a sooty deco hotel towering above like an unstable zigzag of boxes: The Carter.

At the Carter, which then housed a bar called Sally's II, the figure pulled open one of the glass doors and ascended a curving staircase past stained red wallpaper. Inside, the atmosphere was raucous. The curls that in this light looked like wood shavings trembled with excitement. Chattering minions rushed up to greet her. Hugs and kisses were lusty and abandoned. Hoots and cackles filled the air. Everybody was there! At the circular bar was that meaty transvestite I saw almost every night, in her leopard print cocktail dress. She had large, soulful eyes and a big blunt nose. Her hair was yanked back into a bun, her eyebrows reduced to penciled lines. I couldn't stop looking at her.

The trannie mouthed hello, then shifted her eyes knowingly to indicate why she too had not darted forward to welcome the newcomer. Next to her was her gargantuan keeper with his heavy brow ridges and lush, rude mouth. Through his crisply rolled, fatigue-print shirt, his muscles curved like armor. Over his bulging shoulders was his fashionable new hunting vest, tightly strapped. The expression on the lips of this soldier of fortune defied anyone to approach his womanly charge. So the leopard lady stayed frozen at the bar stool.

Sally's, as I remember it then, was low-ceilinged and cavernous, suffused with an orange glow. Canned show music blared from cheap giant speakers, and the queens assembled at the tables fronting the stage with its limp, sequined banner. Off to the side, a naked, pancaked shoulder or a hem of tulle poked from the ramshackle dressing room. Then an announcer with a voice of indeterminate sex called out the opening act. The music swelled to a climax. A spot fixed the center of the stage. The figure in black vinyl whom I'd been following through the streets danced frenetically onstage. She whirled about, lip-synching the words to the song that was playing. Her impossibly thin arms gestured like manic snakes. Her teeth glinted sparkling grins at the small crowd of clapping, hooting queens, gay men, and johns. Everyone was caught in the celebration.

Day

But what if a stranger—a day worker—(yourself, perhaps?) was to wander inside. Would the small, festive circle, the rapt eyes, and bright lights still seem the same? For the uninitiated, the celebration would become a grotesque spectacle. The fantastic creature whirling in shiny vinyl would be reduced by sociology. The outsider would be likely to see a skeletal transvestite with the clinical symptoms of AIDS wasting. This out-of-place visitor would appraise all of it with a cluck of the tongue or a sad shake of the head. He'd study their faces for a hint of stubble pushing through the pancake. He'd shrug pityingly at their stoned eyes caught in a narcissistic haze. His would be the harsh, flattening gaze of the daylight.

When time—regular jobs, bank accounts, the discipline of reproduction—walks in on these celebrations, all the beauty is reduced to a grotesque Dance of Death, a medieval masquerade from the plague years. The Children of Times Square lived out of time because they lived in the moment. For them, day was the enemy. But the liquid blackness of night interrupted by isolated pools of brightness set them off in all their hard-edged effrontery. They bloomed in Times Square precisely because life was crumbling and retreating around their image. But did they ever think the Life would disappear entirely?

Now, in 2003, the world of day has triumphed. The bright blandness of the suburbs, the reductive glare of shopping mall lights on cartoon architecture have invaded my terrain, taken over every surface of old Times Square with impartial precision, punished ambiguity or exaggeration. The powerful, expensively maintained cars speed through Times Square to costly Broadway entertainment, then tunnel imperiously through the night streets back to day. In the process, there is no contact and no confusion. The merciless patches of darkness with their bright pools of glory are gone.

Night

Still, like cockroaches after a bomb, fragments of my world remain. It is August 2, 2003, and I'm wandering the streets of Times Square again. At this hour, most Broadway shows are emptying. Against a mailbox, a young man with a wide, curvaceous mouth framed by soft, brushed whiskers stands vigilant as a hawk. One of his narrowed almond eyes under their full eyebrows is a laser that pierces the pollution, dissecting into exploitable parts everyone who passes. The other eye—like a cracked marble—appears to be sightless. The working eye sculpts the buttocks of the nervous woman passing by with her suited husband. Both are holding theater programs. The eye shifts to appraise the partly open clasp of the purse. It then moves across the street to float with a steady, proprietary gaze over the body of another passing woman. As if by chemical reaction, the woman's body stiffens. And as I pass the young man at the mailbox, he suddenly falls into step with me. Peals of calculated chatter spill from his lips. Slowly but surely our steps are in unison. They turn up the avenue and duck inside a bar.

The bar we have entered—just by chance—is a time warp. It's a wide terrain of soft shadows, punctuated now and then by ceiling spots. The air conditioning is aggressive, merciless. Behind the bar is the ovoid face of the bartender with thinned, far-apart eyebrows and a large, mournful mouth. The back of his hands are covered with bruises so large and opaque that they stand out in the darkness. Are they veins ruptured by needles or the lesions from a fistfight?

Like idols in an incense-filled temple, three nearly naked young women are about to bare their breasts on a stage. One of these dancers turns to show her smooth profile to the audience. A large scar pops into the shaft of light.

At the pool table, men are strutting and stooping, striking monumental poses, offering repertories of attitude. With unblinking, predatory eyes, they fix the bodies of the female dancers. A wolfish teenager holds out a dollar bill and touches one of the dancer's legs. The young man I came in with whispers a proposition into my ear. We slip out of the bar.

Dawn

The young man is gone, and I'm lying in bed, hungover, sweating, and full of regret. The air conditioner in this apartment in Hell's Kitchen is broken. Slowly the city is coming alive with people on the street, taxis, and truckdrivers. Life is occurring as if despite me.

Unable to sleep, I go out, light a cigarette. And as the cars and cabs and SUVs spew petroleum exhaust, their removable radios blare out news of no-smoking legislation. At a stoplight, through an open car window, I hear another radio. A talk show host is telling of vigilant citizens hunting beaches and day care centers for abusers. Why does this make me think of bewildered teenagers dreaming of fantastic sex and searching futilely for the Outsider? Why do we buy the blouse with the pattern of tropical colors, drum our fingers to the reggae, or eat the restaurant meal with "exterminator" spices? Occasionally, a journalist complains that all the old transgressive poses have been co-opted. Meanwhile fashion designers, musicians, and advertisers are mining the physicality and dynamism of the poor to package libido for us. The supply seems inexhaustible.

For the rest of the day, thoughts of this nature occur to me, as I stand in line at this or that automated teller or punch in numbers on a phone tree. As I pick up a TV remote. The button is pressed, and the channel is changed. On screen, the passionate fatality of boxing is piped into my living room. Who will win? What do the blows feel like? What social fate awaits the loser? At the end of the day, I climb back between my no-iron sheets, imagining the noses of the originators of all our borrowed energies pressed against our bedroom windows, yearningly fixated on the unobtainable fantasies of our propriety.

Night

It is the middle of a work-day night. A restless, disenfranchised feeling makes me toss and turn. Without any reason, my thoughts stray back into the night. I fear the violence and treachery of this world of night, yet I know that I somehow envy its vitality and dynamism. Why are our children wearing goatees and backwards baseball caps? Why is our daughter dancing to salsa? Has the stranded world of the underclass become our last fresh "material"? The thought follows me into sleep.

But miles away, in the city, as I sleep, as you sleep, the very poor are creating themselves from our leftovers, rummaging through our cultural garbage cans. They have very little ethnic history in their memory. They've built the rituals of super-gangs, the rhythms of rap, and the cartoon legends of prison religions mostly from their own imagination. Their self-written "history" is a pastiche of made-up "facts," historical snippets, and quotes from the Bible and the Koran. It's the Black Israelites or the religion that was forged in prison called the Five-Percenters. That's why I fall asleep with a silent irony compressing my lips. Who are we? Who are the poor? About those poor we do not dare speak ill of, there is now no language to speak about them at all.

Day

The next morning, after writing this, I go out for coffee, head east toward Broadway. The sloppy, corny deco four-story on the corner is a staple of the neighborhood memory. Somewhere in everyone's mind is an image of the peeling metallic paint on a second-story window, announcing a modeling agency that closed three decades ago. There was the floor that had the hairdressing school a few years back and the floor with the still-active boxing gym with the drug-addicted trainer who once held a world title. Now they've built a tall, wooden fence around the building and excavated a pit around it. Is it the Disney Corporation or the Marriot chain that's taken the space over?

But despite the fact that this building is scheduled for destruction, the new light of morning has softened its crumbling contours and restored some of its lost smartness. The light casts blue shadows on large cardboard boxes sheltering a squadron of homeless sleepers half a block away. It turns the liverish pallor of a scrawny, pot-bellied prostitute in hot pants into a faded Technicolor image.

In front of the grocery stands a blowsy dealer with sardonically arched eyebrows, too old to be called a homeboy, tremblingly trying to peel the wrapper of an ice cream bar, unaware of the wrecking ball swinging through the sky a few stories above his head. The ball smashes against the old building with a dull crash that is swallowed by the hazy air. The over-the-hill dealer looks up, startled. The ball begins gouging hunks from the sides of the monolith with a brutality that seems primordial. Bricks tumble down exposing steel beams like a skeleton stripped of flesh. The dealer keeps watching. Then the beams collapse and crash to the ground.

When the dust settles, a great wave of humans pours from the giant mouth of the Port Authority Bus Terminal. They are more or less rested, groomed for the day, carrying the necessary papers, a change of shoes, or account books. Feet pointed in the same direction, they file through the meaningless streets to the sealed places where they make and remake their bread and butter.

Times Square Obituary

This text was written in 1997, when Giuliani's clean-up and the new anti-porn laws had finally finished off most of old Times Square.

IT'S GONE NOW, it's over… At STELLA'S, the cops are forcing male lap dancers to wear tops and bottoms, looking ridiculous in beach outfits in the middle of winter.

One block up from O'NEAL'S, which once served teenage hustlers and working-class johns, but lost half its clientele in 1985 when the drinking age was boosted from eighteen to twenty-one.

Half a block east of FASCINATION, where homeless hustlers could win cartons of cigarettes playing Pac-Man.

Near TAD'S STEAKHOUSE, to which PAUL ROGERS, the Pushcart-prize-winning author of *SAUL'S BOOK*, about a Jewish con and his Puerto Rican hustler, brought underaged tricks to eat, until his "adopted son" bludgeoned him to death in 1986.

One avenue over from the fire station that in 1986 stuck its hose with hostility into the back of the air conditioner at the hustler bar TRIX, which welcomed such stellar clientele as DOG in 1987, who inspired

DOG DAY AFTERNOON, and EGON VON FURSTENBERG, who didn't look away when I stared at him, and DANNY, the beloved international fashion stylist and ex sex worker who finally died of HIV in 1997.

Down the street from which lived JAMES BIDGOOD, the anonymous author of the underground homoerotic film *PINK NARCISSUS*, who built intricate sets from detritus found on the street in 1966 and lived in them with model BOBBY KENDALL during years of painstaking filming with a super-8 camera, until 1970.

Several blocks uptown from COCKTAILS, where the crack was hidden in the ceiling tiles in 1995 and the LATIN KINGS took their female dates and played pool among the johns, with the film *BLOOD IN BLOOD OUT* playing over and over on the video monitor. Two blocks down from the FULTON HOTEL, where, in 1990, VENUS, star of *PARIS IS BURNING*, never got to see the film and wasn't discovered dead under the bed until somebody finally noticed the smell.

And kitty corner from the EROS, where CHI CHI LA RUE recently presented her naked dancers on stage, over which another woman, the NINETY-YEAR-OLD GREEK OWNER of the theater, lived in cloistered luxury among thick carpets and a crystal chandelier but died shortly before her building was condemned in 1997.

Not far from LA FIESTA, in 1985, whose bar mirrors were tilted at an angle that revealed your butt.

Several blocks up from the 43rd Street BLARNEY STONE, with its drunks, crackheads, neighborhood regulars, and gays. Half a block west of BLUES, a Black gay bar where I first heard the song "I WANT A BIG, BIG DICK," after which the bar was raided by cops in 1982, swinging billy clubs that cracked skulls. But then became SALLY'S HIDEAWAY, the drag bar that finally burned in 1989, and in 1990 moved farther east on the block to the CARTER HOTEL to become SALLY'S II, where Dorian Corey, another star of *PARIS IS*

BURNING, performed, then died of AIDS in 1993, after which a murdered corpse that had become a mummy was discovered in her closet, following which SALLY, the owner, and JESSE, the manager, also died in 1996, as well as co-manager JIMMY PEANUTS, who had a stroke a month ago.

Just half a block in from the MINNESOTA STRIP, which was the name for Eighth Avenue between 42nd and 48th streets, because so many runaways arriving at PORT AUTHORITY BUS TERMINAL from Minnesota used it for begging and hustling. When they weren't putting up with the shelter COVENANT HOUSE west on 41st, after which its director FATHER BRUCE RITTER was revealed as something less than a saint, in 1988.

Down the block from THE HAYMARKET, the classic hustler bar that had closed by the early eighties and inspired the ALAN BOWNE play *FORTY-DEUCE*, which was made into a never released film by PAUL MORISSEY and starring KEVIN BACON in 1986. Several blocks up from the old ESCUELITA, which served its clients Latin-style on tables with real cloths until 1995, and where you could buy your own bottle of booze for the night and watch the drag show.

Which went on southeast of HOMBRE on Ninth Avenue, which closed and then reopened secretly in 1996 from 4 a.m. until 10 a.m. each weekend morning and became a magnet for all the leftovers, until the cops busted it and it reopened as SAVOY in 1997 and started welcoming the LATIN KINGS as well as hustlers who would invite their tricks to the pay-by-the-hour hotel around the corner. Near JOHN LA FLEUR'S drag and go-go boy club, in the parking lot of which the six-time world champion boxer EMILE GRIFFITH was beaten within an inch of his life in 1997.

Down the block from PORT AUTHORITY BUS TERMINAL, which used to be open all night but was severely disabled as an unofficial shelter for the homeless in 1996 when the lockers were removed due to worries about terrorism, and out of which at midnight the cops now chase people with the use of barking dogs.

It's gone now, it's over… and you're bound to forget it.

Blackout

HOW MUCH OF OUR PLEASURE comes from others' suffering? The question kept occurring to me as I picked my way through the pitch-black streets; dark, yes, but even more extraordinary, free of a certain aural dimension, free of buzzing street lamps, the barely perceptible hum of distant air conditioners, the muffled sound of a television coming from an upstairs floor—all the sounds we associate with New York on a night in summer. Now they were gone because of the blackout, and more than an absence of light was this lack of subliminal sounds, as if a dimension were missing.

The companion who'd gone out with me into the night when Manhattan was plunged into total darkness was Cara, already a woman of darkness herself. In her late fifties, she sported a head shaved to all but a shock of flaming red hair; and to the side, on the scalp, a tattoo of a spider. As always, her clothes were black, so that all I could glimpse of her as we threaded past other pedestrians carrying candles or flashlights was this shock of red hair and a patch of white scalp, floating eerily in the night. Cara had been traveling throughout the country, sleeping in hostels, appearing unannounced at cabarets, and convincing them to let her perform her special brand of punk jazz vocals, with an S&M flavor. Probably no one else but her would have agreed to go out into the darkness with me, after the lights went out; but like me, urban adventure, mystery, and a slight increase in risk are what gives her energy.

As we reached the corner, what was the odor of singed flesh that reached our nostrils? The glow of coals soon explained that the Puerto Rican and Dominican families in the nearby building had removed all their meat from the freezer, figuring it would spoil before the electricity came back on. They'd brought boomboxes and fresh batteries to the street and were cooking up an enormous barbecue.

A block later, we came to Tompkins Square Park, where couples and small groups sat on blankets illuminated by flickering candles. Then we headed north, toward Stuyvesant Park, where not a single candle or flashlight broke through the darkness. Instead, a wan, glassy light from the night sky brought out the fuzzy outlines of hunched shadows, knotted masses, stooping figures from which issued sucking sounds and soft moans.

Gay guys had been cruising this park for several decades, I knew. During the last New York Blackout, in 1977, this park had been the place of an unbridled orgy. Now, twenty-six years later, it was starting all over again. This time, however, another phantom lurked among the tangle of shadow-limbs, a certain disease that hadn't yet been identified when the old blackout had occurred. Tempted as I was by the spidery fingers that fumbled at my fly, I moved away, joining Cara, who was leaning against a tree, smoking.

We headed south again, blinded temporarily each time the headlights of a car crept by. There were no traffic lights functioning, so the cars hovered at every corner like cowed beasts, then shot recklessly into the intersection.

In the East Village, nearly every bar was open. Packed to the gills, illuminated by candlelight, the bars were host to frenetic drinking bouts. As the shadows played over raucous faces, I turned to Cara and said, "It's like those Dances of Death during the Plague years." And indeed, there was a desperate gayety to the partying hordes, many of whom had brought their drinks out to the street and were dancing disjointedly to the relatively soft music coming from battery-run tape players.

Was it a sense of dread or of guilt that made me suddenly want to listen to the radio? I took out the tiny portable radio I'd brought with me and plugged in its earphone. At the same time, Cara and I headed back toward Tompkins Square park, from which a strange fiery glow emanated.

According to the newscaster, the city was peaceful. Unlike the blackout of 1977, there was no raiding, no increase in crime this time. Instead, there were New Yorkers suffering silently, uncomplainingly. Some had been caught in subways for hours, then led out single file along the rat-infested tracks. Others had spent half the day trapped in elevators without ventilation, waiting for the fire department to arrive and free them. Many who lived in the suburbs had given up all hope of making it home that night. They were sleeping in droves on the sidewalks and the steps of the main post office, using their suit jackets or pocketbooks as pillows. In Brooklyn, a couple of fires had broken out from the use of candles, and in one of them an elderly woman had died. There was no mention of the unspoken fear moving through everyone's mind, that the authorities were lying to us, that this was really another act of terrorism.

In Tompkins Square Park, an enormous throng had gathered. I don't know where they found all the scraps of wood that they began piling into a fire. Higher and higher it blazed toward the treetops, right from the sidewalk from which it spread. Several men had stripped naked, and a few people had brought percussion instruments. Afro-Caribbean rhythms thundered into the blackness, echoed through the flames. More and more people, some half-dressed, danced in a circle around the conflagration. Sparks singed the leaves of the trees. Faces contorted with pleasure. Whoops of celebration filled the air. The lights of New York, those perpetual curtailers of freedom, were gone for the time being.

Unbridled liberty raged, grotesque and uncontrollable, frustrated and desperate, an agony of energy that was doomed to be extinguished by the light of day.

Fear of Fashion

A Black Boxes Alibi

GLINTS FROM THE DOCTOR'S GLASSES are making my eyelids flutter, black boxes are starting to pile up one within the other. I wish the doctor would stop that steam heat. I can't hear her. That hissing noise gets inside my ears. It grinds up every thought into black dots. Now light is spitting out of the dots like pins, everything is going to be shut off suddenly, as if by a switch—

The doctor says I'm not going to faint, that I'm remembering things in a half-waking, half-dreaming state: "Things you normally can't or don't want to remember." That my fall into the spitting black spots is just the normal process of falling into sleep. But the second before unconsciousness is more horrible than any memory, Doctor. And far worse than any daydream or nightmare. A dreadful logic seems to take over, and incidents that have nothing to do with each other creep together into accusations…

"Maybe you're feeling the medication," suggests the doctor. She draws the heel of her shoe against the ankle of the other foot so that the hem is lifted slightly off the knee… and tilts her head to one shoulder… The doctor's mouth opens, closes, as she explains that I'm merely experiencing what's called a hypnogogic state, that the injection she gave me… But her voice can't really be made out, overlapped by the whisper of the radiator… which seems as if it's coming out of me.

"It's your own breathing you're listening to."

The doctor's voice tries to be reassuring before it's ground up by jackhammers. And the air around it congeals into oval swellings… like white swells of skin creased by some tight material… Swellings around a red, smiling mouth that glints like the ruby eye on H's barbaric-looking arm bracelet…

In fact, H *was* smiling at me.

Her frail white knees swayed together, hinting of impatience… of too much to drink, especially with the shoe slipped off the heel of one foot. It hung there like a black teardrop, oval and shiny.

H is smiling, explaining the difficulties in her marriage, owing to her husband's disability. She has gotten into the habit of spending hours alone without telling anyone. Except for me, she tells me. She jabs at the shiny olive in her cocktail with her fingernails, while her black pinpricked pupils spiral into me like drills… or like long, glittering pins…

"Sometimes I'm afraid I've used his sickness to buy my independence," she sighs, "used it as an excuse for a career as a fashion designer."

Her husband is sitting all the way at the other end of the large room. She speaks under her breath. His eyes are focused on the tiny plaque on his lap. He is holding a sharp stylus, absorbed in his miniature engraving of his wife. He looks up. The look hangs between us in midair… until the head sinks down again… while H holds the pose that he has suggested for her, and the hem of her dress begins to creep above her knee.

Clamped between two darkened fingernails, an olive gleams, disappears. Ice clinks. She takes a sip of her fourth drink. A quiver runs through her husband's body. The stylus drops out of his hand… Had he heard…? She gets up, picks up the stylus, puts it back in his hand, sits down again. Clutching a pencil in a thin hand half obscured by a large ring, she continues to speak in the same amiable tone about the gloves she's designed, the ones I'm to display, my reason for being here.

Their living room is filled with her sketches: gloves for all occasions. And with his work: hundreds of tiny miniatures of her.

The hand with the darkened fingernails picks up the cocktail glass… sets it down… lights a cigarette… Slowly the face becomes unfocused in a screen of smoke. The glass rises into the smoke, disappears. The ice clinks… The uninterrupted whisper of steam heat changes the walls to a powder that seems to float in the air. On the powder, H's designs and the miniatures of her etched by her husband are quivering… in the smoke.

She stands up suddenly. What has her husband asked for? Her cotton hands flutter above his head. She takes the engraving from his lap and sets it on the table. Her voice gets louder as she moves toward the dressing room. What is the reason for her sudden excitement?

You ask me what she's saying, Doctor…?

It would only bore you, it would only sound so very banal to you… since it's just a conversation about fashion: small talk about the problem of falling asleep… There is really no substitute for a good night's sleep or afternoon beauty rest, is there? And it's clear that modern life is making it harder and harder to "get away from it all," don't you agree? Perhaps the use of a sleep mask… after all, it's safer than prescription drugs. And it's certainly less expensive than hours spent on a psychiatrist's couch… please don't take offense… To be blindfolded during sleep is astonishingly… refreshing…

To be perfectly honest, sleep is becoming more and more of a problem for me. As soon as the lights are turned off all at once in this wing, everyone is plunged into utter blackness. I lie on my bed listening to others' snores in the ward. The room is blacker than the inside of a camera. The floor falls away, but I'm only sinking into another sort of room, deeper, blacker… a black box. . . And inside it is another, and another…

until an enormous stab of light, too bright to make out the figures it reveals, clubs me into unconsciousness. When I first wake up, I don't know whether I've passed out or fallen asleep. I can't move my arms or legs, my lips are stuck to my teeth. The overhead lights are white coals sitting on my eyes. You're bending over my bed, Doctor, just a pink shape, shiny pearls, a blurred oval of a face… Your glasses, if you're wearing them, are like long tunnels… black boxes piling up… black sparks into which I start to fall all over again.

In fact, these fainting fits got so bad that H's husband suggested I stop visiting them… I'd fainted more than once in front of other guests—I couldn't remember anything when I woke up… But I kept coming back to see them, maybe because H said she sympathized. She too sometimes found it hard to get her breath, to keep her balance, she would tell me—as she mixed me a cocktail and handed it to me and watched me drink it with the same concentration with which she designed the long dark gloves… until the glittering pin in her red hair made me squint, hurt my eyes… Why didn't the police question H about the ingredients in her cocktails, I keep wondering? What I didn't tell them is that they—H and her husband—asked some of us to pose for photos… just as a party game. The same ones they used in court… And sometimes, when I looked at a photo that had been taken, for which I couldn't remember posing—I often couldn't remember what happened before I fainted—no one wanted to say whether the pose was real or faked. Could I really have been doing that? I asked. H let out a loud laugh… and her eyes were like dull pebbles…

The phone's ringing. But you're not answering it, are you? The black phone on your desk is ringing and you're not getting up to answer it. Shiny, black, that phone continues to ring in a sleepless room. A room that I'd never been in with all the lights turned off… H's husband said I'd fainted, and because they were afraid to let me go home alone, they put me on the sofa in the room with all the etchings and tiny engravings.

And they turned out all the lights… and left me alone for what seemed like hours, until I held two cushions against my ears, to get away from the white hiss of the steam heat. And then suddenly the phone rang—would you please answer that phone!—I noiselessly edged the receiver off the hook and I pressed it to my cheek… but there was no voice… nothing. Only a tiny rubbing sound—or was it breathing? yes, breathing—complicated by an occasional thud or squeak… like the noise of H's husband's rubber-tipped crutch on the marble floor of her dressing room. Yes, that's it: light thuds, squeaks, a pause… more of them. And the breathing was interrupted by one sharp, quick moan, after which it started again faster… laced with the powdery whisper of the radiator. While the thuds and squeaks grew faster, louder… Then quieter… after which they suddenly grew louder again.

It was her husband making his way back and forth between the telephone and some other point, with that painful walk of his… bringing her pieces of clothing or a hairbrush, I imagine. She'd said it that night in a low voice: "He just doesn't feel useful anymore. Sometimes I ask him to help me get dressed, just to make him think that he is…" That sideways swing of the hip that seems as if it's going to dislocate the thigh from the socket at each step… I must admit that the thought of H's husband's disability bewilders me. What exactly would it look like if revealed? At times the leg jerks sideways in its socket, so suddenly that it would be impossible to move at all without a crutch, at other times the outward twist of the pelvis is not enough to inhibit forward movement seriously, the walk looks almost normal… except for that horrible squeaking… Only the sound of the attendant's rubber-soled shoes on the tiled floor, you say?

Then what about the conversation? Soon it will begin all over again. The talk about the eye bandage—or sleep mask—or blindfold, whatever she first called it—worn to induce sleep: which is effective, but not nearly so much as one that deadens all sound too. It is as if a familiar story were unfolding itself almost automatically… it being clear that the fast pace of modern life is making it impossible to "get away from it all…" Had she really admitted to a certain pleasure in being blindfolded? Perhaps. It was safer than drugs and cheaper than hours spent on the psychiatrist's couch… Through the thick smoke her expression could barely be made out. The face looked like a blurred moon… or as if there were no face, merely a luminous space under the swollen coils of hair…

I'll show you what it seemed like. Give me those scissors, the points are blunt—I couldn't possibly hurt anyone with them. Let me have that ladies' magazine over there…

You take a model advertising a common household product, like this one… And you cut away the face… no! you cut away everything else, instead, like this… the product, all the words, the setting. And you lay the figure on this black table. Like this. Her smile is horribly compelling, isn't it? Now you don't know why she's smiling like that, do you? In imitating emotions—feelings that the rest of us are simulating when we don't even know that we are—she has at her fingertips enormous opportunities for control. And, if I could only harness that power… Look at the smile and imagine it multiplying, over the table, the floor… my lap—

That light again? Only the reflection from your glasses? Take them off for now, if you don't mind. See what you've done? You've made me nip off part of the model's left leg. That's the one H's husband was having trouble with. He had to get a new brace. This new brace prevented the possibility of the leg dislocating from the hip socket, but it transformed his barely noticeable limp into an exaggerated turnout, even with the use of the crutch…

I saw no reason to tell the police everything that happened that night… when the engraving stylus dropped out of his hand, when he screwed up his face as if he were in pain. Then she went into the dressing room with the muffling curtains to get his medicine and took me with her so that I could see the larger paintings he'd made of her... and sank into the cushioned love seat... explaining that I'd misunderstood, none of the paintings were in this room, I was to watch her posing for one instead... for which she began slowly preparing... covering her mouth with another layer of red lipstick, applying creams and rouges until the face looked like a rigid mask—

Please don't put those glasses back on! You don't need to look at your notes. No, I never said that, stop putting words into my mouth... claiming to be repeating exactly what I've told you. Your voice sounds rehearsed and insincere... Your face... well, it isn't a face at all, but a blinding glare, a faceless oval...

Maybe I should tell the police—and you—how she described the pleasures of being blindfolded... reminding herself of the enormous tests of patience in learning to find her way about the house by the use of touch alone. That was after we went into her beige, silk-curtained dressing room filled with the suffocating froufrou of garments over which her soft, insinuating voice could barely be heard, while her husband waited for his medicine and—

That's not true! That I was never invited into the dressing room to see any paintings, that I let myself in when no one was home, and waited for her in the mammoth closet... until she and her husband came in to get ready for bed... clicking on the tiny nightlight. And every object was softened into buzzing shadows, pulverized into tiny particles. And the sound of congealed breathing could be heard over the whisper of silk and the chatter of plastic bracelets. And her husband's voice croaked, "Are you almost ready?" as he limped toward her...

Do the notes say, Doctor, that pinpricked pupils are drilling into me as I'm watching a skirt fastened about the ankles with a silk cord? That the tiered wig is being attached with a long golden pin to the real hair, which has been pulled back until the temples redden? And that a glove is slowly being pulled up an arm to drain it of color just as the bathrobe falls open and the horrible medical contraption attached to the hip and the thigh is suddenly revealed?

...that the phone rings, again... and that the receiver is placed on the dressing table so that whoever is on the other end can pick up every sound... of the head being covered with a white stocking fastened at the neck, yards of the material wrapped tighter... a black rubber stocking pulled over the bound features until the face suspended above the chair looks like... a blank oval, a giant olive... black, shiny... breath escaping like steam from a broken radiator.

And black boxes are spilling out of your glasses... one within the other, and gasps can be heard coming from the shiny oval, while the figure is straining upright, too upright on the chair. When someone limps forward, it is not to H, to help her, but to me instead, who is sinking rapidly into blackness.

A Fashion Enthusiast

From a novel in progress, *Slaves of Fashion*

BY SEIZING EVERY OPPORTUNITY to work overtime, by keeping to myself and following my own display ideas, I achieved some notoriety. My window decorations began to appear in the evening papers. I merely began to work harder and spent all my lunch hours at home.

I went to hear V., the celebrated designer, speak on the future of men's fashions at a buyer's meeting. A wealthy and powerful family had secured her position in the world of fashion, and she'd risen to control a whole line of evening wear. During her speech, I became nauseous and dizzy and went into the unattended cloakroom. It was dark, for the only source of light, an illuminated wall clock, had been covered by a coat. Probably a coat placed by a woman who was standing there in darkness, or perhaps she'd followed me. Noticing my alarm, she smiled faintly; or rather, I thought she did, since there was barely enough light to see. Then she chatted without encouragement in cordial tones.

She was the daughter of the speaker and was also a designer of gloves. Presently she was working on some designs that had to be displayed with much sensitivity and attention to detail. She continued to talk about her designs and about fashion without any evident reason to do so; then, suddenly, she asked my name. She said she had heard it mentioned and wondered if by any chance I was the window artist whose designs were appearing on the society pages of her favorite newspaper. Had I any specific ideas for the displaying of gloves? Through the door, I could see that her mother had ended her speech and was moving toward the cloakroom. The other woman quickly scrawled an address on a piece of paper and slipped silently away. I left soon after.

At the indicated address, a hotel, I was taken to a suite of rooms by a bellboy. The door had been unlocked and, sitting in an armchair against which leaned a rubber-tipped cane, was a graying man of about sixty. He introduced himself as a G de M and said he was the husband of the woman I had met. He was also involved in the clothing industry, for his family had controlled the crinoline market for over fifty years. Years ago, he had been taken by a severe infection and now had trouble walking.

Trembling slightly, he grasped the arms of his chair and pulled himself eagerly forward to talk. "Painting, sculpting in clay have filled some gaps." Though I was never to see his sculpture, he continued to refer to it. "She's always the subject"—he meant his wife—"and I'm trying to capture her beauty in a very static pose."

His wife appeared for a moment in a black dressing gown. She had gathered her hair and fastened it with one long golden pin. She asked me to forgive her for her lateness and then disappeared.

He and I were alone once more. I faced him in absolute silence. Soon he began to talk again about the paintings, none of which, I noticed, glancing around the room, were present. It seems there was a hopelessness about these studies that provoked a strange impatience about finishing them. Thus, few had been completed. Those that were finished radiated a sense of loss and of the past.

His wife, he said, had been most striking at the age of sixteen and pointed to a framed photograph of her in a school uniform holding a shiny baton. The long, curved fingernails would have made it impossible to handle the instrument successfully.

"But my paintings…" Though I mentioned other things, he kept coming back to them. "They're curiously flawed, but they're meticulously executed." I imagined them and, for some reason, saw the body of the baton twirler—his wife at sixteen—thrust into contorted poses. "I suppose my work is quite a personal thing," he kept saying, almost wincing. He gestured to the picture of his wife. "Between the two of us."

Going on to speak of the great pleasure he took in all the arts, especially visual, he stated they were the only thing that had never disappointed him. He did not believe that art had any transcendent powers. "It's just a way of passing time…"

Soon there were strange lapses of attention. He began to doze. I sat for many moments not knowing what to do but to watch the sleeping figure. Then his wife reappeared, wearing a different outfit I don't find necessary to describe. She glanced at her husband and suggested she and I move into another room to work.

The room was both a studio and bedroom, but unlike one I'd ever seen. Underneath the slanting skylight, the walls had been painted an aggressive saffron, lending color to the more discreet, pearl-colored satin spread that covered the bed in one corner. Nothing else marred these orangey yellow walls in that half of the room except an oversized, gilt-framed mirror.

The other end of the room was her studio. I'd more than expected to see work in progress tacked all over the walls, but the only sign of it was a pedestal holding an oversized ceramic arm, perhaps three times the size of a normal woman's. It was perfectly covered by an emerald kid glove that reached past the elbow, and halfway up its forearm was a heavy, barbaric-looking bracelet of brass and emerald. Employing a model of oversized proportions helped her to work with details and create a better equilibrium among the fingers, palm, and wrist of the model, as she explained. With only this one large sample to show, the enormous room dwarfed the drafting table on whose stool she had sat. Above her, a crystal chandelier, more appropriate for a drawing room, sent flashes of light off the long golden pin in her hair.

She pulled some designs from a large portfolio and spread them on the floor. Clutching a drafting pen in a thin hand half obscured by her large ring, she began speaking in a husky voice—first about the gloves, which were of every variety—but soon about herself. Because there were not often many guests in her home, it was pleasant to have someone to chat with. She continually referred to her relationship with her husband and the problem of his infirmity. She seemed oblivious to the fact that I did not wish her to do so. There were difficulties, she tried to explain, owing to the large difference in age… and his infirmity forced her to be independent.

Since her name was identical to that mentioned in a poem by Rimbaud, "H," I asked permission to refer to her by that single letter; but she could not resist embarrassing me by pointing out that the majority of critics had interpreted his puzzling text to be about masturbation. She heard her husband's cane tapping in the other room and excused herself briskly but with charm, and I went home.

A few days later, H called. She had decided to contract me to display her gloves. She and her husband would expect me for dinner that evening, and afterward, we would discuss the designs in great detail.

The call was complicated by a bad connection and obscured by other noises. I felt I could hear the tapping of his cane and the sound of hair being brushed, or perhaps the friction of material sliding over the receiver. In casual tones, I asked what she was doing at the moment.

"I'm getting dressed for dinner," she explained.

Dinner was served on a veranda protected by glass. He was in good spirits and seemed happy to have someone whom he now termed one of his "rare visits from a friend as a dinner guest." Both of them sat at the table, demonstrating a lack of interest in the food. He did this with the play of a fork in a small saucer of pâté; H traced the rim of a glass with the inside of an index finger, without bothering to drink its contents.

G de M's hunger seemed replaced by an excessive joviality. It animated his tired features, and, though genuine, seemed to be taxing his body to an intolerable degree... Grasping the edge of the table, breathing rapidly, and punctuating his words by shaking his cane, he spoke enthusiastically about current ideas in fashion, but also about today's youth. They could be the only ones who could prevent my most profound dreams from becoming a reality because they had lost an interest in the extremities of beauty.

Without knowing why, I spoke politely of my mother, even my depth of feeling for her. Soon I was confiding that she probably wasn't as alone as I had thought. Although there were visitors, they arrived after I had been put to bed. My father, she said, was supposed to have been French, as was, I supposed, G de M... Suddenly, my words sounded trivial to my own ears, too self-involved. "How silly we are when we are young," G de M gently interrupted. "We always think there's no one like us."

"How true," breathed his wife.

"The thing is to break away from our homes, in order to realize that there exist other worlds." I remember my discomfort. The tip of his cane, in the midst of a gesture, had grazed my wrist.

She was soon talking about her designs, which she hoped would revolutionize the role of the glove so it could be worn in a variety of situations. Was I for or against their removal before a meal? This led to a discussion of fashion in general. Rebellious against foolish clothing taboos forced upon us by our Puritan ancestors, she believed at the same time that many decorative elements were superfluous. The body was no longer anything to be ashamed of; and perhaps one day when climate could be controlled scientifically, clothing could become only a matter of personal expression. We would no longer want to wear our fashions but would carry them with us like handbags or walking paintings. She made reference to her own simple outfit: a yellow suit of a new synthetic material, hair tucked under a tight cap of brown mink.

G de M continued the discussion of fashion by relating it to mystery and silence. It was often an ideal to which our fantasies aspired but never attained. Since full attainment was impossible, we should content ourselves with those few stolen moments during which the ideal actually seemed to move and speak.

Dessert was served despite the fact that they had not touched their food. She had mentioned a small but select group of fashion enthusiasts of which she and her husband were members. Many of the ideas about clothing she had expressed were a result of discussions that took place during their meetings. They enjoyed describing and wearing fashions that they expected were the trends of the future.

"We try to do today what we think others will do tomorrow," she said in summation. Theirs were ultra-modern tastes that often centered on unconventional uses of makeup and clothing. Since these had not yet been accepted in the fashion world, meetings sometimes took on an esoteric or even ritualistic tone.

She offered to bring my name up to the members at the next meeting. Certainly, my reputation as a display engineer would work in my favor...

Sort of a Fashion Journalist

YO, FASHIONISTAS, what's up wid' yoo? The Fall 2001 collections in New York this year loo' like dey thought up by your bookkeeper! I thought you couturiers wuz artistic? I come from a time when fashion was all about bodies, color, and sex. In those days the biz was riddled with orgies, parties, nose candy. As in Halston and his pal Liza Minnelli? Or Calvin Klein cavorting on Fire Island before those cheek implants began to sag? These really were the banquet years: Liza had to have two closets… for the two different weights between which she kept yo-yo-ing.

I was there when Halston showed his famous Spring Collection of 1979. Hey, were you? And were you astonished like me when you saw Halston's numbing plethora of simple shirtwaists cut at the bias, worn by spindly, sneering blonde models with heads the size of softballs? It was a kind of pre-Gwyneth Paltrow look. Yo, Gwyneths, one of you had on pink eye shadow that made you look like you'd been crying all morning. I guess I should have taken the cue then. You were crying about the death of fashion.

Hot-blooded as Halston may have been in his personal life, his fashions would usher in more than twenty years of sullen minimalism. And Calvin Klein would pick up the ball: creating "earth" tones that got less and less earthy. Ralph Lauren would commonize that WASP aesthetic for your everyday man, making American fashion's greatest excess the "equestrian" style.

Sad to say, fashion never did get off that high horse. We'd believed we'd end up with that futurist post-Courrèges look featured in *2001: A Space Odyssey*. But take a look around you. Fashion was booted back into a kind of traditionalism, which became another word for I-got-no-new-ideas-so-fuck-it. This is not the time to "think pink," as in surrealist Schiaparelli, but tweed or parka, as in Klein or Nautica. Sure, there's an eclecticism to the clothing shown at the Fall 2001 collections in New York, but it's all so colorless and oh so yawningly imitative. And sure, I had my fill of über-sexy models striding down the runway in Donna Karan, Anna Sui, or Darryl K—but those crotches seemed more defended than Fort Knox, my pretties!

So spare me the lazy dot.com chic of a Kenneth Cole, let's hightail it to this season's offbeat shows. On the way downtown, we shouldn't miss the ultra-talented Liz Collins, whose slashed-ribbon dresses looked like they've been tailored by Freddie Krueger. Nor the fearlessly iconoclastic Miguel Adrover, whose quiet, near-literal emphasis on traditional Egyptian garb this season brought him before the fashionista firing squad. What he was putting out was too poetic, you see. It just won't sell. Now he's gotta pay and pay.

Not so the less visible *artistes*. Their market's still small, and consequently they're still creative and playful. Take Iranian émigré Morteza Saifi. His show below Canal Street was romantic and mysterious. Models walked single file, hidden by a plywood barrier that allowed tantalizing peeks at stiff hieratic hairstyles over exaggerated turtlenecks. One wore a jacket with a back panel that looped into a flowery neckline. And then there was that exquisite cape jacket that dropped to make a dress.

Happily, there was the always surprising Pierrot, a French émigré who has brought back irony to knitwear. Papering an auditorium in the

Ukrainian National Home with huge photo murals of a Michigan forest, he turned the runway into a real dirt path and placed a statue of a bear, an outhouse, and a lighted tent along the way. During the show, we were treated to a multitude of fauna: Brunhilde-like campers in clinging, full-body camouflage knit jumpsuits, an axe-waving female lumberjack in a red-and-black wool jacket, and a cheerleader in pleated skirt whose sweater emblem featured two guns. The show started as a parody of sappy nature lovers, then turned into a tongue-in-cheek rally for the militia movement. It was orange-and-olive survival knitwear with a sense of humor, a Disney version of the right to bear arms.

And while we're at it, let's not forget the libidinal John Bartlett, who put 100 male models onto army cots in a dark room riddled with the sound of a respirator. Thus, he presented his military-inspired fashions in triage, reminding us not to take it lying down.

So, dear David Chu, you may be the creative director of Nautica, but your sensibility would be better left to engineering. And I may be championing those days when certain designers partied and paid for it by dying of overdoses or AIDS. But ain't that better than being killed by the boredom of your thirty-second season of charcoal-gray cashmere and tweed?

An Eden of Fashion

FOR ME, TOMORROW'S FASHION will be neither of cloth nor of fur, nor even of any new technological material. It will be something impalpable, a totally cerebral and aesthetic system: a kind of halo of pure light.

Accordingly, I see myself totally enveloped—dressed—by virtual projections, micro-devices that translate my most obscure, most unconscious desires. It is a new Edenic form of fashion, of absolute allure, pure desire.

The traditional functions of clothing—protection against cold and wall of modesty—will disappear. In their place will be clouds tailored to our bodies, with more precision than that of the most luxurious couturiers, into which, according to our whims, warm, perfumed vapors will be infused. The new fashion is the end of air conditioning and heating, and perhaps even every form of housing.

For now, I'm a prisoner of my aged body, damaged by my vices, but tomorrow I'll wear images of skin that are suppler and more sinuous than the skin of reptiles. If I want to have breasts like a woman for an evening, I'll have them immediately, and they will be more tender than any breasts you could imagine. My breasts will be completely made of light. Even more astonishing is that at every moment I will be so naked I will experience that nudity as I did when I was born.

In the future, fashion and plastic surgery will be one, which will transform our bodies into something elusive and seemingly transparent. Our totally naked bodies, completely haloed in light, will explode in flashes, like the uninsulated tips of two electric wires, each time they touch.

A Genuine Star Sapphire

THE ENTICEMENT AND ALLURE of ornamentation has only partly to do with the beauty and cost of precious metals and gems. What is more exciting is the contrast between their durability and the vulnerability of human flesh. As has been pointed out by poets from Homer to Baudelaire, there is sadism and power in the wearing of jewelry: something cold, hard, and immutable stamped on the skin's surface, aggressively flashing its ascendancy. Ornamentation cannot be wholly separated from the accoutrements of battle.

I agree, but only to a certain extent. It's true that Nancy Reagan brought imperial fashion back to America after the drab, born-again practicality of the Carter 70s. It's also true that jewelry has in the past been an insignia of the far right. However, I interpret the current taste for jewelry in a more curious light. From the beginning of history, precious stones and cryptic metal geometric patterns have been used not only to symbolize power but to point to the occult. Jewelry is the cold announcement of the flesh's eventual annihilation. It is permanency, mocking our transient nature. But it is also a belief in the impossible. Faith in the ability of crystalline structures to radiate their mysterious energies.

Just two and a half blocks from my home in New York City is a park famous for its desperation. Despite the passing of its more turbulent times, a wide variety of characters can still be found there. One of them has been a fixture for the last two or three years, whenever the weather is warm enough to sit outside. You can always spot him from a distance because of his golden hair and pearl-white skin. He's a runaway, a teenager who made his appearance in the park at the age of fifteen. And on one dirty, soft white hand, the back of which is covered with delicate blue veins, is a very large genuine star-sapphire ring. It sits in strange contrast to the crude, artlessly sketched tattoo of an anarchist star on the back of his hand.

For months I sat in the park, shifting my gaze between this magnificent ring and the teenager's equally magnificent face. It wasn't so much his aquiline features, worthy of a beautiful girl, his plush pink mouth, or sharp, winged cheekbones accentuating the heart-shaped lines of his skull that caught my attention. It was his eyes. And it wasn't the fact that his eyes were large and richly colored, unnaturally wide, spaced-apart ovals, but the fact that they also looked like star sapphires—blue and milky, glinting with mysterious lights. Dirt stained as both face and hands became from his homeless nights, this triplet of blue always shown forth in purity, glimmering with hidden darts of fire.

There was, however, another feature of these features that was really the reason for my fascination. It was that his eyes didn't match. Whereas one blue orb was soft and limpid, the other was always hard and vigilant. It seemed to change only with the movement of his head; but when he was still, it was fixed, cold, and staring. Thus, he seemed to look at me with a double nature: one soft and vulnerable, the other hard and threatening.

One day, after months of staring, I got the courage to sit next to him. The voice that came from his soft ivory throat was a damaged one, already graveled from the ravages of crack. And his speech contradicted the clear constancy of the icy blue stars on his finger and in his eye sockets because his thoughts had been muddled by drugs for some time. He spoke incessantly and obsessively of his two sapphires, which he said he had taken from his physically abusive parents in order to "steal their power." He had, in fact, a surprisingly advanced knowledge of the occult power of jewels—their protective nature, their ability to bring good luck or bad, their relationship to astrology—and made reference to many sources, including the Egyptians. My two sapphires, he kept repeating, and he held them responsible for the fact that he was still alive; they had protected him from all the dangers faced by a soft, young runaway in a hostile city. But two? I finally asked. Two sapphires? Where is the other?

It was then he stuck his child's finger into the corner of the cold, staring eye, and popped out a round orb. This isn't glass, he claimed, balancing the gleaming orb on his outstretched palm. At least, not the blue center. It's a genuine star sapphire. It has power. Then, lapsing into a mawkish grin, he claimed he could see out of it, too.

DANGEROUS MINDS

Gore

SHUT UP, GORE VIDAL, and rest in peace for once. I'm in awe that we've lived to see the demise of that energetic old whore, a Wife of Bath who lived as long as Methuselah and still coveted the limelight. A lousy novelist, because he refused to take second place to his characters, as all novelists must do, and a provocative essayist, who put strategically sensationalist political commentary he didn't really believe in at the service of his narcissism and grandiosity—to the great delight of all his readers, including me. "Gore is a man without an unconscious," his friend, the Italian writer Italo Calvino, once said. Mr. Vidal said of himself: "I'm exactly as I appear. There is no warm, lovable person inside. Beneath my cold exterior, once you break the ice, you find cold water." May you have the last laugh, you old curmudgeon, and finally get a little peace of mind.

My Body: Design and Architecture

THANK YOU VERY MUCH for your interest in reassigning my body. First of all, let me say that, in conjunction with your very contemporary approach, there is no need to worry about any prudishness on my part, any embarrassment. I intend to reveal my history, express all my desires as well as insecurities.

And now, may I explain how I think I developed such a severe body dysmorphic disorder, or would you call it gender dysfunction? You're the doctors, so you tell me. I can only state that I feel I can remember nearly the exact moment when my mother first allowed me into her bedroom as she was dressing. It was in the summer, before my third birthday, which is in August, so I'd suspect it was in… July. We were, in fact, spending our very first summer on that crystalline lake in upstate New York, which local legend described as the clearest and cleanest spring-fed lake in the world! And we were there because we had money, you know, it was such a posh town, no Jews and all that…

I remember the soft pixilated effect of the very blue water of that lake as seen through the screen covering Mother's bedroom window, because at that very moment, she was placing a soft cone-shape, created with swirls of Georgette, on her head and adjusting the veil that covered half her face.

Do you remember the veils on hats women wore in those days? Perhaps you've seen pictures? Given the tendency for heavy foundation makeup at the time, along with the abundant use of rouge, and the passion for very, very red lipstick *(Love that Red!, Bricktop, Fire and Ice,* I remember all the names!), such veils gave the effect of concealing something very hierarchical, even precious, and maybe a bit evil (although I'm just referring to an effect). Surprisingly, the use of eye shadow or mascara was still restrained in those days, but my mother—may we call her "Ayesha," or "Lucretia," for purposes of anonymity, though unfortunately, her name happened to be a lot drabber than that?—had *enormous* eyes!

…Hm, now where was I? Something about…. Oh, yes, the veil. There *was* something about it covering her rather deliciously remote (should I say, "maddeningly remote"?) enormous green eyes and producing the same effect as the screen that shielded me from the icy, (the lake was spring fed, you see) blue, blue, blue *purity* of the lake. But the strangest thing is, I can't remember the name of that lake, though we lived on it every summer for about ten years… No, I can't. It's one of many seemingly essential things I can't remember.

I do, however, recall how that veil intrigued, how I wished that Ayesha would (or could?) *never* take it off, and the thrill of imagining Lucretia eating with the veil on, bringing a corner of the crisp white napkin to the corner of flamingly red lips at intervals, as she sometimes did, after which the napkin was stained by a shocking spot of red… or lifting the very thin edge of a sparkling glass to those lips, as the edge of the veil grazed the glass's bulbous, transparent surface…

Surface, don't you love that word?

Where was I? Merely saying that perhaps the only activity I couldn't visualize being performed in that veil (I'm sure there were others, but remember, I wasn't quite three) was Ayesha *asleep* in it, a non-actuality that greatly disturbed me, for some reason.

Much more *important* than hats or veils, more closely related to the reason I sit before you today, was Lucretia's *corset. Black,* you see—not, of course, when she was in her white summer dresses, but almost all the other times…

Can you remember, for example, the proverbial *little black dress?* But—this was at a later age—I knew that every single other mother wore a *white* girdle. I'd even seen one or two at the homes of friends, after our play led us into their mothers' closets while the moms were downstairs preparing a snack or something like that. And I always took the initiative in play, and would encircle the soft, thin wrist of a playmate with my thumb and forefinger (I chose children much smaller than me with whom to play), and lead "it" into the closet (I mean "the child," but— except in the case of my mother—I simply detest gendered adjectival pronouns, or that awkward contemporary solution of using both with "or," or even worse, "they," as if employing the plural incorrectly would solve the problem)… and then lead that child deep into recesses of the closet, where there was always *that powdery scent* (mixed with a hint of old perspiration, I suppose, though how could I have identified it as such since I still had no odor—which is why children certainly don't ever wear deodorant, correct?)… to experience a thrilling intimation of *suffo-cation,* caused by the cool, superficial caress of dry satin or nylon against my mouth, and the gentle abrasion of tulle applique. And shrouded in these… *fabbbb-rrrrics,* I'd clasp the frail little body about the waist and press *it* (yes, I prefer an article here, too) against my (oh, I do want to say *its* here, as well!) larger body.

Strange? Remember, I was only a child. But I still think this is where it started, the notion *(you'd* call it an illusion) that I already was what I desperately wanted to be: a thing, frail but lithe, and perhaps… *blond?*… without the slightest hint of hair anywhere on its trunk, on its legs, but-tocks… arms, unless maybe it was a faint blond down that is barely visible on the delicate skin…

Hmm… Does the image appeal to you? Perhaps you should ask yourself why. On the other hand, my description is so faulty. That wasn't what I wanted to be at all. It wasn't just the quality of *surface* (that word again!) that I was re-envisioning. It was the *structure*. Are you shocked? Yes, at times, I know, you yourselves must deal with structure, when it comes to *gender reassignment*, for example. And even when you're dealing with surface appearance, which is most of the time, you sometimes find your scalpel probing deeper, deeper, into the muscular structure… but as for me, I wanted to be more than what I've just described, I wanted to escape *all signification*, because it's "wrong." Have you considered the fact that anything that sticks out of you—that is salient, shall we say?— is under the threat of cultural interpretation (a kind of decapitation, isn't it)?

I don't have to tell you *that*. You've read your *theory*, etc. So I suppose what *it* (there I go again! you know I mean "I") wanted to be was little more than a *surface*. And what would one call such an *entity*? Something larval? Or a mollusk. But even that—right away, because it has three dimensions—leads to a womblike connotation. Is there no way to escape *both* phallic and receptive implications and communicate? Well, there must be, I've always thought. But then what do you become? Are you even an *object*? The moment there are more than two dimensions you become something beyond your control.

I can see this is disturbing you. So I'll resort to a euphemism, an abstraction. I'll say that I wanted to escape being "architectural." Is that any more palatable? It was the only way to escape all the silly categories in which our culture places us, wouldn't you agree? And besides, my mother… Hmm… *Lucretia*, forbade any subjects other than herself. *And perhaps I agreed with her!* You decide.

Yes, I am getting into theory. At the same time as being personal. But if you don't mind. I'd like to get *out of it*. And get out of it I *did*. For quite a while I think I'd managed to escape any implications of gender.

It was something that went way beyond my activities with children, which I'd begun to detest—not for cliché reasons, I have no sentimentality about the protection of children, and I even believe that their egos develop at such an early stage that they are indeed capable of "choice." After all, there are *children who murder*, aren't there?

Excuse me. I didn't mean to offend anyone. I don't wish to break the law any more, either. At any rate, you must know all about this, it must be in my file… that soon I began to suspect there was a consciousness beyond all of this that represented a far more dramatic state of regression. It was a thrilling discovery: the concept that real freedom resides in *regression*, not in the further development of signs, significations, complexes, and other socially interwoven patterns… A way of escaping the fact that a life has essentially been a *hollowness* supported by a traditional structure. Yes, I actually thought I could escape the net of karma, and still go on "living."

Paraphilic infantilism seemed to provide that for a while. People speak of it as if it's some kind of sexual fetish, but actually, it's a better mind-emptier than the most advanced systems of meditation. With or without diapers. The evaporation of the will into the capable, burdened arms of another, the rocking motion… The lapse into powerlessness and *sexual innocence*, the evaporation of any self-consciousness or *gender anxiety*.

Hmm… it was during one of these sessions that the idea came to me that there could be a more radical way to cut short the generation of representations—at least for a few moments, and discover *smoothness*. I know it was a dangerous idea. You must understand that the only place I could find such services I am now discussing was in a dungeon run by an unpleasant novelist-madam, and because I was such a faithful customer of paraphilic infantilism, or perhaps because the novelist found me a *resource to mine*, or perhaps only because all they wanted was to laugh at me, once a session was over and I had resumed a social identity by getting dressed, I'd be asked to stay, perhaps to have a drink with the novelist, around whom sometimes milled a couple of off-duty "workers."

During one of those downtimes, I overheard a rather heated discussion between the madam-novelist and one of the workers. It seems that the former wanted a certain client-service provided by the latter to *cease*. It involved—rather astonishingly, I thought at the time—a "client" who insisted on having pressure applied to the carotid artery, carrier of the principal blood supply to the brain! Before and after, the client was quite vocal about the exquisiteness of the experience, and it (well, "he") used the word *release*. But the madam-novelist greatly feared an *accident*, a scandal involving the police…

It wasn't difficult at all to time my leaving one day when the expert on applying pressure to the carotid artery was leaving as well. And of course, I was impelled to do so by the intimation that pressure services might lead, temporarily of course, to the erasure of all *qualities*. But there was one major *impediment*. The pressure expert was an Oriental. And no matter how sublime this transcendent experience promised to be, I absolutely refused to be degraded in such a way.

Ahem… hmm. So you see, I am not entirely without principles.

There was, however, a solution close at hand. With the usual sense of accommodation, with which such individuals are "gifted," the pressure expert suggested a more acceptable colleague, who showed up at my apartment the very next day.

I told you that I had no intention of succumbing to any unnecessary prudery in talking to you, so I'll admit to you that I anticipated our meeting with an excitement that can only be described as *nuptial*. I had requested, as well, that she (yes, in this case I am more than happy to employ such a discriminative pronoun!) obscure half her face with a veil. Surely the pre-phallic wholeness inaccessible to all of us once we are capable of expressing a desire for it was about to be returned by some magic, if only *for a few precious moments!*

Hmm… Yes.

But wait! I sense a lasciviousness coming over all of you! I can feel it pressing against me like the flesh of a cold fish. Be forewarned that I am neither an object of desire nor a procurer of it! Neither role interests me…

Do you understand? Then, to go on:

…As anyone who has indulged in erotic strangulation can tell you, the complimentary stimulation of "organs residing down there" (suddenly, I feel too—shall we say, "maidenly," for lack of a better term— to be any more precise) and denial of blood to the brain produces a sensual transcendence that has little to do with language or form, and doubtlessly not at all that much to do with what we call existence. From this opiated pinnacle brought on by the pressure, I felt myself swiftly pouring into *nothingness…*

And that, apparently, was how I ended up here and eventually found my way to you. I must have plunged too far into non being, and my glimpse of a consciousness minus the obfuscations of symbolism was indeed brief and is of course partly alien to memory, that *cesspool of corpse-symbols.*

Please realize that I have not delved into these personal secrets for any idle reason! I am, instead, hoping you will now understand my urgency to accomplish the surgery I have in mind as soon as possible, in fact… to achieve a form of existence that is equal to a poreless surface *impregnable to meaning.* I've grown to detest every appendage of the body and its phallic implications, from so-called "fingers and toes" to limbs, not to mention that builder of destructive mental structures, the tongue, and its coarser, even more betraying brother at the southern extremities. So, all of them must go. I know what I'm asking you is radical: to restore me from my dysmorphic disorder to an antimorphic *naught.* But let's start the surgery as soon as possible. I'm not demanding any "complete makeover," as you are used to providing, but just a complete *unmaking*, the anti-creation of a subject *without qualities*. I imagine that this will be your *masterpiece*! No salience will be immune to your amputating artistry. Begin your work with a scalpel with no restraint whatsoever! Show me the perfect roundness of *zero*—the circularity of Ayesha's arms!

Intern's Incantation

UH-OH: IS THAT A CIGARETTE, sadist? When you know I quit last week but on days like this… okay, let me have one, I deserve it, my head is splitting. We'll take a break, too. But you got to let me know when fifteen minutes are up 'cause I left my beeper at the goddamn nurse's station…

…What you think about 606B, dementia or lesions? Nobody can stand that raving anymore. The brain scan looked normal, so I doubt it's lesions from an opportunistic organism. And you know, once the virus starts getting past the blood-brain barrier, sensory areas can lapse for hours at a time. Then bingo, back to normal…

…Who knows what the hell's going on in his head, if he's in pain. Or maybe nature's taking care of him, he's out of it. I kind of liked that guy when he got admitted, before the tube went up his nose. He's a graphic designer or something. But you know what I don't get about these gay guys? The thousand or more sexual contacts. I mean what kind of person could have that kind of need?

…Whoa, wait a minute, let me see, is that a real Rolex? I got one, too. My mother-in-law sent me one for my birthday, see. So normally I don't like these pretentious name brands. But I figure what the hell, I could use a good watch, and I'm not totally averse to the status either…

…So I'm at Robbins Ice Cream, the one down the block and across from Emergency. I mean I just had such a lust for ice cream. I was coming in on a call, a kidney stone, but I hadn't had lunch, and I just wanted to stop for a quick one. How was I to know she sent me a fake from Florida?

Because when I got to the Op room, they were already wheeling him out. Weinstein was livid. So much for my mother-in-law's watches.

Hello, honey. (Her ass drives me bananas.) Listen, got any Tylenol? I haven't slept a full hour in two days. I'll stop by the station in a minute to pick up a couple. Shit, my head is killing me. Wonder if I'm getting a brain tumor. To tell you the truth, this gig is getting to me after all. Seeing them wheel 'em in and wheel 'em out one after the other.

It's a lost cause, and we know it. How many years has it been, nine? And they still don't have a convincing explanation for route of infection… Somebody swallows the stuff, okay? You'd think barring any ulcerations, it'd make a clean entry right to the stomach and die, seeing it's supposed to be so fragile.

Hear it? There he goes again. Sounds like he's fucking cursing, or calling for his mother. Let's keep walking. I wish somebody would shut him up. Let me have a light, will you?

Anyway, it looks like it's no go on that condo. The maintenance is just not worth it. I spent all last night figuring out that the best deal right now is to stick with the share, then get out of this city. I'm thinking California, but who isn't? Who isn't thinking every goddamn thing before you are in this fucking competitive world we live in? You want to be a doctor? Right. So do two million other people!

I don't know, though. I did one thing right. I mean going into this radiology thing. It's the least messy. You look at X rays all day, occasionally you got to touch a body. Except the first six months, I thought I'd go crazy. They did everything they could to knock the wind out of me. You think this stuff is arbitrary, but big brother is up there, pulling the strings, looking for your weak points. I'm convinced they put me on this ward 'cause they thought I was some kind of fag basher. And to tell you the truth, I've never felt too easy about homos.

So every time they got a fag lying there who's so wasted he ran out of veins, they call me in. Call him, they told the nurses, he can get blood from a stone. I start talking to these guys to calm them down, and before I know it, we've got a rapport going. You know me. And what I begin to realize is that most of them are people who've taken good care of their bodies, you know? athletes like me. Then one day I'm standing over this stretcher, and this skeleton looks up at me and smiles. I take a good look, and I realize it's this guy I used to jog with, only there's not that much of him left right now. Well the guy looks so thrilled to see me. He sticks his hand out from under the sheet and grabs my arm, won't let go. And me, I said the stupidest thing, ha ha, you know how it is in a situation like that, I said to him, I haven't seen you at the quarter mile lately. I mean what a stupid thing to say. And the guy says to me, you got to help me. So I tell him I'm doing the best I can. He says to tell the nurses to leave, and then he says shut the door and come here, so what am I supposed to do? So I go over to the bed and out comes the claw again, he grabs my arm like in a death grip, see? Like this! I couldn't believe he still had that much strength. And he grits his teeth and stares me in the eye, says, you got to help me. You got to get me some medicine to get me out of this. Well, nobody can get you out of this, brother, I tell him. You can, he disagrees. He wants me to put him over the edge. Well, I got nothing against this guy, obviously, I mean I used to jog with him, but I never knew he was gay or anything, and now he wants me to jeopardize my career, you know, sneak in something to put the poor guy out of his misery. No way, brother, I got to say. But he won't let go the claw and starts pleading with me, saying please please, and when that doesn't work, telling me I'm a fucking hypocrite and coming out with every curse word he can think of. And then finally, you know what he did? You won't believe this, but I'm not shitting you, I don't even like to think about it, he spits at me! Right in my face. And when that spit hit me, I went wild for a split second and I landed him one across the face. Maybe that's how the watch broke. And the claw sank away from my arm and ran out of gas. And I ran out of there. I don't even like to think about it.

I don't know… A lot of careers are going to be made or lost on this one, I mean the money pouring into some of these foundations is fantastic! But with all the competition, you could get lost in the crowd. My old man doesn't understand it. After all the money he sunk into this, why I don't have a sure future. Come back home, he says, and hang up a shingle. He never heard of negligence insurance, the way he talks. Did you see in that article in the *Times* by the girl M.D. from Boston, the gynecologist? She figured it all out. With insurance rates rising the same as they have in the last ten years, and rents too, we'll be out of business. And that's what we're doing thirty-four-hour shifts for, so we can give it up and get jobs as waiters? Gimme a break.

You see, the other day I was waiting in line for something, the bank, the supermarket, the drugstore, what the fuck difference does it make? Maybe it was just the heat or just a feeling that had been building up. It was a really horrible feeling, the feeling that I couldn't be waiting in line anymore. I've got to get out of here, I kept thinking, whatever it is I'm waiting for, I have to have it right away, I deserve it! But somehow, I feel I'm being discriminated against. The indifference of these other people in line is maddening. I mean what is there about them that they have to bottle themselves up and withdraw forever from any meaningful human contact, I kept thinking. I mean even the clothes they have put on their bodies are steeped in contempt. They have chosen these clothes to wear because they hate their own bodies and their bodies' similarities to other humans'.

It was a crazy feeling. My chest felt shallow, as if my heart was beating right at the surface. I can't wait here a minute longer because my legs are turning to water. I have to sit down right here on the floor. Or I have to feel my body pressed against the cool sheets. Something is forcing me to spread my legs apart, one hand on the small of my back, my belly pressed against the sheet. I don't want to, but a voice that is at once soothing and authoritative keeps demanding it. I can't exactly see the face but it is the representative of a racial type. I'm going to pierce you. It's the voice talking. I'm afraid it will hurt a little. Some warmth from your body has infused mine with strength and longing. It is as if your blood is flowing into mine. But it is so dark in here, part of what you imagine I can see, part of what seems obvious to us is lost in shadow: the smooth, golden skin, the thick, corded neck, the square chin. He thinks he knows the sound of my sharp intake of breath, the pleasure that courses through my muscles without my looking up, as his belt whisks against his jeans, the heavy buckle landing with a dull clank on the floor, the dry sounds the jeans make as they slide down against the hard legs.

In some way, he is about to be kind to me. But no one must see this, not even the two of us in a way. Still my eyes secretly study each half-gesture, looking for a sign of empathy, tenderness. Thank you for subtly disguising this. That we wish we would never be allowed to touch, to admire, to kiss the flat ripples of the stomach, the erect nipples, and dark tuft of hair. What it would feel like to touch that face, that hard, uncaring mask, eyes like bright pebbles, nostrils flared, lips pursed, a frozen mask of indifference that is usually lost in shadow.

Do not come to me at once, to where I am kneeling, huddled, crouched on the cold floor. Do not come to me, hold yourself back. He lifts his head and throws it back haughtily, probably imagines how this looks to me and is pleased.

Go inside us, be us, imagine how we would want it to be and become it.

He walks forward, finally. Erect cock, scrotum jiggling slightly.

Then he lets us touch him. There's barely time to catch my breath. I'm forced to accept it. He supposes we must be thinking this. The odor of his leather belt is still coming from his hard belly. The moaning that travels to my ears, the hopelessness, has nothing to do with it at all. We do not exist, and neither do our cocks and bodies. Only this hard cock throbbing.

But I know he is not responsible for this feeling of emptiness. That I am only a human being like you. Maybe I just need to feel him demanding that I give up.

Well, fifteen minutes are up, I guess. Let's get back to our station.

Friday the Thirteenth

THE NOTION OF FRIDAY the thirteenth is so ingrained in our minds that few of us ever stop to think about the people needed to cause all that alleged bad luck. So, my question is: Is Friday the thirteenth a *good-luck day* for them?

I rarely go to a bar or club on Friday the thirteenth for the simple and obvious reason that those drinking with me would either have to be masochists waiting for some ill fortune to befall them or those who cause misfortune to others. This is why I had a feeling of misgiving as I made my way to a small bar in the East Village, which itself has had its share of unlucky incarnations. It has moved twice at the insistence of the police, who seem to object to the amount of flesh shown by its male go-go dancers, the heavy traffic in cocaine running through its restrooms, and its percentage of drinkers without ID.

On the other hand, this particular Friday the thirteenth seemed no more sordid than normal. A line of poorly fed dancers, their ringed eyes and sallow skin betraying a habit of drug abuse, were dancing desultorily on top of the shellacked bar. As usual, the exposure of certain features of their bodies was potentially flagrant enough to irritate law enforcers.

Unlike most of today's go-go boys, who tend to wear overly tight bikinis, these young men were wearing briefs at least two sizes too large for them, which tended to sabotage the standard function of such garments—the cupping, containment and concealment of the private parts—and were so loose in the thigh that the wearer's "package" tended to slip out at certain swinging movements of the hips. Correspondingly, the stretched-out waistbands of the briefs caused sliding below the waist, exposing the globes of the buttocks each time a dancer indolently turned with the intention of offering a back view.

Those not used to such an atmosphere may be puzzled by the fact of my choosing to drink by standing at such a bar; but on the one hand, it offered a place to put my elbows, and on the other, allowed me easy access to the bartender, whereas I would have had to fight my way through the crowd to refill my glass each time if I had given up the post. Thirdly, the position allowed me a rather uniquely intimate view of the dancers' charms, despite the fact that it involved a great deal of neck craning; and if I became motivated to show my appreciation by tipping one of them, his drooping waistband, past which one was invited to plunge the tip-holding hand, was within easy reach. The only logistical problem involved the exchange of money and drinks across the bar.

Quite late in the evening, my attention began to focus rather exaggeratedly on the two teardrop-shaped buttocks of the nearest dancer. And each time I threaded an arm between his legs to receive another drink from the bartender, I wasn't exactly vigilant about not letting my wrist graze against them. This would elicit a gentle leer from the dancer, and because he was quite aware of the section of anatomy I seemed to favor, he obligingly turned his back to me and bent his knees to lower the object of desire nearer.

I suppose I shouldn't have brought my head so close to it during my minute examination of its particularities—but the effort seemed well worth the verification of the silken skin encasing the two perfectly shaped orbs of flesh. However, if my eyes—and ears—had been in a more elevated position, I might have noticed that the squatting dancer was having a heated lover's quarrel with the bartender. To show his frustration during this argument, the latter must have pushed him with excessive and sudden force, for I suddenly found myself stretched out on my back on the floor, my face serving as a makeshift cushion for the part of the anatomy I had so admired and that belonged to the currently toppled dancer.

English and French versions of these texts have appeared in
the following magazines, anthologies, and literary journals:

Actuel Magazine
Airs de Paris (Centre Pompidou)
American Book Jam
American Letters and Commentary
Animal Shelter 1
Apollo (Maas Verlag)
Beaux Arts Magazine
Benzene
Between C&D
Between Men
Big Trips: More Good Gay Travel Writing
Bil Bo K
Brothers of the Night
Butt Magazine
Central Park
D.T.V.
Dreamworks
Dutch
Exotic
Flesh and the Word 4
Frank
Happily Ever After: Erotic Fairy Tales for Men
In the Language of Barbarians, I Would Tell You Stories (Edgewise)
Index Magazine
Konkret Magazine
New York Rage (L'Incertain)
Maatstaf
Meet Me at the Baths (Gay Parisian Press)
Men on Men 3
Men on Men 6
nerve.com
nest Magazine
Noirotica
Noirotica 2: Pulp Friction
Out Magazine
Pacific Agony (Semiotext(e))
Prague Literary Review
Pretending to Say No (Plume)
Pugzine
Purple Magazine
Put A Egg on It
Q
My Body: Design and Architecture and Convalescence (Red Dust Books)
Sans Nom: La Revue des Moeurs

Satanica
Shout Magazine
Slightly West Literary Journal (The Evergreen State College)
Take My Advice (Simon & Schuster)
The Edgier Waters: 5 Years of 3:AM
The Fiction Review
The Literary Review
The Portable Lower East Side
The Review of Contemporary Fiction
The Soho Press Book of 80s Short Fiction
Unbearables
Up Is Up, But So Is Down: New York's Downtown Literary Scene, 1974-1992
User (Dutton/Plume)
Van Gogh's Ear
Verbal Abuse
XXX Fruit

ABOUT THE AUTHOR

BRUCE BENDERSON is most known for his seventh book, a memoir called *The Romanian: Story of an Obsession* (Tarcher/Penguin, 2006), which won France's prestigious literary award, the Prix de Flore, in translation.

He is also the author of the novels *User* (Dutton, 1994) and *Pacific Agony* (Semiotext(e) 2009) as well as the story collection *Pretending to Say No* (Plume, 1990). A collection of his essays, *Sex and Isolation*, was published by University of Wisconsin Press in 2008.

Benderson is bilingual, writes in both English and French, and all eight of his books have been republished in translation by Editions Payot & Rivages in France.

As a journalist, Benderson has written in English or French for *The New York Times Magazine*, *The Wall Street Journal*, *The Village Voice*, *nest*, *French Vogue*, *Vogue Hommes*, *Beaux Arts Magazine*, *L'Humanité*, *Madame Figaro*, *Blackbook*, *and Libération*, among others. For five years, he was the author of a monthly column for the French gay magazine *Têtu*.

Benderson is a literary translator from the French. His numerous published translations include works by Grégoire Bouiller, Martin Page, Tony Duvert, David Foenkinos, Philippe Djian, Alain Robbe-Grillet, Philippe Sollers, and Beatrix Preciado. His most recent translation was an 1100-page biography, *Jean Renoir*.

In 2007, Benderson published a personal encyclopedia of the American counterculture for a French audience, entitled *Concentré de Counterculture* (Scali). His book *Transhumain*, about The Singularity and the future interfacing of technology and biology, which he wrote directly in French, was published by Payot in 2010. A satirical essay, *Against*

Marriage (Semiotexte, 2014), was published to become part of an installation at the Whitney Biennale.

Benderson has also worked closely with three Hollywood personalities: Leslie Caron, for her 2010 memoir *Thank Heaven*; Hill Harper, for his 2013 book *Letters to an Incarcerated Brother;* and Raquel Welch, for her book *Raquel: Beyond the Cleavage*. In 2014 he wrote the subtitles for the French film *Race d'ep*.

He has taught creative writing, urban culture, and French literature during three separate terms at Deep Springs College in Dyer, Nevada. He has also lectured or taught workshops at Brown University, Evergreen College, and Sarah Lawrence. Benderson is the literary executor of fiction writer and translator Ursule Molinaro.

BOOKS BY ITNA

Crashing Cathedrals: Edmund White by the Book
Tom Cardamone

Tiny Fish that Only Want to Kiss
Gary Indiana

Victims
Travis Jeppesen

Everything Must Go
Lauren John Joseph

The Beads
David McConnell

The Virtuous Ones
Christopher Stoddard